Varney the Vampire or; The Feast of Blood
A Romance of Exciting Interest
By Thomas Preskett Prest
Edited by Anthony Uyl

Devoted Publishing
Woodstock, Ontario, 2017

Varney the Vampire or; The Feast of Blood

A Romance of Exciting Interest

By Thomas Preskett Prest (1810-1859)

The Author of
"Grace Rivers, or, The Merchant's Daughter."

Edited by Anthony Uyl

Originally Published from 1845-1847

Originally Published by:
London: Printed and Published by E. Lloyd, 12, Salisbury-Square, Fleet-Street

"Art thou a spirit of health or goblin damned?"

What kind of stories do you have?
Let us know!

Contact us at: devotedpub@hotmail.com
Visit our shop on Facebook: @DevotedPublishing

Published in Woodstock, Ontario, Canada 2017.

For bulk educational rates, please contact us at the above email address.

ISBN: 978-1-77356-046-5

PREFACE

The unprecedented success of the romance of "Varney the Vampyre," leaves the Author but little to say further, than that he accepts that success and its results as gratefully as it is possible for any one to do popular favours.

A belief in the existence of Vampyres first took its rise in Norway and Sweden, from whence it rapidly spread to more southern regions, taking a firm hold of the imaginations of the more credulous portion of mankind.

The following romance is collected from seemingly the most authentic sources, and the Author must leave the question of credibility entirely to his readers, not even thinking that he is peculiarly called upon to express his own opinion upon the subject.

Nothing has been omitted in the life of the unhappy Varney, which could tend to throw a light upon his most extraordinary career, and the fact of his death just as it is here related, made a great noise at the time through Europe and is to be found in the public prints for the year 1713.

With these few observations, the Author and Publisher, are well content to leave the work in the hands of a public, which has stamped it with an approbation far exceeding their most sanguine expectations, and which is calculated to act as the strongest possible incentive to the production of other works, which in a like, or perchance a still further degree may be deserving of public patronage and support.

To the whole of the Metropolitan Press for their laudatory notices, the Author is peculiarly obliged.

London Sep. 1847

CHAPTER I

"How graves give up their dead.
And how the night air hideous grows
With shrieks!"

MIDNIGHT.--THE HAIL-STORM.--THE DREADFUL VISITOR.--THE VAMPYRE

The solemn tones of an old cathedral clock have announced midnight--the air is thick and heavy--a strange, death like stillness pervades all nature. Like the ominous calm which precedes some more than usually terrific outbreak of the elements, they seem to have paused even in their ordinary fluctuations, to gather a terrific strength for the great effort. A faint peal of thunder now comes from far off. Like a signal gun for the battle of the winds to begin, it appeared to awaken them from their lethargy, and one awful, warring hurricane swept over a whole city, producing more devastation in the four or five minutes it lasted, than would a half century of ordinary phenomena.

It was as if some giant had blown upon some toy town, and scattered many of the buildings before the hot blast of his terrific breath; for as suddenly as that blast of wind had come did it cease, and all was as still and calm as before.

Sleepers awakened, and thought that what they had heard must be the confused chimera of a dream. They trembled and turned to sleep again.

All is still--still as the very grave. Not a sound breaks the magic of repose. What is that--a strange, pattering noise, as of a million of fairy feet? It is hail--yes, a hail-storm has burst over the city. Leaves are dashed from the trees, mingled with small boughs; windows that lie most opposed to the direct fury of the pelting particles of ice are broken, and the rapt repose that before was so remarkable in its intensity, is exchanged for a noise which, in its accumulation, drowns every cry of surprise or consternation which here and there arose from persons who found their houses invaded by the storm.

Now and then, too, there would come a sudden gust of wind that in its strength, as it blew laterally, would, for a moment, hold millions of the hailstones suspended in mid air, but it was only to dash them with redoubled force in some new direction, where more mischief was to be done.

Oh, how the storm raged! Hail--rain--wind. It was, in very truth, an awful night.

***

There is an antique chamber in an ancient house. Curious and quaint carvings adorn the walls, and the large chimney-piece is a curiosity of itself. The ceiling is low, and a large bay window, from roof to floor, looks to the west. The window is latticed, and filled with curiously painted glass and rich stained pieces, which send in a strange, yet beautiful light, when sun or moon shines into the apartment. There is but one portrait in that room, although the walls seem panelled for the express purpose of containing a series of pictures. That portrait is of a young man, with a pale face, a stately brow, and a strange expression about the eyes, which no one cared to look on twice.

There is a stately bed in that chamber, of carved walnut-wood is it made, rich in design and elaborate in execution; one of those works of art which owe their existence to the Elizabethan era. It is hung with heavy silken and damask furnishing; nodding feathers are at its corners--covered with dust are they, and they lend a funereal aspect to the room. The floor is of polished oak.

God! how the hail dashes on the old bay window! Like an occasional discharge of mimic musketry, it comes clashing, beating, and cracking upon the small panes; but they resist it--their small size saves them; the wind, the hail, the rain, expend their fury in vain.

The bed in that old chamber is occupied. A creature formed in all fashions of loveliness lies in a half sleep upon that ancient couch--a girl young and beautiful as a spring morning. Her long hair has escaped from its confinement and streams over the blackened coverings of the bedstead; she has been restless in her sleep, for the clothing of the bed is in much confusion. One arm is over her head, the other hangs nearly off the side of the bed near to which she lies. A neck and bosom that would have formed a study for the rarest sculptor that ever Providence gave genius to, were half disclosed. She moaned slightly in her sleep, and once or twice the lips moved as if in prayer--at least one might judge so, for the name of Him who suffered for all came once faintly from them.

She has endured much fatigue, and the storm does not awaken her; but it can disturb the slumbers it does not possess the power to destroy entirely. The turmoil of the elements wakes the senses, although it cannot entirely break the repose they have lapsed into.

Oh, what a world of witchery was in that mouth, slightly parted, and exhibiting within the pearly teeth that glistened even in the faint light that came from that bay window. How sweetly the long silken eyelashes lay upon the cheek. Now she moves, and one shoulder is entirely visible--whiter, fairer than the spotless clothing of the bed on which she lies, is the smooth skin of that fair creature, just budding into womanhood, and in that transition state which presents to us all the charms of the girl--almost of the child, with the more matured beauty and gentleness of advancing years.

Was that lightning? Yes--an awful, vivid, terrifying flash--then a roaring peal of thunder, as if a thousand mountains were rolling one over the other in the blue vault of Heaven! Who sleeps now in that ancient city? Not one living soul. The dread trumpet of eternity could not more effectually have awakened any one.

The hail continues. The wind continues. The uproar of the elements seems at its height. Now she awakens--that beautiful girl on the antique bed; she opens those eyes of celestial blue, and a faint cry of alarm bursts from her lips. At least it is a cry which, amid the noise and turmoil without, sounds but faint and weak. She sits upon the bed and presses her hands upon her eyes. Heavens! what a wild torrent of wind, and rain, and hail! The thunder likewise seems intent upon awakening sufficient echoes to last until the next flash of forked lightning should again produce the wild concussion of the air. She murmurs a prayer--a prayer for those she loves best; the names of those dear to her gentle heart come from her lips; she weeps and prays; she thinks then of what devastation the storm must surely produce, and to the great God of Heaven she prays for all living things. Another flash--a wild, blue, bewildering flash of lightning streams across that bay window, for an instant bringing out every colour in it with terrible distinctness. A shriek bursts from the lips of the young girl, and then, with eyes fixed upon that window, which, in another moment, is all darkness, and with such an expression of terror upon her face as it had never before known, she trembled, and the perspiration of intense fear stood upon her brow.

"What--what was it?" she gasped; "real, or a delusion? Oh, God, what was it? A figure tall and gaunt, endeavouring from the outside to unclasp the window. I saw it. That flash of lightning revealed it to me. It stood the whole length of the window."

There was a lull of the wind. The hail was not falling so thickly--moreover, it now fell, what there was of it, straight, and yet a strange clattering sound came upon the glass of that long window. It could not be a delusion--she is awake, and she hears it. What can produce it? Another flash of lightning--another shriek--there could be now no delusion.

A tall figure is standing on the ledge immediately outside the long window. It is its finger-nails upon the glass that produces the sound so like the hail, now that the hail has ceased. Intense fear paralysed the limbs of that beautiful girl. That one shriek is all she can utter--with hands clasped, a face of marble, a heart beating so wildly in her bosom, that each moment it seems as if it would break its confines, eyes distended and fixed upon the window, she waits, froze with horror. The pattering and clattering of the nails continue. No word is spoken, and now she fancies she can trace the darker form of that figure against the window, and she can see the long arms moving to and fro, feeling for some mode of entrance. What strange light is that which now gradually creeps up into the air? red and terrible--brighter and brighter it grows. The lightning has set fire to a mill, and the reflection of the rapidly consuming building falls upon that long window. There can be no mistake. The figure is there, still feeling for an entrance, and clattering against the glass with its long nails, that appear as if the growth of many years had been untouched. She tries to scream again but a choking sensation comes over her, and she cannot. It is too dreadful--she tries to move--each limb seems weighed down by tons of lead--she can but in a hoarse faint whisper cry,--

"Help--help--help--help!"

And that one word she repeats like a person in a dream. The red glare of the fire continues. It throws up the tall gaunt figure in hideous relief against the long window. It shows, too, upon the one portrait that is in the chamber, and that portrait appears to fix its eyes upon the attempting intruder, while the flickering light from the fire makes it look fearfully life-like. A small pane of glass is broken, and the form from without introduces a long gaunt hand, which seems utterly destitute of flesh. The fastening is removed, and one-half of the window, which opens like folding doors, is swung wide open upon its hinges.

And yet now she could not scream--she could not move. "Help!--help!--help!" was all she could say. But, oh, that look of terror that sat upon her face, it was dreadful--a look to haunt the memory for a lifetime--a look to obtrude itself upon the happiest moments, and turn them to bitterness.

The figure turns half round, and the light falls upon the face. It is perfectly white--perfectly bloodless. The eyes look like polished tin; the lips are drawn back, and the principal feature next to those dreadful eyes is the teeth--the fearful looking teeth--projecting like those of some wild animal, hideously, glaringly white, and fang-like. It approaches the bed with a strange, gliding movement. It clashes together the long nails that literally appear to hang from the finger ends. No sound comes from its lips. Is she going mad--that young and beautiful girl exposed to so much terror? she has drawn up all her limbs; she cannot even now say help. The power of articulation is gone, but the power of movement has returned to her; she can draw herself slowly along to the other side of the bed from that towards which the hideous appearance is coming.

But her eyes are fascinated. The glance of a serpent could not have produced a greater effect upon her than did the fixed gaze of those awful, metallic-looking eyes that were bent on her face. Crouching down so that the gigantic height was lost, and the horrible, protruding, white face was the most prominent object, came on the figure. What was it?--what did it want there?--what made it look so hideous--so unlike an inhabitant of the earth, and yet to be on it?

Now she has got to the verge of the bed, and the figure pauses. It seemed as if when it paused she lost the power to proceed. The clothing of the bed was now clutched in her hands with unconscious power. She drew her breath short and thick. Her bosom heaves, and her limbs tremble, yet she cannot withdraw her eyes from that marble-looking face. He holds her with his glittering eye.

The storm has ceased--all is still. The winds are hushed; the church clock proclaims the hour of one: a hissing sound comes from the throat of the hideous being, and he raises his long, gaunt arms--the lips move. He advances. The girl places one small foot from the bed on to the floor. She is unconsciously dragging the clothing with her. The door of the room is in that direction--can she reach it? Has she power to walk?--can she withdraw her eyes from the face of the intruder, and so break the hideous charm? God of Heaven! is it real, or some dream so like reality as to nearly overturn the judgment for ever?

The figure has paused again, and half on the bed and half out of it that young girl lies trembling. Her long hair streams across the entire width of the bed. As she has slowly moved along she has left it streaming across the pillows. The pause lasted about a minute--oh, what an age of agony. That minute was, indeed, enough for madness to do its full work in.

With a sudden rush that could not be foreseen--with a strange howling cry that was enough to awaken terror in every breast, the figure seized the long tresses of her hair, and twining them round his bony hands he held her to the bed. Then she screamed--Heaven granted her then power to scream. Shriek followed shriek in rapid succession. The bed-clothes fell in a heap by the side of the bed--she was dragged by her long silken hair completely on to it again. Her beautifully rounded limbs quivered with the agony of her soul. The glassy, horrible eyes of the figure ran over that angelic form with a hideous satisfaction--horrible profanation. He drags her head to the bed's edge. He forces it back by the long hair still entwined in his grasp. With a plunge he seizes her neck in his fang-like teeth--a gush of blood, and a hideous sucking noise follows. The girl has swooned, and the vampyre is at his hideous repast!

CHAPTER II

THE ALARM.--THE PISTOL SHOT.--THE PURSUIT AND ITS CONSEQUENCES

Lights flashed about the building, and various room doors opened; voices called one to the other. There was an universal stir and commotion among the inhabitants.

"Did you hear a scream, Harry?" asked a young man, half-dressed, as he walked into the chamber of another about his own age.

"I did--where was it?"

"God knows. I dressed myself directly."

"All is still now."

"Yes; but unless I was dreaming there was a scream."

"We could not both dream there was. Where did you think it came from?"

"It burst so suddenly upon my ears that I cannot say."

There was a tap now at the door of the room where these young men were, and a female voice said,--

"For God's sake, get up!"

"We are up," said both the young men, appearing.

"Did you hear anything?"

"Yes, a scream."

"Oh, search the house--search the house; where did it come from--can you tell?"

"Indeed we cannot, mother."

Another person now joined the party. He was a man of middle age, and, as he came up to them, he said,--

"Good God! what is the matter?"

Scarcely had the words passed his lips, than such a rapid succession of shrieks came upon their ears, that they felt absolutely stunned by them. The elderly lady, whom one of the young men had called mother, fainted, and would have fallen to the floor of the corridor in which they all stood, had she not been promptly supported by the last comer, who himself staggered, as those piercing cries came upon the night air. He, however, was the first to recover, for the young men seemed paralysed.

"Henry," he cried, "for God's sake support your mother. Can you doubt that these cries come from Flora's room?"

The young man mechanically supported his mother, and then the man who had just spoken darted back to his own bed-room, from whence he returned in a moment with a pair of pistols, and shouting,--

"Follow me, who can!" he bounded across the corridor in the direction of the antique apartment, from whence the cries proceeded, but which were now hushed.

That house was built for strength, and the doors were all of oak, and of considerable thickness. Unhappily, they had fastenings within, so that when the man reached the chamber of her who so much required help, he was helpless, for the door was fast.

"Flora! Flora!" he cried; "Flora, speak!"

All was still.

"Good God!" he added; "we must force the door."

"I hear a strange noise within," said the young man, who trembled violently.

"And so do I. What does it sound like?"

"I scarcely know; but it nearest resembles some animal eating, or sucking some liquid."

"What on earth can it be? Have you no weapon that will force the door? I shall go mad if I am kept here."

"I have," said the young man. "Wait here a moment."

He ran down the staircase, and presently returned with a small, but powerful, iron crow-bar.

"This will do," he said.

"It will, it will.--Give it to me."

"Has she not spoken?"

"Not a word. My mind misgives me that something very dreadful must have happened to her."

"And that odd noise!"

"Still goes on. Somehow, it curdles the very blood in my veins to hear it."

The man took the crow-bar, and with some difficulty succeeded in introducing it between the door and the side of the wall--still it required great strength to move it, but it did move, with a harsh, crackling sound.

"Push it!" cried he who was using the bar, "push the door at the same time."

The younger man did so. For a few moments the massive door resisted. Then, suddenly, something gave way with a loud snap--it was a part of the lock,--and the door at once swung wide open.

How true it is that we measure time by the events which happen within a given space of it, rather than by its actual duration.

To those who were engaged in forcing open the door of the antique chamber, where slept the young girl whom they named Flora, each moment was swelled into an hour of agony; but, in reality, from the first moment of the alarm to that when the loud cracking noise heralded the destruction of the fastenings of the door, there had elapsed but very few minutes indeed.

"It opens--it opens," cried the young man.

"Another moment," said the stranger, as he still plied the crowbar--"another moment, and we shall have free ingress to the chamber. Be patient."

This stranger's name was Marchdale; and even as he spoke, he succeeded in throwing the massive door wide open, and clearing the passage to the chamber.

To rush in with a light in his hand was the work of a moment to the young man named Henry; but the very rapid progress he made into the apartment prevented him from observing accurately what it contained, for the wind that came in from the open window caught the flame of the candle, and although it did not actually extinguish it, it blew it so much on one side, that it was comparatively useless as a light.

"Flora--Flora!" he cried.

Then with a sudden bound something dashed from off the bed. The concussion against him was so sudden and so utterly unexpected, as well as so tremendously violent, that he was thrown down, and, in his fall, the light was fairly extinguished.

All was darkness, save a dull, reddish kind of light that now and then, from the nearly consumed mill in the immediate vicinity, came into the room. But by that light, dim, uncertain, and flickering as it was, some one was seen to make for the window.

Henry, although nearly stunned by his fall, saw a figure, gigantic in height, which nearly reached from the floor to the ceiling. The other young man, George, saw it, and Mr. Marchdale likewise saw it, as did the lady who had spoken to the two young men in the corridor when first the screams of the young girl awakened alarm in the breasts of all the inhabitants of that house.

The figure was about to pass out at the window which led to a kind of balcony, from whence there was an easy descent to a garden.

Before it passed out they each and all caught a glance of the side-face, and they saw that the lower part of it and the lips were dabbled in blood. They saw, too, one of those fearful-looking, shining, metallic eyes which presented so terrible an appearance of unearthly ferocity.

No wonder that for a moment a panic seized them all, which paralysed any exertions they might otherwise have made to detain that hideous form.

But Mr. Marchdale was a man of mature years; he had seen much of life, both in this and in foreign lands; and he, although astonished to the extent of being frightened, was much more likely to recover sooner than his younger companions, which, indeed, he did, and acted promptly enough.

"Don't rise, Henry," he cried. "Lie still."

Almost at the moment he uttered these words, he fired at the figure, which then occupied the window, as if it were a gigantic figure set in a frame.

The report was tremendous in that chamber, for the pistol was no toy weapon, but one made for actual service, and of sufficient length and bore of barrel to carry destruction along with the bullets that came from it.

"If that has missed its aim," said Mr. Marchdale, "I'll never pull a trigger again."

As he spoke he dashed forward, and made a clutch at the figure he felt convinced he had shot.

The tall form turned upon him, and when he got a full view of the face, which he did at that moment, from the opportune circumstance of the lady returning at the instant with a light she had been to her own chamber to procure, even he, Marchdale, with all his courage, and that was great, and all his nervous energy, recoiled a step or two, and uttered the exclamation of, "Great God!"

That face was one never to be forgotten. It was hideously flushed with colour--the colour of fresh blood; the eyes had a savage and remarkable lustre; whereas, before, they had looked like polished tin--they now wore a ten times brighter aspect, and flashes of light seemed to dart from them. The mouth was open, as if, from the natural formation of the countenance, the lips receded much from the large canine looking teeth.

A strange howling noise came from the throat of this monstrous figure, and it seemed upon the point of rushing upon Mr. Marchdale. Suddenly, then, as if some impulse had seized upon it, it uttered a wild and terrible shrieking kind of laugh; and then turning, dashed through the window, and in one instant disappeared from before the eyes of those who felt nearly annihilated by its fearful presence.

"God help us!" ejaculated Henry.

Mr. Marchdale drew a long breath, and then, giving a stamp on the floor, as if to recover himself from the state of agitation into which even he was thrown, he cried,--

"Be it what or who it may, I'll follow it"

"No--no--do not," cried the lady.

"I must, I will. Let who will come with me--I follow that dreadful form."

As he spoke, he took the road it took, and dashed through the window into the balcony.

"And we, too, George," exclaimed Henry; "we will follow Mr. Marchdale. This dreadful affair concerns us more nearly than it does him."

The lady who was the mother of these young men, and of the beautiful girl who had been so awfully visited, screamed aloud, and implored of them to stay. But the voice of Mr. Marchdale was heard exclaiming aloud,--

"I see it--I see it; it makes for the wall."

They hesitated no longer, but at once rushed into the balcony, and from thence dropped into the garden.

The mother approached the bed-side of the insensible, perhaps the murdered girl; she saw her, to all appearance, weltering in blood, and, overcome by her emotions, she fainted on the floor of the room.

When the two young men reached the garden, they found it much lighter than might have been fairly expected; for not only was the morning rapidly approaching, but the mill was still burning, and those mingled lights made almost every object plainly visible, except when deep shadows were thrown from some gigantic trees that had stood for centuries in that sweetly wooded spot. They heard the voice of Mr. Marchdale, as he cried,--

"There--there--towards the wall. There--there--God! how it bounds along."

The young men hastily dashed through a thicket in the direction from whence his voice sounded, and then they found him looking wild and terrified, and with something in his hand which looked like a portion of clothing.

"Which way, which way?" they both cried in a breath.

He leant heavily on the arm of George, as he pointed along a vista of trees, and said in a low voice,--

"God help us all. It is not human. Look there--look there--do you not see it?"

They looked in the direction he indicated. At the end of this vista was the wall of the garden. At that point it was full twelve feet in height, and as they looked, they saw the hideous, monstrous form they had traced from the chamber of their sister, making frantic efforts to clear the obstacle.

Then they saw it bound from the ground to the top of the wall, which it very nearly reached, and then each time it fell back again into the garden with such a dull, heavy sound, that the earth seemed to shake again with the concussion. They trembled--well indeed they might, and for some minutes they watched the figure making its fruitless efforts to leave the place.

"What--what is it?" whispered Henry, in hoarse accents. "God, what can it possibly be?"

"I know not," replied Mr. Marchdale. "I did seize it. It was cold and clammy like a corpse. It cannot be human."

"Not human?"

"Look at it now. It will surely escape now."

"No, no--we will not be terrified thus--there is Heaven above us. Come on, and, for dear Flora's sake, let us make an effort yet to seize this bold intruder."

"Take this pistol," said Marchdale. "It is the fellow of the one I fired. Try its efficacy."

"He will be gone," exclaimed Henry, as at this moment, after many repeated attempts and fearful falls, the figure reached the top of the wall, and then hung by its long arms a moment or two, previous to dragging itself completely up.

The idea of the appearance, be it what it might, entirely escaping, seemed to nerve again Mr. Marchdale, and he, as well as the two young men, ran forward towards the wall. They got so close to the figure before it sprang down on the outer side of the wall, that to miss killing it with the bullet from the pistol was a matter of utter impossibility, unless wilfully.

Henry had the weapon, and he pointed it full at the tall form with a steady aim. He pulled the trigger--the explosion followed, and that the bullet did its office there could be no manner of doubt, for the figure gave a howling shriek, and fell headlong from the wall on the outside.

"I have shot him," cried Henry, "I have shot him."

CHAPTER III

THE DISAPPEARANCE OF THE BODY.--FLORA'S RECOVERY AND MADNESS.--THE OFFER OF ASSISTANCE FROM SIR FRANCIS VARNEY

"He is human!" cried Henry; "I have surely killed him."

"It would seem so," said Mr. Marchdale. "Let us now hurry round to the outside of the wall, and see where he lies."

This was at once agreed to, and the whole three of them made what expedition they could towards a gate which led into a paddock, across which they hurried, and soon found themselves clear of the garden wall, so that they could make way towards where they fully expected to find the body of him who had worn so unearthly an aspect, but who it would be an excessive relief to find was human.

So hurried was the progress they made, that it was scarcely possible to exchange many words as they went; a kind of breathless anxiety was upon them, and in the speed they disregarded every obstacle, which would, at any other time, have probably prevented them from taking the direct road they sought.

It was difficult on the outside of the wall to say exactly which was the precise spot which it might be supposed the body had fallen on; but, by following the wall in its entire length, surely they would come upon it.

They did so; but, to their surprise, they got from its commencement to its further extremity without finding any dead body, or even any symptoms of one having lain there.

At some parts close to the wall there grew a kind of heath, and, consequently, the traces of blood would be lost among it, if it so happened that at the precise spot at which the strange being had seemed to topple over, such vegetation had existed. This was to be ascertained; but now, after traversing the whole length of the wall twice, they came to a halt, and looked wonderingly in each other's faces.

"There is nothing here," said Harry.

"Nothing," added his brother.

"It could not have been a delusion," at length said Mr. Marchdale, with a shudder.

"A delusion?" exclaimed the brother! "That is not possible; we all saw it."

"Then what terrible explanation can we give?"

"By heavens! I know not," exclaimed Henry. "This adventure surpasses all belief, and but for the great interest we have in it, I should regard it with a world of curiosity."

"It is too dreadful," said George; "for God's sake, Henry, let us return to ascertain if poor Flora is killed."

"My senses," said Henry, "were all so much absorbed in gazing at that horrible form, that I never once looked towards her further than to see that she was, to appearance, dead. God help her! poor--poor, beautiful Flora. This is, indeed, a sad, sad fate for you to come to. Flora--Flora--"

"Do not weep, Henry," said George. "Rather let us now hasten home, where we may find that tears are premature. She may yet be living and restored to us."

"And," said Mr. Marchdale, "she may be able to give us some account of this dreadful visitation."

"True--true," exclaimed Henry; "we will hasten home."

They now turned their steps homeward, and as they went they much blamed themselves for all leaving home together, and with terror pictured what might occur in their absence to those who were now totally unprotected.

"It was a rash impulse of us all to come in pursuit of this dreadful figure," remarked Mr. Marchdale; "but do not torment yourself, Henry. There may be no reason for your fears."

At the pace they went, they very soon reached the ancient house, and when they came in sight of it, they saw lights flashing from the windows, and the shadows of faces moving to and fro, indicating that the whole household was up, and in a state of alarm.

Henry, after some trouble, got the hall door opened by a terrified servant, who was trembling so much that she could scarcely hold the light she had with her.

"Speak at once, Martha," said Henry. "Is Flora living?"

"Yes; but--"

"Enough--enough! Thank God she lives; where is she now?"

"In her own room, Master Henry. Oh, dear--oh, dear, what will become of us all?"

Henry rushed up the staircase, followed by George and Mr. Marchdale, nor paused he once until he reached the room of his sister.

"Mother," he said, before he crossed the threshold, "are you here?"

"I am, my dear--I am. Come in, pray come in, and speak to poor Flora."

"Come in, Mr. Marchdale," said Henry--"come in; we make no stranger of you."

They all then entered the room.

Several lights had been now brought into that antique chamber, and, in addition to the mother of the beautiful girl who had been so fearfully visited, there were two female domestics, who appeared to be in the greatest possible fright, for they could render no assistance whatever to anybody.

The tears were streaming down the mother's face, and the moment she saw Mr. Marchdale, she clung to his arm, evidently unconscious of what she was about, and exclaimed,--

"Oh, what is this that has happened--what is this? Tell me, Marchdale! Robert Marchdale, you whom I have known even from my childhood, you will not deceive me. Tell me the meaning of all this?"

"I cannot," he said, in a tone of much emotion. "As God is my judge, I am as much puzzled and amazed at the scene that has taken place here to-night as you can be."

The mother wrung her hands and wept.

"It was the storm that first awakened me," added Marchdale; "and then I heard a scream."

The brothers tremblingly approached the bed. Flora was placed in a sitting, half-reclining posture, propped up by pillows. She was quite insensible, and her face was fearfully pale; while that she breathed at all could be but very faintly seen. On some of her clothing, about the neck, were spots of blood, and she looked more like one who had suffered some long and grievous illness, than a young girl in the prime of life and in the most robust health, as she had been on the day previous to the strange scene we have recorded.

"Does she sleep?" said Henry, as a tear fell from his eyes upon her pallid cheek.

"No," replied Mr. Marchdale. "This is a swoon, from which we must recover her."

Active measures were now adopted to restore the languid circulation, and, after persevering in them for some time, they had the satisfaction of seeing her open her eyes.

Her first act upon consciousness returning, however, was to utter a loud shriek, and it was not until Henry implored her to look around her, and see that she was surrounded by none but friendly faces, that she would venture again to open her eyes, and look timidly from one to the other. Then she shuddered, and burst into tears as she said,--

"Oh, Heaven, have mercy upon me--Heaven, have mercy upon me, and save me from that dreadful form."

"There is no one here, Flora," said Mr. Marchdale, "but those who love you, and who, in defence of you, if needs were would lay down their lives."

"Oh, God! Oh, God!"

"You have been terrified. But tell us distinctly what has happened? You are quite safe now."

She trembled so violently that Mr. Marchdale recommended that some stimulant should be given to her, and she was persuaded, although not without considerable difficulty, to swallow a small portion of some wine from a cup. There could be no doubt but that the stimulating effect of the wine was beneficial, for a slight accession of colour visited her cheeks, and she spoke in a firmer tone as she said,--

"Do not leave me. Oh, do not leave me, any of you. I shall die if left alone now. Oh, save me--save me. That horrible form! That fearful face!"

"Tell us how it happened, dear Flora?" said Henry.

"Or would you rather endeavour to get some sleep first?" suggested Mr. Marchdale.

"No--no--no," she said, "I do not think I shall ever sleep again."

"Say not so; you will be more composed in a few hours, and then you can tell us what has occurred."

"I will tell you now. I will tell you now."

She placed her hands over her face for a moment, as if to collect her scattered, thoughts, and then she added,--

"I was awakened by the storm, and I saw that terrible apparition at the window. I think I screamed, but I could not fly. Oh, God! I could not fly. It came--it seized me by the hair. I know no more. I know no more."

She passed her hand across her neck several times, and Mr. Marchdale said, in an anxious voice,--

"You seem, Flora, to have hurt your neck--there is a wound."

"A wound!" said the mother, and she brought a light close to the bed, where all saw on the side of Flora's neck a small punctured wound; or, rather two, for there was one a little distance from the other.

It was from these wounds the blood had come which was observable upon her night clothing.

"How came these wounds?" said Henry.

"I do not know," she replied. "I feel very faint and weak, as if I had almost bled to death."

"You cannot have done so, dear Flora, for there are not above half-a-dozen spots of blood to be seen at all."

Mr. Marchdale leaned against the carved head of the bed for support, and he uttered a deep groan. All eyes were turned upon him, and Henry said, in a voice of the most anxious inquiry,--

"You have something to say, Mr. Marchdale, which will throw some light upon this affair."

"No, no, no, nothing!" cried Mr. Marchdale, rousing himself at once from the appearance of depression that had come over him. "I have nothing to say, but that I think Flora had better get some sleep if she can."

"No sleep-no sleep for me," again screamed Flora. "Dare I be alone to sleep?"

"But you shall not be alone, dear Flora," said Henry. "I will sit by your bedside and watch you."

She took his hand in both hers, and while the tears chased each other down her cheeks, she said,--

"Promise me, Henry, by all your hopes of Heaven, you will not leave me."

"I promise!"

She gently laid herself down, with a deep sigh, and closed her eyes.

"She is weak, and will sleep long," said Mr. Marchdale.

"You sigh," said Henry. "Some fearful thoughts, I feel certain, oppress your heart."

"Hush-hush!" said Mr. Marchdale, as he pointed to Flora. "Hush! not here--not here."

"I understand," said Henry.

"Let her sleep."

There was a silence of some few minutes duration. Flora had dropped into a deep slumber. That silence was first broken by George, who said,--

"Mr. Marchdale, look at that portrait."

He pointed to the portrait in the frame to which we have alluded, and the moment Marchdale looked at it he sunk into a chair as he exclaimed,--

"Gracious Heaven, how like!"

"It is--it is," said Henry. "Those eyes--"

"And see the contour of the countenance, and the strange shape of the mouth."

"Exact--exact."

"That picture shall be moved from here. The sight of it is at once sufficient to awaken all her former terrors in poor Flora's brain if she should chance to awaken and cast her eyes suddenly upon it."

"And is it so like him who came here?" said the mother.

"It is the very man himself," said Mr. Marchdale. "I have not been in this house long enough to ask any of you whose portrait that may be?"

"It is," said Henry, "the portrait of Sir Runnagate Bannerworth, an ancestor of ours, who first, by his vices, gave the great blow to the family prosperity."

"Indeed. How long ago?"

"About ninety years."

"Ninety years. 'Tis a long while--ninety years."

"You muse upon it."

"No, no. I do wish, and yet I dread--"

"What?"

"To say something to you all. But not here--not here. We will hold a consultation on this matter to-morrow. Not now--not now."

"The daylight is coming quickly on," said Henry; "I shall keep my sacred promise of not moving from this room until Flora awakens; but there can be no occasion for the detention of any of you. One is sufficient here. Go all of you, and endeavour to procure what rest you can."

"I will fetch you my powder-flask and bullets," said Mr. Marchdale; "and you can, if you please, reload the pistols. In about two hours more it will be broad daylight."

This arrangement was adopted. Henry did reload the pistols, and placed them on a table by the side of the bed, ready for immediate action, and then, as Flora was sleeping soundly, all left the room but himself.

Mrs. Bannerworth was the last to do so. She would have remained, but for the earnest solicitation of Henry, that she would endeavour to get some sleep to make up for her broken night's repose, and she was indeed so broken down by her alarm on Flora's account, that she had not power to resist, but with tears flowing from her eyes, she sought her own chamber.

And now the calmness of the night resumed its sway in that evil-fated mansion; and although no one really slept but Flora, all were still. Busy thought kept every one else wakeful. It was a mockery to lie down at all, and Henry, full of strange and painful feelings as he was, preferred his present position to the anxiety and apprehension on Flora's account which he knew he should feel if she were not within the sphere of his own observation, and she slept as soundly as some gentle infant tired of its playmates and its sports.

CHAPTER IV

THE MORNING.--THE CONSULTATION.--THE FEARFUL SUGGESTION

What wonderfully different impressions and feelings, with regard to the same circumstances, come across the mind in the broad, clear, and beautiful light of day to what haunt the imagination, and often render the judgment almost incapable of action, when the heavy shadow of night is upon all things.

There must be a downright physical reason for this effect--it is so remarkable and so universal. It seems that the sun's rays so completely alter and modify the constitution of the atmosphere, that it produces, as we inhale it, a wonderfully different effect upon the nerves of the human subject.

We can account for this phenomenon in no other way. Perhaps never in his life had he, Henry Bannerworth, felt so strongly this transition of feeling as he now felt it, when the beautiful daylight gradually dawned upon him, as he kept his lonely watch by the bedside of his slumbering sister.

That watch had been a perfectly undisturbed one. Not the least sight or sound of any intrusion had reached his senses. All had been as still as the very grave.

And yet while the night lasted, and he was more indebted to the rays of the candle, which he had placed upon a shelf, for the power to distinguish objects than to the light of the morning, a thousand uneasy and strange sensations had found a home in his agitated bosom.

He looked so many times at the portrait which was in the panel that at length he felt an undefined sensation of terror creep over him whenever he took his eyes off it.

He tried to keep himself from looking at it, but he found it vain, so he adopted what, perhaps, was certainly the wisest, best plan, namely, to look at it continually.

He shifted his chair so that he could gaze upon it without any effort, and he placed the candle so that a faint light was thrown upon it, and there he sat, a prey to many conflicting and uncomfortable feelings, until the daylight began to make the candle flame look dull and sickly.

Solution for the events of the night he could find none. He racked his imagination in vain to find some means, however vague, of endeavouring to account for what occurred, and still he was at fault. All was to him wrapped in the gloom of the most profound mystery.

And how strangely, too, the eyes of that portrait appeared to look upon him--as if instinct with life, and as if the head to which they belonged was busy in endeavouring to find out the secret communings of his soul. It was wonderfully well executed that portrait; so life-like, that the very features seemed to move as you gazed upon them.

"It shall be removed," said Henry. "I would remove it now, but that it seems absolutely painted on the panel, and I should awake Flora in any attempt to do so."

He arose and ascertained that such was the case, and that it would require a workman, with proper tools adapted to the job, to remove the portrait.

"True," he said, "I might now destroy it, but it is a pity to obscure a work of such rare art as this is; I should blame myself if I were. It shall be removed to some other room of the house, however."

Then, all of a sudden, it struck Henry how foolish it would be to remove the portrait from the wall of a room which, in all likelihood, after that night, would be uninhabited; for it was not probable that Flora would choose again to inhabit a chamber in which she had gone through so much terror.

"It can be left where it is," he said, "and we can fasten up, if we please, even the very door of this room, so that no one need trouble themselves any further about it."

The morning was now coming fast, and just as Henry thought he would partially draw a blind across the window, in order to shield from the direct rays of the sun the eyes of Flora, she awoke.

"Help--help!" she cried, and Henry was by her side in a moment.

"You are safe, Flora--you are safe," he said.

"Where is it now?" she said.

"What--what, dear Flora?"

"The dreadful apparition. Oh, what have I done to be made thus perpetually miserable?"

"Think no more of it, Flora."

"I must think. My brain is on fire! A million of strange eyes seem gazing on me."

"Great Heaven! she raves," said Henry.

"Hark--hark--hark! He comes on the wings of the storm. Oh, it is most horrible--horrible!"

Henry rang the bell, but not sufficiently loudly to create any alarm. The sound reached the waking ear of the mother, who in a few moments was in the room.

"She has awakened," said Henry, "and has spoken, but she seems to me to wander in her discourse. For God's sake, soothe her, and try to bring her mind round to its usual state."

"I will, Henry--I will."

"And I think, mother, if you were to get her out of this room, and into some other chamber as far removed from this one as possible, it would tend to withdraw her mind from what has occurred."

"Yes; it shall be done. Oh, Henry, what was it--what do you think it was?"

"I am lost in a sea of wild conjecture. I can form no conclusion; where is Mr. Marchdale?"

"I believe in his chamber."

"Then I will go and consult with him."

Henry proceeded at once to the chamber, which was, as he knew, occupied by Mr. Marchdale; and as he crossed the corridor, he could not but pause a moment to glance from a window at the face of nature.

As is often the case, the terrific storm of the preceding evening had cleared the air, and rendered it deliciously invigorating and life-like. The weather had been dull, and there had been for some days a certain heaviness in the atmosphere, which was now entirely removed.

The morning sun was shining with uncommon brilliancy, birds were singing in every tree and on every bush; so pleasant, so spirit-stirring, health-giving a morning, seldom had he seen. And the effect upon his spirits was great, although not altogether what it might have been, had all gone on as it usually was in the habit of doing at that house. The ordinary little casualties of evil fortune had certainly from time to time, in the shape of illness, and one thing or another, attacked the family of the Bannerworths in common with every other family, but here suddenly had arisen a something at once terrible and inexplicable.

He found Mr. Marchdale up and dressed, and apparently in deep and anxious thought. The moment he saw Henry, he said,--

"Flora is awake, I presume."

"Yes, but her mind appears to be much disturbed."

"From bodily weakness, I dare say."

"But why should she be bodily weak? she was strong and well, ay, as well as she could ever be in all her life. The glow of youth and health was on her cheeks. Is it possible that, in the course of one night, she should become bodily weak to such an extent?"

"Henry," said Mr. Marchdale, sadly, "sit down. I am not, as you know, a superstitious man."

"You certainly are not."

"And yet, I never in all my life was so absolutely staggered as I have been by the occurrences of to-night."

"Say on."

"There is a frightful, a hideous solution of them; one which every consideration will tend to add strength to, one which I tremble to name now, although, yesterday, at this hour, I should have laughed it to scorn."

"Indeed!"

"Yes, it is so. Tell no one that which I am about to say to you. Let the dreadful suggestion remain with ourselves alone, Henry Bannerworth."

"I--I am lost in wonder."

"You promise me?"

"What--what?"

"That you will not repeat my opinion to any one."

"I do."

"On your honour."

"On my honour, I promise."

Mr. Marchdale rose, and proceeding to the door, he looked out to see that there were no listeners near. Having ascertained then that they were quite alone, he returned, and drawing a chair close to that on which Henry sat, he said,--

"Henry, have you never heard of a strange and dreadful superstition which, in some countries, is extremely rife, by which it is supposed that there are beings who never die."

"Never die!"

"Never. In a word, Henry, have you never heard of--of--I dread to pronounce the word."

"Speak it. God of Heaven! let me hear it."

"A vampyre!"

Henry sprung to his feet. His whole frame quivered with emotion; the drops of perspiration stood upon his brow, as, in, a strange, hoarse voice, he repeated the words,--

"A vampyre!"

"Even so; one who has to renew a dreadful existence by human blood--one who lives on for ever, and must keep up such a fearful existence upon human gore--one who eats not and drinks not as other men--a vampyre."

Henry dropped into his scat, and uttered a deep groan of the most exquisite anguish.

"I could echo that groan," said Marchdale, "but that I am so thoroughly bewildered I know not what to think."

"Good God--good God!"

"Do not too readily yield belief in so dreadful a supposition, I pray you."

"Yield belief!" exclaimed Henry, as he rose, and lifted up one of his hands above his head. "No; by Heaven, and the great God of all, who there rules, I will not easily believe aught so awful and so monstrous."

"I applaud your sentiment, Henry; not willingly would I deliver up myself to so frightful a belief--it is too horrible. I merely have told you of that which you saw was on my mind. You have surely before heard of such things."

"I have--I have."

"I much marvel, then, that the supposition did not occur to you, Henry."

"It did not--it did not, Marchdale. It--it was too dreadful, I suppose, to find a home in my heart. Oh! Flora, Flora, if this horrible idea should once occur to you, reason cannot, I am quite sure, uphold you against it."

"Let no one presume to insinuate it to her, Henry. I would not have it mentioned to her for worlds."

"Nor I--nor I. Good God! I shudder at the very thought--the mere possibility; but there is no possibility, there can be none. I will not believe it."

"Nor I."

"No; by Heaven's justice, goodness, grace, and mercy, I will not believe it."

"Tis well sworn, Henry; and now, discarding the supposition that Flora has been visited by a vampyre, let us seriously set about endeavouring, if we can, to account for what has happened in this house."

"I--I cannot now."

"Nay, let us examine the matter; if we can find any natural explanation, let us cling to it, Henry, as the sheet-anchor of our very souls."

"Do you think. You are fertile in expedients. Do you think, Marchdale; and, for Heaven's sake, and for the sake of our own peace, find out some other way of accounting for what has happened, than the hideous one you have suggested."

"And yet my pistol bullets hurt him not; he has left the tokens of his presence on the neck of Flora."

"Peace, oh! peace. Do not, I pray you, accumulate reasons why I should receive such a dismal, awful superstition. Oh, do not, Marchdale, as you love me!"

"You know that my attachment to you," said Marchdale, "is sincere; and yet, Heaven help us!"

His voice was broken by grief as he spoke, and he turned aside his head to hide the bursting tears that would, despite all his efforts, show themselves in his eyes.

"Marchdale," added Henry, after a pause of some moments' duration, "I will sit up to-night with my sister."

"Do--do!"

"Think you there is a chance it may come again?"

"I cannot--I dare not speculate upon the coming of so dreadful a visitor, Henry; but I will hold watch with you most willingly."

"You will, Marchdale?"

"My hand upon it. Come what dangers may, I will share them with you, Henry."

"A thousand thanks. Say nothing, then, to George of what we have been talking about. He is of a highly susceptible nature, and the very idea of such a thing would kill him."

"I will; be mute. Remove your sister to some other chamber, let me beg of you, Henry; the one she now inhabits will always be suggestive of horrible thoughts."

"I will; and that dreadful-looking portrait, with its perfect likeness to him who came last night."

"Perfect indeed. Do you intend to remove it?"

"I do not. I thought of doing so; but it is actually on the panel in the wall, and I would not willingly destroy it, and it may as well remain where it is in that chamber, which I can readily now believe will become henceforward a deserted one in this house."

"It may well become such."

"Who comes here? I hear a step."

There was a tip at the door at this moment, and George made his appearance in answer to the summons to come in. He looked pale and ill; his face betrayed how much he had mentally suffered during that night, and almost directly he got into the bed-chamber he said,--

"I shall, I am sure, be censured by you both for what I am going to say; but I cannot help saying it, nevertheless, for to keep it to myself would destroy me."

"Good God, George! what is it?" said Mr. Marchdale.

"Speak it out!" said Henry.

"I have been thinking of what has occurred here, and the result of that thought has been one of the wildest suppositions that ever I thought I should have to entertain. Have you never heard of a vampyre?"

Henry sighed deeply, and Marchdale was silent.

"I say a vampyre," added George, with much excitement in his manner. "It is a fearful, a horrible supposition; but our poor, dear Flora has been visited by a vampyre, and I shall go completely mad!"

He sat down, and covering his face with his hands, he wept bitterly and abundantly.

"George," said Henry, when he saw that the frantic grief had in some measure abated--"be calm, George, and endeavour to listen to me."

"I hear, Henry."

"Well, then, do not suppose that you are the only one in this house to whom so dreadful a superstition has occurred."

"Not the only one?"

"No; it has occurred to Mr. Marchdale also."

"Gracious Heaven!"

"He mentioned it to me; but we have both agreed to repudiate it with horror."

"To--repudiate--it?"

"Yes, George."

"And yet--and yet--"

"Hush, hush! I know what you would say. You would tell us that our repudiation of it cannot affect the fact. Of that we are aware; but yet will we disbelieve that which a belief in would be enough to drive us mad."

"What do you intend to do?"

"To keep this supposition to ourselves, in the first place; to guard it most zealously from the ears of Flora."

"Do you think she has ever heard of vampyres?"

"I never heard her mention that in all her reading she had gathered even a hint of such a fearful superstition. If she has, we must be guided by circumstances, and do the best we can."

"Pray Heaven she may not!"

"Amen to that prayer, George," said Henry. "Mr. Marchdale and I intend to keep watch over Flora to-night."

"May not I join you?"

"Your health, dear George, will not permit you to engage in such matters. Do you seek your natural repose, and leave it to us to do the best we can in this most fearful and terrible emergency."

"As you please, brother, and as you please, Mr. Marchdale. I know I am a frail reed, and my belief is that this affair will kill me quite. The truth is, I am horrified--utterly and frightfully horrified. Like my poor, dear sister, I do not believe I shall ever sleep again."

"Do not fancy that, George," said Marchdale. "You very much add to the uneasiness which must be your poor mother's portion, by allowing this circumstance to so much affect you. You well know her affection for you all, and let me therefore, as a very old friend of hers, entreat you to wear as cheerful an aspect as you can in her presence."

"For once in my life," said George, sadly, "I will; to my dear mother, endeavour to play the hypocrite."

"Do so," said Henry. "The motive will sanction any such deceit as that, George, be assured."

The day wore on, and Poor Flora remained in a very precarious situation. It was not until mid-day that Henry made up his mind he would call in a medical gentleman to her, and then he rode to the neighbouring market-town, where he knew an extremely intelligent practitioner resided. This gentleman Henry resolved upon, under a promise of secrecy, makings confidant of; but, long before he reached him, he found he might well dispense with the promise of secrecy.

He had never thought, so engaged had he been with other matters, that the servants were cognizant of the whole affair, and that from them he had no expectation of being able to keep the whole story in all its details. Of course such an opportunity for tale-bearing and gossiping was not likely to be lost; and while Henry was thinking over how he had better act in the matter, the news that Flora Bannerworth had been visited in the night by a vampyre--for the servants named the visitation such at once--was spreading all over the county.

As he rode along, Henry met a gentleman on horseback who belonged to the county, and who, reining in his steed, said to him,

"Good morning, Mr. Bannerworth."

"Good morning," responded Henry, and he would have ridden on, but the gentleman added,--

"Excuse me for interrupting you, sir; but what is the strange story that is in everybody's mouth about a vampyre?"

Henry nearly fell off his horse, he was so much astonished, and, wheeling the animal around, he said,--

"In everybody's mouth!"

"Yes; I have heard it from at least a dozen persons."

"You surprise me."

"It is untrue? Of course I am not so absurd as really to believe about the vampyre; but is there no foundation at all for it? We generally find that at the bottom of these common reports there is a something around which, as a nucleus, the whole has formed."

"My sister is unwell."

"Ah, and that's all. It really is too bad, now."

"We had a visitor last night."

"A thief, I suppose?"

"Yes, yes--I believe a thief. I do believe it was a thief, and she was terrified."

"Of course, and upon such a thing is grafted a story of a vampyre, and the marks of his teeth being in her neck, and all the circumstantial particulars."

"Yes, yes."

"Good morning, Mr. Bannerworth."

Henry bade the gentleman good morning, and much vexed at the publicity which the affair had already obtained, he set spurs to his horse, determined that he would speak to no one else upon so uncomfortable a theme. Several attempts were made to stop him, but he only waved his hand and trotted on, nor did he pause in his speed till he reached the door of Mr. Chillingworth, the medical man whom he intended to consult.

Henry knew that at such a time he would be at home, which was the case, and he was soon closeted with the man of drugs. Henry begged his patient hearing, which being accorded, he related to him at full length what had happened, not omitting, to the best of his remembrance, any one particular. When he had concluded his narration, the doctor shifted his position several times, and then said,--

"That's all?"

"Yes--and enough too."

"More than enough, I should say, my young friend. You astonish me."

"Can you form any supposition, sir, on the subject?"

"Not just now. What is your own idea?"

"I cannot be said to have one about it. It is too absurd to tell you that my brother George is impressed with a belief a vampyre has visited the house."

"I never in all my life heard a more circumstantial narrative in favour of so hideous a superstition."

"Well, but you cannot believe--"

"Believe what?"

"That the dead can come to life again, and by such a process keep up vitality."

"Do you take me for a fool?"

"Certainly not."

"Then why do you ask me such questions?"

"But the glaring facts of the case."

"I don't care if they were ten times more glaring, I won't believe it. I would rather believe you were all mad, the whole family of you--that at the full of the moon you all were a little cracked."

"And so would I."

"You go home now, and I will call and see your sister in the course of two hours. Something may turn up yet, to throw some new light upon this strange subject."

With this understanding Henry went home, and he took care to ride as fast as before, in order to avoid questions, so that he got back to his old ancestral home without going through the disagreeable ordeal of having to explain to any one what had disturbed the peace of it.

When Henry reached his home, he found that the evening was rapidly coming on, and before he could permit himself to think upon any other subject, he inquired how his terrified sister had passed the hours during his absence.

He found that but little improvement had taken place in her, and that she had occasionally slept, but to awaken and speak incoherently, as if the shock she had received had had some serious affect upon her nerves. He repaired at once to her room, and, finding that she was awake, he leaned over her, and spoke tenderly to her.

"Flora," he said, "dear Flora, you are better now?"

"Harry, is that you?"

"Yes, dear."

"Oh, tell me what has happened?"

"Have you not a recollection, Flora?"

"Yes, yes, Henry; but what was it? They none of them will tell me what it was, Henry."

"Be calm, dear. No doubt some attempt to rob the house."

"Think you so?"

"Yes; the bay window was peculiarly adapted for such a purpose; but now that you are removed here to this room, you will be able to rest in peace."

"I shall die of terror, Henry. Even now those eyes are glaring on me so hidiously. Oh, it is fearful--it is very fearful, Henry. Do you not pity me, and no one will promise to remain with me at night."

"Indeed, Flora, you are mistaken, for I intend to sit by your bedside armed, and so preserve you from all harm."

She clutched his hand eagerly, as she said,--

"You will, Henry. You will, and not think it too much trouble, dear Henry."

"It can be no trouble, Flora."

"Then I shall rest in peace, for I know that the dreadful vampyre cannot come to me when you are by-"

"The what, Flora!"

"The vampyre, Henry. It was a vampyre."

"Good God, who told you so?"

"No one. I have read of them in the book of travels in Norway, which Mr. Marchdale lent us all."

"Alas, alas!" groaned Henry. "Discard, I pray you, such a thought from your mind."

"Can we discard thoughts. What power have we but from that mind, which is ourselves?"

"True, true."

"Hark, what noise is that? I thought I heard a noise. Henry, when you go, ring for some one first. Was there not a noise?"

"The accidental shutting of some door, dear."

"Was it that?"

"It was."

"Then I am relieved. Henry, I sometimes fancy I am in the tomb, and that some one is feasting on my flesh. They do say, too, that those who in life have been bled by a vampyre, become themselves vampyres, and have the same horrible taste for blood as those before them. Is it not horrible?"

"You only vex yourself by such thoughts, Flora. Mr. Chillingworth is coming to see you."

"Can he minister to a mind diseased?"

"But yours is not, Flora. Your mind is healthful, and so, although his power extends not so far, we will thank Heaven, dear Flora, that you need it not."

She sighed deeply, as she said,--

"Heaven help me! I know not, Henry. The dreadful being held on by my hair. I must have it all taken off. I tried to get away, but it dragged me back--a brutal thing it was. Oh, then at that moment, Henry, I felt as if something strange took place in my brain, and that I was going mad! I saw those glazed eyes close to, mine--I felt a hot, pestiferous breath upon my face--help--help!"

"Hush! my Flora, hush! Look at me."

"I am calm again. It fixed its teeth in my throat. Did I faint away?"

"You did, dear; but let me pray you to refer all this to imagination; or at least the greater part of it."

"But you saw it."

"Yes--"

"All saw it."

"We all saw some man--a housebreaker--It must have been some housebreaker. What more easy, you know, dear Flora, than to assume some such disguise?"

"Was anything stolen?"

"Not that I know of; but there was an alarm, you know."

Flora shook her head, as she said, in a low voice,--

"That which came here was more than mortal. Oh, Henry, if it had but killed me, now I had been happy; but I cannot live--I hear it breathing now."

"Talk of something else, dear Flora," said the much distressed Henry; "you will make yourself much worse, if you indulge yourself in these strange fancies."

"Oh, that they were but fancies!"

"They are, believe me."

"There is a strange confusion in my brain, and sleep comes over me suddenly, when I least expect it. Henry, Henry, what I was, I shall never, never be again."

"Say not so. All this will pass away like a dream, and leave so faint a trace upon your memory, that the time will come when you will wonder it ever made so deep an impression on your mind."

"You utter these words, Henry," she said, "but they do not come from your heart. Ah, no, no, no! Who comes?"

The door was opened by Mrs. Bannerworth, who said,--

"It is only me, my dear. Henry, here is Dr. Chillingworth in the dining-room."

Henry turned to Flora, saying,--

"You will see him, dear Flora? You know Mr. Chillingworth well."

"Yes, Henry, yes, I will see him, or whoever you please."

"Shew Mr. Chillingworth up," said Henry to the servant.

In a few moments the medical man was in the room, and he at once approached the bedside to speak to Flora, upon whose pale countenance he looked with evident interest, while at the same time it seemed mingled with a painful feeling--at least so his own face indicated.

"Well, Miss Bannerworth," he said, "what is all this I hear about an ugly dream you have had?"

"A dream?" said Flora, as she fixed her beautiful eyes on his face.

"Yes, as I understand."

She shuddered, and was silent.

"Was it not a dream, then?" added Mr. Chillingworth.

She wrung her hands, and in a voice of extreme anguish and pathos, said,--

"Would it were a dream--would it were a dream! Oh, if any one could but convince me it was a dream!"

"Well, will you tell me what it was?"

"Yes, sir, it was a vampyre."

Mr. Chillingworth glanced at Henry, as he said, in reply to Flora's words,--

"I suppose that is, after all, another name, Flora, for the nightmare?"

"No--no--no!"

"Do you really, then, persist in believing anything so absurd, Miss Bannerworth?"

"What can I say to the evidence of my own senses?" she replied. "I saw it, Henry saw it, George saw, Mr. Marchdale, my mother--all saw it. We could not all be at the same time the victims of the same delusion."

"How faintly you speak."

"I am very faint and ill."

"Indeed. What wound is that on your neck?"

A wild expression came over the face of Flora; a spasmodic action of the muscles, accompanied with a shuddering, as if a sudden chill had come over the whole mass of blood took place, and she said,--

"It is the mark left by the teeth of the vampyre."

The smile was a forced one upon the face of Mr. Chillingworth.

"Draw up the blind of the window, Mr. Henry," he said, "and let me examine this puncture to which your sister attaches so extraordinary a meaning."

The blind was drawn up, and a strong light was thrown into the room. For full two minutes Mr. Chillingworth attentively examined the two small wounds in the neck of Flora. He took a powerful magnifying glass from his pocket, and looked at them through it, and after his examination was concluded, he said,--

"They are very trifling wounds, indeed."

"But how inflicted?" said Henry.

"By some insect, I should say, which probably--it being the season for many insects--has flown in at the window."

"I know the motive," said Flora "which prompts all these suggestions it is a kind one, and I ought to be the last to quarrel with it; but what I have seen, nothing can make me believe I saw not, unless I am, as once or twice I have thought myself, really mad."

"How do you now feel in general health?"

"Far from well; and a strange drowsiness at times creeps over me. Even now I feel it."

She sunk back on the pillows as she spoke and closed her eyes with a deep sigh.

Mr. Chillingworth beckoned Henry to come with him from the room, but the latter had promised that he would remain with Flora; and as Mrs. Bannerworth had left the chamber because she was unable to control her feelings, he rang the bell, and requested that his mother would come.

She did so, and then Henry went down stairs along with the medical man, whose opinion he was certainly eager to be now made acquainted with.

As soon as they were alone in an old-fashioned room which was called the oak closet, Henry turned to Mr. Chillingworth, and said,--

"What, now, is your candid opinion, sir? You have seen my sister, and those strange indubitable evidences of something wrong."

"I have; and to tell you candidly the truth, Mr. Henry, I am sorely perplexed."

"I thought you would be."

"It is not often that a medical man likes to say so much, nor is it, indeed, often prudent that he should do so, but in this case I own I am much puzzled. It is contrary to all my notions upon all such subjects."

"Those wounds, what do you think of them?"

"I know not what to think. I am completely puzzled as regards them."

"But, but do they not really bear the appearance of being bites?"

"They really do."

"And so far, then, they are actually in favour of the dreadful supposition which poor Flora entertains."

"So far they certainly are. I have no doubt in the world of their being bites; but we not must jump to a conclusion that the teeth which inflicted them were human. It is a strange case, and one which I feel assured must give you all much uneasiness, as, indeed, it gave me; but, as I said before, I will not let my judgment give in to the fearful and degrading superstition which all the circumstances connected with this strange story would seem to justify."

"It is a degrading superstition."

"To my mind your sister seems to be labouring under the effect of some narcotic."

"Indeed!"

"Yes; unless she really has lost a quantity of blood, which loss has decreased the heart's action sufficiently to produce the languor under which she now evidently labours."

"Oh, that I could believe the former supposition, but I am confident she has taken no narcotic; she could not even do so by mistake, for there is no drug of the sort in the house. Besides, she is not heedless by any means. I am quite convinced she has not done so."

"Then I am fairly puzzled, my young friend, and I can only say that I would freely have given half of what I am worth to see that figure you saw last night."

"What would you have done?"

"I would not have lost sight of it for the world's wealth."

"You would have felt your blood freeze with horror. The face was terrible."

"And yet let it lead me where it liked I would have followed it."

"I wish you had been here."

"I wish to Heaven I had. If I though there was the least chance of another visit I would come and wait with patience every night for a month."

"I cannot say," replied Henry. "I am going to sit up to-night with my sister, and I believe, our friend Mr. Marchdale will share my watch with me."

Mr. Chillingworth appeared to be for a few moments lost in thought, and then suddenly rousing himself, as if he found it either impossible to come to any rational conclusion upon the subject, or had arrived at one which he chose to keep to himself, he said,--

"Well, well, we must leave the matter at present as it stands. Time may accomplish something towards its development, but at present so palpable a mystery I never came across, or a matter in which human calculation was so completely foiled."

"Nor I--nor I."

"I will send you some medicines, such as I think will be of service to Flora, and depend upon seeing me by ten o'clock to-morrow morning."

"You have, of course, heard something," said Henry to the doctor, as he was pulling on his gloves, "about vampyres."

"I certainly have, and I understand that in some countries, particularly Norway and Sweden, the superstition is a very common one."

"And in the Levant."

"Yes. The ghouls of the Mahometans are of the same description of beings. All that I have heard of the European vampyre has made it a being which can be killed, but is restored to life again by the rays of a full moon falling on the body."

"Yes, yes, I have heard as much."

"And that the hideous repast of blood has to be taken very frequently, and that if the vampyre gets it not he wastes away, presenting the appearance of one in the last stage of a consumption, and visibly, so to speak, dying."

"That is what I have understood."

"To-night, do you know, Mr. Bannerworth, is the full of the moon."

Henry started.

"If now you had succeeded in killing--. Pshaw, what am I saying. I believe I am getting foolish, and that the horrible superstition is beginning to fasten itself upon me as well as upon all of you. How strangely the fancy will wage war with the judgment in such a way as this."

"The full of the moon," repeated Henry, as he glanced towards the window, "and the night is near at hand."

"Banish these thoughts from your mind," said the doctor, "or else, my young friend, you will make yourself decidedly ill. Good evening to you, for it is evening. I shall see you to-morrow morning."

Mr. Chillingworth appeared now to be anxious to go, and Henry no longer opposed his departure; but when he was gone a sense of great loneliness came over him.

"To-night," he repeated, "is the full of the moon. How strange that this dreadful adventure should have taken place just the night before. 'Tis very strange. Let me see--let me see."

He took from the shelves of a book case the work which Flora had mentioned, entitled, "Travels in Norway," in which work he found some account of the popular belief in vampyres.

He opened the work at random, and then some of the leaves turned over of themselves to a particular place, as the leaves of a book will frequently do when it has been kept open a length of time at that part, and the binding stretched there more than anywhere else. There was a note at the bottom of one of the pages at this part of the book, and Henry read as follows:--

"With regard to these vampyres, it is believed by those who are inclined to give credence to so dreadful a superstition, that they always endeavour to make their feast of blood, for the revival of their bodily powers, on some evening immediately preceding a full moon, because if any accident befal them, such as being shot, or otherwise killed or wounded, they can recover by lying down somewhere where the full moon's rays will fall upon them."

Henry let the book drop from his hands with a groan and a shudder.

CHAPTER V

THE NIGHT WATCH.--THE PROPOSAL.--THE MOONLIGHT.--THE FEARFUL ADVENTURE

A kind of stupefaction came over Henry Bannerworth, and he sat for about a quarter of an hour scarcely conscious of where he was, and almost incapable of anything in the shape of rational thought. It was his brother, George, who roused him by saying, as he laid his hand upon his shoulder,--

"Henry, are you asleep?"

Henry had not been aware of his presence, and he started up as if he had been shot.

"Oh, George, is it you?" he said.

"Yes, Henry, are you unwell?"

"No, no; I was in a deep reverie."

"Alas! I need not ask upon what subject," said George, sadly. "I sought you to bring you this letter."

"A letter to me?"

"Yes, you see it is addressed to you, and the seal looks as if it came from someone of consequence."

"Indeed!"

"Yes, Henry. Read it, and see from whence it comes."

There was just sufficient light by going to the window to enable Henry to read the letter, which he did aloud.

It ran thus:--

"Sir Francis Varney presents his compliments to Mr. Beaumont, and is much concerned to hear that some domestic affliction has fallen upon him. Sir Francis hopes that the genuine and loving sympathy of a neighbour will not be regarded as an intrusion, and begs to proffer any assistance or counsel that may be within the compass of his means.

"Ratford Abbey."

"Sir Francis Varney!" said Henry, "who is he?"

"Do you not remember, Henry," said George, "we were told a few days ago, that a gentleman of that name had become the purchaser of the estate of Ratford Abbey."

"Oh, yes, yes. Have you seen him?"

"I have not."

"I do not wish to make any new acquaintance, George. We are very poor--much poorer indeed than the general appearance of this place, which, I fear, we shall soon have to part with, would warrant any one believing. I must, of course, return a civil answer to this gentleman, but it must be such as one as shall repress familiarity."

"That will be difficult to do while we remain here, when we come to consider the very close proximity of the two properties, Henry."

"Oh, no, not at all. He will easily perceive that we do not want to make acquaintance with him, and then, as a gentleman, which doubtless he is, he will give up the attempt."

"Let it be so, Henry. Heaven knows I have no desire to form any new acquaintance with any one, and more particularly under our present circumstances of depression. And now, Henry, you must permit me, as I have had some repose, to share with you your night watch in Flora's room."

"I would advise you not, George; your health, you know, is very far from good."

"Nay, allow me. If not, then the anxiety I shall suffer will do me more harm than the watchfulness I shall keep up in her chamber."

This was an argument which Henry felt himself the force of too strongly not to admit it in the case of George, and he therefore made no further opposition to his wish to make one in the night watch.

"There will be an advantage," said George, "you see, in three of us being engaged in this matter, because, should anything occur, two can act together, and yet Flora may not be left alone."

"True, true, that is a great advantage."

Now a soft gentle silvery light began to spread itself over the heavens. The moon was rising, and as the beneficial effects of the storm of the preceding evening were still felt in the clearness of the air, the rays appeared to be more lustrous and full of beauty than they commonly were.

Each moment the night grew lighter, and by the time the brothers were ready to take their places in the chamber of Flora, the moon had risen considerably.

Although neither Henry nor George had any objection to the company of Mr. Marchdale, yet they gave him the option, and rather in fact urged him not to destroy his night's repose by sitting up with them; but he said,--

"Allow me to do so; I am older, and have calmer judgment than you can have. Should anything again appear, I am quite resolved that it shall not escape me."

"What would you do?"

"With the name of God upon my lips," said Mr. Marchdale, solemnly, "I would grapple with it."

"You laid hands upon it last night."

"I did, and have forgotten to show you what I tore from it. Look here,--what should you say this was?"

He produced a piece of cloth, on which was an old-fashioned piece of lace, and two buttons. Upon a close inspection, this appeared to be a portion of the lapel of a coat of ancient times, and suddenly, Henry, with a look of intense anxiety, said,--

"This reminds me of the fashion of garments very many years ago, Mr. Marchdale."

"It came away in my grasp as if rotten and incapable of standing any rough usage."

"What a strange unearthly smell it has!"

"Now you mention it yourself," added Mr. Marchdale, "I must confess it smells to me as if it had really come from the very grave."

"It does--it does. Say nothing of this relic of last night's work to any one."

"Be assured I shall not. I am far from wishing to keep up in any one's mind proofs of that which I would fain, very fain refute."

Mr. Marchdale replaced the portion of the coat which the figure had worn in his pocket, and then the whole three proceeded to the chamber of Flora.

***

It was within a very few minutes of midnight, the moon had climbed high in the heavens, and a night of such brightness and beauty had seldom shown itself for a long period of time.

Flora slept, and in her chamber sat the two brothers and Mr. Marchdale, silently, for she had shown symptoms of restlessness, and they much feared to break the light slumber into which she had fallen.

Occasionally they had conversed in whispers, which could not have the effect of rousing her, for the room, although smaller than the one she had before occupied, was still sufficiently spacious to enable them to get some distance from the bed.

Until the hour of midnight now actually struck, they were silent, and when the last echo of the sounds had died away, a feeling of uneasiness came over them, which prompted some conversation to get rid of it.

"How bright the moon is now," said Henry, in a low tone.

"I never saw it brighter," replied Marchdale. "I feel as if I were assured that we shall not to-night be interrupted."

"It was later than this," said Henry.

"It was--it was."

"Do not then yet congratulate us upon no visit."

"How still the house is!" remarked George; "it seems to me as if I had never found it so intensely quiet before."

"It is very still."

"Hush! she moves."

Flora moaned in her sleep, and made a slight movement. The curtains were all drawn closely round the bed to shield her eyes from the bright moonlight which streamed into the room so brilliantly. They might have closed the shutters of the window, but this they did not like to do, as it would render their watch there of no avail at all, inasmuch as they would not be able to see if any attempt was made by any one to obtain admittance.

A quarter of an hour longer might have thus passed when Mr. Marchdale said in a whisper,--

"A thought has just struck me that the piece of coat I have, which I dragged from the figure last night, wonderfully resembles in colour and appearance the style of dress of the portrait in the room which Flora lately slept in."

"I thought of that," said Henry, "when first I saw it; but, to tell the honest truth, I dreaded to suggest any new proof connected with last night's visitation."

"Then I ought not to have drawn your attention to it," said Mr. Marchdale, "and regret I have done so."

"Nay, do not blame yourself on such an account," said Henry. "You are quite right, and it is I who am too foolishly sensitive. Now, however, since you have mentioned it, I must own I have a great desire to test the accuracy of the observation by a comparison with the portrait."

"That may easily be done."

"I will remain here," said George, "in case Flora awakens, while you two go if you like. It is but across the corridor."

Henry immediately rose, saying--

"Come, Mr. Marchdale, come. Let us satisfy ourselves at all events upon this point at once. As George says it is only across the corridor, and we can return directly."

"I am willing," said Mr. Marchdale, with a tone of sadness.

There was no light needed, for the moon stood suspended in a cloudless sky, so that from the house being a detached one, and containing numerous windows, it was as light as day.

Although the distance from one chamber to the other was only across the corridor, it was a greater space than these words might occupy, for the corridor was wide, neither was it directly across, but considerably slanting. However, it was certainly sufficiently close at hand for any sound of alarm from one chamber to reach another without any difficulty.

A few moments sufficed to place Henry and Mr. Marchdale in that antique room, where, from the effect of the moonlight which was streaming over it, the portrait on the panel looked exceedingly life like.

And this effect was probably the greater because the rest of the room was not illuminated by the moon's rays, which came through a window in the corridor, and then at the open door of that chamber upon the portrait.

Mr. Marchdale held the piece of cloth he had close to the dress of the portrait, and one glance was sufficient to show the wonderful likeness between the two.

"Good God!" said Henry, "it is the same."

Mr. Marchdale dropped the piece of cloth and trembled.

"This fact shakes even your scepticism," said Henry.

"I know not what to make of it."

"I can tell you something which bears upon it. I do not know if you are sufficiently aware of my family history to know that this one of my ancestors, I wish I could say worthy ancestors, committed suicide, and was buried in his clothes."

"You--you are sure of that?"

"Quite sure."

"I am more and more bewildered as each moment some strange corroborative fact of that dreadful supposition we so much shrink from seems to come to light and to force itself upon our attention."

There was a silence of a few moments duration, and Henry had turned towards Mr. Marchdale to say something, when the cautious tread of a footstep was heard in the garden, immediately beneath that balcony.

A sickening sensation came over Henry, and he was compelled to lean against the wall for support, as in scarcely articulate accents he said--

"The vampyre--the vampyre! God of heaven, it has come once again!"

"Now, Heaven inspire us with more than mortal courage," cried Mr. Marchdale, and he dashed open the window at once, and sprang into the balcony.

Henry in a moment recovered himself sufficiently to follow him, and when he reached his side in the balcony, Marchdale said, as he pointed below,--

"There is some one concealed there."

"Where--where?"

"Among the laurels. I will fire a random shot, and we may do some execution."

"Hold!" said a voice from below; "don't do any such thing, I beg of you."

"Why, that is Mr. Chillingworth's voice," cried Henry.

"Yes, and it's Mr. Chillingworth's person, too," said the doctor, as he emerged from among some laurel bushes.

"How is this?" said Marchdale.

"Simply that I made up my mind to keep watch and ward to-night outside here, in the hope of catching the vampyre. I got into here by climbing the gate."

"But why did you not let me know?" said Henry.

"Because I did not know myself, my young friend, till an hour and a half ago."

"Have you seen anything?"

"Nothing. But I fancied I heard something in the park outside the wall."

"Indeed!"

"What say you, Henry," said Mr. Marchdale, "to descending and taking a hasty examination of the garden and grounds?"

"I am willing; but first allow me to speak to George, who otherwise might be surprised at our long absence."

Henry walked rapidly to the bed chamber of Flora, and he said to George,--

"Have you any objection to being left alone here for about half an hour, George, while we make an examination of the garden?"

"Let me have some weapon and I care not. Remain here while I fetch a sword from my own room."

Henry did so, and when George returned with a sword, which he always kept in his bed-room, he said,--

"Now go, Henry. I prefer a weapon of this description to pistols much. Do not be longer gone than necessary."

"I will not, George, be assured."

George was then left alone, and Henry returned to the balcony, where Mr. Marchdale was waiting for him. It was a quicker mode of descending to the garden to do so by clambering over the balcony than any other, and the height was not considerable enough to make it very objectionable, so Henry and Mr. Marchdale chose that way of joining Mr. Chillingworth.

"You are, no doubt, much surprised at finding me here," said the doctor; "but the fact is, I half made up my mind to come while I was here; but I had not thoroughly done so, therefore I said nothing to you about it."

"We are much indebted to you," said Henry, "for making the attempt."

"I am prompted to it by a feeling of the strongest curiosity."

"Are you armed, sir?" said Marchdale.

"In this stick," said the doctor, "is a sword, the exquisite temper of which I know I can depend upon, and I fully intended to run through any one whom I saw that looked in the least of the vampyre order."

"You would have done quite right," replied Mr. Marchdale. "I have a brace of pistols here, loaded with ball; will you take one, Henry, if you please, and then we shall be all armed."

Thus, then, prepared for any exigency, they made the whole round of the house; but found all the fastenings secure, and everything as quiet as possible.

"Suppose, now, we take a survey of the park outside the garden wall," said Mr. Marchdale.

This was agreed to; but before they had proceeded far, Mr. Marchdale said,--

"There is a ladder lying on the wall; would it not be a good plan to place it against the very spot the supposed vampyre jumped over last night, and so, from a more elevated position, take a view of the open meadows. We could easily drop down on the outer side, if we saw anything suspicious."

"Not a bad plan," said the doctor. "Shall we do it?"

"Certainly," said Henry; and they accordingly carried the ladder, which had been used for pruning the trees, towards the spot at the end of the long walk, at which the vampyre had made good, after so many fruitless efforts, his escape from the premises.

They made haste down the long vista of trees until they reached the exact spot, and then they placed the ladder as near as possible, exactly where Henry, in his bewilderment on the evening before, had seen the apparition from the grave spring to.

"We can ascend singly," said Marchdale; "but there is ample space for us all there to sit on the top of the wall and make our observations."

This was seen to be the case, and in about a couple of minutes they had taken up their positions on the wall, and, although the height was but trifling, they found that they had a much more extensive view than they could have obtained by any other means.

"To contemplate the beauty of such a night as this," said Mr. Chillingworth, "is amply sufficient compensation for coming the distance I have."

"And who knows," remarked Marchdale, "we may yet see something which may throw a light upon our present perplexities God knows that I would give all I can call mine in the world to relieve you and your sister, Henry Bannerworth, from the fearful effect which last night's proceedings cannot fail to have upon you."

"Of that I am well assured, Mr. Marchdale," said Henry. "If the happiness of myself and family depended upon you, we should be happy indeed."

"You are silent, Mr. Chillingworth," remarked Marchdale, after a slight pause.

"Hush!" said Mr. Chillingworth--"hush--hush!"

"Good God, what do you hear?" cried Henry.

The doctor laid his hand upon Henry's arm as he said,--

"There is a young lime tree yonder to the right."

"Yes--yes."

"Carry your eye from it in a horizontal line, as near as you can, towards the wood."

Henry did so, and then he uttered a sudden exclamation of surprise, and pointed to a rising spot of ground, which was yet, in consequence of the number of tall trees in its vicinity, partially enveloped in shadow.

"What is that?" he said.

"I see something," said Marchdale. "By Heaven! it is a human form lying stretched there."

"It is--as if in death."

"What can it be?" said Chillingworth.

"I dread to say," replied Marchdale; "but to my eyes, even at this distance, it seems like the form of him we chased last night."

"The vampyre?"

"Yes--yes. Look, the moonbeams touch him. Now the shadows of the trees gradually recede. God of Heaven! the figure moves."

Henry's eyes were riveted to that fearful object, and now a scene presented itself which filled them all with wonder and astonishment, mingled with sensations of the greatest awe and alarm.

As the moonbeams, in consequence of the luminary rising higher and higher in the heavens, came to touch this figure that lay extended on the rising ground, a perceptible movement took place in it. The limbs appeared to tremble, and although it did not rise up, the whole body gave signs of vitality.

"The vampyre--the vampyre!" said Mr. Marchdale. "I cannot doubt it now. We must have hit him last night with the pistol bullets, and the moonbeams are now restoring him to a new life."

Henry shuddered, and even Mr. Chillingworth turned pale. But he was the first to recover himself sufficiently to propose some course of action, and he said,--

"Let us descend and go up to this figure. It is a duty we owe to ourselves as much as to society."

"Hold a moment," said Mr. Marchdale, as he produced a pistol. "I am an unerring shot, as you well know, Henry. Before we move from this position we now occupy, allow me to try what virtue may be in a bullet to lay that figure low again."

"He is rising!" exclaimed Henry.

Mr. Marchdale levelled the pistol--he took a sure and deliberate aim, and then, just as the figure seemed to be struggling to its feet, he fired, and, with a sudden bound, it fell again.

"You have hit it," said Henry.

"You have indeed," exclaimed the doctor. "I think we can go now."

"Hush!" said Marchdale--"Hush! Does it not seem to you that, hit it as often as you will, the moonbeams will recover it?"

"Yes--yes," said Henry, "they will--they will."

"I can endure this no longer," said Mr. Chillingworth, as he sprung from the wall. "Follow me or not, as you please, I will seek the spot where this being lies."

"Oh, be not rash," cried Marchdale. "See, it rises again, and its form looks gigantic."

"I trust in Heaven and a righteous cause," said the doctor, as he drew the sword he had spoken of from the stick, and threw away the scabbard. "Come with me if you like, or I go alone."

Henry at once jumped down from the wall, and then Marchdale followed him, saying,--

"Come on; I will not shrink."

They ran towards the piece of rising ground; but before they got to it, the form rose and made rapidly towards a little wood which was in the immediate neighbourhood of the hillock.

"It is conscious of being pursued," cried the doctor. "See how it glances back, and then increases its speed."

"Fire upon it, Henry," said Marchdale.

He did so; but either his shot did not take effect, or it was quite unheeded if it did, by the vampyre, which gained the wood before they could have a hope of getting sufficiently near it to effect, or endeavour to effect, a capture.

"I cannot follow it there," said Marchdale. "In open country I would have pursued it closely; but I cannot follow it into the intricacies of a wood."

"Pursuit is useless there," said Henry. "It is enveloped in the deepest gloom."

"I am not so unreasonable," remarked Mr. Chillingworth, "as to wish you to follow into such a place as that. I am confounded utterly by this affair."

"And I," said Marchdale. "What on earth is to be done?"

"Nothing--nothing!" exclaimed Henry, vehemently; "and yet I have, beneath the canopy of Heaven, declared that I will, so help me God! spare neither time nor trouble in the unravelling of this most fearful piece of business. Did either of you remark the clothing which this spectral appearance wore?"

"They were antique clothes," said Mr. Chillingworth, "such as might have been fashionable a hundred years ago, but not now."

"Such was my impression," added Marchdale.

"And such my own," said Henry, excitedly. "Is it at all within the compass of the wildest belief that what we have seen is a vampyre, and no other than my ancestor who, a hundred years ago, committed suicide?"

There was so much intense excitement, and evidence of mental suffering, that Mr. Chillingworth took him by the arm, saying,--

"Come home--come home; no more of this at present; you will but make yourself seriously unwell."

"No--no--no."

"Come home now, I pray you; you are by far too much excited about this matter to pursue it with the calmness which should be brought to bear upon it."

"Take advice, Henry," said Marchdale, "take advice, and come home at once."

"I will yield to you; I feel that I cannot control my own feelings--I will yield to you, who, as you say, are cooler on this subject than I can be. Oh, Flora, Flora, I have no comfort to bring to you now."

Poor Henry Bannerworth appeared to be in a complete state of mental prostration, on account of the distressing circumstances that had occurred so rapidly and so suddenly in his family, which had had quite enough to contend with without having superadded to every other evil the horror of believing that some preternatural agency was at work to destroy every hope of future happiness in this world, under any circumstances.

He suffered himself to be led home by Mr. Chillingworth and Marchdale; he no longer attempted to dispute the dreadful fact concerning the supposed vampyre; he could not contend now against all the corroborating circumstances that seemed to collect together for the purpose of proving that which, even when proved, was contrary to all his notions of Heaven, and at variance with all that was recorded and established is part and parcel of the system of nature.

"I cannot deny," he said, when they had reached home, "that such things are possible; but the probability will not bear a moment's investigation."

"There are more things," said Marchdale, solemnly, "in Heaven, and on earth, than are dreamed of in our philosophy."

"There are indeed, it appears," said Mr. Chillingworth.

"And are you a convert?" said Henry, turning to him.

"A convert to what?"

"To a belief in--in--these vampyres?"

"I? No, indeed; if you were to shut me up in a room full of vampyres, I would tell them all to their teeth that I defied them."

"But after what we have seen to-night?"

"What have we seen?"

"You are yourself a witness."

"True; I saw a man lying down, and then I saw a man get up; he seemed then to be shot, but whether he was or not he only knows; and then I saw him walk off in a desperate hurry. Beyond that, I saw nothing."

"Yes; but, taking such circumstances into combination with others, have you not a terrible fear of the truth of the dreadful appearance?"

"No--no; on my soul, no. I will die in my disbelief of such an outrage upon Heaven as one of these creatures would most assuredly be."

"Oh! that I could think like you; but the circumstance strikes too nearly to my heart."

"Be of better cheer, Henry--be of better cheer," said Marchdale; "there is one circumstance which we ought to consider, it is that, from all we have seen, there seems to be some things which would favour an opinion, Henry, that your ancestor, whose portrait hangs in the chamber which was occupied by Flora, is the vampyre."

"The dress was the same," said Henry.

"I noted it was."

"And I."

"Do you not, then, think it possible that something might be done to set that part of the question at rest?"

"What--what?"

"Where is your ancestor buried?"

"Ah! I understand you now."

"And I," said Mr. Chillingworth; "you would propose a visit to his mansion?"

"I would," added Marchdale; "anything that may in any way tend to assist in making this affair clearer, and divesting it of its mysterious circumstances, will be most desirable."

Henry appeared to rouse for some moments and then he said,--

"He, in common with many other members of the family, no doubt occupies place in the vault under the old church in the village."

"Would it be possible," asked Marchdale, "to get into that vault without exciting general attention?"

"It would," said Henry; "the entrance to the vault is in the flooring of the pew which belongs to the family in the old church."

"Then it could be done?" asked Mr. Chillingworth.

"Most undoubtedly."

"Will you under take such an adventure?" said Mr. Chillingworth. "It may ease your mind."

"He was buried in the vault, and in his clothes," said Henry, musingly; "I will think of it. About such a proposition I would not decide hastily. Give me leave to think of it until to-morrow."

"Most certainly."

They now made their way to the chamber of Flora, and they heard from George that nothing of an alarming character had occurred to disturb him on his lonely watch. The morning was now again dawning, and Henry earnestly entreated Mr. Marchdale to go to bed, which he did, leaving the two brothers to continue as sentinels by Flora's bed side, until the morning light should banish all uneasy thoughts.

Henry related to George what had taken place outside the house, and the two brothers held a long and interesting conversation for some hours upon that subject, as well as upon others of great importance to their welfare. It was not until the sun's early rays came glaring in at the casement that they both rose, and thought of awakening Flora, who had now slept soundly for so many hours.

CHAPTER VI

A GLANCE AT THE BANNERWORTH FAMILY.--THE PROBABLE CONSEQUENCES OF THE MYSTERIOUS APPARITION'S APPEARANCE

Having thus far, we hope, interested our readers in the fortunes of a family which had become subject to so dreadful a visitation, we trust that a few words concerning them, and the peculiar circumstances in which they are now placed, will not prove altogether out of place, or unacceptable. The Bannerworth family then were well known in the part of the country where they resided. Perhaps, if we were to say they were better known by name than they were liked, on account of that name, we should be near the truth, for it had unfortunately happened that for a very considerable time past the head of the family had been the very worst specimen of it that could be procured. While the junior branches were frequently amiable and most intelligent, and such in mind and manner as were calculated to inspire goodwill in all who knew them, he who held the family property, and who resided in the house now occupied by Flora and her brothers, was a very so--so sort of character.

This state of things, by some strange fatality, had gone on for nearly a hundred years, and the consequence was what might have been fairly expected, namely--that, what with their vices and what with their extravagances, the successive heads of the Bannerworth family had succeeded in so far diminishing the family property that, when it came into the hands of Henry Bannerworth, it was of little value, on account of the numerous encumbrances with which it was saddled.

The father of Henry had not been a very brilliant exception to the general rule, as regarded the head of the family. If he were not quite so bad as many of his ancestors, that gratifying circumstance was to be accounted for by the supposition that he was not quite so bold, and that the change in habits, manners, and laws, which had taken place in a hundred years, made it not so easy for even a landed proprietor to play the petty tyrant.

He had, to get rid of those animal spirits which had prompted many of his predecessors to downright crimes, had recourse to the gaming-table, and, after raising whatever sums he could upon the property which remained, he naturally, and as might have been fully expected, lost them all.

He was found lying dead in the garden of the house one day, and by his side was his pocket-book, on one leaf of which, it was the impression of the family, he had endeavoured to write something previous to his decease, for he held a pencil firmly in his grasp.

The probability was that he had felt himself getting ill, and, being desirous of making some communication to his family which pressed heavily upon his mind, he had attempted to do so, but was stopped by the too rapid approach of the hand of death.

For some days previous to his decease, his conduct had been extremely mysterious. He had announced an intention of leaving England for ever--of selling the house and grounds for whatever they would fetch over and above the sums for which they were mortgaged, and so clearing himself of all encumbrances.

He had, but a few hours before he was found lying dead, made the following singular speech to Henry,--

"Do not regret, Henry, that the old house which has been in our family so long is about to be parted with. Be assured that, if it is but for the first time in my life, I have good and substantial reasons now for what I am about to do. We shall be able to go some other country, and there live like princes of the land."

Where the means were to come from to live like a prince, unless Mr. Bannerworth had some of the German princes in his eye, no one knew but himself, and his sudden death buried with him that most important secret.

There were some words written on the leaf of his pocket-book, but they were of by far too indistinct and ambiguous a nature to lead to anything. They were these:--

"The money is ----------"

And then there was a long scrawl of the pencil, which seemed to have been occasioned by his sudden decease.

Of course nothing could be made of these words, except in the way of a contradiction as the family lawyer said, rather more facetiously than a man of law usually speaks, for if he had written "The money is not," he would have been somewhere remarkably near the truth.

However, with all his vices he was regretted by his children, who chose rather to remember him in his best aspect than to dwell upon his faults.

For the first time then, within the memory of man, the head of the family of the Bannerworths was a gentleman, in every sense of the word. Brave, generous, highly educated, and full of many excellent and noble qualities--for such was Henry, whom we have introduced to our readers under such distressing circumstances.

And now, people said, that the family property having been all dissipated and lost, there would take place a change, and that the Bannerworths would have to take to some course of honourable industry for a livelihood, and that then they would be as much respected as they had before been detested and disliked.

Indeed, the position which Henry held was now a most precarious one--for one of the amazingly clever acts of his father had been to encumber the property with overwhelming claims, so that when Henry administered to the estate, it was doubted almost by his attorney if it were at all desirable to do so.

An attachment, however, to the old house of his family, had induced the young man to hold possession of it as long as he could, despite any adverse circumstance which might eventually be connected with it.

Some weeks, however, only after the decease of his father, and when he fairly held possession, a sudden and a most unexpected offer came to him from a solicitor in London, of whom he knew nothing, to purchase the house and grounds, for a client of his, who had instructed him so to do, but whom he did not mention.

The offer made was a liberal one, and beyond the value of the place. The lawyer who had conducted Henry's affairs for him since his father's decease, advised him by all means to take it; but after a consultation with his mother and sister, and George, they all resolved to hold by their own house as long as they could, and, consequently, he refused the offer.

He was then asked to let the place, and to name his own price for the occupation of it; but that he would not do: so the negotiation went off altogether, leaving only, in the minds of the family, much surprise at the exceeding eagerness of some one, whom they knew not, to get possession of the place on any terms.

There was another circumstance perhaps which materially aided in producing a strong feeling on the minds of the Bannerworths, with regard to remaining where they were.

That circumstance occurred thus: a relation of the family, who was now dead, and with whom had died all his means, had been in the habit, for the last half dozen years of his life, of sending a hundred pounds to Henry, for the express purpose of enabling him and his brother George and his sifter Flora to take a little continental or home tour, in the autumn of the year.

A more acceptable present, or for a more delightful purpose, to young people, could not be found; and, with the quiet, prudent habits of all three of them, they contrived to go far and to see much for the sum which was thus handsomely placed at their disposal.

In one of those excursions, when among the mountains of Italy, an adventure occurred which placed the life of Flora in imminent hazard.

They were riding along a narrow mountain path, and, her horse slipping, she fell over the ledge of a precipice.

In an instant, a young man, a stranger to the whole party, who was travelling in the vicinity, rushed to the spot, and by his knowledge and exertions, they felt convinced her preservation was effected.

He told her to lie quiet; he encouraged her to hope for immediate succour; and then, with much personal exertion, and at immense risk to himself, he reached the ledge of rock on which she lay, and then he supported her until the brothers had gone to a neighbouring house, which, bye-the-bye, was two good English miles off, and got assistance.

There came on, while they were gone, a terrific storm, and Flora felt that but for him who was with her she must have been hurled from the rock, and perished in an abyss below, which was almost too deep for observation.

Suffice it to say that she was rescued; and he who had, by his intrepidity, done so much towards saving her, was loaded with the most sincere and heartfelt acknowledgments by the brothers as well as by herself.

He frankly told them that his name was Holland; that he was travelling for amusement and instruction, and was by profession an artist.

He travelled with them for some time; and it was not at all to be wondered at, under the circumstances, that an attachment of the tenderest nature should spring up between him and the beautiful girl, who felt that she owed to him her life.

Mutual glances of affection were exchanged between them, and it was arranged that when he returned to England, he should come at once as an honoured guest to the house of the family of the Bannerworths.

All this was settled satisfactorily with the full knowledge and acquiescence of the two brothers, who had taken a strange attachment to the young Charles Holland, who was indeed in every way likely to propitiate the good opinion of all who knew him.

Henry explained to him exactly how they were situated, and told him that when he came he would find a welcome from all, except possibly his father, whose wayward temper he could not answer for.

Young Holland stated that he was compelled to be away for a term of two years, from certain family arrangements he had entered into, and that then he would return and hope to meet Flora unchanged as he should be.

It happened that this was the last of the continental excursions of the Bannerworths, for, before another year rolled round, the generous relative who had supplied them with the means of making such delightful trips was no more; and, likewise, the death of the father had occurred in the manner we have related, so that there was no chance as had been anticipated and hoped for by Flora, of meeting Charles Holland on the continent again, before his two years of absence from England should be expired.

Such, however, being the state of things, Flora felt reluctant to give up the house, where he would be sure to come to look for her, and her happiness was too dear to Henry to induce him to make any sacrifice of it to expediency.

Therefore was it that Bannerworth Hall, as it was sometimes called, was retained, and fully intended to be retained at all events until after Charles Holland had made his appearance, and his advice (for he was, by the young people, considered as one of the family) taken, with regard to what was advisable to be done.

With one exception this was the state of affairs at the hall, and that exception relates to Mr. Marchdale.

He was a distant relation of Mrs. Bannerworth, and, in early life, had been sincerely and tenderly attached to her. She, however, with the want of steady reflection of a young girl, as she then was, had, as is generally the case among several admirers, chosen the very worst: that is, the man who treated her with the most indifference, and who paid her the least attention, was of course, thought the most of, and she gave her hand to him.

That man was Mr. Bannerworth. But future experience had made her thoroughly awake to her former error; and, but for the love she bore her children, who were certainly all that a mother's heart could wish, she would often have deeply regretted the infatuation which had induced her to bestow her hand in the quarter she had done so.

About a month after the decease of Mr. Bannerworth, there came one to the hall, who desired to see the widow. That one was Mr. Marchdale.

It might have been some slight tenderness towards him which had never left her, or it might be the pleasure merely of seeing one whom she had known intimately in early life, but, be that as it may, she certainly gave him a kindly welcome; and he, after consenting to remain for some time as a visitor at the hall, won the esteem of the whole family by his frank demeanour and cultivated intellect.

He had travelled much and seen much, and he had turned to good account all he had seen, so that not only was Mr. Marchdale a man of sterling sound sense, but he was a most entertaining companion.

His intimate knowledge of many things concerning which they knew little or nothing; his accurate modes of thought, and a quiet, gentlemanly demeanour, such as is rarely to be met with, combined to make him esteemed by the Bannerworths. He had a small independence of his own, and being completely alone in the world, for he had neither wife nor child, Marchdale owned that he felt a pleasure in residing with the Bannerworths.

Of course he could not, in decent terms, so far offend them as to offer to pay for his subsistence, but he took good care that they should really be no losers by having him as an inmate, a matter which he could easily arrange by little presents of one kind and another, all of which he managed should be such as were not only ornamental, but actually spared his kind entertainers some positive expense which otherwise they must have gone to.

Whether or not this amiable piece of manoeuvring was seen through by the Bannerworths it is not our purpose to inquire. If it was seen through, it could not lower him in their esteem, for it was probably just what they themselves would have felt a pleasure in doing under similar circumstances, and if they did not observe it, Mr. Marchdale would, probably, be all the better pleased.

Such then may be considered by our readers as a brief outline of the state of affairs among the

Bannerworths--a state which was pregnant with changes, and which changes were now likely to be rapid and conclusive.

How far the feelings of the family towards the ancient house of their race would be altered by the appearance at it of so fearful a visitor as a vampyre, we will not stop to inquire, inasmuch as such feelings will develop themselves as we proceed.

That the visitation had produced a serious effect upon all the household was sufficiently evident, as well among the educated as among the ignorant. On the second morning, Henry received notice to quit his service from the three servants he with difficulty had contrived to keep at the hall. The reason why he received such notice he knew well enough, and therefore he did not trouble himself to argue about a superstition to which he felt now himself almost, compelled to give way; for how could he say there was no such thing as a vampyre, when he had, with his own eyes, had the most abundant evidence of the terrible fact?

He calmly paid the servants, and allowed them to leave him at once without at all entering into the matter, and, for the time being, some men were procured, who, however, came evidently with fear and trembling, and probably only took the place, on account of not being able, to procure any other. The comfort of the household was likely to be completely put an end to, and reasons now for leaving the hall appeared to be most rapidly accumulating.

CHAPTER VII

THE VISIT TO THE VAULT OF THE BANNERWORTHS, AND ITS UNPLEASANT RESULT.--THE MYSTERY

Henry and his brother roused Flora, and after agreeing together that it would be highly imprudent to say anything to her of the proceedings of the night, they commenced a conversation with her in encouraging and kindly accents.

"Well, Flora," said Henry, "you see you have been quite undisturbed to-night."

"I have slept long, dear Henry."

"You have, and pleasantly too, I hope."

"I have not had any dreams, and I feel much refreshed, now, and quite well again."

"Thank Heaven!" said George.

"If you will tell dear mother that I am awake, I will get up with her assistance."

The brothers left the room, and they spoke to each other of it as a favourable sign, that Flora did not object to being left alone now, as she had done on the preceding morning.

"She is fast recovering, now, George," said Henry. "If we could now but persuade ourselves that all this alarm would pass away, and that we should hear no more of it, we might return to our old and comparatively happy condition."

"Let us believe, Henry, that we shall."

"And yet, George, I shall not be satisfied in my mind, until I have paid a visit."

"A visit? Where?"

"To the family vault."

"Indeed, Henry! I thought you had abandoned that idea."

"I had. I have several times abandoned it; but it comes across my mind again and again."

"I much regret it."

"Look you, George; as yet, everything that has happened has tended to confirm a belief in this most horrible of all superstitions concerning vampyres."

"It has."

"Now, my great object, George, is to endeavour to disturb such a state of things, by getting something, however slight, or of a negative character, for the mind to rest upon on the other side of the question."

"I comprehend you, Henry."

"You know that at present we are not only led to believe, almost irresistibly that we have been visited here by a vampyre but that that vampyre is our ancestor, whose portrait is on the panel of the wall of the chamber into which he contrived to make his way."

"True, most true."

"Then let us, by an examination of the family vault, George, put an end to one of the evidences. If we find, as most surely we shall, the coffin of the ancestor of ours, who seems, in dress and appearance, so horribly mixed up in this affair, we shall be at rest on that head."

"But consider how many years have elapsed."

"Yes, a great number."

"What then, do you suppose, could remain of any corpse placed in a vault so long ago?"

"Decomposition must of course have done its work, but still there must be a something to show that a corpse has so undergone the process common to all nature. Double the lapse of time surely could not obliterate all traces of that which had been."

"There is reason in that, Henry."

"Besides, the coffins are all of lead, and some of stone, so that they cannot have all gone."

"True, most true."

"If in the one which, from the inscription and the date, we discover to be that of our ancestor whom we seek, we find the evident remains of a corpse, we shall be satisfied that he has rested in his tomb in peace."

"Brother, you seem bent on this adventure," said George; "if you go, I will accompany you."

"I will not engage rashly in it, George. Before I finally decide, I will again consult with Mr.

Marchdale. His opinion will weigh much with me."

"And in good time, here he comes across the garden," said George, as he looked from the window of the room in which they sat.

It was Mr. Marchdale, and the brothers warmly welcomed him as he entered the apartment.

"You have been early afoot," said Henry.

"I have," he said. "The fact is, that although at your solicitation I went to bed, I could not sleep, and I went out once more to search about the spot where we had seen the--the I don't know what to call it, for I have a great dislike to naming it a vampyre."

"There is not much in a name," said George.

"In this instance there is," said Marchdale. "It is a name suggestive of horror."

"Made you any discovery?" said Henry.

"None whatever."

"You saw no trace of any one?"

"Not the least."

"Well, Mr. Marchdale, George and I were talking over this projected visit to the family vault."

"Yes."

"And we agreed to suspend our judgments until we saw you, and learned your opinion."

"Which I will tell you frankly," said Mr. Marchdale, "because I know you desire it freely."

"Do so."

"It is, that you make the visit."

"Indeed."

"Yes, and for this reason. You have now, as you cannot help having, a disagreeable feeling, that you may find that one coffin is untenanted. Now, if you do find it so, you scarcely make matters worse, by an additional confirmation of what already amounts to a strong supposition, and one which is likely to grow stronger by time."

"True, most true."

"On the contrary, if you find indubitable proofs that your ancestor has slept soundly in the tomb, and gone the way of all flesh, you will find yourselves much calmer, and that an attack is made upon the train of events which at present all run one way."

"That is precisely the argument I was using to George," said Henry, "a few moments since."

"Then let us go," said George, "by all means."

"It is so decided then," said Henry.

"Let it be done with caution," replied Mr. Marchdale.

"If any one can manage it, of course we can."

"Why should it not be done secretly and at night? Of course we lose nothing by making a night visit to a vault into which daylight, I presume, cannot penetrate."

"Certainly not."

"Then let it be at night."

"But we shall surely require the concurrence of some of the church authorities."

"Nay, I do not see that," interposed Mr. Marchdale. "It is the vault actually vested in and belonging to yourself you wish to visit, and, therefore, you have right to visit it in any manner or at any time that may be most suitable to yourself."

"But detection in a clandestine visit might produce unpleasant consequences."

"The church is old," said George, "and we could easily find means of getting into it. There is only one objection that I see, just now, and that is, that we leave Flora unprotected."

"We do, indeed," said Henry. "I did not think of that."

"It must be put to herself, as a matter for her own consideration," said Mr. Marchdale, "if she will consider herself sufficiently safe with the company and protection of your mother only."

"It would be a pity were we not all three present at the examination of the coffin," remarked Henry.

"It would, indeed. There is ample evidence," said Mr. Marchdale, "but we must not give Flora a night of sleeplessness and uneasiness on that account, and the more particularly as we cannot well explain to her where we are going, or upon what errand."

"Certainly not."

"Let us talk to her, then, about it," said Henry. "I confess I am much bent upon the plan, and fain would not forego it; neither should I like other than that we three should go together."

"If you determine, then, upon it," said Marchdale, "we will go to-night; and, from your acquaintance with the place, doubtless you will be able to decide what tools are necessary."

"There is a trap-door at the bottom of the pew," said Henry; "it is not only secured down, but it is locked likewise, and I have the key in my possession."

"Indeed!"

"Yes; immediately beneath is a short flight of stone steps, which conduct at once into the vault."

"Is it large?"

"No; about the size of a moderate chamber, and with no intricacies about it."

"There can be no difficulties, then."

"None whatever, unless we meet with actual personal interruption, which I am inclined to think is very far from likely. All we shall require will be a screwdriver, with which to remove the screws, and then something with which to wrench open the coffin."

"Those we can easily provide, along with lights," remarked Mr. Marchdale.

"I hope to Heaven that this visit to the tomb will have the effect of easing your minds, and enabling you to make a successful stand against the streaming torrent of evidence that has poured in upon us regarding this most fearful of apparitions."

"I do, indeed, hope so," added Henry; "and now I will go at once to Flora, and endeavour to convince her she is safe without us to-night."

"By-the-bye, I think," said Marchdale, "that if we can induce Mr. Chillingworth to come with us, it will be a great point gained in the investigation."

"He would," said Henry, "be able to come to an accurate decision with respect to the remains--if any--in the coffin, which we could not."

"Then have him, by all means," said George. "He did not seem averse last night to go on such an adventure."

"I will ask him when he makes his visit this morning upon Flora; and should he not feel disposed to join us, I am quite sure he will keep the secret of our visit."

All this being arranged, Henry proceeded to Flora, and told her that he and George, and Mr. Marchdale wished to go out for about a couple of hours in the evening after dark, if she felt sufficiently well to feel a sense of security without them.

Flora changed colour, and slightly trembled, and then, as if ashamed of her fears, she said,--

"Go, go; I will not detain you. Surely no harm can come to me in presence of my mother."

"We shall not be gone longer than the time I mention to you," said Henry.

"Oh, I shall be quite content. Besides, am I to be kept thus in fear all my life? Surely, surely not. I ought, too, to learn to defend myself."

Henry caught at the idea, as he said,--

"If fire-arms were left you, do you think you would have courage to use them?"

"I do, Henry."

"Then you shall have them; and let me beg of you to shoot any one without the least hesitation who shall come into your chamber."

"I will, Henry. If ever human being was justified in the use of deadly weapons, I am now. Heaven protect me from a repetition of the visit to which I have now been once subjected. Rather, oh, much rather would I die a hundred deaths than suffer what I have suffered."

"Do not allow it, dear Flora, to press too heavily upon your mind in dwelling upon it in conversation. I still entertain a sanguine expectation that something may arise to afford a far less dreadful explanation of what has occurred than what you have put upon it. Be of good cheer, Flora, we shall go one hour after sunset, and return in about two hours from the time at which we leave here, you may be assured."

Notwithstanding this ready and courageous acquiescence of Flora in the arrangement, Henry was not without his apprehension that when the night should come again, her fears would return with it; but he spoke to Mr. Chillingworth upon the subject, and got that gentleman's ready consent to accompany them.

He promised to meet them at the church porch exactly at nine o'clock, and matters were all arranged, and Henry waited with much eagerness and anxiety now for the coming night, which he hoped would dissipate one of the fearful deductions which his imagination had drawn from recent circumstances.

He gave to Flora a pair of pistols of his own, upon which he knew he could depend, and he took good care to load them well, so that there could be no likelihood whatever of their missing fire at a critical moment.

"Now, Flora," he said, "I have seen you use fire-arms when you were much younger than you are now, and therefore I need give you no instructions. If any intruder does come, and you do fire, be sure you take a good aim, and shoot low."

"I will, Henry, I will; and you will be back in two hours?"

"Most assuredly I will."

The day wore on, evening came, and then deepened into night. It turned out to be a cloudy night, and therefore the moon's brilliance was nothing near equal to what it had been on the preceding night Still, however, it had sufficient power over the vapours that frequently covered it for many minutes together, to produce a considerable light effect upon the face of nature, and the night was consequently very far, indeed, from what might be called a dark one.

George, Henry, and Marchdale, met in one of the lower rooms of the house, previous to starting upon their expedition; and after satisfying themselves that they had with them all the tools that were necessary, inclusive of the same small, but well-tempered iron crow-bar with which Marchdale had, on the night of the visit of the vampyre, forced open the door of Flora's chamber, they left the hall, and proceeded at a rapid pace towards the church.

"And Flora does not seem much alarmed," said Marchdale, "at being left alone?"

"No," replied Henry, "she has made up her mind with a strong natural courage which I knew was in her disposition to resist as much as possible the depressing effects of the awful visitation she has endured."

"It would have driven some really mad."

"It would, indeed; and her own reason tottered on its throne, but, thank Heaven, she has recovered."

"And I fervently hope that, through her life," added Marchdale, "she may never have such another trial."

"We will not for a moment believe that such a thing can occur twice."

"She is one among a thousand. Most young girls would never at all have recovered the fearful shock to the nerves."

"Not only has she recovered," said Henry, "but a spirit, which I am rejoiced to see, because it is one which will uphold her, of resistance now possesses her."

"Yes, she actually--I forgot to tell you before--but she actually asked me for arms to resist any second visitation."

"You much surprise me."

"Yes, I was surprised, as well as pleased, myself."

"I would have left her one of my pistols had I been aware of her having made such a request. Do you know if she can use fire-arms?"

"Oh, yes; well."

"What a pity. I have them both with me."

"Oh, she is provided."

"Provided?"

"Yes; I found some pistols which I used to take with me on the continent, and she has them both well loaded, so that if the vampyre makes his appearance, he is likely to meet with rather a warm reception."

"Good God! was it not dangerous?"

"Not at all, I think."

"Well, you know best, certainly, of course. I hope the vampyre may come, and that we may have the pleasure, when we return, of finding him dead. By-the-bye, I--I--. Bless me, I have forgot to get the materials for lights, which I pledged myself to do."

"How unfortunate."

"Walk on slowly, while I run back and get them."

"Oh, we are too far--"

"Hilloa!" cried a man at this moment, some distance in front of them.

"It is Mr. Chillingworth," said Henry.

"Hilloa," cried the worthy doctor again. "Is that you, my friend, Henry Bannerworth?"

"It is," cried Henry.

Mr. Chillingworth now came up to them and said,--

"I was before my time, so rather than wait at the church porch, which would have exposed me to observation perhaps, I thought it better to walk on, and chance meeting with you."

"You guessed we should come this way?'

"Yes, and so it turns out, really. It is unquestionably your most direct route to the church."

"I think I will go back," said Mr Marchdale.

"Back!" exclaimed the doctor; "what for?"

"I forgot the means of getting lights. We have candles, but no means of lighting them."

"Make yourselves easy on that score," said Mr. Chillingworth. "I am never without some chemical matches of my own manufacture, so that as you have the candles, that can be no bar to our going on a once."

"That is fortunate," said Henry.

"Very," added Marchdale; "for it seems a mile's hard walking for me, or at least half a mile from the hall. Let us now push on."

They did push on, all four walking at a brisk pace. The church, although it belonged to the village, was not in it. On the contrary, it was situated at the end of a long lane, which was a mile nearly from the village, in the direction of the hall, therefore, in going to it from the hall, that amount of distance was saved, although it was always called and considered the village church.

It stood alone, with the exception of a glebe house and two cottages, that were occupied by persons who held situations about the sacred edifice, and who were supposed, being on the spot, to keep watch and ward over it.

It was an ancient building of the early English style of architecture, or rather Norman, with one of those antique, square, short towers, built of flint stones firmly embedded in cement, which, from time, had acquired almost the consistency of stone itself. There were numerous arched windows, partaking something of the more florid gothic style, although scarcely ornamental enough to be called such. The edifice stood in the centre of a grave-yard, which extended over a space of about half an acre, and altogether it was one of the prettiest and most rural old churches within many miles of the spot.

Many a lover of the antique and of the picturesque, for it was both, went out of his way while travelling in the neighbourhood to look at it, and it had an extensive and well-deserved reputation as a fine specimen of its class and style of building.

In Kent, to the present day, are some fine specimens of the old Roman style of church, building; and, although they are as rapidly pulled down as the abuse of modern architects, and the cupidity of speculators, and the vanity of clergymen can possibly encourage, in older to erect flimsy, Italianised structures in their stead, yet sufficient of them remain dotted over England to interest the traveller. At Walesden there is a church of this description which will well repay a visit. This, then, was the kind of building into which it was the intention of our four friends to penetrate, not on an unholy, or an unjustifiable errand, but on one which, proceeding from good and proper motives, it was highly desirable to conduct in as secret a manner as possible.

The moon was more densely covered by clouds than it had yet been that evening, when they reached the little wicket-gate which led into the churchyard, through which was a regularly used thoroughfare.

"We have a favourable night," remarked Henry, "for we are not so likely to be disturbed."

"And now, the question is, how are we to get in?" said Mr. Chillingworth, as he paused, and glanced up at the ancient building.

"The doors," said George, "would effectually resist us."

"How can it be done, then?"

"The only way I can think of," said Henry, "is to get out one of the small diamond-shaped panes of glass from one of the low windows, and then we can one of us put in our hands, and undo the fastening, which is very simple, when the window opens like a door, and it is but a step into the church."

"A good way," said Marchdale. "We will lose no time."

They walked round the church till they came to a very low window indeed, near to an angle of the wall, where a huge abutment struck far out into the burial-ground.

"Will you do it, Henry?" said George.

"Yes. I have often noticed the fastenings. Just give me a slight hoist up, and all will be right."

George did so, and Henry with his knife easily bent back some of the leadwork which held in one of the panes of glass, and then got it out whole. He handed it down to George, saying,--

"Take this, George. We can easily replace it when we leave, so that there can be no signs left of any one having been here at all."

George took the piece of thick, dim-coloured glass, and in another moment Henry had succeeded in opening the window, and the mode of ingress to the old church was fair and easy before them all, had there been ever so many.

"I wonder," said Marchdale, "that a place so inefficiently protected has never been robbed."

"No wonder at all," remarked Mr. Chillingworth. "There is nothing to take that I am aware of that would repay anybody the trouble of taking."

"Indeed!"

"Not an article. The pulpit, to be sure, is covered with faded velvet; but beyond that, and an old box, in which I believe nothing is left but some books, I think there is no temptation."

"And that, Heaven knows, is little enough, then."

"Come on," said Henry. "Be careful; there is nothing beneath the window, and the depth is about two feet."

Thus guided, they all got fairly into the sacred edifice, and then Henry closed the window, and fastened it on the inside as he said,--

"We have nothing to do now but to set to work opening a way into the vault, and I trust that Heaven will pardon me for thus desecrating the tomb of my ancestors, from a consideration of the object I have in view by so doing."

"It does seem wrong thus to tamper with the secrets of the tomb," remarked Mr. Marchdale.

"The secrets of a fiddlestick!" said the doctor. "What secrets has the tomb I wonder?"

"Well, but, my dear sir--"

"Nay, my dear sir, it is high time that death, which is, then, the inevitable fate of us all, should be regarded with more philosophic eyes than it is. There are no secrets in the tomb but such as may well be endeavoured to be kept secret."

"What do you mean?"

"There is one which very probably we shall find unpleasantly revealed."

"Which is that?"

"The not over pleasant odour of decomposed animal remains--beyond that I know of nothing of a secret nature that the tomb can show us."

"Ah, your profession hardens you to such matters."

"And a very good thing that it does, or else, if all men were to look upon a dead body as something almost too dreadful to look upon, and by far too horrible to touch, surgery would lose its value, and crime, in many instances of the most obnoxious character, would go unpunished."

"If we have a light here," said Henry, "we shall run the greatest chance in the world of being seen, for the church has many windows."

"Do not have one, then, by any means," said Mr. Chillingworth. "A match held low down in the pew may enable us to open the vault."

"That will be the only plan."

Henry led them to the pew which belonged to his family, and in the floor of which was the trap door.

"When was it last opened?" inquired Marchdale.

"When my father died," said Henry; "some ten months ago now, I should think."

"The screws, then, have had ample time to fix themselves with fresh rust."

"Here is one of my chemical matches," said Mr. Chillingworth, as he suddenly irradiated the pew with a clear and beautiful flame, that lasted about a minute.

The heads of the screws were easily discernible, and the short time that the light lasted had enabled Henry to turn the key he had brought with him in the lock.

"I think that without a light now," he said, "I can turn the screws well."

"Can you?"

"Yes; there are but four."

"Try it, then."

Henry did so, and from the screws having very large heads, and being made purposely, for the convenience of removal when required, with deep indentations to receive the screw-driver, he found no difficulty in feeling for the proper places, and extracting the screws without any more light than was afforded to him from the general whitish aspect of the heavens.

"Now, Mr. Chillingworth," he said "another of your matches, if you please. I have all the screws so loose that I can pick them up with my fingers."

"Here," said the doctor.

In another moment the pew was as light as day, and Henry succeeded in taking out the few screws, which he placed in his pocket for their greater security, since, of course, the intention was to replace everything exactly as it was found, in order that not the least surmise should arise in the mind of any person that the vault had been opened, and visited for any purpose whatever, secretly or otherwise.

"Let us descend," said Henry. "There is no further obstacle, my friends. Let us descend."

"If any one," remarked George, in a whisper, as they slowly descended the stairs which conducted into the vault--"if any one had told me that I should be descending into a vault for the purpose of ascertaining if a dead body, which had been nearly a century there, was removed or not, and had become a vampyre, I should have denounced the idea as one of the most absurd that ever entered the brain of a human being."

"We are the very slaves of circumstances," said Marchdale, "and we never know what we may do, or what we may not. What appears to us so improbable as to border even upon the impossible at one time, is at another the only course of action which appears feasibly open to us to attempt to pursue."

They had now reached the vault, the floor of which was composed of flat red tiles, laid in tolerable order the one beside the other. As Henry had stated, the vault was by no means of large extent. Indeed, several of the apartments for the living, at the hall, were much larger than was that one destined for the dead.

The atmosphere was dump and noisome, but not by any means so bad as might have been expected, considering the number of months which had elapsed since last the vault was opened to receive one of its ghastly and still visitants.

"Now for one of your lights. Mr. Chillingworth. You say you have the candles, I think, Marchdale, although you forgot the matches."

"I have. They are here."

Marchdale took from his pocket a parcel which contained several wax candles, and when it was opened, a smaller packet fell to the ground.

"Why, these are instantaneous matches," said Mr. Chillingworth, as he lifted the small packet up.

"They are; and what a fruitless journey I should have had back to the hall," said Mr. Marchdale, "if you had not been so well provided as you are with the means of getting a light. These matches, which I thought I had not with me, have been, in the hurry of departure, enclosed, you see, with the candles. Truly, I should have hunted for them at home in vain."

Mr. Chillingworth lit the wax candle which was now handed to him by Marchdale, and in another moment the vault from one end of it to the other was quite clearly discernible.

CHAPTER VIII

THE COFFIN.--THE ABSENCE OF THE DEAD.--THE MYSTERIOUS CIRCUMSTANCE, AND THE CONSTERNATION OF GEORGE

They were all silent for a few moments as they looked around them with natural feelings of curiosity. Two of that party had of course never been in that vault at all, and the brothers, although they had descended into it upon the occasion, nearly a year before, of their father being placed in it, still looked upon it with almost as curious eyes as they who now had their first sight of it.

If a man be at all of a thoughtful or imaginative cast of mind, some curious sensations are sure to come over him, upon standing in such a place, where he knows around him lie, in the calmness of death, those in whose veins have flowed kindred blood to him--who bore the same name, and who preceded him in the brief drama of his existence, influencing his destiny and his position in life probably largely by their actions compounded of their virtues and their vices.

Henry Bannerworth and his brother George were just the kind of persons to feel strongly such sensations. Both were reflective, imaginative, educated young men, and, as the light from the wax candle flashed upon their faces, it was evident how deeply they felt the situation in which they were placed.

Mr. Chillingworth and Marchdale were silent. They both knew what was passing in the minds of the brothers, and they had too much delicacy to interrupt a train of thought which, although from having no affinity with the dead who lay around, they could not share in, yet they respected. Henry at length, with a sudden start, seemed to recover himself from his reverie.

"This is a time for action, George," he said, "and not for romantic thought. Let us proceed."

"Yes, yes," said George, and he advanced a step towards the centre of the vault.

"Can you find out among all these coffins, for there seem to be nearly twenty," said Mr. Chillingworth, "which is the one we seek?"

"I think we may," replied Henry. "Some of the earlier coffins of our race, I know, were made of marble, and others of metal, both of which materials, I expect, would withstand the encroaches of time for a hundred years, at least."

"Let us examine," said George.

There were shelves or niches built into the walls all round, on which the coffins were placed, so that there could not be much difficulty in a minute examination of them all, the one after the other.

When, however, they came to look, they found that "decay's offensive fingers" had been more busy than they could have imagined, and that whatever they touched of the earlier coffins crumbled into dust before their very fingers.

In some cases the inscriptions were quite illegible, and, in others, the plates that had borne them had fallen on to the floor of the vault, so that it was impossible to say to which coffin they belonged.

Of course, the more recent and fresh-looking coffins they did not examine, because they could not have anything to do with the object of that melancholy visit.

"We shall arrive at no conclusion," said George. "All seems to have rotted away among those coffins where we might expect to find the one belonging to Marmaduke Bannerworth, our ancestor."

"Here is a coffin plate," said Marchdale, taking one from the floor.

He handed it to Mr. Chillingworth, who, upon an inspection of it, close to the light, exclaimed,--

"It must have belonged to the coffin you seek."

"What says it?"

"Ye mortale remains of Marmaduke Bannerworth, Yeoman. God reste his soule. A.D. 1540."

"It is the plate belonging to his coffin," said Henry, "and now our search is fruitless."

"It is so, indeed," exclaimed George, "for how can we tell to which of the coffins that have lost the plates this one really belongs?"

"I should not be so hopeless," said Marchdale. "I have, from time to time, in the pursuit of antiquarian lore, which I was once fond of, entered many vaults, and I have always observed that an inner coffin of metal was sound and good, while the outer one of wood had rotted away, and yielded at once to the touch of the first hand that was laid upon it."

"But, admitting that to be the case," said Henry, "how does that assist us in the identification of a coffin?"

"I have always, in my experience, found the name and rank of the deceased engraved upon the lid of the inner coffin, as well as being set forth in a much more perishable manner on the plate which was secured to the outer one."

"He is right," said Mr. Chillingworth. "I wonder we never thought of that. If your ancestor was buried in a leaden coffin, there will be no difficulty in finding which it is."

Henry seized the light, and proceeding to one of the coffins, which seemed to be a mass of decay, he pulled away some of the rotted wood work, and then suddenly exclaimed,--

"You are quite right. Here is a firm strong leaden coffin within, which, although quite black, does not otherwise appear to have suffered."

"What is the inscription on that?" said George.

With difficulty the name on the lid was deciphered, but it was found not to be the coffin of him whom they sought.

"We can make short work of this," said Marchdale, "by only examining those leaden coffins which have lost the plates from off their outer cases. There do not appear to be many in such a state."

He then, with another light, which he lighted from the one that Henry now carried, commenced actively assisting in the search, which was carried on silently for more than ten minutes.

Suddenly Mr. Marchdale cried, in a tone of excitement,--

"I have found it. It is here."

They all immediately surrounded the spot where he was, and then he pointed to the lid of a coffin, which he had been rubbing with his handkerchief, in order to make the inscription more legible, and said,--

"See. It is here."

By the combined light of the candles they saw the words,--

"Marmaduke Bannerworth, Yeoman, 1640."

"Yes, there can be no mistake here," said Henry. "This is the coffin, and it shall be opened."

"I have the iron crowbar here," said Marchdale. "It is an old friend of mine, and I am accustomed to the use of it. Shall I open the coffin?"

"Do so--do so," said Henry.

They stood around in silence, while Mr. Marchdale, with much care, proceeded to open the coffin, which seemed of great thickness, and was of solid lead.

It was probably the partial rotting of the metal, in consequence of the damps of that place, that made it easier to open the coffin than it otherwise would have been, but certain it was that the top came away remarkably easily. Indeed, so easily did it come off, that another supposition might have been hazarded, namely, that it had never at all been effectually fastened.

The few moments that elapsed were ones of very great suspense to every one there present; and it would, indeed, be quite sure to assert, that all the world was for the time forgotten in the absorbing interest which appertained to the affair which was in progress.

The candles were now both held by Mr. Chillingworth, and they were so held as to cast a full and clear light upon the coffin. Now the lid slid off, and Henry eagerly gazed into the interior.

There lay something certainly there, and an audible "Thank God!" escaped his lips.

"The body is there!" exclaimed George.

"All right," said Marchdale, "here it is. There is something, and what else can it be?"

"Hold the lights," said Mr. Chillingworth; "hold the lights, some of you; let us be quite certain."

George took the lights, and Mr. Chillingworth, without any hesitation, dipped his hands at once into the coffin, and took up some fragments of rags which were there. They were so rotten, that they fell to pieces in his grasp, like so many pieces of tinder.

There was a death-like pause for some few moments, and then Mr. Chillingworth said, in a low voice,--

"There is not the least vestige of a dead body here."

Henry gave a deep groan, as he said,--

"Mr. Chillingworth, can you take upon yourself to say that no corpse has undergone the process of decomposition in this coffin?"

"To answer your question exactly, as probably in your hurry you have worded it," said Mr.

Chillingworth, "I cannot take upon myself to say any such thing; but this I can say, namely, that in this coffin there are no animal remains, and that it is quite impossible that any corpse enclosed here could, in any lapse of time, have so utterly and entirely disappeared."

"I am answered," said Henry.

"Good God!" exclaimed George, "and has this but added another damning proof, to those we have already on our minds, of one of the must dreadful superstitions that ever the mind of man conceived?"

"It would seem so," said Marchdale, sadly.

"Oh, that I were dead! This is terrible. God of heaven, why are these things? Oh, if I were but dead, and so spared the torture of supposing such things possible."

"Think again, Mr. Chillingworth; I pray you think again," cried Marchdale.

"If I were to think for the remainder of my existence," he replied, "I could come to no other conclusion. It is not a matter of opinion; it is a matter of fact."

"You are positive, then," said Henry, "that the dead body of Marmaduke Bannerworth is not rested here?"

"I am positive. Look for yourselves. The lead is but slightly discoloured; it looks tolerably clean and fresh; there is not a vestige of putrefaction--no bones, no dust even."

They did all look for themselves, and the most casual glance was sufficient to satisfy the most sceptical.

"All is over," said Henry; "let us now leave this place; and all I can now ask of you, my friends, is to lock this dreadful secret deep in your own hearts."

"It shall never pass my lips," said Marchdale.

"Nor mine, you may depend," said the doctor. "I was much in hopes that this night's work would have had the effect of dissipating, instead of adding to, the gloomy fancies that now possess you."

"Good heavens!" cried George, "can you call them fancies, Mr. Chillingworth?"

"I do, indeed."

"Have you yet a doubt?"

"My young friend, I told you from the first, that I would not believe in your vampyre; and I tell you now, that if one was to come and lay hold of me by the throat, as long as I could at all gasp for breath I would tell him he was a d----d impostor."

"This is carrying incredulity to the verge of obstinacy."

"Far beyond it, if you please."

"You will not be convinced?" said Marchdale.

"I most decidedly, on this point, will not."

"Then you are one who would doubt a miracle, if you saw it with your own eyes."

"I would, because I do not believe in miracles. I should endeavour to find some rational and some scientific means of accounting for the phenomenon, and that's the very reason why we have no miracles now-a-days, between you and I, and no prophets and saints, and all that sort of thing."

"I would rather avoid such observations in such a place as this," said Marchdale.

"Nay, do not be the moral coward," cried Mr. Chillingworth, "to make your opinions, or the expression of them, dependent upon any certain locality."

"I know not what to think," said Henry; "I am bewildered quite. Let us now come away."

Mr. Marchdale replaced the lid of the coffin, and then the little party moved towards the staircase. Henry turned before he ascended, and glanced back into the vault.

"Oh," he said, "if I could but think there had been some mistake, some error of judgment, on which the mind could rest for hope."

"I deeply regret," said Marchdale, "that I so strenuously advised this expedition. I did hope that from it would have resulted much good."

"And you had every reason so to hope," said Chillingworth. "I advised it likewise, and I tell you that its result perfectly astonishes me, although I will not allow myself to embrace at once all the conclusions to which it would seem to lead me."

"I am satisfied," said Henry; "I know you both advised me for the best. The curse of Heaven seems now to have fallen upon me and my house."

"Oh, nonsense!" said Chillingworth. "What for?"

"Alas! I know not."

"Then you may depend that Heaven would never act so oddly. In the first place, Heaven don't curse anybody; and, in the second, it is too just to inflict pain where pain is not amply deserved."

They ascended the gloomy staircase of the vault. The countenances of both George and Henry were very much saddened, and it was quite evident that their thoughts were by far too busy to enable them to enter into any conversation. They did not, and particularly George, seem to hear all that was said to them. Their intellects seemed almost stunned by the unexpected circumstance of the disappearance of the body of their ancestor.

All along they had, although almost unknown to themselves, felt a sort of conviction that they must find some remains of Marmaduke Bannerworth, which would render the supposition, even in the most superstitious minds, that he was the vampyre, a thing totally and physically impossible.

But now the whole question assumed a far more bewildering shape. The body was not in its coffin--it had not there quietly slept the long sleep of death common to humanity. Where was it then? What had become of it? Where, how, and under what circumstances had it been removed? Had it itself burst the bands that held it, and hideously stalked forth into the world again to make one of its seeming inhabitants, and kept up for a hundred years a dreadful existence by such adventures as it had consummated at the hall, where, in the course of ordinary human life, it had once lived?

All these were questions which irresistibly pressed themselves upon the consideration of Henry and his brother. They were awful questions.

And yet, take any sober, sane, thinking, educated man, and show him all that they had seen, subject him to all to which they had been subjected, and say if human reason, and all the arguments that the subtlest brain could back it with, would be able to hold out against such a vast accumulation of horrible evidences, and say--"I don't believe it."

Mr. Chillingworth's was the only plan. He would not argue the question. He said at once,--

"I will not believe this thing--upon this point I will yield to no evidence whatever."

That was the only way of disposing of such a question; but there are not many who could so dispose of it, and not one so much interested in it as were the brothers Bannerworth, who could at all hope to get into such a state of mind.

The boards were laid carefully down again, and the screws replaced. Henry found himself unequal to the task, so it was done by Marchdale, who took pains to replace everything in the same state in which they had found it, even to the laying even the matting at the bottom of the pew.

Then they extinguished the light, and, with heavy hearts, they all walked towards the window, to leave the sacred edifice by the same means they had entered it.

"Shall we replace the pane of glass?" said Marchdale.

"Oh, it matters not--it matters not," said Henry, listlessly; "nothing matters now. I care not what becomes of me--I am getting weary of a life which now must be one of misery and dread."

"You must not allow yourself to fall into such a state of mind as this," said the doctor, "or you will become a patient of mine very quickly."

"I cannot help it."

"Well, but be a man. If there are serious evils affecting you, fight out against them the best way you can."

"I cannot."

"Come, now, listen to me. We need not, I think, trouble ourselves about the pane of glass, so come along."

He took the arm of Henry and walked on with him a little in advance of the others.

"Henry," he said, "the best way, you may depend, of meeting evils, be they great or small, is to get up an obstinate feeling of defiance against them. Now, when anything occurs which is uncomfortable to me, I endeavour to convince myself, and I have no great difficulty in doing so, that I am a decidedly injured man."

"Indeed!"

"Yes; I get very angry, and that gets up a kind of obstinacy, which makes me not feel half so much mental misery as would be my portion, if I were to succumb to the evil, and commence whining over it, as many people do, under the pretence of being resigned."

"But this family affliction of mine transcends anything that anybody else ever endured."

"I don't know that; but it is a view of the subject which, if I were you, would only make me more obstinate."

"What can I do?"

"In the first place, I would say to myself, 'There may or there may not be supernatural beings, who, from some physical derangement of the ordinary nature of things, make themselves obnoxious to living people; if there are, d--n them! There may be vampyres; and if there are, I defy them.' Let the imagination paint its very worst terrors; let fear do what it will and what it can in peopling the mind with horrors. Shrink from nothing, and even then I would defy them all."

"Is not that like defying Heaven?"

"Most certainly not; for in all we say and in all we do we act from the impulses of that mind which is given to us by Heaven itself. If Heaven creates an intellect and a mind of a certain order, Heaven will not quarrel that it does the work which it was adapted to do."

"I know these are your opinions. I have heard you mention them before."

"They are the opinions of every rational person. Henry Bannerworth, because they will stand the test of reason; and what I urge upon you is, not to allow yourself to be mentally prostrated, even if a vampyre has paid a visit to your house. Defy him, say I--fight him. Self-preservation is a great law of nature, implanted in all our hearts; do you summon it to your aid."

"I will endeavour to think as you would have me. I thought more than once of summoning religion to my aid."

"Well, that is religion."

"Indeed!"

"I consider so, and the most rational religion of all. All that we read about religion that does not seem expressly to agree with it, you may consider as an allegory."

"But, Mr. Chillingworth, I cannot and will not renounce the sublime truths of Scripture. They may be incomprehensible; they may be inconsistent; and some of them may look ridiculous; but still they are sacred and sublime, and I will not renounce them although my reason may not accord with them, because they are the laws of Heaven."

No wonder this powerful argument silenced Mr. Chillingworth, who was one of those characters in society who hold most dreadful opinions, and who would destroy religious beliefs, and all the different sects in the world, if they could, and endeavour to introduce instead some horrible system of human reason and profound philosophy.

But how soon the religious man silences his opponent; and let it not be supposed that, because his opponent says no more upon the subject, he does so because he is disgusted with the stupidity of the other; no, it is because he is completely beaten, and has nothing more to say.

The distance now between the church and the hall was nearly traversed, and Mr. Chillingworth, who was a very good man, notwithstanding his disbelief in certain things of course paved the way for him to hell, took a kind leave of Mr. Marchdale and the brothers, promising to call on the following morning and see Flora.

Henry and George then, in earnest conversation with Marchdale, proceeded homewards. It was evident that the scene in the vault had made a deep and saddening impression upon them, and one which was not likely easily to be eradicated.

CHAPTER IX

THE OCCURRENCES OF THE NIGHT AT THE HALL.--THE SECOND APPEARANCE OF THE VAMPYRE, AND THE PISTOL-SHOT

Despite the full and free consent which Flora had given to her brothers to entrust her solely to the care of her mother and her own courage at the hall, she felt greater fear creep over her after they were gone than she chose to acknowledge.

A sort of presentiment appeared to come over her that some evil was about to occur, and more than once she caught herself almost in the act of saying,--

"I wish they had not gone."

Mrs. Bannerworth, too, could not be supposed to be entirely destitute of uncomfortable feelings, when she came to consider how poor a guard she was over her beautiful child, and how much terror might even deprive of the little power she had, should the dreadful visitor again make his appearance.

"But it is but for two hours," thought Flora, "and two hours will soon pass away."

There was, too, another feeling which gave her some degree of confidence, although it arose from a bad source, inasmuch as it was one which showed powerfully how much her mind was dwelling on the particulars of the horrible belief in the class of supernatural beings, one of whom she believed had visited her.

That consideration was this. The two hours of absence from the hall of its male inhabitants, would be from nine o'clock until eleven, and those were not the two hours during which she felt that she would be most timid on account of the vampyre.

"It was after midnight before," she thought, "when it came, and perhaps it may not be able to come earlier. It may not have the power, until that time, to make its hideous visits, and, therefore, I will believe myself safe."

She had made up her mind not to go to bed until the return of her brothers, and she and her mother sat in a small room that was used as a breakfast-room, and which had a latticed window that opened on to the lawn.

This window had in the inside strong oaken shutters, which had been fastened as securely as their construction would admit of some time before the departure of the brothers and Mr. Marchdale on that melancholy expedition, the object of which, if it had been known to her, would have added so much to the terrors of poor Flora.

It was not even guessed at, however remotely, so that she had not the additional affliction of thinking, that while she was sitting there, a prey to all sorts of imaginative terrors, they were perhaps gathering fresh evidence, as, indeed, they were, of the dreadful reality of the appearance which, but for the collateral circumstances attendant upon its coming and its going, she would fain have persuaded herself was but the vision of a dream.

It was before nine that the brothers started, but in her own mind Flora gave them to eleven, and when she heard ten o'clock sound from a clock which stood in the hall, she felt pleased to think that in another hour they would surely be at home.

"My dear," said her mother, "you look more like yourself, now."

"Do, I, mother?"

"Yes, you are well again."

"Ah, if I could forget--"

"Time, my dear Flora, will enable you to do so, and all the fear of what made you so unwell will pass away. You will soon forget it all."

"I will hope to do so."

"Be assured that, some day or another, something will occur, as Henry says, to explain all that has happened, in some way consistent with reason and the ordinary nature of things, my dear Flora."

"Oh, I will cling to such a belief; I will get Henry, upon whose judgment I know I can rely, to tell me so, and each time that I hear such words from his lips, I will contrive to dismiss some portion of the terror which now, I cannot but confess, clings to my heart."

Flora laid her hand upon her mother's arm, and in a low, anxious tone of voice, said,--"Listen, mother."

Mrs. Bannerworth turned pale, as she said,--"Listen to what, dear?"

"Within these last ten minutes," said Flora, "I have thought three or four times that I heard a slight noise without. Nay, mother, do not tremble--it may be only fancy."

Flora herself trembled, and was of a death-like paleness; once or twice she passed her hand across her brow, and altogether she presented a picture of much mental suffering.

They now conversed in anxious whispers, and almost all they said consisted in anxious wishes for the return of the brothers and Mr. Marchdale.

"You will be happier and more assured, my dear, with some company," said Mrs. Bannerworth. "Shall I ring for the servants, and let them remain in the room with us, until they who are our best safeguards next to Heaven return?"

"Hush--hush--hush, mother!"

"What do you hear?"

"I thought--I heard a faint sound."

"I heard nothing, dear."

"Listen again, mother. Surely I could not be deceived so often. I have now, at least, six times heard a sound as if some one was outside by the windows."

"No, no, my darling, do not think; your imagination is active and in a state of excitement."

"It is, and yet--"

"Believe me, it deceives you."

"I hope to Heaven it does!"

There was a pause of some minutes' duration, and then Mrs. Bannerworth again urged slightly the calling of some of the servants, for she thought that their presence might have the effect of giving a different direction to her child's thoughts; but Flora saw her place her hand upon the bell, and she said,--

"No, mother, no--not yet, not yet. Perhaps I am deceived."

Mrs. Bannerworth upon this sat down, but no sooner had she done so than she heartily regretted she had not rung the bell, for, before, another word could be spoken, there came too perceptibly upon their ears for there to be any mistake at all about it, a strange scratching noise upon the window outside.

A faint cry came from Flora's lips, as she exclaimed, in a voice of great agony,--

"Oh, God!--oh, God! It has come again!"

Mrs. Bannerworth became faint, and unable to move or speak at all; she could only sit like one paralysed, and unable to do more than listen to and see what was going on.

The scratching noise continued for a few seconds, and then altogether ceased. Perhaps, under ordinary circumstances, such a sound outside the window would have scarcely afforded food for comment at all, or, if it had, it would have been attributed to some natural effect, or to the exertions of some bird or animal to obtain admittance to the house.

But there had occurred now enough in that family to make any little sound of wonderful importance, and these things which before would have passed completely unheeded, at all events without creating much alarm, were now invested with a fearful interest.

When the scratching noise ceased, Flora spoke in a low, anxious whisper, as she said,--

"Mother, you heard it then?"

Mrs. Bannerworth tried to speak, but she could not; and then suddenly, with a loud clash, the bar, which on the inside appeared to fasten the shutters strongly, fell as if by some invisible agency, and the shutters now, but for the intervention of the window, could be easily pushed open from without.

Mrs. Bannerworth covered her face with her hands, and, after rocking to and fro for a moment, she fell off her chair, having fainted with the excess of terror that came over her.

For about the space of time in which a fast speaker could count twelve, Flora thought her reason was leaving her, but it did not. She found herself recovering; and there she sat, with her eyes fixed upon the window, looking more like some exquisitely-chiselled statue of despair than a being of flesh and blood, expecting each moment to have its eyes blasted by some horrible appearance, such as might be supposed to drive her to madness.

And now again came the strange knocking or scratching against the glass of the window.

This continued for some minutes, during which it appeared likewise to Flora that some confusion was going on at another part of the house, for she fancied she heard voices and the banging of doors.

It seemed to her as if she must have sat looking at the shutters of that window a long time before she saw them shake, and then one wide hinged portion of them slowly opened.

Once again horror appeared to be on the point of producing madness in her brain, and then, as before, a feeling of calmness rapidly ensued.

She was able to see plainly that something was by the window, but what it was she could not plainly discern, in consequence of the lights she had in the room. A few moments, however, sufficed to settle that mystery, for the window was opened and a figure stood before her.

One glance, one terrified glance, in which her whole soul was concentrated, sufficed to shew her who and what the figure was. There was the tall, gaunt form--there was the faded ancient apparel--the lustrous metallic-looking eyes--its half-opened month, exhibiting the tusk-like teeth! It was--yes, it was--the vampyre!

It stood for a moment gazing at her, and then in the hideous way it had attempted before to speak, it apparently endeavoured to utter some words which it could not make articulate to human ears. The pistols lay before Flora. Mechanically she raised one, and pointed it at the figure. It advanced a step, and then she pulled the trigger.

A stunning report followed. There was a loud cry of pain, and the vampyre fled. The smoke and the confusion that was incidental to the spot prevented her from seeing if the figure walked or ran away. She thought she heard a crashing sound among the plants outside the window, as if it had fallen, but she did not feel quite sure.

It was no effort of any reflection, but a purely mechanical movement, that made her raise the other pistol, and discharge that likewise in the direction the vampyre had taken. Then casting the weapon away, she rose, and made a frantic rush from the room. She opened the door, and was dashing out, when she found herself caught in the circling arms of some one who either had been there waiting, or who had just at that moment got there.

The thought that it was the vampyre, who by some mysterious means, had got there, and was about to make her his prey, now overcame her completely, and she sunk into a state of utter insensibility on the moment.

CHAPTER X

THE RETURN FROM THE VAULT.--THE ALARM, AND THE SEARCH AROUND THE HALL

It so happened that George and Henry Bannerworth, along with Mr. Marchdale, had just reached the gate which conducted into the garden of the mansion when they all were alarmed by the report of a pistol. Amid the stillness of the night, it came upon them with so sudden a shock, that they involuntarily paused, and there came from the lips of each an expression of alarm.

"Good heavens!" cried George, "can that be Flora firing at any intruder?"

"It must be," cried Henry; "she has in her possession the only weapons in the house."

Mr. Marchdale turned very pale, and trembled slightly, but he did not speak.

"On, on," cried Henry; "for God's sake, let us hasten on."

As he spoke, he cleared the gate at a bound, and at a terrific pace he made towards the house, passing over beds, and plantations, and flowers heedlessly, so that he went the most direct way to it.

Before, however, it was possible for any human speed to accomplish even half of the distance, the report of the other shot came upon his ears, and he even fancied he heard the bullet whistle past his head in tolerably close proximity. This supposition gave him a clue to the direction at all events from whence the shots proceeded, otherwise he knew not from which window they were fired, because it had not occurred to him, previous to leaving home, to inquire in which room Flora and his mother were likely to be seated waiting his return.

He was right as regarded the bullet. It was that winged messenger of death which had passed his head in such very dangerous proximity, and consequently he made with tolerable accuracy towards the open window from whence the shots had been fired.

The night was not near so dark as it had been, although even yet it was very far from being a light one, and he was soon enabled to see that there was a room, the window of which was wide open, and lights burning on the table within. He made towards it in a moment, and entered it. To his astonishment, the first objects he beheld were Flora and a stranger, who was now supporting her in his arms. To grapple him by the throat was the work of a moment, but the stranger cried aloud in a voice which sounded familiar to Harry,--

"Good God, are you all mad?"

Henry relaxed his hold, and looked in his face.

"Gracious heavens, it is Mr. Holland!" he said.

"Yes; did you not know me?"

Henry was bewildered. He staggered to a seat, and, in doing so, he saw his mother, stretched apparently lifeless upon the floor. To raise her was the work of a moment, and then Marchdale and George, who had followed him as fast as they could, appeared at the open window.

Such a strange scene as that small room now exhibited had never been equalled in Bannerworth Hall. There was young Mr. Holland, of whom mention has already been made, as the affianced lover of Flora, supporting her fainting form. There was Henry doing equal service to his mother; and on the floor lay the two pistols, and one of the candles which had been upset in the confusion; while the terrified attitudes of George and Mr. Marchdale at the window completed the strange-looking picture.

"What is this--oh! what has happened?" cried George.

"I know not--I know not," said Henry. "Some one summon the servants; I am nearly mad."

Mr. Marchdale at once rung the bell, for George looked so faint and ill as to be incapable of doing so; and he rung it so loudly and so effectually, that the two servants who had been employed suddenly upon the others leaving came with much speed to know what was the matter.

"See to your mistress," said Henry. "She is dead, or has fainted. For God's sake, let who can give me some account of what has caused all this confusion here."

"Are you aware, Henry," said Marchdale, "that a stranger is present in the room?"

He pointed to Mr. Holland as he spoke, who, before Henry could reply, said,--

"Sir, I may be a stranger to you, as you are to me, and yet no stranger to those whose home this is."

"No, no," said Henry, "you are no stranger to us, Mr. Holland, but are thrice welcome--none can be more welcome. Mr. Marchdale, this is Mr Holland, of whom you have heard me speak."

"I am proud to know you, sir," said Marchdale.

"Sir, I thank you," replied Holland, coldly.

It will so happen; but, at first sight, it appeared as if those two persons had some sort of antagonistic feeling towards each other, which threatened to prevent effectually their ever becoming intimate friends.

The appeal of Henry to the servants to know if they could tell him what had occurred was answered in the negative. All they knew was that they had heard two shots fired, and that, since then, they had remained where they were, in a great fright, until the bell was rung violently. This was no news at all and, therefore, the only chance was, to wait patiently for the recovery of the mother, or of Flora, from one or the other of whom surely some information could be at once then procured.

Mrs. Bannerworth was removed to her own room, and so would Flora have been; but Mr. Holland, who was supporting her in his arms, said,--

"I think the air from the open window is recovering her, and it is likely to do so. Oh, do not now take her from me, after so long an absence. Flora, Flora, look up; do you not know me? You have not yet given me one look of acknowledgment. Flora, dear Flora!"

The sound of his voice seemed to act as the most potent of charms in restoring her to consciousness; it broke through the death-like trance in which she lay, and, opening her beautiful eyes, she fixed them upon his face, saying,--

"Yes, yes; it is Charles--it is Charles."

She burst into a hysterical flood of tears, and clung to him like some terrified child to its only friend in the whole wide world.

"Oh, my dear friends," cried Charles Holland, "do not deceive me; has Flora been ill?"

"We have all been ill," said George.

"All ill?"

"Ay, and nearly mad," exclaimed Harry.

Holland looked from one to the other in surprise, as well he might, nor was that surprise at all lessened when Flora made an effort to extricate herself from his embrace, as she exclaimed,--

"You must leave me--you must leave me, Charles, for ever! Oh! never, never look upon my face again!"

"I--I am bewildered," said Charles.

"Leave me, now," continued Flora; "think me unworthy; think what you will, Charles, but I cannot, I dare not, now be yours."

"Is this a dream?"

"Oh, would it were. Charles, if we had never met, you would be happier--I could not be more wretched."

"Flora, Flora, do you say these words of so great cruelty to try my love?"

"No, as Heaven is my judge, I do not."

"Gracious Heaven, then, what do they mean?"

Flora shuddered, and Henry, coming up to her, took her hand in his tenderly, as he said,--

"Has it been again?"

"It has."

"You shot it?"

"I fired full upon it, Henry, but it fled."

"It did--fly?"

"It did, Henry, but it will come again--it will be sure to come again."

"You--you hit it with the bullet?" interposed Mr. Marchdale. "Perhaps you killed it?"

"I think I must have hit it, unless I am mad."

Charles Holland looked from one to the other with such a look of intense surprise, that George remarked it, and said at once to him,--

"Mr. Holland, a full explanation is due to you, and you shall have it."

"You seem the only rational person here," said Charles. "Pray what is it that everybody calls 'it?'"

"Hush--hush!" said Henry; "you shall hear soon, but not at present."

"Hear me, Charles," said Flora. "From this moment mind, I do release you from every vow, from every promise made to me of constancy and love; and if you are wise, Charles, and will be advised, you will now this moment leave this house never to return to it."

"No," said Charles--"no; by Heaven I love you, Flora! I have come to say again all that in another clime I said with joy to you. When I forget you, let what trouble may oppress you, may God forget me, and my own right hand forget to do me honest service."

"Oh! no more--no more!" sobbed Flora.

"Yes, much more, if you will tell me of words which shall be stronger than others in which to paint my love, my faith, and my constancy."

"Be prudent," said Henry. "Say no more."

"Nay, upon such a theme I could speak for ever. You may cast me off, Flora; but until you tell me you love another, I am yours till the death, and then with a sanguine hope at my heart that we shall meet again, never, dearest, to part."

Flora sobbed bitterly.

"Oh!" she said, "this is the unkindest blow of all--this is worse than all."

"Unkind!" echoed Holland.

"Heed her not," said Henry; "she means not you."

"Oh, no--no!" she cried. "Farewell, Charles--dear Charles."

"Oh, say that word again!" he exclaimed, with animation. "It is the first time such music has met my ears."

"It must be the last."

"No, no--oh, no."

"For your own sake I shall be able now, Charles, to show you that I really loved you."

"Not by casting me from you?"

"Yes, even so. That will be the way to show you that I love you."

She held up her hands wildly, as she added, in an excited voice,--

"The curse of destiny is upon me! I am singled out as one lost and accursed. Oh, horror--horror! would that I were dead!"

Charles staggered back a pace or two until he came to the table, at which he clutched for support. He turned very pale as he said, in a faint voice,--

"Is--is she mad, or am I?"

"Tell him I am mad, Henry," cried Flora. "Do not, oh, do not make his lonely thoughts terrible with more than that. Tell him I am mad."

"Come with me," whispered Henry to Holland. "I pray you come with me at once, and you shall know all."

"I--will."

"George, stay with Flora for a time. Come, come, Mr. Holland, you ought, and you shall know all; then you can come to a judgment for yourself. This way, sir. You cannot, in the wildest freak of your imagination, guess that which I have now to tell you."

Never was mortal man so utterly bewildered by the events of the last hour of his existence as was now Charles Holland, and truly he might well be so. He had arrived in England, and made what speed he could to the house of a family whom he admired for their intelligence, their high culture, and in one member of which his whole thoughts of domestic happiness in this world were centered, and he found nothing but confusion, incoherence, mystery, and the wildest dismay.

Well might he doubt if he were sleeping or waking--well might he ask if he or they were mad.

And now, as, after a long, lingering look of affection upon the pale, suffering face of Flora, he followed Henry from the room, his thoughts were busy in fancying a thousand vague and wild imaginations with respect to the communication which was promised to be made to him.

But, as Henry had truly said to him, not in the wildest freak of his imagination could he conceive of any thing near the terrible strangeness and horror of that which he had to tell him, and consequently he found himself closeted with Henry in a small private room, removed from the domestic part of the hall, to the full in as bewildered a state as he had been from the first.

CHAPTER XI

THE COMMUNICATIONS TO THE LOVER.--THE HEART'S DESPAIR

Consternation is sympathetic, and any one who had looked upon the features of Charles Holland, now that he was seated with Henry Bannerworth, in expectation of a communication which his fears told him was to blast all his dearest and most fondly cherished hopes for ever, would scarce have recognised in him the same young man who, one short hour before, had knocked so loudly, and so full of joyful hope and expectation, at the door of the hall.

But so it was. He knew Henry Bannerworth too well to suppose that any unreal cause could blanch his cheek. He knew Flora too well to imagine for one moment that caprice had dictated the, to him, fearful words of dismissal she had uttered to him.

Happier would it at that time have been for Charles Holland had she acted capriciously towards him, and convinced him that his true heart's devotion had been cast at the feet of one unworthy of so really noble a gift. Pride would then have enabled him, no doubt, successfully to resist the blow. A feeling of honest and proper indignation at having his feelings trifled with, would, no doubt, have sustained him, but, alas! the case seemed widely different.

True, she implored him to think of her no more--no longer to cherish in his breast the fond dream of affection which had been its guest so long; but the manner in which she did so brought along with it an irresistible conviction, that she was making a noble sacrifice of her own feelings for him, from some cause which was involved in the profoundest mystery.

But now he was to hear all. Henry had promised to tell him, and as he looked into his pale, but handsomely intellectual face, he half dreaded the disclosure he yet panted to hear.

"Tell me all, Henry--tell me all," he said. "Upon the words that come from your lips I know I can rely."

"I will have no reservations with you," said Henry, sadly. "You ought to know all, and you shall. Prepare yourself for the strangest revelation you ever heard."

"Indeed!"

"Ay. One which in hearing you may well doubt; and one which, I hope, you will never find an opportunity of verifying."

"You speak in riddles."

"And yet speak truly, Charles. You heard with what a frantic vehemence Flora desired you to think no more of her?"

"I did--I did."

"She was right. She is a noble-hearted girl for uttering those words. A dreadful incident in our family has occurred, which might well induce you to pause before uniting your fate with that of any member of it."

"Impossible. Nothing can possibly subdue the feelings of affection I entertain for Flora. She is worthy of any one, and, as such, amid all changes--all mutations of fortune, she shall be mine."

"Do not suppose that any change of fortune has produced the scene you were witness to."

"Then, what else?"

"I will tell you, Holland. In all your travels, and in all your reading, did you ever come across anything about vampyres?"

"About what?" cried Charles, drawing his chair forward a little. "About what?"

"You may well doubt the evidence of your own ears, Charles Holland, and wish me to repeat what I said. I say, do you know anything about vampyres?"

Charles Holland looked curiously in Henry's face, and the latter immediately added,--

"I can guess what is passing in your mind at present, and I do not wonder at it. You think I must be mad."

"Well, really, Henry, your extraordinary question--"

"I knew it. Were I you, I should hesitate to believe the tale; but the fact is, we have every reason to believe that one member of our own family is one of those horrible preternatural beings called vampyres."

"Good God, Henry, can you allow your judgment for a moment to stoop to such a supposition?"

"That is what I have asked myself a hundred times; but, Charles Holland, the judgment, the feelings, and all the prejudices, natural and acquired, must succumb to actual ocular demonstration. Listen to me, and do not interrupt me. You shall know all, and you shall know it circumstantially."

Henry then related to the astonished Charles Holland all that had occurred, from the first alarm of Flora, up to that period when he, Holland, caught her in his arms as she was about to leave the room.

"And now," he said, in conclusion, "I cannot tell what opinion you may come to as regards these most singular events. You will recollect that here is the unbiassed evidence of four or five people to the facts, and, beyond that, the servants, who have seen something of the horrible visitor."

"You bewilder me, utterly," said Charles Holland.

"As we are all bewildered."

"But--but, gracious Heaven! it cannot be."

"It is."

"No--no. There is--there must be yet some dreadful mistake."

"Can you start any supposition by which we can otherwise explain any of the phenomena I have described to you? If you can, for Heaven's sake do so, and you will find no one who will cling to it with more tenacity than I."

"Any other species or kind of supernatural appearance might admit of argument; but this, to my perception, is too wildly improbable--too much at variance with all we see and know of the operations of nature."

"It is so. All that we have told ourselves repeatedly, and yet is all human reason at once struck down by the few brief words of--'We have seen it.'"

"I would doubt my eyesight."

"One might; but many cannot be labouring under the same delusion."

"My friend, I pray you, do not make me shudder at the supposition that such a dreadful thing as this is at all possible."

"I am, believe me, Charles, most unwilling to oppress anyone with the knowledge of these evils; but you are so situated with us, that you ought to know, and you will clearly understand that you may, with perfect honour, now consider yourself free from all engagements you have entered into with Flora."

"No, no! By Heaven, no!"

"Yes, Charles. Reflect upon the consequences now of a union with such a family."

"Oh, Henry Bannerworth, can you suppose me so dead to all good feeling, so utterly lost to honourable impulses, as to eject from my heart her who has possession of it entirely, on such a ground as this?"

"You would be justified."

"Coldly justified in prudence I might be. There are a thousand circumstances in which a man may be justified in a particular course of action, and that course yet may be neither honourable nor just. I love Flora; and were she tormented by the whole of the supernatural world, I should still love her. Nay, it becomes, then, a higher and a nobler duty on my part to stand between her and those evils, if possible."

"Charles--Charles," said Henry, "I cannot of course refuse to you my meed of praise and admiration for your generosity of feeling; but, remember, if we are compelled, despite all our feelings and all our predilections to the contrary, to give in to a belief in the existence of vampyres, why may we not at once receive as the truth all that is recorded of them?"

"To what do you allude?"

"To this. That one who has been visited by a vampyre, and whose blood has formed a horrible repast for such a being, becomes, after death, one of the dreadful race, and visits others in the same way."

"Now this must be insanity," cried Charles.

"It bears the aspect of it, indeed," said Henry; "oh, that you could by some means satisfy yourself that I am mad."

"There may be insanity in this family," thought Charles, with such an exquisite pang of misery, that he groaned aloud.

"Already," added Henry, mournfully, "already the blighting influence of the dreadful tale is upon you, Charles. Oh, let me add my advice to Flora's entreaties. She loves you, and we all esteem you; fly, then, from us, and leave us to encounter our miseries alone. Fly from us, Charles Holland, and take with you our best wishes for happiness which you cannot know here."

"Never," cried Charles; "I devote my existence to Flora. I will not play the coward, and fly from one whom I love, on such grounds. I devote my life to her."

Henry could not speak for emotion for several minutes, and when at length, in a faltering voice, he could utter some words, he said,--

"God of heaven, what happiness is marred by these horrible events? What have we all done to be the victims of such a dreadful act of vengeance?"

"Henry, do not talk in that way," cried Charles. "Rather let us bend all our energies to overcoming the evil, than spend any time in useless lamentations. I cannot even yet give in to a belief in the existence of such a being as you say visited Flora."

"But the evidences."

"Look you here, Henry: until I am convinced that some things have happened which it is totally impossible could happen by any human means whatever, I will not ascribe them to supernatural influence."

"But what human means, Charles, could produce what I have now narrated to you?"

"I do not know, just at present, but I will give the subject the most attentive consideration. Will you accommodate me here for a time?"

"You know you are as welcome here as if the house were your own, and all that it contains."

"I believe so, most truly. You have no objection, I presume, to my conversing with Flora upon this strange subject?"

"Certainly not. Of course you will be careful to say nothing which can add to her fears."

"I shall be most guarded, believe me. You say that your brother George, Mr. Chillingworth, yourself, and this Mr. Marchdale, have all been cognisant of the circumstances."

"Yes--yes."

"Then with the whole of them you permit me to hold free communication upon the subject?"

"Most certainly."

"I will do so then. Keep up good heart, Henry, and this affair, which looks so full of terror at first sight, may yet be divested of some of its hideous aspect."

"I am rejoiced, if anything can rejoice me now," said Henry, "to see you view the subject with so much philosophy."

"Why," said Charles, "you made a remark of your own, which enabled me, viewing the matter in its very worst and most hideous aspect, to gather hope."

"What was that?"

"You said, properly and naturally enough, that if ever we felt that there was such a weight of evidence in favour of a belief in the existence of vampyres that we are compelled to succumb to it, we might as well receive all the popular feelings and superstitions concerning them likewise."

"I did. Where is the mind to pause, when once we open it to the reception of such things?"

"Well, then, if that be the case, we will watch this vampyre and catch it."

"Catch it?"

"Yes; surely it can be caught; as I understand, this species of being is not like an apparition, that may be composed of thin air, and utterly impalpable to the human touch, but it consists of a revivified corpse."

"Yes, yes."

"Then it is tangible and destructible. By Heaven! if ever I catch a glimpse of any such thing, it shall drag me to its home, be that where it may, or I will make it prisoner."

"Oh, Charles! you know not the feeling of horror that will come across you when you do. You have no idea of how the warm blood will seem to curdle in your veins, and how you will be paralysed in every limb."

"Did you feel so?"

"I did."

"I will endeavour to make head against such feelings. The love of Flora shall enable me to vanquish them. Think you it will come again to-morrow?"

"I can have no thought the one way or the other."

"It may. We must arrange among us all, Henry, some plan of watching which, without completely prostrating our health and strength, will always provide that one shall be up all night and on the alert."

"It must be done."

"Flora ought to sleep with the consciousness now that she has ever at hand some intrepid and well-armed protector, who is not only himself prepared to defend her, but who can in a moment give an alarm to us all, in case of necessity requiring it."

"It would be a dreadful capture to make to seize a vampyre," said Henry.

"Not at all; it would be a very desirable one. Being a corpse revivified, it is capable of complete destruction, so as to render it no longer a scourge to any one."

"Charles, Charles, are you jesting with me, or do you really give any credence to the story?"

"My dear friend, I always make it a rule to take things at their worst, and then I cannot be disappointed. I am content to reason upon this matter as if the fact of the existence of a vampyre were thoroughly established, and then to think upon what is best to be done about it."

"You are right."

"If it should turn out then that there is an error in the fact, well and good--we are all the better off; but if otherwise, we are prepared, and armed at all points."

"Let it be so, then. It strikes me, Charles, that you will be the coolest and the calmest among us all on this emergency; but the hour now waxes late, I will get them to prepare a chamber for you, and at least to-night, after what has occurred already, I should think we can be under no apprehension."

"Probably not. But, Henry, if you would allow me to sleep in that room where the portrait hangs of him whom you suppose to be the vampyre, I should prefer it."

"Prefer it!"

"Yes; I am not one who courts danger for danger's sake, but I would rather occupy that room, to see if the vampyre, who perhaps has a partiality for it, will pay me a visit."

"As you please, Charles. You can have the apartment. It is in the same state as when occupied by Flora. Nothing has been, I believe, removed from it."

"You will let me, then, while I remain here, call it my room?"

"Assuredly."

This arrangement was accordingly made to the surprise of all the household, not one of whom would, indeed, have slept, or attempted to sleep there for any amount of reward. But Charles Holland had his own reasons for preferring that chamber, and he was conducted to it in the course of half an hour by Henry, who looked around it with a shudder, as he bade his young friend good night.

CHAPTER XII

CHARLES HOLLAND'S SAD FEELINGS.--THE PORTRAIT.--THE OCCURRENCE OF THE NIGHT AT THE HALL

Charles Holland wished to be alone, if ever any human being had wished fervently to be so. His thoughts were most fearfully oppressive.

The communication that had been made to him by Henry Bannerworth, had about it too many strange, confirmatory circumstances to enable him to treat it, in his own mind, with the disrespect that some mere freak of a distracted and weak imagination would, most probably, have received from him.

He had found Flora in a state of excitement which could arise only from some such terrible cause as had been mentioned by her brother, and then he was, from an occurrence which certainly never could have entered into his calculations, asked to forego the bright dream of happiness which he had held so long and so rapturously to his heart.

How truly he found that the course of true love ran not smooth; and yet how little would any one have suspected that from such a cause as that which now oppressed his mind, any obstruction would arise.

Flora might have been fickle and false; he might have seen some other fairer face, which might have enchained his fancy, and woven for him a new heart's chain; death might have stepped between him and the realization of his fondest hopes; loss of fortune might have made the love cruel which would have yoked to its distresses a young and beautiful girl, reared in the lap of luxury, and who was not, even by those who loved her, suffered to feel, even in later years, any of the pinching necessities of the family.

All these things were possible--some of them were probable; and yet none of them had occurred. She loved him still; and he, although he had looked on many a fair face, and basked in the sunny smiles of beauty, had never for a moment forgotten her faith, or lost his devotion to his own dear English girl.

Fortune he had enough for both; death had not even threatened to rob him of the prize of such a noble and faithful heart which he had won. But a horrible superstition had arisen, which seemed to place at once an impassable abyss between them, and to say to him, in a voice of thundering denunciation,--

"Charles Holland, will you have a vampyre for your bride?"

The thought was terrific. He paced the gloomy chamber to and fro with rapid strides, until the idea came across his mind that by so doing he might not only be proclaiming to his kind entertainers how much he was mentally distracted, but he likewise might be seriously distracting them.

The moment this occurred to him he sat down, and was profoundly still for some time. He then glanced at the light which had been given to him, and he found himself almost unconsciously engaged in a mental calculation as to how long it would last him in the night.

Half ashamed, then, of such terrors, as such a consideration would seem to indicate, he was on the point of hastily extinguishing it, when he happened to cast his eyes on the now mysterious and highly interesting portrait in the panel.

The picture, as a picture, was well done, whether it was a correct likeness or not of the party whom it represented. It was one of those kind of portraits that seem so life-like, that, as you look at them, they seem to return your gaze fully, and even to follow you with their eyes from place to place.

By candle-light such an effect is more likely to become striking and remarkable than by daylight; and now, as Charles Holland shaded his own eyes from the light, so as to cast its full radiance upon the portrait, he felt wonderfully interested in its life-like appearance.

"Here is true skill," he said; "such as I have not before seen. How strangely this likeness of a man whom I never saw seems to gaze upon me."

Unconsciously, too, he aided the effect, which he justly enough called life-like, by a slight movement of the candle, such as any one not blessed with nerves of iron would be sure to make, and such a movement made the face look as if it was inspired with vitality.

Charles remained looking at the portrait for a considerable period of time. He found a kind of fascination in it which prevented him from drawing his eyes away from it. It was not fear which induced him to continue gazing on it, but the circumstance that it was a likeness of the man who, after death, was supposed to have borrowed so new and so hideous an existence, combined with its artistic merits, chained him to the spot.

"I shall now," he said, "know that face again, let me see it where I may, or under what circumstances I may. Each feature is now indelibly fixed upon my memory--I never can mistake it."

He turned aside as he uttered these words, and as he did so his eyes fell upon a part of the ornamental frame which composed the edge of the panel, and which seemed to him to be of a different colour from the surrounding portion.

Curiosity and increased interest prompted him at once to make a closer inquiry into the matter; and, by a careful and diligent scrutiny, he was almost induced to come to the positive opinion, that it no very distant period in time past, the portrait had been removed from the place it occupied.

When once this idea, even vague and indistinct as it was, in consequence of the slight grounds he formed it on, had got possession of his mind, he felt most anxious to prove its verification or its fallacy.

He held the candle in a variety of situations, so that its light fell in different ways on the picture; and the more he examined it, the more he felt convinced that it must have been moved lately.

It would appear as if, in its removal, a piece of the old oaken carved framework of the panel had been accidentally broken off, which caused the new look of the fracture, and that this accident, from the nature of the broken bit of framing, could have occurred in any other way than from an actual or attempted removal of the picture, he felt was extremely unlikely.

He set down the candle on a chair near at hand, and tried if the panel was fast in its place. Upon the very first touch, he felt convinced it was not so, and that it easily moved. How to get it out, though, presented a difficulty, and to get it out was tempting.

"Who knows," he said to himself, "what may be behind it? This is an old baronial sort of hall, and the greater portion of it was, no doubt, built at a time when the construction of such places as hidden chambers and intricate staircases were, in all buildings of importance, considered a disiderata."

That he should make some discovery behind the portrait, now became an idea that possessed him strongly, although he certainly had no definite grounds for really supposing that he should do so.

Perhaps the wish was more father to the thought than he, in the partial state of excitement he was in, really imagined; but so it was. He felt convinced that he should not be satisfied until he had removed that panel from the wall, and seen what was immediately behind it.

After the panel containing the picture had been placed where it was, it appeared that pieces of moulding had been inserted all around, which had had the effect of keeping it in its place, and it was a fracture of one of these pieces which had first called Charles Holland's attention to the probability of the picture having been removed. That he should have to get two, at least, of the pieces of moulding away, before he could hope to remove the picture, was to him quite apparent, and he was considering how he should accomplish such a result, when he was suddenly startled by a knock at his chamber door.

Until that sudden demand for admission at his door came, he scarcely knew to what a nervous state he had worked himself up. It was an odd sort of tap--one only--a single tap, as if some one demanded admittance, and wished to awaken his attention with the least possible chance of disturbing any one else.

"Come in," said Charles, for he knew he had not fastened his door; "come in."

There was no reply, but after a moment's pause, the same sort of low tap came again.

Again he cried "come in," but, whoever it was, seemed determined that the door should be opened for him, and no movement was made from the outside. A third time the tap came, and Charles was very close to the door when he heard it, for with a noiseless step he had approached it intending to open it. The instant this third mysterious demand for admission came, he did open it wide. There was no one there! In an instant he crossed the threshold into the corridor, which ran right and left. A window at one end of it now sent in the moon's rays, so that it was tolerably light, but he could see no one. Indeed, to look for any one, he felt sure was needless, for he had opened his chamber-door almost simultaneously with the last knock for admission.

"It is strange," he said, as he lingered on the threshold of his room door for some moments; "my imagination could not so completely deceive me. There was most certainly a demand for admission."

Slowly, then, he returned to his room again, and closed the door behind him.

"One thing is evident," he said, "that if I am in this apartment to be subjected to these annoyances, I shall get no rest, which will soon exhaust me."

This thought was a very provoking one, and the more he thought that he should ultimately find a necessity for giving up that chamber he had himself asked as a special favour to be allowed to occupy, the more vexed he became to think what construction might be put upon his conduct for so doing.

"They will all fancy me a coward," he thought, "and that I dare not sleep here. They may not, of course, say so, but they will think that my appearing so bold was one of those acts of bravado which I have not courage to carry fairly out."

Taking this view of the matter was just the way to enlist a young man's pride in staying, under all circumstances, where he was, and, with a slight accession of colour, which, even although he was alone, would visit his cheeks, Charles Holland said aloud,--

"I will remain the occupant of this room come what may, happen what may. No terrors, real or unsubstantial, shall drive me from it: I will brave them all, and remain here to brave them."

Tap came the knock at the door again, and now, with more an air of vexation than fear, Charles turned again towards it, and listened. Tap in another minute again succeeded, and much annoyed, he walked close to the door, and laid his hand upon the lock, ready to open it at the precise moment of another demand for admission being made.

He had not to wait long. In about half a minute it came again, and, simultaneously with the sound, the door flew open. There was no one to be seen; but, as he opened the door, he heard a strange sound in the corridor--a sound which scarcely could be called a groan, and scarcely a sigh, but seemed a compound of both, having the agony of the one combined with the sadness of the other. From what direction it came he could not at the moment decide, but he called out,--

"Who's there? who's there?"

The echo of his own voice alone answered him for a few moments, and then he heard a door open, and a voice, which he knew to be Henry's, cried,--

"What is it? who speaks?"

"Henry," said Charles.

"Yes--yes--yes."

"I fear I have disturbed you."

"You have been disturbed yourself, or you would not have done so. I shall be with you in a moment."

Henry closed his door before Charles Holland could tell him not to come to him, as he intended to do, for he felt ashamed to have, in a manner of speaking, summoned assistance for so trifling a cause of alarm as that to which he had been subjected. However, he could not go to Henry's chamber to forbid him from coming to his, and, more vexed than before, he retired to his room again to await his coming.

He left the door open now, so that Henry Bannerworth, when he had got on some articles of dress, walked in at once, saying,--

"What has happened, Charles?"

"A mere trifle, Henry, concerning which I am ashamed you should have been at all disturbed."

"Never mind that, I was wakeful."

"I heard a door open, which kept me listening, but I could not decide which door it was till I heard your voice in the corridor."

"Well, it was this door; and I opened it twice in consequence of the repeated taps for admission that came to it; some one has been knocking at it, and, when I go to it, lo! I can see nobody."

"Indeed!"

"Such is the case."

"You surprise me."

"I am very sorry to have disturbed you, because, upon such a ground, I do not feel that I ought to have done so; and, when I called out in the corridor, I assure you it was with no such intention."

"Do not regret it for a moment," said Henry; "you were quite justified in making an alarm on such an occasion."

"It's strange enough, but still it may arise from some accidental cause; admitting, if we did but know it, of some ready enough explanation."

"It may, certainly, but, after what has happened already, we may well suppose a mysterious connexion between any unusual sight or sound, and the fearful ones we have already seen."

"Certainly we may."

"How earnestly that strange portrait seems to look upon us, Charles."

"It does, and I have been examining it carefully. It seems to have been removed lately."

"Removed!"

"Yes, I think, as far as I can judge, that it has been taken from its frame; I mean, that the panel on which it is painted has been taken out."

"Indeed!"

"If you touch it you will find it loose, and, upon a close examination, you will perceive that a piece of the moulding which holds it in its place has been chipped off, which is done in such a place that I think it could only have arisen during the removal of the picture."

"You must be mistaken."

"I cannot, of course, take upon myself, Henry, to say precisely such is the case," said Charles.

"But there is no one here to do so."

"That I cannot say. Will you permit me and assist me to remove it? I have a great curiosity to know what is behind it."

"If you have, I certainly will do so. We thought of taking it away altogether, but when Flora left this room the idea was given up as useless. Remain here a few moments, and I will endeavour to find something which shall assist us in its removal."

Henry left the mysterious chamber in order to search in his own for some means of removing the frame-work of the picture, so that the panel would slip easily out, and while he was gone, Charles Holland continued gazing upon it with greater interest, if possible, than before.

In a few minutes Henry returned, and although what he had succeeded in finding were very inefficient implements for the purpose, yet with this aid the two young men set about the task.

It is said, and said truly enough, that "where there is a will there is a way," and although the young men had no tools at all adapted for the purpose, they did succeed in removing the moulding from the sides of the panel, and then by a little tapping at one end of it, and using a knife at a lever at the other end of the panel, they got it fairly out.

Disappointment was all they got for their pains. On the other side there was nothing but a rough wooden wall, against which the finer and more nicely finished oak panelling of the chamber rested.

"There is no mystery here," said Henry.

"None whatever," said Charles, as he tapped the wall with his knuckles, and found it all hard and sound. "We are foiled."

"We are indeed."

"I had a strange presentiment, now," added Charles, "that we should make some discovery that would repay us for our trouble. It appears, however, that such is not to be the case; for you see nothing presents itself to us but the most ordinary appearances."

"I perceive as much; and the panel itself, although of more than ordinary thickness, is, after all, but a bit of planed oak, and apparently fashioned for no other object than to paint the portrait on."

"True. Shall we replace it?"

Charles reluctantly assented, and the picture was replaced in its original position. We say Charles reluctantly assented, because, although he had now had ocular demonstration that there was really nothing behind the panel but the ordinary woodwork which might have been expected from the construction of the old house, yet he could not, even with such a fact staring him in the face, get rid entirely of the feeling that had come across him, to the effect that the picture had some mystery or another.

"You are not yet satisfied," said Henry, as he observed the doubtful look of Charles Holland's face.

"My dear friend," said Charles, "I will not deceive you. I am much disappointed that we have made no discovery behind that picture."

"Heaven knows we have mysteries enough in our family," said Henry.

Even as he spoke they were both startled by a strange clattering noise at the window, which was accompanied by a shrill, odd kind of shriek, which sounded fearful and preternatural on the night air.

"What is that?" said Charles.

"God only knows," said Henry.

The two young men naturally turned their earnest gaze in the direction of the window, which we have before remarked was one unprovided with shutters, and there, to their intense surprise, they saw, slowly rising up from the lower part of it, what appeared to be a human form. Henry would have dashed forward, but Charles restrained him, and drawing quickly from its case a large holster pistol, he levelled it carefully at the figure, saying in a whisper,--

"Henry, if I don't hit it, I will consent to forfeit my head."

He pulled the trigger--a loud report followed--the room was filled with smoke, and then all was still. A circumstance, however, had occurred, as a consequence of the concussion of air produced by the discharge of the pistol, which neither of the young men had for the moment calculated upon, and that was the putting out of the only light they there had.

In spite of this circumstance, Charles, the moment he had discharged the pistol, dropped it and sprung forward to the window. But here he was perplexed, for he could not find the old fashioned, intricate fastening which held it shut, and he had to call to Henry,--

"Henry! For God's sake open the window for me, Henry! The fastening of the window is known to you, but not to me. Open it for me."

Thus called upon, Henry sprung forward, and by this time the report of the pistol had effectually alarmed the whole household. The flashing of lights from the corridor came into the room, and in another minute, just as Henry succeeded in getting the window wide open, and Charles Holland had made his way on to the balcony, both George Bannerworth and Mr. Marchdale entered the chamber, eager to know what had occurred. To their eager questions Henry replied,--

"Ask me not now;" and then calling to Charles, he said,--"Remain where you are, Charles, while I run down to the garden immediately beneath the balcony."

"Yes--yes," said Charles.

Henry made prodigious haste, and was in the garden immediately below the bay window in a wonderfully short space of time. He spoke to Charles, saying,--

"Will you now descend? I can see nothing here; but we will both make a search."

George and Mr. Marchdale were both now in the balcony, and they would have descended likewise, but Henry said,--

"Do not all leave the house. God only knows, now, situated as we are, what might happen."

"I will remain, then," said George. "I have been sitting up to-night as the guard, and, therefore, may as well continue to do so."

Marchdale and Charles Holland clambered over the balcony, and easily, from its insignificant height, dropped into the garden. The night was beautiful, and profoundly still. There was not a breath of air sufficient to stir a leaf on a tree, and the very flame of the candle which Charles had left burning in the balcony burnt clearly and steadily, being perfectly unruffled by any wind.

It cast a sufficient light close to the window to make everything very plainly visible, and it was evident at a glance that no object was there, although had that figure, which Charles shot at, and no doubt hit, been flesh and blood, it must have dropped immediately below.

As they looked up for a moment after a cursory examination of the ground, Charles exclaimed,--

"Look at the window! As the light is now situated, you can see the hole made in one of the panes of glass by the passage of the bullet from my pistol."

They did look, and there the clear, round hole, without any starring, which a bullet discharged close to a pane of glass will make in it, was clearly and plainly discernible.

"You must have hit him," said Henry.

"One would think so," said Charles; "for that was the exact place where the figure was."

"And there is nothing here," added Marchdale. "What can we think of these events--what resource has the mind against the most dreadful suppositions concerning them?"

Charles and Henry were both silent; in truth, they knew not what to think, and the words uttered by Marchdale were too strikingly true to dispute for a moment. They were lost in wonder.

"Human means against such an appearance as we saw to-night," said Charles, "are evidently useless."

"My dear young friend," said Marchdale, with much emotion, as he grasped Henry Bannerworth's hand, and the tears stood in his eyes as he did so,--"my dear young friend, these constant alarms will kill you. They will drive you, and all whose happiness you hold dear, distracted. You must control these dreadful feelings, and there is but one chance that I can see of getting now the better of these."

"What is that?"

"By leaving this place for ever."

"Alas! am I to be driven from the home of my ancestors from such a cause as this? And whither am I to fly? Where are we to find a refuge? To leave here will be at once to break up the establishment which is now held together, certainly upon the sufferance of creditors, but still to their advantage, inasmuch as I am doing what no one else would do, namely, paying away to within the scantiest pittance the whole proceeds of the estate that spreads around me."

"Heed nothing but an escape from such horrors as seem to be accumulating now around you."

"If I were sure that such a removal would bring with it such a corresponding advantage, I might, indeed, be induced to risk all to accomplish it."

"As regards poor dear Flora," said Mr. Marchdale, "I know not what to say, or what to think; she has been attacked by a vampyre, and after this mortal life shall have ended, it is dreadful to think there may be a possibility that she, with all her beauty, all her excellence and purity of mind, and all those virtues and qualities which should make her the beloved of all, and which do, indeed, attach all hearts towards her, should become one of that dreadful tribe of beings who cling to existence by feeding, in the most dreadful manner, upon the life blood of others--oh, it is too dreadful to contemplate! Too horrible--too horrible!"

"Then wherefore speak of it?" said Charles, with some asperity. "Now, by the great God of Heaven, who sees all our hearts, I will not give in to such a horrible doctrine! I will not believe it; and were death itself my portion for my want of faith, I would this moment die in my disbelief of anything so truly fearful!"

"Oh, my young friend," added Marchdale, "if anything could add to the pangs which all who love, and admire, and respect Flora Bannerworth must feel at the unhappy condition in which she is placed, it would be the noble nature of you, who, under happier auspices, would have been her guide through life, and the happy partner of her destiny."

"As I will be still."

"May Heaven forbid it! We are now among ourselves, and can talk freely upon such a subject. Mr. Charles Holland, if you wed, you would look forward to being blessed with children--those sweet ties which bind the sternest hearts to life with so exquisite a bondage. Oh, fancy, then, for a moment, the mother of your babes coming at the still hour of midnight to drain from their veins the very life blood she gave to them. To drive you and them mad with the expected horror of such visitations--to make your nights hideous--your days but so many hours of melancholy retrospection. Oh, you know not the world of terror, on the awful brink of which you stand, when you talk of making Flora Bannerworth a wife."

"Peace! oh, peace!" said Henry.

"Nay, I know my words are unwelcome," continued Mr. Marchdale. "It happens, unfortunately for human nature, that truth and some of our best and holiest feelings are too often at variance, and hold a sad contest--"

"I will hear no more of this," cried Charles Holland.--"I will hear no more."

"I have done," said Mr. Marchdale.

"And 'twere well you had not begun."

"Nay, say not so. I have but done what I considered was a solemn duty."

"Under that assumption of doing duty--a solemn duty--heedless of the feelings and the opinions of others," said Charles, sarcastically, "more mischief is produced--more heart-burnings and anxieties caused, than by any other two causes of such mischievous results combined. I wish to hear no more of this."

"Do not be angered with Mr. Marchdale, Charles," said Henry. "He can have no motive but our welfare in what he says. We should not condemn a speaker because his words may not sound pleasant to our ears."

"By Heaven!" said Charles, with animation, "I meant not to be illiberal; but I will not because I cannot see a man's motives for active interference in the affairs of others, always be ready, merely on account of such ignorance, to jump to a conclusion that they must be estimable."

"To-morrow, I leave this house," said Marchdale.

"Leave us?" exclaimed Henry.

"Ay, for ever."

"Nay, now, Mr. Marchdale, is this generous?"

"Am I treated generously by one who is your own guest, and towards whom I was willing to hold out the honest right hand of friendship?"

Henry turned to Charles Holland, saying,--

"Charles, I know your generous nature. Say you meant no offence to my mother's old friend."

"If to say I meant no offence," said Charles, "is to say I meant no insult, I say it freely."

"Enough," cried Marchdale; "I am satisfied."

"But do not," added Charles, "draw me any more such pictures as the one you have already presented to my imagination, I beg of you. From the storehouse of my own fancy I can find quite enough to make me wretched, if I choose to be so; but again and again do I say I will not allow this monstrous superstition to tread me down, like the tread of a giant on a broken reed. I will contend against it while I have life to do so."

"Bravely spoken."

"And when I desert Flora Bannerworth, may Heaven, from that moment, desert me!"

"Charles!" cried Henry, with emotion, "dear Charles, my more than friend--brother of my heart--noble Charles!"

"Nay, Henry, I am not entitled to your praises. I were base indeed to be other than that which I purpose to be. Come weal or woe--come what may, I am the affianced husband of your sister, and she, and she only, can break asunder the tie that binds me to her."

CHAPTER XIII

THE OFFER FOR THE HALL.--THE VISIT TO SIR FRANCIS VARNEY.--THE STRANGE RESEMBLANCE.--A DREADFUL SUGGESTION

The party made a strict search through every nook and corner of the garden, but it proved to be a fruitless one: not the least trace of any one could be found. There was only one circumstance, which was pondered over deeply by them all, and that was that, beneath the window of the room in which Flora and her mother sat while the brothers were on their visit to the vault of their ancestors, were visible marks of blood to a considerable extent.

It will be remembered that Flora had fired a pistol at the spectral appearance, and that immediately upon that it had disappeared, after uttering a sound which might well be construed into a cry of pain from a wound.

That a wound then had been inflicted upon some one, the blood beneath the window now abundantly testified; and when it was discovered, Henry and Charles made a very close examination indeed of the garden, to discover what direction the wounded figure, be it man or vampyre, had taken.

But the closest scrutiny did not reveal to them a single spot of blood, beyond the space immediately beneath the window;--there the apparition seemed to have received its wound, and then, by some mysterious means, to have disappeared.

At length, wearied with the continued excitement, combined with want of sleep, to which they had been subjected, they returned to the hall.

Flora, with the exception of the alarm she experienced from the firing of the pistol, had met with no disturbance, and that, in order to spare her painful reflections, they told her was merely done as a precautionary measure, to proclaim to any one who might be lurking in the garden that the inmates of the house were ready to defend themselves against any aggression.

Whether or not she believed this kind deceit they knew not. She only sighed deeply, and wept. The probability is, that she more than suspected the vampyre had made another visit, but they forbore to press the point; and, leaving her with her mother, Henry and George went from her chamber again--the former to endeavour to seek some repose, as it would be his turn to watch on the succeeding night, and the latter to resume his station in a small room close to Flora's chamber, where it had been agreed watch and ward should be kept by turns while the alarm lasted.

At length, the morning again dawned upon that unhappy family, and to none were its beams more welcome.

The birds sang their pleasant carols beneath the window. The sweet, deep-coloured autumnal sun shone upon all objects with a golden luster; and to look abroad, upon the beaming face of nature, no one could for a moment suppose, except from sad experience, that there were such things as gloom, misery, and crime, upon the earth.

"And must I," said Henry, as he gazed from a window of the hall upon the undulating park, the majestic trees, the flowers, the shrubs, and the many natural beauties with which the place was full,--"must I be chased from this spot, the home of my self and of my kindred, by a phantom--must I indeed seek refuge elsewhere, because my own home has become hideous?"

It was indeed a cruel and a painful thought! It was one he yet would not, could not be convinced was absolutely necessary. But now the sun was shining: it was morning; and the feelings, which found a home in his breast amid the darkness, the stillness, and the uncertainty of night, were chased away by those glorious beams of sunlight, that fell upon hill, valley, and stream, and the thousand sweet sounds of life and animation that filled that sunny air!

Such a revulsion of feeling was natural enough. Many of the distresses and mental anxieties of night vanish with the night, and those which oppressed the heart of Henry Bannerworth were considerably modified.

He was engaged in these reflections when he heard the sound of the lodge bell, and as a visitor was now somewhat rare at this establishment, he waited with some anxiety to see to whom he was indebted for so early a call.

In the course of a few minutes, one of the servants came to him with a letter in her hand.

It bore a large handsome seal, and, from its appearance, would seem to have come from some personage of consequence. A second glance at it shewed him the name of "Varney" in the corner, and, with some degree of vexation, he muttered to himself,

"Another condoling epistle from the troublesome neighbour whom I have not yet seen."

"If you please, sir," said the servant who had brought him the letter, "as I'm here, and you are here, perhaps you'll have no objection to give me what I'm to have for the day and two nights as I've been here, cos I can't stay in a family as is so familiar with all sorts o' ghostesses: I ain't used to such company."

"What do you mean?" said Henry.

The question was a superfluous one--: too well he knew what the woman meant, and the conviction came across his mind strongly that no domestic would consent to live long in a house which was subject to such dreadful visitations.

"What does I mean!" said the woman,--"why, sir, if it's all the same to you, I don't myself come of a wampyre family, and I don't choose to remain in a house where there is sich things encouraged. That's what I means, sir."

"What wages are owing to you?" said Henry.

"Why, as to wages, I only comed here by the day."

"Go, then, and settle with my mother. The sooner you leave this house, the better."

"Oh, indeed. I'm sure I don't want to stay."

This woman was one of those who were always armed at all points for a row, and she had no notion of concluding any engagement, of any character whatever, without some disturbance; therefore, to see Henry take what she said with such provoking calmness was aggravating in the extreme; but there was no help for such a source of vexation. She could find no other ground of quarrel than what was connected with the vampyre, and, as Henry would not quarrel with her on such a score, she was compelled to give it up in despair.

When Henry found himself alone, and free from the annoyance of this woman, he turned his attention to the letter he held in his hand, and which, from the autograph in the corner, he knew came from his new neighbour, Sir Francis Varney, whom, by some chance or another, he had never yet seen.

To his great surprise, he found that the letter contained the following words:--

Dear Sir,--"As a neighbour, by purchase of an estate contiguous to your own, I am quite sure you have excused, and taken in good part, the cordial offer I made to you of friendship and service some short time since; but now, in addressing to you a distinct proposition, I trust I shall meet with an indulgent consideration, whether such proposition be accordant with your views or not.

"What I have heard from common report induces me to believe that Bannerworth Hall cannot be a desirable residence for yourself, or your amiable sister. If I am right in that conjecture, and you have any serious thought of leaving the place, I would earnestly recommend you, as one having some experience in such descriptions of property, to sell it at once.

"Now, the proposition with which I conclude this letter is, I know, of a character to make you doubt the disinterestedness of such advice; but that it is disinterested, nevertheless, is a fact of which I can assure my own heart, and of which I beg to assure you. I propose, then, should you, upon consideration, decide upon such a course of proceeding, to purchase of you the Hall. I do not ask for a bargain on account of any extraneous circumstances which may at the present time depreciate the value of the property, but I am willing to give a fair price for it. Under these circumstances, I trust, sir, that you will give a kindly consideration to my offer, and even if you reject it, I hope that, as neighbours, we may live long in peace and amity, and in the interchange of those good offices which should subsist between us. Awaiting your reply,

"Believe me to be, dear sir,
"Your very obedient servant,
"FRANCIS VARNEY.
"To Henry Bannerworth, Esq."

Henry, after having read this most unobjectionable letter through, folded it up again, and placed it in his pocket. Clasping his hands, then, behind his back, a favourite attitude of his when he was in deep contemplation, he paced to and fro in the garden for some time in deep thought.

"How strange," he muttered. "It seems that every circumstance combines to induce me to leave my old ancestral home. It appears as if everything now that happened had that direct tendency. What can be the meaning of all this? 'Tis very strange--amazingly strange. Here arise circumstances which are enough to induce any man to leave a particular place. Then a friend, in whose single-mindedness and judgment I know I can rely, advises the step, and immediately upon the back of that comes a fair and candid offer."

There was an apparent connexion between all these circumstances which much puzzled Henry. He walked to and fro for nearly an hour, until he heard a hasty footstep approaching him, and upon looking in the direction from whence it came, he saw Mr. Marchdale.

"I will seek Marchdale's advice," he said, "upon this matter. I will hear what he says concerning it."

"Henry," said Marchdale, when he came sufficiently near to him for conversation, "why do you remain here alone?"

"I have received a communication from our neighbour, Sir Francis Varney," said Henry.

"Indeed!"

"It is here. Peruse it for yourself, and then tell me, Marchdale, candidly what you think of it."

"I suppose," said Marchdale, as he opened the letter, "it is another friendly note of condolence on the state of your domestic affairs, which, I grieve to say, from the prattling of domestics, whose tongues it is quite impossible to silence, have become food for gossip all over the neighbouring villages and estates."

"If anything could add another pang to those I have already been made to suffer," said Henry, "it would certainly arise from being made the food of vulgar gossip. But read the letter, Marchdale. You will find its contents of a more important character than you anticipate."

"Indeed!" said Marchdale, as he ran his eyes eagerly over the note.

When he had finished it he glanced at Henry, who then said,--

"Well, what is your opinion?"

"I know not what to say, Henry. You know that my own advice to you has been to get rid of this place."

"It has."

"With the hope that the disagreeable affair connected with it now may remain connected with it as a house, and not with you and yours as a family."

"It may be so."

"There appears to me every likelihood of it."

"I do not know," said Henry, with a shudder. "I must confess, Marchdale, that to my own perceptions it seems more probable that the infliction we have experienced from the strange visitor, who seems now resolved to pester us with visits, will rather attach to a family than to a house. The vampyre may follow us."

"If so, of course the parting with the Hall would be a great pity, and no gain."

"None in the least."

"Henry, a thought has struck me."

"Let's hear it, Marchdale."

"It is this:--Suppose you were to try the experiment of leaving the Hall without selling it. Suppose for one year you were to let it to some one, Henry."

"It might be done."

"Ay, and it might, with very great promise and candour, be proposed to this very gentleman, Sir Francis Varney, to take it for one year, to see how he liked it before becoming the possessor of it. Then if he found himself tormented by the vampyre, he need not complete the purchase, or if you found that the apparition followed you from hence, you might yourself return, feeling that perhaps here, in the spots familiar to your youth, you might be most happy, even under such circumstances as at present oppress you."

"Most happy!" ejaculated Henry.

"Perhaps I should not have used that word."

"I am sure you should not," said Henry, "when you speak of me."

"Well--well; let us hope that the time may not be very far distant when I may use the term happy, as applied to you, in the most conclusive and the strongest manner it can be used."

"Oh," said Henry, "I will hope; but do not mock me with it now, Marchdale, I pray you."

"Heaven forbid that I should mock you!"

"Well--well; I do not believe you are the man to do so to any one. But about this affair of the house."

"Distinctly, then, if I were you, I would call upon Sir Francis Varney, and make him an offer to become a tenant of the Hall for twelve months, during which time you could go where you please, and test the fact of absence ridding you or not ridding you of the dreadful visitant who makes the night here truly hideous."

"I will speak to my mother, to George, and to my sister of the matter. They shall decide."

Mr. Marchdale now strove in every possible manner to raise the spirits of Henry Bannerworth, by painting to him the future in far more radiant colours than the present, and endeavouring to induce a belief in his mind that a short period of time might after all replace in his mind, and in the minds of those who were naturally so dear to him, all their wonted serenity.

Henry, although he felt not much comfort from these kindly efforts, yet could feel gratitude to him who made them; and after expressing such a feeling to Marchdale, in strong terms, he repaired to the house, in order to hold a solemn consultation with those whom he felt ought to be consulted as well as himself as to what steps should be taken with regard to the Hall.

The proposition, or rather the suggestion, which had been made by Marchdale upon the proposition of Sir Francis Varney, was in every respect so reasonable and just, that it met, as was to be expected, with the concurrence of every member of the family.

Flora's cheeks almost resumed some of their wonted colour at the mere thought now of leaving that home to which she had been at one time so much attached.

"Yes, dear Henry," she said, "let us leave here if you are agreeable so to do, and in leaving this house, we will believe that we leave behind us a world of terror."

"Flora," remarked Henry, in a tone of slight reproach, "if you were so anxious to leave Bannerworth Hall, why did you not say so before this proposition came from other mouths? You know your feelings upon such a subject would have been laws to me."

"I knew you were attached to the old house," said Flora; "and, besides, events have come upon us all with such fearful rapidity, there has scarcely been time to think."

"True--true."

"And you will leave, Henry?"

"I will call upon Sir Francis Varney myself, and speak to him upon the subject."

A new impetus to existence appeared now to come over the whole family, at the idea of leaving a place which always would be now associated in their minds with so much terror. Each member of the family felt happier, and breathed more freely than before, so that the change which had come over them seemed almost magical. And Charles Holland, too, was much better pleased, and he whispered to Flora,--

"Dear Flora, you will now surely no longer talk of driving from you the honest heart that loves you?"

"Hush, Charles, hush!" she said; "meet me an hour hence in the garden, and we will talk of this."

"That hour will seem an age," he said.

Henry, now, having made a determination to see Sir Francis Varney, lost no time in putting it into execution. At Mr. Marchdale's own request, he took him with him, as it was desirable to have a third person present in the sort of business negotiation which was going on. The estate which had been so recently entered upon by the person calling himself Sir Francis Varney, and which common report said he had purchased, was a small, but complete property, and situated so close to the grounds connected with Bannerworth Hall, that a short walk soon placed Henry and Mr. Marchdale before the residence of this gentleman, who had shown so kindly a feeling towards the Bannerworth family.

"Have you seen Sir Francis Varney?" asked Henry of Mr. Marchdale, as he rung the gate-bell.

"I have not. Have you?"

"No; I never saw him. It is rather awkward our both being absolute strangers to his person."

"We can but send in our names, however; and, from the great vein of courtesy that runs through his letter, I have no doubt but we shall receive the most gentlemanly reception from him."

A servant in handsome livery appeared at the iron-gates, which opened upon a lawn in the front of Sir Francis Varney's house, and to this domestic Henry Bannerworth handed his card, on which he had written, in pencil, likewise the name of Mr. Marchdale.

"If your master," he said, "is within, we shall be glad to see him."

"Sir Francis is at home, sir," was the reply, "although not very well. If you will be pleased to walk in, I will announce you to him."

Henry and Marchdale followed the man into a handsome enough reception-room, where they were desired to wait while their names were announced.

"Do you know if this gentleman be a baronet," said Henry, "or a knight merely?"

"I really do not; I never saw him in my life, or heard of him before he came into this neighbourhood."

"And I have been too much occupied with the painful occurrences of this hall to know anything of our neighbours. I dare say Mr. Chillingworth, if we had thought to ask him, would have known something concerning him."

"No doubt."

This brief colloquy was put an end to by the servant, who said,--

"My master, gentlemen, is not very well; but he begs me to present his best compliments, and to say he is much gratified with your visit, and will be happy to see you in his study."

Henry and Marchdale followed the man up a flight of stone stairs, and then they were conducted through a large apartment into a smaller one. There was very little light in this small room; but at the moment of their entrance a tall man, who was seated, rose, and, touching the spring of a blind that was to the window, it was up in a moment, admitting a broad glare of light. A cry of surprise, mingled with terror, came from Henry Bannerworth's lip. The original of the portrait on the panel stood before him! There was the lofty stature, the long, sallow face, the slightly projecting teeth, the dark, lustrous, although somewhat sombre eyes; the expression of the features--all were alike.

"Are you unwell, sir?" said Sir Francis Varney, in soft, mellow accents, as he handed a chair to the bewildered Henry.

"God of Heaven!" said Henry; "how like!"

"You seem surprised, sir. Have you ever seen me before?"

Sir Francis drew himself up to his full height, and cast a strange glance upon Henry, whose eyes were rivetted upon his face, as if with a species of fascination which he could not resist.

"Marchdale," Henry gasped; "Marchdale, my friend, Marchdale. I--I am surely mad."

"Hush! be calm," whispered Marchdale.

"Calm--calm--can you not see? Marchdale, is this a dream? Look--look--oh! look."

"For God's sake, Henry, compose yourself."

"Is your friend often thus?" said Sir Francis Varney, with the same mellifluous tone which seemed habitual to him.

"No, sir, he is not; but recent circumstances have shattered his nerves; and, to tell the truth, you bear so strong a resemblance to an old portrait, in his house, that I do not wonder so much as I otherwise should at his agitation."

"Indeed."

"A resemblance!" said Henry; "a resemblance! God of Heaven! it is the face itself."

"You much surprise me," said Sir Francis.

Henry sunk into the chair which was near him, and he trembled violently. The rush of painful thoughts and conjectures that came through his mind was enough to make any one tremble. "Is this the vampyre?" was the horrible question that seemed impressed upon his very brain, in letters of flame. "Is this the vampyre?"

"Are you better, sir?" said Sir Francis Varney, in his bland, musical voice. "Shall I order any refreshment for you?"

"No--no," gasped Henry; "for the love of truth tell me! Is--is your name really Varney!"

"Sir?"

"Have you no other name to which, perhaps, a better title you could urge?"

"Mr. Bannerworth, I can assure you that I am too proud of the name of the family to which I belong to exchange it for any other, be it what it may."

"How wonderfully like!"

"I grieve to see you so much distressed. Mr. Bannerworth. I presume ill health has thus shattered your nerves?"

"No; ill health has not done the work. I know not what to say, Sir Francis Varney, to you; but recent events in my family have made the sight of you full of horrible conjectures."

"What mean you, sir?"

"You know, from common report, that we have had a fearful visitor at our house."

"A vampyre, I have heard," said Sir Francis Varney, with a bland, and almost beautiful smile, which displayed his white glistening teeth to perfection.

"Yes; a vampyre, and--and--"

"I pray you go on, sir; you surely are far above the vulgar superstition of believing in such matters?"

"My judgment is assailed in too many ways and shapes for it to hold out probably as it ought to do against so hideous a belief, but never was it so much bewildered as now."

"Why so?"

"Because--"

"Nay, Henry," whispered Mr. Marchdale, "it is scarcely civil to tell Sir Francis to his face, that he resembles a vampyre."

"I must, I must."

"Pray, sir," interrupted Varney to Marchdale, "permit Mr. Bannerworth to speak here freely. There is nothing in the whole world I so much admire as candour."

"Then you so much resemble the vampyre," added Henry, "that--that I know not what to think."

"Is it possible?" said Varney.

"It is a damning fact."

"Well, it's unfortunate for me, I presume? Ah!"

Varney gave a twinge of pain, as if some sudden bodily ailment had attacked him severely.

"You are unwell, sir?" said Marchdale.

"No, no--no," he said; "I--hurt my arm, and happened accidentally to touch the arm of this chair with it."

"A hurt?" said Henry.

"Yes, Mr. Bannerworth."

"A--a wound?"

"Yes, a wound, but not much more than skin deep. In fact, little beyond an abrasion of the skin."

"May I inquire how you came by it?"

"Oh, yes. A slight fall."

"Indeed."

"Remarkable, is it not? Very remarkable. We never know a moment when, from same most trifling cause, we may receive really some serious bodily harm. How true it is, Mr. Bannerworth, that in the midst of life we are in death."

"And equally true, perhaps," said Henry, "that in the midst of death there may be found a horrible life."

"Well, I should not wonder. There are really so many strange things in this world, that I have left off wondering at anything now."

"There are strange things," said Henry. "You wish to purchase of me the Hall, sir?"

"If you wish to sell."

"You--you are perhaps attached to the place? Perhaps you recollected it, sir, long ago?"

"Not very long," smiled Sir Francis Varney. "It seems a nice comfortable old house; and the grounds, too, appear to be amazingly well wooded, which, to one of rather a romantic temperament like myself, is always an additional charm to a place. I was extremely pleased with it the first time I beheld it, and a desire to call myself the owner of it took possession of my mind. The scenery is remarkable for its beauty, and, from what I have seen of it, it is rarely to be excelled. No doubt you are greatly attached to it."

"It has been my home from infancy," returned Henry, "and being also the residence of my ancestors for centuries, it is natural that I should be so."

"True--true."

"The house, no doubt, has suffered much," said Henry, "within the last hundred years."

"No doubt it has. A hundred years is a tolerable long space of time, you know."

"It is, indeed. Oh, how any human life which is spun out to such an extent, must lose its charms, by losing all its fondest and dearest associations."

"Ah, how true," said Sir Francis Varney. He had some minutes previously touched a bell, and at this moment a servant brought in on a tray some wine and refreshments.

CHAPTER XIV

HENRY'S AGREEMENT WITH SIR FRANCIS VARNEY.--THE SUDDEN ARRIVAL AT THE HALL.--FLORA'S ALARM

On the tray which the servant brought into the room, were refreshments of different kinds, including wine, and after waving his hand for the domestic to retire, Sir Francis Varney said,--

"You will be better, Mr. Bannerworth, for a glass of wine after your walk, and you too, sir. I am ashamed to say, I have quite forgotten your name."

"Marchdale."

"Mr. Marchdale. Ay, Marchdale. Pray, sir, help yourself."

"You take nothing yourself?" said Henry.

"I am under a strict regimen," replied Varney. "The simplest diet alone does for me, and I have accustomed myself to long abstinence."

"He will not eat or drink," muttered Henry, abstractedly.

"Will you sell me the Hall?" said Sir Francis Varney.

Henry looked in his face again, from which he had only momentarily withdrawn his eyes, and he was then more struck than ever with the resemblance between him and the portrait on the panel of what had been Flora's chamber. What made that resemblance, too, one about which there could scarcely be two opinions, was the mark or cicatrix of a wound in the forehead, which the painter had slightly indented in the portrait, but which was much more plainly visible on the forehead of Sir Francis Varney. Now that Henry observed this distinctive mark, which he had not done before, he could feel no doubt, and a sickening sensation came over him at the thought that he was actually now in the presence of one of those terrible creatures, vampyres.

"You do not drink," said Varney. "Most young men are not so modest with a decanter of unimpeachable wine before them. I pray you help yourself."

"I cannot."

Henry rose as he spoke, and turning to Marchdale, he said, in addition,--

"Will you come away?"

"If you please," said Marchdale, rising.

"But you have not, my dear sir," said Varney, "given me yet any answer about the Hall?"

"I cannot yet," answered Henry, "I will think. My present impression is, to let you have it on whatever terms you may yourself propose, always provided you consent to one of mine."

"Name it."

"That you never show yourself in my family."

"How very unkind. I understand you have a charming sister, young, beautiful, and accomplished. Shall I confess, now, that I had hopes of making myself agreeable to her?"

"You make yourself agreeable to her? The sight of you would blast her for ever, and drive her to madness."

"Am I so hideous?"

"No, but--you are--"

"What am I?"

"Hush, Henry, hush," cried Marchdale. "Remember you are in this gentleman's house."

"True, true. Why does he tempt me to say these dreadful things? I do not want to say them."

"Come away, then--come away at once. Sir Francis Varney, my friend, Mr. Bannerworth, will think over your offer, and let you know. I think you may consider that your wish to become the purchaser of the Hall will be complied with."

"I wish to have it," said Varney, "and I can only say, that if I am master of it, I shall be very happy to see any of the family on a visit at any time."

"A visit!" said Henry, with a shudder. "A visit to the tomb were far more desirable. Farewell, sir."

"Adieu," said Sir Francis Varney, and he made one of the most elegant bows in the world, while there came over his face a peculiarity of expression that was strange, if not painful, to contemplate. In another minute Henry and Marchdale were clear of the house, and with feelings of bewilderment and horror, which beggar all description, poor Henry allowed himself to be led by the arm by Marchdale to some distance, without uttering a word. When he did speak, he said,--

"Marchdale, it would be charity of some one to kill me."

"To kill you!"

"Yes, for I am certain otherwise that I must go mad."

"Nay, nay; rouse yourself."

"This man, Varney, is a vampyre."

"Hush! hush!"

"I tell you, Marchdale," cried Henry, in a wild, excited manner, "he is a vampyre. He is the dreadful being who visited Flora at the still hour of midnight, and drained the life-blood from her veins. He is a vampyre. There are such things. I cannot doubt now. Oh, God, I wish now that your lightnings would blast me, as here I stand, for over into annihilation, for I am going mad to be compelled to feel that such horrors can really have existence."

"Henry--Henry."

"Nay, talk not to me. What can I do? Shall I kill him? Is it not a sacred duty to destroy such a thing? Oh, horror--horror. He must be killed--destroyed--burnt, and the very dust to which he is consumed must be scattered to the winds of Heaven. It would be a deed well done, Marchdale."

"Hush! hush! These words are dangerous."

"I care not."

"What if they were overheard now by unfriendly ears? What might not be the uncomfortable results? I pray you be more cautious what you say of this strange man."

"I must destroy him."

"And wherefore?"

"Can you ask? Is he not a vampyre?"

"Yes; but reflect, Henry, for a moment upon the length to which you might carry out so dangerous an argument. It is said that vampyres are made by vampyres sucking the blood of those who, but for that circumstance, would have died and gone to decay in the tomb along with ordinary mortals; but that being so attacked during life by a vampyre, they themselves, after death, become such."

"Well--well, what is that to me?"

"Have you forgotten Flora?"

A cry of despair came from poor Henry's lips, and in a moment he seemed completely, mentally and physically, prostrated.

"God of Heaven!" he moaned, "I had forgotten her!"

"I thought you had."

"Oh, if the sacrifice of my own life would suffice to put an end to all this accumulating horror, how gladly would I lay it down. Ay, in any way--in any way. No mode of death should appal me. No amount of pain make me shrink. I could smile then upon the destroyer, and say, 'welcome--welcome--most welcome.'"

"Rather, Henry, seek to live for those whom you love than die for them. Your death would leave them desolate. In life you may ward off many a blow of fate from them."

"I may endeavour so to do."

"Consider that Flora may be wholly dependent upon such kindness as you may be able to bestow upon her."

"Charles clings to her."

"Humph!"

"You do not doubt him?"

"My dear friend, Henry Bannerworth, although I am not an old man, yet I am so much older than you that I have seen a great deal of the world, and am, perhaps, far better able to come to accurate judgments with regard to individuals."

"No doubt--no doubt; but yet--"

"Nay, hear me out. Such judgments, founded upon experience, when uttered have all the character of prophecy about them. I, therefore, now prophecy to you that Charles Holland will yet be so stung with horror at the circumstance of a vampyre visiting Flora, that he will never make her his wife."

"Marchdale, I differ from you most completely," said Henry. "I know that Charles Holland is the very soul of honour."

"I cannot argue the matter with you. It has not become a thing of fact. I have only sincerely to hope that I am wrong."

"You are, you may depend, entirely wrong. I cannot be deceived in Charles. From you such words produce no effect but one of regret that you should so much err in your estimate of any one. From any one but yourself they would have produced in me a feeling of anger I might have found it difficult to smother."

"It has often been my misfortune through life," said Mr. Marchdale, sadly, "to give the greatest offence where I feel the truest friendship, because it is in such quarters that I am always tempted to speak too freely."

"Nay, no offence," said Henry. "I am distracted, and scarcely know what I say. Marchdale, I know you are my sincere friend--but, as I tell you, I am nearly mad."

"My dear Henry, be calmer. Consider upon what is to be said concerning this interview at home."

"Ay; that is a consideration."

"I should not think it advisable to mention the disagreeable fact, that in your neighbour you think you have found out the nocturnal disturber of your family."

"No--no."

"I would say nothing of it. It is not at all probable that, after what you have said to him this Sir Francis Varney, or whatever his real name may be will obtrude himself upon you."

"If he should he die."

"He will, perhaps, consider that such a step would be dangerous to him."

"It would be fatal, so help me. However, and then would I take especial care that no power of resuscitation should ever enable that man again to walk the earth."

"They say that only way of destroying a vampyre is to fix him to the earth with a stake, so that he cannot move, and then, of course, decomposition will take its course, as in ordinary cases."

"Fire would consume him, and be a quicker process," said Henry. "But these are fearful reflections, and, for the present, we will not pursue them. Now to play the hypocrite, and endeavour to look composed and serene to my mother, and to Flora while my heart is breaking."

The two friends had by this time reached the hall, and leaving his friend Marchdale, Henry Bannerworth, with feelings of the most unenviable description, slowly made his way to the apartment occupied by his mother and sister.

CHAPTER XV

THE OLD ADMIRAL AND HIS SERVANT.--THE COMMUNICATION FROM THE LANDLORD OF THE NELSON'S ARMS

While those matters of most grave and serious import were going on at the Hall, while each day, and almost each hour in each day, was producing more and more conclusive evidence upon a matter which at first had seemed too monstrous to be at all credited, it may well be supposed what a wonderful sensation was produced among the gossip-mongers of the neighbourhood by the exaggerated reports that had reached them.

The servants, who had left the Hall on no other account, as they declared, but sheer fright at the awful visits of the vampyre, spread the news far and wide, so that in the adjoining villages and market-towns the vampyre of Bannerworth Hall became quite a staple article of conversation.

Such a positive godsend for the lovers of the marvellous had not appeared in the country side within the memory of that sapient individual--the oldest inhabitant.

And, moreover, there was one thing which staggered some people of better education and maturer judgments, and that was, that the more they took pains to inquire into the matter, in order, if possible, to put an end to what they considered a gross lie from the commencement, the more evidence they found to stagger their own senses upon the subject.

Everywhere then, in every house, public as well as private, something was being continually said of the vampyre. Nursery maids began to think a vampyre vastly superior to "old scratch and old bogie" as a means of terrifying their infant charges into quietness, if not to sleep, until they themselves became too much afraid upon the subject to mention it.

But nowhere was gossiping carried on upon the subject with more systematic fervour than at an inn called the Nelson's Arms, which was in the high street of the nearest market town to the Hall.

There, it seemed as if the lovers of the horrible made a point of holding their head quarters, and so thirsty did the numerous discussions make the guests, that the landlord was heard to declare that he, from his heart, really considered a vampyre as very nearly equal to a contested election.

It was towards evening of the same day that Marchdale and Henry made their visit to Sir Francis Varney, that a postchaise drew up to the inn we have mentioned. In the vehicle were two persons of exceedingly dissimilar appearance and general aspect.

One of these people was a man who seemed fast verging upon seventy years of age, although, from his still ruddy and embrowned complexion and stentorian voice, it was quite evident he intended yet to keep time at arm's-length for many years to come.

He was attired in ample and expensive clothing, but every article had a naval animus about it, if we may be allowed such an expression with regard to clothing. On his buttons was an anchor, and the general assortment and colour of the clothing as nearly assimilated as possible to the undress naval uniform of an officer of high rank some fifty or sixty years ago.

His companion was a younger man, and about his appearance there was no secret at all. He was a genuine sailor, and he wore the shore costume of one. He was hearty-looking, and well dressed, and evidently well fed.

As the chaise drove up to the door of the inn, this man made an observation to the other to the following effect,--

"A-hoy!"

"Well, you lubber, what now?" cried the other.

"They call this the Nelson's Arms; and you know, shiver me, that for the best half of his life he had but one."

"D--n you!" was the only rejoinder he got for this observation; but, with that, he seemed very well satisfied.

"Heave to!" he then shouted to the postilion, who was about to drive the chaise into the yard. "Heave to, you lubberly son of a gun! we don't want to go into dock."

"Ah!" said the old man, "let's get out, Jack. This is the port; and, do you hear, and be cursed to you, let's have no swearing, d--n you, nor bad language, you lazy swab."

"Aye, aye," cried Jack; "I've not been ashore now a matter o' ten years, and not larnt a little shore-going politeness, admiral, I ain't been your walley de sham without larning a little about land reckonings. Nobody would take me for a sailor now, I'm thinking, admiral."

"Hold your noise!"

"Aye, aye, sir."

Jack, as he was called, bundled out of the chaise when the door was opened, with a movement so closely resembling what would have ensued had he been dragged out by the collar, that one was tempted almost to believe that such a feat must have been accomplished all at once by some invisible agency.

He then assisted the old gentleman to alight, and the landlord of the inn commenced the usual profusion of bows with which a passenger by a postchaise is usually welcomed in preference to one by a stage coach.

"Be quiet, will you!" shouted the admiral, for such indeed he was. "Be quiet."

"Best accommodation, sir--good wine--well-aired beds--good attendance--fine air--"

"Belay there," said Jack; and he gave the landlord what no doubt he considered a gentle admonition, but which consisted of such a dig in the ribs, that he made as many evolutions as the clown in a pantomime when he vociferates hot codlings.

"Now, Jack, where's the sailing instructions?" said his master.

"Here, sir, in the locker," said Jack, as he took from his pocket a letter, which he handed to the admiral.

"Won't you step in, sir?" said the landlord, who had begun now to recover a little from the dig in the ribs.

"What's the use of coming into port and paying harbour dues, and all that sort of thing, till we know if it's the right, you lubber, eh?"

"No; oh, dear me, sir, of course--God bless me, what can the old gentleman mean?"

The admiral opened the letter, and read:--

"If you stop at the Nelson's Aims at Uxotter, you will hear of me, and I can be sent for, when I will tell you more.

"Yours, very obediently and humbly,
"JOSIAH CRINKLES."

"Who the deuce is he?"

"This is Uxotter, sir," said the landlord; "and here you are, sir, at the Nelson's Arms. Good beds--good wine--good--"

"Silence!"

"Yes, sir--oh, of course"

"Who the devil is Josiah Crinkles?"

"Ha! ha! ha! ha! Makes me laugh, sir. Who the devil indeed! They do say the devil and lawyers, sir, know something of each other--makes me smile."

"I'll make you smile on the other side of that d----d great hatchway of a mouth of yours in a minute. Who is Crinkles?"

"Oh, Mr. Crinkles, sir, everybody knows, most respectable attorney, sir, indeed, highly respectable man, sir."

"A lawyer?"

"Yes, sir, a lawyer."

"Well, I'm d----d!"

Jack gave a long whistle, and both master and man looked at each other aghast.

"Now, hang me!" cried the admiral, "if ever I was so taken in in all my life."

"Ay, ay, sir," said Jack.

"To come a hundred and seventy miles see a d----d swab of a rascally lawyer."

"Ay, ay, sir."

"I'll smash him--Jack!"

"Yer honour?"

"Get into the chaise again."

"Well, but where's Master Charles? Lawyers, in course, sir, is all blessed rogues; but, howsomdever, he may have for once in his life this here one of 'em have told us of the right channel, and if so be as he has, don't be the Yankee to leave him among the pirates. I'm ashamed on you."

"You infernal scoundrel; how dare you preach to me in such a way, you lubberly rascal?"

"Cos you desarves it."

"Mutiny--mutiny--by Jove! Jack, I'll have you put in irons--you're a scoundrel, and no seaman."

"No seaman!--no seaman!"

"Not a bit of one."

"Very good. It's time, then, as I was off the purser's books. Good bye to you; I only hopes as you may get a better seaman to stick to you and be your walley de sham nor Jack Pringle, that's all the harm I wish you. You didn't call me no seaman in the Bay of Corfu, when the bullets were scuttling our nobs."

"Jack, you rascal, give us your fin. Come here, you d----d villain. You'll leave me, will you?"

"Not if I know it."

"Come in, then"

"Don't tell me I'm no seaman. Call me a wagabone if you like, but don't hurt my feelings. There I'm as tender as a baby, I am.--Don't do it."

"Confound you, who is doing it?"

"The devil."

"Who is?"

"Don't, then."

Thus wrangling, they entered the inn, to the great amusement of several bystanders, who had collected to hear the altercation between them.

"Would you like a private room, sir?" said the landlord.

"What's that to you?" said Jack.

"Hold your noise, will you?" cried his master. "Yes, I should like a private room, and some grog."

"Strong as the devil!" put in Jack.

"Yes, sir-yes, sir. Good wines--good beds--good--"

"You said all that before, you know," remarked Jack, as he bestowed upon the landlord another terrific dig in the ribs.

"Hilloa!" cried the admiral, "you can send for that infernal lawyer, Mister Landlord."

"Mr. Crinkles, sir?"

"Yes, yes."

"Who may I have the honour to say, sir, wants to see him?"

"Admiral Bell."

"Certainly, admiral, certainly. You'll find him a very conversible, nice, gentlemanly little man, sir."

"And tell him as Jack Pringle is here, too," cried the seaman.

"Oh, yes, yes--of course," said the landlord, who was in such a state of confusion from the digs in the ribs he had received and the noise his guests had already made in his house, that, had he been suddenly put upon his oath, he would scarcely have liked to say which was the master and which was the man.

"The idea now, Jack," said the admiral, "of coming all this way to see a lawyer."

"Ay, ay, sir."

"If he'd said he was a lawyer, we would have known what to do. But it's a take in, Jack."

"So I think. Howsomdever, we'll serve him out when we catch him, you know."

"Good--so we will."

"And, then, again, he may know something about Master Charles, sir, you know. Lord love him, don't you remember when he came aboard to see you once at Portsmouth?"

"Ah! I do, indeed."

"And how he said he hated the French, and quite a baby, too. What perseverance and sense. 'Uncle,' says he to you, 'when I'm a big man, I'll go in a ship, and fight all the French in a heap,' says he. 'And beat 'em, my boy, too,' says you; cos you thought he'd forgot that; and then he says, 'what's the use of saying that, stupid?--don't we always beat 'em?'"

The admiral laughed and rubbed his hands, as he cried aloud,--

"I remember, Jack--I remember him. I was stupid to make such a remark."

"I know you was--a d----d old fool I thought you."

"Come, come. Hilloa, there!"

"Well, then, what do you call me no seaman for?"

"Why, Jack, you bear malice like a marine."

"There you go again. Goodbye. Do you remember when we were yard arm to yard arm with those two Yankee frigates, and took 'em both! You didn't call me a marine then, when the scuppers were running with blood. Was I a seaman then?"

"You were, Jack--you were; and you saved my life."

"I didn't."

"You did."

"I say I didn't--it was a marlin-spike."

"But I say you did, you rascally scoundrel.--I say you did, and I won't be contradicted in my own ship."

"Call this your ship?"

"No, d--n it--I--"

"Mr. Crinkles," said the landlord, flinging the door wide open, and so at once putting an end to the discussion which always apparently had a tendency to wax exceedingly warm.

"The shark, by G--d!" said Jack.

A little, neatly dressed man made his appearance, and advanced rather timidly into the room. Perhaps he had heard from the landlord that the parties who had sent for him were of rather a violent sort.

"So you are Crinkles, are you?" cried the admiral. "Sit down, though you are a lawyer."

"Thank you, sir. I am an attorney, certainly, and my name as certainly is Crinkles."

"Look at that."

The admiral placed the letter in the little lawyer's hands, who said,--

"Am I to read it?"

"Yes, to be sure."

"Aloud?"

"Read it to the devil, if you like, in a pig's whisper, or a West India hurricane."

"Oh, very good, sir. I--I am willing to be agreeable, so I'll read it aloud, if it's all the same to you."

He then opened the letter, and read as follows:--

"To Admiral Bell.

"Admiral,--Being, from various circumstances, aware that you take a warm and a praiseworthy interest in your nephew, Charles Holland, I venture to write to you concerning a matter in which your immediate and active co-operation with others may rescue him from a condition which will prove, if allowed to continue, very much to his detriment, and ultimate unhappiness.

"You are, then, hereby informed, that he, Charles Holland, has, much earlier than he ought to have done, returned to England, and that the object of his return is to contract a marriage into a family in every way objectionable, and with a girl who is highly objectionable.

"You, admiral, are his nearest and almost his only relative in the world; you are the guardian of his property, and, therefore, it becomes a duty on your part to interfere to save him from the ruinous consequences of a marriage, which is sure to bring ruin and distress upon himself and all who take an interest in his welfare.

"The family he wishes to marry into is named Bannerworth, and the young lady's name is Flora Bannerworth. When, however, I inform you that a vampyre is in that family, and that if he marries into it, he marries a vampyre, and will have vampyres for children, I trust I have said enough to warn you upon the subject, and to induce you to lose no time in repairing to the spot.

"If you stop at the Nelson's Arms at Uxotter, you will hear of me. I can be sent for, when I will tell you more.

"Yours, very obediently and humbly,

"JOSIAH CRINKLES."

"P.S. I enclose you Dr. Johnson's definition of a vampyre, which is as follows:

"VAMPYRE (a German blood-sucker)--by which you perceive how many vampyres, from time immemorial, must have been well entertained at the expense of John Bull, at the court of St. James, where no thing hardly is to be met with but German blood-suckers."

***

The lawyer ceased to read, and the amazed look with which he glanced at the face of Admiral Bell would, under any other circumstances, have much amused him. His mind, however, was by far too much engrossed with a consideration of the danger of Charles Holland, his nephew, to be amused at anything; so, when he found that the little lawyer said nothing, he bellowed out,--

"Well, sir?"

"We--we--well," said the attorney.

"I've sent for you, and here you are, and here I am, and here's Jack Pringle. What have you got to say?"

"Just this much," said Mr. Crinkles, recovering himself a little, "just this much, sir, that I never saw that letter before in all my life."

"You--never--saw--it?"

"Never."

"Didn't you write it?"

"On my solemn word of honour, sir, I did not."

Jack Pringle whistled, and the admiral looked puzzled. Like the admiral in the song, too, he "grew paler," and then Mr. Crinkles added,--

"Who has forged my name to a letter such as this, I cannot imagine. As for writing to you, sir, I never heard of your existence, except publicly, as one of those gallant officers who have spent a long life in nobly fighting their country's battles, and who are entitled to the admiration and the applause of every Englishman."

Jack and the admiral looked at each other in amazement, and then the latter exclaimed,--

"What! This from a lawyer?"

"A lawyer, sir," said Crinkles, "may know how to appreciate the deeds of gallant men, although he may not be able to imitate them. That letter, sir, is a forgery, and I now leave you, only much gratified at the incident which has procured me the honour of an interview with a gentleman, whose name will live in the history of his country. Good day, sir! Good day!"

"No! I'm d----d if you go like that," said Jack, as he sprang to the door, and put his back against it. "You shall take a glass with me in honour of the wooden walls of Old England, d----e, if you was twenty lawyers."

"That's right, Jack," said the admiral. "Come, Mr. Crinkles, I'll think, for your sake, there may be two decent lawyers in the world, and you one of them. We must have a bottle of the best wine the ship--I mean the house--can afford together."

"If it is your command, admiral, I obey with pleasure," said the attorney; "and although I assure you, on my honour, I did not write that letter, yet some of the matters mentioned in it are so generally notorious here, that I can afford you information concerning them."

"Can you?"

"I regret to say I can, for I respect the parties."

"Sit down, then--sit down. Jack, run to the steward's room and get the wine. We will go into it now starboard and larboard. Who the deuce could have written that letter?"

"I have not the least idea, sir."

"Well--well, never mind; it has brought me here, that's something, so I won't grumble much at it. I didn't know my nephew was in England, and I dare say he didn't know I was; but here we both are, and I won't rest till I've seen him, and ascertained how the what's-its-name--"

"The vampyre."

"Ah! the vampyre."

"Shiver my timbers!" said Jack Pringle, who now brought in some wine much against the remonstrances of the waiters of the establishment, who considered that he was treading upon their vested interests by so doing.--"Shiver my timbers, if I knows what a wamphigher is, unless he's some distant relation to Davy Jones!"

"Hold your ignorant tongue," said the admiral; "nobody wants you to make a remark, you great lubber!"

"Very good," said Jack, and he sat down the wine on the table, and then retired to the other end of the room, remarking to himself that he was not called a great lubber on a certain occasion, when bullets were scuttling their nobs, and they were yard arm and yard arm with God knows who.

"Now, mister lawyer," said Admiral Bell, who had about him a large share of the habits of a rough sailor. "Now, mister lawyer, here is a glass first to our better acquaintance, for d----e, if I don't like you!"

"You are very good, sir."

"Not at all. There was a time, when I'd just as soon have thought of asking a young shark to supper with me in my own cabin as a lawyer, but I begin to see that there may be such a thing as a decent, good sort of a fellow seen in the law; so here's good luck to you, and you shall never want a friend or a bottle while Admiral Bell has a shot in the locker."

"Gammon," said Jack.

"D--n you, what do you mean by that?" roared the admiral, in a furious tone.

"I wasn't speaking to you," shouted Jack, about two octaves higher. "It's two boys in the street as is pretending they're a going to fight, and I know d----d well they won't."

"Hold your noise."

"I'm going. I wasn't told to hold my noise, when our nobs were being scuttled off Beyrout."

"Never mind him, mister lawyer," added the admiral. "He don't know what he's talking about. Never mind him. You go on and tell me all you know about the--the--"

"The vampyre!"

"Ah! I always forget the names of strange fish. I suppose, after all, it's something of the mermaid order?"

"That I cannot say, sir; but certainly the story, in all its painful particulars, has made a great sensation all over the country."

"Indeed!"

"Yes, sir. You shall hear how it occurred. It appears that one night Miss Flora Bannersworth, a young lady of great beauty, and respected and admired by all who knew her was visited by a strange being who came in at the window."

"My eye," said Jack, "it waren't me, I wish it had a been."

"So petrified by fear was she, that she had only time to creep half out of the bed, and to utter one cry of alarm, when the strange visitor seized her in his grasp."

"D--n my pig tail," said Jack, "what a squall there must have been, to be sure."

"Do you see this bottle?" roared the admiral.

"To be sure, I does; I think as it's time I seed another."

"You scoundrel, I'll make you feel it against that d----d stupid head of yours, if you interrupt this gentleman again."

"Don't be violent."

"Well, as I was saying," continued the attorney, "she did, by great good fortune, manage to scream, which had the effect of alarming the whole house. The door of her chamber, which was fast, was broken open."

"Yes, yes--"

"Ah," cried Jack.

"You may imagine the horror and the consternation of those who entered the room to find her in the grasp of a fiend-like figure, whose teeth were fastened on her neck, and who was actually draining her veins of blood."

"The devil!"

"Before any one could lay hands sufficiently upon the figure to detain it, it had fled precipitately from its dreadful repast. Shots were fired after it in vain."

"And they let it go?"

"They followed it, I understand, as well as they were able, and saw it scale the garden wall of the premises; there it escaped, leaving, as you may well imagine, on all their minds, a sensation of horror difficult to describe."

"Well, I never did hear anything the equal of that. Jack, what do you think of it?"

"I haven't begun to think, yet," said Jack.

"But what about my nephew, Charles?" added the admiral.

"Of him I know nothing."

"Nothing?"

"Not a word, admiral. I was not aware you had a nephew, or that any gentleman bearing that, or any other relationship to you, had any sort of connexion with these mysterious and most unaccountable circumstances. I tell you all I have gathered from common report about this vampyre business. Further I know not, I assure you."

"Well, a man can't tell what he don't know. It puzzles me to think who could possibly have written me this letter."

"That I am completely at a loss to imagine," said Crinkles. "I assure you, my gallant sir, that I am much hurt at the circumstance of any one using my name in such a way. But, nevertheless, as you are here, permit me to say, that it will be my pride, my pleasure, and the boast of the remainder of my existence, to be of some service to so gallant a defender of my country, and one whose name, along with the memory of his deeds, is engraved upon the heart of every Briton."

"Quite ekal to a book, he talks," said Jack. "I never could read one myself, on account o' not knowing how, but I've heard 'em read, and that's just the sort o' incomprehensible gammon."

"We don't want any of your ignorant remarks," said the admiral, "so you be quiet."

"Ay, ay, sir."

"Now, Mister Lawyer, you are an honest fellow, and an honest fellow is generally a sensible fellow."

"Sir, I thank you."

"If so be as what this letter says is true, my nephew Charles has got a liking for this girl, who has had her neck bitten by a vampyre, you see."

"I perceive, sir."

"Now what would you do?"

"One of the most difficult, as well, perhaps, as one of the most ungracious of tasks," said the attorney, "is to interfere with family affairs. The cold and steady eye of reason generally sees things in such very different lights to what they appear to those whose feelings and whose affections are much compromised in their results."

"Very true. Go on."

"Taking, my dear sir, what in my humble judgment appears to be a reasonable view of this subject, I should say it would be a dreadful thing for your nephew to marry into a family any member of which was liable to the visitations of a vampyre."

"It wouldn't be pleasant."

"The young lady might have children."

"Oh, lots," cried Jack.

"Hold your noise, Jack."

"Ay, ay, sir."

"And she might herself actually, when after death she became a vampyre, come and feed on her own children."

"Become a vampyre! What, is she going to be a vampyre too?"

"My dear sir, don't you know that it is a remarkable fact, as regards the physiology of vampyres, that whoever is bitten by one of those dreadful beings, becomes a vampyre?"

"The devil!"

"It is a fact, sir."

"Whew!" whistled Jack; "she might bite us all, and we should be a whole ship's crew o' wamphighers. There would be a confounded go!"

"It's not pleasant," said the admiral, as he rose from his chair, and paced to and fro in the room, "it's not pleasant. Hang me up at my own yard-arm if it is."

"Who said it was?" cried Jack.

"Who asked you, you brute?"

"Well, sir," added Mr. Crinkles, "I have given you all the information I can; and I can only repeat what I before had the honour of saying more at large, namely, that I am your humble servant to command, and that I shall be happy to attend upon you at any time."

"Thank ye--thank ye, Mr.--a--a--"

"Crinkles."

"Ah, Crinkles. You shall hear from me again, sir, shortly. Now that I am down here, I will see to the very bottom of this affair, were it deeper than fathom ever sounded. Charles Holland was my poor sister's son; he's the only relative I have in the wide world, and his happiness is dearer to my heart than my own."

Crinkles turned aside, and, by the twinkle of his eyes, one might premise that the honest little lawyer was much affected.

"God bless you, sir," he said; "farewell."

"Good day to you."

"Good-bye, lawyer," cried Jack. "Mind how you go. D--n me, if you don't seem a decent sort of fellow, and, after all, you may give the devil a clear berth, and get into heaven's straits with a flowing sheet, provided as you don't, towards the end of the voyage, make any lubberly blunders."

The old admiral threw himself into a chair with a deep sigh.

"Jack," said he.

"Aye, aye, sir."

"What's to be done now?"

Jack opened the window to discharge the superfluous moisture from an enormous quid he had indulged himself with while the lawyer was telling about the vampyre, and then again turning his face towards his master, he said,--

"Do! What shall we do? Why, go at once and find out Charles, our nevy, and ask him all about it, and see the young lady, too, and lay hold o' the wamphigher if we can, as well, and go at the whole affair broadside to broadside, till we make a prize of all the particulars, after which we can turn it over in our minds agin, and see what's to be done."

"Jack, you are right. Come along."

"I knows I am. Do you know now which way to steer?"

"Of course not. I never was in this latitude before, and the channel looks intricate. We will hail a pilot, Jack, and then we shall be all right, and if we strike it will be his fault."

"Which is a mighty great consolation," said Jack. "Come along."

CHAPTER XVI

THE MEETING OF THE LOVERS IN THE GARDEN.--AN AFFECTING SCENE.--THE SUDDEN APPEARANCE OF SIR FRANCIS VARNEY

Our readers will recollect that Flora Bannerworth had made an appointment with Charles Holland in the garden of the hall. This meeting was looked forward to by the young man with a variety of conflicting feelings, and he passed the intermediate time in a most painful state of doubt as to what would be its result.

The thought that he should be much urged by Flora to give up all thoughts of making her his, was a most bitter one to him, who loved her with so much truth and constancy, and that she would say all she could to induce such a resolution in his mind he felt certain. But to him the idea of now abandoning her presented itself in the worst of aspects.

"Shall I," he said, "sink so low in my own estimation, as well as in hers, and in that of all honourable-minded persons, as to desert her now in the hour of affliction? Dare I be so base as actually or virtually to say to her, 'Flora, when your beauty was undimmed by sorrow--when all around you seemed life and joy, I loved you selfishly for the increased happiness which you might bestow upon me; but now the hand of misfortune presses heavily upon you--you are not what you were, and I desert you? Never--never--never!"

Charles Holland, it will be seen by some of our more philosophic neighbours, felt more acutely than he reasoned; but let his errors of argumentation be what they may, can we do other than admire the nobility of soul which dictated such a self denying generous course as that he was pursuing?

As for Flora, Heaven only knows if at that precise time her intellect had completely stood the test of the trying events which had nearly overwhelmed it.

The two grand feelings that seemed to possess her mind were fear of the renewed visit of the vampyre, and an earnest desire to release Charles Holland from his repeated vows of constancy towards her.

Feeling, generosity, and judgment, all revolted holding a young man to such a destiny as hers. To link him to her fate, would be to make him to a real extent a sharer in it, and the more she heard fall from his lips in the way of generous feelings of continued attachment to her, the more severely did she feel that he would suffer most acutely if united to her.

And she was right. The very generosity of feeling which would have now prompted Charles Holland to lead Flora Bannerworth to the altar, even with the marks of the vampyre's teeth upon her throat, gave an assurance of a depth of feeling which would have made him an ample haven in all her miseries, in all her distresses and afflictions.

What was familiarly in the family at the Hall called the garden, was a semicircular piece of ground shaded in several directions by trees, and which was exclusively devoted to the growth of flowers. The piece of ground was nearly hidden from the view of the house, and in its centre was a summer-house, which at the usual season of the year was covered with all kinds of creeping plants of exquisite perfumes, and rare beauty. All around, too, bloomed the fairest and sweetest of flowers, which a rich soil and a sheltered situation could produce.

Alas! though, of late many weeds had straggled up among their more estimable floral culture, for the decayed fortunes of the family had prevented them from keeping the necessary servants, to place the Hall and its grounds in a state of neatness, such as it had once been the pride of the inhabitants of the place to see them. It was then in this flower-garden that Charles and Flora used to meet.

As may be supposed, he was on the spot before the appointed hour, anxiously expecting the appearance of her who was so really and truly dear to him. What to him were the sweet flowers that there grew in such happy luxuriance and heedless beauty? Alas, the flower that to his mind was fairer than them all, was blighted, and in the wan cheek of her whom he loved, he sighed to see the lily usurping the place of the radiant rose.

"Dear, dear Flora," he ejaculated, "you must indeed be taken from this place, which is so full of the most painful remembrance; now, I cannot think that Mr. Marchdale somehow is a friend to me, but that conviction, or rather impression, does not paralyze my judgment sufficiently to induce me not to acknowledge that his advice is good. He might have couched it in pleasanter words--words that would not, like daggers, each have brought a deadly pang home to my heart, but still I do think that in his conclusion he was right."

A light sound, as of some fairy footstep among the flowers, came upon his ears, and turning instantly to the direction from whence the sound proceeded, he saw what his heart had previously assured him of, namely, that it was his Flora who was coming.

Yes, it was she; but, ah, how pale, how wan--how languid and full of the evidences of much mental suffering was she. Where now was the elasticity of that youthful step? Where now was that lustrous beaming beauty of mirthfulness, which was wont to dawn in those eyes?

Alas, all was changed. The exquisite beauty of form was there, but the light of joy which had lent its most transcendent charms to that heavenly face, was gone. Charles was by her side in a moment. He had her hand clasped in his, while his disengaged one was wound tenderly around her taper waist.

"Flora, dear, dear Flora," he said, "you are better. Tell me that you feel the gentle air revives you?"

She could not speak. Her heart was too full of woe.

"Oh; Flora, my own, my beautiful," he added, in those tones which come so direct from the heart, and which are so different from any assumption of tenderness. "Speak to me, dear, dear Flora--speak to me if it be but a word."

"Charles," was all she could say, and then she burst into a flood of tears, and leant so heavily upon his arm, that it was evident but for that support she must have fallen.

Charles Holland welcomed those, although, they grieved him so much that he could have accompanied them with his own, but then he knew that she would be soon now more composed, and that they would relieve the heart whose sorrows called them into existence.

He forbore to speak to her until he found this sudden gush of feeling was subsiding into sobs, and then in low, soft accents, he again endeavoured to breathe comfort to her afflicted and terrified spirit.

"My Flora," he said, "remember that there are warm hearts that love you. Remember that neither time nor circumstance can change such endearing affection as mine. Ah, Flora, what evil is there in the whole world that love may not conquer, and in the height of its noble feelings laugh to scorn."

"Oh, hush, hush, Charles, hush."

"Wherefore, Flora, would you still the voice of pure affection? I love you surely, as few have ever loved. Ah, why would you forbid me to give such utterance as I may to those feelings which fill up my whole heart?"

"No--no--no."

"Flora, Flora, wherefore do you say no?"

"Do not, Charles, now speak to me of affection or love. Do not tell me you love me now."

"Not tell you I love you! Ah, Flora, if my tongue, with its poor eloquence to give utterance to such a sentiment, were to do its office, each feature of my face would tell the tale. Each action would show to all the world how much I loved you."

"I must not now hear this. Great God of Heaven give me strength to carry out the purpose of my soul."

"What purpose is it, Flora, that you have to pray thus fervently for strength to execute? Oh, if it savour aught of treason against love's majesty, forget it. Love is a gift from Heaven. The greatest and the most glorious gift it ever bestowed upon its creatures. Heaven will not aid you in repudiating that which is the one grand redeeming feature that rescues human nature from a world of reproach."

Flora wrung her hands despairingly as she said,--

"Charles, I know I cannot reason with you. I know I have not power of language, aptitude of illustration, nor depth of thought to hold a mental contention with you."

"Flora, for what do I contend?"

"You, you speak of love."

"And I have, ere this, spoken to you of love unchecked."

"Yes, yes. Before this."

"And now, wherefore not now? Do not tell me you are changed."

"I am changed, Charles. Fearfully changed. The curse of God has fallen upon me, I know not why. I know not that in word or in thought I have done evil, except perchance unwittingly, and yet--the vampyre."

"Let not that affright you."

"Affright me! It has killed me."

"Nay, Flora,--you think too much of what I still hope to be susceptible of far more rational explanation."

"By your own words, then, Charles, I must convict you. I cannot, I dare not be yours, while such a dreadful circumstance is hanging over me, Charles; if a more rational explanation than the hideous one which my own fancy gives to the form that visits me can be found, find it, and rescue me from despair and from madness."

They had now reached the summer-house, and as Flora uttered these words she threw herself on to a seat, and covering her beautiful face with her hands, she sobbed convulsively.

"You have spoken," said Charles, dejectedly. "I have heard that which you wished to say to me."

"No, no. Not all, Charles."

"I will be patient, then, although what more you may have to add should tear my very heart-strings."

"I--I have to add, Charles," she said, in a tremulous voice, "that justice, religion, mercy--every human attribute which bears the name of virtue, calls loudly upon me no longer to hold you to vows made under different auspices."

"Go on, Flora."

"I then implore you, Charles, finding me what I am, to leave me to the fate which it has pleased Heaven to cast upon me. I do not ask you, Charles, not to love me."

"'Tis well. Go on, Flora."

"Because I should like to think that, although I might never see you more, you loved me still. But you must think seldom of me, and you must endeavour to be happy with some other--"

"You cannot, Flora, pursue the picture you yourself would draw. These words come not from your heart."

"Yes--yes--yes."

"Did you ever love me?"

"Charles, Charles, why will you add another pang to those you know must already rend my heart?"

"No, Flora, I would tear my own heart from my bosom ere I would add one pang to yours. Well I know that gentle maiden modesty would seal your lips to the soft confession that you loved me. I could not hope the joy of hearing you utter these words. The tender devoted lover is content to see the truthful passion in the speaking eyes of beauty. Content is he to translate it from a thousand acts, which, to eyes that look not so acutely as a lover's, bear no signification; but when you tell me to seek happiness with another, well may the anxious question burst from my throbbing heart of, 'Did you ever love me, Flora?'"

Her senses hung entranced upon his words. Oh, what a witchery is in the tongue of love. Some even of the former colour of her cheek returned as forgetting all for the moment but that she was listening to the voice of him, the thoughts of whom had made up the day dream of her happiness, she gazed upon his face.

His voice ceased. To her it seemed as if some music had suddenly left off in its most exquisite passage. She clung to his arm--she looked imploringly up to him. Her head sunk upon his breast as she cried,

"Charles, Charles, I did love you. I do love you now."

"Then let sorrow and misfortune shake their grisly locks in vain," he cried. "Heart to heart--hand to hand with me, defy them."

He lifted up his arms towards Heaven as he spoke, and at the moment came such a rattling peal of thunder, that the very earth seemed to shake upon its axis.

A half scream of terror burst from the lips of Flora, as she cried,--

"What was that?"

"Only thunder," said Charles, calmly.

"'Twas an awful sound."

"A natural one."

"But at such a moment, when you were defying Fate to injure us. Oh! Charles, is it ominous?"

"Flora, can you really give way to such idle fancies?"

"The sun is obscured."

"Ay, but it will shine all the brighter for its temporary eclipse. The thunder-storm will clear the air of many noxious vapours; the forked lightning has its uses as well as its powers of mischief. Hark! there again!"

Another peal, of almost equal intensity to the other, shook the firmament. Flora trembled.

"Charles," she said, "this is the voice of Heaven. We must part--we must part for ever. I cannot be yours."

"Flora, this is madness. Think again, dear Flora. Misfortunes for a time will hover over the best and most fortunate of us; but, like the clouds that now obscure the sweet sunshine, will pass away, and leave no trace behind them. The sunshine of joy will shine on you again."

There was a small break in the clouds, like a window looking into Heaven. From it streamed one beam of sunlight, so bright, so dazzling, and so beautiful, that it was a sight of wonder to look upon. It fell upon the face of Flora; it warmed her cheek; it lent lustre to her pale lips and tearful eyes; it illumined that little summer-house as if it had been the shrine of some saint.

"Behold!" cried Charles, "where is your omen now?"

"God of Heaven!'" cried Flora; and she stretched out her arms.

"The clouds that hover over your spirit now," said Charles, "shall pass away. Accept this beam of sunlight as a promise from God."

"I will--I will. It is going."

"It has done its office."

The clouds closed over the small orifice, and all was gloom again as before.

"Flora," said Charles, "you will not ask me now to leave you?"

She allowed him to clasp her to his heart. It was beating for her, and for her only.

"You will let me, Flora, love you still?"

Her voice, as she answered him, was like the murmur of some distant melody the ears can scarcely translate to the heart.

"Charles we will live, love, and die together."

And now there was a wrapt stillness in that summer-house for many minutes--a trance of joy. They did not speak, but now and then she would look into his face with an old familiar smile, and the joy of his heart was near to bursting in tears from his eyes.

A shriek burst from Flora's lips--a shriek so wild and shrill that it awakened echoes far and near. Charles staggered back a step, as if shot, and then in such agonised accents as he was long indeed in banishing the remembrance of, she cried,--

"The vampyre! the vampyre!"

CHAPTER XVII

THE EXPLANATION.--THE ARRIVAL OF THE ADMIRAL AT THE HOUSE.--A SCENE OF CONFUSION, AND SOME OF ITS RESULTS

So sudden and so utterly unexpected a cry of alarm from Flora, at such a time might well have the effect of astounding the nerves of any one, and no wonder that Charles was for a few seconds absolutely petrified and almost unable to think.

Mechanically, then, he turned his eyes towards the door of the summer-house, and there he saw a tall, thin man, rather elegantly dressed, whose countenance certainly, in its wonderful resemblance to the portrait on the panel, might well appal any one.

The stranger stood in the irresolute attitude on the threshold of the summer-house of one who did not wish to intrude, but who found it as awkward, if not more so now, to retreat than to advance.

Before Charles Holland could summon any words to his aid, or think of freeing himself from the clinging grasp of Flora, which was wound around him, the stranger made a very low and courtly bow, after which he said, in winning accents,--

"I very much fear that I am an intruder here. Allow me to offer my warmest apologies, and to assure you, sir, and you, madam, that I had no idea any one was in the arbour. You perceive the rain is falling smartly, and I made towards here, seeing it was likely to shelter me from the shower."

These words were spoken in such a plausible and courtly tone of voice, that they might well have become any drawing-room in the kingdom.

Flora kept her eyes fixed upon him during the utterance of these words; and as she convulsively clutched the arm of Charles, she kept on whispering,--

"The vampyre! the vampyre!"

"I much fear," added the stranger, in the same bland tones, "that I have been the cause of some alarm to the young lady!"

"Release me," whispered Charles to Flora. "Release me; I will follow him at once."

"No, no--do not leave me--do not leave me. The vampyre--the dreadful vampyre!"

"But, Flora--"

"Hush--hush--hush! It speaks again."

"Perhaps I ought to account for my appearance in the garden at all," added the insinuating stranger. "The fact is, I came on a visit--"

Flora shuddered.

"To Mr. Henry Bannerworth," continued the stranger; "and finding the garden-gate open, I came in without troubling the servants, which I much regret, as I can perceive I have alarmed and annoyed the lady. Madam, pray accept of my apologies."

"In the name of God, who are you?" said Charles.

"My name is Varney."

"Oh, yes. You are the Sir Francis Varney, residing close by, who bears so fearful a resemblance to--"

"Pray go on, sir. I am all attention."

"To a portrait here."

"Indeed! Now I reflect a moment, Mr. Henry Bannerworth did incidentally mention something of the sort. It's a most singular coincidence."

The sound of approaching footsteps was now plainly heard, and in a few moments Henry and George, along with Mr. Marchdale, reached the spot. Their appearance showed that they had made haste, and Henry at once exclaimed,--

"We heard, or fancied we heard, a cry of alarm."

"You did hear it," said Charles Holland. "Do you know this gentleman?"

"It is Sir Francis Varney."

"Indeed!"

Varney bowed to the new comers, and was altogether as much at his ease as everybody else seemed quite the contrary. Even Charles Holland found the difficulty of going up to such a well-bred, gentlemanly man, and saying, "Sir, we believe you to be a vampyre"--to be almost, if not insurmountable.

"I cannot do it," he thought, "but I will watch him."

"Take me away," whispered Flora. "'Tis he--'tis he. Oh, take me away, Charles."

"Hush, Flora, hush. You are in some error; the accidental resemblance should not make us be rude to this gentleman."

"The vampyre!--it is the vampyre!"

"Are you sure, Flora?"

"Do I know your features--my own--my brother's? Do not ask me to doubt--I cannot. I am quite sure. Take me from his hideous presence, Charles."

"The young lady, I fear, is very much indisposed," remarked Sir Francis Varney, in a sympathetic tone of voice. "If she will accept of my arm, I shall esteem it a great honour."

"No--no--no!--God! no," cried Flora.

"Madam, I will not press you."

He bowed, and Charles led Flora from the summer-house towards the hall.

"Flora," he said, "I am bewildered--I know not what to think. That man most certainly has been fashioned after the portrait which is on the panel in the room you formerly occupied; or it has been painted from him."

"He is my midnight visitor!" exclaimed Flora. "He is the vampyre;--this Sir Francis Varney is the vampyre."

"Good God! What can be done?"

"I know not. I am nearly distracted."

"Be calm, Flora. If this man be really what you name him, we now know from what quarter the mischief comes, which is, at all events, a point gained. Be assured we shall place a watch upon him."

"Oh, it is terrible to meet him here."

"And he is so wonderfully anxious, too, to possess the Hall."

"He is--he is."

"It looks strange, the whole affair. But, Flora, be assured of one thing, and that is, of your own safety."

"Can I be assured of that?"

"Most certainly. Go to your mother now. Here we are, you see, fairly within doors. Go to your mother, dear Flora, and keep yourself quiet. I will return to this mysterious man now with a cooler judgment than I left him."

"You will watch him, Charles?"

"I will, indeed."

"And you will not let him approach the house here alone?"

"I will not."

"Oh, that the Almighty should allow such beings to haunt the earth!"

"Hush, Flora, hush! we cannot judge of his allwise purpose."

"'Tis hard that the innocent should be inflicted with its presence."

Charles bowed his head in mournful assent.

"Is it not very, very dreadful?"

"Hush--hush! Calm yourself, dearest, calm yourself. Recollect that all we have to go upon in this matter is a resemblance, which, after all, may be accidental. But leave it all to me, and be assured that now I have some clue to this affair, I will not lose sight of it, or of Sir Francis Varney."

So saying, Charles surrendered Flora to the care of her mother, and then was hastening back to the summer-house, when he met the whole party coming towards the Hall, for the rain was each moment increasing in intensity.

"We are returning," remarked Sir Francis Varney, with a half bow and a smile, to Charles.

"Allow me," said Henry, "to introduce you, Mr. Holland, to our neighbour, Sir Francis Varney."

Charles felt himself compelled to behave with courtesy, although his mind was so full of conflicting feelings as regarded Varney; but there was no avoiding, without such brutal rudeness as was inconsistent with all his pursuits and habits, replying in something like the same strain to the extreme courtly politeness of the supposed vampyre.

"I will watch him closely," thought Charles. "I can do no more than watch him closely."

Sir Francis Varney seemed to be a man of the most general and discursive information. He talked fluently and pleasantly upon all sorts of topics, and notwithstanding he could not but have heard what Flora had said of him, he asked no questions whatever upon that subject.

This silence as regarded a matter which would at once have induced some sort of inquiry from any other man, Charles felt told much against him, and he trembled to believe for a moment that, after all, it really might be true.

"Is he a vampyre?" he asked himself. "Are there vampyres, and is this man of fashion--this courtly, talented, educated gentleman one?" It was a perfectly hideous question.

"You are charmingly situated here," remarked Varney, as, after ascending the few steps that led to the hall door, he turned and looked at the view from that slight altitude.

"The place has been much esteemed," said Henry, "for its picturesque beauties of scenery."

"And well it may be. I trust, Mr. Holland, the young lady is much better?"

"She is, sir," said Charles.

"I was not honoured by an introduction."

"It was my fault," said Henry, who spoke to his extraordinary guest with an air of forced hilarity. "It was my fault for not introducing you to my sister."

"And that was your sister?"

"It was, sir."

"Report has not belied her--she is beautiful. But she looks rather pale, I thought. Has she bad health?"

"The best of health."

"Indeed! Perhaps the little disagreeable circumstance, which is made so much food for gossip in the neighbourhood, has affected her spirits?"

"It has."

"You allude to the supposed visit here of a vampyre?" said Charles, as he fixed his eyes upon Varney's face.

"Yes, I allude to the supposed appearance of a supposed vampyre in this family," said Sir Francis Varney, as he returned the earnest gaze of Charles, with such unshrinking assurance, that the young man was compelled, after about a minute, nearly to withdraw his own eyes.

"He will not be cowed," thought Charles. "Use has made him familiar to such cross-questioning."

It appeared now suddenly to occur to Henry that he had said something at Varney's own house which should have prevented him from coming to the Hall, and he now remarked,--

"We scarcely expected the pleasure of your company here, Sir Francis Varney."

"Oh, my dear sir, I am aware of that; but you roused my curiosity. You mentioned to me that there was a portrait here amazingly like me."

"Did I?"

"Indeed you did, or how could I know it? I wanted to see if the resemblance was so perfect."

"Did you hear, sir," added Henry, "that my sister was alarmed at your likeness to that portrait?"

"No, really."

"I pray you walk in, and we will talk more at large upon that matter."

"With great pleasure. One leads a monotonous life in the country, when compared with the brilliancy of a court existence. Just now I have no particular engagement. As we are near neighbours I see no reason why we should not be good friends, and often interchange such civilities as make up the amenities of existence, and which, in the country, more particularly, are valuable."

Henry could not be hypocrite enough to assent to this; but still, under the present aspect of affairs, it was impossible to return any but a civil reply; so he said,--

"Oh, yes, of course--certainly. My time is very much occupied, and my sister and mother see no company."

"Oh, now, how wrong."

"Wrong, sir?"

"Yes, surely. If anything more than another tends to harmonize individuals, it is the society of that fairer half of the creation which we love for their very foibles. I am much attached to the softer sex--to young persons full of health. I like to see the rosy checks, where the warm blood mantles in the superficial veins, and all is loveliness and life."

Charles shrank back, and the word "Demon" unconsciously escaped his lips.

Sir Francis took no manner of notice of the expression, but went on talking, as if he had been on the very happiest terms with every one present.

"Will you follow me, at once, to the chamber where the portrait hangs," said Henry, "or will you partake of some refreshment first?"

"No refreshment for me," said Varney. "My dear friend, if you will permit me to call you such, this is a time of the day at which I never do take any refreshment."

"Nor at any other," thought Henry.

They all went to the chamber where Charles had passed one very disagreeable night, and when they arrived, Henry pointed to the portrait on the panel, saying--

"There, Sir Francis Varney, is your likeness."

He looked, and, having walked up to it, in an under tone, rather as if he were conversing with himself than making a remark for any one else to hear, he said--

"It is wonderfully like."

"It is, indeed," said Charles.

"If I stand beside it, thus," said Varney, placing himself in a favourable attitude for comparing the two faces, "I dare say you will be more struck with the likeness than before."

So accurate was it now, that the same light fell upon his face as that under which the painter had executed the portrait, that all started back a step or two.

"Some artists," remarked Varney, "have the sense to ask where a portrait is to be hung before they paint it, and then they adapt their lights and shadows to those which would fall upon the original, were it similarly situated."

"I cannot stand this," said Charles to Henry; "I must question him farther."

"As you please, but do not insult him."

"I will not."

"He is beneath my roof now, and, after all, it is but a hideous suspicion we have of him."

"Rely upon me."

Charles stepped forward, and once again confronting Varney, with an earnest gaze, he said--

"Do you know, sir, that Miss Bannerworth declares the vampyre she fancies to have visited this chamber to be, in features, the exact counterpart of this portrait?"

"Does she indeed?"

"She does, indeed."

"And perhaps, then, that accounts for her thinking that I am the vampyre, because I bear a strong resemblance to the portrait."

"I should not be surprised," said Charles.

"How very odd."

"Very."

"And yet entertaining. I am rather amused than otherwise. The idea of being a vampyre. Ha! ha! If ever I go to a masquerade again, I shall certainly assume the character of a vampyre."

"You would do it well."

"I dare say, now, I should make quite a sensation."

"I am certain you would. Do you not think, gentlemen, that Sir Francis Varney would enact the character to the very life? By Heavens, he would do it so well that one might, without much difficulty, really imagine him a vampyre."

"Bravo--bravo," said Varney, as he gently folded his hands together, with that genteel applause that may even be indulged in in a box at the opera itself. "Bravo. I like to see young persons enthusiastic; it looks as if they had some of the real fire of genius in their composition. Bravo--bravo."

This was, Charles thought, the very height and acme of impudence, and yet what could he do? What could he say? He was foiled by the downright coolness of Varney.

As for Henry, George, and Mr. Marchdale, they had listened to what was passing between Sir Francis and Charles in silence. They feared to diminish the effect of anything Charles might say, by adding a word of their own; and, likewise, they did not wish to lose one observation that might come from the lips of Varney.

But now Charles appeared to have said all he had to say, he turned to the window and looked out. He seemed like a man who had made up his mind, for a time, to give up some contest in which he had been engaged.

And, perhaps, not so much did he give it up from any feeling or consciousness of being beaten, as from a conviction that it could be the more effectually, at some other and far more eligible opportunity, renewed.

Varney now addressed Henry, saying,--

"I presume the subject of our conference, when you did me the honour of a call, is no secret to any one here?"

"None whatever," said Henry.

"Then, perhaps, I am too early in asking you if you have made up your mind?"

"I have scarcely, certainly, had time to think."

"My dear sir, do not let me hurry you; I much regret, indeed, the intrusion."

"You seem anxious to possess the Hall," remarked Mr. Marchdale, to Varney.

"I am."

"Is it new to you?"

"Not quite. I have some boyish recollections connected with this neighbourhood, among which Bannerworth Hall stands sufficiently prominent."

"May I ask how long ago that was?" said Charles Howard, rather abruptly.

"I do not recollect, my enthusiastic young friend," said Varney. "How old are you?"

"Just about twenty-one."

"You are, then, for your age, quite a model of discretion."

It would have been difficult for the most accurate observer of human nature to have decided whether this was said truthfully or ironically, so Charles made no reply to it whatever.

"I trust," said Henry, "we shall induce you, as this is your first visit, Sir Francis Varney, to the Hall, to partake of some thing."

"Well, well, a cup of wine--"

"Is at your service."

Henry now led the way to a small parlour, which, although by no means one of the showiest rooms of the house, was, from the care and exquisite carving with which it abounded, much more to the taste of any who possessed an accurate judgment in such works of art.

Then wine was ordered, and Charles took an opportunity of whispering to Henry,--

"Notice well if he drinks."

"I will."

"Do you see that beneath his coat there is a raised place, as if his arm was bound up?"

"I do."

"There, then, was where the bullet from the pistol fired by Flora, when we were at the church, hit him."

"Hush! for God's sake, hush! you are getting into a dreadful state of excitement, Charles; hush! hush!"

"And can you blame--"

"No, no; but what can we do?"

"You are right. Nothing can we do at present. We have a clue now, and be it our mutual inclination, as well as duty, to follow it. Oh, you shall see how calm I will be!"

"For Heaven's sake, be so. I have noted that his eyes flash upon yours with no friendly feeling."

"His friendship were a curse."

"Hush! he drinks!"

"Watch him."

"I will."

"Gentlemen all," said Sir Francis Varney, in such soft, dulcet tones, that it was quite a fascination to hear him speak; "gentlemen all, being as I am, much delighted with your company, do not accuse me of presumption, if I drink now, poor drinker as I am, to our future merry meetings."

He raised the wine to his lips, and seemed to drink, after which he replaced the glass upon the table.

Charles glanced at it, it was still full.

"You have not drank, Sir Francis Varney," he said.

"Pardon me, enthusiastic young sir," said Varney, "perhaps you will have the liberality to allow me to take my wine how I please and when I please."

"Your glass is full."

"Well, sir?"

"Will you drink it?"

"Not at any man's bidding, most certainly. If the fair Flora Bannerworth would grace the board with her sweet presence, methinks I could then drink on, on, on."

"Hark you, sir," cried Charles, "I can bear no more of this. We have had in this house most horrible and damning evidence that there are such things as vampyres."

"Have you really? I suppose you eat raw pork at supper, and so had the nightmare?"

"A jest is welcome in its place, but pray hear me out, sir, if it suit your lofty courtesy to do so."

"Oh, certainly."

"Then I say we believe, as far as human judgment has a right to go, that a vampyre has been here."

"Go on, it's interesting. I always was a lover of the wild and the wonderful."

"We have, too," continued Charles, "some reason to believe that you are the man."

Varney tapped his forehead as he glanced at Henry, and said,--

"Oh, dear, I did not know. You should have told me he was a little wrong about the brain; I might have quarreled with the lad. Dear me, how lamentable for his poor mother."

"This will not do, Sir Francis Varney alias Bannerworth."

"Oh--oh! Be calm--be calm."

"I defy you to your teeth, sir! No, God, no! Your teeth!"

"Poor lad! Poor lad!"

"You are a cowardly demon, and here I swear to devote myself to your destruction."

Sir Francis Varney drew himself up to his full height, and that was immense, as he said to Henry,--

"I pray you, Mr. Bannerworth, since I am thus grievously insulted beneath your roof, to tell me if your friend here be mad or sane?"

"He's not mad."

"Then--"

"Hold, sir! The quarrel shall be mine. In the name of my persecuted sister--in the name of Heaven. Sir Francis Varney, I defy you."

Sir Francis, in spite of his impenetrable calmness, appeared somewhat moved, as he said,--

"I have already endured insult sufficient--I will endure no more. If there are weapons at hand--"

"My young friend," interrupted Mr. Marchdale, stepping between the excited men, "is carried away by his feelings, and knows not what he says. You will look upon it in that light, Sir Francis."

"We need no interference," exclaimed Varney, his hitherto bland voice changing to one of fury. "The hot blooded fool wishes to fight, and he shall--to the death--to the death."

"And I say he shall not," exclaimed Mr. Marchdale, taking Henry by the arm. "George," he added, turning to the young man, "assist me in persuading your brother to leave the room. Conceive the agony of your sister and mother if anything should happen to him."

Varney smiled with a devilish sneer, as he listened to these words, and then he said,--

"As you will--as you will. There will be plenty of time, and perhaps better opportunity, gentlemen. I bid you good day."

And with provoking coolness, he then moved towards the door, and quitted the room.

"Remain here," said Marchdale; "I will follow him, and see that he quits the premises."

He did so, and the young men, from the window, beheld Sir Francis walking slowly across the garden, and then saw Mr. Marchdale follow on his track.

While they were thus occupied, a tremendous ringing came at the gate, but their attention was so rivetted to what was passing in the garden, that they paid not the least attention to it.

CHAPTER XVIII

THE ADMIRAL'S ADVICE.--THE CHALLENGE TO THE VAMPYRE.--THE NEW SERVANT AT THE HALL

The violent ringing of the bell continued uninterruptedly until at length George volunteered to answer it. The fact was, that now there was no servant at all in the place for, after the one who had recently demanded of Henry her dismissal had left, the other was terrified to remain alone, and had precipitately gone from the house, without even going through the ceremony of announcing her intention to. To be sure, she sent a boy for her money afterwards, which may be considered a great act of condescension.

Suspecting, then, this state of things, George himself hastened to the gate, and, being not over well pleased at the continuous and unnecessary ringing which was kept up at it, he opened it quickly, and cried, with more impatience, by a vast amount, than was usual with him.

"Who is so impatient that he cannot wait a seasonable time for the door to be opened?"

"And who the d----l are you?" cried one who was immediately outside.

"Who do you want?" cried George.

"Shiver my timbers!" cried Admiral Bell, for it was no other than that personage. "What's that to you?"

"Ay, ay," added Jack, "answer that if you can, you shore-going-looking swab."

"Two madmen, I suppose," ejaculated George, and he would have closed the gate upon them; but Jack introduced between it and the post the end of a thick stick, saying,--

"Avast there! None of that; we have had trouble enough to get in. If you are the family lawyer, or the chaplain, perhaps you'll tell us where Mister Charley is."

"Once more I demand of you who you want?" said George, who was now perhaps a little amused at the conduct of the impatient visitors.

"We want the admiral's nevey" said Jack.

"But how do I know who is the admiral's nevey as you call him."

"Why, Charles Holland, to be sure. Have you got him aboard or not?"

"Mr. Charles Holland is certainly here; and, if you had said at once, and explicitly, that you wished to see him, I could have given you a direct answer."

"He is here?" cried the admiral.

"Most certainly."

"Come along, then; yet, stop a bit. I say, young fellow, just before we go any further, tell us if he has maimed the vampyre?"

"The what?

"The wamphigher," said Jack, by way of being, as he considered, a little more explanatory than the admiral.

"I do not know what you mean," said George; "if you wish to see Mr. Charles Holland walk in and see him. He is in this house; but, for myself, as you are strangers to me, I decline answering any questions, let their import be what they may."

"Hilloa! who are they?" suddenly cried Jack, as he pointed to two figures some distance off in the meadows, who appeared to be angrily conversing.

George glanced in the direction towards which Jack pointed, and there he saw Sir Francis Varney and Mr. Marchdale standing within a few paces of each other, and apparently engaged in some angry discussion.

His first impulse was to go immediately towards them; but, before he could execute even that suggestion of his mind, he saw Varney strike Marchdale, and the latter fell to the ground.

"Allow me to pass," cried George, as he endeavoured to get by the rather unwieldy form of the admiral. But, before he could accomplish this, for the gate was narrow, he saw Varney, with great swiftness, make off, and Marchdale, rising to his feet, came towards the Hall.

When Marchdale got near enough to the garden-gate to see George, he motioned to him to remain where he was, and then, quickening his pace, he soon came up to the spot.

"Marchdale," cried George, "you have had an encounter with Sir Francis Varney."

"I have," said Marchdale, in an excited manner. "I threatened to follow him, but he struck me to the earth as easily as I could a child. His strength is superhuman."

"I saw you fall."

"I believe, but that he was observed, he would have murdered me."

"Indeed!"

"What, do you mean to say that lankey, horse-marine looking fellow is as bad as that!" said the admiral.

Marchdale now turned his attention to the two new comers, upon whom he looked with some surprise, and then, turning to George, he said,--

"Is this gentleman a visitor?"

"To Mr. Holland, I believe he is," said George; "but I have not the pleasure of knowing his name."

"Oh, you may know my name as soon as you like," cried the admiral. "The enemies of old England know it, and I don't care if all the world knows it. I'm old Admiral Bell, something of a hulk now, but still able to head a quarter-deck if there was any need to do so."

"Ay, ay," cried Jack, and taking from his pocket a boatswain's whistle, he blew a blast so long, and loud, and shrill, that George was fain to cover his ears with his hands to shut out the brain-piercing, and, to him unusual sound.

"And are you, then, a relative," said Marchdale, "of Mr. Holland's, sir, may I ask?"

"I'm his uncle, and be d----d to him, if you must know, and some one has told me that the young scamp thinks of marrying a mermaid, or a ghost, or a vampyre, or some such thing, so, for the sake of the memory of his poor mother, I've come to say no to the bargain, and d--n me, who cares."

"Come in, sir," said George, "I will conduct you to Mr. Holland. I presume this is your servant?"

"Why, not exactly. That's Jack Pringle, he was my boatswain, you see, and now he's a kind o' something betwixt and between. Not exactly a servant."

"Ay, ay, sir," said Jack. "Have it all your own way, though we is paid off."

"Hold your tongue, you audacious scoundrel, will you."

"Oh, I forgot, you don't like anything said about paying off, cos it puts you in mind of--"

"Now, d--n you, I'll have you strung up to the yard-arm, you dog, if you don't belay there."

"I'm done. All's right."

By this time the party, including the admiral, Jack, George Bannerworth, and Marchdale, had got more than half-way across the garden, and were observed by Charles Holland and Henry, who had come to the steps of the hall to see what was going on. The moment Charles saw the admiral a change of colour came over his face, and he exclaimed,--

"By all that's surprising, there is my uncle!"

"Your uncle!" said Henry.

"Yes, as good a hearted a man as ever drew breath, and yet, withal, as full of prejudices, and as ignorant of life, as a child."

Without waiting for any reply from Henry, Charles Holland rushed forward, and seizing his uncle by the hand, he cried, in tones of genuine affection,--

"Uncle, dear uncle, how came you to find me out?"

"Charley, my boy," cried the old man, "bless you; I mean, confound your d----d impudence; you rascal, I'm glad to see you; no, I ain't, you young mutineer. What do you mean by it, you ugly, ill-looking, d----d fine fellow--my dear boy. Oh, you infernal scoundrel."

All this was accompanied by a shaking of the hand, which was enough to dislocate anybody's shoulder, and which Charles was compelled to bear as well as he could.

It quite prevented him from speaking, however, for a few moments, for it nearly shook the breath out of him. When, then, he could get in a word, he said,--

"Uncle, I dare say you are surprised."

"Surprised! D--n me, I am surprised."

"Well, I shall be able to explain all to your satisfaction, I am sure. Allow me now to introduce you to my friends."

Turning then to Henry, Charles said,--

"This is Mr. Henry Bannerworth, uncle; and this Mr. George Bannerworth, both good friends of mine; and this is Mr. Marchdale, a friend of theirs, uncle."

"Oh, indeed!"

"And here you see Admiral Bell, my most worthy, but rather eccentric uncle."

"Confound your impudence."

"What brought him here I cannot tell; but he is a brave officer, and a gentleman."

"None of your nonsense," said the admiral.

"And here you sees Jack Pringle," said that individual, introducing himself, since no one appeared inclined to do that office for him, "a tar for all weathers. One as hates the French, and is never so happy as when he's alongside o' some o' those lubberly craft blazing away."

"That's uncommonly true," remarked the admiral.

"Will you walk in, sir?" said Henry, courteously. "Any friend of Charles Holland's is most welcome here. You will have much to excuse us for, because we are deficient in servants at present, in consequence of come occurrences in our family, which your nephew has our full permission to explain to you in full."

"Oh, very good, I tell you what it is, all of you, what I've seen of you, d----e, I like, so here goes. Come along, Jack."

The admiral walked into the house, and as he went, Charles Holland said to him,--

"How came you to know I was here, uncle?"

"Some fellow wrote me a despatch."

"Indeed!"

"Yes, saying at you was a going to marry some odd sort of fish as it wasn't at all the thing to introduce into the family."

"Was--was a vampyre mentioned?"

"That's the very thing."

"Hush, uncle--hush."

"What for?"

"Do not, I implore, hint at such a thing before these kind friends of mine. I will take an opportunity within the next hour of explaining all to you, and you shall form your own kind and generous judgement upon circumstances in which my honour and my happiness are so nearly concerned."

"Gammon," said the admiral.

"What, uncle?"

"Oh, I know you want to palaver me into saying it's all right. I suppose if my judgment and generosity don't like it, I shall be an old fool, and a cursed goose?"

"Now, uncle."

"Now, nevey."

"Well, well--no more at present. We will talk over this at leisure. You promise me to say nothing about it until you have heard my explanation, uncle?"

"Very good. Make it as soon as you can, and as short as you can, that's all I ask of you."

"I will, I will."

Charles was to the full as anxious as his uncle could be to enter upon the subject, some remote information of which, he felt convinced, had brought the old man down to the Hall. Who it could have been that so far intermeddled with his affairs as to write to him, he could not possibly conceive.

A very few words will suffice to explain the precise position in which Charles Holland was. A considerable sum of money had been left to him, but it was saddled with the condition that he should not come into possession of it until he was one year beyond the age which is usually denominated that of discretion, namely, twenty-one. His uncle, the admiral, was the trustee of his fortune, and he, with rare discretion, had got the active and zealous assistance of a professional gentleman of great honour and eminence to conduct the business for him.

This gentleman had advised that for the two years between the ages of twenty and twenty-two, Charles Holland should travel, inasmuch as in English society he would find himself in an awkward position, being for one whole year of age, and yet waiting for his property.

Under such circumstances, reasoned the lawyer, a young man, unless he is possessed of very rare discretion indeed, is almost sure to get fearfully involved with money-lenders. Being of age, his notes, and bills, and bonds would all be good, and he would be in a ten times worse situation than a wealthy minor.

All this was duly explained to Charles, who, rather eagerly than otherwise, caught at the idea of a two years wander on the continent, where he could visit so many places, which to a well read young man like himself, and one of a lively imagination, were full of the most delightful associations.

But the acquaintance with Flora Bannerworth effected a great revolution in his feelings. The dearest, sweetest spot on earth became that which she inhabited. When the Bannerworths left him abroad, he knew not what to do with himself. Everything, and every pursuit in which he had before taken a delight, became most distasteful to him. He was, in fact, in a short time, completely "used up," and then he determined upon returning to England, and finding out the dear object of his attachment at once. This resolution was no sooner taken, than his health and spirits returned to him, and with what rapidity he could, he now made his way to his native shores.

The two years were so nearly expired, that he made up his mind he would not communicate either with his uncle, the admiral, or the professional gentleman upon whose judgment he set so high and so just a value. And at the Hall he considered he was in perfect security from any interruption, and so he would have been, but for that letter which was written to Admiral Bell, and signed Josiah Crinkles, but which Josiah Crinkles so emphatically denied all knowledge of. Who wrote it, remains at present one of those mysteries which time, in the progress of our narrative, will clear up.

The opportune, or rather the painful juncture at which Charles Holland had arrived at Bannerworth Hall, we are well cognisant of. Where he expected to find smiles he found tears, and the family with whom he had fondly hoped he should pass a time of uninterrupted happiness, he found plunged in the gloom incidental to an occurrence of the most painful character.

Our readers will perceive, too, that coming as he did with an utter disbelief in the vampyre, Charles had been compelled, in some measure, to yield to the overwhelming weight of evidence which had been brought to bear upon the subject, and although he could not exactly be said to believe in the existence and the appearance of the vampyre at Bannerworth Hall, he was upon the subject in a most painful state of doubt and indecision.

Charles now took an opportunity to speak to Henry privately, and inform him exactly how he stood with his uncle, adding--

"Now, my dear friend, if you forbid me, I will not tell my uncle of this sad affair, but I must own I would rather do so fully and freely, and trust to his own judgment upon it."

"I implore you to do so," said Henry. "Conceal nothing. Let him know the precise situation and circumstances of the family by all means. There is nothing so mischievous as secrecy: I have the greatest dislike to it. I beg you tell him all."

"I will; and with it, Henry, I will tell him that my heart is irrevocably Flora's."

"Your generous clinging to one whom your heart saw and loved, under very different auspices," said Henry, "believe me, Charles, sinks deep into my heart. She has related to me something of a meeting she had with you."

"Oh, Henry, she may tell you what I said; but there are no words which can express the depth of my tenderness. 'Tis only time which can prove how much I love her."

"Go to your uncle," said Henry, in a voice of emotion. "God bless you, Charles. It is true you would have been fully justified in leaving my sister; but the nobler and the more generous path you have chosen has endeared you to us all."

"Where is Flora now?" said Charles.

"She is in her own room. I have persuaded her, by some occupation, to withdraw her mind from a too close and consequently painful contemplation of the distressing circumstances in which she feels herself placed."

"You are right. What occupation best pleases her?"

"The pages of romance once had a charm for her gentle spirit."

"Then come with me, and, from among the few articles I brought with me here, I can find some papers which may help her to pass some merry hours."

Charles took Henry to his room, and, unstrapping a small valise, he took from it some manuscript papers, one of which he handed to Henry, saying--

"Give that to her: it contains an account of a wild adventure, and shows that human nature may suffer much more--and that wrongfully too--than came ever under our present mysterious affliction."

"I will," said Henry; "and, coming from you, I am sure it will have a more than ordinary value in her eyes."

"I will now," said Charles, "seek my uncle. I will tell him how I love her; and at the end of my narration, if he should not object, I would fain introduce her to him, that he might himself see that, let what beauty may have met his gaze, her peer he never yet met with, and may in vain hope to do so."

"You are partial, Charles."

"Not so. 'Tis true I look upon her with a lover's eyes, but I look still with those of truthful observation."

"Well, I will speak to her about seeing your uncle, and let you know. No doubt, he will not be at all averse to an interview with any one who stands high in your esteem."

The young men now separated--Henry, to seek his beautiful sister; and Charles, to communicate to his uncle the strange particulars connected with Varney, the Vampyre.

CHAPTER XIX

FLORA IN HER CHAMBER.--HER FEARS.--THE MANUSCRIPT.--AN ADVENTURE

Henry found Flora in her chamber. She was in deep thought when he tapped at the door of the room, and such was the state of nervous excitement in which she was that even the demand for admission made by him to the room was sufficient to produce from her a sudden cry of alarm.

"Who--who is there?" she then said, in accents full of terror.

"'Tis I, dear Flora," said Henry.

She opened the door in an instant, and, with a feeling of grateful relief, exclaimed--

"Oh, Henry, is it only you?"

"Who did you suppose it was, Flora?"

She shuddered.

"I--I--do not know; but I am so foolish now, and so weak-spirited, that the slightest noise is enough to alarm me."

"You must, dear Flora, fight up, as I had hoped you were doing, against this nervousness."

"I will endeavour. Did not some strangers come a short time since, brother?"

"Strangers to us, Flora, but not to Charles Holland. A relative of his--an uncle whom he much respects, has found him out here, and has now come to see him."

"And to advise him," said Flora, as she sunk into a chair, and wept bitterly; "to advise him, of course, to desert, as he would a pestilence, a vampyre bride."

"Hush, hush! for the sake of Heaven, never make use of such a phrase, Flora. You know not what a pang it brings to my heart to hear you."

"Oh, forgive me, brother."

"Say no more of it, Flora. Heed it not. It may be possible--in fact, it may well be supposed as more than probable--that the relative of Charles Holland may shrink from sanctioning the alliance, but do you rest securely in the possession of the heart which I feel convinced is wholly yours, and which, I am sure, would break ere it surrendered you."

A smile of joy came across Flora's pale but beautiful face, as she cried,--

"And you, dear brother--you think so much of Charles's faith?"

"As Heaven is my judge, I do."

"Then I will bear up with what strength God may give me against all things that seek to depress me; I will not be conquered."

"You are right, Flora; I rejoice to find in you such a disposition. Here is some manuscript which Charles thinks will amuse you, and he bade me ask you if you would be introduced to his uncle."

"Yes, yes--willingly."

"I will tell him so; I know he wishes it, and I will tell him so. Be patient, dear Flora, and all may yet be well."

"But, brother, on your sacred word, tell me do you not think this Sir Francis Varney is the vampyre?"

"I know not what to think, and do not press me for a judgment now. He shall be watched."

Henry left his sister, and she sat for some moments in silence with the papers before her that Charles had sent her.

"Yes," she then said, gently, "he loves me--Charles loves me; I ought to be very, very happy. He loves me. In those words are concentrated a whole world of joy--Charles loves me--he will not forsake me. Oh, was there ever such dear love--such fond devotion?--never, never. Dear Charles. He loves me--he loves me!"

The very repetition of these words had a charm for Flora--a charm which was sufficient to banish much sorrow; even the much-dreaded vampyre was forgotten while the light of love was beaming upon her, and she told herself,--

"He is mine!--he is mine! He loves me truly."

After a time, she turned to the manuscript which her brother had brought her, and, with a far greater concentration of mind than she had thought it possible she could bring to it, considering the many painful subjects of contemplation that she might have occupied herself with, she read the pages with very great pleasure and interest.

The tale was one which chained her attention both by its incidents and the manner of its recital. It commenced as follows, and was entitled, "Hugo de Verole; or, the Double Plot."

In a very mountainous part of Hungary lived a nobleman whose paternal estates covered many a mile of rock and mountain land, as well as some fertile valleys, in which reposed a hardy and contented peasantry. The old Count de Hugo de Verole had quitted life early, and had left his only son, the then Count Hugo de Verole, a boy of scarcely ten years, under the guardianship of his mother, an arbitrary and unscrupulous woman.

The count, her husband, had been one of those quiet, even-tempered men, who have no desire to step beyond the sphere in which they are placed; he had no cares, save those included in the management of his estate, the prosperity of his serfs, and the happiness of those, around him.

His death caused much lamentation throughout his domains, it was so sudden and unexpected, being in the enjoyment of his health and strength until a few hours previous, and then his energies became prostrated by pain and disease. There was a splendid funeral ceremony, which, according to the usages of his house, took place by torch-light.

So great and rapid were the ravages of disease, that the count's body quickly became a mass of corruption. All were amazed at the phenomena, and were heartily glad when the body was disposed of in the place prepared for its reception in the vaults of his own castle. The guests who came to witness the funeral, and attend the count's obsequies, and to condole with the widow on the loss she had sustained, were entertained sumptuously for many days.

The widow sustained her part well. She was inconsolable for the loss of her husband, and mourned his death bitterly. Her grief appeared profound, but she, with difficulty, subdued it to within decent bounds, that she might not offend any of her numerous guests.

However, they left her with the assurances of their profound regard, and then when they were gone, when the last guest had departed, and were no longer visible to the eye of the countess, as she gazed from the battlements, then her behaviour changed totally.

She descended from the battlements, and then with an imperious gesture she gave her orders that all the gates of the castle should be closed, and a watch set. All signs of mourning she ordered to be laid on one side save her own, which she wore, and then she retired to her own apartment, where she remained unseen.

Here the countess remained in profound meditation for nearly two days, during which time the attendants believed she was praying for the welfare of the soul of their deceased master, and they feared she would starve herself to death if she remained any longer.

Just as they had assembled together for the purpose of either recalling her from her vigils or breaking open the door, they were amazed to see the countess open the room-door, and stand in the midst of them.

"What do you here?" she demanded, in a stern voice.

The servants were amazed and terrified at her contracted brow, and forgot to answer the question she put to them.

"What do you do here?"

"We came, my lady, to see--see--if--if you were well."

"And why?"

"Because we hadn't seen your ladyship these two days, and we thought that your grief was so excessive that we feared some harm might befall you."

The countess's brows contracted for a few seconds, and she was about to make a hasty reply, but she conquered the desire to do so, and merely said,--

"I am not well, I am faint; but, had I been dying, I should not have thanked you for interfering to prevent me; however, you acted for the best, but do so no more. Now prepare me some food."

The servants, thus dismissed, repaired to their stations, but with such a degree of alacrity, that they sufficiently showed how much they feared their mistress.

The young count, who was only in his sixth year, knew little about the loss he had sustained; but after a day or two's grief, there was an end of his sorrow for the time.

That night there came to the castle-gate a man dressed in a black cloak, attended by a servant. They were both mounted on good horses, and they demanded to be admitted to the presence of the Countess de Hugo de Verole.

The message was carried to the countess, who started, but said,--

"Admit the stranger."

Accordingly the stranger was admitted, and shown into the apartment where the countess was sitting.

At a signal the servants retired, leaving the countess and the stranger alone. It was some moments ere they spoke, and then the countess said in a low tone,--

"You are come?"

"I am come."

"You cannot now, you see, perform your threat. My husband, the count, caught a putrid disease, and he is no more."

"I cannot indeed do what I intended, inform your husband of your amours; but I can do something as good, and which will give you as much annoyance."

"Indeed."

"Aye, more, it will cause you to be hated. I can spread reports."

"You can."

"And these may ruin you."

"They may."

"What do you intend to do? Do you intend that I shall be an enemy or a friend? I can be either, according to my will."

"What, do you desire to be either?" inquired the countess, with a careless tone.

"If you refuse my terms, you can make me an implacable enemy, and if you grant them, you can make me a useful friend and auxiliary," said the stranger.

"What would you do if you were my enemy?" inquired the countess.

"It is hardly my place," said the stranger, "to furnish you with a knowledge of my intentions, but I will say this much, that the bankrupt Count of Morven is your lover."

"Well?"

"And in the second place, that you were the cause of the death of your husband."

"How dare you, sir--"

"I dare say so much, and I dare say, also, that the Count of Morven bought the drug of me, and that he gave it to you, and that you gave it to the count your husband."

"And what could you do if you were my friend?" inquired the countess, in the same tone, and without emotion.

"I should abstain from doing all this; should be able to put any one else out of your way for you, when you get rid of this Count of Morven, as you assuredly will; for I know him too well not to be sure of that."

"Get rid of him!"

"Exactly, in the same manner you got rid of the old count."

"Then I accept your terms."

"It is agreed, then?"

"Yes, quite."

"Well, then, you must order me some rooms in a tower, where I can pursue my studies in quiet."

"You will be seen--and noticed--all will be discovered."

"No, indeed, I will take care of that, I can so far disguise myself that he will not recognise me, and you can give out I am a philosopher or necromancer, or what you will; no one will come to me--they will be terrified."

"Very well."

"And the gold?"

"Shall be forthcoming as soon as I can get it. The count has placed all his gold in safe keeping, and all I can seize are the rents as they become due."

"Very well; but let me have them. In the meantime you must provide for me, as I have come here with the full intention of staying here, or in some neighbouring town."

"Indeed!"

"Yes; and my servant must be discharged, as I want none here."

The countess called to an attendant and gave the necessary orders, and afterwards remained some time with the stranger, who had thus so unceremoniously thrust himself upon her, and insisted upon staying under such strange and awful circumstances.

***

The Count of Morven came a few weeks after, and remained some days with the countess. They were ceremonious and polite until they had a moment to retire from before people, when the countess changed her cold disdain to a cordial and familiar address.

"And now, my dear Morven," she exclaimed, as soon as they were unobserved--"and now, my dear Morven, that we are not seen, tell me, what have you been doing with yourself?"

"Why, I have been in some trouble. I never had gold that would stay by me. You know my hand was always open."

"The old complaint again."

"No; but having come to the end of my store, I began to grow serious."

"Ah, Morven!' said the countess, reproachfully.

"Well, never mind; when my purse is low my spirits sink, as the mercury does with the cold. You used to say my spirits were mercurial--I think they were."

"Well, what did you do?"

"Oh, nothing."

"Was that what you were about to tell me?" inquired the countess.

"Oh, dear, no. You recollect the Italian quack of whom I bought the drug you gave to the count, and which put an end to his days--he wanted more money. Well, as I had no more to spare, I could spare no more to him, and he turned vicious, and threatened. I threatened, too, and he knew I was fully able and willing to perform any promise I might make to him on that score. I endeavoured to catch him, as he had already began to set people off on the suspicious and marvellous concerning me, and if I could have come across him, I would have laid him very low indeed."

"And you could not find him?"

"No, I could not."

"Well, then, I will tell you where he is at this present moment."

"You?"

"Yes, I."

"I can scarcely credit my senses at what you say," said Count Morven. "My worthy doctor, you are little better than a candidate for divine honours. But where is he?"

"Will you promise to be guided by me?" said the countess.

"If you make it a condition upon which you grant the information, I must."

"Well, then, I take that as a promise."

"You may. Where--oh, where is he?"

"Remember your promise. Your doctor is at this moment in this castle."

"This castle?"

"Yes, this castle."

"Surely there must be some mistake; it is too much fortune at once."

"He came here for the same purpose he went to you."

"Indeed!"

"Yes, to get more money by extortion, and a promise to poison anybody I liked."

"D--n! it is the offer he made to me, and he named you."

"He named you to me, and said I should be soon tired of you."

"You have caged him?"

"Oh, dear, no; he has a suite of apartments in the eastern tower, where he passes for a philosopher, or a wizard, as people like best."

"How?"

"I have given him leave there."

"Indeed!"

"Yes; and what is more amazing is, that he is to aid me in poisoning you when I have become tired of you."

"This is a riddle I cannot unravel; tell me the solution."

"Well, dear, listen,--he came to me and told me of something I already knew, and demanded money and a residence for his convenience, and I have granted him the asylum."

"You have?"

"I have."

"I see; I will give him an inch or two of my Andrea Ferrara."

"No--no."

"Do you countenance him?"

"For a time. Listen--we want men in the mines; my late husband sent very few to them of late years, and therefore they are getting short of men there."

"Aye, aye."

"The thing will be for you to feign ignorance of the man, and then you will be able to get him seized, and placed in the mines, for such men as he are dangerous, and carry poisoned weapons."

"Would he not be better out of the world at once; there would be no escape, and no future contingencies?"

"No--no. I will have no more lives taken; and he will be made useful; and, moreover, he will have time to reflect upon the mistake he had made in threatening me."

"He was paid for the job, and he had no future claim. But what about the child?"

"Oh, he may remain for some time longer here with us."

"It will be dangerous to do so," said the count; "he is now ten years old, and there is no knowing what may be done for him by his relatives."

"They dare not enter the gates of this castle Morven."

"Well, well; but you know he might have travelled the same road as his father, and all would be settled."

"No more lives, as I told you; but we can easily secure him some other way, and we shall be equally as free from him and them."

"That is enough--there are dungeons, I know, in this castle, and he can be kept there safe enough."

"He can; but that is not what I propose. We can put him into the mines and confine him as a lunatic."

"Excellent!"

"You see, we must make those mines more productive somehow or other; they would be so, but the count would not hear of it; he said it was so inhuman, they were so destructive of life."

"Paha! what were the mines intended for if not for use?"

"Exactly--I often said so, but he always put a negative to it."

"We'll make use of an affirmative, my dear countess, and see what will be the result in a change of policy. By the way, when will our marriage be celebrated?"

"Not for some months."

"How, so long? I am impatient."

"You must restrain your impatience--but we must have the boy settled first, and the count will have been dead a longer time then, and we shall not give so much scandal to the weak-minded fools that were his friends, for it will be dangerous to have so many events happen about the same period."

"You shall act as you think proper--but the first thing to be done will be, to get this cunning doctor quietly out of the way."

"Yes."

"I must contrive to have him seized, and carried to the mines."

"Beneath the tower in which he lives is a trap-door and a vault, from which, by means of another trap and vault, is a long subterranean passage that leads to a door that opens into one end of the mines; near this end live several men whom you must give some reward to, and they will, by concert, seize him, and set him to work."

"And if he will not work?"

"Why, they will scourge him in such a manner, that he would be afraid even of a threat of a repetition of the same treatment."

"That will do. But I think the worthy doctor will split himself with rage and malice, he will be like a caged tiger."

"But he will be denuded of his teeth and claws," replied the countess, smiling "therefore he will have leisure to repent of having threatened his employers."

***

Some weeks passed over, and the Count of Morven contrived to become acquainted with the doctor. They appeared to be utter strangers to each other, though each knew the other; the doctor having disguised himself, he believed the disguise impenetrable and therefore sat at ease.

"Worthy doctor," said the count to him, one day; "you have, no doubt, in your studies, become acquainted with many of the secrets of science."

"I have, my lord count; I may say there are few that are not known to Father Aldrovani. I have spent many years in research."

"Indeed!"

"Yes; the midnight lamp has burned till the glorious sun has reached the horizon, and brings back the day, and yet have I been found beside my books."

"'Tis well; men like you should well know the value of the purest and most valuable metals the earth produces?"

"I know of but one--that is gold!"

"'Tis what I mean."

"But 'tis hard to procure from the bowels of the earth--from the heart of these mountains by which we are surrounded."

"Yes, that is true. But know you not the owners of this castle and territory possess these mines and work them?"

"I believe they do; but I thought they had discontinued working them some years."

"Oh, no! that was given out to deceive the government, who claimed so much out of its products."

"Oh! ah! aye, I see now."

"And ever since they have been working it privately, and storing bars of gold up in the vaults of this--"

"Here, in this castle?"

"Yes; beneath this very tower--it being the least frequented--the strongest, and perfectly inaccessible from all sides, save the castle--it was placed there for the safest deposit."

"I see; and there is much gold deposited in the vaults?"

"I believe there is an immense quantity in the vaults."

"And what is your motive for telling me of this hoard of the precious metal?"

"Why, doctor, I thought that you or I could use a few bars; and that, if we acted in concert, we might be able to take away, at various times, and secrete, in some place or other, enough to make us rich men for all our lives."

"I should like to see this gold before I said anything about it," replied the doctor, thoughtfully.

"As you please; do you find a lamp that will not go out by the sudden draughts of air, or have the means of relighting it, and I will accompany you."

"When?"

"This very night, good doctor, when you shall see such a golden harvest you never yet hoped for, or even believed in."

"To-night be it, then," replied the doctor. "I will have a lamp that will answer our purpose, and some other matters."

"Do, good doctor," and the count left the philosopher's cell.

***

"The plan takes," said the count to the countess, "give me the keys, and the worthy man will be in safety before daylight."

"Is he not suspicious?"

"Not at all."

***

That night, about an hour before midnight,--the Count Morven stole towards the philosopher's room. He tapped at the door.

"Enter," said the philosopher.

The count entered, and saw the philosopher seated, and by him a lamp of peculiar construction, and incased in gauze wire, and a cloak.

"Are you ready?" inquired the count.

"Quite," he replied.

"Is that your lamp?"

"It is."

"Follow me, then, and hold the lamp tolerably high, as the way is strange, and the steps steep."

"Lead on."

"You have made up your mind, I dare say, as to what share of the undertaking you will accept of with me."

"And what if I will not?" said the philosopher, coolly.

"It falls to the ground, and I return the keys to their place."

"I dare say I shall not refuse, if you have not deceived me as to the quantity and purity of the metal they have stored up."

"I am no judge of these metals, doctor. I am no assayest; but I believe you will find what I have to show you will far exceed your expectations on that head."

"'Tis well: proceed."

They had now got to the first vault, in which stood the first door, and, with some difficulty, they opened the vault door.

"It has not been opened for some time," said the philosopher.

"I dare say not, they seldom used to go here, from what I can learn, though it is kept a great secret."

"And we can keep it so, likewise."

"True."

They now entered the vault, and came to the second door, which opened into a kind of flight of steps, cut out of the solid rock, and then along a passage cut out of the mountain, of some kind of stone, but not so hard as the rock itself.

"You see," said the count, "what care has been taken to isolate the place, and detach it from the castle, so that it should not be dependent upon the possessor of the castle. This is the last door but one, and now prepare yourself for a surprise, doctor, this will be an extraordinary one."

So saying, the count opened the door, and stepped on one side, when the doctor approached the place, and was immediately thrust forward by the count and he rolled down some steps into the mine, and was immediately seized by some of the miners, who had been stationed there for that purpose, and carried to a distant part of the mine, there to work for the remainder of his life.

The count, seeing all secure, refastened the doors, and returned to the castle. A few weeks after this the body of a youth, mangled and disfigured, was brought to the castle, which the countess said was her son's body.

The count had immediately secured the real heir, and thrust him into the mines, there to pass a life of labour and hopeless misery.

***

There was a high feast held. The castle gates were thrown open, and everybody who came were entertained without question.

This was on the occasion of the count's and countess's marriage. It seemed many months after the death of her son, whom she affected to mourn for a long time.

However, the marriage took place, and in all magnificence and splendour. The countess again appeared arrayed in splendour and beauty: she was proud and haughty, and the count was imperious.

In the mean time, the young Count de Hugo de Verole was confined in the mines, and the doctor with him.

By a strange coincidence, the doctor and the young count became companions, and the former, meditating projects of revenge, educated the young count as well as he was able for several years in the mines, and cherished in the young man a spirit of revenge. They finally escaped together, and proceeded to Leyden, where the doctor had friends, and where he placed his pupil at the university, and thus made him a most efficient means of revenge, because the education of the count gave him a means of appreciating the splendour and rank he had been deprived of. He, therefore, determined to remain at Leyden until he was of age, and then apply to his father's friends, and then to his sovereign, to dispossess and punish them both for their double crime.

The count and countess lived on in a state of regal splendour. The immense revenue of his territory, and the treasure the late count had amassed, as well as the revenue that the mines brought in, would have supported a much larger expenditure than even their tastes disposed them to enjoy.

They had heard nothing of the escape of the doctor and the young count. Indeed, those who knew of it held their peace and said nothing about it, for they feared the consequences of their negligence. The first intimation they received was at the hands of a state messenger, summoning them to deliver up the castle revenues and treasure of the late count.

This was astounding to them, and they refused to do so, but were soon after seized upon by a regiment of cuirassiers sent to take them, and they were accused of the crime of murder at the instance of the doctor.

They were arraigned and found guilty, and, as they were of the patrician order, their execution was delayed, and they were committed to exile. This was done out of favour to the young count, who did not wish to have his family name tainted by a public execution, or their being confined like convicts.

The count and countess quitted Hungary, and settled in Italy, where they lived upon the remains of the Count of Morven's property, shorn of all their splendour but enough to keep them from being compelled to do any menial office.

The young count took possession of his patrimony and his treasure at last, such as was left by his mother and her paramour.

The doctor continued to hide his crime from the young count, and the perpetrators denying all knowledge of it, he escaped; but he returned to his native place, Leyden, with a reward for his services from the young count.

Flora rose from her perusal of the manuscript, which here ended, and even as she did so, she heard a footstep approaching her chamber door.

CHAPTER XX

THE DREADFUL MISTAKE.--THE TERRIFIC INTERVIEW IN THE CHAMBER.--THE ATTACK OF THE VAMPYRE

The footstep which Flora, upon the close of the tale she had been reading, heard approaching her apartment, came rapidly along the corridor.

"It is Henry, returned to conduct me to an interview with Charles's uncle," she said. "I wonder, now, what manner of man he is. He should in some respects resemble Charles; and if he do so, I shall bestow upon him some affection for that alone."

Tap--tap came upon the chamber door. Flora was not at all alarmed now, as she had been when Henry brought her the manuscript. From some strange action of the nervous system, she felt quite confident, and resolved to brave everything. But then she felt quite sure that it was Henry, and before the knocking had taken her by surprise.

"Come in," she said, in a cheerful voice. "Come in."

The door opened with wonderful swiftness--a figure stepped into the room, and then closed it as rapidly, and stood against it. Flora tried to scream, but her tongue refused its office; a confused whirl of sensations passed through her brain--she trembled, and an icy coldness came over her. It was Sir Francis Varney, the vampyre!

He had drawn up his tall, gaunt frame to its full height, and crossed his arms upon his breast; there was a hideous smile upon his sallow countenance, and his voice was deep and sepulchral, as he said,--

"Flora Bannerworth, hear that which I have to say, and hear it calmly. You need have nothing to fear. Make an alarm--scream, or shout for help, and, by the hell beneath us, you are lost!"

There was a death-like, cold, passionless manner about the utterance of these words, as if they were spoken mechanically, and came from no human lips.

Flora heard them, and yet scarcely comprehended them; she stepped slowly back till she reached a chair, and there she held for support. The only part of the address of Varney that thoroughly reached her ears, was that if she gave any alarm some dreadful consequences were to ensue. But it was not on account of these words that she really gave no alarm; it was because she was utterly unable to do so.

"Answer me," said Varney. "Promise that you will hear that which I have to say. In so promising you commit yourself to no evil, and you shall hear that which shall give you much peace."

It was in vain she tried to speak; her lips moved, but she uttered no sound.

"You are terrified," said Varney, "and yet I know not why. I do not come to do you harm, although harm have you done me. Girl, I come to rescue you from a thraldom of the soul under which you now labour."

There was a pause of some moments' duration, and then, faintly, Flora managed to say,--

"Help! help! Oh, help me, Heaven!"

Varney made a gesture of impatience, as he said,--

"Heaven works no special matters now. Flora Bannerworth, if you have as much intellect as your nobility and beauty would warrant the world in supposing, you will listen to me."

"I--I hear," said Flora, as she still, dragging the chair with her, increased the distance between them.

"'Tis well. You are now more composed."

She fixed her eyes upon the face of Varney with a shudder. There could be no mistake. It was the same which, with the strange, glassy looking eyes, had glared upon her on that awful night of the storm when she was visited by the vampyre. And Varney returned that gaze unflinchingly There was a hideous and strange contortion of his face now as he said,--

"You are beautiful. The most cunning statuary might well model some rare work of art from those rounded limbs, that were surely made to bewitch the gazer. Your skin rivals the driven snow--what a face of loveliness, and what a form of enchantment."

She did not speak, but a thought came across her mind, which at once crimsoned her cheek--

she knew she had fainted on the first visit of the vampyre, and now he, with a hideous reverence, praised beauties which he might have cast his demoniac eyes over at such a time.

"You understand me," he said. "Well, let that pass. I am something allied to humanity yet."

"Speak your errand," gasped Flora, "or come what may, I scream for help to those who will not be slow to render it."

"I know it."

"You know I will scream?"

"No; you will hear me. I know they would not be slow to tender help to you, but you will not call for it; I will present to you no necessity."

"Say on--say on."

"You perceive I do not attempt to approach you; my errand is one of peace."

"Peace from you! Horrible being, if you be really what even now my appalled imagination shrinks from naming you, would not even to you absolute annihilation be a blessing?"

"Peace, peace. I came not here to talk on such a subject. I must be brief, Flora Bannerworth, for time presses. I do not hate you. Wherefore should I? You are young, and you are beautiful, and you bear a name which should command, and does command, some portion of my best regard."

"There is a portrait," said Flora, "in this house."

"No more--no more. I know what you would say."

"It is yours."

"The house, and all within, I covet," he said, uneasily. "Let that suffice. I have quarrelled with your brother--I have quarrelled with one who just now fancies he loves you."

"Charles Holland loves me truly."

"It does not suit me now to dispute that point with you. I have the means of knowing more of the secrets of the human heart than common men. I tell you, Flora Bannerworth, that he who talks to you of love, loves you not but with the fleeting fancy of a boy; and there is one who hides deep in his heart a world of passion, one who has never spoken to you of love, and yet who loves you with a love as far surpassing the evanescent fancy of this boy Holland, as does the mighty ocean the most placid lake that ever basked in idleness beneath a summer's sun."

There was a wonderful fascination in the manner now of Varney. His voice sounded like music itself. His words flowed from his tongue, each gently and properly accented, with all the charm of eloquence.

Despite her trembling horror of that man--despite her fearful opinion, which might be said to amount to a conviction of what he really was, Flora felt an irresistible wish to hear him speak on. Ay, despite too, the ungrateful theme to her heart which he had now chosen as the subject of his discourse, she felt her fear of him gradually dissipating, and now when he made a pause, she said,--

"You are much mistaken. On the constancy and truth of Charles Holland, I would stake my life."

"No doubt, no doubt."

"Have you spoken now that which you had to say?"

"No, no. I tell you I covet this place, I would purchase it, but having with your bad-tempered brothers quarrelled, they will hold no further converse with me."

"And well they may refuse."

"Be, that as it may, sweet lady, I come to you to be my mediator. In the shadow of the future I can see many events which are to come."

"Indeed."

"It is so. Borrowing some wisdom from the past, and some from resources I would not detail to you, I know that if I have inflicted much misery upon you, I can spare you much more. Your brother or your lover will challenge me."

"Oh, no, no."

"I say such will happen, and I can kill either. My skill as well as my strength is superhuman."

"Mercy! mercy!" gasped Flora. "I will spare either or both on a condition."

"What fearful condition?"

"It is not a fearful one. Your terrors go far before the fact. All I wish, maiden, of you is to induce these imperious brothers of yours to sell or let the Hall to me."

"Is that all?"

"It is. I ask no more, and, in return, I promise you not only that I will not fight with them, but that you shall never see me again. Rest securely, maiden, you will be undisturbed by me."

"Oh, God! that were indeed an assurance worth the striving for," said Flora.

"It is one you may have. But--"

"Oh, I knew--my heart told me there was yet some fearful condition to come."

"You are wrong again. I only ask of you that you keep this meeting a secret."

"No, no, no--I cannot."

"Nay, what so easy?"

"I will not; I have no secrets from those I love."

"Indeed, you will find soon the expediency of a few at least; but if you will not, I cannot urge it longer. Do as your wayward woman's nature prompts you."

There was a slight, but a very slight, tone of aggravation in these words, and the manner in which they were uttered.

As he spoke, he moved from the door towards the window, which opened into a kitchen garden. Flora shrunk as far from him as possible, and for a few moments they regarded each other in silence.

"Young blood," said Varney, "mantles in your veins."

She shuddered with terror.

"Be mindful of the condition I have proposed to you. I covet Bannerworth Hall."

"I--I hear."

"And I must have it. I will have it, although my path to it be through a sea of blood. You understand me, maiden? Repeat what has passed between us or not, as you please. I say, beware of me, if you keep not the condition I have proposed."

"Heaven knows that this place is becoming daily more hateful to us all," said Flora.

"Indeed!"

"You well might know so much. It is no sacrifice to urge it now. I will urge my brother."

"Thanks--a thousand thanks. You may not live to regret even having made a friend of Varney--"

"The vampyre!" said Flora.

He advanced towards her a step, and she involuntarily uttered a scream of terror.

In an instant his hand clasped her waist with the power of an iron vice; she felt hit hot breath flushing on her cheek. Her senses reeled, and she found herself sinking. She gathered all her breath and all her energies into one piercing shriek, and then she fell to the floor. There was a sudden crash of broken glass, and then all was still.

CHAPTER XXI

THE CONFERENCE BETWEEN THE UNCLE AND NEPHEW, AND THE ALARM

Meanwhile Charles Holland had taken his uncle by the arm, and led him into a private room.

"Dear uncle," he said, "be seated, and I will explain everything without reserve."

"Seated!--nonsense! I'll walk about," said the admiral. "D--n me! I've no patience to be seated, and very seldom had or have. Go on now, you young scamp."

"Well--well; you abuse me, but I am quite sure, had you been in my situation, you would have acted precisely as I have done."

"No, I shouldn't."

"Well, but, uncle--"

"Don't think to come over me by calling me uncle. Hark you, Charles--from this moment I won't be your uncle any more."

"Very well, sir."

"It ain't very well. And how dare you, you buccaneer, call me sir, eh? I say, how dare you?"

"I will call you anything you like."

"But I won't be called anything I like. You might as well call me at once Morgan, the Pirate, for he was called anything he liked. Hilloa, sir! how dare you laugh, eh? I'll teach you to laugh at me. I wish I had you on board ship--that's all, you young rascal. I'd soon teach you to laugh at your superior officer, I would."

"Oh, uncle, I did not laugh at you."

"What did you laugh at, then?"

"At the joke."

"Joke. D--n me, there was no joke at all!"

"Oh, very good."

"And it ain't very good."

Charles knew very well that, this sort of humour, in which was the old admiral, would soon pass away, and then that he would listen to him comfortably enough; so he would not allow the least exhibition of petulance or mere impatience to escape himself, but contented himself by waiting until the ebullition of feeling fairly worked itself out.

"Well, well," at length said the old man, "you have dragged me here, into a very small and a very dull room, under pretence of having something to tell me, and I have heard nothing yet."

"Then I will now tell you," said Charles. "I fell in love--"

"Bah!"

"With Flora Bannerworth, abroad; she is not only the most beautiful of created beings--"

"Bah!"

"But her mind is of the highest order of intelligence, honour, candour, and all amiable feelings--"

"Bah!"

"Really, uncle, if you say 'Bah!' to everything, I cannot go on."

"And what the deuce difference, sir, does it make to you, whether I say 'Bah!' or not?"

"Well, I love her. She came to England, and, as I could not exist, but was getting ill, and should, no doubt, have died if I had not done so, I came to England."

"But d----e, I want to know about the mermaid."

"The vampyre, you mean, sir?"

"Well, well, the vampyre."

"Then, uncle, all I can tell you is, that it is supposed a vampyre came one night and inflicted a wound upon Flora's neck with his teeth, and that he is still endeavouring to renew his horrible existence from the young, pure blood that flows through her veins."

"The devil he is!"

"Yes. I am bewildered, I must confess, by the mass of circumstances that have combined to give the affair a horrible truthfulness. Poor Flora is much injured in health and spirits; and when I came home, she, at once, implored me to give her up, and think of her no more, for she could not think of allowing me to unite my fate with hers, under such circumstances."

"She did?"

"Such were her words, uncle. She implored me--she used that word, 'implore'--to fly from her, to leave her to her fate, to endeavour to find happiness with some one else."

"Well?"

"But I saw her heart was breaking."

"What o' that?"

"Much of that, uncle. I told her that when I deserted her in the hour of misfortune that I hoped Heaven would desert me. I told her that if her happiness was wrecked, to cling yet to me, and that with what power and what strength God had given me, I would stand between her and all ill."

"And what then?"

"She--she fell upon my breast and wept and blessed me. Could I desert her--could I say to her, 'My dear girl, when you were full of health and beauty, I loved you, but now that sadness is at your heart I leave you?' Could I tell her that, uncle, and yet call myself a man?"

"No!" roared the old admiral, in a voice that made the room echo again; "and I tell you what, if you had done so, d--n you, you puppy, I'd have braced you, and--and married the girl myself. I would, d----e, but I would."

"Dear uncle!"

"Don't dear me, sir. Talk of deserting a girl when the signal of distress, in the shape of a tear, is in her eye!"

"But I--"

"You are a wretch--a confounded lubberly boy--a swab--a d----d bad grampus."

"You mistake, uncle."

"No, I don't. God bless you, Charles, you shall have her--if a whole ship's crew of vampyres said no, you shall have her. Let me see her--just let me see her."

The admiral gave his lips a vigorous wipe with his sleeve, and Charles said hastily,--

"My dear uncle, you will recollect that Miss Bannerworth is quite a young lady."

"I suppose she is."

"Well, then, for God's sake, don't attempt to kiss her."

"Not kiss her! d----e, they like it. Not kiss her, because she's a young lady! D----e, do you think I'd kiss a corporal of marines?"

"No, uncle; but you know young ladies are very delicate."

"And ain't I delicate--shiver my timbers, ain't I delicate? Where is she? that's what I want to know."

"Then you approve of what I have done?"

"You are a young scamp, but you have got some of the old admiral's family blood in you, so don't take any credit for acting like an honest man--you couldn't help it."

"But if I had not so acted," said Charles, with a smile, "what would have become of the family blood, then?"

"What's that to you? I would have disowned you, because that very thing would have convinced me you were an impostor, and did not belong to the family at all."

"Well, that would have been one way of getting over the difficulty."

"No difficulty at all. The man who deserts the good ship that carries him through the waves, or the girl that trusts her heart to him, ought to be chopped up into meat for wild monkeys."

"Well, I think so to."

"Of course you do."

"Why, of course?"

"Because it's so d----d reasonable that, being a nephew of mine, you can't possibly help it."

"Bravo, uncle! I had no idea you were so argumentative."

"Hadn't you, spooney; you'd be an ornament to the gun-room, you would; but where's the 'young lady' who is so infernal delicate--where is she, I say?"

"I will fetch her, uncle."

"Ah, do; I'll be bound, now, she's one of the right build--a good figure-head, and don't make too much stern-way."

"Well, well, whatever you do, now don't pay her any compliments, for your efforts in that line are of such a very doubtful order, that I shall dread to hear you."

"You be off, and mind your own business; I haven't been at sea forty years without picking up some out-and-out delicate compliments to say to a young lady."

"But do you really imagine, now, that the deck of a man-of-war is a nice place to pick up courtly compliments in?"

"Of course I do. There you hear the best of language, d----e! You don't know what you are talking about, you fellows that have stuck on shore all your lives; it's we seamen who learn life."

"Well, well--hark!"

"What's that?"

"A cry--did you not hear a cry?"

"A signal of distress, by G--d!"

In their efforts to leave the room, the uncle and nephew for about a minute actually blocked up the door-way, but the superior bulk of the admiral prevailed, and after nearly squeezing poor Charles flat, he got out first.

But this did not avail him, for he knew not where to go. Now, the second scream which Flora had uttered when the vampyre had clasped her waist came upon their ears, and, as they were outside the room, it acted well as a guide in which direction to come.

Charles fancied correctly enough at once that it proceeded from the room which was called "Flora's own room," and thitherward accordingly he dashed at tremendous speed.

Henry, however, happened to be nearer at hand, and, moreover, he did not hesitate a moment, because he knew that Flora was in her own room; so he reached it first, and Charles saw him rush in a few moments before he could reach the room.

The difference of time, however, was very slight, and Henry had only just raised Flora from the floor as Charles appeared.

"God of Heaven!" cried the latter, "what has happened?"

"I know not," said Henry; "as God is my judge, I know not. Flora, Flora, speak to us! Flora! Flora!"

"She has fainted!" cried Charles. "Some water may restore her. Oh, Henry, Henry, is not this horrible?"

"Courage! courage!" said Henry although his voice betrayed what a terrible state of anxiety he was himself in; "you will find water in that decanter, Charles. Here is my mother, too! Another visit! God help us!"

Mrs. Bannerworth sat down on the edge of the sofa which was in the room, and could only wring her hands and weep.

"Avast!" cried the admiral, making his appearance. "Where's the enemy, lads?"

"Uncle," said Charles, "uncle, uncle, the vampyre has been here again--the dreadful vampyre!"

"D--n me, and he's gone, too, and carried half the window with him. Look there!"

It was literally true; the window, which was a long latticed one, was smashed through.

"Help! oh, help!" said Flora, as the water that was dashed in her face began to recover her.

"You are safe!" cried Henry, "you are safe!"

"Flora," said Charles; "you know my voice, dear Flora? Look up, and you will see there are none here but those who love you."

Flora opened her eyes timidly as the said,--

"Has it gone?"

"Yes, yes, dear," said Charles. "Look around you; here are none but true friends."

"And tried friends, my dear," said Admiral Bell, "excepting me; and whenever you like to try me, afloat or ashore, d--n me, shew me Old Nick himself, and I won't shrink--yard arm and yard arm--grapnel to grapnel--pitch pots and grenades!"

"This is my uncle, Flora," said Charles.

"I thank you, sir," said Flora, faintly.

"All right!" whispered the admiral to Charles; "what a figure-head, to be sure! Poll at Swansea would have made just about four of her, but she wasn't so delicate, d--n me!"

"I should think not."

"You are right for once in a way, Charley."

"What was it that alarmed you?" said Charles, tenderly, as he now took one of Flora's hands in his.

"Varney--Varney, the vampyre."

"Varney!" exclaimed Henry; "Varney here!"

"Yes, he came in at that door: and when I screamed, I suppose--for I hardly was conscious--he darted out through the window."

"This," said Henry, "is beyond all human patience. By Heaven! I cannot and will not endure it."

"It shall be my quarrel," said Charles; "I shall go at once and defy him. He shall meet me."

"Oh, no, no, no," said Flora, as she clung convulsively to Charles. "No, no; there is a better way."

"What way?"

"The place has become full of terrors. Let us leave it. Let him, as he wishes, have it."

"Let him have it?"

"Yes, yes. God knows, if it purchase an immunity from these visits, we may well be overjoyed. Remember that we have ample reason to believe him more than human. Why should you allow yourselves to risk a personal encounter with such a man, who might be glad to kill you that he might have an opportunity of replenishing his own hideous existence from your best heart's blood?"

The young men looked aghast.

"Besides," added Flora, "you cannot tell what dreadful powers of mischief he may have, against which human courage might be of no avail."

"There is truth and reason," said Mr. Marchdale, stepping forward, "in what Flora says."

"Only let me come across him, that's all," said Admiral Bell, "and I'll soon find out what he is. I suppose he's some long slab of a lubber after all, ain't he, with no strength."

"His strength is immense," said Marchdale. "I tried to seize him, and I fell beneath his arm as if I had been struck by the hammer of a Cyclops."

"A what?" cried the admiral.

"A Cyclops."

"D--n me, I served aboard the Cyclops eleven years, and never saw a very big hammer aboard of her."

"What on earth is to be done?" said Henry.

"Oh," chimed in the admiral, "there's always a bother about what's to be done on earth. Now, at sea, I could soon tell you what was to be done."

"We must hold a solemn consultation over this matter," said Henry. "You are safe now, Flora."

"Oh, be ruled by me. Give up the Hall."

"You tremble."

"I do tremble, brother, for what may yet ensue. I implore you to give up the Hall. It is but a terror to us now--give it up. Have no more to do with it. Let us make terms with Sir Francis Varney. Remember, we dare not kill him."

"He ought to be smothered," said the admiral.

"It is true," remarked Henry, "we dare not, even holding all the terrible suspicions we do, take his life."

"By foul means certainly not," said Charles, "were he ten times a vampyre. I cannot, however, believe that he is so invulnerable as he is represented."

"No one represents him here," said Marchdale. "I speak, sir, because I saw you glance at me. I only know that, having made two unsuccessful attempts to seize him, he eluded me, once by leaving in my grasp a piece of his coat, and the next time he struck me down, and I feel yet the effects of the terrific blow."

"You hear?" said Flora.

"Yes, I hear," said Charles.

"For some reason," added Marchdale, in a tone of emotion, "what I say seems to fall always badly upon Mr. Holland's ear. I know not why; but if it will give him any satisfaction, I will leave Bannerworth Hall to-night."

"No, no, no," said Henry; "for the love of Heaven, do not let us quarrel."

"Hear, hear," cried the admiral. "We can never fight the enemy well if the ship's crew are on bad terms. Come now, you Charles, this appears to be an honest, gentlemanly fellow--give him your hand."

"If Mr. Charles Holland," said Marchdale, "knows aught to my prejudice in any way, however slight, I here beg of him to declare it at once, and openly."

"I cannot assert that I do," said Charles.

"Then what the deuce do you make yourself so disagreeable for, eh?" cried the admiral.

"One cannot help one's impression and feelings," said Charles; "but I am willing to take Mr. Marchdale's hand."

"And I yours, young sir," said Marchdale, "in all sincerity of spirit, and with good will towards you."

They shook hands; but it required no conjuror to perceive that it was not done willingly or cordially. It was a handshaking of that character which seemed to imply on each side, "I don't like you, but I don't know positively any harm of you."

"There now," said the admiral, "that's better."

"Now, let us hold counsel about this Varney," said Henry. "Come to the parlour all of you, and we will endeavour to come to some decided arrangement."

"Do not weep, mother," said Flora. "All may yet be well. We will leave this place."

"We will consider that question, Flora," said Henry; "and believe me your wishes will go a long way with all of us, as you may well suppose they always would."

They left Mrs. Bannerworth with Flora, and proceeded to the small oaken parlour, in which were the elaborate and beautiful carvings which have been before mentioned.

Henry's countenance, perhaps, wore the most determined expression of all. He appeared now as if he had thoroughly made up his mind to do something which should have a decided tendency to put a stop to the terrible scenes which were now day by day taking place beneath that roof.

Charles Holland looked serious and thoughtful, as if he were revolving some course of action in his mind concerning which he was not quite clear.

Mr. Marchdale was more sad and depressed, to all appearance, than any of them.

As for the admiral, he was evidently in a state of amazement, and knew not what to think. He was anxious to do something, and yet what that was to be he had not the most remote idea, any more than as if he was not at all cognisant of any of those circumstances, every one of which was so completely out of the line of his former life and experience.

George had gone to call on Mr. Chillingworth, so he was not present at the first part of this serious council of war.

CHAPTER XXII

THE CONSULTATION.--THE DETERMINATION TO LEAVE THE HALL

This was certainly the most seriously reasonable meeting which had been held at Bannerworth Hall on the subject of the much dreaded vampyre. The absolute necessity for doing something of a decisive character was abundantly apparent, and when Henry promised Flora that her earnest wish to leave the house should not be forgotten as an element in the discussion which was about to ensue, it was with a rapidly growing feeling on his own part, to the effect that that house, associated even as it was with many endearing recollections, was no home for him.

Hence he was the more inclined to propose a departure from the Hall if it could possibly be arranged satisfactorily in a pecuniary point of view. The pecuniary point of view, however, in which Henry was compelled to look at the subject, was an important and a troublesome one.

We have already hinted at the very peculiar state of the finances of the family; and, in fact, although the income derivable from various sources ought to have been amply sufficient to provide Henry, and those who were dependent upon him, with a respectable livelihood, yet it was nearly all swallowed up by the payment of regular instalments upon family debts incurred by his father. And the creditors took great credit to themselves that they allowed of such an arrangement, instead of sweeping off all before them, and leaving the family to starve.

The question, therefore, or, at all events, one of the questions, now was, how far would a departure from the Hall of him, Henry, and the other branches of the family, act upon that arrangement?

During a very few minutes' consideration, Henry, with the frank and candid disposition which was so strong a characteristic of his character, made up his mind to explain all this fully to Charles Holland and his uncle.

When once he formed such a determination he was not likely to be slow in carrying it into effect, and no sooner, then, were the whole of them seated in the small oaken parlour than he made an explicit statement of his circumstances.

"But," said Mr. Marchdale, when he had done, "I cannot see what right your creditors have to complain of where you live, so long as you perform your contract to them."

"True; but they always expected me, I knew, to remain at the Hall, and if they chose, why, of course, at any time, they could sell off the whole property for what it would fetch, and pay themselves as far as the proceeds would go. At all events, I am quite certain there could be nothing at all left for me."

"I cannot imagine," added Mr. Marchdale, "that any men could be so unreasonable."

"It is scarcely to be borne," remarked Charles Holland, with more impatience than he usually displayed, "that a whole family are to be put to the necessity of leaving their home for no other reason than the being pestered by such a neighbour as Sir Francis Varney. It makes one impatient and angry to reflect upon such a state of things."

"And yet they are lamentably true," said Henry. "What can we do?"

"Surely there must be some sort of remedy."

"There is but one that I can imagine, and that is one we all alike revolt from. We might kill him."

"That is out of the question."

"Of course my impression is that he bears the same name really as myself, and that he is my ancestor, from whom was painted the portrait on the panel."

"Have circumstances really so far pressed upon you," said Charles Holland, "as at length to convince you that this man is really the horrible creature we surmise he may be?"

"Dare we longer doubt it?" cried Henry, in a tone of excitement. "He is the vampyre."

"I'll be hanged if I believe it," said Admiral Bell! "Stuff and nonsense! Vampyre, indeed! Bother the vampyre."

"Sir," said Henry, "you have not had brought before you, painfully, as we have, all the circumstances upon which we, in a manner, feel compelled to found this horrible belief. At first incredulity was a natural thing. We had no idea that ever we could be brought to believe in such a thing."

"That is the case," added Marchdale. "But, step by step, we have been driven from utter disbelief in this phenomenon to a trembling conviction that it must be true."

"Unless we admit that, simultaneously, the senses of a number of persons have been deceived."

"That is scarcely possible."

"Then do you mean really to say there are such fish?" said the admiral.

"We think so."

"Well, I'm d----d! I have heard all sorts of yarns about what fellows have seen in one ocean and another; but this does beat them all to nothing."

"It is monstrous," exclaimed Charles.

There was a pause of some few moments' duration, and then Mr. Marchdale said, in a low voice,--

"Perhaps I ought not to propose any course of action until you, Henry, have yourself done so; but even at the risk of being presumptuous, I will say that I am firmly of opinion you ought to leave the Hall."

"I am inclined to think so, too," said Henry.

"But the creditors?" interposed Charles.

"I think they might be consulted on the matter beforehand," added Marchdale, "when no doubt they would acquiesce in an arrangement which could do them no harm."

"Certainly, no harm," said Henry, "for I cannot take the estate with me, as they well know."

"Precisely. If you do not like to sell it, you can let it."

"To whom?"

"Why, under the existing circumstances, it is not likely you would get any tenant for it than the one who has offered himself."

"Sir Francis Varney?"

"Yes. It seems to be a great object with him to live here, and it appears to me, that notwithstanding all that has occurred, it is most decidedly the best policy to let him."

Nobody could really deny the reasonableness of this advice, although it seemed strange, and was repugnant to the feelings of them all, as they heard it. There was a pause of some seconds' duration, and then Henry said,--

"It does, indeed, seem singular, to surrender one's house to such a being."

"Especially," said Charles, "after what has occurred."

"True."

"Well," said Mr. Marchdale, "if any better plan of proceeding, taking the whole case into consideration, can be devised, I shall be most happy."

"Will you consent to put off all proceedings for three days?" said Charles Holland, suddenly.

"Have you any plan, my dear sir?" said Mr. Marchdale.

"I have, but it is one which I would rather say nothing about for the present."

"I have no objection," said Henry, "I do not know that three days can make any difference in the state of affairs. Let it be so, if you wish, Charles."

"Then I am satisfied," said Charles. "I cannot but feel that, situated as I am regarding Flora, this is almost more my affair than even yours, Henry."

"I cannot see that," said Henry. "Why should you take upon yourself more of the responsibility of these affairs than I, Charles? You induce in my mind a suspicion that you have some desperate project in your imagination, which by such a proposition you would seek to reconcile me to."

Charles was silent, and Henry then added,--

"Now, Charles, I am quite convinced that what I have hinted at is the fact. You have conceived some scheme which you fancy would be much opposed by us?"

"I will not deny that I have," said Charles. "It is one, however, which you must allow me for the present to keep locked in my own breast."

"Why will you not trust us?"

"For two reasons."

"Indeed!"

"The one is, that I have not yet thoroughly determined upon the course I project; and the other is, that it is one in which I am not justified in involving any one else."

"Charles, Charles," said Henry, despondingly; "only consider for a moment into what new misery you may plunge poor Flora, who is, Heaven knows, already sufficiently afflicted, by attempting an enterprise which even we, who are your friends, may unwittingly cross you in the performance of."

"This is one in which I fear no such result. It cannot so happen. Do not urge me."

"Can't you say at once what you think of doing?" said the old admiral. "What do you mean by turning your sails in all sorts of directions so oddly? You sneak, why don't you be what do you call it--explicit?"

"I cannot, uncle."

"What, are you tongue-tied?"

"All here know well," said Charles, "that if I do not unfold my mind fully, it is not that I fear to trust any one present, but from some other most special reason."

"Charles, I forbear to urge you further," said Henry, "and only implore you to be careful."

At this moment the room door opened, and George Bannerworth, accompanied by Mr. Chillingworth, came in.

"Do not let me intrude," said the surgeon; "I fear, as I see you seated, gentlemen, that my presence must be a rudeness and a disturbance to some family consultation among yourselves?"

"Not at all, Mr. Chillingworth," said Henry. "Pray be seated; we are very glad indeed to see you. Admiral Bell, this is a friend on whom we can rely--Mr. Chillingworth."

"And one of the right sort, I can see," said the admiral, as he shook Mr. Chillingworth by the hand.

"Sir, you do me much honour," said the doctor.

"None at all, none at all; I suppose you know all about this infernal odd vampyre business?"

"I believe I do, sir."

"And what do you think of it?"

"I think time will develop the circumstances sufficiently to convince us all that such things cannot be."

"D--n me, you are the most sensible fellow, then, that I have yet met with since I have been in this neighbourhood; for everybody else is so convinced about the vampyre, that they are ready to swear by him."

"It would take much more to convince me. I was coming over here when I met Mr. George Bannerworth coming to my house."

"Yes," said George, "and Mr. Chillingworth has something to tell us of a nature confirmatory of our own suspicions."

"It is strange," said Henry; "but any piece of news, come it from what quarter it may, seems to be confirmatory, in some degree or another, of that dreadful belief in vampyres."

"Why," said the doctor, "when Mr. George says that my news is of such a character, I think he goes a little too far. What I have to tell you, I do not conceive has anything whatever to do with the fact, or one fact of there being vampyres."

"Let us hear it," said Henry.

"It is simply this, that I was sent for by Sir Francis Varney myself."

"You sent for?"

"Yes; he sent for me by a special messenger to come to him, and when I went, which, under the circumstances, you may well guess, I did with all the celerity possible, I found it was to consult me about a flesh wound in his arm, which was showing some angry symptoms."

"Indeed."

"Yes, it was so. When I was introduced to him I found him lying on a couch, and looking pale and unwell. In the most respectful manner, he asked me to be seated, and when I had taken a chair, he added,--

"'Mr. Chillingworth, I have sent for you in consequence of a slight accident which has happened to my arm. I was incautiously loading some fire-arms, and discharged a pistol so close to me that the bullet inflicted a wound on my arm.'

"'If you will allow me," said I, 'to see the wound, I will give you my opinion.'

"He then showed me a jagged wound, which had evidently been caused by the passage of a bullet, which, had it gone a little deeper, must have inflicted serious injury. As it was, the wound was but trifling.

"He had evidently been attempting to dress it himself, but finding some considerable inflammation, he very likely got a little alarmed."

"You dressed the wound?"

"I did."

"And what do you think of Sir Francis Varney, now that you have had so capital an opportunity," said Henry, "of a close examination of him?"

"Why, there is certainly something odd about him which I cannot well define, but, take him altogether, he can be a very gentlemanly man indeed."

"So he can."

"His manners are easy and polished; he has evidently mixed in good society, and I never, in all my life, heard such a sweet, soft, winning voice."

"That is strictly him. You noticed, I presume, his great likeness to the portrait on the panel?"

"I did. At some moments, and viewing his face in some particular lights, it showed much more strongly than at others. My impression was that he could, when he liked, look much more like the portrait on the panel than when he allowed his face to assume its ordinary appearance."

"Probably such an impression would be produced upon your mind," said Charles, "by some accidental expression of the countenance which even he was not aware of, and which often occurs in families."

"It may be so."

"Of course you did not hint, sir, at what has passed here with regard to him?" said Henry.

"I did not. Being, you see, called in professionally, I had no right to take advantage of that circumstance to make any remarks to him about his private affairs."

"Certainly not."

"It was all one to me whether he was a vampyre or not, professionally, and however deeply I might feel, personally, interested in the matter, I said nothing to him about it, because, you see, if I had, he would have had a fair opportunity of saying at once, 'Pray, sir, what is that to you?' and I should have been at a loss what to reply."

"Can we doubt," said Henry, "but that this very wound has been inflicted upon Sir Francis Varney, by the pistol-bullet which was discharged at him by Flora?"

"Everything leads to such an assumption certainly," said Charles Holland.

"And yet you cannot even deduce from that the absolute fact of Sir Francis Varney being a vampyre?"

"I do not think, Mr. Chillingworth," said Marchdale, "anything would convince you but a visit from him, and an actual attempt to fasten upon some of your own veins."

"That would not convince me," said Chillingworth.

"Then you will not be convinced?"

"I certainly will not. I mean to hold out to the last. I said at the first, and I say so still, that I never will give way to this most outrageous superstition."

"I wish I could think with you," said Marchdale, with a shudder; "but there may be something in the very atmosphere of this house which has been rendered hideous by the awful visits that have been made to it, which forbids me to disbelieve in those things which others more happily situated can hold at arm's length, and utterly repudiate."

"There may be," said Henry; "but as to that, I think, after the very strongly expressed wish of Flora, I will decide upon leaving the house."

"Will you sell it or let it?"

"The latter I should much prefer," was the reply.

"But who will take it now, except Sir Francis Varney? Why not at once let him have it? I am well aware that this does sound odd advice, but remember, we are all the creatures of circumstances, and that, in some cases where we least like it, we must swim with the stream."

"That you will not decide upon, however, at present," said Charles Holland, as he rose.

"Certainly not; a few days can make no difference."

"None for the worse, certainly, and possibly much for the better."

"Be it so; we will wait."

"Uncle," said Charles, "will you spare me half an hour of your company?"

"An hour, my boy, if you want it," said the admiral, rising from his chair.

"Then this consultation is over," said Henry, "and we quite understand that to leave the Hall is a matter determined on, and that in a few days a decision shall be come to as to whether Varney the Vampyre shall be its tenant or not."

CHAPTER XXIII

THE ADMIRAL'S ADVICE TO CHARLES HOLLAND.--THE CHALLENGE TO THE VAMPYRE

When Charles Holland got his uncle into a room by themselves, he said,--

"Uncle, you are a seaman, and accustomed to decide upon matters of honour. I look upon myself as having been most grievously insulted by this Sir Francis Varney. All accounts agree in representing him as a gentleman. He goes openly by a title, which, if it were not his, could easily be contradicted; therefore, on the score of position in life, there is no fault to find with him. What would you do if you were insulted by a gentleman?"

The old admiral's eyes sparkled, and he looked comically in the face of Charles, as he said,--

"I know now where you are steering."

"What would you do, uncle?"

"Fight him!"

"I knew you would say so, and that's just what I want to do as regards Sir Francis Varney."

"Well, my boy, I don't know that you can do better. He must be a thundering rascal, whether he is a vampyre or not; so if you feel that he has insulted you, fight him by all means, Charles."

"I am much pleased, uncle, to find that you take my view of the subject," said Charles. "I knew that if I mentioned such a thing to the Bannerworths, they would endeavour all in their power to pursuade me against it."

"Yes, no doubt; because they are all impressed with a strange fear of this fellow's vampyre powers. Besides, if a man is going to fight, the fewer people he mentions it to most decidedly the better, Charles."

"I believe that is the fact, uncle. Should I overcome Varney, there will most likely be at once an end to the numerous and uncomfortable perplexities of the Bannerworths as regards him; and if he overcome me, why, then, at all events, I shall have made an effort to rescue Flora from the dread of this man."

"And then he shall fight me," added the admiral, "so he shall have two chances, at all events, Charles."

"Nay, uncle, that would, you know, scarcely be fair. Besides, if I should fall, I solemnly bequeath Flora Bannerworth to your good offices. I much fear that the pecuniary affairs of poor Henry,--from no fault of his, Heaven knows,--are in a very bad state, and that Flora may yet live to want some kind and able friend."

"Never fear, Charles. The young creature shall never want while the old admiral has got a shot in the locker."

"Thank you, uncle, thank you. I have ample cause to know, and to be able to rely upon your kind and generous nature. And now about the challenge?"

"You write it, boy, and I'll take it."

"Will you second me, uncle?"

"To be sure I will. I wouldn't trust anybody else to do so on any account. You leave all the arrangements with me, and I'll second you as you ought to be seconded."

"Then I will write it at once, for I have received injuries at the hands of that man, or devil, be he what he may, that I cannot put up with. His visit to the chamber of her whom I love would alone constitute ample ground of action."

"I should say it rather would, my boy."

"And after this corroborative story of the wound, I cannot for a moment doubt that Sir Francis Varney is the vampyre, or the personifier of the vampyre."

"That's clear enough, Charles. Come, just you write your challenge, my boy, at once, and let me have it."

"I will, uncle."

Charles was a little astonished, although pleased, at his uncle's ready acquiescence in his fighting a vampyre, but that circumstance he ascribed to the old man's habits of life, which made him so familiar with strife and personal contentions of all sorts, that he did not ascribe to it that amount of importance which more peaceable people did. Had he, while he was writing the note to Sir Francis Varney, seen the old admiral's face, and the exceedingly cunning look it wore, he might have suspected that the acquiescence in the duel was but a seeming acquiescence. This, however, escaped him, and in a few moments he read to his uncle the following note:--

"To SIR FRANCIS VARNEY.

"Sir,--The expressions made use of towards me by you, as well as general circumstances, which I need not further allude to here, induce me to demand of you that satisfaction due from one gentleman to another. My uncle, Admiral Bell, is the bearer of this note, and will arrange preliminaries with any friend you may choose to appoint to act in your behalf. I am, sir, yours, &c.

"CHARLES HOLLAND."

"Will that do?" said Charles.

"Capital!" said the admiral.

"I am glad you like it."

"Oh, I could not help liking it. The least said and the most to the purpose, always pleases me best; and this explains nothing, and demands all you want--which is a fight; so it's all right, you see, and nothing can be possibly better."

Charles did glance in his uncle's face, for he suspected, from the manner in which these words were uttered, that the old man was amusing himself a little at his expense. The admiral, however, looked so supernaturally serious that Charles was foiled.

"I repeat, it's a capital letter," he said.

"Yes, you said so."

"Well, what are you staring at?"

"Oh, nothing."

"Do you doubt my word?"

"Not at all, uncle; only I thought there was a degree of irony in the manner in which you spoke."

"None at all, my boy. I never was more serious in all my life."

"Very good. Then you will remember that I leave my honour in this affair completely in your hands."

"Depend upon me, my boy."

"I will, and do."

"I'll be off and see the fellow at once."

The admiral bustled out of the room, and in a few moments Charles heard him calling loudly,--

"Jack--Jack Pringle, you lubber, where are you?--Jack Pringle, I say."

"Ay, ay, sir," said Jack, emerging from the kitchen, where he had been making himself generally useful in assisting Mrs. Bannerworth, there being no servant in the house, to cook some dinner for the family.

"Come on, you rascal, we are going for a walk."

"The rations will be served out soon," growled Jack.

"We shall be back in time, you cormorant, never fear. You are always thinking of eating and drinking, you are, Jack; and I'll be hanged if I think you ever think of anything else. Come on, will you; I'm going on rather a particular cruise just now, so mind what you are about."

"Aye, aye, sir," said the tar, and these two originals, who so perfectly understood each other, walked away, conversing as they went, and their different voices coming upon the ear of Charles, until distance obliterated all impression of the sound.

Charles paced to and fro in the room where he had held this brief and conclusive conversation with his uncle. He was thoughtful, as any one might well be who knew not but that the next four-and-twenty hours would be the limit of his sojourn in this world.

"Oh, Flora--Flora!" he at length said, "how happy we might to have been together--how happy we might have been! but all is past now, and there seems nothing left us but to endure. There it but one chance, and that is in my killing this fearful man who is invested with so dreadful an existence. And if I do kill him in fair and in open fight, I will take care that his mortal frame has no power again to revisit the glimpses of the moon."

It was strange to imagine that such was the force of many concurrent circumstances, that a young man like Charles Holland, of first-rate abilities and education, should find it necessary to give in so far to a belief which was repugnant to all his best feelings and habits of thought, as to be reasoning with himself upon the best means of preventing the resuscitation of the corpse of a vampyre. But so it was. His imagination had yielded to a succession of events which very few persons indeed could have held out against.

"I have heard and read," he said, as he continued his agitated and uneasy walk, "of how these dreadful beings are to be in their graves. I have heard of stakes being driven through the body so as to pin it to the earth until the gradual progress of decay has rendered its revivification a thing of utter and total impossibility. Then, again," he added, after a slight pause, "I have heard of their being burned, and the ashes gathered to the winds of Heaven to prevent them from ever again uniting or assuming human form."

These were disagreeable and strange fancies, and he shuddered while he indulged in them. He felt a kind of trembling horror come over him even at the thought of engaging in conflict with a being, who perhaps, had lived more than a hundred years.

"That portrait," he thought, "on the panel, is the portrait of a man in the prime of life. If it be the portrait of Sir Francis Varney, by the date which the family ascribe to it he must be nearly one hundred and fifty years of age now."

This was a supposition which carried the imagination to a vast amount of strange conjectures.

"What changes he must have witnessed about him in that time," thought Charles. "How he must have seen kingdoms totter and fall, and how many changes of habits, of manners, and of customs must he have become a spectator of. Renewing too, ever and anon, his fearful existence by such fearful means."

This was a wide field of conjecture for a fertile imagination, and now that he was on the eve of engaging with such a being in mortal combat, on behalf of her he loved, the thoughts it gave rise to came more strongly and thickly upon him than ever they had done before.

"But I will fight him," he suddenly said, "for Flora's sake, were he a hundred times more hideous a being than so many evidences tend to prove him. I will fight with him, and it may be my fate to rid the world of such a monster in human form."

Charles worked himself up to a kind of enthusiasm by which he almost succeeded in convincing himself that, in attempting the destruction of Sir Francis Varney, he was the champion of human nature.

It would be aside from the object of these pages, which is to record facts as they occurred, to enter into the metaphysical course of reasoning which came across Charles's mind; suffice it to say that he felt nothing shaken as regarded his resolve to meet Varney the Vampyre, and that he made up his mind the conflict should be one of life or death.

"It must be so," he said. "It must be so. Either he or I must fall in the fight which shall surely be."

He now sought Flora, for how soon might he now be torn from her for ever by the irresistible hand of death. He felt that, during the few brief hours which now would only elapse previous to his meeting with Sir Francis Varney, he could not enjoy too much of the society of her who reigned supreme in his heart, and held in her own keeping his best affections.

But while Charles is thus employed, let us follow his uncle and Jack Pringle to the residence of Varney, which, as the reader is aware, was so near at hand that it required not many minutes' sharp walking to reach it.

The admiral knew well he could trust Jack with any secret, for long habits of discipline and deference to the orders of superiors takes off the propensity to blabbing which, among civilians who are not accustomed to discipline, is so very prevalent. The old man therefore explained to Jack what he meant to do, and it received Jack's full approval; but as in the enforced detail of other matters it must come out, we will not here prematurely enter into the admiral's plans.

When they reached the residence of Sir Francis Varney, they were received courteously enough, and the admiral desired Jack to wait for him in the handsome hall of the house, while he was shewn up stairs to the private room of the vampyre.

"Confound the fellow!" muttered the old admiral, "he is well lodged at all events. I should say he was not one of those sort of vampyres who have nowhere to go to but their own coffins when the evening comes."

The room into which the admiral was shewn had green blinds to it, and they were all drawn down. It is true that the sun was shining brightly outside, although transiently, but still a strange green tinge was thrown over everything in the room, and more particularly did it appear to fall upon the face of Varney, converting his usually sallow countenance into a still more hideous and strange colour. He was sitting upon a couch, and, when the admiral came in, he rose, and said, in a deep-toned voice, extremely different to that he usually spoke in,--

"My humble home is much honoured, sir, by your presence in it."

"Good morning," said the admiral. "I have come to speak to you, sir, rather seriously."

"However abrupt this announcement may sound to me," said Varney, "I am quite sure I shall always hear, with the most profound respect, whatever Admiral Bell may have to say."

"There is no respect required," said the admiral, "but only a little attention."

Sir Francis bowed in a stately manner, saying,--

"I shall be quite unhappy if you will not be seated, Admiral Bell."

"Oh, never mind that, Sir Francis Varney, if you be Sir Francis Varney; for you may be the devil himself, for all I know. My nephew, Charles Holland, considers that, one way and another, he has a very tolerable quarrel with you."

"I much grieve to hear it."

"Do you?"

"Believe me, I do. I am most scrupulous in what I say; and an assertion that I am grieved, you may thoroughly and entirely depend upon."

"Well, well, never mind that; Charles Holland is a young man just entering into life. He loves a girl who is, I think, every way worthy of him."

"Oh, what a felicitous prospect!"

"Just hear me out, if you please."

"With pleasure, sir--with pleasure."

"Well, then, when a young, hot-headed fellow thinks he has a good ground of quarrel with anybody, you will not be surprised at his wanting to fight it out."

"Not at all."

"Well, then, to come to the point, my nephew, Charles Holland, has a fancy for fighting with you."

"Ah!"

"You take it d----d easy."

"My dear sir, why should I be uneasy? He is not my nephew, you know. I shall have no particular cause, beyond those feelings of common compassion which I hope inhabit my breast as well as every one else's."

"What do you mean?"

"Why, he is a young man just, as you say, entering into life, and I cannot help thinking it would be a pity to cut him off like a flower in the bud, so very soon."

"Oh, you make quite sure, then, of settling him, do you?"

"My dear sir, only consider; he might be very troublesome, indeed; you know young men are hot-headed and troublesome. Even if I were only to maim him, he might be a continual and never-ceasing annoyance to me. I think I should be absolutely, in a manner of speaking, compelled to cut him off."

"The devil you do!"

"As you say, sir."

"D--n your assurance, Mr. Vampyre, or whatever odd fish you may be."

"Admiral Bell, I never called upon you and received a courteous reception, and then insulted you."

"Then why do you talk of cutting off a better man than yourself? D--n it, what would you say to him cutting you off?"

"Oh, as for me, my good sir, that's quite another thing. Cutting me off is very doubtful."

Sir Francis Varney gave a strange smile as he spoke, and shook his head, as if some most extraordinary and extravagant proposition had been mooted, which it was scarcely worth the while of anybody possessed of common sense to set about expecting.

Admiral Bell felt strongly inclined to get into a rage, but he repressed the idea as much as he could, although, but for the curious faint green light that came through the blinds, his heightened colour would have sufficiently proclaimed what state of mind he was in.

"Mr. Varney," he said, "all this is quite beside the question; but, at all events, if it have any weight at all, it ought to have a considerable influence in deciding you to accept of what terms I propose."

"What are they, sir?"

"Why, that you permit me to espouse my nephew Charles's quarrel, and meet you instead of him."

"You meet me?"

"Yes; I've met a better man more than once before. It can make no difference to you."

"I don't know that, Admiral Bell. One generally likes, in a duel, to face him with whom one has had the misunderstanding, be it on what grounds it may."

"There's some reason, I know, in what you say; but, surely, if I am willing, you need not object."

"And is your nephew willing thus to shift the danger and the job of resenting his own quarrels on to your shoulders?"

"No; he knows nothing about it. He has written you a challenge, of which I am the bearer, but I voluntarily, and of my own accord, wish to meet you instead."

"This is a strange mode of proceeding."

"If you will not accede to it, and fight him first, and any harm comes to him, you shall fight me afterwards."

"Indeed."

"Yes, indeed you shall, however surprised you may look."

"As this appears to be quite a family affair, then," said Sir Francis Varney, "it certainly does appear immaterial which of you I fight with first."

"Quite so; now you take a sensible view of the question. Will you meet me?"

"I have no particular objection. Have you settled all your affairs, and made your will?"

"What's that to you?"

"Oh, I only asked, because there is generally so much food for litigation if a man dies intestate, and is worth any money."

"You make devilish sure," said the admiral, "of being the victor. Have you made your will?"

"Oh, my will," smiled Sir Francis; "that, my good sir, is quite an indifferent affair."

"Well, make it or not, as you like. I am old, I know, but I can pull a trigger as well as any one."

"Do what?"

"Pull a trigger."

"Why, you don't suppose I resort to any such barbarous modes of fighting?"

"Barbarous! Why, how do you fight then?"

"As a gentleman, with my sword."

"Swords! Oh, nonsense! nobody fights with swords now-a-days. That's all exploded."

"I cling to the customs and the fashions of my youth," said Varney. "I have been, years ago, accustomed always to wear a sword, and to be without one now vexes me."

"Pray, how many years ago?"

"I am older than I look, but that is not the question. I am willing to meet you with swords if you like. You are no doubt aware that, as the challenged party, I am entitled to the choice of weapons."

"I am."

"Then you cannot object to my availing myself of the one in the use of which I am perfectly unequalled."

"Indeed."

"Yes, I am, I think, the first swordsman in Europe; I have had immense practice."

"Well, sir, you have certainly made a most unexpected choice of weapons. I can use a sword still, but am by no means a master of fencing. However, it shall not be said that I went back from my word, and let the chances be as desperate as they may, I will meet you."

"Very good."

"With swords?"

"Ay, with swords; but I must have everything properly arranged, so that no blame can rest on me, you know. As you will be killed, you are safe from all consequences, but I shall be in a very different position; so, if you please, I must have this meeting got up in such a manner as shall enable me to prove, to whoever may question me on the subject, that you had fair play."

"Oh, never fear that."

"But I do fear it. The world, my good sir, is censorious, and you cannot stop people from saying extremely ill-natured things."

"What do you require, then?"

"I require you to send me a friend with a formal challenge."

"Well?"

"Then I shall refer him to a friend of mine, and they two must settle everything between them."

"Is that all?"

"Not quite. I will have a surgeon on the ground, in case, when I pink you, there should be a chance of saving your life. It always looks humane."

"When you pink me?"

"Precisely."

"Upon my word, you take these affairs easy. I suppose you have had a few of them?"

"Oh, a good number. People like yourself worry me into them, I don't like the trouble, I assure you; it is no amusement to me. I would rather, by a great deal, make some concession than fight, because I will fight with swords, and the result is then so certain that there is no danger in the matter to me."

"Hark you, Sir Francis Varney. You are either a very clever actor, or a man, as you say, of such skill with your sword, that you can make sure of the result of a duel. You know, therefore, that it is not fair play on your part to fight a duel with that weapon."

"Oh, I beg your pardon there. I never challenge anybody, and when foolish people will call me out, contrary to my inclination, I think I am bound to take what care of myself I can."

"D--n me, there's some reason in that, too," said the admiral; "but why do you insult people?"

"People insult me first."

"Oh, nonsense!"

"How should you like to be called a vampyre, and stared at as if you were some hideous natural phenomenon?"

"Well, but--"

"I say, Admiral Bell, how should you like it? I am a harmless country gentleman, and because, in the heated imaginations of some member of a crack-brained family, some housebreaker has been converted into a vampyre, I am to be pitched upon as the man, and insulted and persecuted accordingly."

"But you forget the proofs."

"What proofs?"

"The portrait, for one."

"What! Because there is an accidental likeness between me and an old picture, am I to be set down as a vampyre? Why, when I was in Austria last, I saw an old portrait of a celebrated court fool, and you so strongly resemble it, that I was quite struck when I first saw you with the likeness; but I was not so unpolite as to tell you that I considered you were the court fool turned vampyre."

"D--n your assurance!"

"And d--n yours, if you come to that."

The admiral was fairly beaten. Sir Francis Varney was by far too long-headed and witty for him. After now in vain endeavouring to find something to say, the old man buttoned up his coat in a great passion, and looking fiercely at Varney, he said,--"I don't pretend to a gift of the gab. D--n me, it ain't one of my peculiarities; but though you may talk me down, you sha'n't keep me down."

"Very good, sir."

"It is not very good. You shall hear from me."

"I am willing."

"I don't care whether you are willing or not. You shall find that when once I begin to tackle an enemy, I don't so easily leave him. One or both of us, sir, is sure to sink."

"Agreed."

"So say I. You shall find that I'm a tar for all weathers, and if you were a hundred and fifty vampires all rolled into one, I'd tackle you somehow."

The admiral walked to the door in high dudgeon; when he was near to it, Varney said, in some of his most winning and gentle accents,--

"Will you not take some refreshment, sir before you go from my humble house?"

"No!" roared the admiral.

"Something cooling?"

"No!"

"Very good, sir. A hospitable host can do no more than offer to entertain his guests."

Admiral Bell turned at the door, and said, with some degree of intense bitterness,

"You look rather poorly. I suppose, to-night, you will go and suck somebody's blood, you shark--you confounded vampyre! You ought to be made to swallow a red-hot brick, and then let dance about till it digests."

Varney smiled as he rang the bell, and said to a servant,--

"Show my very excellent friend Admiral Bell out. He will not take any refreshments."

The servant bowed, and preceded the admiral down the staircase; but, to his great surprise, instead of a compliment in the shape of a shilling or half-a-crown for his pains, he received a tremendous kick behind, with a request to go and take it to his master, with his compliments.

The fume that the old admiral was in beggars all description. He walked to Bannerworth Hall at such a rapid pace, that Jack Pringle had the greatest difficulty in the world to keep up with him, so as to be at all within speaking distance.

"Hilloa, Jack," cried the old man, when they were close to the Hall. "Did you see me kick that fellow?"

"Ay, ay, sir."

"Well, that's some consolation, at any rate, if somebody saw it. It ought to have been his master, that's all I can say to it, and I wish it had."

"How have you settled it, sir?"

"Settled what?"

"The fight, sir."

"D--n me, Jack, I haven't settled it at all."

"That's bad, sir."

"I know it is; but it shall be settled for all that, I can tell him, let him vapour as much as he may about pinking me, and one thing and another."

"Pinking you, sir?"

"Yes. He wants to fight with cutlasses, or toasting-forks, d--n me, I don't know exactly which, and then he must have a surgeon on the ground, for fear when he pinks me I shouldn't slip my cable in a regular way, and he should be blamed."

Jack gave a long whistle, as he replied,--

"Going to do it, sir?"

"I don't know now what I'm going to do. Mind, Jack, mum is the word."

"Ay, ay, sir."

"I'll turn the matter over in my mind, and then decide upon what had best be done. If he pinks me, I'll take d----d good care he don't pink Charles."

"No, sir, don't let him do that. A wamphigher, sir, ain't no good opponent to anybody. I never seed one afore, but it strikes me as the best way to settle him, would be to shut him up in some little bit of a cabin, and then smoke him with brimstone, sir."

"Well, well, I'll consider, Jack, I'll consider. Something must be done, and that quickly too. Zounds, here's Charles--what the deuce shall I say to him, by way of an excuse, I wonder, for not arranging his affair with Varney? Hang me, if I ain't taken aback now, and don't know where to place a hand."

CHAPTER XXIV

THE LETTER TO CHARLES.--THE QUARREL.--THE ADMIRAL'S NARRATIVE.--THE MIDNIGHT MEETING

It was Charles Holland who now advanced hurriedly to meet the admiral. The young man's manner was anxious. He was evidently most intent upon knowing what answer could be sent by Sir Francis Varney to his challenge.

"Uncle," he said, "tell me at once, will he meet me? You can talk of particulars afterwards, but now tell me at once if he will meet me?"

"Why, as to that," said the admiral, with a great deal of fidgetty hesitation, "you see, I can't exactly say."

"Not say!"

"No. He's a very odd fish. Don't you think he's a very odd fish, Jack Pringle'?"

"Ay, ay, sir."

"There, you hear, Charles, that Jack is of my opinion that your opponent is an odd fish."

"But, uncle, why trifle with my impatience thus? Have you seen Sir Francis Varney?"

"Seen him. Oh, yes."

"And what did he say?"

"Why, to tell the truth, my lad, I advise you not to fight with him at all."

"Uncle, is this like you? This advice from you, to compromise my honour, after sending a man a challenge?"

"D--n it all, Jack, I don't know how to get out of it," said the admiral. "I tell you what it is, Charles, he wants to fight with swords; and what on earth is the use of your engaging with a fellow who has been practising at his weapon for more than a hundred years?"

"Well, uncle, if any one had told me that you would be terrified by this Sir Francis Varney into advising me not to fight, I should have had no hesitation whatever in saying such a thing was impossible."

"I terrified?"

"Why, you advise me not to meet this man, even after I have challenged him."

"Jack," said the admiral, "I can't carry it on, you see. I never could go on with anything that was not as plain as an anchor, and quite straightforward. I must just tell all that has occurred."

"Ay, ay, sir. The best way."

"You think so, Jack?"

"I know it is, sir, always axing pardon for having a opinion at all, excepting when it happens to be the same as yourn, sir."

"Hold your tongue, you libellous villain! Now, listen to me, Charles. I got up a scheme of my own."

Charles gave a groan, for he had a very tolerable appreciation of his uncle's amount of skill in getting up a scheme of any kind or description.

"Now here am I," continued the admiral, "an old hulk, and not fit for use anymore. What's the use of me, I should like to know? Well, that's settled. But you are young and hearty, and have a long life before you. Why should you throw away your life upon a lubberly vampyre?"

"I begin to perceive now, uncle," said Charles, reproachfully, "why you, with such apparent readiness, agreed to this duel taking place."

"Well, I intended to fight the fellow myself, that's the long and short of it, boy."

"How could you treat me so?"

"No nonsense, Charles. I tell you it was all in the family. I intended to fight him myself. What was the odds whether I slipped my cable with his assistance, or in the regular course a little after this? That's the way to argufy the subject; so, as I tell you, I made up my mind to fight him myself."

Charles looked despairingly, but said,--

"What was the result?"

"Oh, the result! D--n me, I suppose that's to come. The vagabond won't fight like a Christian. He says he's quite willing to fight anybody that calls him out, provided it's all regular."

"Well--well."
"And he, being the party challenged--for he says he never himself challenges anybody, as he is quite tired of it--must have his choice of weapons."
"He is entitled to that; but it is generally understood now-a-days that pistols are the weapons in use among gentlemen for such purposes."
"Ah, but he won't understand any such thing, I tell you. He will fight with swords."
"I suppose he is, then, an adept at the use of the sword?"
"He says he is."
"No doubt--no doubt. I cannot blame a man for choosing, when he has the liberty of choice, that weapon in the use of which he most particularly, from practice, excels."
"Yes; but if he be one half the swordsman he has had time enough, according to all accounts, to be, what sort of chance have you with him?"
"Do I hear you reasoning thus?"
"Yes, to be sure you do. I have turned wonderfully prudent, you see: so I mean to fight him myself, and mind, now, you have nothing whatever to do with it."
"An effort of prudence that, certainly."
"Well, didn't I say so?"
"Come--come, uncle, this won't do. I have challenged Sir Francis Varney, and I must meet him with any weapon he may, as the challenged party, choose to select. Besides, you are not, I dare say, aware that I am a very good fencer, and probably stand as fair a chance as Varney in a contest with swords."
"Indeed!"
"Yes, uncle. I could not be so long on the continent as I have been without picking up a good knowledge of the sword, which is so popular all over Germany."
"Humph! but only consider, this d----d fellow is no less than a hundred and fifty years old."
"I care not."
"Yes, but I do."
"Uncle, uncle, I tell you I will fight with him; and if you do not arrange matters for me so that I can have the meeting with this man, which I have myself sought, and cannot, even if I wished, now recede from with honour, I must seek some other less scrupulous friend to do so."
"Give me an hour or two to think of it, Charles," said the admiral. "Don't speak to any one else, but give me a little time. You shall have no cause of complaint. Your honour cannot suffer in my hands."
"I will wait your leisure, uncle; but remember that such affairs as these, when once broached, had always better be concluded with all convenient dispatch."
"I know that, boy--I know that."
The admiral walked away, and Charles, who really felt much fretted at the delay which had taken place, returned to the house.
He had not been there long, when a lad, who had been temporarily hired during the morning by Henry to answer the gate, brought him a note, saying,--
"A servant, sir, left this for you just now."
"For me?" said Charles, as he glanced at the direction. "This is strange, for I have no acquaintance about here. Does any one wait?"
"No, sir."
The note was properly directed to him, therefore Charles Holland at once opened it. A glance at the bottom of the page told him that it came from his enemy, Sir Francis Varney, and then he read it with much eagerness. It ran thus:--

"SIR,--Your uncle, as he stated himself to be, Admiral Bell, was the bearer to me, as I understood him this day, of a challenge from you. Owing to some unaccountable hallucination of intellect, he seemed to imagine that I intended to set myself up as a sort of animated target, for any one to shoot at who might have a fancy so to do.
"According to this eccentric view of the case, the admiral had the kindness to offer to fight me first, when, should he not have the good fortune to put me out of the world, you were to try your skill, doubtless.
"I need scarcely say that I object to these family arrangements. You have challenged me, and, fancying the offence sufficient, you defy me to mortal combat. If, therefore, I fight with any one at all, it must be with you.
"You will clearly understand me, sir, that I do not accuse you of being at all party to this freak of intellect of your uncle's. He, no doubt, alone conceived it, with a laudable desire on his part of serving you. If, however, to meet me, do so to-night, in the middle of the park surrounding your own friends estate.

"There is a pollard oak growing close to a small pool; you, no doubt, have noticed the spot often. Meet me there, if you please, and any satisfaction you like I will give you, at twelve o'clock this night.

"Come alone, or you will not see me. It shall be at your own option entirely, to convert the meeting into a hostile one or not. You need send me no answer to this. If you are at the place I mention at the time I have named, well and good. If you an not, I can only, if I please, imagine that you shrink from a meeting with

"FRANCIS VARNEY."

Charles Holland read this letter twice over carefully, and then folding it up, and placing it in his pocket, he said,--

"Yes, I will meet him; he may be assured that I will meet him. He shall find that I do not shrink from Francis Varney In the name of honour, love, virtue, and Heaven, I will meet this man, and it shall go hard with me but I will this night wring from him the secret of what he really is. For the sake of her who is so dear to me--for her sake, I will meet this man, or monster, be he what he may."

It would have been far more prudent had Charles informed Henry Bannerworth or George of his determination to meet the vampyre that evening, but he did not do so. Somehow he fancied it would be some reproach against his courage if he did not go, and go alone, too, for he could not help suspecting that, from the conduct of his uncle, Sir Francis Varney might have got up an opinion inimical to his courage.

With all the eager excitement of youth, there was nothing that arrayed itself to his mind in such melancholy and uncomfortable colours as an imputation upon his courage.

"I will show this vampyre, if he be such," he said, "that I am not afraid to meet him, and alone, too, at his own hour--at midnight, even when, if his preternatural powers be of more avail to him than at any other time, he can attempt, if he dare, to use them."

Charles resolved upon going armed, and with the greatest care he loaded his pistols, and placed them aside ready for action, when the time should come to set out to meet the vampyre at the spot in the park which had been particularly alluded to in his letter.

This spot was perfectly well known to Charles; indeed, no one could be a single day at Bannerworth Hall without noticing it, so prominent an object was that pollard oak, standing, as it did, alone, with the beautiful green sward all around it. Near to it was the pool which hid been mentioned, which was, in reality, a fish-pond, and some little distance off commenced the thick plantation, among the intricacies of which Sir Francis Varney, or the vampyre, had been supposed to disappear, after the revivification of his body at the full of the moon.

This spot was in view of several of the windows of the house, so that if the night should happen to be a very light one, and any of the inhabitants of the Hall should happen to have the curiosity to look from those particular windows, no doubt the meeting between Charles Holland and the vampyre would be seen.

This, however, was a contingency which was nothing to Charles, whatever it might be to Sir Francis Varney, and he scarcely at all considered it as worth consideration. He felt more happy and comfortable now that everything seemed to be definitively arranged by which he could come to some sort of explanation with that mysterious being who had so effectually, as yet, succeeded in destroying his peace of mind and his prospects of happiness.

"I will this night force him to declare himself," thought Charles. "He shall tell me who and what he really is, and by some means I will endeavour to put an end to those frightful persecutions which Flora has suffered."

This was a thought which considerably raised Charles's spirits, and when he sought Flora again, which he now did, she was surprised to see him so much more easy and composed in his mind, which was sufficiently shown by his manner, than he had been but so short a time before.

"Charles," she said, "what has happened to give such an impetus to your spirits?"

"Nothing, dear Flora, nothing; but I have been endeavouring to throw from my mind all gloomy thoughts, and to convince myself that in the future you and I, dearest, may yet be very happy."

"Oh, Charles, if I could but think so."

"Endeavour, Flora, to think so. Remember how much our happiness is always in our own power, Flora, and that, let fate do her worst, so long as we are true to each other, we have a recompense for every ill."

"Oh, indeed, Charles, that is a dear recompense."

"And it is well that no force of circumstances short of death itself can divide us."

"True, Charles, true, and I am more than ever now bound to look upon you with a loving heart; for have you not clung to me generously under circumstances which, if any at all could have justified you in rending asunder every tie which bound us together, surely would have done so most fully."

"It is misfortune and distress that tries love," said Charles. "It is thus that the touchstone is applied to see if it be current gold indeed, or some base metal, which by a superficial glitter imitates it."

"And your love is indeed true gold."

"I am unworthy of one glance from those dear eyes if it were not."

"Oh, if we could but go from here I think then we might be happy. A strong impression is upon my mind, and has been so for some time, that these persecutions to which I have been subjected are peculiar to this house."

"Think you so?"

"I do, indeed!"

"It may be so, Flora. You are aware that your brother has made up his mind that he will leave the Hall."

"Yes, yes."

"And that only in deference to an expressed wish of mine he put off the carrying such a resolve into effect for a few days."

"He said so much."

"Do not, however, imagine, dearest Flora, that those few days will be idly spent."

"Nay, Charles, I could not imagine so."

"Believe me, I have some hopes that in that short space of time I shall be able to accomplish yet something which shall have a material effect upon the present posture of affairs."

"Do not run into danger, Charles."

"I will not. Believe me, Flora, I have too much appreciation of the value of an existence which is blessed by your love, to encounter any needless risks."

"You say needless. Why do you not confide in me, and tell me if the object you have in view to accomplish in the few days delay is a dangerous one at all."

"Will you forgive me, Flora, if for once I keep a secret from you?"

"Then, Charles, along with the forgiveness I must conjure up a host of apprehensions."

"Nay, why so?"

"You would tell me if there were no circumstances that you feared would fill me with alarm."

"Now, Flora, your fears and not your judgment condemn me. Surely you cannot think me so utterly heedless as to court danger for danger's sake."

"No, not so--"

"You pause."

"And yet you have a sense of what you call honour, which, I fear, would lead you into much risk."

"I have a sense of honour; but not that foolish one which hangs far more upon the opinions of others than my own. If I thought a course of honour lay before me, and all the world, in a mistaken judgment, were to condemn it as wrong, I would follow it."

"You are right, Charles; you are right. Let me pray of you to be careful, and, at all events, to interpose no more delay to our leaving this house than you shall feel convinced is absolutely necessary for some object of real and permanent importance."

Charles promised Flora Bannerworth that for her sake, as well as his own, he would be most specially careful of his safety; and then in such endearing conversation as may be well supposed to be dictated by such hearts as theirs another happy hour was passed away.

They pictured to themselves the scene where first they met, and with a world of interest hanging on every word they uttered, they told each other of the first delightful dawnings of that affection which had sprung up between them, and which they fondly believed neither time nor circumstance would have the power to change or subvert.

In the meantime the old admiral was surprised that Charles was so patient, and had not been to him to demand the result of his deliberation.

But he knew not on what rapid pinions time flies, when in the presence of those whom we love. What was an actual hour, was but a fleeting minute to Charles Holland, as he sat with Flora's hand clasped in his, and looking at her sweet face.

At length a clock striking reminded him of his engagement with his uncle, and he reluctantly rose.

"Dear Flora," he said, "I am going to sit up to watch to-night, so be under no sort of apprehension."

"I will feel doubly safe," she said.

"I have now something to talk to my uncle about, and must leave you."

Flora smiled, and held out her hand to him. He pressed it to his heart. He knew not what impulse came over him then, but for the first time he kissed the cheek of the beautiful girl.

With a heightened colour she gently repulsed him. He took a long lingering look at her as he passed out of the room, and when the door was closed between them, the sensation he experienced was as if some sudden cloud had swept across the face of the sun, dimming to a vast extent its precious lustre.

A strange heaviness came across his spirits, which before had been so unaccountably raised. He felt as if the shadow of some coming evil was resting on his soul--as if some momentous calamity was preparing for him, which would almost be enough to drive him to madness, and irredeemable despair.

"What can this be," he exclaimed, "that thus oppresses me? What feeling is this that seems to tell me, I shall never again see Flora Bannerworth?"

Unconsciously he uttered these words, which betrayed the nature of his worst forebodings.

"Oh, this is weakness," he then added. "I must fight out against this; it is mere nervousness. I must not endure it, I will not suffer myself thus to become the sport of imagination. Courage, courage, Charles Holland. There are real evils enough, without your adding to them by those of a disordered fancy. Courage, courage, courage."

CHAPTER XXV

THE ADMIRAL'S OPINION.--THE REQUEST OF CHARLES

Charles then sought the admiral, whom he found with his hands behind him, pacing to and fro in one of the long walks of the garden, evidently in a very unsettled state of mind. When Charles appeared, he quickened his pace, and looked in such a state of unusual perplexity that it was quite ridiculous to observe him.

"I suppose, uncle, you have made up your mind thoroughly by this time?"

"Well, I don't know that."

"Why, you have had long enough surely to think over it. I have not troubled you soon."

"Well, I cannot exactly say you have, but, somehow or another, I don't think very fast, and I have an unfortunate propensity after a time of coming exactly round to where I began."

"Then, to tell the truth, uncle, you can come to no sort of conclusion."

"Only one."

"And what may that be?"

"Why, that you are right in one thing, Charles, which is, that having sent a challenge to this fellow of a vampyre, you must fight him."

"I suspect that that is a conclusion you had from the first, uncle?"

"Why so?"

"Because it is an obvious and a natural one. All your doubts, and trouble, and perplexities, have been to try and find some excuse for not entertaining that opinion, and now that you really find it in vain to make it, I trust that you will accede as you first promised to do, and not seek by any means to thwart me."

"I will not thwart you, my boy, although in my opinion you ought not to fight with a vampyre."

"Never mind that. We cannot urge that as a valid excuse, so long as he chooses to deny being one. And after all, if he be really wrongfully suspected, you must admit that he is a very injured man."

"Injured!--nonsense. If he is not a vampyre, he's some other out-of-the-way sort of fish, you may depend. He's the oddest-looking fellow ever I came across in all my born days, ashore or afloat."

"Is he?"

"Yes, he is: and yet, when I come to look at the thing again in my mind, some droll sights that I have seen come across my memory. The sea is the place for wonders and for mysteries. Why, we see more in a day and a night there, than you landsmen could contrive to make a whole twelvemonth's wonder of."

"But you never saw a vampyre, uncle?"

"Well, I don't know that. I didn't know anything about vampyres till I came here; but that was my ignorance, you know. There might have been lots of vampyres where I've been, for all I know."

"Oh, certainly; but as regards this duel, will you wait now until to-morrow morning, before you take any further steps in the matter?"

"Till to-morrow morning?"

"Yes, uncle."

"Why, only a little while ago, you were all eagerness to have something done off-hand."

"Just so; but now I have a particular reason for waiting until to-morrow morning."

"Have you? Well, as you please, boy--as you please. Have everything your own way."

"You are very kind, uncle; and now I have another favour to ask of you."

"What is it?"

"Why, you know that Henry Bannerworth receives but a very small sum out of the whole proceeds of the estate here, which ought, but for his father's extravagance, to be wholly at his disposal."

"So I have heard."

"I am certain he is at present distressed for money, and I have not much. Will you lend me fifty pounds, uncle, until my own affairs are sufficiently arranged to enable you to pay yourself again?"

"Will I! of course I will."

"I wish to offer that sum as an accommodation to Henry. From me, I dare say he will receive it freely, because he must be convinced how freely it is offered; and, besides, they look upon me now almost as a member of the family in consequence of my engagement with Flora."

"Certainly, and quite correct too: there's a fifty-pound note, my boy; take it, and do what you like with it, and when you want any more, come to me for it."

"I knew I could trespass thus far on your kindness, uncle."

"Trespass! It's no trespass at all."

"Well, we will not fall out about the terms in which I cannot help expressing my gratitude to you for many favours. To-morrow, you will arrange the duel for me."

"As you please. I don't altogether like going to that fellow's house again."

"Well, then, we can manage, I dare say, by note."

"Very good. Do so. He puts me in mind altogether of a circumstance that happened a good while ago, when I was at sea, and not so old a man as I am now."

"Puts you in mind of a circumstance, uncle?"

"Yes; he's something like a fellow that figured in an affair that I know a good deal about; only I do think as my chap was more mysterious by a d----d sight than this one."

"Indeed!"

"Oh, dear, yes. When anything happens in an odd way at sea, it is as odd again as anything that occurs on land, my boy, you may depend."

"Oh, you only fancy that, uncle, because you have spent so long a time at sea."

"No, I don't imagine it, you rascal. What can you have on shore equal to what we have at sea? Why, the sights that come before us would make you landsmen's hairs stand up on end, and never come down again."

"In the ocean, do you mean, that you see those sights, uncle?"

"To be sure. I was once in the southern ocean, in a small frigate, looking out for a seventy-four we were to join company with, when a man at the mast-head sung out that he saw her on the larboard bow. Well, we thought it was all right enough, and made away that quarter, when what do you think it turned out to be?"

"I really cannot say."

"The head of a fish."

"A fish!"

"Yes! a d----d deal bigger than the hull of a vessel. He was swimming along with his head just what I dare say he considered a shaving or so out of the water."

"But where were the sails, uncle?"

"The sails?"

"Yes; your man at the mast-head must have been a poor seaman not to have missed the sails."

"All, that's one of your shore-going ideas, now. You know nothing whatever about it. I'll tell you where the sails were, master Charley."

"Well, I should like to know."

"The spray, then, that he dashed up with a pair of fins that were close to his head, was in such a quantity, and so white, that they looked just like sails."

"Oh!"

"Ah! you may say 'oh!' but we all saw him--the whole ship's crew; and we sailed alongside of him for some time, till he got tired of us, and suddenly dived down, making such a vortex in the water, that the ship shook again, and seemed for about a minute as if she was inclined to follow him to the bottom of the sea."

"And what do you suppose it was, uncle?"

"How should I know?"

"Did you ever see it again?"

"Never; though others have caught a glimpse of him now and then in the same ocean, but never came so near him as we did, that ever I heard of, at all events. They may have done so."

"It is singular!"

"Singular or not, it's a fool to what I can tell you. Why, I've seen things that, if I were to set about describing them to you, you would say I was making up a romance."

"Oh, no; it's quite impossible, uncle, any one could ever suspect you of such a thing."

"You'd believe me, would you?"

"Of course I would."

"Then here goes. I'll just tell you now of a circumstance that I haven't liked to mention to anybody yet."

"Indeed! why so?"

"Because I didn't want to be continually fighting people for not believing it; but here you have it:--"

We were outward bound; a good ship, a good captain, and good messmates, you know, go far towards making a prosperous voyage a pleasant and happy one, and on this occasion we had every reasonable prospect of all.

Our hands were all tried men--they had been sailors from infancy; none of your French craft, that serve an apprenticeship and then become land lubbers again. Oh, no, they were stanch and true, and loved the ocean as the sluggard loves his bed, or the lover his mistress.

Ay, and for the matter of that, the love was a more enduring and a more healthy love, for it increased with years, and made men love one another, and they would stand by each other while they had a limb to lift--while they were able to chew a quid or wink an eye, leave alone wag a pigtail.

We were outward bound for Ceylon, with cargo, and were to bring spices and other matters home from the Indian market. The ship was new and good--a pretty craft; she sat like a duck upon the water, and a stiff breeze carried her along the surface of the waves without your rocking, and pitching, and tossing, like an old wash-tub at a mill-tail, as I have had the misfortune to sail in more than once afore.

No, no, we were well laden, and well pleased, and weighed anchor with light hearts and a hearty cheer.

Away we went down the river, and soon rounded the North Foreland, and stood out in the Channel. The breeze was a steady and stiff one, and carried us through the water as though it had been made for us.

"Jack," said I to a messmate of mine, as he stood looking at the skies, then at the sails, and finally at the water, with a graver air than I thought was at all consistent with the occasion or circumstances.

"Well," he replied.

"What ails you? You seem as melancholy as if we were about to cast lots who should be eaten first. Are you well enough?"

"I am hearty enough, thank Heaven," he said, "but I don't like this breeze."

"Don't like the breeze!" said I; "why, mate, it is as good and kind a breeze as ever filled a sail. What would you have, a gale?"

"No, no; I fear that."

"With such a ship, and such a set of hearty able seamen, I think we could manage to weather out the stiffest gale that ever whistled through a yard."

"That may be; I hope it is, and I really believe and think so."

"Then what makes you so infernally mopish and melancholy?"

"I don't know, but can't help it. It seems to me as though there was something hanging over us, and I can't tell what."

"Yes, there are the colours, Jack, at the masthead; they are flying over us with a hearty breeze."

"Ah! ah!" said Jack, looking up at the colours, and then went away without saying anything more, for he had some piece of duty to perform.

I thought my messmate had something on his mind that caused him to feel sad and uncomfortable, and I took no more notice of it; indeed, in the course of a day or two he was as merry as any of the rest, and had no more melancholy that I could perceive, but was as comfortable as anybody.

We had a gale off the coast of Biscay, and rode it out without the loss of a spar or a yard; indeed, without the slightest accident or rent of any kind.

"Now, Jack, what do you think of our vessel?" said I.

"She's like a duck upon water, rises and falls with the waves, and doesn't tumble up and down like a hoop over stones."

"No, no; she goes smoothly and sweetly; she is a gallant craft, and this is her first voyage, and I predict a prosperous one."

"I hope so," he said.

Well, we went on prosperously enough for about three weeks; the ocean was as calm and as smooth as a meadow, the breeze light but good, and we stemmed along majestically over the deep blue waters, and passed coast after coast, though all around was nothing but the apparently pathless main in sight.

"A better sailer I never stepped into," said the captain one day; "it would be a pleasure to live and die in such a vessel."

Well, as I said, we had been three weeks or thereabouts, when one morning, after the sun was up and the decks washed, we saw a strange man sitting on one of the water-casks that were on deck, for, being full, we were compelled to stow some of them on deck.

You may guess those on deck did a little more than stare at this strange and unexpected apparition. By jingo, I never saw men open their eyes wider in all my life, nor was I any exception to the rule. I stared, as well I might; but we said nothing for some minutes, and the stranger looked calmly on us, and then cocked his eye with a nautical air up at the sky, as if he expected to receive a twopenny-post letter from St. Michael, or a billet doux from the Virgin Mary.

"Where has he come from?" said one of the men in a low tone to his companion, who was standing by him at that moment.

"How can I tell?" replied his companion. "He may have dropped from the clouds; he seems to be examining the road; perhaps he is going back."

The stranger sat all this time with the most extreme and provoking coolness and unconcern; he deigned us but a passing notice, but it was very slight.

He was a tall, spare man--what is termed long and lathy--but he was evidently a powerful man. He had a broad chest, and long, sinewy arms, a hooked nose, and a black, eagle eye. His hair was curly, but frosted by age; it seemed as though it had been tinged with white at the extremities, but he was hale and active otherwise, to judge from appearances.

Notwithstanding all this, there was a singular repulsiveness about him that I could not imagine the cause, or describe; at the same time there was an air of determination in his wild and singular-looking eyes, and over their whole there was decidedly an air and an appearance so sinister as to be positively disagreeable.

"Well," said I, after we had stood some minutes, "where did you come from, shipmate?"

He looked at me and then up at the sky, in a knowing manner.

"Come, come, that won't do; you have none of Peter Wilkins's wings, and couldn't come on the aerial dodge; it won't do; how did you get here?"

He gave me an awful wink, and made a sort of involuntary movement, which jumped him up a few inches, and he bumped down again on the water-cask.

"That's as much as to say," thought I, "that he's sat himself on it."

"I'll go and inform the captain," said I, "of this affair; he'll hardly believe me when I tell him, I am sure."

So saying, I left the deck and went to the cabin, where the captain was at breakfast, and related to him what I had seen respecting the stranger. The captain looked at me with an air of disbelief, and said,--

"What?--do you mean to say there's a man on board we haven't seen before?"

"Yes, I do, captain. I never saw him afore, and he's sitting beating his heels on the water-cask on deck."

"The devil!"

"He is, I assure you, sir; and he won't answer any questions."

"I'll see to that. I'll see if I can't make the lubber say something, providing his tongue's not cut out. But how came he on board? Confound it, he can't be the devil, and dropped from the moon."

"Don't know, captain," said I. "He is evil-looking enough, to my mind, to be the father of evil, but it's ill bespeaking attentions from that quarter at any time."

"Go on, lad; I'll come up after you."

I left the cabin, and I heard the captain coming after me. When I got on deck, I saw he had not moved from the place where I left him. There was a general commotion among the crew when they heard of the occurrence, and all crowded round him, save the man at the wheel, who had to remain at his post.

The captain now came forward, and the men fell a little back as he approached. For a moment the captain stood silent, attentively examining the stranger, who was excessively cool, and stood the scrutiny with the same unconcern that he would had the captain been looking at his watch.

"Well, my man," said the captain, "how did you come here?"

"I'm part of the cargo," he said, with an indescribable leer.

"Part of the cargo be d----d!" said the captain, in sudden rage, for he thought the stranger was coming his jokes too strong. "I know you are not in the bills of lading."

"I'm contraband," replied the stranger; "and my uncle's the great chain of Tartary."

The captain stared, as well he might, and did not speak for some minutes; all the while the stranger kept kicking his heels against the water-casks and squinting up at the skies; it made us feel very queer.

"Well, I must confess you are not in the regular way of trading."

"Oh, no," said the stranger; "I am contraband--entirely contraband."

"And how did you come on board?"

At this question the stranger again looked curiously up at the skies, and continued to do so for more than a minute; he then turned his gaze upon the captain.

"No, no," said the captain; "eloquent dumb show won't do with me; you didn't come, like Mother Shipton, upon a birch broom. How did you come on board my vessel?"

"I walked on board," said the stranger.

"You walked on board; and where did you conceal yourself?"

"Below."

"Very good; and why didn't you stay below altogether?"

"Because I wanted fresh air. I'm in a delicate state of health, you see; it doesn't do to stay in a confined place too long."

"Confound the binnacle!" said the captain; it was his usual oath when anything bothered him, and he could not make it out. "Confound the binnacle!--what a delicate-looking animal you are. I wish you had stayed where you were; your delicacy would have been all the same to me. Delicate, indeed!"

"Yes, very," said the stranger, coolly.

There was something so comic in the assertion of his delicateness of health, that we should all have laughed; but we were somewhat scared, and had not the inclination.

"How have you lived since you came on board?" inquired the captain.

"Very indifferently."

"But how? What have you eaten? and what have you drank?"

"Nothing, I assure you. All I did while was below was--"

"What?"

"Why, I sucked my thumbs like a polar bear in its winter quarters."

And as he spoke the stranger put his two thumbs into his mouth, and extraordinary thumbs they were, too, for each would have filled an ordinary man's mouth.

"These," said the stranger, pulling them out, and gazing at them wistfully, and with a deep sigh he continued,--

"These were thumbs at one time; but they are nothing now to what they were."

"Confound the binnacle!" muttered the captain to himself, and then he added, aloud,--

"It's cheap living, however; but where are you going to, and why did you come aboard?"

"I wanted a cheap cruise, and I am going there and back."

"Why, that's where we are going," said the captain.

"Then we are brothers," exclaimed the stranger, hopping off the water-cask like a kangaroo, and bounding towards the captain, holding out his hand as though he would have shaken hands with him.

"No, no," said the captain; "I can't do it."

"Can't do it!" exclaimed the stranger, angrily. "What do you mean?"

"That I can't have anything to do with contraband articles; I am a fair trader, and do all above board. I haven't a chaplain on board, or he should offer up prayers for your preservation, and the recovery of your health, which seems so delicate."

"That be--"

The stranger didn't finish the sentence; he merely screwed his mouth up into an incomprehensible shape, and puffed out a lot of breath, with some force, and which sounded very much like a whistle: but, oh, what thick breath he had, it was as much like smoke as anything I ever saw, and so my shipmate said.

"I say, captain," said the stranger, as he saw him pacing the deck.

"Well."

"Just send me up some beef and biscuit, and some coffee royal--be sure it's royal, do you hear, because I'm partial to brandy, it's the only good thing there is on earth."

I shall not easily forget the captain's look as he turned towards the stranger, and gave his huge shoulders a shrug, as much as to say,--

"Well, I can't help it now; he's here, and I can't throw him overboard."

The coffee, beef, and biscuit were sent him, and the stranger seemed to eat them with great gout, and drank the coffee with much relish, and returned the things, saying,

"Your captain is an excellent cook; give him my compliments."

I thought the captain would think that was but a left-handed compliment, and look more angry than pleased, but no notice was taken of it.

It was strange, but this man had impressed upon all in the vessel some singular notion of his being more than he should be--more than a mere mortal, and not one endeavoured to interfere with him; the captain was a stout and dare-devil a fellow as you would well met with, yet he seemed tacitly to acknowledge more than he would say, for he never after took any further notice of the stranger nor he of him.

They had barely any conversation, simply a civil word when they first met, and so forth; but there was little or no conversation of any kind between them.

The stranger slept upon deck, and lived upon deck entirely; he never once went below after we saw him, and his own account of being below so long.

This was very well, but the night-watch did not enjoy his society, and would have willingly dispensed with it at that hour so particularly lonely and dejected upon the broad ocean, and perhaps a thousand miles away from the nearest point of land.

At this dread and lonely hour, when no sound reaches the ear and disturbs the wrapt stillness of the night, save the whistling of the wind through the cordage, or an occasional dash of water against the vessel's side, the thoughts of the sailor are fixed on far distant objects--his own native land and the friends and loved ones he has left behind him.

He then thinks of the wilderness before, behind, and around him; of the immense body of water, almost in places bottomless; gazing upon such a scene, and with thoughts as strange and indefinite as the very boundless expanse before him, it is no wonder if he should become superstitious; the time and place would, indeed unbidden, conjure up thoughts and feelings of a fearful character and intensity.

The stranger at such times would occupy his favourite seat on the water cask, and looking up at the sky and then on the ocean, and between whiles he would whistle a strange, wild, unknown melody.

The flesh of the sailors used to creep up in knots and bumps when they heard it; the wind used to whistle as an accompaniment and pronounce fearful sounds to their ears.

The wind had been highly favourable from the first, and since the stranger had been discovered it had blown fresh, and we went along at a rapid rate, stemming the water, and dashing the spray off from the bows, and cutting the water like a shark.

This was very singular to us, we couldn't understand it, neither could the captain, and we looked very suspiciously at the stranger, and wished him at the bottom, for the freshness of the wind now became a gale, and yet the ship came through the water steadily, and away we went before the wind, as if the devil drove us; and mind I don't mean to say he didn't.

The gale increased to a hurricane, and though we had not a stitch of canvass out, yet we drove before the gale as if we had been shot out of the mouth of a gun.

The stranger still sat on the water casks, and all night long he kept up his infernal whistle. Now, sailors don't like to hear any one whistle when there's such a gale blowing over their heads--it's like asking for more; but he would persist, and the louder and stronger the wind blew, the louder he whistled.

At length there came a storm of rain, lightning, and wind. We were tossed mountains high, and the foam rose over the vessel, and often entirely over our heads, and the men were lashed to their posts to prevent being washed away.

But the stranger still lay on the water casks, kicking his heels and whistling his infernal tune, always the same. He wasn't washed away nor moved by the action of the water; indeed, we heartily hoped and expected to see both him and the water cask floated overboard at every minute; but, as the captain said,--

"Confound the binnacle! the old water tub seems as if it were screwed on to the deck, and won't move off and he on the top of it."

There was a strong inclination to throw him overboard, and the men conversed in low whispers, and came round the captain, saying,--

"We have come, captain, to ask you what you think of this strange man who has come so mysteriously on board?"

"I can't tell what to think, lads; he's past thinking about--he's something above my comprehension altogether, I promise you."

"Well, then, we are thinking much of the same thing, captain."

"What do you mean?"

"That he ain't exactly one of our sort."

"No, he's no sailor, certainly; and yet, for a land lubber, he's about as rum a customer as ever I met with."

"So he is, sir."

"He stands salt water well; and I must say that I couldn't lay a top of those water casks in that style very well."

"Nor nobody amongst us, sir."

"Well, then, he's in nobody's way, it he?--nobody wants to take his berth, I suppose?"

The men looked at each other somewhat blank; they didn't understand the meaning at all--far from it; and the idea of any one's wanting to take the stranger's place on the water casks was so outrageously ludicrous, that at any other time they would have considered it a devilish good joke and have never ceased laughing at it.

He paused some minutes, and then one of them said,--

"It isn't that we envy him his berth, captain, 'cause nobody else could live there for a moment. Any one amongst us that had been there would have been washed overboard a thousand times over."

"So they would," said the captain.

"Well, sir, he's more than us."

"Very likely; but how can I help that?"

"We think he's the main cause of all this racket in the heavens--the storm and hurricane; and that, in short, if he remains much longer we shall all sink."

"I am sorry for it. I don't think we are in any danger, and had the strange being any power to prevent it, he would assuredly do so, lest he got drowned."

"But we think if he were thrown overboard all would be well."

"Indeed!"

"Yes, captain, you may depend upon it he's the cause of all the mischief. Throw him overboard and that's all we want."

"I shall not throw him overboard, even if I could do such a thing; and I am by no means sure of anything of the kind."

"We do not ask it, sir."

"What do you desire?"

"Leave to throw him overboard--it is to save our own lives."

"I can't let you do any such thing; he's in nobody's way."

"But he's always a whistling. Only hark now, and in such a hurricane as this, it is dreadful to think of it. What else can we do, sir?--he's not human."

At this moment, the stranger's whistling came clear upon their ears; there was the same wild, unearthly notes as before, but the cadences were stronger, and there was a supernatural clearness in all the tones.

"There now," said another, "he's kicking the water cask with his heels."

"Confound the binnacle!" said the captain; "it sounds like short peals of thunder. Go and talk to him, lads."

"And if that won't do, sir, may we--"

"Don't ask me any questions. I don't think a score of the best men that were ever born could move him."

"I don't mind trying," said one.

Upon this the whole of the men moved to the spot where the water casks were standing and the stranger lay.

There was he, whistling like fury, and, at the same time, beating his heels to the tune against the empty casks. We came up to him, and he took no notice of us at all, but kept on in the same way.

"Hilloa!" shouted one.

"Hilloa!" shouted another.

No notice, however, was taken of us, and one of our number, a big, herculean fellow, an Irishman, seized him by the leg, either to make him get up, or, as we thought, to give him a lift over our heads into the sea.

However, he had scarcely got his fingers round the calf of the leg, when the stranger pinched his leg so tight against the water cask, that he could not move, and was as effectually pinned as if he had been nailed there. The stranger, after he had finished a bar of the music, rose gradually to a sitting posture, and without the aid of his hands, and looking the unlucky fellow in the face, he said,--

"Well, what do you want?"

"My hand," said the fellow.

"Take it then," he said.

He did take it, and we saw that there was blood on it.

The stranger stretched out his left hand, and taking him by the breech, he lifted him, without any effort, upon the water-cask beside him.

We all stared at this, and couldn't help it; and we were quite convinced we could not throw him overboard, but he would probably have no difficulty in throwing us overboard.

"Well, what do you want?" he again exclaimed to us all.

We looked at one another, and had scarce courage to speak; at length I said,--

"We wish you to leave off whistling."

"Leave off whistling!" he said. "And why should I do anything of the kind?"

"Because it brings the wind."

"Ha! ha! why, that's the very reason I am whistling, to bring the wind."

"But we don't want so much."

"Pho! pho! you don't know what's good for you--it's a beautiful breeze, and not a bit too stiff."

"It's a hurricane."

"Nonsense."

"But it is."

"Now you see how I'll prove you are wrong in a minute. You see my hair, don't you?" he said, after he took off his cap. "Very well, look now."

He got up on the water-cask, and stood bolt upright; and running his fingers through his hair, made it all stand straight on end.

"Confound the binnacle!" said the captain, "if ever I saw the like."

"There," said the stranger, triumphantly, "don't tell me there's any wind to signify; don't you see, it doesn't even move one of my grey hairs; and if it blew as hard as you say, I am certain it would move a hair."

"Confound the binnacle!" muttered the captain as he walked away. "D--n the cabouse, if he ain't older than I am--he's too many for me and everybody else."

"Are you satisfied?"

What could we say?--we turned away and left the place, and stood at our quarters--there was no help for it--we were impelled to grin and abide by it.

As soon as we had left the place he put his cap on again and sat down on the water-casks, and then took leave of his prisoner, whom he set free, and there lay at full length on his back, with his legs hanging down. Once more he began to whistle most furiously, and beat time with his feet.

For full three weeks did he continue at this game night and day, without any interruption, save such as he required to consume enough coffee royal, junk, and biscuit, as would have served three hearty men.

Well, about that time, one night the whistling ceased and he began to sing--oh! it was singing--such a voice! Gog and Magog in Guildhall, London, when they spoke were nothing to him--it was awful; but the wind calmed down to a fresh and stiff breeze. He continued at this game for three whole days and nights, and on the fourth it ceased, and when we went to take his coffee royal to him he was gone.

We hunted about everywhere, but he was entirely gone, and in three weeks after we safely cast anchor, having performed our voyage in a good month under the usual time; and had it been an old vessel she would have leaked and stinted like a tub from the straining; however, we were glad enough to get in, and were curiously inquisitive as to what was put in our vessel to come back with, for as the captain said,--

"Confound the binnacle! I'll have no more contraband articles if I can help it."

CHAPTER XXVI

THE MEETING BY MOONLIGHT IN THE PARK.--THE TURRET WINDOW IN THE HALL.--THE LETTERS

The old admiral showed such a strong disposition to take offence at Charles if he should presume, for a moment, to doubt the truth of the narrative that was thus communicated to him, that the latter would not anger him by so doing, but confined his observations upon it to saying that he considered it was very wonderful, and very extraordinary, and so on, which very well satisfied the old man.

The day was now, however, getting far advanced, and Charles Holland began to think of his engagement with the vampyre. He read and read the letter over and over again, but he could not come to a correct conclusion as to whether it intended to imply that he, Sir Francis Varney, would wish to fight him at the hour and place mentioned, or merely give him a meeting as a preliminary step.

He was rather, on the whole, inclined to think that some explanation would be offered by Varney, but at all events he persevered in his determination of going well armed, lest anything in the shape of treachery should be intended.

As nothing of any importance occurred now in the interval of time till nearly midnight, we will at once step to that time, and our readers will suppose it to be a quarter to twelve o'clock at night, and young Charles Holland on the point of leaving the house, to keep his appointment by the pollard oak, with the mysterious Sir Francis Varney.

He placed his loaded pistols conveniently in his pocket, so that at a moment's notice he could lay hands on them, and then wrapping himself up in a travelling cloak he had brought with him to Bannerworth Hall, he prepared to leave his chamber.

The moon still shone, although now somewhat on the wane, and although there were certainly many clouds in the sky they were but of a light fleecy character, and very little interrupted the rays of light that came from the nearly full disc of the moon.

From his window he could not perceive the spot in the park where he was to meet Varney, because the room in which he was occupied not a sufficiently high place in the house to enable him to look over a belt of trees that stopped the view. From almost any of the upper windows the pollard oak could be seen.

It so happened now that the admiral had been placed in a room immediately above the one occupied by his nephew, and, as his mind was full of how he should manage with regard to arranging the preliminaries of the duel between Charles and Varney on the morrow, he found it difficult to sleep; and after remaining in bed about twenty minutes, and finding that each moment he was only getting more and more restless, he adopted a course which he always did under such circumstances.

He rose and dressed himself again, intending to sit up for an hour and then turn into bed and try a second time to get to sleep. But he had no means of getting a light, so he drew the heavy curtain from before the window, and let in as much of the moonlight as he could.

This window commanded a most beautiful and extensive view, for from it the eye could carry completely over the tops of the tallest trees, so that there was no interruption whatever to the prospect, which was as extensive as it was delightful.

Even the admiral, who never would confess to seeing much beauty in scenery where water formed not a large portion of it, could not resist opening his window and looking out, with a considerable degree of admiration, upon wood and dale, as they were illuminated by the moon's rays, softened, and rendered, if anything, more beautiful by the light vapours, through which they had to struggle to make their way.

Charles Holland, in order to avoid the likelihood of meeting with any one who would question him as to where he was going, determined upon leaving his room by the balcony, which, as we are aware, presented ample facilities for his so doing.

He cast a glance at the portrait in the panel before he left the apartment, and then saying,--

"For you, dear Flora, for you I essay this meeting with the fearful original of that portrait," he immediately opened his window, and stepped out on to the balcony.

Young and active as was Charles Holland, to descend from that balcony presented to him no difficulty whatever, and he was, in a very few moments, safe in the garden of Bannerworth Hall.

He never thought, for a moment, to look up, or he would, in an instant, have seen the white head of his old uncle, as it was projected over the sill of the window of his chamber.

The drop of Charles from the balcony of his window, just made sufficient noise to attract the admiral's attention, and, then, before he could think of making any alarm, he saw Charles walking hastily across a grass plot, which was sufficiently in the light of the moon to enable the admiral at once to recognise him, and leave no sort of doubt as to his positive identity.

Of course, upon discovering that it was Charles, the necessity for making an alarm no longer existed, and, indeed, not knowing what it was that had induced him to leave his chamber, a moment's reflection suggested to him the propriety of not even calling to Charles, lest he should defeat some discovery which he might be about to make.

"He has heard something, or seen something," thought the admiral, "and is gone to find out what it is. I only wish I was with him; but up here I can do nothing at all, that's quite clear."

Charles, he saw, walked very rapidly, and like a man who has some fixed destination which he wishes to reach as quickly as possible.

When he dived among the trees which skirted one side of the flower gardens, the admiral was more puzzled than ever, and he said--

"Now where on earth is he off to? He is fully dressed, and has his cloak about him."

After a few moments' reflection he decided that, having seen something suspicious, Charles must have got up, and dressed himself, to fathom it.

The moment this idea became fairly impressed upon his mind, he left his bedroom, and descended to where one of the brothers he knew was sitting up, keeping watch during the night. It was Henry who was so on guard; and when the admiral came into the room, he uttered an expression of surprise to find him up, for it was now some time past twelve o'clock.

"I have come to tell you that Charles has left the house," said the admiral.

"Left the house?"

"Yes; I saw him just now go across the garden."

"And you are sure it was he?"

"Quite sure. I saw him by the moonlight cross the green plot."

"Then you may depend he has seen or heard something, and gone alone to find out what it is rather than give any alarm."

"That is just what I think."

"It must be so. I will follow him, if you can show me exactly which way he went."

"That I can easily. And in case I should have made any mistake, which it is not at all likely, we can go to his room first and see if it is empty."

"A good thought, certainly; that will at once put an end to all doubt upon the question."

They both immediately proceeded to Charles's room, and then the admiral's accuracy of identification of his nephew was immediately proved by finding that Charles was not there, and that the window was wide open.

"You see I am right," said the admiral.

"You are," cried Henry; "but what have we here?"

"Where?"

"Here on the dressing-table. Here are no less than three letters, all laid as it on purpose to catch the eye of the first one who might enter the room."

"Indeed!"

"You perceive them?"

Henry held them to the light, and after a moment's inspection of them, he said, in a voice of much surprise,--

"Good God! what is the meaning of this?"

"The meaning of what?"

"The letters are addressed to parties in the house here. Do you not see?"

"To whom?"

"One to Admiral Bell--"

"The deuce!"

"Another to me, and the third to my sister Flora. There is some new mystery here."

The admiral looked at the superscription of one of the letters which was handed to him in silent amazement. Then he cried,--

"Set down the light, and let us read them."

Henry did so, and then they simultaneously opened the epistles which were severally addressed to them. There was a silence, as of the very grave, for some moments, and then the old admiral staggered to a seat, as he exclaimed,--

"Am I dreaming--am I dreaming?"

"Is this possible?" said Henry, in a voice of deep emotion, as he allowed the note addressed to him to drop on to the floor.

"D--n it, what does yours say?" cried the old admiral, in a louder tone.

"Read it--what says yours?"

"Read it--I'm amazed."

The letters were exchanged, and read by each with the same breathless attention they had bestowed upon their own; after which, they both looked at each other in silence, pictures of amazement, and the most absolute state of bewilderment.

Not to keep our readers in suspense, we at once transcribe each of these letters.

The one to the admiral contained these words,--

"MY DEAR UNCLE,

"Of course you will perceive the prudence of keeping this letter to yourself, but the fact is, I have now made up my mind to leave Bannerworth Hall.

"Flora Bannerworth is not now the person she was when first I knew her and loved her. Such being the case, and she having altered, not I, she cannot accuse me of fickleness.

"I still love the Flora Bannerworth I first knew, but I cannot make my wife one who is subject to the visitations of a vampyre.

"I have remained here long enough now to satisfy myself that this vampyre business is no delusion. I am quite convinced that it is a positive fact, and that, after death, Flora will herself become one of the horrible existences known by that name.

"I will communicate to you from the first large city on the continent whither I am going, at which I make any stay, and in the meantime, make what excuses you like at Bannerworth Hall, which I advise you to leave as quickly as you can, and believe me to be, my dear uncle, yours truly,

"CHARLES HOLLAND."

Henry's letter was this:--

"MY DEAR SIR,

"If you calmly and dispassionately consider the painful and distressing circumstances in which your family are placed, I am sure that, far from blaming me for the step which this note will announce to you I have taken, you will be the first to give me credit for acting with an amount of prudence and foresight which was highly necessary under the circumstances.

"If the supposed visits of a vampyre to your sister Flora had turned out, as first I hoped they would, a delusion and been in any satisfactory manner explained away I should certainly have felt pride and pleasure in fulfilling my engagement to that young lady.

"You must, however, yourself feel that the amount of evidence in favour of a belief that an actual vampyre has visited Flora, enforces a conviction of its truth.

"I cannot, therefore, make her my wife under such very singular circumstances.

"Perhaps you may blame me for not taking at once advantage of the permission given me to forego my engagement when first I came to your house; but the fact is, I did not then in the least believe in the existence of the vampyre, but since a positive conviction of that most painful fact has now forced itself upon me, I beg to decline the honour of an alliance which I had at one time looked forward to with the most considerable satisfaction.

"I shall be on the continent as fast as conveyances can take me, therefore, should you entertain any romantic notions of calling me to an account for a course of proceeding I think perfectly and fully justifiable, you will not find me.

"Accept the assurances of my respect for yourself and pity for your sister, and believe me to be, my dear sir, your sincere friend,

"CHARLES HOLLAND."

These two letters might well make the admiral stare at Henry Bannerworth, and Henry stare at him.

An occurrence so utterly and entirely unexpected by both of them, was enough to make them doubt the evidence of their own senses. But there were the letters, as a damning evidence of the outrageous fact, and Charles Holland was gone.

It was the admiral who first recovered from the stunning effect of the epistles, and he, with a gesture of perfect fury, exclaimed,--

"The scoundrel--the cold-blooded villain! I renounce him for ever! he is no nephew of mine; he is some d----d imposter! Nobody with a dash of my family blood in his veins would have acted so to save himself from a thousand deaths."

"Who shall we trust now," said Henry, "when those whom we take to our inmost hearts deceive us thus? This is the greatest shock I have yet received. If there be a pang greater than another, surely it is to be found in the faithlessness and heartlessness of one we loved and trusted."

"He is a scoundrel!" roared the admiral. "D--n him, he'll die on a dunghill, and that's too good a place for him. I cast him off--I'll find him out, and old as I am, I'll fight him--I'll wring his neck, the rascal; and, as for poor dear Miss Flora, God bless her! I'll--I'll marry her myself, and make her an admiral.--I'll marry her myself. Oh, that I should be uncle to such a rascal!"

"Calm yourself," said Henry, "no one can blame you."

"Yes, you can; I had no right to be his uncle, and I was an old fool to love him."

The old man sat down, and his voice became broken with emotion as he said,--

"Sir, I tell you I would have died willingly rather than this should have happened. This will kill me now,--I shall die now of shame and grief."

Tears gushed from the admiral's eyes and the sight of the noble old man's emotion did much to calm the anger of Henry which, although he said but little, was boiling at his heart like a volcano.

"Admiral Bell," he said, "you have nothing to do with this business; we can not blame you for the heartlessness of another. I have but one favour to ask of you."

"What--what can I do?"

"Say no more about him at all."

"I can't help saying something about him. You ought to turn me out of the house."

"Heaven forbid! What for?"

"Because I'm his uncle--his d----d old fool of an uncle, that always thought so much of him."

"Nay, my good sir, that was a fault on the right side, and cannot discredit you. I thought him the most perfect of human beings."

"Oh, if I could but have guessed this."

"It was impossible. Such duplicity never was equalled in this world--it was impossible to foresee it."

"Hold--hold! did he give you fifty pounds?"

"What?"

"Did he give you fifty pounds?"

"Give me fifty pounds! Most decidedly not; what made you think of such a thing?"

"Because to-day he borrowed fifty pounds of me, he said, to lend to you."

"I never heard of the transaction until this moment."

"The villain!"

"No, doubt, sir, he wanted that amount to expedite his progress abroad."

"Well, now, damme, if an angel had come to me and said 'Hilloa! Admiral Bell, your nephew, Charles Holland, is a thundering rogue,' I should have said 'You're a liar!'"

"This is fighting against facts, my dear sir. He is gone--mention him no more; forget him, as I shall endeavour myself to do, and persuade my poor sister to do."

"Poor girl! what can we say to her?"

"Nothing, but give her all the letters, and let her be at once satisfied of the worthlessness of him she loved."

"The best way. Her woman's pride will then come to her help."

"I hope it will. She is of an honourable race, and I am sure she will not condescend to shed a tear for such a man as Charles Holland has proved himself to be."

"D--n him, I'll find him out, and make him fight you. He shall give you satisfaction."

"No, no."

"No? But he shall."

"I cannot fight with him."

"You cannot?"

"Certainly not. He is too far beneath me now. I cannot fight on honourable terms with one whom I despise as too dishonourable to contend with. I have nothing now but silence and contempt."

"I have though, for I'll break his neck when I see him, or he shall break mine. The villain! I'm ashamed to stay here, my young friend."

"How mistaken a view you take of this matter, my dear sir. As Admiral Bell, a gentleman, a brave officer, and a man of the purest and most unblemished honour, you confer a distinction upon us by your presence here."

The admiral wrung Henry by the hand, as he said,--

"To-morrow--wait till to-morrow; we will talk over this matter to morrow--I cannot to-night, I have not patience; but to-morrow, my dear boy, we will have it all out. God bless you. Good night."

CHAPTER XXVII

THE NOBLE CONFIDENCE OF FLORA BANNERWORTH IN HER LOVER.--HER OPINION OF THE THREE LETTERS.--THE ADMIRAL'S ADMIRATION

To describe the feelings of Henry Bannerworth on the occasion of this apparent defalcation from the path of rectitude and honour by his friend, as he had fondly imagined Charles Holland to be, would be next to impossible.

If, as we have taken occasion to say, it be a positive fact, that a noble and a generous mind feels more acutely any heartlessness of this description from one on whom it has placed implicit confidence, than the most deliberate and wicked of injuries from absolute strangers, we can easily conceive that Henry Bannerworth was precisely the person to feel most acutely the conduct which all circumstances appeared to fix upon Charles Holland, upon whose faith, truth, and honour, he would have staked his very existence but a few short hours before.

With such a bewildered sensation that he scarcely knew where he walked or whither to betake himself, did he repair to his own chamber, and there he strove, with what energy he was able to bring to the task, to find out some excuses, if he could, for Charles's conduct. But he could find none. View it in what light he would, it presented but a picture of the most heartless selfishness it had ever been his lot to encounter.

The tone of the letters, too, which Charles had written, materially aggravated the moral delinquency of which he had been guilty; belief, far better, had he not attempted an excuse at all than have attempted such excuses as were there put down in those epistles.

A more cold blooded, dishonourable proceeding could not possibly be conceived.

It would appear, that while he entertained a doubt with regard to the reality of the visitation of the vampyre to Flora Bannerworth, he had been willing to take to himself abundance of credit for the most honourable feelings, and to induce a belief in the minds of all that an exalted feeling of honour, as well as a true affection that would know no change, kept him at the feet of her whom he loved.

Like some braggart, who, when there is no danger, is a very hero, but who, the moment he feels convinced he will be actually and truly called upon for an exhibition of his much-vaunted prowess, had Charles Holland deserted the beautiful girl who, if anything, had now certainly, in her misfortunes, a far higher claim upon his kindly feeling than before.

Henry could not sleep, although, at the request of George, who offered to keep watch for him the remainder of the night he attempted to do so.

He in vain said to himself, "I will banish from my mind this most unworthy subject. I have told Admiral Bell that contempt is the only feeling I can now have for his nephew, and yet I now find myself dwelling upon him, and upon his conduct, with a perseverance which is a foe to my repose."

At length came the welcome and beautiful light of day, and Henry rose fevered and unrefreshed.

His first impulse now was to hold a consultation with his brother George, as to what was to be done, and George advised that Mr. Marchdale, who as yet knew nothing of the matter, should be immediately informed of it, and consulted, as being probably better qualified than either of them to come to a just, a cool, and a reasonable opinion upon the painful circumstance, which it could not be expected that either of them would be able to view calmly.

"Let it be so, then," said Henry; "Mr. Marchdale shall decide for us."

They at once sought this friend of the family, who was in his own bed-room, and when Henry knocked at the door, Marchdale opened it hurriedly, eagerly inquiring what was the matter.

"There is no alarm," said Henry. "We have only come to tell you of a circumstance which has occurred during the night, and which will somewhat surprise you."

"Nothing calamitous, I hope?"

"Vexatious; and yet, I think it is a matter upon which we ought almost to congratulate ourselves. Read those two letters, and give us your candid opinion upon them."

Henry placed in Mr. Marchdale's hands the letter addressed to himself, as well as that to the admiral.

Marchdale read them both with marked attention, but he did not exhibit in his countenance so much surprise as regret.

When he had finished, Henry said to him,--

"Well, Marchdale, what think you of this new and extraordinary episode in our affairs?"

"My dear young friends," said Marchdale, in a voice of great emotion, "I know not what to say to you. I have no doubt but that you are both of you much astonished at the receipt of these letters, and equally so at the sudden absence of Charles Holland."

"And are not you?"

"Not so much as you, doubtless, are. The fact is, I never did entertain a favourable opinion of the young man, and he knew it. I have been accustomed to the study of human nature under a variety of aspects; I have made it a matter of deep, and I may add, sorrowful, contemplation, to study and remark those minor shades of character which commonly escape observation wholly. And, I repeat, I always had a bad opinion of Charles Holland, which he guessed, and hence he conceived a hatred to me, which more than once, as you cannot but remember, showed itself in little acts of opposition and hostility."

"You much surprise me."

"I expected to do so. But you cannot help remembering that at one time I was on the point of leaving here solely on his account."

"You were so."

"Indeed I should have done so, but that I reasoned with myself upon the subject, and subdued the impulse of the anger which some years ago, when I had not seen so much of the world, would have guided me."

"But why did you not impart to us your suspicions? We should at least, then, have been prepared for such a contingency as has occurred."

"Place yourself in my position, and then yourself what you would have done. Suspicion is one of those hideous things which all men should be most specially careful not only how they entertain at all, but how they give expression to. Besides, whatever may be the amount of one's own internal conviction with regard to the character of any one, there is just a possibility that one may be wrong."

"True, true."

"That possibility ought to keep any one silent who has nothing but suspicion to go upon, however cautious it may make him, as regards his dealings with the individual. I only suspected from little minute shades of character, that would peep out in spite of him, that Charles Holland was not the honourable man he would fain have had everybody believe him to be."

"And had you from the first such a feeling?"

"I had."

"It is very strange."

"Yes; and what is more strange still, is that he from the first seemed to know it; and despite a caution which I could see he always kept uppermost in his thoughts, he could not help speaking tartly to me at times."

"I have noticed that," said George.

"You may depend it is a fact," added Marchdale, "that nothing so much excites the deadly and desperate hatred of a man who is acting a hypocritical part, as the suspicion, well grounded or not, that another sees and understands the secret impulses of his dishonourable heart."

"I cannot blame you, or any one else, Mr. Marchdale," said Henry, "that you did not give utterance to your secret thoughts, but I do wish that you had done so."

"Nay, dear Henry," replied Mr. Marchdale, "believe me, I have made this matter a subject of deep thought, and have abundance of reasons why I ought not to have spoken to you upon the subject."

"Indeed!"

"Indeed I have, and not among the least important is the one, that if I had acquainted you with my suspicions, you would have found yourself in the painful position of acting a hypocritical part yourself towards this Charles Holland, for you must either have kept the secret that he was suspected, or you must have shewn it to him by your behaviour."

"Well, well. I dare say, Marchdale, you acted for the best. What shall we do now?"

"Can you doubt?"

"I was thinking of letting Flora at once know the absolute and complete worthlessness of her lover, so that she could have no difficulty in at once tearing herself from him by the assistance of the natural pride which would surely come to her aid, upon finding herself so much deceived."

"The test may be possible."

"You think so?"

"I do, indeed."

"Here is a letter, which of course remains unopened, addressed to Flora by Charles Holland. The admiral rather thought it would hurt her feelings to deliver her such an epistle, but I must confess I am of a contrary opinion upon that point, and think now the more evidence she has of the utter worthlessness of him who professed to love her with so much disinterested affection, the better it will be for her."

"You could not, possibly, Henry, have taken a more sensible view of the subject."

"I am glad you agree with me."

"No reasonable man could do otherwise, and from what I have seen of Admiral Bell, I am sure, upon reflection, he will be of the same opinion."

"Then it shall be so. The first shock to poor Flora may be severe, but we shall then have the consolation of knowing that it is the only one, and that in knowing the very worst, she has no more on that score to apprehend. Alas, alas! the hand of misfortune now appears to have pressed heavily upon us indeed. What in the name of all that is unlucky and disastrous, will happen next, I wonder?"

"What can happen?" said Marchdale; "I think you have now got rid of the greatest evil of all--a false friend."

"We have, indeed."

"Go, then, to Flora; assure her that in the affection of others who know no falsehood, she will find a solace from every ill. Assure her that there are hearts that will place themselves between her and every misfortune."

Mr. Marchdale was much affected as he spoke. Probably he felt deeper than he chose to express the misfortunes of that family for whom he entertained so much friendship. He turned aside his head to hide the traces of emotion which, despite even his great powers of self-command, would shew themselves upon his handsome and intelligent countenance. Then it appeared as if his noble indignation had got, for a few brief moments, the better of all prudence, and he exclaimed,--

"The villain! the worse than villain! who would, with a thousand artifices, make himself beloved by a young, unsuspecting, and beautiful girl, but then to leave her to the bitterness of regret, that she had ever given such a man a place in her esteem. The heartless ruffian!"

"Be calm, Mr. Marchdale, I pray you be calm," said George; "I never saw you so much moved."

"Excuse me," he said, "excuse me; I am much moved, and I am human. I cannot always, let me strive my utmost, place a curb upon my feelings."

"They are feelings which do you honour."

"Nay, nay, I am foolish to have suffered myself to be led away into such a hasty expression of them. I am accustomed to feel acutely and to feel deeply, but it is seldom I am so much overcome as this."

"Will you accompany us to the breakfast room at once, Mr. Marchdale, where we will make this communication to Flora; you will then be able to judge by her manner of receiving it, what it will be best to say to her."

"Come, then, and pray be calm. The least that is said upon this painful and harassing subject, after this morning, will be the best."

"You are right--you are right."

Mr. Marchdale hastily put on his coat. He was dressed, with the exception of that one article of apparel, when the brothers came to his chamber, and then he came to the breakfast-parlour where the painful communication was to be made to Flora of her lover's faithlessness.

Flora was already seated in that apartment. Indeed, she had been accustomed to meet Charles Holland there before others of the family made their appearance, but, alas! this morning the kind and tender lover was not there.

The expression that sat upon the countenances of her brothers, and of Mr. Marchdale, was quite sufficient to convince her that something more serious than usual had occurred, and she at the moment turned very pale. Marchdale observed this change of change of countenance in her, and he advanced towards her, saying,--

"Calm yourself, Flora, we have something to communicate to you, but it is a something which should excite indignation, and no other feeling, in your breast."

"Brother, what is the meaning of this?" said Flora, turning aside from Marchdale, and withdrawing the hand which he would have taken.

"I would rather have Admiral Bell here before I say anything," said Henry, "regarding a matter in which he cannot but feel much interested personally."

"Here he is," said the admiral, who at that moment had opened the door of the breakfast room. "Here he is, so now fire away, and don't spare the enemy."

"And Charles?" said Flora, "where is Charles?"

"D--n Charles!" cried the admiral, who had not been much accustomed to control his feelings.

"Hush! hush!" said Henry; "my dear sir, hush! do not indulge now in any invectives. Flora, here are three letters; you will see that the one which is unopened is addressed to yourself. However, we wish you to read the whole three of them, and then to form your own free and unbiased opinion."

Flora looked as pale as a marble statue, when she took the letters into her hands. She let the two that were open fall on the table before her, while she eagerly broke the seal of that which was addressed to herself.

Henry, with an instinctive delicacy, beckoned every one present to the window, so that Flora had not the pain of feeling that any eyes were fixed upon her but those of her mother, who had just come into the room, while she was perusing those documents which told such a tale of heartless dissimulation.

"My dear child," said Mrs. Bannerworth, "you are ill."

"Hush! mother--hush!" said Flora, "let me know all."

She read the whole of the letters through, and then, as the last one dropped from her grasp, she exclaimed,--

"Oh, God! oh, God! what is all that has occurred compared to this? Charles--Charles--Charles!"

"Flora!" exclaimed Henry, suddenly turning from the window. "Flora, is this worthy of you?"

"Heaven now support me!"

"Is this worthy of the name you bear Flora? I should have thought, and I did hope, that woman's pride would have supported you."

"Let me implore you," added Marchdale, "to summon indignation to your aid, Miss Bannerworth."

"Charles--Charles--Charles!" she again exclaimed, as she wrung her hands despairingly.

"Flora, if anything could add a sting to my already irritated feelings," said Henry, "this conduct of yours would."

"Henry--brother, what mean you? Are you mad?"

"Are you, Flora?"

"God, I wish now that I was."

"You have read those letters, and yet you call upon the name of him who wrote them with frantic tenderness."

"Yes, yes," she cried; "frantic tenderness is the word. It is with frantic tenderness I call upon his name, and ever will.--Charles! Charles!--dear Charles!"

"This surpasses all belief," said Marchdale.

"It is the frenzy of grief," added George; "but I did not expect it of her. Flora--Flora, think again."

"Think--think--the rush of thought distracts. Whence came these letters?--where did you find these most disgraceful forgeries?"

"Forgeries!" exclaimed Henry; and he staggered back, as if someone had struck him a blow.

"Yes, forgeries!" screamed Flora. "What has become of Charles Holland? Has he been murdered by some secret enemy, and then these most vile fabrications made up in his name? Oh, Charles, Charles, are you lost to me for ever?"

"Good God!" said Henry; "I did not think of that"

"Madness!--madness!" cried Marchdale.

"Hold!" shouted the admiral. "Let me speak to her."

He pushed every one aside, and advanced to Flora. He seized both her hands in his own, and in a tone of voice that was struggling with feeling, he cried,--

"Look at me, my dear; I'm an old man old enough to be your grandfather, so you needn't mind looking me steadily in the face. Look at me, I want to ask you a question."

Flora raised her beautiful eyes, and looked the old weather-beaten admiral full in the face.

Oh! what a striking contrast did those two persons present to each other. That young and beautiful girl, with her small, delicate, childlike hands clasped, and completely hidden in the huge ones of the old sailor, the white, smooth skin contrasting wonderfully with his wrinkled, hardened features.

"My dear," he cried, "you have read those--those d----d letters, my dear?"

"I have, sir."

"And what do you think of them?"

"They were not written by Charles Holland, your nephew."

A choking sensation seemed to come over the old man, and he tried to speak, but in vain. He shook the hands of the young girl violently, until he saw that he was hurting her, and then, before she could be aware of what he was about, he gave her a kiss on the cheek, as he cried,--

"God bless you--God bless you! You are the sweetest, dearest little creature that ever was, or that ever will be, and I'm a d----d old fool, that's what I am. These letters were not written by my nephew, Charles. He is incapable of writing them, and, d--n me, I shall take shame to myself as long as I live for ever thinking so."

"Dear sir," said Flora, who somehow or another did not seem at all offended at the kiss which the old man had given her; "dear sir, how could you believe, for one moment, that they came from him? There has been some desperate villany on foot. Where is he?--oh, find him, if he be yet alive. If they who have thus striven to steal from him that honour, which is the jewel of his heart, have murdered him, seek them out, sir, in the sacred name of justice, I implore you."

"I will--I will. I don't renounce him; he is my nephew still--Charles Holland--my own dear sister's son; and you are the best girl, God bless you, that ever breathed. He loved you--he loves you still; and if he's above ground, poor fellow, he shall yet tell you himself he never saw those infamous letters."

"You--you will seek for him?" sobbed Flora, and the tears gushed from her eyes. "Upon you, sir, who, as I do, feel assured of his innocence, I alone rely. If all the world say he is guilty, we will not think so."

"I'm d----d if we do."

Henry had sat down by the table, and, with his hands clasped together, seemed in an agony of thought.

He was now roused by a thump on the back by the admiral, who cried,--

"What do you think, now, old fellow? D--n it, things look a little different now."

"As God is my judge," said Henry, holding up his hands, "I know not what to think, but my heart and feelings all go with you and with Flora, in your opinion of the innocence of Charles Holland."

"I knew you would say that, because you could not possibly help it, my dear boy. Now we are all right again, and all we have got to do is to find out which way the enemy has gone, and then give chase to him."

"Mr. Marchdale, what do you think of this new suggestion," said George to that gentleman.

"Pray, excuse me," was his reply; "I would much rather not be called upon to give an opinion."

"Why, what do you mean by that?" said the admiral.

"Precisely what I say, sir."

"D--n me, we had a fellow once in the combined fleets, who never had an opinion till after something had happened, and then he always said that was just what he thought."

"I was never in the combined, or any other fleet, sir," said Marchdale, coldly.

"Who the devil said you were?" roared the admiral.

Marchdale merely hawed.

"However," added the admiral, "I don't care, and never did, for anybody's opinion, when I know I am right. I'd back this dear girl here for opinions, and good feelings, and courage to express them, against all the world, I would, any day. If I was not the old hulk I am, I would take a cruise in any latitude under the sun, if it was only for the chance of meeting with just such another."

"Oh, lose no time!" said Flora. "If Charles is not to be found in the house, lose no time in searching for him, I pray you; seek him, wherever there is the remotest probability he may chance to be. Do not let him think he is deserted."

"Not a bit of it," cried the admiral. "You make your mind easy, my dear. If he's above ground, we shall find him out, you may depend upon it. Come along master Henry, you and I will consider what had best be done in this uncommonly ugly matter."

Henry and George followed the admiral from the breakfast-room, leaving Marchdale there, who looked serious and full of melancholy thought.

It was quite clear that he considered Flora had spoken from the generous warmth of her affection as regarded Charles Holland, and not from the convictions which reason would have enforced her to feel.

When he was now alone with her and Mrs. Bannerworth, he spoke in a feeling and affectionate tone regarding the painful and inexplicable events which had transpired.

CHAPTER XXVIII

MR. MARCHDALE'S EXCULPATION OF HIMSELF.--THE SEARCH THROUGH THE GARDENS.--THE SPOT OF THE DEADLY STRUGGLE.--THE MYSTERIOUS PAPER

It was, perhaps, very natural that, with her feelings towards Charles Holland, Flora should shrink from every one who seemed to be of a directly contrary impression, and when Mr. Marchdale now spoke, she showed but little inclination to hear what he had to say in explanation.

The genuine and unaffected manner, however, in which he spoke, could not but have its effect upon her, and she found herself compelled to listen, as well as, to a great extent, approve of the sentiments that fell from his lips.

"Flora," he said, "I beg that you will here, in the presence of your mother, give me a patient hearing. You fancy that, because I cannot join so glibly as the admiral in believing that these letters are forgeries, I must be your enemy."

"Those letters," said Flora, "were not written by Charles Holland."

"That is your opinion."

"It is more than an opinion. He could not write them."

"Well, then, of course, if I felt inclined, which Heaven alone knows I do not, I could not hope successfully to argue against such a conviction. But I do not wish to do so. All I want to impress upon you is, that I am not to be blamed for doubting his innocence; and, at the same time, I wish to assure you that no one in this house would feel more exquisite satisfaction than I in seeing it established."

"I thank you for so much," said Flora; "but as, to my mind, his innocence has never been doubted, it needs to me no establishing."

"Very good. You believe these letters forgeries?"

"I do."

"And that the disappearance of Charles Holland is enforced, and not of his own free will?"

"I do."

"Then you may rely upon my unremitting exertions night and day to find him and any suggestion you can make, which is likely to aid in the search, shall, I pledge myself, be fully carried out."

"I thank you, Mr. Marchdale."

"My dear," said the mother, "rely on Mr. Marchdale."

"I will rely on any one who believe Charles Holland innocent of writing those odious letters, mother--I rely upon the admiral. He will aid me heart and hand."

"And so will Mr. Marchdale."

"I am glad to hear it."

"And yet doubt it, Flora," said Marchdale, dejectedly. "I am very sorry that such should be the case; I will not, however, trouble you any further, nor, give me leave to assure you, will I relax in my honest endeavours to clear up this mystery."

So saying, Mr. Marchdale bowed, and left the room, apparently more vexed than he cared to express at the misconstruction which had been put upon his conduct and motives. He at once sought Henry and the admiral, to whom he expressed his most earnest desire to aid in attempting to unravel the mysterious circumstances which had occurred.

"This strongly-expressed opinion of Flora," he remarked, "is of course amply sufficient to induce us to pause before we say one word more that shall in any way sound like a condemnation of Mr. Holland. Heaven forbid that I should."

"No," said the admiral; "don't."

"I do not intend."

"I would not advise anybody."

"Sir, if you use that as a threat--"

"A threat?"

"Yes; I must say, it sounded marvellously like one."

"Oh, dear, no--quite a mistake. I consider that every man has a fair right to the enjoyment of his opinion. All I have to remark is, that I shall, after what has occurred, feel myself called upon to fight anybody who says those letters were written by my nephew."

"Indeed, sir!"

"Ah, indeed."

"You will permit me to say such is a strange mode of allowing every one the free enjoyment of his opinion."

"Not at all."

"Whatever pains and penalties may be the result, Admiral Bell, of differing with so infallible authority as yourself, I shall do so whenever my judgment induces me."

"You will?"

"Indeed I will."

"Very good. You know the consequences."

"As to fighting you, I should refuse to do so."

"Refuse?"

"Yes; most certainly."

"Upon what ground?"

"Upon the ground that you were a madman."

"Come," now interposed Henry, "let me hope that, for my sake as well as for Flora's, this dispute will proceed no further."

"I have not courted it," said Marchdale. "I have much temper, but I am not a stick or a stone."

"D----e, if I don't think," said the admiral, "you are a bit of both."

"Mr. Henry Bannerworth," said Marchdale, "I am your guest, and but for the duty I feel in assisting in the search for Mr. Charles Holland, I should at once leave your house."

"You need not trouble yourself on my account," said the admiral; "if I find no clue to him in the neighbourhood for two or three days, I shall be off myself."

"I am going," said Henry, rising, "to search the garden and adjoining meadows; if you two gentlemen choose to come with me, I shall of course be happy of your company; if, however, you prefer remaining here to wrangle, you can do so."

This had the effect, at all events, of putting a stop to the dispute for the present, and both the admiral and Mr. Marchdale accompanied Henry on his search. That search was commenced immediately under the balcony of Charles Holland's window, from which the admiral had seen him emerge.

There was nothing particular found there, or in the garden. Admiral Bell pointed out accurately the route he had seen Charles take across the grass plot just before he himself left his chamber to seek Henry.

Accordingly, this route was now taken, and it led to a low part of the garden wall, which any one of ordinary vigour could easily have surmounted.

"My impression is," said the admiral, "that he got over here."

"The ivy appears to be disturbed," remarked Henry.

"Suppose we mark the spot, and then go round to it on the outer side?" suggested George.

This was agreed to; for, although the young man might have chosen rather to clamber over the wall than go round, it was doubtful if the old admiral could accomplish such a feat.

The distance round, however, was not great, and as they had cast over the wall a handful of flowers from the garden to mark the precise spot, it was easily discoverable.

The moment they reached it, they were panic-stricken by the appearances which it presented. The grass was for some yards round about completely trodden up, and converted into mud. There were deep indentations of feet-marks in all directions, and such abundance of evidence that some most desperate struggle had recently taken place there, that the most sceptical person in the world could not have entertained any doubt upon the subject.

Henry was the first to break the silence with which they each regarded the broken ground.

"This is conclusive to my mind," he said, with a deep sigh. "Here has poor Charles been attacked."

"God keep him!" exclaimed Marchdale, "and pardon me my doubts--I am now convinced."

The old admiral gazed about him like one distracted. Suddenly he cried--

"They have murdered him. Some fiends in the shape of men have murdered him, and Heaven only knows for what."

"It seems but too probable," said Henry. "Let us endeavour to trace the footsteps. Oh! Flora, Flora, what terrible news this will be to you."

"A horrible supposition comes across my mind," said George. "What if he met the vampyre?"

"It may have been so," said Marchdale, with a shudder. "It is a point which we should endeavour to ascertain, and I think we may do so."

"How!"

"By some inquiry as to whether Sir Francis Varney was from home at midnight last night."

"True; that might be done."

"The question, suddenly put to one of his servants, would, most probably, be answered as a thing of course."

"It would."

"Then that shall be decided upon. And now, my friends, since you have some of you thought me luke-warm in this business, I pledge myself that, should it be ascertained that Varney was from home at midnight last evening, I will defy him personally, and meet him hand to hand."

"Nay, nay," said Henry, "leave that course to younger hands."

"Why so?"

"It more befits me to be his challenger."

"No, Henry. You are differently situated to what I am."

"How so?"

"Remember, that I am in the world a lone man; without ties or connexions. If I lose my life, I compromise no one by my death; but you have a mother and a bereaved sister to look to who will deserve your care."

"Hilloa," cried the admiral, "what's this?"

"What?" cried each, eagerly, and they pressed forward to where the admiral was stooping to the ground to pick up something which was nearly completely trodden into the grass.

He with some difficulty raised it. It was a small slip of paper, on which was some writing, but it was so much covered with mud as not to be legible.

"If this be washed," said Henry, "I think we shall be able to read it clearly."

"We can soon try that experiment," said George. "And as the footsteps, by some mysterious means, show themselves nowhere else but in this one particular spot, any further pursuit of inquiry about here appears useless."

"Then we will return to the house," said Henry, "and wash the mud from this paper."

"There is one important point," remarked Marchdale, "which it appears to me we have all overlooked."

"Indeed!"

"Yes."

"What may that be?"

"It is this. Is any one here sufficiently acquainted with the handwriting of Mr. Charles Holland to come to an opinion upon the letters?"

"I have some letters from him," said Henry, "which we received while on the continent, and I dare say Flora has likewise."

"Then they should be compared with the alleged forgeries."

"I know his handwriting well," said the admiral. "The letters bear so strong a resemblance to it that they would deceive anybody."

"Then you may depend," remarked Henry, "some most deep-laid and desperate plot is going on."

"I begin," added Marchdale, "to dread that such must be the case. What say you to claiming the assistance of the authorities, as well as offering a large reward for any information regarding Mr. Charles Holland?"

"No plan shall be left untried, you may depend."

They had now reached the house, and Henry having procured some clean water, carefully washed the paper which had been found among the trodden grass. When freed from the mixture of clay and mud which had obscured it, they made out the following words,--

"--it be so well. At the next full moon seek a convenient spot, and it can be done. The signature is, to my apprehension, perfect. The money which I hold, in my opinion, is much more in amount than you imagine, must be ours; and as for--"

Here the paper was torn across, and no further words were visible upon it.

Mystery seemed now to be accumulating upon mystery; each one, as it showed itself darkly, seeming to bear some remote relation to what preceded it; and yet only confusing it the more.

That this apparent scrap of a letter had dropped from some one's pocket during the fearful struggle, of which there were such ample evidences, was extremely probable; but what it related to, by whom it was written, or by whom dropped, were unfathomable mysteries.

In fact, no one could give an opinion upon these matters at all; and after a further series of conjectures, it could only be decided, that unimportant as the scrap of paper appeared now to be, it should be preserved, in case it should, as there was a dim possibility that it might become a connecting link in some chain of evidence at another time.

"And here we are," said Henry, "completely at fault, and knowing not what to do."

"Well, it is a hard case," said the admiral, "that, with all the will in the world to be up and doing something, we are lying here like a fleet of ships in a calm, as idle as possible."

"You perceive we have no evidence to connect Sir Francis Varney with this affair, either nearly or remotely," said Marchdale.

"Certainly not," replied Henry.

"But yet, I hope you will not lose sight of the suggestion I proposed, to the effect of ascertaining if he were from home last night."

"But how is that to be carried out?"

"Boldly."

"How boldly?"

"By going at once, I should advise, to his house, and asking the first one of his domestics you may happen to see."

"I will go over," cried George; "on such occasions as these one cannot act upon ceremony."

He seized his hat, and without waiting for a word from any one approving or condemning his going, off he went.

"If," said Henry, "we find that Varney has nothing to do with the matter, we are completely at fault."

"Completely," echoed Marchdale.

"In that case, admiral, I think we ought to defer to your feelings upon the subject, and do whatever you suggest should be done."

"I shall offer a hundred pounds reward to any one who can and will bring any news of Charles."

"A hundred pounds is too much," said Marchdale.

"Not at all; and while I am about it, since the amount is made a subject of discussion, I shall make it two hundred, and that may benefit some rascal who is not so well paid for keeping the secret as I will pay him for disclosing it."

"Perhaps you are right," said Marchdale.

"I know I am, as I always am."

Marchdale could not forbear a smile at the opinionated old man, who thought no one's opinion upon any subject at all equal to his own; but he made no remark, and only waited, as did Henry, with evident anxiety for the return of George.

The distance was not great, and George certainly performed his errand quickly, for he was back in less time than they had thought he could return in. The moment he came into the room, he said, without waiting for any inquiry to be made of him,--

"We are at fault again. I am assured that Sir Francis Varney never stirred from home after eight o'clock last evening."

"D--n it, then," said the admiral, "let us give the devil his due. He could not have had any hand in this business."

"Certainly not."

"From whom, George, did you get your information?" asked Henry, in a desponding tone.

"From, first of all, one of his servants, whom I met away from the house, and then from one whom I saw at the house."

"There can be no mistake, then?"

"Certainly none. The servants answered me at once, and so frankly that I cannot doubt it."

The door of the room was slowly opened, and Flora came in. She looked almost the shadow of what she had been but a few weeks before. She was beautiful, but she almost realised the poet's description of one who had suffered much, and was sinking into an early grave, the victim of a broken heart:--

"She was more beautiful than death,
And yet as sad to look upon."

Her face was of a marble paleness, and as she clasped her hands, and glanced from face to face, to see if she could gather hope and consolation from the expression of any one, she might have been taken for some exquisite statue of despair.

"Have you found him?" she said. "Have you found Charles?"

"Flora, Flora," said Henry, as he approached her.

"Nay, answer me; have you found him? You went to seek him. Dead or alive, have you found him?"

"We have not, Flora."

"Then I must seek him myself. None will search for him as I will search; I must myself seek him. 'Tis true affection that can alone be successful in such a search."

"Believe me, dear Flora, that all has been done which the shortness of the time that has elapsed would permit. Further measures will now immediately be taken. Rest assured, dear sister, that all will be done that the utmost zeal can suggest."

"They have killed him! they have killed him!" she said, mournfully. "Oh, God, they have killed him! I am not now mad, but the time will come when I must surely be maddened. The vampyre has killed Charles Holland--the dreadful vampyre!"

"Nay, now, Flora, this is frenzy."

"Because he loved me has he been destroyed. I know it, I know it. The vampyre has doomed me to destruction. I am lost, and all who loved me will be involved in one common ruin on my account. Leave me all of you to perish. If, for iniquities done in our family, some one must suffer to appease the divine vengeance, let that one be me, and only me."

"Hush, sister, hush!" cried Henry. "I expected not this from you. The expressions you use are not your expressions. I know you better. There is abundance of divine mercy, but no divine vengeance. Be calm, I pray you."

"Calm! calm!"

"Yes. Make an exertion of that intellect we all know you to possess. It is too common a thing with human nature, when misfortune overtakes it, to imagine that such a state of things is specially arranged. We quarrel with Providence because it does not interfere with some special miracle in our favour; forgetting that, being denizens of this earth, and members of a great social system; We must be subject occasionally to the accidents which will disturb its efficient working."

"Oh, brother, brother!" she exclaimed, as she dropped into a seat, "you have never loved."

"Indeed!"

"No; you have never felt what it was to hold your being upon the breath of another. You can reason calmly, because you cannot know the extent of feeling you are vainly endeavouring to combat."

"Flora, you do me less than justice. All I wish to impress upon your mind is, that you are not in any way picked out by Providence to be specially unhappy--that there is no perversion of nature on your account."

"Call you that hideous vampyre form that haunts me no perversion of ordinary nature?"

"What is is natural," said Marchdale.

"Cold reasoning to one who suffers as I suffer. I cannot argue with you; I can only know that I am most unhappy--most miserable."

"But that will pass away, sister, and the sun of your happiness may smile again."

"Oh, if I could but hope!"

"And wherefore should you deprive yourself of that poorest privilege of the most unhappy?"

"Because my heart tells me to despair."

"Tell it you won't, then," cried Admiral Bell. "If you had been at sea as long as I have, Miss Bannerworth, you would never despair of anything at all."

"Providence guarded you," said Marchdale.

"Yes, that's true enough, I dare say, I was in a storm once off Cape Ushant, and it was only through Providence, and cutting away the mainmast myself, that we succeeded in getting into port."

"You have one hope," said Marchdale to Flora, as he looked in her wan face.

"One hope?"

"Yes. Recollect you have one hope."

"What is that?"

"You think that, by removing from this place, you may find that peace which is here denied you."

"No, no, no."

"Indeed. I thought that such was your firm conviction."

"It was; but circumstances have altered."

"How?"

"Charles Holland has disappeared here, and here must I remain to seek for him."

"True he may have disappeared here," remarked Marchdale; "and yet that may be no argument for supposing him still here."

"Where, then, is he?"

"God knows how rejoiced I should be if I were able to answer your question. I must seek him, dead or alive! I must see him yet before I bid adieu to this world, which has now lost all its charms for me."

"Do not despair," said Henry; "I will go to the town now at once, to make known our suspicions that he has met with some foul play. I will set every means in operation that I possibly can to discover him. Mr. Chillingworth will aid me, too; and I hope that not many days will elapse, Flora, before some intelligence of a most satisfactory nature shall be brought to you on Charles Holland's account."

"Go, go, brother; go at once."

"I go now at once."

"Shall I accompany you?" said Marchdale.

"No. Remain here to keep watch over Flora's safety while I am gone; I can alone do all that can be done."

"And don't forget to offer the two hundred pounds reward," said the admiral, "to any one who can bring us news of Charles, on which we can rely."

"I will not."

"Surely--surely something must result from that," said Flora, as she looked in the admiral's face, as if to gather encouragement in her dawning hopes from its expression.

"Of course it will, my dear," he said. "Don't you be downhearted; you and I are of one mind in this affair, and of one mind we will keep. We won't give up our opinions for anybody."

"Our opinions," she said, "of the honour and honesty of Charles Holland. That is what we will adhere to."

"Of course we will."

"Ah, sir, it joys me, even in the midst of this, my affliction, to find one at least who is determined to do him full justice. We cannot find such contradictions in nature as that a mind, full of noble impulses, should stoop to such a sudden act of selfishness as those letters would attribute to Charles Holland. It cannot--cannot be."

"You are right, my dear. And now, Master Henry, you be off, will you, if you please."

"I am off now. Farewell, Flora, for a brief space."

"Farewell, brother; and Heaven speed you on your errand."

"Amen to that," cried the admiral; "and now, my dear, if you have got half an hour to spare, just tuck your arm under mine, and take a walk with me in the garden, for I want to say something to you."

"Most willingly," said Flora.

"I would not advise you to stray far from the house, Miss Bannerworth," said Marchdale.

"Nobody asked you for advice," said the admiral. "D----e, do you want to make out that I ain't capable of taking care of her?"

"No, no; but--"

"Oh, nonsense! Come along, my dear; and if all the vampyres and odd fish that were ever created were to come across our path, we would settle them somehow or another. Come along, and don't listen to anybody's croaking."

CHAPTER XXIX

A PEEP THROUGH AN IRON GRATING.--THE LONELY PRISONER IN HIS DUNGEON.--THE MYSTERY

Without forestalling the interest of our story, or recording a fact in its wrong place, we now call our readers' attention to a circumstance which may, at all events, afford some food for conjecture.

Some distance from the Hall, which, from time immemorial, had been the home and the property of the Bannerworth family, was an ancient ruin known by the name of the Monks' Hall.

It was conjectured that this ruin was the remains of some one of those half monastic, half military buildings which, during the middle ages, were so common in almost every commanding situation in every county of England.

At a period of history when the church arrogated to itself an amount of political power which the intelligence of the spirit of the age now denies to it, and when its members were quite ready to assert at any time the truth of their doctrines by the strong arm of power, such buildings as the one, the old grey ruins of which were situated near to Bannerworth Hall, were erected.

Ostensibly for religious purposes, but really as a stronghold for defence, as well as for aggression, this Monks' Hall, as it was called, partook quite as much of the character of a fortress, as of an ecclesiastical building.

The ruins covered a considerable extent, of ground, but the only part which seemed successfully to have resisted the encroaches of time, at least to a considerable extent, was a long, hall in which the jolly monks no doubt feasted and caroused.

Adjoining to this hall, were the walls of other parts of the building, and at several places there were small, low, mysterious-looking doors that led, heaven knows where, into some intricacies and labyrinths beneath the building, which no one had, within the memory of man, been content to run the risk of losing himself in.

It was related that among these subterranean passages and arches there were pitfalls and pools of water; and whether such a statement was true or not, it certainly acted as a considerable damper upon the vigour of curiosity.

This ruin was so well known in the neighbourhood, and had become from earliest childhood so familiar to the inhabitants of Bannerworth Hall, that one would as soon expect an old inhabitant of Ludgate-hill to make some remark about St. Paul's, as any of them to allude to the ruins of Monks' Hall.

They never now thought of going near to it, for in infancy they had spoiled among its ruins, and it had become one of those familiar objects which, almost, from that very familiarity, cease to hold a place in the memories of those who know it so well.

It is, however, to this ruin we would now conduct our readers, premising that what we have to say concerning it now, is not precisely in the form of a connected portion of our narrative.

***

It is evening--the evening of that first day of heart loneliness to poor Flora Bannerworth. The lingering rays of the setting sun are gilding the old ruins with a wondrous beauty. The edges of the decayed stones seem now to be tipped with gold, and as the rich golden refulgence of light gleams upon the painted glass which still adorned a large window of the hall, a flood of many-coloured beautiful light was cast within, making the old flag-stones, with which the interior was paved, look more like some rich tapestry, laid down to do honour to a monarch.

So picturesque and so beautiful an aspect did the ancient ruin wear, that to one with a soul to appreciate the romantic and the beautiful, it would have amply repaid the fatigue of a long journey now to see it.

And as the sun sank to rest, the gorgeous colours that it cast upon the mouldering wall, deepened from an appearance of burnished gold to a crimson hue, and from that again the colour changed to a shifting purple, mingling with the shadows of the evening, and so gradually fading away into absolute darkness.

The place is as silent as the tomb--a silence far more solemn than could have existed, had there been no remains of a human habitation; because even these time-worn walls were suggestive of what once had been; and the wrapt stillness which now pervaded them brought with them a melancholy feeling for the past.

There was not even the low hum of insect life to break the stillness of these ancient ruins.

And now the last rays of the sun are gradually fading away. In a short time all will be darkness. A low gentle wind is getting up, and beginning slightly to stir the tall blades of grass that have shot up between some of the old stones. The silence is broken, awfully broken, by a sudden cry of despair; such a cry as might come from some imprisoned spirit, doomed to waste an age of horror in a tomb.

And yet it was scarcely to be called a scream, and not all a groan. It might have come from some one on the moment of some dreadful sacrifice, when the judgment had not sufficient time to call courage to its aid, but involuntarily had induced that sound which might not be repeated.

A few startled birds flew from odd holes and corners about the ruins, to seek some other place of rest. The owl hooted from a corner of what had once been a belfry, and a dreamy-looking bat flew out from a cranny and struck itself headlong against a projection.

Then all was still again. Silence resumed its reign, and if there had been a mortal ear to drink in that sudden sound, the mind might well have doubted if fancy had not more to do with the matter than reality.

From out a portion of the ruins that was enveloped in the deepest gloom, there now glides a figure. It is of gigantic height, and it moves along with a slow and measured tread. An ample mantle envelopes the form, which might well have been taken for the spirit of one of the monks who, centuries since, had made that place their home.

It walked the whole length of the ample hall we have alluded to, and then, at the window from which had streamed the long flood of many coloured light, it paused.

For more than ten minutes this mysterious looking figure there stood.

At length there passed something on the outside of the window, that looked like the shadow of a human form.

Then the tall, mysterious, apparition-looking man turned, and sought a side entrance to the hall.

Then he paused, and, in about a minute, he was joined by another who must have been he who had so recently passed the stained glass window on the outer side.

There was a friendly salutation between these two beings, and they walked to the centre of the hall, where they remained for some time in animated conversation.

From the gestures they used, it was evident that the subject of their discourse was one of deep and absorbing interest to both. It was one, too, upon which, after a time, they seemed a little to differ, and more than once they each assumed attitudes of mutual defiance.

This continued until the sun had so completely sunk, that twilight was beginning sensibly to wane, and then gradually the two men appeared to have come to a better understanding, and whatever might be the subject of their discourse, there was some positive result evidently arrived at now.

They spoke in lower tones. They used less animated gestures than before; and, after a time, they both walked slowly down the hull towards the dark spot from whence the first tall figure had so mysteriously emerged.

***

There it a dungeon--damp and full of the most unwholesome exhalations--deep under ground it seems, and, in its excavations, it would appear as if some small land springs had been liberated, for the earthen floor was one continued extent of moisture.

From the roof, too, came perpetually the dripping of water, which fell with sullen, startling splashes in the pool below.

At one end, and near to the roof,--so near that to reach it, without the most efficient means from the inside, was a matter of positive impossibility--is a small iron grating, and not much larger than might be entirely obscured by any human face that might be close to it from the outside of the dungeon.

That dreadful abode is tenanted. In one corner, on a heap of straw, which appears freshly to have been cast into the place, lies a hopeless prisoner.

It is no great stretch of fancy to suppose, that it is from his lips came the sound of terror and of woe that had disturbed the repose of that lonely spot.

The prisoner is lying on his back; a rude bandage round his head, on which were numerous spots of blood, would seem to indicate that he had suffered personal injury in some recent struggle. His eyes were open. They were fixed desparingly, perhaps unconsciously, upon that small grating which looked into the upper world.

That grating slants upwards, and looks to the west, so that any one confined in that dreary dungeon might be tantalized, on a sweet summer's day, by seeing the sweet blue sky, and occasionally the white clouds flitting by in that freedom which he cannot hope for.

The carol of a bird, too, might reach him there. Alas! sad remembrance of life, and joy, and liberty.

But now all is deepening gloom. The prisoner sees nothing--hears nothing; and the sky is not quite dark. That small grating looks like a strange light-patch in the dungeon wall.

Hark! some footstep sounds upon his ear. The creaking of a door follows--a gleam of light shines into the dungeon, and the tall mysterious-looking figure in the cloak stands before the occupant of that wretched place.

Then comes in the other man, and he carries in his hand writing materials. He stoops to the stone couch on which the prisoner lies, and offers him a pen, as he raises him partially from the miserable damp pallet.

But there is no speculation in the eyes of that oppressed man. In vain the pen is repeatedly placed in his grasp, and a document of some length, written on parchment, spread out before him to sign. In vain is he held up now by both the men, who have thus mysteriously sought him in his dungeon; he has not power to do as they would wish him. The pen falls from his nerveless grasp, and, with a deep sigh, when they cease to hold him up, he falls heavily back upon the stone couch.

Then the two men looked at each other for about a minute silently; after which he who was the shorter of the two raised one hand, and, in a voice of such concentrated hatred and passion as was horrible to hear, he said,--

"D--n!"

The reply of the other was a laugh; and then he took the light from the floor, and motioned the one who seemed so little able to control his feelings of bitterness and disappointment to leave the place with him.

With a haste and vehemence, then, which showed how much angered he was, the shorter man of the two now rolled up the parchment, and placed it in a breast-pocket of his coat.

He cast a withering look of intense hatred on the form of the nearly-unconscious prisoner, and then prepared to follow the other.

But when they reached the door of the dungeon, the taller man of the two paused, and appeared for a moment or two to be in deep thought; after which he handed the lamp he carried to his companion, and approached the pallet of the prisoner.

He took from his pocket a small bottle, and, raising the head of the feeble and wounded man, he poured some portion of the contents into his mouth, and watched him swallow it.

The other looked on in silence, and then they both slowly left the dreary dungeon.

***

The wind rose, and the night had deepened into the utmost darkness. The blackness of a night, unillumined by the moon, which would not now rise for some hours, was upon the ancient ruins. All was calm and still, and no one would have supposed that aught human was within those ancient, dreary looking walls.

Time will show who it was who lay in that unwholesome dungeon, as well as who were they who visited him so mysteriously, and retired again with feelings of such evident disappointment with the document it seemed of such importance, at least to one of them, to get that unconscious man to sign.

CHAPTER XXX

THE VISIT OF FLORA TO THE VAMPYRE.--THE OFFER.--THE SOLEMN ASSEVERATION

Admiral Bell had, of course, nothing particular to communicate to Flora in the walk he induced her to take with him in the gardens of Bannerworth Hall, but he could talk to her upon a subject which was sure to be a welcome one, namely, of Charles Holland.

And not only could he talk to her of Charles, but he was willing to talk of him in the style of enthusiastic commendation which assimilated best with her own feelings. No one but the honest old admiral, who was as violent in his likes and his dislikes as any one could possibly be, could just then have conversed with Flora Bannerworth to her satisfaction of Charles Holland.

He expressed no doubts whatever concerning Charles's faith, and to his mind, now that he had got that opinion firmly fixed in his mind, everybody that held a contrary one he at once denounced as a fool or a rogue.

"Never you mind, Miss Flora," he said; "you will find, I dare say, that all will come right eventually. D--n me! the only thing that provokes me in the whole business is, that I should have been such an old fool as for a moment to doubt Charles."

"You should have known him better, sir."

"I should, my dear, but I was taken by surprise, you see, and that was wrong, too, for a man who has held a responsible command."

"But the circumstances, dear sir, were of a nature to take every one by surprise."

"They were, they were. But now, candidly speaking, and I know I can speak candidly to you; do you really think this Varney is the vampyre?"

"I do."

"You do? Well, then, somebody must tackle him, that's quite clear; we can't put up with his fancies always."

"What can be done?"

"Ah, that I don't know, but something must be done, you know. He wants this place; Heaven only knows why or wherefore he has taken such a fancy to it; but he has done so, that is quite clear. If it had a good sea view, I should not be so much surprised; but there's nothing of the sort, so it's no way at all better than any other shore-going stupid sort of house, that you can see nothing but land from."

"Oh, if my brother would but make some compromise with him to restore Charles to us and take the house, we might yet be happy."

"D--n it! then you still think that he has a hand in spiriting away Charles?"

"Who else could do so?"

"I'll be hanged if I know. I do feel tolerably sure, and I have good deal of reliance upon your opinion, my dear; I say, I do feel tolerably sure: but, if I was d----d sure, now, I'd soon have it out of him."

"For my sake, Admiral Bell, I wish now to extract one promise from you."

"Say your say, my dear, and I'll promise you."

"You will not then expose yourself to the danger of any personal conflict with that most dreadful man, whose powers of mischief we do not know, and therefore cannot well meet or appreciate."

"Whew! is that what you mean?"

"Yes; you will, I am sure, promise me so much."

"Why, my dear, you see the case is this. In affairs of fighting, the less ladies interfere the better."

"Nay, why so?"

"Because--because, you see, a lady has no reputation for courage to keep up. Indeed, it's rather the other way, for we dislike a bold woman as much as we hold in contempt a cowardly man."

"But if you grant to us females that in consequence of our affections, we are not courageous, you must likewise grant how much we are doomed to suffer from the dangers of those whom we esteem."

"You would be the last person in the world to esteem a coward."

"Certainly. But there is more true courage often in not fighting than in entering into a contest."

"You are right enough there, my dear."

"Under ordinary circumstances, I should not oppose your carrying out the dictates of your honour, but now, let me entreat you not to meet this dreadful man, if man he can be called, when you know not how unfair the contest may be."

"Unfair?"

"Yes. May he not have some means of preventing you from injuring him, and of overcoming you, which no mortal possesses?"

"He may."

"Then the supposition of such a case ought to be sufficient ground for at once inducing you to abandon all idea of meeting with him."

"My dear, I'll consider of this matter."

"Do so."

"There is another thing, however, which now you will permit me to ask of you as a favour."

"It is granted ere it is spoken."

"Very good. Now you must not be offended with what I am going to say, because, however it may touch that very proper pride which you, and such as you, are always sure to possess, you are fortunately at all times able to call sufficient judgment to your aid to enable you to see what is really offensive and what is not."

"You alarm me by such a preface."

"Do I? then here goes at once. Your brother Henry, poor fellow, has enough to do, has he not, to make all ends meet."

A flush of excitement came over Flora's cheek as the old admiral thus bluntly broached a subject of which she already knew the bitterness to such a spirit as her brother's.

"You are silent," continued the old man; "by that I guess I am not wrong in my I supposition; indeed it is hardly a supposition at all, for Master Charles told me as much, and no doubt he had it from a correct quarter."

"I cannot deny it, sir."

"Then don't. It ain't worth denying, my dear. Poverty is no crime, but, like being born a Frenchman, it's a d----d misfortune."

Flora could scarcely refuse a smile, as the nationality of the old admiral peeped out even in the midst of his most liberal and best feelings.

"Well," he continued, "I don't intend that he shall have so much trouble as he has had. The enemies of his king and his country shall free him from his embarrassments."

"The enemies?"

"Yes; who else?"

"You speak in riddles, sir."

"Do I? Then I'll soon make the riddles plain. When I went to sea I was worth nothing--as poor as a ship's cat after the crew had been paid off for a month. Well, I began fighting away as hard and fast as I could, and the more I fought, and the more hard knocks I gave and took, the more money I got."

"Indeed."

"Yes; prize after prize we hauled into port, and at last the French vessels wouldn't come out of their harbours."

"What did you do then?"

"What did we do then? Why what was the most natural thing in the whole world for us to do, we did."

"I cannot guess."

"Well, I am surprised at that. Try again."

"Oh, yes; I can guess now. How could I have been so dull? You went and took them out."

"To be sure we did--to be sure we did, my dear; that's how we managed them. And, do you see, at the end of the war I found myself with lots of prize money, all wrung from old England's enemies, and I intend that some of it shall find it's way to your brother's pocket; and you see that will bear out just what I said, that the enemies of his king and his country shall free him from his difficulties--don't you see?"

"I see your noble generosity, admiral."

"Noble fiddlestick! Now I have mentioned this matter to you, my dear, and I don't so much mind talking to you about such matters as I should to your brother, I want you to do me the favour of managing it all for me."

"How, sir?"

"Why, just this way. You must find out how much money will free your brother just now from a parcel of botherations that beset him, and then I will give it to you, and you can hand it to him, you see, so I need not say anything about it; and if he speaks to me on the subject at all, I can put him down at once by saying, 'avast there, it's no business of mine.'"

"And can you, dear admiral, imagine that I could conceal the generous source from where so much assistance came?"

"Of course; it will come from you. I take a fancy to make you a present of a sum of money; you do with it what you please--it's yours, and I have no right and no inclination to ask you what use you put it to."

Tears gushed from the eyes of Flora as she tried to utter some word, but could not. The admiral swore rather fearfully, and pretended to wonder much what on earth she could be crying for. At length, after the first gush of feeling was over, she said,--

"I cannot accept of so much generosity, sir--I dare not"

"Dare not!"

"No; I should think meanly of myself were I to take advantage of the boundless munificence of your nature."

"Take advantage! I should like to see anybody take advantage of me, that's all."

"I ought not to take the money of you. I will speak to my brother, and well I know how much he will appreciate the noble, generous offer, my dear sir."

"Well, settle it your own way, only remember I have a right to do what I like with my own money."

"Undoubtedly."

"Very good. Then as that is undoubted, whatever I lend to him, mind I give to you, so it's as broad as it's long, as the Dutchman said, when he looked at the new ship that was built for him, and you may as well take it yourself you see, and make no more fuss about it."

"I will consider," said Flora, with much emotion--"between this time and the same hour to-morrow I will consider, sir, and if you can find any words more expressive of heartfelt gratitude than others, pray imagine that I have used them with reference to my own feelings towards you for such an unexampled offer of friendship."

"Oh, bother--stuff."

The admiral now at once changed the subject, and began to talk of Charles--a most grateful theme to Flora, as may well be supposed. He related to her many little particulars connected with him which all tended to place his character in a most amiable light, and as her ears drank in the words of commendation of him she loved, what sweeter music could there be to her than the voice of that old weather-beaten rough-spoken man.

"The idea," he added, to a warm eulogium he had uttered concerning Charles--"the idea that he could write those letters my dear, is quite absurd."

"It is, indeed. Oh, that we could know what had become of him!"

"We shall know. I don't think but what he's alive. Something seems to assure me that we shall some of these days look upon his face again."

"I am rejoiced to hear you say so."

"We will stir heaven and earth to find him. If he were killed, do you see, there would have been some traces of him now at hand; besides, he would have been left lying where the rascals attacked him."

Flora shuddered.

"But don't you fret yourself. You may depend that the sweet little cherub that sits up aloft has looked after him."

"I will hope so."

"And now, my dear, Master Henry will soon be home, I am thinking, and as he has quite enough disagreeables on his own mind to be able to spare a few of them, you will take the earliest opportunity, I am sure, of acquainting him with the little matter we have been talking about, and let me know what he says."

"I will--I will."

"That's right. Now, go in doors, for there's a cold air blowing here, and you are a delicate plant rather just now--go in and make yourself comfortable and easy. The worst storm must blow over at last."

CHAPTER XXXI

SIR FRANCIS VARNEY AND HIS MYSTERIOUS VISITOR.--THE STRANGE CONFERENCE

Sir Francis Varney is in what he calls his own apartment. It is night, and a dim and uncertain light from a candle which has been long neglected, only serves to render obscurity more perplexing. The room is a costly one. One replete with all the appliances of refinement and luxury which the spirit and the genius of the age could possibly supply him with, but there is upon his brow the marks of corroding care, and little does that most mysterious being seem to care for all the rich furnishing of that apartment in which he sits.

His cadaverous-looking face is even paler and more death-like-looking than usual; and, if it can be conceived possible that such an one can feel largely interested in human affairs, to look at him, we could well suppose that some interest of no common magnitude was at stake.

Occasionally, too, he muttered some unconnected words, no doubt mentally filling up the gaps, which rendered the sentences incomplete, and being unconscious, perhaps, that he was giving audible utterance to any of his dark and secret meditations.

At length he rose, and with an anxious expression of countenance, he went to the window, and looked out into the darkness of the night. All was still, and not an object was visible. It was that pitchy darkness without, which, for some hours, when the moon is late in lending her reflected beams, comes over the earth's surface.

"It is near the hour," he muttered. "It is now very near the hour; surely he will come, and yet I know not why I should fear him, although I seem to tremble at the thought of his approach. He will surely come. Once a year--only once does he visit me, and then 'tis but to take the price which he has compelled me to pay for that existence, which but for him had been long since terminated. Sometimes I devoutly wish it were."

With a shudder he returned to the seat he had so recently left, and there for some time he appeared to meditate in silence.

Suddenly now, a clock, which was in the hall of that mansion he had purchased, sounded the hour loudly.

"The time has come," said Sir Francis. "The time has come. He will surely soon be here. Hark! hark!"

Slowly and distinctly he counted the strokes of the clock, and, when they had ceased, he exclaimed, with sudden surprise--

"Eleven! But eleven! How have I been deceived. I thought the hour of midnight was at hand."

He hastily consulted the watch he wore, and then he indeed found, that whatever he had been looking forward to with dread for some time past, as certain to ensue, at or about twelve o clock, had yet another hour in which to prey upon his imagination.

"How could I have made so grievous an error?" he exclaimed. "Another hour of suspense and wonder as to whether that man be among the living or the dead. I have thought of raising my hand against his life, but some strange mysterious feeling has always staid me; and I have let him come and go freely, while an opportunity might well have served me to put such a design into execution. He is old, too--very old, and yet he keeps death at a distance. He looked pale, but far from unwell or failing, when last I saw him. Alas! a whole hour yet to wait. I would that this interview were over."

That extremely well known and popular disease called the fidgets, now began, indeed, to torment Sir Francis Varney. He could not sit--he could not walk, and, somehow or another, he never once seemed to imagine that from the wine cup he should experience any relief, although, upon a side table, there stood refreshments of that character. And thus some more time passed away, and he strove to cheat it of its weariness by thinking of a variety of subjects; but as the fates would have it, there seemed not one agreeable reminiscence in the mind of that most inexplicable man, and the more he plunged into the recesses of memory the more uneasy, not to say almost terrified, he looked and became. A shuddering nervousness came across him, and, for a few moments, he sat as if he were upon the point of fainting. By a vigorous effort, however, he shook this off, and then placing before him the watch, which now indicated about the quarter past eleven, he strove with a calmer aspect to wait the coming of him whose presence, when he did come, would really be a great terror, since the very thought beforehand produced so much hesitation and apparent dismay.

In order too, if possible, then to further withdraw himself from a too painful consideration of those terrors, which in due time the reader will be acquainted with the cause of, he took up a book, and plunging at random into its contents, he amused his mind for a time with the following brief narrative:--

The wind howled round the gable ends of Bridport House in sudden and furious gusts, while the inmates sat by the fire-side, gazing in silence upon the blazing embers of the huge fire that shed a red and bright light all over the immense apartment in which they all sat.

It was an ancient looking place, very large, end capable of containing a number of guests. Several were present.

An aged couple were seated in tall high straight-backed chairs. They were the owners of that lordly mansion, and near them sat two young maidens of surpassing beauty; they were dissimilar, and yet there was a slight likeness, but of totally different complexions.

The one had tresses of raven black; eyebrows, eyelashes, and eyes were all of the same hue; she was a beautiful and proud-looking girl, her complexion clear, with the hue of health upon her cheeks, while a smile played around her lips. The glance of the eye was sufficient to thrill through the whole soul.

The other maiden was altogether different; her complexion altogether fairer--her hair of sunny chestnut, and her beautiful hazel eyes were shaded by long brown eyelashes, while a playful smile also lit up her countenance. She was the younger of the two.

The attention of the two young maidens had been directed to the words of the aged owner of the house, for he had been speaking a few moments before.

There were several other persons present, and at some little distance were many of the domestics who were not denied the privilege of warmth and rest in the presence of their master.

These were not the times, when, if servants sat down, they were deemed idle; but the daily task done, then the evening hour was spent by the fire-side.

"The wind howls and moans," said an aged domestic, "in an awful manner. I never heard the like."

"It seems as though some imprisoned spirit was waiting for the repose that had been denied on earth," said the old lady as she shifted her seat and gazed steadily on the fire.

"Ay," said her aged companion, "it is a windy night, and there will be a storm before long, or I'm mistaken."

"It was just such a night as that my son Henry left his home," said Mrs. Bradley, "just such another--only it had the addition of sleet and rain."

The old man sighed at the mention of his son's name, a tear stood in the eyes of the maidens, while one looked silently at the other, and seemed to exchange glances.

"I would that I might again see him before my body seeks its final home in the cold remorseless grave."

"Mother," said the fairest of the two maidens, "do not talk thus, let us hope that we yet may have many years of happiness together."

"Many, Emma?"

"Yes, mamma, many."

"Do you know that I am very old, Emma, very old indeed, considering what I have suffered, such a life of sorrow and ill health is at least equal to thirty years added to my life."

"You may have deceived yourself, aunt," said the other maiden; "at all events, you cannot count upon life as certain, for the strongest often go first, while those who seem much more likely to fall, by care, as often live in peace and happiness."

"But I lead no life of peace and happiness, while Henry Bradley is not here; besides, my life might be passed without me seeing him again."

"It is now two years since he was here last," said the old man,

"This night two years was the night on which he left."

"This night two years?"

"Yes."

"It was this night two years," said one of the servant men, "because old Dame Poutlet had twins on that night."

"A memorable circumstance."

"And one died at a twelvemonth old," said the man; "and she had a dream which foretold the event."

"Ay, ay."

"Yes, and moreover she's had the same dream again last Wednesday was a week," said the man.

"And lost the other twin?"

"Yes sir, this morning."

"Omens multiply," said the aged man; "I would that it would seem to indicate the return of Henry to his home."

"I wonder where he can have gone to, or what he could have done all this time; probably he may not be in the land of the living."

"Poor Henry," said Emma.

"Alas, poor boy! We may never see him again--it was a mistaken act of his, and yet he knew not otherwise how to act or escape his father's displeasure."

"Say no more--say no more upon that subject; I dare not listen to it. God knows I know quite enough," said Mr. Bradley; "I knew not he would have taken my words so to heart as he did."

"Why," said the old woman, "he thought you meant what you said."

There was a long pause, during which all gazed at the blazing fire, seemingly wrapt in their own meditation.

Henry Bradley, the son of the apparently aged couple, had left that day two years, and wherefore had he left the home of his childhood? wherefore had he, the heir to large estates, done this?

He had dared to love without his father's leave, and had refused the offer his father made him of marrying a young lady whom he had chosen for him, but whom he could not love.

It was as much a matter of surprise to the father that the son should refuse, as it was to the son that his father should contemplate such a match.

"Henry," said the father, "you have been thought of by me, I have made proposals for marrying you to the daughter of our neighbour, Sir Arthur Onslow."

"Indeed, father!"

"Yes; I wish you to go there with me to see the young lady."

"In the character of a suitor?"

"Yes," replied the father, "certainly; it's high time you were settled."

"Indeed, I would rather not go, father; I have no intention of marrying just yet. I do not desire to do so."

This was an opposition that Mr. Bradley had not expected from his son, and which his imperious temper could ill brook, and with a darkened brow he said,--

"It is not much, Henry, that I trespass upon your obedience; but when I do so, I expect that you will obey me."

"But, father, this matter affects me for my whole life."

"That is why I have deliberated so long and carefully over it."

"But it is not unreasonable that I should have a voice in the affair, father, since it may render me miserable."

"You shall have a voice."

"Then I say no to the whole regulation," said Henry, decisively.

"If you do so you forfeit my protection, much more favour; but you had better consider over what you have said. Forget it, and come with me."

"I cannot."

"You will not?"

"No, father; I cannot do as you wish me; my mind is fully made up upon that matter."

"And so is mine. You either do as I would have you, or you leave the house, and seek your own living, and you are a beggar."

"I should prefer being such," said Henry, "than to marry any young lady, and be unable to love her."

"That is not required."

"No! I am astonished! Not necessary to love the woman you marry!"

"Not at all; if you act justly towards her she ought to be grateful; and it is all that is requisite in the marriage state. Gratitude will beget love, and love in one begets love in the other."

"I will not argue with you, father, upon the matter. You are a better judge than I; you have had more experience."

"I have."

"And it would be useless to speak upon the subject; but of this I can speak--my own resolve--that I will not marry the lady in question."

The son had all the stern resolve of the father, but he had also very good reasons for what he did. He loved, and was beloved in return; and hence he would not break his faith with her whom he loved.

To have explained this to his father would have been to gain nothing except an accession of anger, and he would have made a new demand upon his (the son's) obedience, by ordering him to discard from his bosom the image that was there indelibly engraven.

"You will not marry her whom I have chosen for your bride?"

"I cannot."

"Do not talk to me of can and can't, when I speak of will and wont. It Is useless to disguise the fact. You have your free will in the matter. I shall take no answer but yes or no."

"Then, no, father."

"Good, sir; and now we are strangers."

With that Mr. Bradley turned abruptly from his son, and left him to himself.

It was the first time they had any words of difference together, and it was sudden and soon terminated.

Henry Bradley was indignant at what had happened; he did not think his father would have acted as he had done in this instance; but he was too much interested in the fate of another to hesitate for a moment. Then came the consideration as to what he should do, now that he had arrived at such a climax.

His first thoughts turned to his mother and sister. He could not leave the house without bidding them good-bye. He determined to see his mother, for his father had left the Hall upon a visit.

Mrs. Bradley and Emma were alone when he entered their apartment, and to them he related all that had passed between himself and father.

They besought him to stay, to remain there, or at least in the neighbourhood; but he was resolved to quit the place altogether for a time, as he could do nothing there, and he might chance to do something elsewhere.

Upon this, they got together all the money and such jewels as they could spare, which in all amounted to a considerable sum; then taking an affectionate leave of his mother and sister, Henry left the Hall--not before he had taken a long and affectionate farewell of one other who lived within those walls.

This was no other than the raven-eyed maiden who sat by the fire side, and listened attentively to the conversation that was going on. She was his love--she, a poor cousin. For her sake he had braved all his father's anger, and attempted to seek his fortune abroad.

This done, he quietly left the Hall, without giving any one any intimation of where he was going.

Old Mr. Bradley, when he had said so much to his son, was highly incensed at what he deemed his obstinacy; and he thought the threat hanging over him would have had a good effect; but he was amazed when he discovered that Henry had indeed left the Hall, and he knew not whither.

For some time he comforted himself with the assurance that he would, he must return, but, alas! he came not, and this was the second anniversary of that melancholy day, which no one more repented of and grieved for, than did poor Mr. Bradley.

"Surely, surely he will return, or let us know where he is," he said; "he cannot be in need, else he would have written to us for aid."

"No, no," said Mrs. Bradley; "it is, I fear, because he has not written, that he is in want; he would never write if he was in poverty, lest he should cause us unhappiness at his fate. Were he doing well, we should hear of it, for he would be proud of the result of his own unaided exertions."

"Well, well," said Mr. Bradley, "I can say no more; if I was hasty, so was he; but it is passed. I would forgive all the past, if I could but see him once again--once again!"

"How the wind howls," added the aged man; "and it's getting worse and worse."

"Yes, and the snow is coming down now in style," said one of the servants, who brought in some fresh logs which were piled up on the fire, and he shook the white flakes off his clothes.

"It will be a heavy fall before morning," said one of the men.

"Yes, it has been gathering for some days; it will be much warmer than it has been when it is all down."

"So it will--so it will."

At that moment there was a knocking at the gate, and the dogs burst into a dreadful uproar from their kennels.

"Go, Robert," said Mr. Bradley, "and see who it is that knocks such a night as this; it is not fit or safe that a dog should be out in it."

The man went out, and shortly returned, saying,--

"So please you, sir, there is a traveller that has missed his way, and desires to know if he can obtain shelter here, or if any one can be found to guide him to the nearest inn."

"Bid him come in; we shall lose no warmth because there is one more before the fire."

The stranger entered, and said,--"I have missed my way, and the snow comes down so thick and fast, and is whirled in such eddies, that I fear, by myself, I should fall into some drift, and perish before morning."

"Do not speak of it, sir," said Mr. Bradley; "such a night as this is a sufficient apology for the request you make, and an inducement to me to grant it most willingly."

"Thanks," replied the stranger; "the welcome is most seasonable."

"Be seated, sir; take your seat by the ingle; it is warm."

The stranger seated himself, and seemed lost in reflection, as he gazed intently on the blazing logs. He was a robust man, with great whiskers and beard, and, to judge from his outward habiliments, he was a stout man.

"Have you travelled far?"

"I have, sir."

"You appear to belong to the army, if I mistake not?"

"I do, sir."

There was a pause; the stranger seemed not inclined to speak of himself much; but Mr. Bradley continued,--

"Have you come from foreign service, sir? I presume you have."

"Yes; I have not been in this country more than six days."

"Indeed; shall we have peace think you?"

"I do so, and I hope it may be so, for the sake of many who desire to return to their native land, and to those they love best."

Mr. Bradley heaved a deep sigh, which was echoed softly by all present, and the stranger looked from one to another, with a hasty glance, and then turned his gaze upon the fire.

"May I ask, sir, if you have any person whom you regard in the army--any relative?"

"Alas! I have--perhaps, I ought to say I had a son. I know not, however, where he is gone."

"Oh! a runaway; I see."

"Oh, no; he left because there were some family differences, and now, I would, that he were once more here."

"Oh!" said the stranger, softly, "differences and mistakes will happen now and then, when least desired."

At this moment, an old hound who had lain beside Ellen Mowbray, she who wore the coal-black tresses, lifted his head at the difference in sound that was noticed in the stranger's voice. He got up and slowly walked up to him, and began to smell around him, and, in another moment, he rushed at him with a cry of joy, and began to lick and caress him in the most extravagant manner. This was followed by a cry of joy in all present.

"It is Henry!" exclaimed Ellen Mowbray, rising and rushing into his arms.

It was Henry, and he threw off the several coats he had on, as well as the large beard he wore to disguise himself.

The meeting was a happy one; there was not a more joyful house than that within many miles around. Henry was restored to the arms of those who loved him, and, in a month, a wedding was celebrated between him and his cousin Ellen.

***

Sir Francis Varney glanced at his watch. It indicated but five minutes to twelve o'clock, and he sprang to his feet. Even as he did so, a loud knocking at the principal entrance to his house awakened every echo within its walls.

CHAPTER XXXII

THE THOUSAND POUNDS.--THE STRANGER'S PRECAUTIONS

Varney moved not now, nor did he speak, but, like a statue, he stood, with his unearthly looking eyes rivetted upon the door of the apartment.

In a few moments one of his servants came, and said--

"Sir, a person is here, who says he wants to see you. He desired me to say, that he had ridden far, and that moments were precious when the tide of life was ebbing fast."

"Yes! yes!" gasped Varney; "admit him, I know him! Bring him here? It is--an--old friend--of mine."

He sank into a chair, and still he kept his eyes fixed upon that door through which his visitor must come. Surely some secret of dreadful moment must be connected with him whom Sir Francis expected--dreaded--and yet dared not refuse to see. And now a footstep approaches--a slow and a solemn footstep--it pauses a moment at the door of the apartment, and then the servant flings it open, and a tall man enters. He is enveloped in the folds of a horseman's cloak, and there is the clank of spurs upon his heels as he walks into the room.

Varney rose again, but he said not a word and for a few moments they stood opposite each other in silence. The domestic has left the room, and the door is closed, so that there was nothing to prevent them from conversing; and, yet, silent they continued for some minutes. It seemed as if each was most anxious that the other should commence the conversation, first.

And yet there was nothing so very remarkable in the appearance of that stranger which should entirely justify Sir Francis Varney, in feeling so much alarm at his presence. He certainly was a man past the prime of life; and he looked like one who had battled much with misfortune, and as if time had not passed so lightly over his brow, but that it had left deep traces of its progress. The only thing positively bad about his countenance, was to be found in his eyes. There there was a most ungracious and sinister expression, a kind of lurking and suspicions look, as if he were always resolving in his mind some deep laid scheme, which might be sufficient to circumvent the whole of mankind.

Finding, probably, that Varney would not speak first, he let his cloak fall more loosely about him, and in a low, deep tone, he said,

"I presume I was expected?"

"You were," said Varney. "It is the day, and it is the hour."

"You are right. I like to see you so mindful. You don't improve in looks since--"

"Hush--hush! no more of that; can we not meet without a dreadful allusion to the past! There needs nothing to remind me of it; and your presence here now shows that you are not forgetful. Speak not of that fearful episode. Let no words combine to place it in a tangible shape to human understanding. I cannot, dare not, hear you speak of that."

"It is well," said the stranger; "as you please. Let our interview be brief. You know my errand?"

"I do. So fearful a drag upon limited means, is not likely to be readily forgotten."

"Oh, you are too ingenious--too full of well laid schemes, and to apt and ready in their execution, to feel, as any fearful drag, the conditions of our bargain. Why do you look at me so earnestly?"

"Because," said Varney--and he trembled as he spoke--"because each lineament of your countenance brings me back to the recollection of the only scene in life that made me shudder, and which I cannot think of, even with the indifference of contempt. I see it all before my mind's eye, coming in frightful panoramic array, those incidents, which even to dream of, are sufficient to drive the soul to madness; the dread of this annual visit, hangs upon me like a dark cloud upon my very heart; it sits like some foul incubus, destroying its vitality and dragging me, from day to day, nearer to that tomb, from whence not as before, I can emerge."

"You have been among the dead?" said the stranger.

"I have."

"And yet are mortal."

"Yes," repeated Varney, "yes, and yet am mortal."

"It was I that plucked you back to that world, which, to judge from your appearance, has had since that eventful period but few charms for you. By my faith you look like--"

"Like what I am," interrupted Varney.

"This is a subject that once a year gets frightfully renewed between us. For weeks before your visit I am haunted by frightful recollections, and it takes me many weeks after you are gone, before I can restore myself to serenity. Look at me; am I not an altered man?"

"In faith you are," said the stranger "I have no wish to press upon you painful recollections. And yet 'tis strange to me that upon such a man as you, the event to which you allude should produce so terrible an impression."

"I have passed through the agony of death," said Varney, "and have again endured the torture--for it is such--of the re-union of the body and the soul; not having endured so much, not the faintest echo of such feelings can enter into your imagination."

"There may be truth in that, and yet, like a fluttering moth round a flame, it seems to me, that when I do see you, you take a terrific kind of satisfaction in talking of the past."

"That is strictly true," said Varney; "the images with which my mind is filled are frightful. Pent up do they remain for twelve long months. I can speak to you, and you only, without disguise, and thus does it seem to me that I get rid of the uneasy load of horrible imaginings. When you are gone, and have been gone a sufficient lapse of time, my slumbers are not haunted with frightful images--I regain a comparative peace, until the time slowly comes around again, when we are doomed to meet."

"I understand you. You seem well lodged here?"

"I have ever kept my word, and sent to you, telling you where I am."

"You have, truly. I have no shadow of complaint to make against you. No one, could have more faithfully performed his bond than you have. I give you ample credit for all that, and long may you live still to perform your conditions."

"I dare not deceive you, although to keep such faith I may be compelled to deceive a hundred others."

"Of that I cannot judge. Fortune seems to smile upon you; you have not as yet disappointed me."

"And will not now," said Varney. "The gigantic and frightful penalty of disappointing you, stares me in the face. I dare not do so."

He took from his pocket, as he spoke, a clasped book, from which he produced several bank notes, which he placed before the stranger.

"A thousand pounds," he said; "that is the agreement."

"It is to the very letter. I do not return to you a thousand thanks--we understand each other better than to waste time with idle compliment. Indeed I will go quite as far as to say, truthfully, that did not my necessities require this amount from you, you should have the boon, for which you pay that price at a much cheaper rate."

"Enough! enough!" said Varney. "It is strange, that your face should have been the last I saw, when the world closed upon me, and the first that met my eyes when I was again snatched back to life! Do you pursue still your dreadful trade?"

"Yes," said the stranger, "for another year, and then, with such a moderate competence as fortune has assigned me, I retire, to make way for younger and abler spirits."

"And then," said Varney, "shall you still require of me such an amount as this?"

"No; this is my last visit but one. I shall be just and liberal towards you. You are not old; and I have no wish to become the clog of your existence. As I have before told you, it is my necessity, and not my inclination, that sets the value upon the service I rendered you."

"I understand you, and ought to thank you. And in reply to so much courtesy, be assured, that when I shudder at your presence, it is not that I regard you with horror, as an individual, but it is because the sight of you awakens mournfully the remembrance of the past."

"It is clear to me," said the stranger; "and now I think we part with each other in a better spirit than we ever did before; and when we meet again, the remembrance that it is the last time, will clear away the gloom that I now find hanging over you."

"It may! it may! With what an earnest gaze you still regard me!"

"I do. It does appear to me most strange, that time should not have obliterated the effects which I thought would have ceased with their cause. You are no more the man that in my recollection you once were, than I am like a sporting child."

"And I never shall be," said Varney; "never--never again! This self-same look which the hand of death had placed upon me, I shall ever wear. I shudder at myself, and as I oft perceive the eye of idle curiosity fixed steadfastly upon me, I wonder in my inmost heart, if even the wildest guesser hits upon the cause why I am not like unto other men?"

"No. Of that you may depend there is no suspicion; but I will leave you now; we part such friends, as men situated as we are can be. Once again shall we meet, and then farewell for ever."

"Do you leave England, then?"

"I do. You know my situation in life. It is not one which offers me inducements to remain. In some other land, I shall win the respect and attention I may not hope for here. There my wealth will win many golden opinions; and casting, as best I may, the veil of forgetfulness over my former life, my declining years may yet be happy. This money, that I have had of you from time to time, has been more pleasantly earned than all beside. Wrung, as it has been, from your fears, still have I taken it with less reproach. And now, farewell!"

Varney rang for a servant to show the stranger from the house, and without another word they parted.

Then, when he was alone, that mysterious owner of that costly home drew a long breath of apparently exquisite relief.

"That is over!--that is over!" he said. "He shall have the other thousand pounds, perchance, sooner than he thinks. With all expedition I will send it to him. And then on that subject I shall be at peace. I shall have paid a large sum; but that which I purchased was to me priceless. It was my life!--it was my life itself! That possession which the world's wealth cannot restore! And shall I grudge these thousands, which have found their way into this man's hands? No! 'Tis true, that existence, for me, has lost some of its most resplendent charms. 'Tis true, that I have no earthly affections, and that shunning companionship with all, I am alike shunned by all; and yet, while the life-blood still will circulate within my shrunken veins, I cling to vitality."

He passed into an inner room, and taking from a hook, on which it hung, a long, dark-coloured cloak, he enveloped his tall, unearthly figure within its folds.

Then, with his hat in his hand, he passed out of his house, and appeared to be taking his way towards Bannerworth House.

Surely it must be guilt of no common die that could oppress a man so destitute of human sympathies as Sir Francis Varney. The dreadful suspicions that hovered round him with respect to what he was, appeared to gather confirmation from every act of his existence.

Whether or not this man, to whom he felt bound to pay annually so large a sum, was in the secret, and knew him to be something more than earthly, we cannot at present declare; but it would seem from the tenor of their conversation as if such were the fact.

Perchance he had saved him from the corruption of the tomb, by placing out, on some sylvan spot, where the cold moonbeams fell, the apparently lifeless form, and now claimed so large a reward for such a service, and the necessary secrecy contingent upon it.

We say this may be so, and yet again some more natural and rational explanation may unexpectedly present itself; and there may be yet a dark page in Sir Francis Varney's life's volume, which will place him in a light of superadded terrors to our readers.

Time, and the now rapidly accumulating incidents of our tale, will soon tear aside the veil of mystery that now envelopes some of our dramatis personae.

And let us hope that in the development of those incidents we shall be enabled to rescue the beautiful Flora Bannerworth from the despairing gloom that is around her. Let us hope and even anticipate that we shall see her smile again; that the roseate hue of health will again revisit her cheeks, the light buoyancy of her step return, and that as before she may be the joy of all around her, dispensing and receiving happiness.

And, he too, that gallant fearless lover, he whom no chance of time or tide could sever from the object of his fond affections, he who listened to nothing but the dictates of his heart's best feelings, let us indulge a hope that he will have a bright reward, and that the sunshine of a permanent felicity will only seem the brighter for the shadows that for a time have obscured its glory.

CHAPTER XXXIII

THE STRANGE INTERVIEW.--THE CHASE THROUGH THE HALL

It was with the most melancholy aspect that anything human could well bear, that Sir Francis Varney took his lonely walk, although perhaps in saying so much, probably we are instituting a comparison which circumstances scarcely empower us to do; for who shall say that that singular man, around whom a very atmosphere of mystery seemed to be perpetually increasing, was human?

Averse as we are to believe in the supernatural, or even to invest humanity with any preternatural powers, the more than singular facts and circumstances surrounding the existence and the acts of that man bring to the mind a kind of shuddering conviction, that if he be indeed really mortal he still must possess some powers beyond ordinary mortality, and be walking the earth for some unhallowed purposes, such as ordinary men with the ordinary attributes of human nature can scarcely guess at.

Silently and alone he took his way through that beautiful tract of country, comprehending such picturesque charms of hill and dale which lay between his home and Bannerworth Hall. He was evidently intent upon reaching the latter place by the shortest possible route, and in the darkness of that night, for the moon had not yet risen, he showed no slight acquaintance with the intricacies of that locality, that he was at all enabled to pursue so undeviatingly a tract as that which he took.

He muttered frequently to himself low, indistinct words as he went, and chiefly did they seem to have reference to that strange interview he had so recently had with one who, from some combination of circumstances scarcely to be guessed at, evidently exercised a powerful control over him, and was enabled to make a demand upon his pecuniary resources of rather startling magnitude.

And yet, from a stray word or two, which were pronounced more distinctly, he did not seem to be thinking in anger over that interview; but it would appear that it rather had recalled to his remembrance circumstances of a painful and a degrading nature, which time had not been able entirely to obliterate from his recollection.

"Yes, yes," he said, as he paused upon the margin of the wood, to the confines of which he, or what seemed to be he, had once been chased by Marchdale and the Bannerworths--"yes, the very sight of that man recalls all the frightful pageantry of a horrible tragedy, which I can never--never forget. Never can it escape my memory, as a horrible, a terrific fact; but it is the sight of this man alone that can recall all its fearful minutiae to my mind, and paint to my imagination, in the most vivid colours, every, the least particular connected with that time of agony. These periodical visits much affect me. For months I dread them, and for months I am but slowly recovering from the shocks they give me. 'But once more,' he says--'but once more,' and then we shall not meet again. Well, well; perchance before that time arrives, I may be able to possess myself of those resources which will enable me to forestall his visit, and so at least free myself from the pang of expecting him."

He paused at the margin of the wood, and glanced in the direction of Bannerworth Hall. By the dim light which yet showed from out the light sky, he could discern the ancient gable ends, and turret-like windows; he could see the well laid out gardens, and the grove of stately firs that shaded it from the northern blasts, and, as he gazed, a strong emotion seemed to come over him, such as no one could have supposed would for one moment have possessed the frame of one so apparently unconnected with all human sympathies.

"I know this spot well," he said, "and my appearance here on that eventful occasion, when the dread of my approach induced a crime only second to murder itself, was on such a night as this, when all was so still and calm around, and when he who, at the merest shadow of my presence, rather chose to rush on death than be assured it was myself. Curses on the circumstances that so foiled me! I should have been most wealthy. I should have possessed the means of commanding the adulation of those who now hold me but cheaply; but still the time may come. I have a hope yet, and that greatness which I have ever panted for, that magician-like power over my kind, which the possession of ample means alone can give, may yet be mine."

Wrapping his cloak more closely around him, he strode forward with that long, noiseless step which was peculiar to him. Mechanically he appeared to avoid those obstacles of hedge and ditch which impeded his pathway. Surely he had come that road often, or he would not so easily have pursued his way. And now he stood by the edge of a plantation which in some measure protected from trespassers the more private gardens of the Hall, and there he paused, as if a feeling of irresolution had come over him, or it might be, as indeed it seemed from his subsequent conduct, that he had come without any fixed intention, or if with a fixed intention, without any regular plan of carrying it into effect.

Did he again dream of intruding into any of the chambers of that mansion, with the ghastly aspect of that terrible creation with which, in the minds of its inhabitants, he seemed to be but too closely identified? He was pale, attenuated, and trembled. Could it be that so soon it had become necessary to renew the life-blood in his veins in the awful manner which it is supposed the vampyre brood are compelled to protract their miserable existence?

It might be so, and that he was even now reflecting upon how once more he could kindle the fire of madness in the brain of that beautiful girl, who he had already made so irretrievably wretched.

He leant against an aged tree, and his strange, lustrous-looking eyes seemed to collect every wandering scintillation of light that was around, and to shine with preternatural intensity.

"I must, I will," he said, "be master of Bannerworth Hall. It must come to that. I have set an existence upon its possession, and I will have it; and then, if with my own hands I displace it brick by brick and stone by stone, I will discover that hidden secret which no one but myself now dreams of. It shall be done by force or fraud, by love or by despair, I care not which; the end shall sanctify all means. Ay, even if I wade through blood to my desire, I say it shall be done."

There was a holy and a still calmness about the night much at variance with the storm of angry passion that appeared to be momentarily gathering power in the breast of that fearful man. Not the least sound came from Bannerworth Hall, and it was only occasionally that from afar off on the night air there came the bark of some watchdog, or the low of distant cattle. All else was mute save when the deep sepulchral tones of that man, if man he was, gave an impulse to the soft air around him.

With a strolling movement as if he were careless if he proceeded in that direction or not, he still went onward toward the house, and now he stood by that little summer-house once so sweet and so dear a retreat, in which the heart-stricken Flora had held her interview with him whom she loved with a devotion unknown to meaner minds.

This spot scarcely commanded any view of the house, for so enclosed was it among evergreens and blooming flowers, that it seemed like a very wilderness of nature, upon which, with liberal hand, she had showered down in wild luxuriance her wildest floral beauties.

In and around that spot the night air was loaded with sweets. The mingled perfume of many flowers made that place seem a very paradise. But oh, how sadly at variance with that beauty and contentedness of nature was he who stood amidst such beauty! All incapable as he was of appreciating its tenderness, or of gathering the faintest moral from its glory.

"Why am I here?" he said. "Here, without fixed design or stability of purpose, like some miser who has hidden his own hoards so deeply within the bowels of the earth he cannot hope that he shall ever again be able to bring them to the light of day. I hover around this spot which I feel--which I know--contains my treasure, though I cannot lay my hands upon it, or exult in its glistening beauty."

Even as he spoke he cowered down like some guilty thing, for he heard a faint footstep upon the garden path. So light, so fragile was the step, that, in the light of day, the very hum of summer insects would have drowned the noise; but he heard it, that man of crime--of unholy and awful impulses. He heard it, and he shrunk down among the shrubs and flowers till he was hidden completely from observation amid a world of fragrant essences.

Was it some one stealthily in that place even as he was, unwelcome or unknown? or was it one who had observed him intrude upon the privacy of those now unhappy precincts, and who was coming to deal upon him that death which, vampyre though he might be, he was yet susceptible of from mortal hands?

The footstep advanced, and lower down he shrunk until his coward-heart beat against the very earth itself. He knew that he was unarmed, a circumstance rare with him, and only to be accounted for by the disturbance of his mind consequent upon the visit of that strange man to his house, whose presence had awakened so many conflicting emotions.

Nearer and nearer still came that light footstep, and his deep-seated fears would not let him perceive that it was not the step of caution or of treachery, but owed its lightness to the natural grace and freedom of movement of its owner.

The moon must have arisen, although obscured by clouds, through which it cast but a dim radiance, for the night had certainly grown lighter; so that although there were no strong shadows cast, a more diffused brightness was about all things, and their outlines looked not so dancing, and confused the one with the other.

He strained his eyes in the direction whence the sounds proceeded, and then his fears for his personal safety vanished, for he saw it was a female form that was slowly advancing towards him.

His first impulse was to rise, for with the transient glimpse he got of it, he knew that it must be Flora Bannerworth; but a second thought, probably one of intense curiosity to know what could possibly have brought her to such a spot at such a time, restrained him, and he was quiet. But if the surprise of Sir Francis Varney was great to see Flora Bannerworth at such a time in such a place, we have no doubt, that with the knowledge which our readers have of her, their astonishment would more than fully equal his; and when we come to consider, that since that eventful period when the sanctity of her chamber had been so violated by that fearful midnight visitant, it must appear somewhat strange that she could gather courage sufficient to wander forth alone at such an hour.

Had she no dread of meeting that unearthly being? Did the possibility that she might fall into his ruthless grasp, not come across her mind with a shuddering consciousness of its probability? Had she no reflection that each step she took, was taking her further and further from those who would aid her in all extremities? It would seem not, for she walked onward, unheeding, and apparently unthinking of the presence, possible or probable, of that bane of her existence.

But let us look at her again. How strange and spectral-like she moves along; there seems no speculation in her countenance, but with a strange and gliding step, she walks like some dim shadow of the past in that ancient garden. She is very pale, and on her brow there is the stamp of suffering; her dress is a morning robe, she holds it lightly round her, and thus she moves forward towards that summer-house which probably to her was sanctified by having witnessed those vows of pure affection, which came from the lips of Charles Holland, about whose fate there now hung so great a mystery.

Has madness really seized upon the brain of that beautiful girl? Has the strong intellect really sunk beneath the oppressions to which it has been subjected? Does she now walk forth with a disordered intellect, the queen of some fantastic realm, viewing the material world with eyes that are not of earth; shunning perhaps that which she should have sought, and, perchance, in her frenzy, seeking that which in a happier frame of mind she would have shunned.

Such might have been the impression of any one who had looked upon her for a moment, and who knew the disastrous scenes through which she had so recently passed; but we can spare our readers the pangs of such a supposition. We have bespoken their love for Flora Bannerworth, and we are certain that she has it; therefore would we spare them, even for a few brief moments, from imagining that cruel destiny had done its worst, and that the fine and beautiful spirit we have so much commended had lost its power of rational reflection. No; thank Heaven, such is not the case. Flora Bannerworth is not mad, but under the strong influence of some eccentric dream, which has pictured to her mind images which have no home but in the airy realms of imagination. She has wandered forth from her chamber to that sacred spot where she had met him she loved, and heard the noblest declaration of truth and constancy that ever flowed from human lips.

Yes, she is sleeping; but, with a precision such as the somnambulist so strangely exerts, she trod the well-known paths slowly, but surely, toward that summer's bower, where her dreams had not told her lay crouching that most hideous spectre of her imagination, Sir Francis Varney. He who stood between her and her heart's best joy; he who had destroyed all hope of happiness, and who had converted her dearest affections into only so many causes of greater disquietude than the blessings they should have been to her.

Oh! could she have imagined but for one moment that he was there, with what an eagerness of terror would she have flown back again to the shelter of those walls, where at least was to be found some protection from the fearful vampyre's embrace, and where she would be within hail of friendly hearts, who would stand boldly between her and every thought of harm.

But she knew it not, and onwards she went until the very hem of her garment touched the face of Sir Francis Varney.

And he was terrified--he dared not move--he dared not speak! The idea that she had died, and that this was her spirit, come to wreak some terrible vengeance upon him, for a time possessed him, and so paralysed with fear was he, that he could neither move nor speak.

It had been well if, during that trance of indecision in which his coward heart placed him, Flora had left the place, and again sought her home; but unhappily such an impulse came not over her; she sat upon that rustic seat, where she had reposed when Charles had clasped her to his heart, and through her very dream the remembrance of that pure affection came across her, and in the tenderest and most melodious accents, she said,--

"Charles! Charles! and do you love me still? No--no; you have not forsaken me. Save me, save me from the vampyre!"

She shuddered, and Sir Francis Varney heard her weeping.

"Fool that I am," he muttered, "to be so terrified. She sleeps. This is one of the phases which a disordered imagination oft puts on. She sleeps, and perchance this may be an opportunity of further increasing the dread of my visitation, which shall make Bannerworth Hall far too terrible a dwelling-place for her; and well I know, if she goes, they will all go. It will become a deserted house, and that is what I want. A house, too, with such an evil reputation, that none but myself, who have created that reputation, will venture within its walls:--a house, which superstition will point out as the abode of evil spirits;--a house, as it were, by general opinion, ceded to the vampyre. Yes, it shall be my own; fit dwelling-place for a while for me. I have sworn it shall be mine, and I will keep my oath, little such as I have to do with vows."

He rose, and moved slowly to the narrow entrance of the summer-house; a movement he could make, without at all disturbing Flora, for the rustic seat, on which she sat, was at its further extremity. And there he stood, the upper part of his gaunt and hideous form clearly defined upon the now much lighter sky, so that if Flora Bannerworth had not been in that trance of sleep in which she really was, one glance upward would let her see the hideous companion she had, in that once much-loved spot--a spot hitherto sacred to the best and noblest feelings, but now doomed for ever to be associated with that terrific spectre of despair.

But she was in no state to see so terrible a sight. Her hands were over her face, and she was weeping still.

"Surely, he loves me," she whispered; "he has said he loved me, and he does not speak in vain. He loves me still, and I shall again look upon his face, a Heaven to me! Charles! Charles! you will come again? Surely, they sin against the divinity of love, who would tell me that you love me not!"

"Ha!" muttered Varney, "this passion is her first, and takes a strong hold on her young heart--she loves him--but what are human affections to me? I have no right to count myself in the great muster-roll of humanity. I look not like an inhabitant of the earth, and yet am on it. I love no one, expect no love from any one, but I will make humanity a slave to me; and the lip-service of them who hate me in their hearts, shall be as pleasant jingling music to my ear, as if it were quite sincere! I will speak to this girl; she is not mad--perchance she may be."

There was a diabolical look of concentrated hatred upon Varney's face, as he now advanced two paces towards the beautiful Flora.

CHAPTER XXXIV

THE THREAT.--ITS CONSEQUENCES.--THE RESCUE, AND SIR FRANCIS VARNEY'S DANGER

Sir Francis Varney now paused again, and he seemed for a few moments to gloat over the helpless condition of her whom he had so determined to make his victim; there was no look of pity in his face, no one touch of human kindness could be found in the whole expression of those diabolical features; and if he delayed making the attempt to strike terror into the heart of that unhappy, but beautiful being, it could not be from any relenting feeling, but simply, that he wished for a few moments to indulge his imagination with the idea of perfecting his villany more effectually.

Alas! and they who would have flown to her rescue,--they, who for her would have chanced all accidents, ay, even life itself, were sleeping, and knew not of the loved one's danger. She was alone, and far enough from the house, to be driven to that tottering verge where sanity ends, and the dream of madness, with all its terrors, commences.

But still she slept--if that half-waking sleep could indeed be considered as any thing akin to ordinary slumber--still she slept, and called mournfully upon her lover's name; and in tender, beseeching accents, that should have melted even the stubbornest hearts, did she express her soul's conviction that he loved her still.

The very repetition of the name of Charles Holland seemed to be galling to Sir Francis Varney. He made a gesture of impatience, as she again uttered it, and then, stepping forward, he stood within a pace of where she sat, and in a fearfully distinct voice he said,--

"Flora Bannerworth, awake! awake! and look upon me, although the sight blast and drive you to despair. Awake! awake!"

It was not the sound of the voice which aroused her from that strange slumber. It is said that those who sleep in that eccentric manner, are insensible to sounds, but that the lightest touch will arouse them in an instant; and so it was in this case, for Sir Francis Varney, as he spoke, laid upon the hand of Flora two of his cold, corpse-like looking fingers. A shriek burst from her lips, and although the confusion of her memory and conceptions was immense, yet she was awake, and the somnambulistic trance had left her.

"Help, help!" she cried. "Gracious Heavens! Where am I?"

Varney spoke not, but he spread out his long, thin arms in such a manner that he seemed almost to encircle her, while he touched her not, so that escape became a matter of impossibility, and to attempt to do so, must have been to have thrown herself into his hideous embrace.

She could obtain but a single view of the face and figure of him who opposed her progress, but, slight as that view was, it more than sufficed. The very extremity of fear came across her, and she sat like one paralysed; the only evidence of existence she gave consisting in the words,--

"The vampyre--the vampyre!"

"Yes," said Varney, "the vampyre. You know me, Flora Bannerworth--Varney, the vampyre; your midnight guest at that feast of blood. I am the vampyre. Look upon me well; shrink not from my gaze. You will do well not to shun me, but to speak to me in such a shape that I may learn to love you."

Flora shook as in a convulsion, and she looked as white as any marble statue.

"This is horrible!" she said. "Why does not Heaven grant me the death I pray for?"

"Hold!" said Varney. "Dress not up in the false colours of the imagination that which in itself is sufficiently terrific to need none of the allurements of romance. Flora Bannerworth, you are persecuted--persecuted by me, the vampyre. It is my fate to persecute you; for there are laws to the invisible as well as the visible creation that force even such a being as I am to play my part in the great drama of existence. I am a vampyre; the sustenance that supports this frame must be drawn from the life-blood of others."

"Oh, horror--horror!"

"But most I do affect the young and beautiful. It is from the veins of such as thou art, Flora Bannerworth, that I would seek the sustenance I'm compelled to obtain for my own exhausted energies. But never yet, in all my long career--a career extending over centuries of time--never yet have I felt the soft sensation of human pity till I looked on thee, exquisite piece of excellence. Even at the moment when the reviving fluid from the gushing fountain of your veins was warming at my heart, I pitied and I loved you. Oh, Flora! even I can now feel the pang of being what I am!"

There was a something in the tone, a touch of sadness in the manner, and a deep sincerity in these words, that in some measure disabused Flora of her fears. She sobbed hysterically, and a gush of tears came to her relief, as, in almost inarticulate accents, she said,--

"May the great God forgive even you!"

"I have need of such a prayer," exclaimed Varney--"Heaven knows I have need of such a prayer. May it ascend on the wings of the night air to the throne of Heaven. May it be softly whispered by ministering angels to the ear of Divinity. God knows I have need of such a prayer!"

"To hear you speak in such a strain," said Flora, "calms the excited fancy, and strips even your horrible presence of some of its maddening influence."

"Hush," said the vampire, "you must hear more--you must know more ere you speak of the matters that have of late exercised an influence of terror over you."

"But how came I here?" said Flora, "tell me that. By what more than earthly power have you brought me to this spot? If I am to listen to you, why should it not be at some more likely time and place?"

"I have powers," said Varney, assuming from Flora's words, that she would believe such arrogance--"I have powers which suffice to bend many purposes to my will--powers incidental to my position, and therefore is it I have brought you here to listen to that which should make you happier than you are."

"I will attend," said Flora. "I do not shudder now; there's an icy coldness through my veins, but it is the night air--speak, I will attend you."

"I will. Flora Bannerworth, I am one who has witnessed time's mutations on man and on his works, and I have pitied neither; I have seen the fall of empires, and sighed not that high reaching ambition was toppled to the dust. I have seen the grave close over the young and the beautiful--those whom I have doomed by my insatiable thirst for human blood to death, long ere the usual span of life was past, but I never loved till now."

"Can such a being as you," said Flora "be susceptible of such an earthly passion?"

"And wherefore not?"

"Love is either too much of heaven, or too much of earth to find a home with thee."

"No, Flora, no! it may be that the feeling is born of pity. I will save you--I will save you from a continuance of the horrors that are assailing you."

"Oh! then may Heaven have mercy in your hour of need!"

"Amen!"

"May you even yet know peace and joy above."

"It is a faint and straggling hope--but if achieved, it will be through the interposition of such a spirit as thine, Flora, which has already exercised so benign an influence upon my tortured soul, as to produce the wish within my heart, to do a least one unselfish action."

"That wish," said Flora, "shall be father to the deed. Heaven has boundless mercy yet."

"For thy sweet sake, I will believe so much, Flora Bannerworth; it is a condition with my hateful race, that if we can find one human heart to love us, we are free. If, in the face of Heaven, you will consent to be mine, you will snatch me from a continuance of my frightful doom, and for your pure sake, and on your merits, shall I yet know heavenly happiness. Will you be mine?"

A cloud swept from off the face of the moon, and a slant ray fell upon the hideous features of the vampire. He looked as if just rescued from some charnel-house, and endowed for a space with vitality to destroy all beauty and harmony in nature, and drive some benighted soul to madness.

"No, no, no!" shrieked Flora, "never!"

"Enough," said Varney, "I am answered. It was a bad proposal. I am a vampyre still."

"Spare me! spare me!"

"Blood!"

Flora sank upon her knees, and uplifted her hands to heaven. "Mercy, mercy!" she said.

"Blood!" said Varney, and she saw his hideous, fang-like teeth. "Blood! Flora Bannerworth, the vampyre's motto. I have asked you to love me, and you will not--the penalty be yours."

"No, no!" said Flora. "Can it be possible that even you, who have already spoken with judgment and precision, can be so unjust? you must feel that, in all respects, I have been a victim, most gratuitously--a sufferer, while there existed no just cause that I should suffer; one who has been tortured, not from personal fault, selfishness, lapse of integrity, or honourable feelings, but because you have found it necessary, for the prolongation of your terrific existence, to attack me as you have done. By what plea of honour, honesty, or justice, can I be blamed for not embracing an alternative which is beyond all human control?--I cannot love you."

"Then be content to suffer. Flora Bannerworth, will you not, even for a time, to save yourself and to save me, become mine?"

"Horrible proposition!"

"Then am I doomed yet, perhaps, for many a cycle of years, to spread misery and desolation around me; and yet I love you with a feeling which has in it more of gratefulness and unselfishness than ever yet found a home within my breast. I would fain have you, although you cannot save me; there may yet be a chance, which shall enable you to escape from the persecution of my presence."

"Oh! glorious chance!" said Flora. "Which way can it come? tell me how I may embrace it, and such grateful feelings as a heart-stricken mourner can offer to him who has rescued her from her deep affliction, shall yet be yours."

"Hear me, then, Flora Bannerworth, while I state to you some particulars of mysterious existence, of such beings as myself, which never yet have been breathed to mortal ears."

Flora looked intently at him, and listened, while, with a serious earnestness of manner, he detailed to her something of the physiology of the singular class of beings which the concurrence of all circumstances tended to make him appear.

"Flora," he said, "it is not that I am so enamoured of an existence to be prolonged only by such frightful means, which induces me to become a terror to you or to others. Believe me, that if my victims, those whom my insatiable thirst for blood make wretched, suffer much, I, the vampyre, am not without my moments of unutterable agony. But it is a mysterious law of our nature, that as the period approaches when the exhausted energies of life require a new support from the warm, gushing fountain of another's veins, the strong desire to live grows upon us, until, in a paroxysm of wild insanity, which will recognise no obstacles, human or divine, we seek a victim."

"A fearful state!" said Flora.

"It is so; and, when the dreadful repast is over, then again the pulse beats healthfully, and the wasted energies of a strange kind of vitality are restored to us, we become calm again, but with that calmness comes all the horror, all the agony of reflection, and we suffer far more than tongue can tell."

"You have my pity," said Flora; "even you have my pity."

"I might well demand it, if such a feeling held a place within your breast. I might well demand your pity, Flora Bannerworth, for never crawled an abject wretch upon the earth's rotundity, so pitiable as I."

"Go on, go on."

"I will, and with such brief conclusions as I may. Having once attacked any human being, we feel a strange, but terribly impulsive desire again to seek that person for more blood. But I love you, Flora; the small amount of sensibility that still lingers about my preternatural existence, acknowledges in you a pure and better spirit. I would fain save you."

"Oh! tell me how I may escape the terrible infliction."

"That can only be done by flight. Leave this place, I implore you! leave it as quickly as the movement may be made. Linger not--cast not one regretful look behind you on your ancient home. I shall remain in this locality for years. Let me lose sight of you, I will not pursue you; but, by force of circumstances, I am myself compelled to linger here. Flight is the only means by which you may avoid a doom as terrific as that which I endure."

"But tell me," said Flora, after a moment's pause, during which she appeared to be endeavouring to gather courage to ask some fearful question; "tell me if it be true that those who have once endured the terrific attack of a vampyre, become themselves, after death, one of that dread race?"

"It is by such means," said Varney, "that the frightful brood increases; but time and circumstances must aid the development of the new and horrible existence. You, however, are safe."

"Safe! Oh! say that word again."

"Yes, safe; not once or twice will the vampyre's attack have sufficient influence on your mortal frame, as to induce a susceptibility on your part to become coexistent with such as he. The attacks must be often repeated, and the termination of mortal existence must be a consequence essential, and direct from those attacks, before such a result may be anticipated."

"Yes, yes; I understand."

"If you were to continue my victim from year to year, the energies of life would slowly waste away, and, till like some faint taper's gleam, consuming more sustenance than it received, the veriest accident would extinguish your existence, and then, Flora Bannerworth, you might become a vampyre."

"Oh! horrible! most horrible!"

"If by chance, or by design, the least glimpse of the cold moonbeams rested on your apparently lifeless remains, you would rise again and be one of us--a terror to yourself and a desolation to all around."

"Oh! I will fly from here," said Flora. "The hope of escape from so terrific and dreadful a doom shall urge me onward; if flight can save me--flight from Bannerworth Hall, I will pause not until continents and oceans divide us."

"It is well. I'm able now thus calmly to reason with you. A few short months more and I shall feel the languor of death creeping over me, and then will come that mad excitement of the brain, which, were you hidden behind triple doors of steel, would tempt me again to seek your chamber--again to seize you in my full embrace--again to draw from your veins the means of prolonged life--again to convulse your very soul with terror."

"I need no incentives," said Flora, with a shudder, "in the shape of descriptions of the past, to urge me on."

"You will fly from Bannerworth Hall?"

"Yes, yes!" said Flora, "it shall be so; its very chambers now are hideous with the recollection of scenes enacted in them. I will urge my brothers, my mother, all to leave, and in some distant clime we will find security and shelter. There even we will learn to think of you with more of sorrow than of anger--more pity than reproach--more curiosity than loathing."

"Be it so," said the vampyre; and he clasped his hands, as if with a thankfulness that he had done so much towards restoring peace at least to one, who, in consequence of his acts, had felt such exquisite despair. "Be it so; and even I will hope that the feelings which have induced so desolated and so isolated a being as myself to endeavour to bring peace to one human heart, will plead for me, trumpet-tongued, to Heaven!"

"It will--it will," said Flora.

"Do you think so?"

"I do; and I will pray that the thought may turn to certainty in such a cause."

The vampyre appeared to be much affected; and then he added,--

"Flora, you know that this spot has been the scene of a catastrophe fearful to look back upon, in the annals of your family?"

"It has," said Flora. "I know to what you allude; 'tis a matter of common knowledge to all--a sad theme to me, and one I would not court."

"Nor would I oppress you with it. Your father, here, on this very spot, committed that desperate act which brought him uncalled for to the judgment seat of God. I have a strange, wild curiosity upon such subjects. Will you, in return for the good that I have tried to do you, gratify it?"

"I know not what you mean," said Flora.

"To be more explicit, then, do you remember the day on which your father breathed his last?"

"Too well--too well."

"Did you see him or converse with him shortly before that desperate act was committed?"

"No; he shut himself up for some time in a solitary chamber."

"Ha! what chamber?"

"The one in which I slept myself on the night--"

"Yes, yes; the one with the portrait--that speaking portrait--the eyes of which seem to challenge an intruder as he enters the apartment."

"The same."

"For hours shut up there!" added Varney, musingly; "and from thence he wandered to the garden, where, in this summer-house, he breathed his last?"

"It was so."

"Then, Flora, ere I bid you adieu--"

These words were scarcely uttered, when there was a quick, hasty footstep, and Henry Bannerworth appeared behind Varney, in the very entrance of the summer-house.

"Now," he cried, "for revenge! Now, foul being, blot upon the earth's surface, horrible imitation of humanity, if mortal arm can do aught against you, you shall die!"

A shriek came from the lips of Flora, and flinging herself past Varney, who stepped aside, she clung to her brother, who made an unavailing pass with his sword at the vampyre. It was a critical moment; and had the presence of mind of Varney deserted him in the least, unarmed as he was, he must have fallen beneath the weapon of Henry. To spring, however, up the seat which Flora had vacated, and to dash out some of the flimsy and rotten wood-work at the back of the summer-house by the propulsive power of his whole frame, was the work of a moment; and before Henry could free himself from the clinging embrace of Flora, Varney, the vampyre was gone, and there was no greater chance of his capture than on a former occasion, when he was pursued in vain from the Hall to the wood, in the intricacies of which he was so entirely lost.

CHAPTER XXXV

THE EXPLANATION.--MARCHDALE'S ADVICE.--THE PROJECTED REMOVAL, AND THE ADMIRAL'S ANGER

This extremely sudden movement on the part of Varney was certainly as unexpected as it was decisive. Henry had imagined, that by taking possession of the only entrance to the summer-house, he must come into personal conflict with the being who had worked so much evil for him and his; and that he should so suddenly have created for himself another mode of exit, certainly never occurred to him.

"For Heaven's sake, Flora," he said, "unhand me; this is a time for action."

"But, Henry, Henry, hear me."

"Presently, presently, dear Flora; I will yet make another effort to arrest the headlong flight of Varney."

He shook her off, perhaps with not more roughness than was necessary to induce her to forego her grasp of him, but in a manner that fully showed he intended to be free; and then he sprang through the same aperture whence Varney had disappeared, just as George and Mr. Marchdale arrived at the door of the summer-house.

It was nearly morning, so that the fields were brightening up with the faint radiance of the coming day; and when Henry reached a point which he knew commanded an extensive view, he paused, and ran his eye eagerly along the landscape, with a hope of discovering some trace of the fugitive.

Such, however, was not the case; he saw nothing, heard nothing of Sir Francis Varney; and then he turned, and called loudly to George to join him, and was immediately replied to by his brother's presence, accompanied by Marchdale.

Before, however, they could exchange a word, a rattling discharge of fire-arms took place from one of the windows, and they heard the admiral, in a loud voice, shouting,--

"Broadside to broadside! Give it them again, Jack! Hit them between wind and water!"

Then there was another rattling discharge, and Henry exclaimed,--

"What is the meaning of that firing?"

"It comes from the admiral's room," said Marchdale. "On my life, I think the old man must be mad. He has some six or eight pistols ranged in a row along the window-sill, and all loaded, so that by the aid of a match they can be pretty well discharged as a volley, which he considers the only proper means of firing upon the vampyre."

"It is so," replied George; "and, no doubt, hearing an alarm, he has commenced operations by firing into the enemy."

"Well, well," said Henry; "he must have his way. I have pursued Varney thus far, and that he has again retreated to the wood, I cannot doubt. Between this and the full light of day, let us at least make an effort to discover his place of retreat. We know the locality as well as he can possibly, and I propose now that we commence an active search."

"Come on, then," said Marchdale. "We are all armed; and I, for one, shall feel no hesitation in taking the life, if it be possible to do so, of that strange being."

"Of that possibility you doubt?" said George, as they hurried on across the meadows.

"Indeed I do, and with reason too. I'm certain that when I fired at him before I hit him; and besides, Flora must have shot him upon the occasion when we were absent, and she used your pistols Henry, to defend herself and her mother."

"It would seem so," said Henry; "and disregarding all present circumstances, if I do meet him, I will put to the proof whether he be mortal or not."

The distance was not great, and they soon reached the margin of the wood; they then separated agreeing to meet within it, at a well-spring, familiar to them all: previous to which each was to make his best endeavour to discover if any one was hidden among the bush-wood or in the hollows of the ancient trees they should encounter on their line of march.

The fact was, that Henry finding that he was likely to pass an exceedingly disturbed, restless night, through agitation of spirits, had, after tossing to and fro on his couch for many hours, wisely at length risen, and determined to walk abroad in the gardens belonging to the mansion, in preference to continuing in such a state of fever and anxiety, as he was in, in his own chamber.

Since the vampyre's dreadful visit, it had been the custom of both the brothers, occasionally, to tap at the chamber door of Flora, who, at her own request, now that she had changed her room, and dispensed with any one sitting up with her, wished occasionally to be communicated with by some member of the family.

Henry, then, after rapidly dressing, as he passed the door of her bedroom, was about to tap at it, when to his surprise he found it open, and upon hastily entering it he observed that the bed was empty, and a hasty glance round the apartment convinced him that Flora was not there.

Alarm took possession of him, and hastily arming himself, he roused Marchdale and George, but without waiting for them to be ready to accompany him, he sought the garden, to search it thoroughly in case she should be anywhere there concealed.

Thus it was he had come upon the conference so strangely and so unexpectedly held between Varney and Flora in the summer-house. With what occurred upon that discovery the readers are acquainted.

Flora had promised George that she would return immediately to the house, but when, in compliance with the call of Henry, George and Marchdale had left her alone, she felt so agitated and faint that she began to cling to the trellis work of the little building for a few moments before she could gather strength to reach the mansion.

Two or three minutes might thus have elapsed, and Flora was in such a state of mental bewilderment with all that had occurred, that she could scarce believe it real, when suddenly a slight sound attracted her attention, and through the gap which had been made in the wall of the summer-house, with an appearance of perfect composure, again appeared Sir Francis Varney.

"Flora," he said, quietly resuming the discourse which had been broken off, "I am quite convinced now that you will be much the happier for the interview."

"Gracious Heaven!" said Flora, "whence have you come from?"

"I have never left," said Varney.

"But I saw you fly from this spot."

"You did; but it was only to another immediately outside the summer house. I had no idea of breaking off our conference so abruptly."

"Have you anything to add to what you have already stated?"

"Absolutely nothing, unless you have a question to propose to me--I should have thought you had, Flora. Is there no other circumstance weighing heavily upon your mind, as well as the dreadful visitation I have subjected you to?"

"Yes," said Flora. "What has become of Charles Holland?"

"Listen. Do not discard all hope; when you are far from here you will meet with him again."

"But he has left me."

"And yet he will be able, when you again encounter him, so far to extenuate his seeming perfidy, that you shall hold him as untouched in honour as when first he whispered to you that he loved you."

"Oh, joy! joy!" said Flora; "by that assurance you have robbed misfortune of its sting, and richly compensated me for all that I have suffered."

"Adieu!" said the vampyre. "I shall now proceed to my own home by a different route to that taken by those who would kill me."

"But after this," said Flora, "there shall be no danger; you shall be held harmless, and our departure from Bannerworth Hall shall be so quick, that you will soon be released from all apprehension of vengeance from my brother, and I shall taste again of that happiness which I thought had fled from me for ever."

"Farewell," said the vampire; and folding his cloak closely around him, he strode from the summer-house, soon disappearing from her sight behind the shrubs and ample vegetation with which that garden abounded.

Flora sunk upon her knees, and uttered a brief, but heartfelt thanksgiving to Heaven for this happy change in her destiny. The hue of health faintly again visited her cheeks, and as she now, with a feeling of more energy and strength than she had been capable of exerting for many days, walked towards the house, she felt all that delightful sensation which the mind experiences when it is shaking off the trammels of some serious evil which it delights now to find that the imagination has attired in far worse colours than the facts deserved.

It is scarcely necessary, after this, to say that the search in the wood for Sir Francis Varney was an unproductive one, and that the morning dawned upon the labours of the brother and of Mr. Marchdale, without their having discovered the least indication of the presence of Varney. Again puzzled and confounded, they stood on the margin of the wood, and looked sadly towards the brightening windows of Bannerworth Hall, which were now reflecting with a golden radiance the slant rays of the morning sun.

"Foiled again," remarked Henry, with a gesture of impatience; "foiled again, and as completely as before. I declare that I will fight this man, let our friend the admiral say what he will against such a measure I will meet him in mortal combat; he shall consummate his triumph over our whole family by my death, or I will rid the world and ourselves of so frightful a character."

"Let us hope," said Marchdale, "that some other course may be adopted, which shall put an end to these proceedings."

"That," exclaimed Henry, "is to hope against all probability; what other course can be pursued? Be this Varney man or devil, he has evidently marked us for his prey."

"Indeed, it would seem so," remarked George; "but yet he shall find that we will not fall so easily; he shall discover that if poor Flora's gentle spirit has been crushed by these frightful circumstances, we are of a sterner mould."

"He shall," said Henry; "I for one will dedicate my life to this matter. I will know no more rest than is necessary to recruit my frame, until I have succeeded in overcoming this monster; I will seek no pleasure here, and will banish from my mind, all else that may interfere with that one fixed pursuit. He or I must fall."

"Well spoken," said Marchdale; "and yet I hope that circumstances may occur to prevent such a necessity of action, and that probably you will yet see that it will be wise and prudent to adopt a milder and a safer course."

"No, Marchdale, you cannot feel as we feel. You look on more as a spectator, sympathising with the afflictions of either, than feeling the full sting of those afflictions yourself."

"Do I not feel acutely for you? I'm a lonely man in the world, and I have taught myself now to centre my affections in your family; my recollections of early years assist me in so doing. Believe me, both of you, that I am no idle spectator of your griefs, but that I share them fully. If I advise you to be peaceful, and to endeavour by the gentlest means possible to accomplish your aims, it is not that I would counsel you cowardice; but having seen so much more of the world than either of you have had time or opportunity of seeing, I do not look so enthusiastically upon matters, but, with a cooler, calmer judgment, I do not say a better, I proffer to you my counsel."

"We thank you," said Henry; "but this is a matter in which action seems specially called for. It is not to be borne that a whole family is to be oppressed by such a fiend in human shape as that Varney."

"Let me," said Marchdale, "counsel you to submit to Flora's decision in this business; let her wishes constitute the rules of action. She is the greatest sufferer, and the one most deeply interested in the termination of this fearful business. Moreover she has judgment and decision of character--she will advise you rightly, be assured."

"That she would advise us honourably," said Henry, "and that we should feel every disposition in the world to defer to her wishes our proposition, is not to be doubted; but little shall be done without her counsel and sanction. Let us now proceed homeward, for I am most anxious to ascertain how it came about that she and Sir Francis Varney were together in that summer-house at so strange an hour."

They all three walked together towards the house, conversing in a similar strain as they went.

CHAPTER XXXVI

THE CONSULTATION.--THE DUEL AND ITS RESULTS

Independent of this interview which Flora had had with the much dreaded Sir Francis Varney, the circumstances in which she and all who were dear to her, happened at that moment to be placed, certainly required an amount of consideration, which could not be too soon bestowed.

By a combination of disagreeables, everything that could possibly occur to disturb the peace of the family seemed to have taken place at once; like Macbeth's, their troubles had truly come in battalions, and now that the serenity of their domestic position was destroyed, minor evils and annoyances which that very serenity had enabled them to hold at arm's-length became gigantic, and added much to their distress.

The small income, which, when all was happiness, health and peace, was made to constitute a comfortable household, was now totally inadequate to do so--the power to economise and to make the most of a little, had flown along with that contentedness of spirit which the harmony of circumstances alone could produce.

It was not to be supposed that poor Mrs. Bannerworth could now, as she had formerly done, when her mind was free from anxiety, attend to those domestic matters which make up the comforts of a family--distracted at the situation of her daughter, and bewildered by the rapid succession of troublesome events which so short a period of time had given birth to, she fell into an inert state of mind as different as anything could possibly be, from her former active existence.

It has likewise been seen how the very domestics fled from Bannerworth Hall in dismay, rather than remain beneath the same roof with a family believed to be subject to the visitations of so awful a being as a vampyre.

Among the class who occupy positions of servitude, certainly there might have been found some, who, with feelings and understandings above such considerations, would have clung sympathetically to that family in distress, which they had known under a happier aspect; but it had not been the good fortune of the Bannerworths to have such as these about them; hence selfishness had its way, and they were deserted. It was not likely, then, that strangers would willingly accept service in a family so situated, without some powerful impulse in the shape of a higher pecuniary consideration, as was completely out of the power of the Bannerworths to offer.

Thus was it, then, that most cruelly, at the very time that they had most need of assistance and of sympathy, this unfortunate family almost became isolated from their kind; and, apart from every other consideration, it would have been almost impossible for them to continue inhabitants of the Hall, with anything like comfort, or advantage.

And then, although the disappearance of Charles Holland no longer awakened those feelings of indignation at his supposed perfidy which were first produced by that event; still, view it in which way they might, it was a severe blow of fate, and after it, they one and all found themselves still less able to contend against the sea of troubles that surrounded them.

The reader, too, will not have failed to remark that there was about the whole of the family that pride of independence which induced them to shrink from living upon extraneous aid; and hence, although they felt and felt truly, that when Admiral Bell, in his frank manner, offered them pecuniary assistance, that it was no idle compliment, yet with a sensitiveness such as they might well be expected to feel, they held back, and asked each other what prospect there was of emerging from such a state of things, and if it were justifiable to commence a life of dependence, the end of which was not evident or tangible.

Notwithstanding, too, the noble confidence of Flora in her lover, and notwithstanding that confidence had been echoed by her brothers, there would at times obtrude into the minds of the latter, a feeling of the possibility, that after all they might be mistaken; and Charles Holland might, from some sudden impulse, fancying his future happiness was all at stake, have withdrawn himself from the Hall, and really written the letters attributed to him.

We say this only obtruded itself occasionally, for all their real feelings and aspirations were the other way, although Mr. Marchdale, they could perceive, had his doubts, and they could not but confess that he was more likely to view the matter calmly and dispassionately than they.

In fact, the very hesitation with which he spoke upon the subject, convinced them of his doubt; for they attributed that hesitation to a fear of giving them pain, or of wounding the prejudices of Admiral Bell, with whom he had already had words so nearly approaching to a quarrel.

Henry's visit to Mr. Chillingworth was not likely to be productive of any results beyond those of a conjectural character. All that that gentleman could do was to express a willingness to be directed by them in any way, rather than suggest any course of conduct himself upon circumstances which he could not be expected to judge of as they who were on the spot, and had witnessed their actual occurrence.

And now we will suppose that the reader is enabled with us to look into one of the principal rooms of Bannerworth Hall. It is evening, and some candles are shedding a sickly light on the ample proportions of the once handsome apartment. At solemn consultation the whole of the family are assembled. As well as the admiral, Mr. Chillingworth, and Marchdale, Jack Pringle, too, walked in, by the sufferance of his master, as if he considered he had a perfect right to do so.

The occasion of the meeting had been a communication which Flora had made concerning her most singular and deeply interesting interview with the vampyre. The details of this interview had produced a deep effect upon the whole of the family. Flora was there, and she looked better, calmer, and more collected than she had done for some days past.

No doubt the interview she had had with Varney in the summer-house in the garden had dispelled a host of imaginary terrors with which she had surrounded him, although it had confirmed her fully that he and he only was the dreadful being who had caused her so much misery.

That interview had tended to show her that about him there was yet something human, and that there was not a danger of her being hunted down from place to place by so horrible an existence.

Such a feeling as this was, of course, a source of deep consolation; and with a firmer voice, and more of her old spirit of cheerfulness about her than she had lately exhibited, she again detailed the particulars of the interview to all who had assembled, concluding by saying,--

"And this has given me hope of happier days. If it be a delusion, it is a happy one; and now that but a frightful veil of mystery still hangs over the fate of Charles Holland, I how gladly would I bid adieu to this place, and all that has made it terrible. I could almost pity Sir Francis Varney, rather than condemn him."

"That may be true," said Henry, "to a certain extent, sister; but we never can forget the amount of misery he has brought upon us. It is no slight thing to be forced from our old and much-loved home, even if such proceeding does succeed in freeing us from his persecutions."

"But, my young friend," said Marchdale, "you must recollect, that through life it is continually the lot of humanity to be endeavouring to fly from great evils to those which do not present themselves to the mind in so bad an aspect. It is something, surely, to alleviate affliction, if we cannot entirely remove it."

"That is true," said Mr. Chillingworth, "to a considerable extent, but then it takes too much for granted to please me."

"How so, sir?"

"Why, certainly, to remove from Bannerworth Hall is a much less evil than to remain at Bannerworth Hall, and be haunted by a vampyre; but then that proposition takes for granted that vampyre business, which I will never grant. I repeat, again and again, it is contrary to all experience, to philosophy, and to all the laws of ordinary nature."

"Facts are stubborn things," said Marchdale.

"Apparently," remarked Mr. Chillingworth.

"Well, sir; and here we have the fact of a vampyre."

"The presumed fact. One swallow don't make a summer, Mr. Marchdale."

"This is waste of time," said Henry--"of course, the amount of evidence that will suffice to bring conviction to one man's mind will fail in doing so to another. The question is, what are we to do?"

All eyes were turned upon Flora, as if this question was more particularly addressed to her, and it behoved her, above all others, to answer it. She did so; and in a firm, clear voice, she said,--

"I will discover the fate of Charles Holland, and then leave the Hall."

"The fate of Charles Holland!" said Marchdale. "Why, really, unless that young gentleman chooses to be communicative himself upon so interesting a subject, we may be a long while discovering his fate. I know that it is not a romantic view to take of the question, to suppose simply that he wrote the three letters found upon his dressing-table, and then decamped; but to my mind, it savours most wonderfully of matter-of-fact. I now speak more freely than I have otherwise done, for I am now upon the eve of my departure. I have no wish to remain here, and breed dissension in any family, or to run a tilt against anybody's prejudices." Here he looked at Admiral Bell. "I leave this house to-night."

"You're a d----d lubberly thief," said the admiral; "the sooner you leave it the better. Why, you bad-looking son of a gun, what do you mean? I thought we'd had enough of that."

"I fully expected this abuse," said Marchdale.

"Did you expect that?" said the admiral, as he snatched up an inkstand, and threw at Marchdale, hitting him a hard knock on the chin, and bespattering its contents on his breast. "Now I'll give you satisfaction, you lubber. D--me, if you ain't a second Jones, and enough to sink the ship. Shiver my timbers if I sha'n't say something strong presently."

"I really," said Henry, "must protest, Admiral Bell, against this conduct."

"Protest and be d----d."

"Mr. Marchdale may be right, sir, or he may be wrong, it's a matter of opinion."

"Oh, never mind," said Marchdale; "I look upon this old nautical ruffian as something between a fool and a madman. If he were a younger man I should chastise him upon the spot; but as it is I live in hopes yet of getting him into some comfortable lunatic asylum."

"Me into an asylum!" shouted the admiral. "Jack, did you hear that?"

"Ay, ay, sir."

"Farewell all of you," said Marchdale; "my best wishes be with this family. I cannot remain under this roof to be so insulted."

"A good riddance," cried the admiral. "I'd rather sail round the world with a shipload of vampyres than with such a humbugging son of a gun as you are. D----e, you're worse than a lawyer."

"Nay, nay," cried they, "Mr. Marchdale, stay."

"Stay, stay," cried George, and Mrs. Bannerworth, likewise, said stay; but at the moment Flora stepped forward, and in a clear voice she said,--

"No, let him go, he doubts Charles Holland; let all go who doubt Charles Holland. Mr. Marchdale, Heaven forgive you this injustice you are doing. We may never meet again. Farewell, sir!"

These words were spoken in so decided a tone, that no one contradicted them. Marchdale cast a strange kind of look round upon the family circle, and in another instant he was gone.

"Huzza!" shouted Jack Pringle; "that's one good job."

Henry looked rather resentful, which the admiral could not but observe, and so, less with the devil-may-care manner in which he usually spoke, the old man addressed him.

"Hark ye, Mr. Henry Bannerworth, you ain't best pleased with me, and in that case I don't know that I shall stay to trouble you any longer, as for your friend who has left you, sooner or later you'll find him out--I tell you there's no good in that fellow. Do you think I've been cruizing about for a matter of sixty years, and don't know an honest man when I see him. But never mind, I'm going on a voyage of discovery for my nephew, and you can do as you like."

"Heaven only knows, Admiral Bell," said Henry, "who is right and who is wrong. I do much regret that you have quarrelled with Mr. Marchdale; but what is done can't be undone."

"Do not leave us," said Flora; "let me beg of you, Admiral Bell, not to leave us; for my sake remain here, for to you I can speak freely and with confidence, of Charles, when probably I can do so to no one else. You knew him well and have a confidence in him, which no one else can aspire to. I pray you, therefore, to stay with us."

"Only on one condition," said the admiral.

"Name it--name it!

"You think of letting the Hall?"

"Yes, yes."

"Let me have it, then, and let me pay a few years in advance. If you don't, I'm d----d if I stay another night in the place. You must give me immediate possession, too, and stay here as my guests until you suit yourselves elsewhere. Those are my terms and conditions. Say yes, and all's right; say no, and I'm off like a round shot from a carronade. D----me, that's the thing, Jack, isn't it?"

"Ay, ay, sir."

There was a silence of some few moments after this extraordinary offer had been made, and then they spoke, saying,--

"Admiral Bell, your generous offer, and the feelings which dictated it, are by far too transparent for us to affect not to understand them. Your actions, Admiral--"

"Oh, bother my actions! what are they to you? Come, now, I consider myself master of the house, d--n you! I invite you all to dinner, or supper, or to whatever meal comes next. Mrs. Bannerworth, will you oblige me, as I'm an old fool in family affairs, by buying what's wanted for me and my guests? There's the money, ma'am. Come along, Jack, we'll take a look over our new house. What do you think of it?"

"Wants some sheathing, sir, here and there."

"Very like; but, however, it will do well enough for us; we're in port, you know. Come along."

"Ay, ay, sir."

And off went the admiral and Jack, after leaving a twenty pound note in Mrs. Bannerworth's lap.

CHAPTER XXXVII

SIR FRANCIS VARNEY'S SEPARATE OPPONENTS.--THE INTERPOSITION OF FLORA

The old admiral so completely overcame the family of the Bannerworths by his generosity and evident single-mindedness of his behaviour, that although not one, except Flora, approved of his conduct towards Mr. Marchdale, yet they could not help liking him; and had they been placed in a position to choose which of the two they would have had remain with them, the admiral or Marchdale, there can be no question they would have made choice of the former.

Still, however, it was not pleasant to find a man like Marchdale virtually driven from the house, because he presumed to differ in opinion upon a very doubtful matter with another of its inmates. But as it was the nature of the Bannerworth family always to incline to the most generous view of subjects, the frank, hearty confidence of the old admiral in Charles Holland pleased them better than the calm and serious doubting of Marchdale.

His ruse of hiring the house of them, and paying the rent in advance, for the purpose of placing ample funds in their hands for any contingency, was not the less amiable because it was so easily seen through; and they could not make up their minds to hurt the feelings of the old man by the rejection of his generous offer.

When he had left, this subject was canvassed among them, and it was agreed that he should have his own way in the matter for the present, although they hoped to hear something from Marchdale, which should make his departure appear less abrupt and uncomfortable to the whole of the family.

During the course of this conversation, it was made known to Flora with more distinctness than under any other circumstances it would have been, that George Holland had been on the eve of fighting a duel with Sir Francis Varney, previous to his mysterious disappearance.

When she became fully aware of this fact, to her mind it seemed materially to add to the suspicions previously to then entertained, that foul means had been used in order to put Charles out of the way.

"Who knows," she said, "that this Varney may not shrink with the greatest terror from a conflict with any human being, and feeling one was inevitable with Charles Holland, unless interrupted by some vigorous act of his own, he or some myrmidons of his may have taken Charles's life!"

"I do not think, Flora," said Henry, "that he would have ventured upon so desperate an act; I cannot well believe such a thing possible. But fear not; he will find, if he have really committed any such atrocity, that it will not save him."

These words of Henry, though it made no impression at the time upon Flora, beyond what they carried upon their surface, they really, however, as concerned Henry himself, implied a settled resolution, which he immediately set about reducing to practice.

When the conference broke up, night, as it still was, he, without saying anything to any one, took his hat and cloak, and left the Hall, proceeding by the nearest practicable route to the residence of Sir Francis Varney, where he arrived without any interruption of any character.

Varney was at first denied to him, but before he could leave the house, a servant came down the great staircase, to say it was a mistake; and that Sir Francis was at home, and would be happy to see him.

He was ushered into the same apartment where Sir Francis Varney had before received his visitors; and there sat the now declared vampyre, looking pale and ghastly by the dim light which burned in the apartment, and, indeed, more like some spectre of the tomb, than one of the great family of man.

"Be seated, sir," said Varney; "although my eyes have seldom the pleasure of beholding you within these walls, be assured you are a honoured guest."

"Sir Francis Varney," said Henry, "I came not here to bandy compliments with you; I have none to pay to you, nor do I wish to hear any of them from your lips."

"An excellent sentiment, young man," said Varney, "and well delivered. May I presume, then, without infringing too far upon your extreme courtesy, to inquire, to what circumstances I am indebted for your visit?"

"To one, Sir Francis, that I believe you are better acquainted with than you will have the candour to admit."

"Indeed, sir," said Varney, coldly; "you measure my candour, probably, by a standard of your own; in which case I fear, I may be no gainer; and yet that may be of itself a circumstance that should afford little food for surprise, but proceed, sir--since we have so few compliments to stand between us and our purpose, we shall in all due time arrive at it."

"Yes, in due time, Sir Francis Varney, and that due time has arrived. Know you anything of my friend, Mr. Charles Holland?" said Henry, in marked accents; and he gazed on Sir Francis Varney with earnestness, that seemed to say not even a look should escape his observation.

Varney, however, returned the gaze as steadily, but coldly, as he replied in his measured accents,--

"I have heard of the young gentleman."

"And seen him?"

"And seen him too, as you, Mr. Bannerworth, must be well aware. Surely you have not come all this way, merely to make such an inquiry; but, sir, you are welcome to the answer."

Henry had something of a struggle to keep down the rising anger, at these cool taunts of Varney; but he succeeded--and then he said,--

"I suspect Charles Holland, Sir Francis Varney, has met with unfair treatment, and that he has been unfairly dealt with, for an unworthy purpose."

"Undoubtedly," said Varney, "if the gentleman you allude to, has been unfairly dealt with, it was for a foul purpose; for no good or generous object, my young sir, could be so obtained--you acknowledge so much, I doubt not?"

"I do, Sir Francis Varney; and hence the purpose of my visit here--for this reason I apply to you--"

"A singular object, supported by a singular reason. I cannot see the connection, young sir; pray proceed to enlighten me upon this matter, and when you have done that, may I presume upon your consideration, to inquire in what way I can be of any service to you?"

"Sir Francis," said Henry, his anger raising his tones--"this will not serve you--I have come to exact an account of how you have disposed of my friend; and I will have it."

"Gently, my good sir; you are aware I know nothing of your friend; his motions are his own; and as to what I have done with him; my only answer is, that he would permit me to do nothing with him, had I been so inclined to have taken the liberty."

"You are suspected, Sir Francis Varney, of having made an attempt upon the life or liberty of Charles Holland; you, in fact, are suspected of being his murderer--and, so help me Heaven! if I have not justice, I will have vengeance!"

"Young sir, your words are of grave import, and ought to be coolly considered before they are uttered. With regard to justice and vengeance, Mr. Bannerworth, you may have both; but I tell you, of Charles Holland, or what has become of him, I know nothing. But wherefore do you come to so unlikely a quarter to learn something of an individual of whom I know nothing?"

"Because Charles Holland was to have fought a duel with you: but before that had time to take place, he has suddenly become missing. I suspect that you are the author of his disappearance, because you fear an encounter with a mortal man."

"Mr. Bannerworth, permit me to say, in my own defence, that I do not fear any man, however foolish he may be; and wisdom is not an attribute I find, from experience in all men, of your friend. However, you must be dreaming, sir--a kind of vivid insanity has taken possession of your mind, which distorts--"

"Sir Francis Varney!" exclaimed Henry, now perfectly uncontrollable.

"Sir," said Varney, as he filled up the pause, "proceed; I am all attention. You do me honour."

"If," resumed Henry, "such was your object in putting Mr. Holland aside, by becoming personally or by proxy an assassin, you are mistaken in supposing you have accomplished your object."

"Go on, sir," said Sir Francis Varney, in a bland and sweet tone; "I am all attention; pray proceed."

"You have failed; for I now here, on this spot, defy you to mortal combat. Coward, assassin as you are, I challenge you to fight."

"You don't mean on the carpet here?" said Varney, deliberately.

"No, sir; but beneath the canopy of heaven, in the light of the day. And then, Sir Francis, we shall see who will shrink from the conflict."

"It is remarkably good, Mr. Bannerworth, and, begging your pardon, for I do not wish to give any offence, my honoured sir, it would rehearse before an audience; in short, sir, it is highly dramatic."

"You shrink from the combat, do you? Now, indeed, I know you."

"Young man--young man," said Sir Francis, calmly, and shaking his head very deliberately, and the shadows passed across his pale face, "you know me not, if you think Sir Francis Varney shrinks from any man, much less one like yourself."

"You are a coward, and worse, if you refuse my challenge."

"I do not refuse it; I accept it," said Varney, calmly, and in a dignified manner; and then, with a sneer, he added,--"You are well acquainted with the mode in which gentlemen generally manage these matters, Mr. Bannerworth, and perhaps I am somewhat confined in my knowledge in the ways of the world, because you are your own principal and second. In all my experience, I never met with a similar case."

"The circumstances under which it is given are as unexampled, and will excuse the mode of the challenge," said Henry, with much warmth.

"Singular coincidence--the challenge and mode of it is most singular! They are well matched in that respect. Singular, did I say? The more I think of it, Mr. Bannerworth, the more I am inclined to think this positively odd."

"Early to-morrow, Sir Francis, you shall hear from me."

"In that case, you will not arrange preliminaries now? Well, well; it is very unusual for the principals themselves to do so; and yet, excuse my freedom, I presumed, as you had so far deserted the beaten track, that I had no idea how far you might be disposed to lead the same route."

"I have said all I intended to say, Sir Francis Varney; we shall see each other again."

"I may not detain you, I presume, to taste aught in the way of refreshment?"

Henry made no reply, but turned towards the door, without even making an attempt to return the grave and formal bow that Sir Francis Varney made as he saw him about to quit the apartment; for Henry saw that his pale features were lighted up with a sarcastic smile, most disagreeable to look upon as well as irritating to Henry Bannerworth.

He now quitted Sir Francis Varney's abode, being let out by a servant who had been rung for for that purpose by his master.

Henry walked homeward, satisfied that he had now done all that he could under the circumstances.

"I will send Chillingworth to him in the morning, and then I shall see what all this will end in. He must meet me, and then Charles Holland, if not discovered, shall be, at least, revenged."

There was another person in Bannerworth Hall who had formed a similar resolution. That person was a very different sort of person to Henry Bannerworth, though quite as estimable in his way.

This was no other than the old admiral. It was singular that two such very different persons should deem the same steps necessary, and both keep the secret from each other; but so it was, and, after some internal swearing, he determined upon challenging Varney in person.

"I'd send Jack Pringle, but the swab would settle the matter as shortly as if a youngster was making an entry in a log, and heard the boatswain's whistle summoning the hands to a mess, and feared he would lose his grog.

"D--n my quarters! but Sir Francis Varney, as he styles himself, sha'n't make any way against old Admiral Bell. He's as tough as a hawser, and just the sort of blade for a vampyre to come athwart. I'll pitch him end-long, and make a plank of him afore long. Cus my windpipe! what a long, lanky swab he is, with teeth fit to unpick a splice; but let me alone, I'll see if I can't make a hull of his carcass, vampyre or no vampyre.

"My nevy, Charles Holland, can't be allowed to cut away without nobody's leave or licence. No, no; I'll not stand that anyhow. 'Never desert a messmate in the time of need,' is the first maxim of a seaman, and I ain't the one as 'll do so."

Thus self-communing, the old admiral marched along until he came to Sir Francis Varney's house, at the gate of which he gave the bell what he called a long pull, a strong pull, and a pull altogether, that set it ringing with a fury, the like of which had never certainly been heard by the household.

A minute or two scarcely elapsed before the domestics hurried to answer so urgent a summons; and when the gate was opened, the servant who answered it inquired his business.

"What's that to you, snob? Is your master, Sir Francis Varney, in? because, if he be, let him know old Admiral Bell wants to speak to him. D'ye hear?"

"Yes, sir," replied the servant, who had paused a few moments to examine the individual who gave this odd kind of address.

In another minute word was brought to him that Sir Francis Varney would be very happy to see Admiral Bell.

"Ay, ay," he muttered; "just as the devil likes to meet with holy water, or as I like any water save salt water."

He was speedily introduced to Sir Francis Varney, who was seated in the same posture as he had been left by Henry Bannerworth not many minutes before.

"Admiral Bell," said Sir Francis, rising, and bowing to that individual in the most polite, calm, and dignified manner imaginable, "permit me to express the honour I feel at this unexpected visit."

"None of your gammon."

"Will you be seated. Allow me to offer you such refreshments as this poor house affords."

"D--n all this! You know, Sir Francis, I don't want none o' this palaver. It's for all the world like a Frenchman, when you are going to give him a broadside; he makes grimaces, throws dust in your eyes, and tries to stab you in the back. Oh, no! none of that for me."

"I should say not, Admiral Bell. I should not like it myself, and I dare say you are a man of too much experience not to perceive when you are or are not imposed upon."

"Well, what is that to you? D--n me, I didn't come here to talk to you about myself."

"Then may I presume upon your courtesy so far as to beg that you will enlighten me upon the object of your visit!"

"Yes; in pretty quick time. Just tell me where you have stowed away my nephew, Charles Holland?"

"Really, I--"

"Hold your slack, will you, and hear me out; if he's living, let him out, and I'll say no more about it; that's liberal, you know; it ain't terms everybody would offer you."

"I must, in truth, admit they are not; and, moreover, they quite surprise even me, and I have learned not to be surprised at almost anything."

"Well, will you give him up alive? but, hark ye, you mustn't have made very queer fish of him, do ye see?"

"I hear you," said Sir Francis, with a bland smile, passing one hand gently over the other, and showing his front teeth in a peculiar manner; "but I really cannot comprehend all this; but I may say, generally, that Mr. Holland is no acquaintance of mine, and I have no sort of knowledge where he may be."

"That won't do for me," said the admiral, positively, shaking his head.

"I am particularly sorry, Admiral Bell, that it will not, seeing that I have nothing else to say."

"I see how it is; you've put him out of the way, and I'm d----d if you shan't bring him to life, whole and sound, or I'll know the reason why."

"With that I have already furnished you, Admiral Bell," quietly rejoined Varney; "anything more on that head is out of my power, though my willingness to oblige a person of such consideration as yourself, is very great; but, permit me to add, this is a very strange and odd communication from one gentleman to another. You have lost a relative, who has, very probably, taken some offence, or some notion into his head, of which nobody but himself knows anything, and you come to one yet more unlikely to know anything of him, than even yourself.

"Gammon again, now, Sir Francis Varney, or Blarney."

"Varney, if you please, Admiral Bell; I was christened Varney."

"Christened, eh?"

"Yes, christened--were you not christened? If not, I dare say you understand the ceremony well enough."

"I should think I did; but, as for christening, a--"

"Go on, sir."

"A vampyre! why I should as soon think of reading the burial service of a pig."

"Very possible; but what has all this to do with your visit to me?"

"This much, you lubber. Now, d--n my carcass from head to stern, if I don't call you out."

"Well, Admiral Bell," slid Varney, mildly, "in that case, I suppose I must come out; but why do you insist that I have any knowledge of your nephew, Mr. Charles Holland?"

"You were to have fought a duel with him, and now he's gone."

"I am here," said Varney.

"Ay," said the admiral, "that's as plain as a purser's shirt upon a handspike; but that's the very reason why my nevey ain't here, and that's all about it."

"And that's marvellous little, so far as the sense is concerned," said Varney, without the movement of a muscle.

"It is said that people of your class don't like fighting mortal men; now you have disposed of him, lest he should dispose of you."

"That is explicit, but it is to no purpose, since the gentleman in question hasn't placed himself at my disposal."

"Then, d----e, I will; fish, flesh, or fowl, I don't care; all's one to Admiral Bell. Come fair or fowl, I'm a tar for all men; a seaman ever ready to face a foe, so here goes, you lubberly moon manufactured calf."

"I hear, admiral, but it is scarcely civil, to say the least of it; however, as you are somewhat eccentric, and do not, I dare say, mean all your words imply, I am quite willing to make every allowance."

"I don't want any allowance; d--n you and your allowance, too; nothing but allowance of grog, and a pretty good allowance, too, will do for me, and tell you, Sir Francis Varney," said the admiral, with much wrath, "that you are a d----d lubberly hound, and I'll fight you; yes, I'm ready to hammer away, or with anything from a pop-gun to a ship's gun; you don't come over me with your gammon, I tell you. You've murdered Charles Holland because you couldn't face him--that's the truth of it."

"With the other part of your speech, Admiral Bell, allow me to say, you have mixed up a serious accusation--one I cannot permit to pass lightly."

"Will you or not fight?"

"Oh, yes; I shall be happy to serve you any way that I can. I hope this will be an answer to your accusation, also."

"That's settled, then."

"Why, I am not captious, Admiral Bell, but it is not generally usual for the principals to settle the preliminaries themselves; doubtless you, in your career of fame and glory, know something of the manner in which gentlemen demean themselves on these occasions."

"Oh, d--n you! Yes, I'll send some one to do all this. Yes, yes, Jack Pringle will be the man, though Jack ain't a holiday, shore-going, smooth-spoken swab, but as good a seaman as ever trod deck or handled a boarding-pike."

"Any friend of yours," said Varney, blandly, "will be received and treated as such upon an errand of such consequence; and now our conference has, I presume, concluded."

"Yes, yes, I've done--d----e, no--yes--no. I will keel-haul you but I'll know something of my neavy, Charles Holland."

"Good day, Admiral Bell." As Varney spoke, he placed his hand upon the bell which he had near him, to summon an attendant to conduct the admiral out. The latter, who had said a vast deal more than he ever intended, left the room in a great rage, protesting to himself that he would amply avenge his nephew, Charles Holland.

He proceeded homeward, considerably vexed and annoyed that he had been treated with so much calmness, and all knowledge of his nephew denied.

When he got back, he quarrelled heartily with Jack Pringle--made it up--drank grog--quarrelled--made it up, and finished with grog again--until he went to bed swearing he should like to fire a broadside at the whole of the French army, and annihilate it at once.

With this wish, he fell asleep.

Early next morning, Henry Bannerworth sought Mr. Chillingworth, and having found him, he said in a serious tone,--

"Mr. Chillingworth, I have rather a serious favour to ask you, and one which you may hesitate in granting."

"It must be very serious indeed," said Mr. Chillingworth, "that I should hesitate to grant it to you; but pray inform me what it is that you deem so serious?"

"Sir Francis Varney and I must have a meeting," said Henry.

"Have you really determined upon such a course?" said Mr. Chillingworth; "you know the character of your adversary?"

"That is all settled,--I have given a challenge, and he has accepted it; so all other considerations verge themselves into one--and that is the when, where, and how."

"I see," said Mr. Chillingworth. "Well, since it cannot be helped on your part, I will do what is requisite for you--do you wish anything to be done or insisted on in particular in this affair."

"Nothing with regard to Sir Francis Varney that I may not leave to your discretion. I feel convinced that he is the assassin of Charles Holland, whom he feared to fight in duel."

"Then there remains but little else to do, but to arrange preliminaries, I believe. Are you prepared on every other point?"

"I am--you will see that I am the challenger, and that he must now fight. What accident may turn up to save him, I fear not, but sure I am, that he will endeavour to take every advantage that may arise, and so escape the encounter."

"And what do you imagine he will do now he has accepted your challenge?" said Mr. Chillingworth; "one would imagine he could not very well escape."

"No--but he accepted the challenge which Charles Holland sent him--a duel was inevitable, and it seems to me to be a necessary consequence that he disappeared from amongst us, for Mr. Holland would never have shrunk from the encounter."

"There can be no sort of suspicion about that," remarked Chillingworth; "but allow me to advise you that you take care of yourself, and keep a watchful eye upon every one--do not be seen out alone."

"I fear not."

"Nay, the gentleman who has disappeared was, I am sure, fearless enough; but yet that has not saved him. I would not advise you to be fearful, only watchful; you have now an event awaiting upon you, which it is well you should go through with, unless circumstances should so turn out, that it is needless; therefore I say, when you have the suspicions you do entertain of this man's conduct, beware, be cautious, and vigilant."

"I will do so--in the mean time, I trust myself confidently in your hands--you know all that is necessary."

"This affair is quite a secret from all of the family?"

"Most certainly so, and will remain so--I shall be at the Hall."

"And there I will see you--but be careful not to be drawn into any adventure of any kind--it is best to be on the safe side under all circumstances."

"I will be especially careful, be assured, but farewell; see Sir Francis Varney as early as you can, and let the meeting be as early as you can, and thus diminish the chance of accident."

"That I will attend to. Farewell for the present."

Mr. Chillingworth immediately set about the conducting of the affair thus confided to him; and that no time might be lost, he determined to set out at once for Sir Francis Varney's residence.

"Things with regard to this family seem to have gone on wild of late," thought Mr. Chillingworth; "this may bring affairs to a conclusion, though I had much rather they had come to some other. My life for it, there is a juggle or a mystery somewhere; I will do this, and then we shall see what will come of it; if this Sir Francis Varney meets him--and at this moment I can see no reason why he should not do so--it will tend much to deprive him of the mystery about him; but if, on the other hand, he refuse--but then that's all improbable, because he has agreed to do so. I fear, however, that such a man as Varney is a dreadful enemy to encounter--he is cool and unruffled--and that gives him all the advantage in such affairs; but Henry's nerves are not bad, though shaken by these untowards events; but time will show--I would it were all over."

With these thoughts and feelings strangely intermixed, Mr. Chillingworth set forward for Sir Francis Varney's house.

***

Admiral Bell slept soundly enough though, towards morning, he fell into a strange dream, and thought he was yard arm and yard arm with a strange fish--something of the mermaid species.

"Well," exclaimed the admiral, after a customary benediction of his eyes and limbs, "what's to come next? may I be spliced to a shark if I understand what this is all about. I had some grog last night, but then grog, d'y'see, is--is--a seaman's native element, as the newspapers say, though I never read 'em now, it's such a plague."

He lay quiet for a short time, considering in his own mind what was best to be done, and what was the proper course to pursue, and why he should dream.

"Hilloa, hilloa, hil--loa! Jack a-hoy! a-hoy!" shouted the admiral, as a sudden recollection of his challenge came across his memory; "Jack Pringle a-hoy? d--n you, where are you?--you're never at hand when you are wanted. Oh, you lubber,--a-hoy!"

"A-hoy!" shouted a voice, as the door opened, and Jack thrust his head in; "what cheer, messmate? what ship is this?"

"Oh, you lubberly--"

The door was shut in a minute, and Jack Pringle disappeared.

"Hilloa, Jack Pringle, you don't mean to say you'll desert your colours, do you, you dumb dog?"

"Who says I'll desert the ship as she's sea-worthy!"

"Then why do you go away?"

"Because I won't be called lubberly. I'm as good a man as ever swabbed a deck, and don't care who says to the contrary. I'll stick to the ship as long as she's seaworthy," said Jack.

"Well, come here, and just listen to the log, and be d----d to you."

"What's the orders now, admiral?" said Jack, "though, as we are paid off--"

"There, take that, will you?" said Admiral Bell, as he flung a pillow at Jack, being the only thing in the shape of a missile within reach.

Jack ducked, and the pillow produced a clatter in the washhand-stand among the crockery, as Jack said,--

"There's a mutiny in the ship, and hark how the cargo clatters; will you have it back again?"

"Come, will you? I've been dreaming, Jack."

"Dreaming! what's that?"

"Thinking of something when you are asleep, you swab."

"Ha, ha, ha!" laughed Jack; "never did such a thing in my life--ha, ha, ha! what's the matter now?"

"I'll tell you what's the matter. Jack Pringle, you are becoming mutinous, and I won't have it; if you don't hold your jaw and draw in your slacks, I'll have another second."

"Another second! what's in the wind, now?" said Jack. "Is this the dream?"

"If ever I dream when I'm alongside a strange craft, then it is a dream; but old Admiral Bell ain't the man to sleep when there's any work to be done."

"That's uncommon true," said Jack, turning a quid.

"Well, then, I'm going to fight."

"Fight!" exclaimed Jack. "Avast, there, I don't see where's the enemy--none o' that gammon; Jack Pringle can fight, too, and will lay alongside his admiral, but he don't see the enemy anywhere."

"You don't understand these things, so I'll tell you. I have had a bit of talk with Sir Francis Varney, and I am going to fight him."

"What the wamphigher?" remarked Jack, parenthetically.

"Yes."

"Well, then," resumed Jack, "then we shall see another blaze, at least afore we die; but he's an odd fish--one of Davy Jones's sort."

"I don't care about that; he may be anything he likes; but Admiral Bell ain't a-going to have his nephew burned and eaten, and sucked like I don't know what, by a vampyre, or by any other confounded land-shark."

"In course," said Jack, "we ain't a-going to put up with nothing of that sort, and if so be as how he has put him out of the way, why it's our duty to send him after him, and square the board."

"That's the thing, Jack; now you know you must go to Sir Francis Varney and tell him you come from me."

"I don't care if I goes on my own account," said Jack.

"That won't do; I've challenged him and I must fight him."

"In course you will," returned Jack, "and, if he blows you away, why I'll take your place, and have a blaze myself."

The admiral gave a look at Jack of great admiration, and then said,--

"You are a d----d good seaman, Jack, but he's a knight, and might say no to that, but do you go to him, and tell him that you come from me to settle the when and the where this duel is to be fought."

"Single fight?" said Jack.

"Yes; consent to any thing that is fair," said the admiral, "but let it be as soon as you can. Now, do you understand what I have said?"

"Yes, to be sure; I ain't lived all these years without knowing your lingo."

"Then go at once; and don't let the honour of Admiral Bell and old England suffer, Jack. I'm his man, you know, at any price."

"Never fear," said Jack; "you shall fight him, at any rate. I'll go and see he don't back out, the warmint."

"Then go along, Jack; and mind don't you go blazing away like a fire ship, and letting everybody know what's going on, or it'll be stopped."

"I'll not spoil sport," said Jack, as he left the room, to go at once to Sir Francis Varney, charged with the conducting of the important cartel of the admiral. Jack made the best of his way with becoming gravity and expedition until he reached the gate of the admiral's enemy.

Jack rang loudly at the gate; there seemed, if one might judge by his countenance, a something on his mind, that Jack was almost another man. The gate was opened by the servant, who inquired what he wanted there.

"The wamphigher."

"Who?"

"The wamphigher."

The servant frowned, and was about to say something uncivil to Jack, who winked at him very hard, and then said,--

"Oh, may be you don't know him, or won't know him by that name: I wants to see Sir Francis Varney."

"He's at home," said the servant; "who are you?"

"Show me up, then. I'm Jack Pringle, and I'm come from Admiral Bell; I'm the Admiral's friend, you see, so none of your black looks."

The servant seemed amazed, as well as rather daunted, at Jack's address; he showed him, however, into the hall, where Mr. Chillingworth had just that moment arrived, and was waiting for an interview with Varney.

CHAPTER XXXVIII

MARCHDALE'S OFFER.--THE CONSULTATION AT BANNERWORTH HALL.--THE MORNING OF THE DUEL

Mr. Chillingworth was much annoyed to see Jack Pringle in the hall, and Jack was somewhat surprised at seeing Mr. Chillingworth there at that time in the rooming; they had but little time to indulge in their mutual astonishment, for a servant came to announce that Sir Francis Varney would see them both.

Without saying anything to the servant or each other, they ascended the staircase, and were shown into the apartment where Sir Francis Varney received them.

"Gentlemen," said Sir Francis, in his usual bland tone, "you are welcome."

"Sir Francis," said Mr. Chillingworth, "I have come upon matters of some importance; may I crave a separate audience?"

"And I too," said Jack Pringle; "I come as the friend of Admiral Bell, I want a private audience; but, stay, I don't care a rope's end who knows who I am, or what I come about; say you are ready to name time and place, and I'm as dumb as a figure-head; that is saying something, at all events; and now I'm done."

"Why, gentlemen," said Sir Francis, with a quiet smile, "as you have both come upon the same errand, and as there may arise a controversy upon the point of precedence, you had better be both present, as I must arrange this matter myself upon due inquiry."

"I do not exactly understand this," said Mr. Chillingworth; "do you, Mr. Pringle? perhaps you can enlighten me?"

"It," said Jack, "as how you came here upon the same errand as I, and I as you, why we both come about fighting Sir Francis Varney."

"Yes," said Sir Francis; "what Mr. Pringle says, is, I believe correct to a letter. I have a challenge from both your principals, and am ready to give you both the satisfaction you desire, provided the first encounter will permit me the honour of joining in the second. You, Mr. Pringle, are aware of the chances of war?"

"I should say so," said Jack, with a wink and a nod of a familiar character. "I've seen a few of them."

"Will you proceed to make the necessary agreement between you both, gentlemen? My affection for the one equals fully the good will I bear the other, and I cannot give a preference in so delicate a matter; proceed gentlemen."

Mr. Chillingworth looked at Jack, and Jack Pringle looked at Mr. Chillingworth, and then the former said,--

"Well, the admiral means fighting, and I am come to settle the necessaries; pray let me know what are your terms, Mr. What-d'ye-call'em."

"I am agreeable to anything that is at all reasonable--pistols, I presume?"

"Sir Francis Varney," said Mr. Chillingworth, "I cannot consent to carry on this office, unless you can appoint a friend who will settle these matters with us--myself, at least."

"And I too," said Jack Pringle; "we don't want to bear down an enemy. Admiral Bell ain't the man to do that, and if he were, I'm not the man to back him in doing what isn't fair or right; but he won't do it."

"But, gentlemen, this must not be; Mr. Henry Bannerworth must not be disappointed, and Admiral Bell must not be disappointed. Moreover, I have accepted the two cartels, and I am ready and willing to fight;--one at a time, I presume?"

"Sir Francis, after what you have said, I must take upon myself, on the part of Mr. Henry Bannerworth, to decline meeting you, if you cannot name a friend with whom I can arrange this affair."

"Ah!" said Jack Pringle, "that's right enough. I recollect very well when Jack Mizeu fought Tom Foremast, they had their seconds. Admiral Bell can't do anything in the dark. No, no, d----e! all must be above board."

"Gentlemen," said Sir Francis Varney, "you see the dilemma I am in. Your principals have both challenged me. I am ready to fight any one, or both of them, as the case may be. Distinctly understand that; because it is a notion of theirs that I will not do so, or that I shrink from them; but I am a stranger in this neighbourhood, and have no one whom I could call upon to relinquish so much, as they run the risk of doing by attending me to the field."

"Then your acquaintances are no friends, d----e!" said Jack Pringle, spitting through his teeth into the bars of a beautifully polished grate. "I'd stick to anybody--the devil himself, leave alone a vampyre--if so be as how I had been his friends and drunk grog from the same can. They are a set of lubbers."

"I have not been here long enough to form any such friendships, Mr. Chillingworth; but can confidently rely upon your honour and that of your principal, and will freely and fairly meet him."

"But, Sir Francis, you forget the fact, in transacting, myself for Mr. Bannerworth, and this person or Admiral Bell, we do match, and have our own characters at stake; nay more, our lives and fortunes. These may be small; but they are everything to us. Allow me to say, on my own behalf, that I will not permit my principal to meet you unless you can name a second, as is usual with gentlemen on such occasions."

"I regret, while I declare to you my entire willingness to meet you, that I cannot comply through utter inability to do so, with your request. Let this go forth to the world as I have stated it, and let it be an answer to any aspersions that may be uttered as to my unwillingness to fight."

There was a pause of some moments. Mr. Chillingworth was resolved that, come of it what would, he would not permit Henry to fight, unless Sir Francis Varney himself should appoint a friend, and then they could meet upon equal terms.

Jack Pringle whistled, and spit, and chewed and turned his quid--hitched up his trousers, and looked wistfully from one to the other, as he said,--

"So then it's likely to be no fight at all, Sir Francis what's-o'-name?"

"It seems like it, Mr. Pringle," replied Varney, with a meaning smile; "unless you can be more complaisant towards myself, and kind towards the admiral."

"Why, not exactly that," said Jack; "it's a pity to stop a good play in the beginning, just because some little thing is wrong in the tackling."

"Perhaps your skill and genius may enable us to find some medium course that we may pursue with pleasure and profit. What say you, Mr. Pringle?"

"All I know about genius, as you call it is the Flying Dutchman, or some such odd out of the way fish. But, as I said, I am not one to spoil sport, nor more is the admiral. Oh, no, we is all true men and good."

"I believe it," said Varney, bowing politely.

"You needn't keep your figure-head on the move; I can see you just as well. Howsoever, as I was saying, I don't like to spoil sport, and sooner than both parties should be disappointed, my principal shall become your second, Sir Francis."

"What, Admiral Bell?" exclaimed Varney, lifting his eyebrows with surprise.

"What, Charles Holland's uncle!" exclaimed Mr. Chillingworth, in accents of amazement.

"And why not?" said Jack, with great gravity. "I will pledge my word--Jack Pringle's word--that Admiral Bell shall be second to Sir Francis Varney, during his scrimmage with Mr. Henry Bannerworth. That will let the matter go on; there can be no back-out then, eh?" continued Jack Pringle, with a knowing nod at Chillingworth as he spoke.

"That will, I hope, remove your scruples, Mr. Chillingworth," said Varney, with a courteous smile.

"But will Admiral Bell do this?"

"His second says so, and has, I daresay, influence enough with him to induce that person to act in conformity with his promise."

"In course he will. Do you think he would be the man to hang back? Oh, no; he would be the last to leave Jack Pringle in the lurch--no. Depend upon it, Sir Francis, he'll be as sure to do what I say, as I have said it."

"After that assurance, I cannot doubt it," said Sir Francis Varney; "this act of kindness will, indeed, lay me under a deep and lasting obligation to Admiral Bell, which I fear I shall never be able to pay."

"You need not trouble yourself about that," said Jack Pringle; "the admiral will credit all, and you can pay off old scores when his turn comes in the field."

"I will not forget," said Varney; "he deserves every consideration; but now, Mr. Chillingworth, I presume that we may come to some understanding respecting this meeting, which you were so kind as to do me the honour of seeking."

"I cannot object to its taking place. I shall be most happy to meet your second in the field, and will arrange with him."

"I imagine that, under the circumstances, that it will be barely necessary to go to that length of ceremony. Future interviews can be arranged later; name the time and place, and after that we can settle all the rest on the ground."

"Yes," said Jack; "it will be time enough, surely, to see the admiral when we are upon the ground. I'll warrant the old buffer is a true brick as ever was: there's no flinching about him."

"I am satisfied," said Varney.

"And I also," said Chillingworth; "but, understand, Sir Francis, any default for seconds makes the meeting a blank."

"I will not doubt Mr. Pringle's honour so much as to believe it possible."

"I'm d----d," said Jack, "if you ain't a trump-card, and no mistake; it's a great pity as you is a wamphigher."

"The time, Mr. Chillingworth?"

"To-morrow, at seven o'clock," replied that gentleman.

"The place, sir?"

"The best place that I can think of is a level meadow half-way between here and Bannerworth Hall; but that is your privilege, Sir Francis Varney."

"I waive it, and am much obliged to you for the choice of the spot; it seems of the best character imaginable. I will be punctual."

"I think we have nothing further to arrange now," said Mr. Chillingworth. "You will meet with Admiral Bell."

"Certainly. I believe there is nothing more to be done; this affair is very satisfactorily arranged, and much better than I anticipated."

"Good morning, Sir Francis," said Mr. Chillingworth. "Good morning."

"Adieu," said Sir Francis, with a courteous salutation. "Good day, Mr. Pringle, and commend me to the admiral, whose services will be of infinite value to me."

"Don't mention it," said Jack; "the admiral's the man as'd lend any body a helping hand in case of distress like the present; and I'll pledge my word--Jack Pringle's too, as that he'll do what's right, and give up his turn to Mr. Henry Bannerworth; cause you see he can have his turn arterwards, you know--it's only waiting awhile."

"That's all," said Sir Francis.

Jack Pringle made a sea bow and took his leave, as he followed Mr. Chillingworth, and they both left the house together, to return to Bannerworth Hall.

"Well," said Mr. Chillingworth, "I am glad that Sir Francis Varney has got over the difficulty of having no seconds; for it would not be proper or safe to meet a man without a friend for him."

"It ain't the right thing," said Jack hitching up his trousers; "but I was afeard as how he would back out, and that would be just the wrong thing for the admiral; he'd go raving mad."

They had got but very few paces from Sir Francis Varney's house, when they were joined by Marchdale.

"Ah," he said, as he came up, "I see you have been to Sir Francis Varney's, if I may judge from the direction whence you're coming, and your proximity."

"Yes, we have," said Mr. Chillingworth. "I thought you had left these parts?"

"I had intended to do so," replied Marchdale; "but second thoughts are sometimes best, you know."

"Certainly."

"I have so much friendship for the family at the hall, that notwithstanding I am compelled to be absent from the mansion itself, yet I cannot quit the neighbourhood while there are circumstances of such a character hanging about them. I will remain, and see if there be not something arising, in which I may be useful to them in some matter."

"It is very disinterested of you; you will remain here for some time, I suppose?"

"Yes, undoubtedly; unless, as I do not anticipate, I should see any occasion to quit my present quarters."

"I tell you what it is," said Jack Pringle; "if you had been here half-an-hour earlier you could have seconded the wamphigher."

"Seconded!"

"Yes, we're here to challenge."

"A double challenge?"

"Yes; but in confiding this matter to you, Mr. Marchdale, you will make no use of it to the exploding of this affair. By so doing you will seriously damage the honour of Mr. Henry Bannerworth."

"I will not, you may rely upon it; but Mr. Chillingworth, do I not see you in the character of a second?"

"You do, sir."

"To Mr. Henry?"

"The same, sir."

"Have you reflected upon the probable consequences of such an act, should any serious mischief occur?"

"What I have undertaken, Mr. Marchdale, I will go through with; the consequences I have duly considered, and yet you see me in the character of Mr. Henry Bannerworth's friend."

"I am happy to see you as such, and I do not think Henry could find a better. But this is beside the question. What induced me to make the remark was this,--had I been at the hall, you will admit that Henry Bannerworth would have chosen myself, without any disparagement to you, Mr. Chillingworth."

"Well sir, what then?"

"Why I am a single man, I can live, reside and go any where; one country will suit me as well as another. I shall suffer no loss, but as for you, you will be ruined in every particular; for if you go in the character of a second, you will not be excused; for all the penalties incurred your profession of a surgeon will not excuse you."

"I see all that, sir."

"What I propose is, that you should accompany the parties to the field, but in your own proper character of surgeon, and permit me to take that of second to Mr. Bannerworth."

"This cannot be done, unless by Mr. Henry Bannerworth's consent," said Mr. Chillingworth.

"Then I will accompany you to Bannerworth Hall, and see Mr. Henry, whom I will request to permit me to do what I have mentioned to you."

Mr. Chillingworth could not but admit the reasonableness of this proposal, and it was agreed they should return to Bannerworth Hall in company.

Here they arrived in a very short time after, and entered together.

"And now," said Mr. Chillingworth, "I will go and bring our two principals, who will be as much astonished to find themselves engaged in the same quarrel, as I was to find myself sent on a similar errand to Sir Francis with our friend Mr. John Pringle."

"Oh, not John--Jack Pringle, you mean," said that individual.

Chillingworth now went in search of Henry, and sent him to the apartment where Mr. Marchdale was with Jack Pringle, and then he found the admiral waiting the return of Jack with impatience.

"Admiral!" he said, "I perceive you are unwell this morning."

"Unwell be d----d," said the admiral, starting up with surprise. "Who ever heard that old admiral Bell looked ill just afore he was going into action? I say it's a scandalous lie."

"Admiral, admiral, I didn't say you were ill; only you looked ill--a--a little nervous, or so. Rather pale, eh? Is it not so?"

"Confound you, do you think I want to be physicked? I tell you, I have not a little but a great inclination to give you a good keelhauling. I don't want a doctor just yet."

"But it may not be so long, you know, admiral; but there is Jack Pringle a-waiting you below. Will you go to him? There is a particular reason; he has something to communicate from Sir Francis Varney, I believe."

The admiral gave a look of some amazement at Mr. Chillingworth, and then he said, muttering to himself,--

"If Jack Pringle should have betrayed me--but, no; he could not do that, he is too true. I'm sure of Jack; and how did that son of a gallipot hint about the odd fish I sent Jack to?"

Filled with a dubious kind of belief which he had about something he had heard of Jack Pringle, he entered the room, where he met Marchdale, Jack Pringle, and Henry Bannerworth. Immediately afterwards, Mr. Chillingworth entered the apartment.

"I have," said he, "been to Sir Francis Varney, and there had an interview with him, and with Mr. Pringle; when I found we were both intent upon the same object, namely, an encounter with the knight by our principals."

"Eh?" said the admiral.

"What!" exclaimed Henry; "had he challenged you, admiral?"

"Challenged me!" exclaimed Admiral Bell, with a round oath. "I--however--since it comes to this, I must admit I challenged him."

"That's what I did," said Henry Bannerworth, after a moment's thought; "and I perceive we have both fallen into the same line of conduct."

"That is the fact," said Mr. Chillingworth. "Both Mr. Pringle and I went there to settle the preliminaries, and we found an insurmountable bar to any meeting taking place at all."

"He wouldn't fight, then?" exclaimed Henry. "I see it all now."

"Not fight!" said Admiral Bell, with a sort of melancholy disappointment. "D--n the cowardly rascal! Tell me, Jack Pringle, what did the long horse-marine-looking slab say to it? He told me he would fight. Why he ought to be made to stand sentry over the wind."

"You challenged him in person, too, I suppose?" said Henry.

"Yes, confound him! I went there last night."

"And I too."

"It seems to me," said Marchdale, "that this affair has been not indiscretely conducted; but somewhat unusually and strangely, to say the least of it."

"You see," said Chillingworth, "Sir Francis was willing to fight both Henry and the admiral, as he told us."

"Yes," said Jack; "he told us he would fight us both, if so be as his light was not doused in the first brush."

"That was all that was wanted," said the admiral.

"We could expect no more."

"But then he desired to meet you without any second; but, of course, I would not accede to this proposal. The responsibility was too great and too unequally borne by the parties engaged in the rencontre."

"Decidedly," said Henry; "but it is unfortunate--very unfortunate."

"Very," said the admiral--"very. What a rascally thing it is there ain't another rogue in the country to keep him in countenance."

"I thought it was a pity to spoil sport," said Jack Pringle. "It was a pity a good intention should be spoiled, and I promised the wamphigher that if as how he would fight, you should second him, and you'd meet him to do so."

"Eh! who? I!" exclaimed the admiral in some perplexity.

"Yes; that is the truth," said Mr. Chillingworth. "Mr Pringle said you would do so, and he then and there pledged his word that you should meet him on the ground and second him."

"Yes," said Jack "You must do it. I knew you would not spoil sport, and that there had better be a fight than no fight. I believe you'd sooner see a scrimmage than none, and so it's all arranged."

"Very well," said the admiral, "I only wish Mr. Henry Bannerworth had been his second; I think I was entitled to the first meeting."

"No," said Jack, "you warn't, for Mr. Chillingworth was there first; first come first served, you know."

"Well, well, I mustn't grumble at another man's luck; mine'll come in turn; but it had better be so than a disappointment altogether; I'll be second to this Sir Francis Varney; he shall have fair play, as I'm an admiral; but, d----e he shall fight--yes, yes, he shall fight."

"And to this conclusion I would come," said Henry, "I wish him to fight; now I will take care that he shall not have any opportunity of putting me on one side quietly."

"There is one thing," observed Marchdale, "that I wished to propose. After what has passed, I should not have returned, had I not some presentiment that something was going forward in which I could be useful to my friend."

"Oh!" said the admiral, with a huge twist of his countenance.

"What I was about to say was this,--Mr. Chillingworth has much to lose as he is situated, and I nothing as I am placed. I am chained down to no spot of earth. I am above following a profession--my means, I mean, place me above the necessity. Now, Henry, allow me to be your second in this affair; allow Mr. Chillingworth to attend in his professional capacity; he may be of service--of great service to one of the principals; whereas, if he go in any other capacity, he will inevitably have his own safety to consult."

"That is most unquestionably true," said Henry, "and, to my mind, the best plan that can be proposed. What say you, Admiral Bell, will you act with Mr. Marchdale in this affair?"

"Oh, I!--Yes--certainly--I don't care. Mr. Marchdale is Mr. Marchdale, I believe, and that's all I care about. If we quarrel to-day, and have anything to do to-morrow, in course, to-morrow I can put off my quarrel for next day; it will keep,--that's all I have to say at present."

"Then this is a final arrangement?" said Mr. Chillingworth.

"It is."

"But, Mr. Bannerworth, in resigning my character of second to Mr. Marchdale, I only do so because it appears and seems to be the opinion of all present that I can be much better employed in another capacity."

"Certainly, Mr. Chillingworth; and I cannot but feel that I am under the same obligations to you for the readiness and zeal with which you have acted."

"I have done what I have done," said Chillingworth, "because I believed it was my duty to do so."

"Mr. Chillingworth has undoubtedly acted most friendly and efficiently in this affair," said Marchdale; "and he does not relinquish the part for the purpose of escaping a friendly deed, but to perform one in which he may act in a capacity that no one else can."

"That is true," said the admiral.

"And now," said Chillingworth, "you are to meet to-morrow morning in the meadow at the bottom of the valley, half way between here and Sir Francis Varney's house, at seven o'clock in the morning."

More conversation passed among them, and it was agreed that they should meet early the next morning, and that, of course, the affair should be kept a secret.

Marchdale for that night should remain in the house, and the admiral should appear as if little or nothing was the matter; and he and Jack Pringle retired, to talk over in private all the arrangements.

Henry Bannerworth and Marchdale also retired, and Mr. Chillingworth, after a time, retired, promising to be with them in time for the meeting next morning.

Much of that day was spent by Henry Bannerworth in his own apartment, in writing documents and letters of one kind and another; but at night he had not finished, for he had been compelled to be about, and in Flora's presence, to prevent anything from being suspected.

Marchdale was much with him, and in secret examined the arms, ammunition, and bullets, and saw all was right for the next morning; and when he had done, he said,--

"Now, Henry, you must permit me to insist that you take some hours' repose, else you will scarcely be as you ought to be."

"Very good," said Henry. "I have just finished, and can take your advice."

After many thoughts and reflections, Henry Bannerworth fell into a deep sleep, and slept several hours in calmness and quietude, and at an early hour he awoke, and saw Marchdale sitting by him.

"Is it time, Marchdale? I have not overslept myself, have I?"

"No; time enough--time enough," said Marchdale. "I should have let you sleep longer, but I should have awakened you in good time."

It was now the grey light of morning, and Henry arose and began to prepare for the encounter. Marchdale stole to Admiral Bell's chamber, but he and Jack Pringle were ready.

Few words were spoken, and those few were in a whisper, and the whole party left the Hall in as noiseless a manner as possible. It was a mild morning, and yet it was cold at that time of the morning, just as day is beginning to dawn in the east. There was, however, ample time to reach the rendezvous.

It was a curious party that which was now proceeding towards the spot appointed for the duel, the result of which might have so important an effect on the interests of those who were to be engaged in it.

It would be difficult for us to analyse the different and conflicting emotions that filled the breasts of the various individuals composing that party--the hopes and fears--the doubts and surmises that were given utterance to; though we are compelled to acknowledge that though to Henry, the character of the man he was going to meet in mortal fight was of a most ambiguous and undefined nature, and though no one could imagine the means he might be endowed with for protection against the arms of man--Henry, as we said, strode firmly forward with unflinching resolution. His heart was set on recovering the happiness of his sister, and he would not falter.

So far, then, we may consider that at length proceedings of a hostile character were so far clearly and fairly arranged between Henry Bannerworth and that most mysterious being who certainly, from some cause or another, had betrayed no inclination to meet an opponent in that manner which is sanctioned, bad as it is, by the usages of society.

But whether his motive was one of cowardice or mercy, remained yet to be seen. It might be that he feared himself receiving some mortal injury, which would at once put a stop to that preternatural career of existence which he affected to shudder at, and yet evidently took considerable pains to prolong.

Upon the other hand, it is just possible that some consciousness of invulnerability on his own part, or of great power to injure his antagonist, might be the cause why he had held back so long from fighting the duel, and placed so many obstacles in the way of the usual necessary arrangements incidental to such occasions.

Now, however, there would seem to be no possible means of escape. Sir Francis Varney must fight or fly, for he was surrounded by too many opponents.

To be sure he might have appealed to the civil authorities to protect him, and to sanction him in his refusal to commit what undoubtedly is a legal offence; but then there cannot be a question that the whole of the circumstances would come out, and meet the public eye--the result of which would be, his acquisition of a reputation as unenviable as it would be universal.

It had so happened, that the peculiar position of the Bannerworth family kept their acquaintance within extremely narrow limits, and greatly indisposed them to set themselves up as marks for peculiar observation.

Once holding, as they had, a proud position in the county, and being looked upon quite as magnates of the land, they did not now court the prying eye of curiosity to look upon their poverty; but rather with a gloomy melancholy they lived apart, and repelled the advances of society by a cold reserve, which few could break through.

Had this family suffered in any noble cause, or had the misfortunes which had come over them, and robbed their ancestral house of its lustre, been an unavoidable dispensation of providence, they would have borne the hard position with a different aspect; but it must be remembered, that to the faults, the vices, and the criminality of some of their race, was to be attributed their present depressed state.

It has been seen during the progress of our tale, that its action has been tolerably confined to Bannerworth Hall, its adjacent meadows, and the seat of Sir Francis Varney; the only person at any distance, knowing anything of the circumstances, or feeling any interest in them, being Mr. Chillingworth, the surgeon, who, from personal feeling, as well as from professional habit, was not likely to make a family's affairs a subject of gossip.

A change, however, was at hand--a change of a most startling and alarming character to Varney--one which he might expect, yet not be well prepared for.

This period of serenity was to pass away, and he was to become most alarmingly popular. We will not, however, anticipate, but proceed at once to detail as briefly as may be the hostile meeting.

It would appear that Varney, now that he had once consented to the definitive arrangements of a duel, shrunk not in any way from carrying them out, nor in the slightest attempted to retard arrangements which might be fatal to himself.

The early morning was one of those cloudy ones so frequently occurring in our fickle climate, when the cleverest weather prophet would find it difficult to predict what the next hour might produce.

There was a kind of dim gloominess over all objects; and as there were no bright lights, there were no deep shadows--the consequence of which was a sureness of effect over the landscape, that robbed it of many of its usual beauties.

Such was the state of things when Marchdale accompanied Henry and Admiral Bell from Bannerworth Hall across the garden in the direction of the hilly wood, close to which was the spot intended for the scene of encounter.

Jack Pringle came on at a lazy pace behind with his hands in his pockets, and looking as unconcerned as if he had just come out for a morning's stroll, and scarcely knew whether he saw what was going on or not.

The curious contortion into which he twisted his countenance, and the different odd-looking lumps that appeared in it from time to time, may be accounted for by a quid of unusual size, which he seemed to be masticating with a relish quite horrifying to one unused to so barbarous a luxury.

The admiral had strictly enjoined him not to interfere on pain of being considered a lubber and no seaman for the remainder of his existence--threatened penalties which, of course, had their own weight with Jack, and accordingly he came just, to see the row in as quiet a way as possible, perhaps not without a hope, that something might turn up in the shape of a causus belli, that might justify him in adopting a threatening attitude towards somebody.

"Now, Master Henry," said the admiral, "none of your palaver to me as we go along, recollect I don't belong to your party, you know. I've stood friend to two or three fellows in my time; but if anybody had said to me, 'Admiral Bell, the next time you go out on a quiet little shooting party, it will be as second to a vampyre,' I'd have said 'you're a liar' Howsomever, d--me, here you goes, and what I mean to say is this, Mr Henry, that I'd second even a Frenchman rather than he shouldn't fight when he's asked"

"That's liberal of you," said Henry, "at all event"

"I believe you it is," said the admiral, "so mind if you don't hit him, I'm not a-going to tell you how--all you've got to do, is to fire low; but that's no business of mine. Shiver my timbers, I oughtn't to tell you, but d--n you, hit him if you can."

"Admiral," said Henry, "I can hardly think you are even preserving a neutrality in the matter, putting aside my own partisanship as regards your own man."

"Oh, hang him. I'm not going to let him creep out of the thing on such a shabby pretence. I can tell you. I think I ought to have gone to his house this morning; only, as I said I never would cross his threshold again, I won't."

"I wonder if he'll come," said Mr Marchdale to Henry. "After all, you know he may take to flight, and shun an encounter which, it is evident, he has entered into but tardily."

"I hope not," said Henry, "and yet I must own that your supposition has several times crossed my mind. If, however, he do not meet me, he never can appear at all in the country, and we should, at least, be rid of him, and all his troublesome importunities concerning the Hall. I would not allow that man, on any account, to cross the threshold of my house, as its tenant or its owner."

"Why, it ain't usual," said the admiral, "to let ones house to two people at once, unless you seem quite to forget that I've taken yours. I may as well remind you of it."

"Hurra" said Jack Pringle, at this moment.

"What's the matter with you? Who told you to hurra?"

"Enemy in the offing," said Jack, "three or four pints to the sou-west."

"So he is, by Jove! dodging about among the trees. Come, now, this vampyre's a decenter fellow than I thought him. He means, after all, to let us have a pop at him."

They had now reached so close to the spot, that Sir Francis Varney, who, to all appearance, had been waiting, emerged from among the trees, rolled up in his dismal-looking cloak, and, if possible, looking longer and thinner than ever he had looked before.

His face wore a singular cadaverous looking aspect. His very lips were white and there was a curious, pinkish-looking circle round each of his eyes, that imparted to his whole countenance a most uninviting appearance. He turned his eyes from one to the other of those who were advancing towards him, until he saw the admiral, upon which he gave such a grim and horrible smile, that the old man exclaimed,--

"I say, Jack, you lubber, there's a face for a figure head."

"Ay, ay, sir."

"Did you ever see such a d----d grin as that in your life, in any latitude?"

"Ay, ay, sir."

"You did you swab."

"I should think so."

"It's a lie, and you know it."

"Very good," said Jack, "don't you recollect when that ere iron bullet walked over your head, leaving a nice little nick, all the way off Bergen-ap-Zoom, that was the time--blessed if you didn't give just such a grin as that."

"I didn't, you rascal."

"And I say you did."

"Mutiny, by God!"

"Go to blazes!"

How far this contention might have gone, having now reached its culminating point, had the admiral and Jack been alone, it is hard to say; but as it was, Henry and Marchdale interfered, and so the quarrel was patched up for the moment, in order to give place to more important affairs.

Varney seemed to think, that after the smiling welcome he had given to his second, he had done quite enough; for there he stood, tall, and gaunt, and motionless, if we may except an occasional singular movement of the mouth, and a clap together of his teeth, at times, which was enough to make anybody jump to hear.

"For Heaven's sake," said Marchdale, "do not let us trifle at such a moment as this. Mr. Pringle, you really had no business here."

"Mr. who?" said Jack.

"Pringle, I believe, is your name?" returned Marchdale.

"It were; but blowed if ever I was called mister before."

The admiral walked up to Sir Francis Varney, and gave him a nod that looked much more like one of defiance than of salutation, to which the vampyre replied by a low, courtly bow.

"Oh, bother!" muttered the old admiral. "If I was to double up my backbone like that, I should never get it down straight again. Well, all's right; you've come; that's all you could do, I suppose."

"I am here," said Varney, "and therefore it becomes a work of supererogation to remark that I've come."

"Oh! does it? I never bolted a dictionary, and, therefore, I don't know exactly what you mean."

"Step aside with me a moment, Admiral Bell, and I will tell you what you are to do with me after I am shot, if such should be my fate."

"Do with you! D----d if I'll do anything with you."

"I don't expect you will regret me; you will eat."

"Eat!"

"Yes, and drink as usual, no doubt, notwithstanding being witness to the decease of a fellow-creature."

"Belay there; don't call yourself a fellow-creature of mine; I ain't a vampyre."

"But there's no knowing what you may be; and now listen to my instructions; for as you're my second, you cannot very well refuse to me a few friendly offices. Rain is falling. Step beneath this ancient tree, and I will talk to you."

CHAPTER XXXIX

THE STORM AND THE FIGHT.-THE ADMIRAL'S REPUDIATION OF HIS PRINCIPAL

"Well," said the admiral, when they were fairly under the tree, upon the leaves of which the pattering rain might be heard falling: "well--what is it?"

"If your young friend, Mr. Bannerworth, should chance to send a pistol-bullet through any portion of my anatomy, prejudicial to the prolongation of my existence, you will be so good as not to interfere with anything I may have about me, or to make any disturbance whatever."

"You may depend I sha'n't."

"Just take the matter perfectly easy--as a thing of course."

"Oh! I mean d----d easy."

"Ha! what a delightful thing is friendship! There is a little knoll or mound of earth midway between here and the Hall. Do you happen to know it? There is one solitary tree glowing near its summit--an oriental looking tree, of the fir tribe, which, fan-like, spreads its deep green leaves; across the azure sky."

"Oh! bother it; it's a d----d old tree, growing upon a little bit of a hill, I suppose you mean?"

"Precisely; only much more poetically expressed. The moon rises at a quarter past four to-night, or rather to-morrow, morning."

"Does it?"

"Yes; and if I should happen to be killed, you will have me removed gently to this mound of earth, and there laid beneath this tree, with my face upwards; and take care that it is done before the moon rises. You can watch that no one interferes."

"A likely job. What the deuce do you take me for? I tell you what it is, Mr. Vampyre, or Varney, or whatever's your name, if you should chance to be hit, where-ever you chance to fall, there you'll lie."

"How very unkind."

"Uncommon, ain't it?"

"Well, well, since that is your determination, I must take care of myself in another way. I can do so, and I will."

"Take care of yourself how you like, for all I care; I've come here to second you, and to see that, on the honour of a seaman, if you are put out of the world, it's done in a proper manner, that's all I have to do with you--now you know."

Sir Francis Varney looked after him with a strange kind of smile, as he walked away to make the necessary preparation with Marchdale for the immediate commencement of the contest.

These were simple and brief. It was agreed that twelve paces should be measured out, six each way, from a fixed point; one six to be paced by the admiral, and the other by Marchdale; then they were to draw lots, to see at which end of this imaginary line Varney was to be placed; after this the signal for firing was to be one, two, three--fire!

A few minutes sufficed to complete these arrangements; the ground was measured in the manner we have stated, and the combatants placed in their respective positions, Sir Francis Varney occupying the same spot where he had at first stood, namely, that nearest to the little wood, and to his own residence.

It is impossible that under such circumstances the bravest and the calmest of mankind could fail to feel some slight degree of tremour or uneasiness; and, although we can fairly claim for Henry Bannerworth that he was as truly courageous as any right feeling Christian man could wish to be, yet when it was possible that he stood within, as it were, a hair's breadth of eternity, a strange world of sensation and emotions found a home in his heart, and he could not look altogether undaunted on that future which might, for all he knew to the contrary, be so close at hand, as far as he was concerned.

It was not that he feared death, but that he looked with a decent gravity upon so grave a change as that from this world to the next, and hence was it that his face was pale, and that he looked all the emotion which he really felt.

This was the aspect and the bearing of a brave but not a reckless man; while Sir Francis

Varney, on the other hand, seemed, now that he had fairly engaged in the duel, to look upon it and its attendant circumstances with a kind of smirking satisfaction, as if he were far more amused than personally interested.

This was certainly the more extraordinary after the manner in which he had tried to evade the fight, and, at all events, was quite a sufficient proof that cowardice had not been his actuating motive in so doing.

The admiral, who stood on a level with him, could not see the sort of expression he wore, or, probably, he would have been far from well pleased; but the others did, and they found something inexpressibly disagreeable in the smirking kind of satisfaction with which the vampyre seemed to regard now the proceedings.

"Confound him," whispered Marchdale to Henry, "one would think he was quite delighted, instead, as we had imagined him, not well pleased, at these proceedings; look how he grins."

"It is no matter," said Henry; "let him wear what aspect he may, it is the same to me; and, as Heaven is my judge, I here declare, if I did not think myself justified in so doing, I would not raise my hand against this man."

"There can be no shadow of a doubt regarding your justification. Have at him, and Heaven protect you."

"Amen!"

The admiral was to give the word to fire, and now he and Marshal having stepped sufficiently on one side to be out of all possible danger from any stray shot, he commenced repeating the signal,--

"Are you ready, gentlemen?--once."

They looked sternly at each other, and each grasped his pistol.

"Twice!"

Sir Francis Varney smiled and looked around him, as if the affair were one of the most common-place description.

"Thrice!"

Varney seemed to be studying the sky rather than attending to the duel.

"Fire!" said the admiral, and one report only struck upon the ear. It was that from Henry's pistol.

All eyes were turned upon Sir Francis Varney, who had evidently reserved his fire, for what purpose could not be devised, except a murderous one, the taking of a more steady aim at Henry.

Sir Francis, however, seemed in no hurry, but smiled significantly, and gradually raised the point of his weapon.

"Did you hear the word, Sir Francis? I gave it loud enough, I am sure. I never spoke plainer in my life; did I ever, Jack?"

"Yes, often," said Jack Pringle; "what's the use of your asking such yarns as them? you know you have done so often enough when you wanted grog."

"You d----d rascal, I'll--I'll have your back scored, I will."

"So you will, when you are afloat again, which you never will be--you're paid off, that's certain."

"You lubberly lout, you ain't a seaman; a seaman would never mutiny against his admiral; howsomever, do you hear, Sir Francis, I'll give the matter up, if you don't pay some attention to me."

Henry looked steadily at Varney, expecting every moment to feel his bullet. Mr. Marchdale hastily exclaimed that this was not according to usage.

Sir Francis Varney took no notice, but went on elevating his weapon; when it was perpendicular to the earth he fired in the air.

"I had not anticipated this," said Marchdale, as he walked to Henry. "I thought he was taking a more deadly aim."

"And I," said Henry.

"Ay, you have escaped, Henry; let me congratulate you."

"Not so fast; we may fire again."

"I can afford to do that," he said, with a smile.

"You should have fired, sir, according to custom," said the admiral; "this is not the proper thing."

"What, fire at your friend?"

"Oh, that's all very well! You are my friend for a time, vampyre as you are, and I intend you shall fire."

"If Mr. Henry Bannerworth demands another fire, I have no objection to it, and will fire at him; but as it is I shall not do so, indeed, it would be quite useless for him to do so--to point mortal weapons at me is mere child's play, they will not hurt me."

"The devil they won't," said the admiral.

"Why, look you here," said Sir Francis Varney, stepping forward and placing his hand to his neckerchief; "look you here; if Mr. Henry Bannerworth should demand another fire, he may do so with the same bullet."

"The same bullet!" said Marchdale, stepping forward--"the same bullet! How is this?"

"My eyes," said Jack; "who'd a thought it; there's a go! Wouldn't he do for a dummy--to lead a forlorn hope, or to put among the boarders?"

"Here," said Sir Francis, handing a bullet to Henry Bannerworth--"here is the bullet you shot at me."

Henry looked at it--it was blackened by powder; and then Marchdale seized it and tried it in the pistol, but found the bullet fitted Henry's weapon.

"By heavens, it is so!" he exclaimed, stepping back and looking at Varney from top to toe in horror and amazement.

"D----e," said the admiral, "if I understand this. Why Jack Pringle, you dog, here's a strange fish."

"On, no! there's plenty on 'um in some countries."

"Will you insist upon another fire, or may I consider you satisfied?"

"I shall object," said Marchdale. "Henry, this affair must go no further; it would be madness--worse than madness, to fight upon such terms."

"So say I," said the admiral. "I will not have anything to do with you, Sir Francis. I'll not be your second any longer. I didn't bargain for such a game as this. You might as well fight with the man in brass armour, at the Lord Mayor's show, or the champion at a coronation."

"Oh!" said Jack Pringle; "a man may as well fire at the back of a halligator as a wamphigher."

"This must be considered as having been concluded," said Mr. Marchdale.

"No!" said Henry.

"And wherefore not?"

"Because I have not received his fire."

"Heaven forbid you should."

"I may not with honour quit the ground without another fire."

"Under ordinary circumstances there might be some shadow of an excuse for your demand; but as it is there is none. You have neither honour nor credit to gain by such an encounter, and, certainly, you can gain no object."

"How are we to decide this affair? Am I considered absolved from the accusation under which I lay, of cowardice?" inquired Sir Francis Varney, with a cold smile.

"Why, as for that," said the admiral, "I should as soon expect credit for fighting behind a wall, as with a man that I couldn't hit any more than the moon."

"Henry; let me implore you to quit this scene; it can do no good."

At this moment, a noise, as of human voices, was heard at a distance; this caused a momentary pause, and, the whole party stood still and listened.

The murmurs and shouts that now arose in the distance were indistinct and confused.

"What can all this mean?" said Marchdale; "there is something very strange about it. I cannot imagine a cause for so unusual an occurrence."

"Nor I," said Sir Francis Varney, looking suspiciously at Henry Bannerworth.

"Upon my honour I know neither what is the cause nor the nature of the sounds themselves."

"Then we can easily see what is the matter from yonder hillock," said the admiral; "and there's Jack Pringle, he's up there already. What's he telegraphing about in that manner, I wonder?"

The fact was, Jack Pringle, hearing the riot, had thought that if he got to the neighbouring eminence he might possibly ascertain what it was that was the cause of what he termed the "row," and had succeeded in some degree.

There were a number of people of all kinds coming out from the village, apparently armed, and shouting. Jack Pringle hitched up his trousers and swore, then took off his hat and began to shout to the admiral, as he said,--

"D----e, they are too late to spoil the sport. Hilloa! hurrah!"

"What's all that about, Jack?" inquired the admiral, as he came puffing along. "What's the squall about?"

"Only a few horse-marines and bumboat-women, that have been startled like a company of penguins."

"Oh! my eyes! wouldn't a whole broadside set 'em flying, Jack?"

"Ay; just as them Frenchmen that you murdered on board the Big Thunderer, as you called it."

"I murder them, you rascal?"

"Yes; there was about five hundred of them killed."

"They were only shot."

"They were killed, only your conscience tells you it's uncomfortable."

"You rascal--you villain! You ought to be keel-hauled and well payed."

"Ay; you're payed, and paid off as an old hulk."

"D----e--you--you--oh! I wish I had you on board ship, I'd make your lubberly carcass like a union jack, full of red and blue stripes."

"Oh! it's all very well; but if you don't take to your heels, you'll have all the old women in the village a whacking on you, that's all I have to say about it. You'd better port your helm and about ship, or you'll be keel-hauled."

"D--n your--"

"What's the matter?" inquired Marchdale, as he arrived.

"What's the cause of all the noise we have heard?" said Sir Francis; "has some village festival spontaneously burst forth among the rustics of this place?"

"I cannot tell the cause of it," said Henry Bannerworth; "but they seem to me to be coming towards this place."

"Indeed!"

"I think so too," said Marchdale.

"With what object?" inquired Sir Francis Varney.

"No peaceable one," observed Henry; "for, as far I can observe, they struck across the country, as though they would enclose something, or intercept somebody."

"Indeed! but why come here?"

"If I knew that I could have at once told the cause."

"And they appear armed with a variety of odd weapons," observed Sir Francis; "they mean an attack upon some one! Who is that man with them? he seems to be deprecating their coming."

"That appears to be Mr. Chillingworth," said Henry; "I think that is he."

"Yes," observed the admiral; "I think I know the build of that craft; he's been in our society before. I always know a ship as soon as I see it."

"Does you, though?" said Jack.

"Yea; what do you mean, eh? let me hear what you've got to say against your captain and your admiral, you mutinous dog; you tell me, I say."

"So I will; you thought you were fighting a big ship in a fog, and fired a dozen broadsides or so, and it was only the Flying Dutchman, or the devil."

"You infernal dog--"

"Well, you know it was; it might a been our own shadow for all I can tell. Indeed, I think it was."

"You think!"

"Yes."

"That's mutiny; I'll have no more to do with you, Jack Pringle; you're no seaman, and have no respect for your officer. Now sheer off, or I'll cut your yards."

"Why, as for my yards, I'll square 'em presently if I like, you old swab; but as for leaving you, very well; you have said so, and you shall be accommodated, d----e; however, it was not so when your nob was nearly rove through with a boarding pike; it wasn't 'I'll have no more to do with Jack Pringle' then, it was more t'other."

"Well, then, why be so mutinous?"

"Because you aggrawates me."

The cries of the mob became more distinct as they drew nearer to the party, who began to evince some uneasiness as to their object.

"Surely," said Marchdale, "Mr. Chillingworth has not named anything respecting the duel that has taken place."

"No, no."

"But he was to have been here this morning," said the admiral. "I understood he was to be here in his own character of a surgeon, and yet I have not seen him; have any of you?"

"No," said Henry.

"Then here he comes in the character of conservator of the public peace," said Varney, coldly; "however, I believe that his errand will be useless since the affair is, I presume, concluded."

"Down with the vampyre!"

"Eh!" said the admiral, "eh, what's that, eh? What did they say?"

"If you'll listen they'll tell you soon enough, I'll warrant."

"May be they will, and yet I'd like to know now."

Sir Francis Varney looked significantly at Marchdale, and then waited with downcast eyes for the repetition of the words.

"Down with the vampyre!" resounded on all sides from the people who came rapidly towards them, and converging towards a centre. "Burn, destroy, and kill the vampyre! No vampyre; burn him out; down with him; kill him!"

Then came Mr. Chillingworth's voice, who, with much earnestness, endeavoured to exhort them to moderation, and to refrain from violence.

Sir Francis Varney became very pale agitated; he immediately turned, and taking the least notice, he made for the wood, which lay between him and his own house, leaving the people in the greatest agitation.

Mr. Marchdale was not unmoved at this occurrence, but stood his ground with Henry Bannerworth, the admiral, and Jack Pringle, until the mob came very near to them, shouting, and uttering cries of vengeance, and death of all imaginable kinds that it was possible to conceive, against the unpopular vampyre.

Pending the arrival of these infuriated persons, we will, in a few words, state how it was that so suddenly a set of circumstances arose productive of an amount of personal danger to Varney, such as, up to that time, had seemed not at all likely to occur.

We have before stated there was but one person out of the family of the Bannerworths who was able to say anything of a positive character concerning the singular and inexplicable proceedings at the Hall; and that that person was Mr. Chillingworth, an individual not at all likely to become garrulous upon the subject.

But, alas! the best of men have their weaknesses, and we much regret to say that Mr. Chillingworth so far in this instance forgot that admirable discretion which commonly belonged to him, as to be the cause of the popular tumult which had now readied such a height.

In a moment of thoughtlessness and confidence, he told his wife. Yes, this really clever man, from whom one would not have expected such a piece of horrible indiscretion, actually told his wife all about the vampyre. But such is human nature; combined with an amount of firmness and reasoning power, that one would have thought to be invulnerable safeguards, we find some weakness which astonishes all calculation.

Such was this of Mr. Chillingworth's. It is true, he cautioned the lady to be secret, and pointed to her the danger of making Varney the vampyre a theme for gossip; but he might as well have whispered to a hurricane to be so good as not to go on blowing so, as request Mrs. Chillingworth to keep a secret.

Of course she burst into the usual fervent declarations of "Who was she to tell? Was she a person who went about telling things? When did she see anybody? Not she, once in a blue moon;" and then, when Mr. Chillingworth went out, like the King of Otaheite, she invited the neighbours round about to come to take some tea.

Under solemn promises of secrecy, sixteen ladies that evening were made acquainted with the full and interesting particulars of the attack of the vampyre on Flora Bannerworth, and all the evidence inculpating Sir Francis Varney as the blood-thirsty individual.

When the mind comes to consider that these sixteen ladies multiplied their information by about four-and-twenty each, we become quite lost in a sea of arithmetic, and feel compelled to sum up the whole by a candid assumption that in four-and-twenty hours not an individual in the whole town was ignorant of the circumstances.

On the morning before the projected duel, there was an unusual commotion in the streets. People were conversing together in little knots, and using rather violent gesticulations. Poor Mr. Chillingworth! he alone was ignorant of the causes of the popular commotion, and so he went to bed wondering that an unusual bustle pervaded the little market town, but not at all guessing its origin.

Somehow or another, however, the populace, who had determined to make a demonstration on the following morning against the vampyre, thought it highly necessary first to pay some sort of compliment to Mr. Chillingworth, and, accordingly, at an early hour, a great mob assembled outside his house, and gave three terrific applauding shouts, which roused him most unpleasantly from his sleep; and induced the greatest astonishment at the cause of such a tumult.

Oh, that artful Mrs. Chillingworth! too well she knew what was the matter; yet she pretended to be so oblivious upon the subject.

"Good God!" cried Mr. Chillingworth, as he started up in bed, "what's all that?"

"All what?" said his wife.

"All what! Do you mean to say you heard nothing?"

"Well, I think I did hear a little sort of something."

"A little sort of something? It shook the house."

"Well, well; never mind. Go to sleep again; it's no business of ours."

"Yes; but it may be, though. It's all very well to say 'go to sleep.' That happens to be a thing I can't do. There's something amiss."

"Well, what's that to you?"

"Perhaps nothing; but, perhaps, everything."

Mr. Chillingworth sprang from his bed, and began dressing, a process which he executed with considerable rapidity, and in which he was much accelerated by two or three supplementary shouts from the people below.

Then, in a temporary lull, a loud voice shouted,--

"Down with the vampyre--down with the vampyre!"

The truth in an instant burst over the mind of Mr. Chillingworth; and, turning to his wife, he exclaimed,--

"I understand it now. You've been gossipping about Sir Francis Varney, and have caused all this tumult."

"I gossip! Well, I never! Lay it on me; it's sure to be my fault. I might have known that beforehand. I always am."

"But you must have spoken of it."

"Who have I got to speak to about it?"

"Did you, or did you not?"

"Who should I tell?"

Mr. Chillingworth was dressed, and he hastened down and entered the street with great desperation. He had a hope that he might be enabled to disperse the crowd, and yet be in time to keep his appointment at the duel.

His appearance was hailed with another shout, for it was considered, of course, that he had come to join in the attack upon Sir Francis Varney. He found assembled a much more considerable mob than he had imagined, and to his alarm he found many armed with all sorts of weapons of offence.

"Hurrah!" cried a great lumpy-looking fellow, who seemed half mad with the prospect of a disturbance. "Hurrah! here's the doctor, he'll tell us all about it as we go along. Come on."

"For Heaven's sake," said Mr. Chillingworth, "stop; What are you about to do all of you?"

"Burn the vampyre--burn the vampyre!"

"Hold--hold! this is folly. Let me implore you all to return to your homes, or you will get into serious trouble on this subject."

This was a piece of advice not at all likely to be adopted; and when the mob found that Mr. Chillingworth was not disposed to encourage and countenance it in its violence, it gave another loud shout of defiance, and moved off through the long straggling streets of the town in a direction towards Sir Francis Varney's house.

It is true that what were called the authorities of the town had become alarmed, and were stirring, but they found themselves in such a frightful minority, that it became out of the question for them to interfere with any effect to stop the lawless proceedings of the rioters, so that the infuriated populace had it all their own way, and in a straggling, disorderly-looking kind of procession they moved off, vowing vengeance as they went against Varney the vampyre.

Hopeless as Mr. Chillingworth thought it was to interfere with any degree of effect in the proceedings of the mob, he still could not reconcile it to himself to be absent from a scene which he now felt certain had been produced by his own imprudence, so he went on with the crowd, endeavouring, as he did so, by every argument that could be suggested to him to induce them to abstain from the acts of violence they contemplated. He had a hope, too, that when they reached Sir Francis Varney's, finding him not within, as probably would be the case, as by that time he would have started to meet Henry Bannerworth on the ground, to fight the duel, he might induce the mob to return and forego their meditated violence.

And thus was it that, urged on by a multitude of persons, the unhappy surgeon was expiating, both in mind and person, the serious mistakes he had committed in trusting a secret to his wife.

Let it not be supposed that we for one moment wish to lay down a general principle as regards the confiding secrets to ladies, because from the beginning of the world it has become notorious how well they keep them, and with what admirable discretion, tact, and forethought this fairest portion of humanity conduct themselves.

We know how few Mrs. Chillingworths there are in the world, and have but to regret that our friend the doctor should, in his matrimonial adventure, have met with such a specimen.

CHAPTER XL

THE POPULAR RIOT.--SIR FRANCIS VARNEY'S DANGER.--THE SUGGESTION AND ITS RESULTS

Such, then, were the circumstances which at once altered the whole aspect of the affairs, and, from private and domestic causes of very deep annoyance, led to public results of a character which seemed likely to involve the whole country-side in the greatest possible confusion.

But while we blame Mr. Chillingworth for being so indiscreet as to communicate the secret of such a person as Varney the vampyre to his wife, we trust in a short time to be enabled to show that he made as much reparation as it was possible to make for the mischief he had unintentionally committed. And now as he struggled onward--apparently onward--first and foremost among the rioters, he was really doing all in his power to quell that tumult which superstition and dread had raised.

Human nature truly delights in the marvellous, and in proportion as a knowledge of the natural phenomena of nature is restricted, and unbridled imagination allowed to give the rein to fathomless conjecture, we shall find an eagerness likewise to believe the marvellous to be the truth.

That dim and uncertain condition concerning vampyres, originating probably as it had done in Germany, had spread itself slowly, but insidiously, throughout the whole of the civilized world.

In no country and in no clime is there not something which bears a kind of family relationship to the veritable vampyre of which Sir Francis Varney appeared to be so choice a specimen.

The ghoul of eastern nations is but the same being, altered to suit habits and localities; and the sema of the Scandinavians is but the vampyre of a more primitive race, and a personification of that morbid imagination which has once fancied the probability of the dead walking again among the living, with all the frightful insignia of corruption and the grave about them.

Although not popular in England, still there had been tales told of such midnight visitants, so that Mrs. Chillingworth, when she had imparted the information which she had obtained, had already some rough material to work upon in the minds of her auditors, and therefore there was no great difficulty in very soon establishing the fact.

Under such circumstances, ignorant people always do what they have heard has been done by some one else before them and in an incredibly short space of time the propriety of catching Sir Francis Varney, depriving him of his vampyre-like existence, and driving a stake through his body, became not at all a questionable proposition.

Alas, poor Mr. Chillingworth! as well might he have attempted King Canute's task of stemming the waves of the ocean as that of attempting to stop the crowd from proceeding to Sir Francis Varney's house.

His very presence was a sort of confirmation of the whole affair. In vain he gesticulated, in vain he begged and prayed that they would go back, and in vain he declared that full and ample justice should be done upon the vampyre, provided popular clamour spared him, and he was left to more deliberate judgment.

Those who were foremost in the throng paid no attention to these remonstrances while those who were more distant heard them not, and, for all they knew, he might be urging the crowd on to violence, instead of deprecating it.

Thus, then, this disorderly rabble soon reached the house of Sir Francis Varney and loudly demanded of his terrified servant where he was to be found.

The knocking at the Hall door was prodigious, and, with a laudable desire, doubtless, of saving time, the moment one was done amusing himself with the ponderous knocker, another seized it; so that until the door was flung open by some of the bewildered and terrified men, there was no cessation whatever of the furious demands for admittance.

"Varney the vampyre--Varney the vampyre!" cried a hundred voices. "Death to the vampyre! Where is he? Bring him out. Varney the vampyre!"

The servants were too terrified to speak for some moments, as they saw such a tumultuous assemblage seeking their master, while so singular a name was applied to him. At length, one more bold than the rest contrived to stammer out,--

"My good people, Sir Francis Varney is not at home. He took an early breakfast, and has been out nearly an hour."

The mob paused a moment in indecision, and then one of the foremost cried,--

"Who'd suppose they'd own he was at home? He's hiding somewhere of course; let's pull him out."

"Ah, pull him out--pull him out!" cried many voices. A rush was made into the hall and in a very few minutes its chambers were ransacked, and all its hidden places carefully searched, with the hope of discovering the hidden form of Sir Francis Varney.

The servants felt that, with their inefficient strength, to oppose the proceedings of an assemblage which seemed to be unchecked by all sort of law or reason, would be madness; they therefore only looked on, with wonder and dismay, satisfied certainly in their own minds that Sir Francis would not be found, and indulging in much conjecture as to what would be the result of such violent and unexpected proceedings.

Mr. Chillingworth hoped that time was being gained, and that some sort of indication of what was going on would reach the unhappy object of popular detestation sufficiently early to enable him to provide for his own safety.

He knew he was breaking his own engagement to be present at the duel between Henry Bannerworth and Sir Francis Varney, and, as that thought recurred to him, he dreaded that his professional services might be required on one side or the other; for he knew, or fancied he knew, that mutual hatred dictated the contest; and he thought that if ever a duel had taken place which was likely to be attended with some disastrous result, that was surely the one.

But how could he leave, watched and surrounded as he was by an infuriated multitude--how could he hope but that his footsteps would be dogged, or that the slightest attempt of his to convey a warning to Sir Francis Varney, would not be the means of bringing down upon his head the very danger he sought to shield him from.

In this state of uncertainty, then, did our medical man remain, a prey to the bitterest reflections, and full of the direst apprehensions, without having the slightest power of himself to alter so disastrous a train of circumstances.

Dissatisfied with their non-success, the crowd twice searched the house of Sir Francis Varney, from the attics to the basement; and then, and not till then, did they begin reluctantly to believe that the servants must have spoken the truth.

"He's in the town somewhere," cried one. "Let's go back to the town."

It is strange how suddenly any mob will obey any impulse, and this perfectly groundless supposition was sufficient to turn their steps back again in the direction whence they came, and they had actually, in a straggling sort of column, reached halfway towards the town, when they encountered a boy, whose professional pursuit consisted in tending sheep very early of a morning, and who at once informed them that he had seen Sir Francis Varney in the wood, half way between Bannerworth Hall and his own home.

This event at once turned the whole tide again, and with renewed clamours, carrying Mr. Chillingworth along with them, they now rapidly neared the real spot, where, probably, had they turned a little earlier, they would have viewed the object of their suspicion and hatred.

But, as we have already recorded, the advancing throng was seen by the parties on the ground, where the duel could scarcely have been said to have been fought; and then had Sir Francis Varney dashed into the wood, which was so opportunely at hand to afford him a shelter from his enemies, and from the intricacies of which--well acquainted with them as he doubtless was,--he had every chance of eluding their pursuit.

The whole affair was a great surprise to Henry and his friends, when they saw such a string of people advancing, with such shouts and imprecations; they could not, for the life of them, imagine what could have excited such a turn out among the ordinarily industrious and quiet inhabitants of a town, remarkable rather for the quietude and steadiness of its population, than for any violent outbreaks of popular feeling.

"What can Mr. Chillingworth be about," said Henry, "to bring such a mob here? has he taken leave of his senses?"

"Nay," said Marchdale; "look again; he seems to be trying to keep them back, although ineffectually, for they will not be stayed."

"D----e," said the admiral, "here's a gang of pirates; we shall be boarded and carried before we know where we are, Jack."

"Ay ay, sir," said Jack.

"And is that all you've got to say, you lubber, when you see your admiral in danger? You'd better go and make terms with the enemy at once."

"Really, this is serious," said Henry; "they shout for Varney. Can Mr. Chillingworth have been so mad as to adopt this means of stopping the duel?"

"Impossible," said Marchdale; "if that had been his intention, he could have done so quietly, through the medium of the civil authorities."

"Hang me!" exclaimed the admiral, "if there are any civil authorities; they talk of smashing somebody. What do they say, Jack? I don't hear quite so well as I used."

"You always was a little deaf," said Jack.

"What?"

"A little deaf, I say."

"Why, you lubberly lying swab, how dare you say so?"

"Because you was."

"You slave-going scoundrel!"

"For Heaven's sake, do not quarrel at such a time as this!" said Henry; "we shall be surrounded in a moment. Come, Mr. Marchdale, let you and I visit these people, and ascertain what it is that has so much excited their indignation."

"Agreed," said Marchdale; and they both stepped forward at a rapid pace, to meet the advancing throng.

The crowd which had now approached to within a short distance of the expectant little party, was of a most motley description, and its appearance, under many circumstances, would cause considerable risibility. Men and women were mixed indiscriminately together, and in the shouting, the latter, if such a thing were possible, exceeded the former, both in discordance and energy.

Every individual composing that mob carried some weapon calculated for defence, such as flails, scythes, sickles, bludgeons, &c., and this mode of arming caused them to wear a most formidable appearance; while the passion that superstition had called up was strongly depicted in their inflamed features. Their fury, too, had been excited by their disappointment, and it was with concentrated rage that they now pressed onward.

The calm and steady advance of Henry and Mr. Marchdale to meet the advancing throng, seemed to have the effect of retarding their progress a little, and they came to a parley at a hedge, which separated them from the meadow in which the duel had been fought.

"You seem to be advancing towards us," said Henry. "Do you seek me or any of my friends; and if so, upon what errand? Mr. Chillingworth, for Heaven's sake, explain what is the cause of all this assault. You seem to be at the head of it."

"Seem to be," said Mr. Chillingworth, "without being so. You are not sought, nor any of your friends?"

"Who, then?"

"Sir Francis Varney," was the immediate reply.

"Indeed! and what has he done to excite popular indignation? of private wrong I can accuse him; but I desire no crowd to take up my cause, or to avenge my quarrels."

"Mr. Bannerworth, it has become known, through my indiscretion, that Sir Francis Varney is suspected of being a vampyre."

"Is this so?"

"Hurrah!" shouted the mob. "Down with the vampyre! hurrah! where is he? Down with him!"

"Drive a stake through him," said a woman; "it's the only way, and the humanest. You've only to take a hedge stake and sharpen it a bit at one end, and char it a little in the fire so as there mayt'n't be no splinters to hurt, and then poke it through his stomach."

The mob gave a great shout at this humane piece of advice, and it was some time before Henry could make himself heard at all, even to those who were nearest to him.

When he did succeed in so doing, he cried, with a loud voice,--

"Hear me, all of you. It is quite needless for me to inquire how you became possessed of the information that a dreadful suspicion hangs over the person of Sir Francis Varney; but if, in consequence of hearing such news, you fancy this public demonstration will be agreeable to me, or likely to relieve those who are nearest or dearest to me from the state of misery and apprehension into which they have fallen, you are much mistaken."

"Hear him, hear him!" cried Mr. Marchdale; "he speaks both wisdom and truth."

"If anything," pursued Henry, "could add to the annoyance of vexation and misery we have suffered, it would assuredly be the being made subjects of every-day gossip, and every-day clamour."

"You hear him?" said Mr. Marchdale.

"Yes, we does," said a man; "but we comes out to catch a vampyre, for all that."

"Oh, to be sure," said the humane woman; "nobody's feelings is nothing to us. Are we to be woke up in the night with vampyres sucking our bloods while we've got a stake in the country?"

"Hurrah!" shouted everybody. "Down with the vampyre! where is he?"

"You are wrong. I assure you, you are all wrong," said Mr. Chillingworth, imploringly; "there is no vampyre here, you see. Sir Francis Varney has not only escaped, but he will take the law of all of you."

This was an argument which appeared to stagger a few, but the bolder spirits pushed them on, and a suggestion to search the wood having been made by some one who was more cunning than his neighbours, that measure was at once proceeded with, and executed in a systematic manner, which made those who knew it to be the hiding-place of Sir Francis Varney tremble for his safety.

It was with a strange mixture of feeling that Henry Bannerworth waited the result of the search for the man who but a few minutes before had been opposed to him in a contest of life or death.

The destruction of Sir Francis Varney would certainly have been an effectual means of preventing him from continuing to be the incubus he then was upon the Bannerworth family; and yet the generous nature of Henry shrank with horror from seeing even such a creature as Varney sacrificed at the shrine of popular resentment, and murdered by an infuriated populace.

He felt as great an interest in the escape of the vampyre as if some great advantage to himself had been contingent upon such an event; and, although he spoke not a word, while the echoes of the little wood were all awakened by the clamorous manner in which the mob searched for their victim, his feelings could be well read upon his countenance.

The admiral, too, without possessing probably the fine feelings of Henry Bannerworth, took an unusually sympathetic interest in the fate of the vampyre; and, after placing himself in various attitudes of intense excitement, he exclaimed,--

"D--n it, Jack, I do hope, after all, the vampyre will get the better of them. It's like a whole flotilla attacking one vessel--a lubberly proceeding at the best, and I'll be hanged if I like it. I should like to pour in a broadside into those fellows, just to let them see it wasn't a proper English mode of fighting. Shouldn't you, Jack?"

"Ay, ay, sir, I should."

"Shiver me, if I see an opportunity, if I don't let some of those rascals know what's what."

Scarcely had these words escaped the lips of the old admiral than there arose a loud shout from the interior of the wood. It was a shout of success, and seemed at the very least to herald the capture of the unfortunate Varney.

"By Heaven!" exclaimed Henry, "they have him."

"God forbid!" said Mr. Marchdale; "this grows too serious."

"Bear a hand, Jack," said the admiral: "we'll have a fight for it yet; they sha'n't murder even a vampyre in cold blood. Load the pistols and send a flying shot or two among the rascals, the moment they appear."

"No, no," said Henry; "no more violence, at least there has been enough--there has been enough."

Even as he spoke there came rushing from among the trees, at the corner of the wood, the figure of a man. There needed but one glance to assure them who it was. Sir Francis Varney had been seen, and was flying before those implacable foes who had sought his life.

He had divested himself of his huge cloak, as well as of his low slouched hat, and, with a speed which nothing but the most absolute desperation could have enabled him to exert, he rushed onward, beating down before him every obstacle, and bounding over the meadows at a rate that, if he could have continued it for any length of time, would have set pursuit at defiance.

"Bravo!" shouted the admiral, "a stern chase is a long chase, and I wish them joy of it--d----e, Jack, did you ever see anybody get along like that?"

"Ay, ay, sir."

"You never did, you scoundrel."

"Yes, I did."

"When and where?"

"When you ran away off the sound."

The admiral turned nearly blue with anger, but Jack looked perfectly imperturbable, as he added,--

"You know you ran away after the French frigates who wouldn't stay to fight you."

"Ah! that indeed. There he goes, putting on every stitch of canvass, I'll be bound."

"And there they come," said Jack, as he pointed to the corner of the wood, and some of the more active of the vampyre's pursuers showed themselves.

It would appear as if the vampyre had been started from some hiding-place in the interior of the wood, and had then thought it expedient altogether to leave that retreat, and make his way to some more secure one across the open country, where there would be more obstacles to his discovery than perseverance could overcome. Probably, then, among the brushwood and trees, for a few moments he had been again lost sight of, until those who were closest upon his track had emerged from among the dense foliage, and saw him scouring across the country at such headlong speed. These were but few, and in their extreme anxiety themselves to capture Varney, whose precipate and terrified flight brought a firm conviction to their minds of his being a vampyre, they did not stop to get much of a reinforcement, but plunged on like greyhounds in his track.

"Jack," said the admiral, "this won't do. Look at that great lubberly fellow with the queer smock-frock."

"Never saw such a figure-head in my life," said Jack.

"Stop him."

"Ay, ay, sir."

The man was coming on at a prodigious rate, and Jack, with all the deliberation in the world, advanced to meet him; and when they got sufficiently close together, that in a few moments they must encounter each other, Jack made himself into as small a bundle as possible, and presented his shoulder to the advancing countryman in such a way, that he flew off it at a tangent, as if he had run against a brick wall, and after rolling head over heels for some distance, safely deposited himself in a ditch, where he disappeared completely for a few moments from all human observation.

"Don't say I hit you," said Jack. "Curse yer, what did yer run against me for? Sarves you right. Lubbers as don't know how to steer, in course runs agin things."

"Bravo," said the admiral; "there's another of them."

The pursuers of Varney the vampyre, however, now came too thick and fast to be so easily disposed of, and as soon as his figure could be seen coursing over the meadows, and springing over road and ditch with an agility almost frightful to look upon, the whole rabble rout was in pursuit of him.

By this time, the man who had fallen into the ditch had succeeded in making his appearance in the visible world again, and as he crawled up the bank, looking a thing of mire and mud, Jack walked up to him with all the carelessness in the world, and said to him,--

"Any luck, old chap?"

"Oh, murder!" said the man, "what do you mean? who are you? where am I? what's the matter? Old Muster Fowler, the fat crowner, will set upon me now."

"Have you caught anything?" said Jack.

"Caught anything?"

"Yes; you've been in for eels, haven't you?"

"D--n!"

"Well, it is odd to me, as some people can't go a fishing without getting out of temper. Have it your own way; I won't interfere with you;" and away Jack walked.

The man cleared the mud out of his eyes, as well as he could, and looked after him with a powerful suspicion that in Jack he saw the very cause of his mortal mishap: but, somehow or other, his immersion in the not over limpid stream had wonderfully cooled his courage, and casting one despairing look upon his begrimed apparel, and another at the last of the stragglers who were pursuing Sir Francis Varney across the fields, he thought it prudent to get home as fast he could, and get rid of the disagreeable results of an adventure which had turned out for him anything but auspicious or pleasant.

Mr. Chillingworth, as though by a sort of impulse to be present in case Sir Francis Varney should really be run down and with a hope of saving him from personal violence, had followed the foremost of the rioters in the wood, found it now quite impossible for him to carry on such a chase as that which was being undertaken across the fields after Sir Francis Varney.

His person was unfortunately but ill qualified for the continuance of such a pursuit, and, although with the greatest reluctance, he at last felt himself compelled to give it up.

In making his way through the intricacies of the wood, he had been seriously incommoded by the thick undergrowth, and he had accidentally encountered several miry pools, with which he had involuntarily made a closer acquaintance than was at all conducive either to his personal appearance or comfort. The doctor's temper, though, generally speaking, one of the most even, was at last affected by his mishaps, and he could not restrain from an execration upon his want of prudence in letting his wife have a knowledge of a secret that was not his own, and the producing an unlooked for circumstance, the termination of which might be of a most disastrous nature.

Tired, therefore, and nearly exhausted by the exertions he had already taken, he emerged now alone from the wood, and near the spot where stood Henry Bannerworth and his friends in consultation.

The jaded look of the surgeon was quite sufficient indication of the trouble and turmoil he had gone through, and some expressions of sympathy for his condition were dropped by Henry, to whom he replied,--

"Nay, my young friend, I deserve it all. I have nothing but my own indiscretion to thank for all the turmoil and tumult that has arisen this morning."

"But to what possible cause can we attribute such an outrage?"

"Reproach me as much as you will, I deserve it. A man may prate of his own secrets if he like, but he should be careful of those of other people. I trusted yours to another, and am properly punished."

"Enough," said Henry; "we'll say no more of that, Mr. Chillingworth. What is done cannot be undone, and we had better spend our time in reflection of how to make the best of what is, than in useless lamentation over its causes. What is to be done?"

"Nay, I know not. Have you fought the duel?"

"Yes; and, as you perceive, harmlessly."

"Thank Heaven for that."

"Nay, I had my fire, which Sir Francis Varney refused to return; so the affair had just ended, when the sound of approaching tumult came upon our ears."

"What a strange mixture," exclaimed Marchdale, "of feelings and passions this Varney appears to be. At one moment acting with the apparent greatest malignity; and another, seeming to have awakened in his mind a romantic generosity which knows no bounds. I cannot understand him."

"Nor I, indeed," said Henry; "but yet I somehow tremble for his fate, and I seem to feel that something ought to be done to save him from the fearful consequences of popular feeling. Let us hasten to the town, and procure what assistance we may: but a few persons, well organised and properly armed, will achieve wonders against a desultory and ill-appointed multitude. There may be a chance of saving him, yet, from the imminent danger which surrounds him."

"That's proper," cried the admiral. "I don't like to see anybody run down. A fair fight's another thing. Yard arm and yard arm--stink pots and pipkins--broadside to broadside--and throw in your bodies, if you like, on the lee quarter; but don't do anything shabby. What do you think of it, Jack?"

"Why, I means to say as how if Varney only keeps on sail as he's been doing, that the devil himself wouldn't catch him in a gale."

"And yet," said Henry, "it is our duty to do the best we can. Let us at once to the town, and summons all the assistance in our power. Come on--come on!"

His friends needed no further urging, but, at a brisk pace, they all proceeded by the nearest footpaths towards the town.

It puzzled his pursuers to think in what possible direction Sir Francis Varney expected to find sustenance or succour, when they saw how curiously he took his flight across the meadows. Instead of endeavouring, by any circuitous path, to seek the shelter of his own house, or to throw himself upon the care of the authorities of the town, who must, to the extent of their power, have protected him, he struck across the fields, apparently without aim or purpose, seemingly intent upon nothing but to distance his pursuers in a long chase, which might possibly tire them, or it might not, according to their or his powers of endurance.

We say this seemed to be the case, but it was not so in reality. Sir Francis Varney had a deeper purpose, and it was scarcely to be supposed that a man of his subtle genius, and, apparently, far-seeing and reflecting intellect, could have so far overlooked the many dangers of his position as not to be fully prepared for some such contingency as that which had just now occurred.

Holding, as he did, so strange a place in society--living among men, and yet possessing so few attributes in common with humanity--he must all along have felt the possibility of drawing upon himself popular violence.

He could not wholly rely upon the secrecy of the Bannerworth family, much as they might well be supposed to shrink from giving publicity to circumstances of so fearfully strange and perilous a nature as those which had occurred amongst them. The merest accident might, at any moment, make him the town's talk. The overhearing of a few chance words by some gossiping domestic--some ebullition of anger or annoyance by some member of the family--or a communication from some friend who had been treated with confidence--might, at any time, awaken around him some such a storm as that which now raged at his heels.

Varney the vampire must have calculated this. He must have felt the possibility of such a state of things; and, as a matter of course, politicly provided himself with some place of refuge.

After about twenty minutes of hard chasing across the fields, there could be no doubt of his intentions. He had such a place of refuge; and, strange a one as it might appear, he sped towards it in as direct a line as ever a well-sped arrow flew towards its mark.

That place of refuge, to the surprise of every one, appeared to be the ancient ruin, of which we have before spoken, and which was so well known to every inhabitant of the county.

Truly, it seemed like some act of mere desperation for Sir Francis Varney to hope there to hide himself. There remained within, of what had once been a stately pile, but a few grey crumbling walls, which the hunted have would have passed unheeded, knowing that not for one instant could he have baffled his pursuers by seeking so inefficient a refuge.

And those who followed hard and fast upon the track of Sir Francis Varney felt so sure of their game, when they saw whither he was speeding, that they relaxed in their haste considerably, calling loudly to each other that the vampire was caught at last, for he could be easily surrounded among the old ruins, and dragged from amongst its moss-grown walls.

In another moment, with a wild dash and a cry of exultation, he sprang out of sight, behind an angle, formed by what had been at one time one of the principal supports of the ancient structure.

Then, as if there was still something so dangerous about him, that only by a great number of hands could he be hoped to be secured, the infuriated peasantry gathered in a dense circle around what they considered his temporary place of refuge, and as the sun, which had now climbed above the tree tops, and dispersed, in a great measure, many of the heavy clouds of morning, shone down upon the excited group, they might have been supposed there assembled to perform some superstitious rite, which time had hallowed as an association of the crumbling ruin around which they stood.

By the time the whole of the stragglers, who had persisted in the chase, had come up, there might have been about fifty or sixty resolute men, each intent upon securing the person of one whom they felt, while in existence, would continue to be a terror to all the weaker and dearer portions of their domestic circles.

There was a pause of several minutes. Those who had come the fleetest were gathering breath, and those who had come up last were looking to their more forward companions for some information as to what had occurred before their arrival.

All was profoundly still within the ruin, and then suddenly, as if by common consent, there arose from every throat a loud shout of "Down with the vampyre! down with the vampyre!"

The echoes of that shout died away, and then all was still as before, while a superstitious feeling crept over even the boldest. It would almost seem as if they had expected some kind of response from Sir Francis Varney to the shout of defiance with which they had just greeted him; but the very calmness, repose, and absolute quiet of the ruin, and all about it, alarmed them, and they looked the one at the other as if the adventure after all were not one of the pleasantest description, and might not fall out so happily as they had expected.

Yet what danger could there be? there were they, more than half a hundred stout, strong men, to cope with one; they felt convinced that he was completely in their power; they knew the ruins could not hide him, and that five minutes time given to the task, would suffice to explore every nook and corner of them.

And yet they hesitated, while an unknown terror shook their nerves, and seemingly from the very fact that they had run down their game successfully, they dreaded to secure the trophy of the chase.

One bold spirit was wanting; and, if it was not a bold one that spoke at length, he might be complimented as being comparatively such. It was one who had not been foremost in the chase, perchance from want of physical power, who now stood forward, and exclaimed,--

"What are you waiting for, now? You can have him when you like. If you want your wives and children to sleep quietly in their beds, you will secure the vampyre. Come on--we all know he's here--why do you hesitate? Do you expect me to go alone and drag him out by the ears?"

Any voice would have sufficed to break the spell which bound them. This did so; and, with one accord, and yells of imprecation, they rushed forward and plunged among the old walls of the ruin.

Less time than we have before remarked would have enabled any one to explore the tottering fabric sufficient to bring a conviction to their minds that, after all, there might have been some mistake about the matter, and Sir Francis Varney was not quite caught yet.

It was astonishing how the fact of not finding him in a moment, again roused all their angry feelings against him, and dispelled every feeling of superstitious awe with which he had been surrounded; rage gave place to the sort of shuddering horror with which they had before contemplated his immediate destruction, when they had believed him to be virtually within their very grasp.

Over and over again the ruins were searched--hastily and impatiently by some, carefully and deliberately by others, until there could be no doubt upon the mind of every one individual, that somehow or somewhere within the shadow of those walls, Sir Francis Varney had disappeared most mysteriously.

Then it would have been a strange sight for any indifferent spectator to have seen how they shrunk, one by one, out of the shadow of those ruins; each seeming to be afraid that the vampyre, in some mysterious manner, would catch him if he happened to be the last within their sombre influence; and, when they had all collected in the bright, open space, some little distance beyond, they looked at each other and at the ruins, with dubious expressions of countenance, each, no doubt, wishing that each would suggest something of a consolatory or practicable character.

"What's to be done, now?" said one.

"Ah! that's it," said another, sententiously. "I'll be hanged if I know."

"He's given us the slip," remarked a third.

"But he can't have given us the slip," said one man, who was particularly famous for a dogmatical spirit of argumentation; "how is it possible? he must be here, and I say he is here."

"Find him, then," cried several at once.

"Oh! that's nothing to do with the argument; he's here, whether we find him or not."

One very cunning fellow laid his finger on his nose, and beckoned to a comrade to retire some paces, where he delivered himself of the following very oracular sentiment:--

"My good friend, you must know Sir Francis Varney is here or he isn't."

"Agreed, agreed."

"Well, if he isn't here it's no use troubling our heads any more about him; but, otherwise, it's quite another thing, and, upon the whole, I must say, that I rather think he is."

All looked at him, for it was evident he was big with some suggestion. After a pause, he resumed,--

"Now, my good friends, I propose that we all appear to give it up, and to go away; but that some one of us shall remain and hide among the ruins for some time, to watch, in case the vampyre makes his appearance from some hole or corner that we haven't found out."

"Oh, capital!" said everybody.

"Then you all agree to that?"

"Yes, yes."

"Very good; that's the only way to nick him. Now, we'll pretend to give it up; let's all of us talk loud about going home."

They did all talk loud about going home; they swore that it was not worth the trouble of catching him, that they gave it up as a bad job; that he might go to the deuce in any way he liked, for all they cared; and then they all walked off in a body, when, the man who had made the suggestion, suddenly cried,--

"Hilloa! hilloa!--stop! stop! you know one of us is to wait?"

"Oh, ay; yes, yes, yes!" said everybody, and still they moved on.

"But really, you know, what's the use of this? who's to wait?"

That was, indeed, a knotty question, which induced a serious consultation, ending in their all, with one accord, pitching upon the author of the suggestion, as by far the best person to hide in the ruins and catch the vampyre.

They then all set off at full speed; but the cunning fellow, who certainly had not the slightest idea of so practically carrying out his own suggestion, scampered off after them with a speed that soon brought him in the midst of the throng again, and so, with fear in their looks, and all the evidences of fatigue about them, they reached the town to spread fresh and more exaggerated accounts of the mysterious conduct of Varney the vampyre.

CHAPTER XLIV

VARNEY'S DANGER, AND HIS RESCUE.--THE PRISONER AGAIN, AND THE SUBTERRANEAN VAULT

We have before slightly mentioned to the reader, and not unadvisedly, the existence of a certain prisoner, confined in a gloomy dungeon, into whose sad and blackened recesses but few and faint glimmering rays of light ever penetrated; for, by a diabolical ingenuity, the narrow loophole which served for a window to that subterraneous abode was so constructed, that, let the sun be at what point it might, during its diurnal course, but a few reflected beams of light could ever find their way into that abode of sorrow.

The prisoner--the same prisoner of whom we before spoke--is there. Despair is in his looks, and his temples are still bound with those cloths, which seemed now for many days to have been sopped in blood, which has become encrusted in their folds.

He still lives, apparently incapable of movement. How he has lived so long seems to be a mystery, for one would think him scarcely in a state, even were nourishment placed to his lips, to enable him to swallow it.

It may be, however, that the mind has as much to do with that apparent absolute prostration of all sort of physical energy as those bodily wounds which he has received at the hands of the enemies who have reduced him to his present painful and hopeless situation.

Occasionally a low groan burst from his lips; it seems to come from the very bottom of his heart, and it sounds as if it would carry with it every remnant of vitality that was yet remaining to him.

Then he moves restlessly, and repeats in hurried accents the names of some who are dear to him, and far away--some who may, perchance, be mourning him, but who know not, guess not, aught of his present sufferings.

As he thus moves, the rustle of a chain among the straw on which he lies gives an indication, that even in that dungeon it has not been considered prudent to leave him master of his own actions, lest, by too vigorous an effort, he might escape from the thraldom in which he is held.

The sound reaches his own ears, and for a few moments, in the deep impatience of his wounded spirit, he heaps malediction on the heads of those who have reduced him to his present state.

But soon a better nature seems to come over him, and gentler words fall from his lips. He preaches patience to himself--he talks not of revenge, but of justice, and in accents of more hopefulness than he had before spoken, he calls upon Heaven to succour him in his deep distress.

Then all is still, and the prisoner appears to have resigned himself once more to the calmness of expectation or of despair; but hark! his sense of hearing, rendered doubly acute by lying so long alone in nearly darkness, and in positive silence, detects sounds which, to ordinary mortal powers of perception, would have been by far too indistinct to produce any tangible effect upon the senses.

It is the sound of feet--on, on they come; far overhead he hears them; they beat the green earth--that sweet, verdant sod, which he may never see again--with an impatient tread. Nearer and nearer still; and now they pause; he listens with all the intensity of one who listens for existence; some one comes; there is a lumbering noise--a hasty footstep; he hears some one labouring for breath--panting like a hunted hare; his dungeon door is opened, and there totters in a man, tall and gaunt; he reels like one intoxicated; fatigue has done more than the work of inebriation; he cannot save himself, and he sinks exhausted by the side of that lonely prisoner.

The captive raises himself as far as his chains will allow him; he clutches the throat of his enervated visitor.

"Villain, monster, vampyre!" he shrieks, "I have thee now;" and locked in a deadly embrace, they roll upon the damp earth, struggling for life together.

***

It is mid-day at Bannerworth Hall, and Flora is looking from the casement anxiously expecting the arrival of her brothers. She had seen, from some of the topmost windows of the Hall, that the whole neighbourhood had been in a state of commotion, but little did she guess the cause of so much tumult, or that it in any way concerned her.

She had seen the peasantry forsaking their work in the fields and the gardens, and apparently intent upon some object of absorbing interest; but she feared to leave the house, for she had promised Henry that she would not do so, lest the former pacific conduct of the vampyre should have been but a new snare, for the purpose of drawing her so far from her home as to lead her into some danger when she should be far from assistance.

And yet more than once was she tempted to forget her promise, and to seek the open country, for fear that those she loved should be encountering some danger for her sake, which she would willingly either share with them or spare them.

The solicitation, however, of her brother kept her comparatively quiet; and, moreover, since her last interview with Varney, in which, at all events, he had shown some feeling for the melancholy situation to which, he had reduced her, she had been more able to reason calmly, and to meet the suggestions of passion and of impulse with a sober judgment.

About midday, then, she saw the domestic party returning--that party, which now consisted of her two brothers, the admiral, Jack Pringle, and Mr. Chillingworth. As for Mr. Marchdale, he had given them a polite adieu on the confines of the grounds of Bannerworth Hall, stating, that although he had felt it to be his duty to come forward and second Henry Bannerworth in the duel with the vampyre, yet that circumstance by no means obliterated from his memory the insults he had received from Admiral Bell, and, therefore, he declined going to Bannerworth Hall, and bade them a very good morning.

To all this, Admiral Bell replied that he might go and be d----d, if he liked, and that he considered him a swab and a humbug, and appealed to Jack Pringle whether he, Jack, ever saw such a sanctified looking prig in his life.

"Ay, ay," says Jack.

This answer, of course, produced the usual contention, which lasted them until they got fairly in the house, where they swore at each other to an extent that was enough to make any one's hair stand on end, until Henry and Mr. Chillingworth interfered, and really begged that they would postpone the discussion until some more fitting opportunity.

The whole of the circumstances were then related to Flora; who, while she blamed her brother much for fighting the duel with the vampyre, found in the conduct of that mysterious individual, as regarded the encounter, yet another reason for believing him to be strictly sincere in his desire to save her from the consequences of his future visits.

Her desire to leave Bannerworth Hall consequently became more and more intense, and as the admiral really now considered himself the master of the house, they offered no amount of opposition to the subject, but merely said,--

"My dear Flora, Admiral Bell shall decide in all these matters, now. We know that he is our sincere friend; and that whatever he says we ought to do, will be dictated by the best possible feelings towards us."

"Then I appeal to you, sir," said Flora, turning to the admiral.

"Very good," replied the old man; "then I say--"

"Nay, admiral," interrupted Mr. Chillingworth; "you promised me, but a short time since, that you would come to no decision whatever upon this question, until you had heard some particulars which I have to relate to you, which, in my humble opinion, will sway your judgment."

"And so I did," cried the admiral; "but I had forgotten all about it. Flora, my dear, I'll be with you in an hour or two. My friend, the doctor, here, has got some sow by the ear, and fancies it's the right one; however, I'll hear what he has got to say, first, before we come to a conclusion. So, come along, Mr. Chillingworth, and let's have it out at once."

"Flora," said Henry, when the admiral had left the room, "I can see that you wish to leave the Hall."

"I do, brother; but not to go far--I wish rather to hide from Varney than to make myself inaccessible by distance."

"You still cling to this neighbourhood?"

"I do, I do; and you know with what hope I cling to it."

"Perfectly; you still think it possible that Charles Holland may be united to you."

"I do, I do."

"You believe his faith."

"Oh, yes; as I believe in Heaven's mercy."

"And I, Flora; I would not doubt him now for worlds; something even now seems to whisper to me that a brighter sun of happiness will yet dawn upon us, and that, when the mists which at present enshroud ourselves and our fortunes pass away, they will disclose a landscape full of beauty, the future of which shall know no pangs."

"Yes, brother," exclaimed Flora, enthusiastically; "this, after all, may be but some trial, grievous while it lasts, but yet tending eventually only to make the future look more bright and beautiful. Heaven may yet have in store for us all some great happiness, which shall spring clearly and decidedly from out these misfortunes."

"Be it so, and may we ever thus banish despair by such hopeful propositions. Lean on my arm, Flora; you are safe with me. Come, dearest, and taste the sweetness of the morning air."

There was, indeed now, a hopefulness about the manner in which Henry Bannerworth spoke, such as Flora had not for some weary months had the pleasure of listening to, and she eagerly rose to accompany him into the garden, which was glowing with all the beauty of sunshine, for the day had turned out to be much finer than the early morning had at all promised it would be.

"Flora," he said, when they had taken some turns to and fro in the garden, "notwithstanding all that has happened, there is no convincing Mr. Chillingworth that Sir Francis Varney is really what to us he appears."

"Indeed!"

"It is so. In the face of all evidence, he neither will believe in vampyres at all, nor that Varney is anything but some mortal man, like ourselves, in his thoughts, talents, feelings, and modes of life; and with no more power to do any one an injury than we have."

"Oh, would that I could think so!"

"And I; but, unhappily, we have by far too many, and too conclusive evidences to the contrary."

"We have, indeed, brother."

"And though, while we respect that strength of mind in our friend which will not allow him, even almost at the last extremity, to yield to what appear to be stern facts, we may not ourselves be so obdurate, but may feel that we know enough to be convinced."

"You have no doubt, brother?"

"Most reluctantly, I must confess, that I feel compelled to consider Varney as something more than mortal."

"He must be so."

"And now, sister, before we leave the place which has been a home to us from earliest life, let us for a few moments consider if there be any possible excuse for the notion of Mr. Chillingworth, to the effect that Sir Francis Varney wants possession of the house for some purpose still more inimical to our peace and prosperity than any he has yet attempted."

"Has he such an opinion?"

"He has."

"'Tis very strange."

"Yes, Flora; he seems to gather from all the circumstances, nothing but an overwhelming desire on the part of Sir Francis Varney to become the tenant of Bannerworth Hall."

"He certainly wishes to possess it."

"Yes; but can you, sister, in the exercise of any possible amount of fancy, imagine any motive for such an anxiety beyond what he alleges?"

"Which is merely that he is fond of old houses."

"Precisely so. That is the reason, and the only one, that can be got from him. Heaven only knows if it be the true one."

"It may be, brother."

"As you say, it may; but there's a doubt, nevertheless, Flora. I much rejoice that you have had an interview with this mysterious being, for you have certainty, since that time, been happier and more composed than I ever hoped to see you again."

"I have indeed."

"It is sufficiently perceivable."

"Somehow, brother, since that interview, I have not had the same sort of dread of Sir Francis Varney which before made the very sound of his name a note of terror to me. His words, and all he said to me during that interview which took place so strangely between us, indeed how I know not, tended altogether rather to make him, to a certain extent, an object of my sympathies rather than my abhorrence."

"That is very strange."

"I own that it is strange, Henry; but when we come for but a brief moment to reflect upon the circumstances which have occurred, we shall, I think, be able to find some cause even to pity Varney the vampyre."

"How?"

"Thus, brother. It is said--and well may I who have been subject to an attack of such a nature, tremble to repeat the saying--that those who have been once subject to the visitations of a vampyre, are themselves in a way to become one of the dreadful and maddening fraternity."

"I have heard so much, sister," replied Henry.

"Yes; and therefore who knows but that Sir Francis Varney may, at one time, have been as innocent as we are ourselves of the terrible and fiendish propensity which now makes him a terror and a reproach to all who know him, or are in any way obnoxious to his attacks."

"That is true."

"There may have been a time--who shall say there was not?--when he, like me, would have shrunk, with a dread as great as any one could have experienced, from the contamination of the touch even of a vampyre."

"I cannot, sister, deny the soundness of your reasoning," said Henry, with a sigh; "but I still no not see anything, even from a full conviction that Varney is unfortunate, which should induce us to tolerate him."

"Nay, brother, I said not tolerate. What I mean is, that even with the horror and dread we must naturally feel at such a being, we may afford to mingle some amount of pity, which shall make us rather seek to shun him, than to cross his path with a resolution of doing him an injury."

"I perceive well, sister, what you mean. Rather than remain here, and make an attempt to defy Sir Francis Varney, you would fly from him, and leave him undisputed master of the field."

"I would--I would."

"Heaven forbid that I or any one should thwart you. You know well, Flora, how dear you are to me; you know well that your happiness has ever been to us all a matter which has assumed the most important of shapes, as regarded our general domestic policy. It is not, therefore, likely now, dear sister, that we should thwart you in your wish to remove from here."

"I know, Henry, all you would say," remarked Flora, as a tear started to her eyes. "I know well all you think, and, in your love for me, I likewise know well I rely for ever. You are attached to this place, as, indeed, we all are, by a thousand happy and pleasant associations; but listen to me further, Henry, I do not wish to wander far."

"Not far, Flora?"

"No. Do I not still cling to a hope that Charles may yet appear? and if he do so, it will assuredly be in this neighbourhood, which he knows is native and most dear to us all."

"True."

"Then do I wish to make some sort of parade, in the way of publicity, of our leaving the Hall."

"Yes, yes."

"And yet not go far. In the neighbouring town, for example, surely we might find some means of living entirely free from remark or observation as to who or what we were."

"That, sister, I doubt. If you seek for that species of solitude which you contemplate, it is only to be found in a desert."

"A desert?"

"Yes; or in a large city."

"Indeed!"

"Ay, Flora; you may well believe me, that it is so. In a small community you can have no possible chance of evading an amount of scrutiny which would very soon pierce through any disguise you could by any possibility assume."

"Then there is no resource. We must go far."

"Nay, I will consider for you, Flora; and although, as a general principle, what I have said I know to be true, yet some more special circumstance may arise that may point a course that, while it enables us, for Charles Holland's sake, to remain in this immediate neighbourhood, yet will procure to us all the secrecy we may desire."

"Dear--dear brother," said Flora, as she flung herself upon Henry's neck, "you speak cheeringly to me, and, what is more, you believe in Charles's faithfulness and truth."

"As Heaven is my judge, I do."

"A thousand, thousand thanks for such an assurance. I know him too well to doubt, for one moment, his faith. Oh, brother! could he--could Charles Holland, the soul of honour, the abode of every noble impulse that can adorn humanity--could he have written those letters? No, no! perish the thought!"

"It has perished."

"Thank God!"

"I only, upon reflection, wonder how, misled for the moment by the concurrence of a number of circumstances, I could ever have suspected him."

"It is like your generous nature, brother to say so; but you know as well as I, that there has been one here who has, far from feeling any sort of anxiety to think as well as possible of poor Charles Holland, has done all that in him lay to take the worst view of his mysterious disappearance, and induce us to do the like."

"You allude to Mr. Marchdale?"

"I do."

"Well, Flora, at the same time that I must admit you have cause for speaking of Mr. Marchdale as you do, yet when we come to consider all things, there may be found for him excuses."

"May there?"

"Yes, Flora; he is a man, as he himself says, past the meridian of life, and the world is a sad as well as a bad teacher, for it soon--too soon, alas! deprives us of our trusting confidence in human nature."

"It may be so; but yet, he, knowing as he did so very little of Charles Holland, judged him hastily and harshly."

"You rather ought to say, Flora, that he did not judge him generously."

"Well, be it so."

"And you must recollect, when you say so, that Marchdale did not love Charles Holland."

"Nay, now," said Flora, while there flashed across her cheek, for a moment, a heightened colour, "you are commencing to jest with me, and, therefore, we will say no more. You know, dear Henry, all my hopes, my wishes, and my feelings, and I shall therefore leave my future destiny in your hands, to dispose of as you please. Look yonder!"

"Where?"

"There. Do you not see the admiral and Mr. Chillingworth walking among the trees?"

"Yes, yes; I do now."

"How very serious and intent they are upon the subject of their discourse. They seem quite lost to all surrounding objects. I could not have imagined any subject that would so completely have absorbed the attention of Admiral Bell."

"Mr. Chillingworth had something to relate to him or to propose, of a nature which, perchance, has had the effect of enchaining all his attention--he called him from the room."

"Yes; I saw that he did. But see, they come towards us, and now we shall, probably, hear what is the subject-matter of their discourse and consultation."

"We shall."

Admiral Bell had evidently seen Henry and his sister, for now, suddenly, as if not from having for the first moment observed them, and, in consequence, broken off their private discourse, but as if they arrived at some point in it which enabled them to come to a conclusion to be communicative, the admiral came towards the brother and sister.

"Well," said the bluff old admiral, when they were sufficiently near to exchange words, "well, Miss Flora, you are looking a thousand times better than you were."

"I thank you, admiral, I am much better."

"Oh, to be sure you are; and you will be much better still, and no sort of mistake. Now, here's the doctor and I have both been agreeing upon what is best for you."

"Indeed!"

"Yes, to be sure. Have we not, doctor?"

"We have, admiral."

"Good; and what, now, Miss Flora, do you suppose it is?"

"I really cannot say."

"Why, it's change of air, to be sure. You must get away from here as quickly as you can, or there will be no peace for you."

"Yes," added Mr. Chillingworth, advancing; "I am quite convinced that change of scene and change of place, and habits, and people, will tend more to your complete recovery than any other circumstances. In the most ordinary cases of indisposition we always find that the invalid recovers much sooner away from the scene of his indisposition, than by remaining in it, even though its general salubrity be much greater than the place to which he may be removed."

"Good," said the admiral.

"Then we are to understand," said Henry, with a smile, "that we are no longer to be your guests, Admiral Bell?"

"Belay there!" cried the admiral; "who told you to understand any such thing, I should like to know?"

"Well, but we shall look upon this house as yours, now; and, that being the case, if we remove from it, of course we cease to be your guests any longer."

"That's all you know about it. Now, hark ye. You don't command the fleet, so don't pretend to know what the admiral is going to do. I have made money by knocking about some of the enemies of old England, and that's the most gratifying manner in the world of making money, so far as I am concerned."

"It is an honourable mode."

"Of course it is. Well, I am going to--what the deuce do you call it?"

"What?"

"That's just what I want to know. Oh, I have it now. I am going to what the lawyers call invest it."

"A prudent step, admiral, and one which it is to be hoped, before now, has occurred to you."

"Perhaps it has and perhaps it hasn't; however, that's my business, and no one's else's. I am going to invest my spare cash in taking houses; so, as I don't care a straw where the houses may be situated, you can look out for one somewhere that will suit you, and I'll take it; so, after all, you will be my guests there just the same as you are here."

"Admiral," said Henry, "it would be imposing upon a generosity as rare as it is noble, were we to allow you to do so much for us as you contemplate."

"Very good."

"We cannot--we dare not."

"But I say you shall. So you have had your say, and I've had mine, after which, if you please, Master Henry Bannerworth, I shall take upon myself to consider the affair as altogether settled. You can commence operations as soon as you like. I know that Miss Flora, here--bless her sweet eyes--don't want to stay at Bannerworth Hall any longer than she can help it."

"Indeed I was urging upon Henry to remove," said Flora; "but yet I cannot help feeling with him, admiral, that we are imposing upon your goodness."

"Go on imposing, then."

"But--"

"Psha! Can't a man be imposed upon if he likes? D--n it, that's a poor privilege for an Englishman to be forced to make a row about. I tell you I like it. I will be imposed upon, so there's an end of that; and now let's come in and see what Mrs. Bannerworth has got ready for luncheon."

***

It can hardly be supposed that such a popular ferment as had been created in the country town, by the singular reports concerning Varney the Vampyre, should readily, and without abundant satisfaction, subside.

An idea like that which had lent so powerful an impulse to the popular mind, was one far easier to set going than to deprecate or extinguish. The very circumstances which had occurred to foil the excited mob in their pursuit of Sir Francis Varney, were of a nature to increase the popular superstition concerning him, and to make him and his acts appear in still more dreadful colours.

Mobs do not reason very closely and clearly; but the very fact of the frantic flight of Sir Francis Varney from the projected attack of the infuriated multitude, was seized hold of as proof positive of the reality of his vampyre-like existence.

Then, again, had he not disappeared in the most mysterious manner? Had he not sought refuge where no human being would think of seeking refuge, namely, in that old, dilapidated ruin, where, when his pursuers were so close upon his track, he had succeeded in eluding their grasp with a facility which looked as if he had vanished into thin air, or as if the very earth had opened to receive him bodily within its cold embraces?

It is not to be wondered at, that the few who fled so precipitately from the ruin, lost nothing of the wonderful story they had to tell, in the carrying it from that place to the town. When they reached their neighbours, they not only told what had really occurred, but they added to it all their own surmises, and the fanciful creation of all their own fears, so that before mid-day, and about the time when Henry Bannerworth was conversing so quietly in the gardens of the Hall with his beautiful sister, there was an amount of popular ferment in the town, of which they had no conception.

All business was suspended, and many persons, now that once the idea had been started concerning the possibility that a vampyre might have been visiting some of the houses in the place, told how, in the dead of the night, they had heard strange noises. How children had shrieked from no apparent cause--doors opened and shut without human agency; and windows rattled that never had been known to rattle before.

Some, too, went so far as to declare that they had been awakened out of their sleep by noises incidental to an effort made to enter their chambers; and others had seen dusky forms of gigantic proportions outside their windows, tampering with their fastenings, and only disappearing when the light of day mocked all attempts at concealment.

These tales flew from mouth to mouth, and all listened to them with such an eager interest, that none thought it worth while to challenge their inconsistencies, or to express a doubt of their truth, because they had not been mentioned before.

The only individual, and he was a remarkably clever man, who made the slightest remark upon the subject of a practical character, hazarded a suggestion that made confusion worse confounded.

He knew something of vampyres. He had travelled abroad, and had heard of them in Germany, as well as in the east, and, to a crowd of wondering and aghast listeners, he said,--

"You may depend upon it, my friends, this has been going on for some time; there have been several mysterious and sudden deaths in the town lately; people have wasted away and died nobody knew how or wherefore."

"Yes--yes," said everybody.

"There was Miles, the butcher; you know how fat he was, and then how fat he wasn't."

A general assent was given to the proposition; and then, elevating one arm in an oratorical manner, the clever fellow continued,--

"I have not a doubt that Miles, the butcher, and every one else who has died suddenly lately, have been victims of the vampyre; and what's more, they'll all be vampyres, and come and suck other people's blood, till at last the whole town will be a town of vampyres."

"But what's to be done?" cried one, who trembled so excessively that he could scarcely stand under his apprehension.

"There is but one plan--Sir Francis Varney must be found, and put out of the world in such a manner that he can't come back to it again; and all those who are dead that we have any suspicion of, should be taken up out of their graves and looked at, to see if they're rotting or not; if they are it's all right; but, if they look fresh and much, as usual, you may depend they're vampyres, and no mistake."

This was a terrific suggestion thrown amongst a mob. To have caught Sir Francis Varney and immolated him at the shrine of popular fury, they would not have shrunk from; but a desecration of the graves of those whom they had known in life was a matter which, however much it had to recommend it, even the boldest stood aghast at, and felt some qualms of irresolution.

There are many ideas, however, which, like the first plunge into a cold bath, are rather uncomfortable for the moment; but which, in a little time, we become so familiarized with, that they become stripped of their disagreeable concomitants, and appear quite pleasing and natural.

So it was with this notion of exhuming the dead bodies of those townspeople who had recently died from what was called a decay of nature, and such other failures of vitality as bore not the tangible name of any understood disease.

From mouth to mouth the awful suggestion spread like wildfire, until at last it grew into such a shape that it almost seemed to become a duty, at all events, to have up Miles the butcher, and see how he looked.

There is, too, about human nature a natural craving curiosity concerning everything connected with the dead. There is not a man of education or of intellectual endowment who would not travel many miles to look upon the exhumation of the remains of some one famous in his time, whether for his vices, his virtues, his knowledge, his talents, or his heroism; and, if this feeling exist in the minds of the educated and refined in a sublimated shape, which lends to it grace and dignity, we may look for it among the vulgar and the ignorant, taking only a grosser and meaner form, in accordance with their habits of thought. The rude materials, of which the highest and noblest feelings of educated minds are formed, will be found amongst the most grovelling and base; and so this vulgar curiosity, which, combined with other feelings, prompted an ignorant and illiterate mob to exhume Miles, the once fat butcher, in a different form tempted the philosophic Hamlet to moralise upon the skull of Yorick.

And it was wonderful to see how, when these people had made up their minds to carry out the singularly interesting, but, at the same, fearful, suggestion, they assumed to themselves a great virtue in so doing--told each other what an absolute necessity there was, for the public good, that it should be done; and then, with loud shouts and cries concerning the vampyre, they proceeded in a body to the village churchyard, where had been lain, with a hope of reposing in peace, the bones of their ancestors.

A species of savage ferocity now appeared to have seized upon the crowd, and the people, in making up their minds to do something which was strikingly at variance with all their preconceived notions of right and wrong, appeared to feel that it was necessary, in order that they might be consistent, to cast off many of the decencies of life, and to become riotous and reckless.

As they proceeded towards the graveyard, they amused themselves by breaking the windows of the tax-gatherers, and doing what passing mischief they could to the habitations of all who held any official situation or authority.

This was something like a proclamation of war against those who might think it their duty to interfere with the lawless proceedings of an ignorant multitude. A public-house or two, likewise, en route, was sacked of some of its inebriating contents, so that, what with the madness of intoxication, and the general excitement consequent upon the very nature of the business which took them to the churchyard, a more wild and infuriated multitude than that which paused at two iron gates which led into the sanctuary of that church could not be imagined.

Those who have never seen a mob placed in such a situation as to have cast off all moral restraint whatever, at the same time that it feels there is no physical power to cope with it, can form no notion of the mass of terrible passions which lie slumbering under what, in ordinary cases, have appeared harmless bosoms, but which now run riot, and overcame every principle of restraint. It is a melancholy fact, but, nevertheless, a fact, despite its melancholy, that, even in a civilised country like this, with a generally well-educated population, nothing but a well-organised physical force keeps down, from the commission of the most outrageous offences, hundreds and thousands of persons.

We have said that the mob paused at the iron gates of the churchyard, but it was more a pause of surprise than one of vacillation, because they saw that those iron gates were closed, which had not been the case within the memory of the oldest among them.

At the first building of the church, and the enclosure of its graveyard, two pairs of these massive gates had been presented by some munificent patron; but, after a time, they hung idly upon their hinges, ornamental certainly, but useless, while a couple of turnstiles, to keep cattle from straying within the sacred precincts, did duty instead, and established, without trouble, the regular thoroughfare, which long habit had dictated as necessary, through the place of sepulture.

But now those gates were closed, and for once were doing duty. Heaven only knows how they had been moved upon their rusty and time-worn hinges. The mob, however, was checked for the moment, and it was clear that the ecclesiastical authorities were resolved to attempt something to prevent the desecration of the tombs.

Those gates were sufficiently strong to resist the first vigorous shake which was given to them by some of the foremost among the crowd, and then one fellow started the idea that they might be opened from the inside, and volunteered to clamber over the wall to do so.

Hoisted up upon the shoulders of several, he grasped the top of the wall, and raised his head above its level, and then something of a mysterious nature rose up from the inside, and dealt him such a whack between the eyes, that down he went sprawling among his coadjutors.

Now, nobody had seen how this injury had been inflicted, and the policy of those in the garrison should have been certainly to keep up the mystery, and leave the invaders in ignorance of what sort of person it was that had so foiled them. Man, however, is prone to indulge in vain glorification, and the secret was exploded by the triumphant waving of the long staff of the beadle, with the gilt knob at the end of it, just over the parapet of the wall, in token of victory.

"It's Waggles! it's Waggles!" cried everybody "it's Waggles, the beadle!"

"Yes," said a voice from within, "it's Waggles, the beadle; and he thinks as he had yer there rather; try it again. The church isn't in danger; oh, no. What do you think of this?"

The staff was flourished more vigorously than ever, and in the secure position that Waggles occupied it seemed not only impossible to attack him, but that he possessed wonderful powers of resistance, for the staff was long and the knob was heavy.

It was a boy who hit upon the ingenious expedient of throwing up a great stone, so that it just fell inside the wall, and hit Waggles a great blow on the head.

The staff was flourished more vigorously than ever, and the mob, in the ecstasy at the fun which was going on, almost forgot the errand which had brought them.

Perhaps after all the affair might have passed off jestingly, had not there been some really mischievous persons among the throng who were determined that such should not be the case, and they incited the multitude to commence an attack upon the gates, which in a few moments must have produced their entire demolition.

Suddenly, however, the boldest drew back, and there was a pause, as the well-known form of the clergyman appeared advancing from the church door, attired in full canonicals.

"There's Mr. Leigh," said several; "how unlucky he should be here."

"What is this?" said the clergyman, approaching the gates. "Can I believe my eyes when I see before me those who compose the worshippers at this church armed, and attempting to enter for the purpose of violence to this sacred place! Oh! let me beseech you, lose not a moment, but return to your homes, and repent of that which you have already done. It is not yet too late; listen, I pray you, to the voice of one with whom you have so often joined in prayer to the throne of the Almighty, who is now looking upon your actions."

This appeal was heard respectfully, but it was evidently very far from suiting the feelings and the wishes of those to whom it was addressed; the presence of the clergyman was evidently an unexpected circumstance, and the more especially too as he appeared in that costume which they had been accustomed to regard with a reverence almost amounting to veneration. He saw the favourable effect he had produced, and anxious to follow it up, he added,--

"Let this little ebullition of feeling pass away, my friends; and, believe me, when I assure you upon my sacred word, that whatever ground there may be for complaint or subject for inquiry, shall be fully and fairly met; and that the greatest exertions shall be made to restore peace and tranquillity to all of you."

"It's all about the vampyre!" cried one fellow--"Mr. Leigh, how should you like a vampyre in the pulpit?"

"Hush, hush! can it be possible that you know so little of the works of that great Being whom you all pretend to adore, as to believe that he would create any class of beings of a nature such as those you ascribe to that terrific word! Oh, let me pray of you to get rid of these superstitions--alike disgraceful to yourselves and afflicting to me."

The clergyman had the satisfaction of seeing the crowd rapidly thinning from before the gates, and he believed his exhortations were having all the effect he wished. It was not until he heard a loud shout behind him, and, upon hastily turning, saw that the churchyard had been scaled at another place by some fifty or sixty persons, that his heart sunk within him, and he began to feel that what he had dreaded would surely come to pass.

Even then he might have done something in the way of pacific exertion, but for the interference of Waggles, the beadle, who spoilt everything.

CHAPTER XLV

THE OPEN GRAVES.--THE DEAD BODIES.--A SCENE OF TERROR

We have said Waggles spoilt everything, and so he did, for before Mr. Leigh could utter a word more, or advance two steps towards the rioters, Waggles charged them staff in hand, and there soon ensued a riot of a most formidable description.

A kind of desperation seemed to have seized the beadle, and certainly, by his sudden and unexpected attack, he achieved wonders. When, however, a dozen hands got hold of the staff, and it was wrenched from him, and he was knocked down, and half-a-dozen people rolled over him, Waggles was not near the man he had been, and he would have been very well content to have lain quiet where he was; this, however, he was not permitted to do, for two or three, who had felt what a weighty instrument of warfare the parochial staff was, lifted him bodily from the ground, and canted him over the wall, without much regard to whether he fell on a hard or a soft place on the other side.

This feat accomplished, no further attention was paid to Mr. Leigh, who, finding that his exhortations were quite unheeded, retired into the church with an appearance of deep affliction about him, and locked himself in the vestry.

The crowd now had entire possession--without even the sort of control that an exhortation assumed over them--of the burying-ground, and soon in a dense mass were these desperate and excited people collected round the well-known spot where lay the mortal remains of Miles, the butcher.

"Silence!" cried a loud voice, and every one obeyed the mandate, looking towards the speaker, who was a tall, gaunt-looking man, attired in a suit of faded black, and who now pressed forward to the front of the throng.

"Oh!" cried one, "it's Fletcher, the ranter. What does he do here?"

"Hear him! hear him!" cried others; "he won't stop us."

"Yes, hear him," cried the tall man, waving his arms about like the sails of a windmill. "Yes, hear him. Sons of darkness, you're all vampyres, and are continually sucking the life-blood from each other. No wonder that the evil one has power over you all. You're as men who walk in the darkness when the sunlight invites you, and you listen to the words of humanity when those of a diviner origin are offered to your acceptance. But there shall be miracles in the land, and even in this place, set apart with a pretended piety that is in itself most damnable, you shall find an evidence of the true light; and the proof that those who will follow me the true path to glory shall be found here within this grave. Dig up Miles, the butcher!"

"Hear, hear, hear, hurra!" said every body. "Mr. Fletcher's not such a fool, after all. He means well."

"Yes, you sinners," said the ranter, "and if you find Miles, the butcher, decaying--even as men are expected to decay whose mortal tabernacles are placed within the bowels of the earth--you shall gather from that a great omen, and a sign that if you follow me you seek the Lord; but I you find him looking fresh and healthy, as if the warm blood was still within his veins, you shall take that likewise as a signification that what I say to you shall be as the Gospel, and that by coming to the chapel of the Little Boozlehum, ye shall achieve a great salvation."

"Very good," said a brawny fellow, advancing with a spade in his hand; "you get out of the way, and I'll soon have him up. Here goes, like blue blazes!"

The first shovelful of earth he took up, he cast over his head into the air, so that it fell in a shower among the mob, which of course raised a shout of indignation; and, as he continued so to dispose of the superfluous earth, a general row seemed likely to ensue. Mr. Fletcher opened his mouth to make a remark, and, as that feature of his face was rather a capacious one, a descending lump of mould, of a clayey consistency, fell into it, and got so wedged among his teeth, that in the process of extracting it he nearly brought some of those essential portions of his anatomy with it.

This was a state of things that could not last long, and he who had been so liberal with his spadesful of mould was speedily disarmed, and yet he was a popular favourite, and had done the thing so good-humouredly, that nobody touched him. Six or eight others, who had brought spades and pickaxes, now pushed forward to the work, and in an incredibly short space of time the grave of Miles, the butcher, seemed to be very nearly excavated.

Work of any kind or nature whatever, is speedily executed when done with a wish to get through it; and never, perhaps, within the memory of man, was a grave opened in that churchyard with such a wonderful celerity. The excitement of the crowd grew intense--every available spot from which a view of the grave could be got, was occupied; for the last few minutes scarcely a remark had been uttered, and when, at last, the spade of one of those who were digging struck upon something that sounded like wood, you might have heard a pin drop, and each one there present drew his breath more shortly than before.

"There he is," said the man, whose spade struck upon the coffin.

Those few words broke the spell, and there was a general murmur, while every individual present seemed to shift his position in his anxiety to obtain a better view of what was about to ensue.

The coffin now having been once found, there seemed to be an increased impetus given to the work; the earth was thrown out with a rapidity that seemed almost the quick result of the working of some machine; and those closest to the grave's brink crouched down, and, intent as they were upon the progress of events, heeded not the damp earth that fell upon them, nor the frail brittle and humid remains of humanity that occasionally rolled to their feet.

It was, indeed, a scene of intense excitement--a scene which only wanted a few prominent features in its foreground of a more intellectual and higher cast than composed the mob, to make it a fit theme for a painter of the highest talent.

And now the last few shovelfuls of earth that hid the top of the coffin were cast from the grave, and that narrow house which contained the mortal remains of him who was so well known, while in life, to almost every one then present, was brought to the gaze of eyes which never had seemed likely to have looked upon him again.

The cry was now for ropes, with which to raise the cumbrous mass; but these were not to be had, no one thought of providing himself with such appliances, so that by main strength, only, could the coffin be raised to the brink.

The difficulty of doing this was immense, for there was nothing tangible to stand upon; and even when the mould from the sides was sufficiently cleared away, that the handles of the coffin could be laid hold of, they came away immediately in the grasp of those who did so.

But the more trouble that presented itself to the accomplishment of the designs of the mob, the more intent that body seemed upon carrying out to the full extent their original designs.

Finding it quite impossible by bodily strength to raise the coffin of the butcher from the position in which it had got imbedded by excessive rains, a boy was hastily despatched to the village for ropes, and never did boy run with such speed before, for all his own curiosity was excited in the issue of an adventure, that to his young imagination was appallingly interesting.

As impatient as mobs usually are, they had not time, in this case, for the exercise of that quality of mind before the boy came back with the necessary means of exerting quite a different species of power against the butcher's coffin.

Strong ropes were slid under the inert mass, and twenty hands at once plied the task of raising that receptacle of the dead from what had been presumed to be its last resting-place. The ropes strained and creaked, and many thought that they would burst asunder sooner than raise the heavy coffin of the defunct butcher.

It is singular what reasons people find for backing their opinion.

"You may depend he's a vampyre," said one, "or it wouldn't be so difficult to get him out of the grave."

"Oh, there can be no mistake about that," said one; "when did a natural Christian's coffin stick in the mud in that way?"

"Ah, to be sure," said another; "I knew no good would come of his goings on; he never was a decent sort of man like his neighbours, and many queer things have been said of him that I have no doubt are true enough, if we did but know the rights of them."

"Ah, but," said a young lad, thrusting his head between the two who were talking, "if he is a vampyre, how does he get out of his coffin of a night with all that weight of mould a top of him?"

One of the men considered for a moment, and then finding no rational answer occur to him, he gave the boy a box on the ear, saying,--

"I should like to know what business that is of yours? Boys, now-a-days, ain't like the boys in my time; they think nothing now of putting their spokes in grown-up people's wheels, just as if their opinions were of any consequence."

Now, by a vigorous effort, those who were tugging at the ropes succeeded in moving the coffin a little, and that first step was all the difficulty, for it was loosened from the adhesive soil in which it lay, and now came up with considerable facility.

There was a half shout of satisfaction at this result, while some of the congregation turned pale, and trembled at the prospect of the sight which was about to present itself; the coffin was dragged from the grave's brink fairly among the long rank grass that flourished in the churchyard, and then they all looked at it for a time, and the men who had been most earnest in raising it wiped the perspiration from their brows, and seemed to shrink from the task of opening that receptacle of the dead now that it was fairly in their power so to do.

Each man looked anxiously in his neighbour's face, and several audibly wondered why somebody else didn't open the coffin.

"There's no harm in it," said one; "if he's a vampyre, we ought to know it; and, if he ain't, we can't do any hurt to a dead man."

"Oughtn't we to have the service for the dead?" said one.

"Yes," said the impertinent boy who had before received the knock on the head, "I think we ought to have that read backwards."

This ingenious idea was recompensed by a great many kicks and cuffs, which ought to have been sufficient to have warned him of the great danger of being a little before his age in wit.

"Where's the use of shirking the job?" cried he who had been so active in shoveling the mud upon the multitude; "why, you cowardly sneaking set of humbugs, you're half afraid, now."

"Afraid--afraid!" cried everybody: "who's afraid."

"Ah, who's afraid?" said a little man, advancing, and assuming an heroic attitude; "I always notice, if anybody's afraid, it's some big fellow, with more bones than brains."

At this moment, the man to whom this reproach was more particularly levelled, raised a horrible shout of terror, and cried out, in frantic accents,--

"He's a-coming--he's a-coming!"

The little man fell at once into the grave, while the mob, with one accord, turned tail, and fled in all directions, leaving him alone with the coffin. Such a fighting, and kicking, and scrambling ensued to get over the wall of the grave-yard, that this great fellow, who had caused all the mischief, burst into such peals of laughter that the majority of the people became aware that it was a joke, and came creeping back, looking as sheepish as possible.

Some got up very faint sorts of laugh, and said "very good," and swore they saw what big Dick meant from the first, and only ran to make the others run.

"Very good," said Dick, "I'm glad you enjoyed it, that's all. My eye, what a scampering there was among you. Where's my little friend, who was so infernally cunning about bones and brains?"

With some difficulty the little man was extricated from the grave, and then, oh, for the consistency of a mob! they all laughed at him; those very people who, heedless of all the amenities of existence, had been trampling upon each other, and roaring with terror, actually had the impudence to laugh at him, and call him a cowardly little rascal, and say it served him right.

But such is popularity!

"Well, if nobody won't open the coffin," said big Dick, "I will, so here goes. I knowed the old fellow when he was alive, and many a time he's d----d me and I've d----d him, so I ain't a-going to be afraid of him now he's dead. We was very intimate, you see, 'cos we was the two heaviest men in the parish; there's a reason for everything."

"Ah, Dick's the fellow to do it," cried a number of persons; "there's nobody like Dick for opening a coffin; he's the man as don't care for nothing."

"Ah, you snivelling curs," said Dick, "I hate you. If it warn't for my own satisfaction, and all for to prove that my old friend, the butcher, as weighed seventeen stone, and stood six feet two and-a-half on his own sole, I'd see you all jolly well--"

"D----d first," said the boy; "open the lid, Dick, let's have a look."

"Ah, you're a rum un," said Dick, "arter my own heart. I sometimes thinks as you must be a nevy, or some sort of relation of mine. Howsomdever, here goes. Who'd a thought that I should ever had a look at old fat and thunder again?--that's what I used to call him; and then he used to request me to go down below, where I needn't turn round to light my blessed pipe."

"Hell--we know," said the boy; "why don't you open the lid, Dick?"

"I'm a going," said Dick; "kim up."

He introduced the corner of a shovel between the lid and the coffin, and giving it a sudden wrench, he loosened it all down one side.

A shudder pervaded the multitude, and, popularly speaking, you might have heard a pin drop in that crowded churchyard at that eventful moment.

Dick then proceeded to the other side, and executed the same manoeuvre.

"Now for it," he said; "we shall see him in a moment, and we'll think we seed him still."

"What a lark!" said the boy.

"You hold yer jaw, will yer? Who axed you for a remark, blow yer? What do you mean by squatting down there, like a cock-sparrow, with a pain in his tail, hanging yer head, too, right over the coffin? Did you never hear of what they call a fluvifium coming from the dead, yer ignorant beast, as is enough to send nobody to blazes in a minute? Get out of the way of the cold meat, will yer?"

"A what, do you say, Dick?"

"Request information from the extreme point of my elbow."

Dick threw down the spade, and laying hold of the coffin-lid with both hands, he lifted it off, and flung it on one side.

There was a visible movement and an exclamation among the multitude. Some were pushed down, in the eager desire of those behind to obtain a sight of the ghastly remains of the butcher; those at a distance were frantic, and the excitement was momentarily increasing.

They might all have spared themselves the trouble, for the coffin was empty--here was no dead butcher, nor any evidence of one ever having been there, not even the grave-clothes; the only thing at all in the receptacle of the dead was a brick.

Dick's astonishment was so intense that his eyes and mouth kept opening together to such an extent, that it seemed doubtful when they would reach their extreme point of elongation. He then took up the brick and looked at it curiously, and turned it over and over, examined the ends and the sides with a critical eye, and at length he said,--

"Well, I'm blowed, here's a transmogrification; he's consolidified himself into a blessed brick--my eye, here's a curiosity."

"But you don't mean to say that's the butcher, Dick?" said the boy.

Dick reached over, and gave him a tap on the head with the brick.

"There!" he said, "that's what I calls occular demonstration. Do you believe it now, you blessed infidel? What's more natural? He was an out-and-out brick while he was alive; and he's turned to a brick now he's dead."

"Give it to me, Dick," said the boy; "I should like to have that brick, just for the fun of the thing."

"I'll see you turned into a pantile first. I sha'n't part with this here, it looks so blessed sensible; it's a gaining on me every minute as a most remarkable likeness, d----d if it ain't."

By this time the bewilderment of the mob had subsided; now that there was no dead butcher to look upon, they fancied themselves most grievously injured; and, somehow or other, Dick, notwithstanding all his exertions in their service, was looked upon in the light of a showman, who had promised some startling exhibition and then had disappointed his auditors.

The first intimation he had of popular vengeance was a stone thrown at him, but Dick's eye happened to be upon the fellow who threw it, and collaring him in a moment, he dealt him a cuff on the side of the head, which confused his faculties for a week.

"Hark ye," he then cried, with a loud voice, "don't interfere with me; you know it won't go down. There's something wrong here; and, as one of yourselves, I'm as much interested in finding out what it is as any of you can possibly be. There seems to be some truth in this vampyre business; our old friend, the butcher, you see, is not in his grave; where is he then?"

The mob looked at each other, and none attempted to answer the question.

"Why, of course, he's a vampyre," said Dick, "and you may all of you expect to see him, in turn, come into your bed-room windows with a burst, and lay hold of you like a million and a half of leeches rolled into one."

There was a general expression of horror, and then Dick continued,--

"You'd better all of you go home; I shall have no hand in pulling up any more of the coffins--this is a dose for me. Of course you can do what you like."

"Pull them all up!" cried a voice; "pull them all up! Let's see how many vampyres there are in the churchyard."

"Well, it's no business of mine," said Dick; "but I wouldn't, if I was you."

"You may depend," said one, "that Dick knows something about it, or he wouldn't take it so easy."

"Ah! down with him," said the man who had received the box on the ears; "he's perhaps a vampyre himself."

The mob made a demonstration towards him, but Dick stood his ground, and they paused again.

"Now, you're a cowardly set," he said; "cause you're disappointed, you want to come upon me. Now, I'll just show what a little thing will frighten you all again, and I warn beforehand it will, so you sha'n't say you didn't know it, and were taken by surprise."

The mob looked at him, wondering what he was going to do.

"Once! twice! thrice!" he said, and then he flung the brick up into the air an immense height, and shouted "heads," in a loud tone.

A general dispersion of the crowd ensued, and the brick fell in the centre of a very large circle indeed.

"There you are again," said Dick; "why, what a nice act you are!"

"What fun!" said the boy. "It's a famous coffin, this, Dick," and he laid himself down in the butcher's last resting-place. "I never was in a coffin before--it's snug enough."

"Ah, you're a rum 'un," said Dick; "you're such a inquiring genius, you is; you'll get your head into some hole one day, and not be able to get it out again, and then I shall see you a kicking. Hush! lay still--don't say anything."

"Good again," said the boy; "what shall I do?"

"Give a sort of a howl and a squeak, when they've all come back again."

"Won't I!" said the boy; "pop on the lid."

"There you are," said Dick; "d----d if I don't adopt you, and bring you up to the science of nothing."

"Now, listen to me, good people all," added Dick; "I have really got something to say to you."

At this intimation the people slowly gathered again round the grave.

"Listen," said Dick, solemnly; "it strikes me there's some tremendous do going on."

"Yes, there is," said several who were foremost.

"It won't be long before you'll all of you be most d--nably astonished; but let me beg of all you not to accuse me of having anything to do with it, provided I tell you all I know."

"No, Dick; we won't--we won't--we won't."

"Good; then, listen. I don't know anything, but I'll tell you what I think, and that's as good; I don't think that this brick is the butcher; but I think, that when you least expect it--hush! come a little closer."

"Yes, yes; we are closer."

"Well, then, I say, when you all least expect it, and when you ain't dreaming of such a thing, you'll hear something of my fat friend as is dead and gone, that will astonish you all."

Dick paused, and he gave the coffin a slight kick, as intimation to the boy that he might as well be doing his part in the drama, upon which that ingenious young gentleman set up such a howl, that even Dick jumped, so unearthly did it sound within the confines of that receptacle of the dead.

But if the effect upon him was great, what must it have been upon those whom it took completely unawares? For a moment or two they seemed completely paralysed, and then they frightened the boy, for the shout of terror that rose from so many throats at once was positively alarming.

This jest of Dick's was final, for, before three minutes had elapsed, the churchyard was clear of all human occupants save himself and the boy, who had played his part so well in the coffin.

"Get out," said Dick, "it's all right--we've done 'em at last; and now you may depend upon it they won't be in a hurry to come here again. You keep your own counsel, or else somebody will serve you out for this. I don't think you're altogether averse to a bit of fun, and if you keep yourself quiet, you'll have the satisfaction of hearing what's said about this affair in every pot-house in the village, and no mistake."

CHAPTER XLVI

THE PREPARATIONS FOR LEAVING BANNERWORTH HALL, AND THE MYSTERIOUS CONDUCT OF THE ADMIRAL AND MR. CHILLINGWORTH

It seemed now, that, by the concurrence of all parties, Bannerworth Hall was to be abandoned; and, notwithstanding Henry was loth--as he had, indeed, from the first shown himself--to leave the ancient abode of his race, yet, as not only Flora, but the admiral and his friend Mr. Chillingworth seemed to be of opinion that it would be a prudent course to adopt, he felt that it would not become him to oppose the measure.

He, however, now made his consent to depend wholly upon the full and free acquiescence of every member of the family.

"If," he said, "there be any among us who will say to me 'Continue to keep open the house in which we have passed so many happy hours, and let the ancient home of our race still afford a shelter to us,' I shall feel myself bound to do so; but if both my mother and my brother agree to a departure from it, and that its hearth shall be left cold and desolate, be it so. I will not stand in the way of any unanimous wish or arrangement."

"We may consider that, then, as settled," said the admiral, "for I have spoken to your brother, and he is of our opinion. Therefore, my boy, we may all be off as soon as we can conveniently get under weigh."

"But my mother?

"Oh, there, I don't know. You must speak to her yourself. I never, if I can help it, interfere with the women folks."

"If she consent, then I am willing."

"Will you ask her?"

"I will not ask her to leave, because I know, then, what answer she would at once give; but she shall hear the proposition, and I will leave her to decide upon it, unbiased in her judgment by any stated opinion of mine upon the matter."

"Good. That'll do; and the proper way to put it, too. There's no mistake about that, I can tell you."

Henry, although he went through the ceremony of consulting his mother, had no sort of doubt before he did so that she was sufficiently aware of the feelings and wishes of Flora to be prepared to yield a ready assent to the proposition of leaving the Hall.

Moreover, Mr. Marchdale had, from the first, been an advocate of such a course of proceeding, and Henry well knew how strong an influence he had over Mrs. Bannerworth's mind, in consequence of the respect in which she held him as an old and valued friend.

He was, therefore, prepared for what his mother said, which was,--

"My dear Henry, you know that the wishes of my children, since they have been grown up and capable of coming to a judgment for themselves, have ever been laws to me. If you, among you all, agree to leave this place, do so."

"But will you leave it freely, mother?"

"Most freely I go with you all; what is it that has made this house and all its appurtenances pleasant in my eyes, but the presence in it of those who are so dear to me? If you all leave it, you take with you the only charms it ever possessed; so it becomes in itself as nothing. I am quite ready to accompany you all anywhere, so that we do but keep together."

"Then, mother, we may consider that as settled."

"As you please."

"'It's scarcely as I please. I must confess that I would fain have clung with a kind of superstitious reverence to this ancient abiding-place of my race, but it may not be so. Those, perchance, who are more practically able to come to correct conclusions, in consequence of their feelings not being sufficiently interested to lead them astray, have decided otherwise; and, therefore, I am content to leave."

"Do not grieve at it, Henry. There has hung a cloud of misfortune over us all since the garden of this house became the scene of an event which we can none of us remember but with terror and shuddering."

"Two generations of our family must live and die before the remembrance of that circumstance can be obliterated. But we will think of it no more."

There can no doubt but that the dreadful circumstance to which both Mrs. Bannerworth and Henry alluded, was the suicide of the father of the family in the gardens which before has been hinted at in the course of this narration, as being a circumstance which had created a great sensation at the time, and cast a great gloom for many months over the family.

The reader will, doubtless, too, recollect that, at his last moments, this unhappy individual was said to have uttered some incoherent words about some hidden money, and that the rapid hand of death alone seemed to prevent him from being explicit upon that subject, and left it merely a matter of conjecture.

As years had rolled on, this affair, even as a subject of speculation, had ceased to occupy the minds of any of the Bannerworth family, and several of their friends, among whom was Mr. Marchdale, were decidedly of opinion that the apparently pointed and mysterious words uttered, were but the disordered wanderings of an intellect already hovering on the confines of eternity.

Indeed, far from any money, of any amount, being a disturbance to the last moments of the dissolute man, whose vices and extravagances had brought his family, to such ruin, it was pretty generally believed that he had committed suicide simply from a conviction of the impossibility of raising any more supplies of cash, to enable him to carry on the career which he had pursued for so long.

But to resume.

Henry at once communicated to the admiral what his mother had said, and then the whole question regarding the removal being settled in the affirmative, nothing remained to be done but to set about it as quickly as possible.

The Bannerworths lived sufficiently distant from the town to be out of earshot of the disturbances which were then taking place; and so completely isolated were they from all sort of society, that they had no notion of the popular disturbance which Varney the vampyre had given rise to.

It was not until the following morning that Mr. Chillingworth, who had been home in the meantime, brought word of what had taken place, and that great commotion was still in the town, and that the civil authorities, finding themselves by far too weak to contend against the popular will, had sent for assistance to a garrison town, some twenty miles distant.

It was a great grief to the Bannerworth family to hear these tidings, not that they were in any way, except as victims, accessory to creating the disturbance about the vampyre, but it seemed to promise a kind of notoriety which they might well shrink from, and which they were just the people to view with dislike.

View the matter how we like, however, it is not to be considered as at all probable that the Bannerworth family would remain long in ignorance of what a great sensation they had created unwittingly in the neighbourhood.

The very reasons which had induced their servants to leave their establishment, and prefer throwing themselves completely out of place, rather than remain in so ill-omened a house, were sure to be bruited abroad far and wide.

And that, perhaps, when they came to consider of it, would suffice to form another good and substantial reason for leaving the Hall, and seeking a refuge in obscurity from the extremely troublesome sort of popularity incidental to their peculiar situation.

Mr. Chillingworth felt uncommonly chary of telling them all that had taken place; although he was well aware that the proceedings of the riotous mob had not terminated with the little disappointment at the old ruin, to which they had so effectually chased Varney the vampyre, but to lose him so singularly when he got there.

No doubt he possessed the admiral with the uproar that was going on in the town, for the latter did hint a little of it to Henry Bannerworth.

"Hilloa!" he said to Henry, as he saw him walking in the garden; "it strikes me if you and your ship's crew continue in these latitudes, you'll get as notorious as the Flying Dutchman in the southern ocean."

"How do you mean?" said Henry.

"Why, it's a sure going proverb to say, that a nod's as good as a wink; but, the fact is, it's getting rather too well known to be pleasant, that a vampyre has struck up rather a close acquaintance with your family. I understand there's a precious row in the town."

"Indeed!"

"Yes; bother the particulars, for I don't know them; but, hark ye, by to-morrow I'll have found a place for you to go to, so pack up the sticks, get all your stores ready to clear out, and make yourself scarce from this place."

"I understand you," said Henry; "We have become the subject of popular rumour; I've only to beg of you, admiral, that you'll say nothing of this to Flora; she has already suffered enough, Heaven knows; do not let her have the additional infliction of thinking that her name is made familiar in every pothouse in the town."

"Leave me alone for that," said the admiral. "Do you think I'm an ass?"

"Ay, ay," said Jack Pringle, who came in at that moment, and thought the question was addressed to him.

"Who spoke to you, you bad-looking horse-marine?"

"Me a horse-marine! didn't you ask a plain question of a fellow, and get a plain answer?"

"Why, you son of a bad looking gun, what do you mean by that? I tell you what it is, Jack; I've let you come sneaking too often on the quarter-deck, and now you come poking your fun at your officers, you rascal!"

"I poking fun!" said Jack; "couldn't think of such a thing. I should just as soon think of you making a joke as me."

"Now, I tell you what it is, I shall just strike you off the ship's books, and you shall just go and cruise by yourself; I've done with you."

"Go and tell that to the marines, if you like," said Jack. "I ain't done with you yet, for a jolly long watch. Why, what do you suppose would become of you, you great babby, without me? Ain't I always a conveying you from place to place, and steering you through all sorts of difficulties?"

"D---n your impudence!"

"Well, then, d---n yours."

"Shiver my timbers!"

"Ay, you may do what you like with your own timbers."

"And you won't leave me?"

"Sartingly not."

"Come here, then?"

Jack might have expected a gratuity, for he advanced with alacrity.

"There," said the admiral, as he laid his stick across his shoulders; "that's your last month's wages; don't spend it all at once."

"Well, I'm d----d!" said Jack; "who'd have thought of that?--he's a turning rumgumtious, and no mistake. Howsomdever, I must turn it over in my mind, and be even with him, somehow--I owes him one for that. I say, admiral."

"What now, you lubber?"

"Nothing; turn that over in your mind;" and away Jack walked, not quite satisfied, but feeling, at least, that he had made a demonstration of attack.

As for the admiral, he considered that the thump he had given Jack with the stick, and it was no gentle one, was a decided balancing of accounts up to that period, and as he remained likewise master of the field, he was upon the whole very well satisfied.

These last few words which had been spoken to Henry by Admiral Bell, more than any others, induced him to hasten his departure from Bannerworth Hall; he had walked away when the altercation between Jack Pringle and the admiral began, for he had seen sufficient of those wordy conflicts between those originals to be quite satisfied that neither of them meant what he said of a discouraging character towards the other, and that far from there being any unfriendly feeling contingent upon those little affairs, they were only a species of friendly sparring, which both parties enjoyed extremely.

He went direct to Flora, and he said to her,--

"Since we are all agreed upon the necessity, or, at all events, upon the expediency of a departure from the Hall, I think, sister, the sooner we carry out that determination the better and the pleasanter for us all it will be. Do you think you could remove so hastily as to-morrow?"

"To-morrow! That is soon indeed."

"I grant you that it is so; but Admiral Bell assures me that he will have everything in readiness, and a place provided for us to go to by then."

"Would it be possible to remove from a house like this so very quickly?"

"Yes, sister. If you look around you, you will see that a great portion of the comforts you enjoy in this mansion belong to it as a part of its very structure, and are not removable at pleasure; what we really have to take away is very little. The urgent want of money during our father's lifetime induced him, as you may recollect even, at various times to part with much that was ornamental, as well as useful, which was in the Hall. You will recollect that we seldom returned from those little continental tours which to us were so delightful, without finding some old familiar objects gone, which, upon inquiry, we found had been turned into money, to meet some more than usually pressing demand."

"That is true, brother; I recollect well."

"So that, upon the whole, sister, there is little to remove."

"Well, well, be it so. I will prepare our mother for this sudden step. Believe me, my heart goes with it; and as a force of vengeful circumstances have induced us to remove from this home, which was once so full of pleasant recollections, it is certainly better, as you say, that the act should be at once consummated, than left hanging in terror over our minds."

"Then I'll consider that as settled," said Henry.

CHAPTER XLVII

THE REMOVAL FROM THE HALL.--THE NIGHT WATCH, AND THE ALARM

Mrs. Bannerworth's consent having been already given to the removal, she said at once, when appealed to, that she was quite ready to go at any time her children thought expedient.

Upon this, Henry sought the admiral, and told him as much, at the same time adding,--

"My sister feared that we should have considerable trouble in the removal, but I have convinced her that such will not be the case, as we are by no means overburdened with cumbrous property."

"Cumbrous property," said the admiral, "why, what do you mean? I beg leave to say, that when I took the house, I took the table and chairs with it. D--n it, what good do you suppose an empty house is to me?"

"The tables and chairs!"

"Yes. I took the house just as it stands. Don't try and bamboozle me out of it. I tell you, you've nothing to move but yourselves and immediate personal effects."

"I was not aware, admiral, that that was your plan."

"Well, then, now you are, listen to me. I've circumvented the enemy too often not to know how to get up a plot. Jack and I have managed it all. To-morrow evening, after dark, and before the moon's got high enough to throw any light, you and your brother, and Miss Flora and your mother, will come out of the house, and Jack and I will lead you where you're to go to. There's plenty of furniture where you're a-going, and so you will get off free, without anybody knowing anything about it."

"Well, admiral, I've said it before, and it is the unanimous opinion of us all, that everything should be left to you. You have proved yourself too good a friend to us for us to hesitate at all in obeying your commands. Arrange everything, I pray you, according to your wishes and feelings, and you will find there shall be no cavilling on our parts."

"That's right; there's nothing like giving a command to some one person. There's no good done without. Now I'll manage it all. Mind you, seven o'clock to-morrow evening everything is to be ready, and you will all be prepared to leave the Hall."

"It shall be so."

"Who's that giving such a thundering ring at the gate?"

"Nay, I know not. We have few visitors and no servants, so I must e'en be my own gate porter."

Henry walked to the gate, and having opened it, a servant in a handsome livery stepped a pace or two into the garden.

"Well," said Henry.

"Is Mr. Henry Bannerworth within, or Admiral Bell?"

"Both," cried the admiral. "I'm Admiral Bell, and this is Mr. Henry Bannerworth. What do you want with us, you d----d gingerbread-looking flunkey?"

"Sir, my master desires his compliments--his very best compliments--and he wants to know how you are after your flurry."

"What?"

"After your--a--a--flurry and excitement."

"Who is your master?" said Henry.

"Sir Francis Varney."

"The devil!" said the admiral; "if that don't beat all the impudence I ever came near. Our flurry! Ah! I like that fellow. Just go and tell him--"

"No, no," said Henry, interposing, "send back no message. Say to your master, fellow, that Mr. Henry Bannerworth feels that not only has he no claim to Sir Francis Varney's courtesy, but that he would rather be without it."

"Oh, ha!" said the footman, adjusting his collar; "very good. This seems a d----d, old-fashioned, outlandish place of yours. Any ale?"

"Now, shiver my hulks!" said the admiral.

"Hush! hush!" said Henry; "who knows but there may be a design in this? We have no ale."

"Oh, ah! dem!--dry as dust, by God! What does the old commodore say? Any message, my ancient Greek?"

"No, thank you," said the admiral; "bless you, nothing. What did you give for that waistcoat, d--n you? Ha! ha! you're a clever fellow."

"Ah! the old gentleman's ill. However, I'll take back his compliments, and that he's much obliged at Sir Francis's condescension. At the same time, I suppose may place in my eye what I may get out of either of you, without hindering me seeing my way back. Ha! ha! Adieu--adieu."

"Bravo!" said the admiral; "that's it--go it--now for it. D--n it, it is a do!"

The admiral's calmness during the latter part of the dialogue arose from the fact that over the flunkey's shoulder, and at some little distance off, he saw Jack Pringle taking off his jacket, and rolling up his sleeves in that deliberate sort of way that seemed to imply a determination of setting about some species of work that combined the pleasant with the useful.

Jack executed many nods to and winks at the livery-servant, and jerked his thumb likewise in the direction of a pump near at hand, in a manner that spoke as plainly as possible, that John was to be pumped upon.

And now the conference was ended, and Sir Francis's messenger turned to go; but Jack Pringle bothered him completely, for he danced round him in such a singular manner, that, turn which way he would, there stood Jack Pringle, in some grotesque attitude, intercepting him; and so he edged him on, till he got him to the pump.

"Jack," said the admiral.

"Ay, ay, sir."

"Don't pump on that fellow now."

"Ay, ay, sir; give us a hand."

Jack laid hold of him by the two ears, and holding him under the pump, kicked his shins until he completely gathered himself beneath the spout. It was in vain that he shouted "Murder! help! fire! thieves!" Jack was inexorable, and the admiral pumped.

Jack turned the fellow's head about in a very scientific manner, so as to give him a fair dose of hydropathic treatment, and in a few minutes, never was human being more thoroughly saturated with moisture than was Sir Francis Varney's servant. He had left off hallooing for aid, for he found that whenever he did so, Jack held his mouth under the spout, which was decidedly unpleasant; so, with a patience that looked like heroic fortitude, he was compelled to wait until the admiral was tired of pumping.

"Very good," at length he said. "Now, Jack, for fear this fellow catcher cold, be so good as to get a horsewhip, and see him off the premises with it."

"Ay, ay, sir," said Jack. "And I say, old fellow, you can take back all our blessed compliments now, and say you've been flurried a little yourself; and if so be as you came here as dry as dust, d----e, you go back as wet as a mop. Won't it do to kick him out, sir?"

"Very well--as you please, Jack."

"Then here goes;" and Jack proceeded to kick the shivering animal from the garden with a vehemence that soon convinced him of the necessity of getting out of it as quickly as possible.

How it was that Sir Francis Varney, after the fearful race he had had, got home again across the fields, free from all danger, and back to his own house, from whence he sent so cool and insolent a message, they could not conceive.

But such must certainly be the fact; somehow or another, he had escaped all danger, and, with a calm insolence peculiar to the man, he had no doubt adopted the present mode of signifying as much to the Bannerworths.

The insolence of his servant was, no doubt, a matter of pre-arrangement with that individual, however he might have set about it con amore. As for the termination of the adventure, that, of course, had not been at all calculated upon; but, like most tools of other people's insolence or ambition, the insolence of the underling had received both his own punishment and his master's.

We know quite enough of Sir Francis Varney to feel assured that he would rather consider it as a good jest than otherwise of his footman, so that with the suffering he endured at the Bannerworths', and the want of sympathy he was likely to find at home, that individual had certainly nothing to congratulate himself upon but the melancholy reminiscence of his own cleverness.

But were the mob satisfied with what had occurred in the churchyard? They were not, and that night was to witness the perpetration of a melancholy outrage, such as the history of the time presents no parallel to.

The finding of a brick in the coffin of the butcher, instead of the body of that individual, soon spread as a piece of startling intelligence all over the place; and the obvious deduction that was drawn from the circumstance, seemed to be that the deceased butcher was unquestionably a vampyre, and out upon some expedition at the time when his coffin was searched.

How he had originally got out of that receptacle for the dead was certainly a mystery; but the story was none the worse for that. Indeed, an ingenious individual found a solution for that part of the business, for, as he said, nothing was more natural, when anybody died who was capable of becoming a vampyre, than for other vampyres who knew it to dig him up, and lay him out in the cold beams of the moonlight, until he acquired the same sort of vitality they themselves possessed, and joined their horrible fraternity.

In lieu of a better explanation--and, after all, it was no bad one--this theory was generally received, and, with a shuddering horror, people asked themselves, if the whole of the churchyard were excavated, how many coffins would be found tenantless by the dead which had been supposed, by simple-minded people, to inhabit them.

The presence, however, of a body of dragoons, towards evening, effectually prevented any renewed attack upon the sacred precincts of the churchyard, and it was a strange and startling thing to see that country town under military surveillance, and sentinels posted at its principal buildings.

This measure smothered the vengeance of the crowd, and insured, for a time, the safety of Sir Francis Varney; for no considerable body of persons could assemble for the purpose of attacking his house again, without being followed; so such a step was not attempted.

It had so happened, however, that on that very day, the funeral of a young man was to have taken place, who had put up for a time at that same inn where Admiral Bell was first introduced to the reader. He had become seriously ill, and, after a few days of indisposition, which had puzzled the country practitioners, breathed his last.

He was to have been buried in the village churchyard on the very day of the riot and confusion incidental to the exhumation of the coffin of the butcher, and probably from that circumstance we may deduce the presence of the clergyman in canonicals at the period of the riot.

When it was found that so disorderly a mob possessed the churchyard, the idea of burying the stranger on that day was abandoned; but still all would have gone on quietly as regarded him, had it not been for the folly of one of the chamber-maids at the tavern.

This woman, with all the love of gossip incidental to her class, had, from the first, entered so fully into all the particulars concerning vampyres, that she fairly might be considered to be a little deranged on that head. Her imagination had been so worked upon, that she was in an unfit state to think of anything else, and if ever upon anybody a stern and revolting superstition was calculated to produce direful effects, it was upon this woman.

The town was tolerably quiet; the presence of the soldiery had frightened some and amused others, and no doubt the night would have passed off serenely, had she not suddenly rushed into the street, and, with bewildered accents and frantic gestures shouted,--

"A vampyre--a vampyre--a vampyre!"

These words soon collected a crowd around her, and then, with screaming accents, which would have been quite enough to convince any reflecting person that she had actually gone distracted upon that point, she cried,--

"Come into the house--come into the house! Look upon the dead body, that should have been in its grave; it's fresher now than it was the day on which it died, and there's a colour in its cheeks! A vampyre--a vampyre--a vampyre! Heaven save us from a vampyre!"

The strange, infuriated, maniacal manner in which these words were uttered, produced an astonishingly exciting effect among the mob. Several women screamed, and some few fainted. The torch was laid again to the altar of popular feeling, and the fierce flame of superstition burnt brightly and fiercely.

Some twenty or thirty persons, with shouts and exclamations, rushed into the inn, while the woman who had created the disturbance still continued to rave, tearing her hair, and shrieking at intervals, until she fell exhausted upon the pavement.

Soon, from a hundred throats, rose the dreadful cry of "A vampyre--a vampyre!" The alarm was given throughout the whole town; the bugles of the military sounded; there was a clash of arms--the shrieks of women; altogether, the premonitory symptoms of such a riot as was not likely to be quelled without bloodshed and considerable disaster.

It is truly astonishing the effect which one weak or vicious-minded person can produce upon a multitude.

Here was a woman whose opinion would have been accounted valueless upon the most common-place subject, and whose word would not have passed for twopence, setting a whole town by the ears by force of nothing but her sheer brutal ignorance.

It is a notorious physiological fact, that after four or five days, or even a week, the bodies of many persons assume an appearance of freshness, such as might have been looked for in vain immediately after death.

It is one of the most insidious processes of that decay which appears to regret with its

"----------- offensive fingers, To mar the lines where beauty lingers."

But what did the chamber-maid know of physiology? Probably, she would have asked if it was anything good to eat; and so, of course, having her head full of vampyres, she must needs produce so lamentable a scene of confusion, the results of which we almost sicken at detailing.

CHAPTER XLVIII

THE STAKE AND THE DEAD BODY

The mob seemed from the first to have an impression that, as regarded the military force, no very serious results would arise from that quarter, for it was not to be supposed that, on an occasion which could not possibly arouse any ill blood on the part of the soldiery, or on which they could have the least personal feeling, they would like to get a bad name, which would stick to them for years to come.

It was no political riot, on which men might be supposed, in consequence of differing in opinion, to have their passions inflamed; so that, although the call of the civil authorities for military aid had been acceded to, yet it was hoped, and, indeed, almost understood by the officers, that their operations would lie confined more to a demonstration of power, than anything else.

Besides, some of the men had got talking to the townspeople, and had heard all about the vampyre story, and not being of the most refined or educated class themselves, they felt rather interested than otherwise in the affair.

Under these circumstances, then, we are inclined to think, that the disorderly mob of that inn had not so wholesome a fear as it was most certainly intended they should have of the redcoats. Then, again, they were not attacking the churchyard, which, in the first case, was the main point in dispute, and about which the authorities had felt so very sore, inasmuch as they felt that, if once the common people found out that the sanctity of such places could be outraged with impunity, they would lose their reverence for the church; that is to say, for the host of persons who live well and get fat in this country by the trade of religion.

Consequently, this churchyard was the main point of defence, and it was zealously looked to when it need not have been done so, while the public-house where there really reigned mischief was half unguarded.

There are always in all communities, whether large or small, a number of persons who really have, or fancy they have, something to gain by disturbance. These people, of course, care not for what pretext the public peace is violated; so long as there is a row, and something like an excuse for running into other people's houses, they are satisfied.

To get into a public-house under such circumstances is an unexpected treat; and thus, when the mob rushed into the inn with such symptoms of fury and excitement, there went with the leaders of the disturbance a number of persons who never thought of getting further than the bar, where they attacked the spirit-taps with an alacrity which showed how great was their love for ardent compounds.

Leaving these persons behind, however, we will follow those who, with a real superstition, and a furious interest in the affair of the vampyre, made their way towards the upper chamber, determining to satisfy themselves if there were truth in the statement so alarmingly made by the woman who had created such an emotion.

It is astonishing what people will do in crowds, in comparison with the acts that they would be able to commit individually. There is usually a calmness, a sanctity, a sublimity about death, which irresistibly induces a respect for its presence, alike from the educated or from the illiterate; and let the object of the fell-destroyer's presence be whom it may, the very consciousness that death has claimed it for its own, invests it with a halo of respect, that, in life, the individual could never aspire to probably.

Let us precede these furious rioters for a few moments, and look upon the chamber of the dead--that chamber, which for a whole week, had been looked upon with a kind of shuddering terror--that chamber which had been darkened by having its sources of light closed, as if it were a kind of disrespect to the dead to allow the pleasant sunshine to fall upon the faded form.

And every inhabitant of that house, upon ascending and descending its intricate and ancient staircases, had walked with a quiet and subdued step past that one particular door.

Even the tones of voice in which they spoke to each other, while they knew that that sad remnant of mortality was in the house, was quiet and subdued, as if the repose of death was but a mortal sleep, and could be broken by rude sounds.

Ay, even some of these very persons, who now with loud and boisterous clamour, had rushed into the place, had visited the house and talked in whispers; but then they were alone, and men will do in throngs acts which, individually, they would shrink from with compunction or cowardice, call it which we will.

The chamber of death is upon the second story of the house. It is a back room, the windows of which command a view of that half garden, half farm-yard, which we find generally belonging to country inns.

But now the shutters were closed, with the exception of one small opening, that, in daylight, would have admitted a straggling ray of light to fall upon the corpse. Now, however, that the sombre shades of evening had wrapped everything in gloom, the room appeared in total darkness, so that the most of those adventurers who had ventured into the place shrunk back until lights were procured from the lower part of the house, with which to enter the room.

A dim oil lamp in a niche sufficiently lighted the staircase, and, by the friendly aid of its glimmering beams, they had found their way up to the landing tolerably well, and had not thought of the necessity of having lights with which to enter the apartments, until they found them in utter darkness.

These requisites, however, were speedily procured from the kitchen of the inn. Indeed, anything that was wanted was laid hold of without the least word of remark to the people of the place, as if might, from that evening forthwith, was understood to constitute right, in that town.

Up to this point no one had taken a very prominent part in the attack upon the inn if attack it could be called; but now the man whom chance, or his own nimbleness, made the first of the throng, assumed to himself a sort of control over his companions and, turning to them, he said,--

"Hark ye, my friends; we'll do everything quietly and properly; so I think we'd better three or four of us go in at once, arm-in-arm."

"Psha!" cried one who had just arrived with a light; "it's your cowardice that speaks. I'll go in first; let those follow me who like, and those who are afraid may remain where they are."

He at once dashed into the room, and this immediately broke the spell of fear which was beginning to creep over the others in consequence of the timid suggestion of the man who, up to that moment, had been first and foremost in the enterprise.

In an instant the chamber was half filled with persons, four or five of whom carried lights; so that, as it was not of very large dimensions, it was sufficiently illuminated for every object in it to be clearly visible.

There was the bed, smooth and unruffled, as if waiting for some expected guest; while close by its side a coffin, supported upon tressles, over which a sheet was partially thrown, contained the sad remains of him who little expected in life that, after death, he should be stigmatised as an example of one of the ghastliest superstitions that ever found a home in the human imagination.

It was evident that some one had been in the room; and that this was the woman whose excited fancy had led her to look upon the face of the corpse there could be no doubt, for the sheet was drawn aside just sufficiently to discover the countenance.

The fact was that the stranger was unknown at the inn, or probably ere this the coffin lid would have been screwed on; but it was hoped, up to the last moment, as advertisements had been put into the county papers, that some one would come forward to identify and claim him.

Such, however, had not been the case, and so his funeral had been determined upon.

The presence of so many persons at once effectually prevented any individual from exhibiting, even if he felt any superstitious fears about approaching the coffin; and so, with one accord, they surrounded it, and looked upon the face of the dead.

There was nothing repulsive in that countenance. The fact was that decomposition had sufficiently advanced to induce a relaxation of the muscles, and a softening of the fibres, so that an appearance of calmness and repose had crept over the face which it did not wear immediately after death.

It happened, too, that the face was full of flesh--for the death had been sudden, and there had not been that wasting away of the muscles and integuments which makes the skin cling, as it were, to the bone, when the ravages of long disease have exhausted the physical frame.

There was, unquestionably, a plumpness, a freshness, and a sort of vitality about the countenance that was remarkable.

For a few moments there was a death-like stillness in the apartment, and then one voice broke the silence by exclaiming,--

"He's a vampyre, and has come here to die. Well he knows he'd be taken up by Sir Francis Varney, and become one of the crew."

"Yes, yes," cried several voices at once; "a vampyre! a vampyre!"

"Hold a moment," cried one; "let us find somebody in the house who has seen him some days ago, and then we can ascertain if there's any difference in his looks."

This suggestion was agreed to, and a couple of stout men ran down stairs, and returned in a few moments with a trembling waiter, whom they had caught in the passage, and forced to accompany them.

This man seemed to think that he was to be made a dreadful example of in some sort of way; and, as he was dragged into the room, he trembled, and looked as pale as death.

"What have I done, gentlemen?" he said; "I ain't a vampyre. Don't be driving a stake through me. I assure you, gentlemen, I'm only a waiter, and have been for a matter of five-and-twenty years."

"You'll be done no harm to," said one of his captors; "you've only got to answer a question that will be put to you."

"Oh, well, certainly, gentlemen; anything you please. Coming--coming, as I always say; give your orders, the waiter's in the room."

"Look upon the fare of that corpse."

"Certainly, certainly--directly."

"Have you ever seen it before?"

"Seen it before! Lord bless you! yes, a dozen of times. I seed him afore he died, and I seed him arter; and when the undertaker's men came, I came up with them and I seed 'em put him in his coffin. You see I kept an eye on 'em, gentlemen, 'cos knows well enough what they is. A cousin of mine was in the trade, and he assures me as one of 'em always brings a tooth-drawing concern in his pocket, and looks in the mouth of the blessed corpse to see if there's a blessed tooth worth pulling out."

"Hold your tongue," said one; "we want none of your nonsense. Do you see any difference now in the face of the corpse to what it was some days since?"

"Well, I don't know; somehow, it don't look so rum."

"Does it look fresher?"

"Well, somehow or another, now you mention it, it's very odd, but it does."

"Enough," cried the man who had questioned him, with considerable excitement of manner. "Neighbours, are we to have our wives and our children scared to death by vampyres?"

"No--no!" cried everybody.

"Is not this, then, one of that dreadful order of beings?"

"Yes--yes; what's to be done?"

"Drive a stake through the body, and so prevent the possibility of anything in the shape of a restoration."

This was a terrific proposition; and even those who felt most strongly upon the subject, and had their fears most awakened, shrank from carrying it into effect. Others, again, applauded it, although they determined, in their own minds, to keep far enough off from the execution of the job, which they hoped would devolve upon others, so that they might have all the security of feeling that such a process had been gone through with the supposed vampyre, without being in any way committed by the dreadful act.

Nothing was easier than to procure a stake from the garden in the rear of the premises; but it was one thing to have the means at hand of carrying into effect so dreadful a proposition, and another actually to do it.

For the credit of human nature, we regret that even then, when civilisation and popular education had by no means made such rapid strides as in our times they have, such a proposition should be entertained for a moment: but so it was; and just as an alarm was given that a party of the soldiers had reached the inn and had taken possession of the doorway with a determination to arrest the rioters, a strong hedge-stake had been procured, and everything was in readiness for the perpetration of the horrible deed.

Even then those in the room, for they were tolerably sober, would have revolted, probably, from the execution of so fearful an act; but the entrance of a party of the military into the lower portion of the tavern, induced those who had been making free with the strong liquors below, to make a rush up-stairs to their companions with the hope of escaping detection of the petty larceny, if they got into trouble on account of the riot.

These persons, infuriated by drink, were capable of anything, and to them, accordingly, the more sober parties gladly surrendered the disagreeable job of rendering the supposed vampyre perfectly innoxious, by driving a hedge-stake through his body--a proceeding which, it was currently believed, inflicted so much physical injury to the frame, as to render his resuscitation out of the question.

The cries of alarm from below, joined now to the shouts of those mad rioters, produced a scene of dreadful confusion.

We cannot, for we revolt at the office, describe particularly the dreadful outrage which was committed upon the corpse; suffice it that two or three, maddened by drink, and incited by the others, plunged the hedge-stake through the body, and there left it, a sickening and horrible spectacle to any one who might cast his eyes upon it.

With such violence had the frightful and inhuman deed been committed, that the bottom of the coffin was perforated by the stake so that the corpse was actually nailed to its last earthly tenement.

Some asserted, that at that moment an audible groan came from the dead man, and that this arose from the extinguishment of that remnant of life which remained in him, on account of his being a vampyre, and which would have been brought into full existence, if the body had been placed in the rays of the moon, when at its full, according to the popular superstition upon that subject.

Others, again, were quite ready to swear that at the moment the stake was used there was a visible convulsion of all the limbs, and that the countenance, before so placid and so calm, became immediately distorted, as if with agony.

But we have done with these horrible surmises; the dreadful deed has been committed, and wild, ungovernable superstition has had, for a time, its sway over the ignorant and debased.

CHAPTER XLIX

THE MOB'S ARRIVAL AT SIR FRANCIS VARNEY'S.--THE ATTEMPT TO GAIN ADMISSION

The soldiery had been sent for from their principal station near the churchyard, and had advanced with some degree of reluctance to quell what they considered as nothing better nor worse than a drunken brawl at a public-house, which they really considered they ought not to be called to interfere with.

When, however, the party reached the spot, and heard what a confusion there was, and saw in what numbers the rioters were assembling, it became evident to them that the case was of a more serious complexion than they had at first imagined, and consequently they felt that their professional dignity was not so much compromised with their interference with the lawless proceedings.

Some of the constabulary of the town were there, and to them the soldiers promised they would hand what prisoners they took, at the same time that they made a distinct condition that they were not to be troubled with their custody, nor in any way further annoyed in the business beyond taking care that they did not absolutely escape, after being once secured.

This was all that the civil authorities of the town required, and, in fact, they hoped that, after making prisoners of a few of the ringleaders of the riotous proceedings, the rest would disperse, and prevent the necessity of capturing them.

Be it known, however, that both military and civil authorities were completely ignorant of the dreadful outrage against all common decency, which had been committed within the public-house.

The door was well guarded, and the question now was how the rioters were to be made to come down stairs, and be captured; and this was likely to remain a question, so long as no means were adopted to make them descend. So that, after a time, it was agreed that a couple of troopers should march up stairs with a constable, to enable him to secure any one who seemed a principal in the riot.

But this only had the effect of driving those who were in the second-floor, and saw the approach of the two soldiers, whom they thought were backed by the whole of their comrades, up a narrow staircase, to a third-floor, rather consisting of lofts than of actual rooms; but still, for the time, it was a refuge; and owing to the extreme narrowness of the approach to it, which consisted of nearly a perpendicular staircase, with any degree of tact or method, it might have been admirably defended.

In the hurry and scramble, all the lights were left behind; and when the two soldiers and constables entered the room where the corpse had lain, they became, for the first time, aware of what a horrible purpose had been carried out by the infuriated mob.

The sight was one of perfect horror, and hardened to scenes which might strike other people as being somewhat of the terrific as these soldiers might be supposed to be by their very profession, they actually sickened at the sight which the mutilated corpse presented, and turned aside with horror.

These feelings soon gave way to anger and animosity against the crowd who could be guilty of such an atrocious outrage; and, for the first time, a strong and interested vengeance against the mob pervaded the breasts of those who were brought to act against it.

One of the soldiers ran down stairs to the door, and reported the scene which was to be seen above. A determination was instantly come to, to capture as many as possible of those who had been concerned in so diabolical an outrage, and leaving a guard of five men at the door, the remainder of the party ascended the staircase, determined upon storming the last refuge of the rioters, and dragging them to justice.

The report, however, of these proceedings that were taking place at the inn, spread quickly over the whole town; and soon as large a mob of the disorderly and the idle as the place could at all afford was assembled outside the inn.

This mob appeared, for a time, inertly to watch the proceedings. It seemed rather a hazardous thing to interfere with the soldiers, whose carbines look formidable and troublesome weapons.

With true mob courage, therefore, they left the minority of their comrades, who were within the house, to their fate; and after a whispered conference from one to the other, they suddenly turned in a body, and began to make for the outskirts of the town.

They then separated, as if by common consent, and straggled out into the open country by twos and threes, consolidating again into a mass when they had got some distance off, and clear of any exertions that could be made by the soldiery to stay them.

The cry then rose of "Down with Sir Francis Varney--slay him--burn his house--death to all vampyres!" and, at a rapid pace, they proceeded in the direction of his mansion.

We will leave this mob, however, for the present, and turn our attention to those who are at the inn, and are certainly in a position of some jeopardy. Their numbers were not great, and they were unarmed; certainly, their best chance would have been to have surrendered at discretion; but that was a measure which, if the sober ones had felt inclined to, those who were infuriated and half maddened with drink would not have acceded to on any account.

A furious resistance was, therefore, fairly to be expected; and what means the soldiery were likely to use for the purpose of storming this last retreat was a matter of rather anxious conjecture.

In the case of a regular enemy, there would not, perhaps, have been much difficulty; but here the capture of certain persons, and not their destruction, was the object; and how that was to be accomplished by fair means, certainly was a question which nobody felt very competent to solve.

Determination, however, will do wonders; and although the rioters numbered over forty, notwithstanding all their desertions, and not above seventeen or eighteen soldiers marched into the inn, we shall perceive that they succeeded in accomplishing their object without any manoeuvring at all.

The space in which the rioters were confined was low, narrow, and inconvenient, as well as dark, for the lights on the staircase cast up that height but very insufficient rays.

Weapons of defence they found but very few, and yet there were some which, to do them but common credit, they used as effectually as possible.

These attics, or lofts, were used as lumber-rooms, and had been so for years, so that there was a collection of old boxes, broken pieces of furniture, and other matters, which will, in defiance of everything and everybody, collect in a house.

These were formidable means of defence, if not of offence, down a very narrow staircase, had they been used with judgment.

Some of the rioters, who were only just drunk enough to be fool-hardy, collected a few of these articles at the top of the staircase, and swore they would smash anybody who should attempt to come up to them, a threat easier uttered than executed.

And besides, after all, if their position had been ever so impregnable, they must come down eventually, or be starved out.

But the soldiers were not at liberty to adopt so slow a process of overcoming their enemy, and up the second-floor staircase they went, with a determination of making short work of the business.

They paused a moment, by word of command, on the landing, and then, after this slight pause, the word was given to advance.

Now when men will advance, in spite of anything and everything, it is no easy matter to stop them, and he who was foremost among the military would as soon thought of hesitating to ascend the narrow staircase before him, when ordered so to do, as paying the national debt. On he went, and down came a great chest, which, falling against his feet, knocked him down as he attempted to scramble over it.

"Fire," said the officer; and it appeared that he had made some arrangements as to how the order was to be obeyed, for the second man fired his carbine, and then scrambled over his prostrate comrade; after which he stooped, and the third fired his carbine likewise, and then hurried forward in the same manner.

At the first sound of the fire arms the rioters were taken completely by surprise; they had not had the least notion of affairs getting to such a length. The smell of the powder, the loud report, and the sensation of positive danger that accompanied these phenomena, alarmed them most terrifically; so that, in point of fact, with the exception of the empty chest that was thrown down in the way of the first soldier, no further idea of defence seemed in any way to find a place in the hearts of the besieged.

They scrambled one over the other in their eagerness to get as far as possible from immediate danger, which, of course, they conceived existed in the most imminent degree the nearest to the door.

Such was the state of terror into which they were thrown, that each one at the moment believed himself shot, and the soldiers had overcome all the real difficulties in getting possession of what might thus be called the citadel of the inn, before those men who had been so valorous a short time since recovered from the tremendous fright into which they had been thrown.

We need hardly say that the carbines were loaded, but with blank cartridges, for there was neither a disposition nor a necessity for taking the lives of these misguided people.

If was the suddenness and the steadiness of the attack that had done all the mischief to their cause; and now, ere they recovered from the surprise of having their position so completely taken by storm, they were handed down stairs, one by one, from soldier to soldier, and into the custody of the civil authorities.

In order to secure the safe keeping of large a body of prisoners, the constables, who were in a great minority, placed handcuffs upon some of the most capable of resistance; so what with those who were thus secured, and those who were terrified into submission, there was not a man of all the lot who had taken refuge in the attics of the public-house but was a prisoner.

At the sound of fire-arms, the women who were outside the inn had, of course, raised a most prodigious clamour.

They believed directly that every bullet must have done some most serious mischief to the townspeople, and it was only upon one of the soldiers, a non-commissioned officer, who was below, assuring them of the innoxious nature of the proceeding which restored anything like equanimity.

"Silence!" he cried: "what are you howling about? Do you fancy that we've nothing better to do than to shoot a parcel of fellows that are not worth the bullets that would be lodged in their confounded carcases?"

"But we heard the gun," said a woman.

"Of course you did; it's the powder that makes the noise, not the bullet. You'll see them all brought out safe wind and limb."

This assurance satisfied the women to a certain extent, and such had been their fear that they should have had to look upon the spectacle of death, or of grievous wounds, that they were comparatively quite satisfied when they saw husbands, fathers, and brothers, only in the custody of the town officers.

And very sheepish some of the fellows looked, when they were handed down and handcuffed, and the more especially when they had been routed only by a few blank cartridges--that sixpenny worth of powder had defeated them.

They were marched off to the town gaol, guarded by the military, who now probably fancied that their night's work was over, and that the most turbulent and troublesome spirits in the town had been secured.

Such, however, was not the case, for no sooner had comparative order been restored, than common observation pointed to a dull red glare in the southern sky.

In a few more minutes there came in stragglers from the open country, shouting "Fire! fire!" with all their might.

CHAPTER L

THE MOB'S ARRIVAL AT SIR FRANCIS VARNEY'S.--THE ATTEMPT TO GAIN ADMISSION

All eyes were directed towards that southern sky which each moment was becoming more and more illuminated by the lurid appearance bespeaking a conflagration, which if it was not extensive, at all events was raging fiercely.

There came, too upon the wind, which set from that direction, strange sounds, resembling shouts of triumph, combined occasionally with sharper cries, indicative of alarm.

With so much system and so quietly had this attack been made upon the house of Sir Francis Varney--for the consequences of it now exhibited themselves most unequivocally--that no one who had not actually accompanied the expedition was in the least aware that it had been at all undertaken, or that anything of the kind was on the tapis.

Now, however, it could be no longer kept a secret, and as the infuriated mob, who had sought this flagrant means of giving vent to their anger, saw the flames from the blazing house rising high in the heavens, they felt convinced that further secrecy was out of the question.

Accordingly, in such cries and shouts as--but for caution's sake--they would have indulged in from the very first, they now gave utterance to their feelings as regarded the man whose destruction was aimed at.

"Death to the vampyre!--death to the vampyre!" was the principal shout, and it was uttered in tones which sounded like those of rage and disappointment.

But it is necessary, now that we have disposed of the smaller number of rioters who committed so serious an outrage at the inn, that we should, with some degree of method, follow the proceedings of the larger number, who went from the town towards Sir Francis Varney's.

These persons either had information of a very positive nature, or a very strong suspicion that, notwithstanding the mysterious and most unaccountable disappearance of the vampyre in the old ruin, he would now be found, as usual, at his own residence.

Perhaps one of his own servants may have thus played the traitor to him; but however it was, there certainly was an air of confidence about some of the leaders of the tumultuous assemblage that induced a general belief that this time, at least, the vampyre would not escape popular vengeance for being what he was.

We have before noticed that these people went out of the town at different points, and did not assemble into one mass until they were at a sufficient distance off to be free from all fear of observation.

Then some of the less observant and cautious of them began to indulge in shouts of rage and defiance; but those who placed themselves foremost succeeded in procuring a halt, and one said,--

"Good friends all, if we make any noise, it can only have one effect, and that is, to warn Sir Francis Varney, and enable him to escape. If, therefore, we cannot go on quietly, I propose that we return to our homes, for we shall accomplish nothing."

This advice was sufficiently and evidently reasonable to meet with no dissension; a death-like stillness ensued, only broken by some two or three voices saying, in subdued tones,--

"That's right--that's right. Nobody speak."

"Come on, then," said he who had given such judicious counsel; and the dark mass of men moved towards Sir Francis Varney's house, as quietly as it was possible for such an assemblage to proceed.

Indeed, saving the sound of the footsteps, nothing could be heard of them at all; and that regular tramp, tramp, would have puzzled any one listening to it from any distance to know in which direction it was proceeding.

In this way they went on until Sir Francis Varney's house was reached, and then a whispered word to halt was given, and all eyes were bent upon the building.

From but one window out of the numerous ones with which the front of the mansion was studded did there shine the least light, and from that there came rather an uncommonly bright reflection, probably arising from a reading lamp placed close to the window.

A general impression, they knew not why exactly, seemed to pervade everybody, that in the room from whence streamed that bright light was Sir Francis Varney.

"The vampyre's room!" said several. "The vampyre's room! That is it!"

"Yes," said he who had a kind of moral control over his comrades; "I have no doubt but he is there."

"What's to be done?" asked several.

"Make no noise whatever, but stand aside, so as not to be seen from the door when it is opened."

"Yes, yes."

"I will knock for admittance, and, the moment it is answered, I will place this stick in such a manner within, that the door cannot be closed again. Upon my saying 'Advance,' you will make a rush forward, and we shall have possession immediately of the house."

All this was agreed to. The mob slunk close to the walls of the house, and out of immediate observation from the hall door, or from any of the windows, and then the leader advanced, and knocked loudly for admission.

The silence was now of the most complete character that could be imagined. Those who came there so bent upon vengeance were thoroughly convinced of the necessity of extreme caution, to save themselves even yet from being completely foiled.

They had abundant faith, from experience, of the resources in the way of escape of Sir Francis Varney, and not one among them was there who considered that there was any chance of capturing him, except by surprise, and when once they got hold of him, they determined he should not easily slip through their fingers.

The knock for admission produced no effect; and, after waiting three or four minutes, it was very provoking to find such a wonderful amount of caution and cunning completely thrown away.

"Try again," whispered one.

"Well, have patience; I am going to try again."

The man had the ponderous old-fashioned knocker in his hand, and was about to make another appeal to Sir Francis Varney's door, when a strange voice said,--

"Perhaps you may as well say at once what you want, instead of knocking there to no purpose."

He gave a start, for the voice seemed to come from the very door itself.

Yet it sounded decidedly human; and, upon a closer inspection, it was seen that a little wicket-gate, not larger than a man's face, had been opened from within.

This was terribly provoking. Here was an extent of caution on the part of the garrison quite unexpected. What was to be done?

"Well?" said the man who appeared at the little opening.

"Oh," said he who had knocked; "I--"

"Well?"

"I--that is to say--ahem! Is Sir Francis Varney within?"

"Well?"

"I say, is Sir Francis Varney within?"

"Well; you have said it!"

"Ah, but you have not answered it."

"No."

"Well, is he at home?"

"I decline saying; so you had better, all of you, go back to the town again, for we are well provided with all material to resist any attack you may be fools enough to make."

As he spoke, the servant shut the little square door with a bang that made his questioner jump again. Here was a dilemma!

CHAPTER LI

THE ATTACK UPON THE VAMPYRE'S HOUSE.--THE STORY OF THE ATTACK.--THE FORCING OF THE DOORS, AND THE STRUGGLE

A council of war was now called among the belligerents, who were somewhat taken aback by the steady refusal of the servant to admit them, and their apparent determination to resist all endeavours on the part of the mob to get into and obtain possession of the house. It argued that they were prepared to resist all attempts, and it would cost some few lives to get into the vampyre's house. This passed through the minds of many as they retired behind the angle of the wall where the council was to be held.

Here they looked in each others' face, as if to gather from that the general tone of the feelings of their companions; but here they saw nothing that intimated the least idea of going back as they came.

"It's all very well, mates, to take care of ourselves, you know," began one tall, brawny fellow; "but, if we bean't to be sucked to death by a vampyre, why we must have the life out of him."

"Ay, so we must."

"Jack Hodge is right; we must kill him, and there's no sin in it, for he has no right to it; he's robbed some poor fellow of his life to prolong his own."

"Ay, ay, that's the way he does; bring him out, I say, then see what we will do with him."

"Yes, catch him first," said one, "and then we can dispose of him afterwards, I say, neighbours, don't you think it would be as well to catch him first?"

"Haven't we come on purpose?"

"Yes, but do it."

"Ain't we trying it?"

"You will presently, when we come to get into the house."

"Well, what's to be done?" said one; "here we are in a fix, I think, and I can't see our way out very clearly."

"I wish we could get in."

"But how is a question I don't very well see," said a large specimen of humanity.

"The best thing that can be done will be to go round and look over the whole house, and then we may come upon some part where it is far easier to get in at than by the front door."

"But it won't do for us all to go round that way," said one; "a small party only should go, else they will have all their people stationed at one point, and if we can divide them, we shall beat them because they have not enough to defend more than one point at a time; now we are numerous enough to make several attacks."

"Oh! that's the way to bother them all round; they'll give in, and then the place is our own."

"No, no," said the big countryman, "I like to make a good rush and drive all afore us; you know what ye have to do then, and you do it, ye know."

"If you can."

"Ay, to be sure, if we can, as you say; but can't we? that's what I want to know."

"To be sure we can."

"Then we'll do it, mate--that's my mind; we'll do it. Come on, and let's have another look at the street-door."

The big countryman left the main body, and resolutely walked up to the main avenue, and approached the door, accompanied by about a dozen or less of the mob. When they came to the door, they commenced knocking and kicking most violently, and assailing it with all kinds of things they could lay their hands upon.

They continued at this violent exercise for some time--perhaps for five minutes, when the little square hole in the door was again opened, and a voice was heard to say,--

"You had better cease that kind of annoyance."

"We want to get in."

"It will cost you more lives to do so than you can afford to spare. We are well armed, and are prepared to resist any effort you can make."

"Oh! it's all very well; but, an you won't open, why we'll make you; that's all about it."

This was said as the big countryman and his companions were leaving the avenue towards the rest of the body.

"Then, take this, as an earnest of what is to follow," said the man, and he discharged the contents of a blunderbuss through the small opening, and its report sounded to the rest of the mob like the report of a field-piece.

Fortunately for the party retiring the man couldn't take any aim, else it is questionable how many of the party would have got off unwounded. As it was, several of them found stray slugs were lodged in various parts of their persons, and accelerated their retreat from the house of the vampyre.

"What luck?" inquired one of the mob to the others, as they came back; "I'm afraid you had all the honour."

"Ay, ay, we have, and all the lead too," replied a man, as he placed his hand upon a sore part of his person, which bled in consequence of a wound.

"Well, what's to be done?"

"Danged if I know," said one.

"Give it up," said another.

"No, no; have him out. I'll never give in while I can use a stick. They are in earnest, and so are we. Don't let us be frightened because they have a gun or two--they can't have many; and besides, if they have, we are too many for them. Besides, we shall all die in our beds."

"Hurrah! down with the vampyre!"

"So say I, lads. I don't want to be sucked to death when I'm a-bed. Better die like a man than such a dog's death as that, and you have no revenge then."

"No, no; he has the better of us then. We'll have him out--we'll burn him--that's the way we'll do it."

"Ay, so we will; only let us get in."

At that moment a chosen party returned who had been round the house to make a reconnaissance.

"Well, well," inquired the mob, "what can be done now--where can we get in?"

"In several places."

"All right; come along then; the place is our own."

"Stop a minute; they are armed at all points, and we must make an attack on all points, else we may fail. A party must go round to the front-door, and attempt to beat it in; there are plenty of poles and things that could be used for such a purpose."

"There is, besides, a garden-door, that opens into the house--a kind of parlour; a kitchen-door; a window in the flower-garden, and an entrance into a store-room; this place appears strong, and is therefore unguarded."

"The very point to make an attack."

"Not quite."

"Why not?"

"Because it can easily be defended, and rendered useless to us. We must make an attack upon all places but that, and, while they are being at those points, we can then enter at that place, and then you will find them desert the other places when they see us inside."

"Hurrah! down with the vampyre!" said the mob, as they listened to this advice, and appreciated the plan.

"Down with the vampyre!"

"Now, then, lads, divide, and make the attack; never mind their guns, they have but very few, and if you rush in upon them, you will soon have the guns yourselves."

"Hurrah! hurrah!" shouted the mob.

The mob now moved away in different bodies, each strong enough to carry the house. They seized upon a variety of poles and stones, and then made for the various doors and windows that were pointed out by those who had made the discovery. Each one of those who had formed the party of observation, formed a leader to the others, and at once proceeded to the post assigned him.

The attack was so sudden and so simultaneous that the servants were unprepared; and though they ran to the doors, and fired away, still they did but little good, for the doors were soon forced open by the enraged rioters, who proceeded in a much more systematic operation, using long heavy pieces of timber which were carried on the shoulders of several men, and driven with the force of battering-rams--which, in fact, they were--against the door.

Bang went the battering-ram, crash went the door, and the whole party rushed headlong in, carried forward by their own momentum and fell prostrate, engine and all, into the passage.

"Now, then, we have them," exclaimed the servants, who began to belabour the whole party with blows, with every weapon they could secure.

Loudly did the fallen men shout for assistance, and but for their fellows who came rushing in behind, they would have had but a sorry time of it.

"Hurrah!" shouted the mob; "the house is our own."

"Not yet," shouted the servants.

"We'll try," said the mob; and they rushed forward to drive the servants back, but they met with a stout resistance, and as some of them had choppers and swords, there were a few wounds given, and presently bang went the blunderbuss.

Two or three of the mob reeled and fell.

This produced a momentary panic, and the servants then had the whole of the victory to themselves, and were about to charge, and clear the passage of their enemies, when a shout behind attracted their attention.

That shout was caused by an entrance being gained in another quarter, whence the servants were flying, and all was disorder.

"Hurrah! hurrah!" shouted the mob.

The servants retreated to the stairs, and here united, they made a stand, and resolved to resist the whole force of the rioters, and they succeeded in doing so, too, for some minutes. Blows were given and taken of a desperate character.

Somehow, there were no deadly blows received by the servants; they were being forced and beaten, but they lost no life; this may be accounted for by the fact that the mob used no more deadly weapons than sticks.

The servants of Sir Francis Varney, on the contrary, were mostly armed with deadly weapons, which, however, they did not use unnecessarily. They stood upon the hall steps--the grand staircase, with long poles or sticks, about the size of quarter-staves, and with these they belaboured those below most unmercifully.

Certainly, the mob were by no means cowards, for the struggle to close with their enemies was as great as ever, and as firm as could well be. Indeed, they rushed on with a desperation truly characteristic of John Bull, and defied the heaviest blows; for as fast as one was stricken down another occupied his place, and they insensibly pressed their close and compact front upon the servants, who were becoming fatigued and harassed.

"Fire, again," exclaimed a voice from among the servants.

The mob made no retrogade movement, but still continued to press onwards, and in another moment a loud report rang through the house, and a smoke hung over the heads of the mob.

A long groan or two escaped some of the men who had been wounded, and a still louder from those who had not been wounded, and a cry arose of,--

"Down with the vampyre--pull down--destroy and burn the whole place--down with them all."

A rush succeeded, and a few more discharges took place, when a shout above attracted the attention of both parties engaged in this fierce struggle. They paused by mutual consent, to look and see what was the cause of that shout.

CHAPTER LII

THE INTERVIEW BETWEEN THE MOB AND SIR FRANCIS VARNEY.--THE MYSTERIOUS DISAPPEARANCE.--THE WINE CELLARS

The shout that had so discomposed the parties who were thus engaged in a terrific struggle came from a party above.

"Hurrah! hurrah!" they shouted a number of times, in a wild strain of delight. "Hurrah! hurrah! hurrah!"

The fact was, a party of the mob had clambered up a verandah, and entered some of the rooms upstairs, whence they emerged just above the landing near the spot where the servants were resisting in a mass the efforts of the mob.

"Hurrah!" shouted the mob below.

"Hurrah!" shouted the mob above.

There was a momentary pause, and the servants divided themselves into two bodies, and one turned to face those above, and the other those who were below.

A simultaneous shout was given by both parties of the mob, and a sudden rush was made by both bodies, and the servants of Sir Francis Varney were broken in an instant. They were instantly separated, and knocked about a good bit, but they were left to shift for themselves, the mob had a more important object in view.

"Down with the vampyre!" they shouted.

"Down with the vampyre!" shouted they, and they rushed helter skelter through the rooms, until they came to one where the door was partially open, and they could see some person very leisurely seated.

"Here he is," they cried.

"Who? who?"

"The vampire."

"Down with him! kill him! burn him!"

"Hurrah! down with the vampire!"

These sounds were shouted out by a score of voices, and they rushed headlong into the room.

But here their violence and headlong precipitancy were suddenly restrained by the imposing and quiet appearance of the individual who was there seated.

The mob entered the room, and there was a sight, that if it did not astonish them, at least, it caused them to pause before the individual who was seated there.

The room was well filled with furniture, and there was a curtain drawn across the room, and about the middle of it there was a table, behind which sat Sir Francis Varney himself, looking all smiles and courtesy.

"Well, dang my smock-frock!" said one, "who'd ha' thought of this? He don't seem to care much about it."

"Well, I'm d----d!" said another; "he seems pretty easy, at all events. What is he going to do?"

"Gentlemen," said Sir Francis Varney, rising, with the blandest smiles, "pray, gentlemen, permit me to inquire the cause of this condescension on your part. The visit is kind."

The mob looked at Sir Francis, and then at each other, and then at Sir Francis again; but nobody spoke. They were awed by this gentlemanly and collected behaviour.

"If you honour me with this visit from pure affection and neighbourly good-will, I thank you."

"Down with the vampyre!" said one, who was concealed behind the rest, and not so much overawed, as he had not seen Sir Francis.

Sir Francis Varney rose to his full height; a light gleamed across his features; they were strongly defined then. His long front teeth, too, showed most strongly when he smiled, as he did now, and said, in a bland voice,--

"Gentlemen, I am at your service. Permit me to say you are welcome to all I can do for you. I fear the interview will be somewhat inconvenient and unpleasant to you. As for myself, I am entirely at your service."

As Sir Francis spoke, he bowed, and folded his hands together, and stepped forwards; but, instead of coming onwards to them, he walked behind the curtain, and was immediately hid from their view.

"Down with the vampyre!" shouted one.

"Down with the vampyre!" rang through the apartment; and the mob now, not awed by the coolness and courtesy of Sir Francis, rushed forward, and, overturning the table, tore down the curtain to the floor; but, to their amazement, there was no Sir Francis Varney present.

"Where is he?"

"Where is the vampyre?"

"Where has he gone?"

These were cries that escaped every one's lips; and yet no one could give an answer to them.

There Sir Francis Varney was not. They were completely thunderstricken. They could not find out where he had gone to. There was no possible means of escape, that they could perceive. There was not an odd corner, or even anything that could, by any possibility, give even a suspicion that even a temporary concealment could take place.

They looked over every inch of flooring and of wainscoting; not the remotest trace could be discovered.

"Where is he?"

"I don't know," said one--"I can't see where he could have gone. There ain't a hole as big as a keyhole."

"My eye!" said one; "I shouldn't be at all surprised, if he were to blow up the whole house."

"You don't say go!"

"I never heard as how vampyres could do so much as that. They ain't the sort of people," said another.

"But if they can do one thing, they can do another."

"That's very true."

"And what's more, I never heard as how a vampyre could make himself into nothing before; yet he has done so."

"He may be in this room now."

"He may."

"My eyes! what precious long teeth he had!"

"Yes; and had he fixed one on 'em in to your arm, he would have drawn every drop of blood out of your body; you may depend upon that," said an old man.

"He was very tall."

"Yes; too tall to be any good."

"I shouldn't like him to have laid hold of me, though, tall as he is; and then he would have lifted me up high enough to break my neck, when he let me fall."

The mob routed about the room, tore everything out of its place, and as the object of their search seemed to be far enough beyond their reach, their courage rose in proportion, and they shouted and screamed with a proportionate increase of noise and bustle; and at length they ran about mad with rage and vexation, doing all the mischief that was in their power to inflict.

Then they became mischievous, and tore the furniture from its place, and broke it in pieces, and then amused themselves with breaking it up, throwing pieces at the pier-glasses, in which they made dreadful holes; and when that was gone, they broke up the frames.

Every hole and corner of the house was searched, but there was no Sir Francis Varney to be found.

"The cellars, the cellars!" shouted a voice.

"The cellars, the cellars!" re-echoed nearly every pair of lips in the whole place; in another moment, there was crushing and crowding to get down into the cellars.

"Hurray!" said one, as he knocked off the neck of the bottle that first came to hand.

"Here's luck to vampyre-hunting! Success to our chase!"

"So say I, neighbour; but is that your manners to drink before your betters?"

So saying, the speaker knocked the other's elbow, while he was in the act of lifting the wine to his mouth; and thus he upset it over his face and eyes.

"D--n it!" cried the man; "how it makes my eyes smart! Dang thee! if I could see, I'd ring thy neck!"

"Success to vampyre-hunting!" said one.

"May we be lucky yet!" said another.

"I wouldn't be luckier than this," said another, as he, too, emptied a bottle. "We couldn't desire better entertainment, where the reckoning is all paid."

"Excellent!"

"Very good!"

"Capital wine this!"

"I say, Huggins!"

"Well," said Huggins.

"What are you drinking?"

"Wine."

"What wine?"

"Danged if I know," was the reply. "It's wine, I suppose; for I know it ain't beer nor spirits; so it must be wine."

"Are you sure it ain't bottled men's blood?"

"Eh?"

"Bottled blood, man! Who knows what a vampyre drinks? It may be his wine. He may feast upon that before he goes to bed of a night, drink anybody's health, and make himself cheerful on bottled blood!"

"Oh, danged! I'm so sick; I wish I hadn't taken the stuff. It may be as you say, neighbour, and then we be cannibals."

"Or vampyres."

"There's a pretty thing to think of."

By this time some were drunk, some were partially so, and the remainder were crowding into the cellars to get their share of the wine.

The servants had now slunk away; they were no longer noticed by the rioters, who, having nobody to oppose them, no longer thought of anything, save the searching after the vampyre, and the destruction of the property. Several hours had been spent in this manner, and yet they could not find the object of their search.

There was not a room, or cupboard, or a cellar, that was capable of containing a cat, that they did not search, besides a part of the rioters keeping a very strict watch on the outside of the house and all about the grounds, to prevent the possibility of the escape of the vampyre.

There was a general cessation of active hostilities at that moment; a reaction after the violent excitement and exertion they had made to get in. Then the escape of their victim, and the mysterious manner in which he got away, was also a cause of the reaction, and the rioters looked in each others' countenances inquiringly.

Above all, the discovery of the wine-cellar tended to withdraw them from violent measures; but this could not last long, there must be an end to such a scene, for there never was a large body of men assembled for an evil purpose, who ever were, for any length of time, peaceable.

To prevent the more alarming effects of drunkenness, some few of the rioters, after having taken some small portion of the wine, became, from the peculiar flavour it possessed, imbued with the idea that it was really blood, and forthwith commenced an instant attack upon the wine and liquors, and they were soon mingling in one stream throughout the cellars.

This destruction was loudly declaimed against by a large portion of the rioters, who were drinking; but before they could make any efforts to save the liquor, the work of destruction had not only been begun, but was ended, and the consequence was, the cellars were very soon evacuated by the mob.

CHAPTER LIII

THE DESTRUCTION OF SIR FRANCIS VARNEY'S HOUSE BY FIRE.--THE ARRIVAL OF THE MILITARY, AND A SECOND MOB

Thus many moments had not elapsed ere the feelings of the rioters became directed into a different channel from that in which it had so lately flowed. When urged about the house and grounds for the vampyre, they became impatient and angry at not finding him. Many believed that he was yet about the house, while many were of opinion that he had flown away by some mysterious means only possessed by vampyres and such like people.

"Fire the house, and burn him out," said one.

"Fire the house!"

"Burn the den!" now arose in shouts from all present, and then the mob were again animated by the love of mischief that seemed to be the strongest feelings that animated them.

"Burn him out--burn him out!" were the only words that could be heard from any of the mob. The words ran through the house like wildfire, nobody thought of anything else, and all were seen running about in confusion.

There was no want of good will on the part of the mob to the undertaking; far from it, and they proceeded in the work con amore. They worked together with right good will, and the result was soon seen by the heaps of combustible materials that were collected in a short time from all parts of the house.

All the old dry wood furniture that could be found was piled up in a heap, and to these were added a number of faggots, and also some shavings that were found in the cellar.

"All right!" exclaimed one man, in exultation.

"Yes," replied a second; "all right--all right! Set light to it, and he will be smoked out if not burned."

"Let us be sure that all are out of the house," suggested one of the bystanders.

"Ay, ay," shouted several; "give them all a chance. Search through the house and give them a warning."

"Very well; give me the light, and then when I come back I will set light to the fire at once, and then I shall know all is empty, and so will you too."

This was at once agreed to by all, with acclamations, and the light being handed to the man, he ascended the stairs, crying out in a loud voice,--

"Come out--come out! the house is on fire!"

"Fire! fire! fire!" shouted the mob as a chorus, every now and then at intervals.

In about ten minutes more, there came a cry of "all right; the house is empty," from up the stairs, and the man descended in haste to the hall.

"Make haste, lads, and fire away, for I see the red coats are leaving the town."

"Hurra! hurra!" shouted the infuriated mob. "Fire--fire--fire the house! Burn out the vampyre! Burn down the house--burn him out, and see if he can stand fire."

Amidst all this tumult there came a sudden blaze upon all around, for the pile had been fired.

"Hurra!" shouted the mob--"hurra!" and they danced like maniacs round the fire; looking, in fact, like so many wild Indians, dancing round their roasting victims, or some demons at an infernal feast.

The torch had been put to twenty different places, and the flames united into one, and suddenly shot up with a velocity, and roared with a sound that caused many who were present to make a precipitate retreat from the hall.

This soon became a necessary measure of self-preservation, and it required no urging to induce them to quit a place that was burning rapidly and even furiously.

"Get the poles and firewood--get faggots," shouted some of the mob, and, lo, it was done almost by magic. They brought the faggots and wood piled up for winter use, and laid them near all the doors, and especially the main entrance. Nay, every gate or door belonging to the outhouses was brought forward and placed upon the fire, which now began to reach the upper stories.

"Hurra--fire! Hurra--fire!"

And a loud shout of triumph came from the mob as they viewed the progress of the flames, as they came roaring and tearing through the house doors and the windows.

Each new victory of the element was a signal to the mob for a cheer; and a hearty cheer, too, came from them.

"Where is the vampyre now?" exclaimed one.

"Ha! where is he?" said another.

"If he be there," said the man, pointing to the flames, "I reckon he's got a warm berth of it, and, at the same time, very little water to boil in his kettle."

"Ha, ha! what a funny old man is Bob Mason; he's always poking fun; he'd joke if his wife were dying."

"There is many a true word spoken in jest," suggested another; "and, to my mind, Bob Mason wouldn't be very much grieved if his wife were to die."

"Die?" said Bob; "she and I have lived and quarrelled daily a matter of five-and-thirty years, and, if that ain't enough to make a man sick of being married, and of his wife, hand me, that's all. I say I am tired."

This was said with much apparent sincerity, and several laughed at the old man's heartiness.

"It's all very well," said the old man; "it's all very well to laugh about matters you don't understand, but I know it isn't a joke--not a bit on it. I tells you what it is, neighbour, I never made but one grand mistake in all my life."

"And what was that?"

"To tie myself to a woman."

"Why, you'd get married to-morrow if your wife were to die to-day," said one.

"If I did, I hope I may marry a vampyre. I should have something then to think about. I should know what's o'clock. But, as for my old woman, lord, lord, I wish Sir Francis Varney had had her for life. I'll warrant when the next natural term of his existence came round again, he wouldn't be in no hurry to renew it; if he did, I should say that vampyres had the happy lot of managing women, which I haven't got."

"No, nor anybody else."

A loud shout now attracted their attention, and, upon looking in the quarter whence it came, they descried a large body of people coming towards them; from one end of the mob could be seen a long string of red coats.

"The red coats!" shouted one.

"The military!" shouted another.

It was plain the military who had been placed in the town to quell disturbances, had been made acquainted with the proceedings at Sir Francis Varney's house, and were now marching to relieve the place, and to save the property.

They were, as we have stated, accompanied by a vast concourse of people, who came out to see what they were going to see, and seeing the flames at Sir Francis Varney's house, they determined to come all the way, and be present.

The military, seeing the disturbance in the distance, and the flames issuing from the windows, made the best of their way towards the scene of tumult with what speed they could make.

"Here they come," said one.

"Yes, just in time to see what is done."

"Yes, they can go back and say we have burned the vampyre's house down--hurra!"

"Hurra!" shouted the mob, in prolonged accents, and it reached the ears of the military.

The officer urged the men onwards, and they responded to his words, by exerting themselves to step out a little faster.

"Oh, they should have been here before this; it's no use, now, they are too late."

"Yes, they are too late."

"I wonder if the vampyre can breathe through the smoke, and live in fire," said one.

"I should think he must be able to do so, if he can stand shooting, as we know he can--you can't kill a vampyre; but yet he must be consumed, if the fire actually touches him, but not unless he can bear almost anything."

"So he can."

"Hurra!" shouted the mob, as a tall flame shot through the top windows of the house.

The fire had got the ascendant now, and no hopes could be entertained, however extravagant, of saving the smallest article that had been left in the mansion.

"Hurra!" shouted the mob with the military, who came up with them.

"Hurra!" shouted the others in reply.

"Quick march!" said the officer; and then, in a loud, commanding tone, he shouted, "Clear the way, there! clear the way."

"Ay, there's room enough for you," said old Mason; "what are you making so much noise about?"

There was a general laugh at the officer, who took no notice of the words, but ordered his men up before the burning pile, which was now an immense mass of flame.

The mob who had accompanied the military now mingled with the mob that had set the house of Sir Francis Varney on fire ere the military had come up with them.

"Halt!" cried out the officer; and the men, obedient to the word of command, halted, and drew up in a double line before the house.

There were then some words of command issued, and some more given to some of the subalterns, and a party of men, under the command of a sergeant, was sent off from the main body, to make a circuit of the house and grounds.

The officer gazed for some moments upon the burning pile without speaking; and then, turning to the next in command, he said in low tones, as he looked upon the mob,--

"We have come too late."

"Yes, much."

"The house is now nearly gutted."

"It is."

"And those who came crowding along with us are inextricably mingled with the others who have been the cause of all this mischief: there's no distinguishing them one from another."

"And if you did, you could not say who had done it, and who had not; you could prove nothing."

"Exactly."

"I shall not attempt to take prisoners, unless any act is perpetrated beyond what has been done."

"It is a singular affair."

"Very."

"This Sir Francis Varney is represented to be a courteous, gentlemanly man," said the officer.

"No doubt about it, but he's beset by a parcel of people who do not mind cutting a throat if they can get an opportunity of doing so."

"And I expect they will."

"Yes, when there is a popular excitement against any man, he had better leave this part at once and altogether. It is dangerous to tamper with popular prejudices; no man who has any value for his life ought to do so. It is a sheer act of suicide."

CHAPTER LIV

THE BURNING OF VARNEY'S HOUSE.--A NIGHT SCENE.--POPULAR SUPERSTITION

The officer ceased to speak, and then the party whom he had sent round the house and grounds returned, and gained the main body orderly enough, and the sergeant went forward to make his report to his superior officer.

After the usual salutation, he waited for the inquiry to be put to him as to what he had seen.

"Well, Scott, what have you done?"

"I went round the premises, sir, according to your instructions, but saw no one either in the vicinity of the house, or in the grounds around it."

"No strangers, eh?"

"No, sir, none."

"You saw nothing at all likely to lead to any knowledge as to who it was that has caused this catastrophe?"

"No, sir."

"Have you learnt anything among the people who are the perpetrators of this fire?"

"No, sir."

"Well, then, that will do, unless there is anything else that you can think of."

"Nothing further, sir, unless it is that I heard some of them say that Sir Francis Varney has perished in the flames."

"Good heavens!"

"So I heard, sir."

"That must be impossible, and yet why should it be so? Go back, Scott, and bring me some person who can give me some information upon this point."

The sergeant departed toward the people, who looked at him without any distrust, for he came single-handed, though they thought he came with the intention of learning what they knew of each other, and so stroll about with the intention of getting up accusations against them. But this was not the case, the officer didn't like the work well enough; he'd rather have been elsewhere.

At length the sergeant came to one man, whom he accosted, and said to him,--

"Do you know anything of yonder fire?"

"Yes: I do know it is a fire."

"Yes, and so do I."

"My friend," said the sergeant, "when a soldier asks a question he does not expect an uncivil answer."

"But a soldier may ask a question that may have an uncivil end to it."

"He may; but it is easy to say so."

"I do say so, then, now."

"Then I'll not trouble you any more."

The sergeant moved on a pace or two more, and then, turning to the mob, he said,--

"Is there any one among you who can tell me anything concerning the fate of Sir Francis Varney?"

"Burnt!"

"Did you see him burnt?"

"No; but I saw him."

"In the flames?"

"No; before the house was on fire."

"In the house?"

"Yes; and he has not been seen to leave it since, and we conclude he must have been burned."

"Will you come and say as much to my commanding officer? It is all I want."

"Shall I be detained?"

"No."

"Then I will go," said the man, and he hobbled out of the crowd towards the sergeant. "I will go and see the officer, and tell him what I know, and that is very little, and can prejudice no one."

"Hurrah!" said the crowd, when they heard this latter assertion; for, at first, they began to be in some alarm lest there should be something wrong about this, and some of them get identified as being active in the fray.

The sergeant led the man back to the spot, where the officer stood a little way in advance of his men.

"Well, Scott," he said, "what have we here?"

"A man who has volunteered a statement, sir."

"Oh! Well, my man, can you say anything concerning all this disturbance that we have here?"

"No, sir."

"Then what did you come here for?"

"I understood the sergeant to want some one who could speak of Sir Francis Varney."

"Well?"

"I saw him."

"Where?"

"In the house."

"Exactly; but have you not seen him out of it?"

"Not since; nor any one else, I believe."

"Where was he?"

"Upstairs, where he suddenly disappeared, and nobody can tell where he may have gone to. But he has not been seen out of the house since, and they say he could not have gone bodily out if they had not seen him."

"He must have been burnt," said the officer, musingly; "he could not escape, one would imagine, without being seen by some one out of such a mob."

"Oh, dear no, for I am told they placed a watch at every hole, window, or door however high, and they saw nothing of him--not even fly out!"

"Fly out! I'm speaking of a man!"

"And I of a vampire!" said the man carelessly.

"A vampyre! Pooh, pooh!"

"Oh no! Sir Francis Varney is a vampyre! There can be no sort of doubt about it. You have only to look at him, and you will soon be satisfied of that. See his great sharp teeth in front, and ask yourself what they are for, and you will soon find the answer. They are to make holes with in the bodies of his victims, through which he can suck their blood!"

The officer looked at the man in astonishment for a few moments, as if he doubted his own ears, and then he said,--

"Are you serious?"

"I am ready to swear to it."

"Well, I have heard a great deal about popular superstition, and thought I had seen something of it; but this is decidedly the worst case that ever I saw or heard of. You had better go home, my man, than, by your presence, countenance such a gross absurdity."

"For all that," said the man, "Sir Francis Varney is a vampyre--a blood-sucker--a human blood-sucker!"

"Get away with you," said the officer, "and do not repeat such folly before any one."

The man almost jumped when he heard the tone in which this was spoken, for the officer was both angry and contemptuous, when he heard the words of the man.

"These people," he added, turning to the sergeant, "are ignorant in the extreme. One would think we had got into the country of vampires, instead of a civilised community."

The day was going down now; the last rays of the setting sun glimmered upwards, and still shone upon the tree-tops. The darkness of night was still fast closing around them. The mob stood a motley mass of human beings, wedged together, dark and sombre, gazing upon the mischief that had been done--the work of their hands. The military stood at ease before the burning pile, and by their order and regularity, presented a contrast to the mob, as strongly by their bright gleaming arms, as by their dress and order.

The flames now enveloped the whole mansion. There was not a window or a door from which the fiery element did not burst forth in clouds, and forked flames came rushing forth with a velocity truly wonderful.

The red glare of the flames fell upon all objects around for some distance--the more especially so, as the sun had sunk, and a bank of clouds rose from beneath the horizon and excluded all his rays; there was no twilight, and there was, as yet, no moon.

The country side was enveloped in darkness, and the burning house could be seen for miles around, and formed a rallying-point to all men's eyes.

The engines that were within reach came tearing across the country, and came to the fire; but they were of no avail. There was no supply of water, save from the ornamental ponds. These they could only get at by means that were tedious and unsatisfactory, considering the emergency of the case.

The house was a lone one, and it was being entirely consumed before they arrived, and therefore there was not the remotest chance of saving the least article. Had they ever such a supply of water, nothing could have been effected by it.

Thus the men stood idly by, passing their remarks upon the fire and the mob.

Those who stood around, and within the influence of the red glare of the flames, looked like so many demons in the infernal regions, watching the progress of lighting the fire, which we are told by good Christians is the doom of the unfortunate in spirit, and the woefully unlucky in circumstances.

It was a strange sight that; and there were many persons who would, without doubt, have rather been snug by their own fire-side than they would have remained there but it happened that no one felt inclined to express his inclination to his neighbour, and, consequently, no one said anything on the subject.

None would venture to go alone across the fields, where the spirit of the vampyre might, for all they knew to the contrary, be waiting to pounce upon them, and worry them.

No, no; no man would have quitted that mob to go back alone to the village; they would sooner have stood there all night through. That was an alternative that none of the number would very willingly accept.

The hours passed away, and the house that had been that morning a noble and well-furnished mansion, was now a smouldering heap of ruins. The flames had become somewhat subdued, and there was now more smoke than flames.

The fire had exhausted itself. There was now no more material that could serve it for fuel, and the flames began to become gradually enough subdued.

Suddenly there was a rush, and then a bright flame shot upward for an instant, so bright and so strong, that it threw a flash of light over the country for miles; but it was only momentary, and it subsided.

The roof, which had been built strong enough to resist almost anything, after being burning for a considerable time, suddenly gave way, and came in with a tremendous crash, and then all was for a moment darkness.

After this the fire might be said to be subdued, it having burned itself out; and the flames that could now be seen were but the result of so much charred wood, that would probably smoulder away for a day or two, if left to itself to do so. A dense mass of smoke arose from the ruins, and blackened the atmosphere around, and told the spectators the work was done.

CHAPTER LV

THE RETURN OF THE MOB AND MILITARY TO THE TOWN.--THE MADNESS OF THE MOB.--THE GROCER'S REVENGE

On the termination of the conflagration, or, rather, the fall of the roof, with the loss of grandeur in the spectacle, men's minds began to be free from the excitement that chained them to the spot, watching the progress of that element which has been truly described as a very good servant, but a very bad master; and of the truth of this every one must be well satisfied.

There was now remaining little more than the livid glare of the hot and burning embers; and this did not extend far, for the walls were too strongly built to fall in from their own weight; they were strong and stout, and intercepted the little light the ashes would have given out.

The mob now began to feel fatigued and chilly. It had been standing and walking about many hours, and the approach of exhaustion could not be put off much longer, especially as there was no longer any great excitement to carry it off.

The officer, seeing that nothing was to be done, collected his men together, and they were soon seen in motion. He had been ordered to stop any tumult that he might have seen, and to save any property. But there was nothing to do now; all the property that could have been saved was now destroyed, and the mob were beginning to disperse, and creep towards their own houses.

The order was then given for the men to take close order, and keep together, and the word to march was given, which the men obeyed with alacrity, for they had no good-will in stopping there the whole of the night.

The return to the village of both the mob and the military was not without its vicissitudes; accidents of all kinds were rife amongst them; the military, however, taking the open paths, soon diminished the distance, and that, too, with little or no accidents, save such as might have been expected from the state of the fields, after they had been so much trodden down of late.

Not so the townspeople or the peasantry; for, by way of keeping up their spirits, and amusing themselves on their way home, they commenced larking, as they called it, which often meant the execution of practical jokes, and these sometimes were of a serious nature.

The night was dark at that hour, especially so when there was a number of persons traversing about, so that little or nothing could be seen.

The mistakes and blunders that were made were numerous. In one place there were a number of people penetrating a path that led only to a hedge and deep ditch; indeed it was a brook very deep and muddy.

Here they came to a stop and endeavoured to ascertain its width, but the little reflected light they had was deceptive, and it did not appear so broad as it was.

"Oh, I can jump it," exclaimed one.

"And so can I," said another. "I have done so before, and why should I not do so now."

This was unanswerable, and as there were many present, at least a dozen were eager to jump.

"If thee can do it, I know I can," said a brawny countryman; "so I'll do it at once.

"The sooner the better," shouted some one behind, "or you'll have no room for a run, here's a lot of 'em coming up; push over as quickly as you can."

Thus urged, the jumpers at once made a rush to the edge of the ditch, and many jumped, and many more, from the prevailing darkness, did not see exactly where the ditch was, and taking one or two steps too many, found themselves up above the waist in muddy water.

Nor were those who jumped much better off, for nearly all jumped short or fell backwards into the stream, and were dragged out in a terrible state.

"Oh, lord! oh, lord!" exclaimed one poor fellow, dripping wet and shivering with cold, "I shall die! oh, the rheumatiz, there'll be a pretty winter for me: I'm half dead."

"Hold your noise," said another, "and help me to get the mud out of my eye; I can't see."

"Never mind," added a third, "considering how you jump, I don't think you want to see."

"This comes a hunting vampyres."

"Oh, it's all a judgment; who knows but he may be in the air: it is nothing to laugh at as I shouldn't be surprised if he were: only think how precious pleasant."

"However pleasant it may be to you," remarked one, "it's profitable to a good many."

"How so?"

"Why, see the numbers, of things that will be spoiled, coats torn, hats crushed, heads broken, and shoes burst. Oh, it's an ill-wind that blows nobody any good."

"So it is, but you may benefit anybody you like, so you don't do it at my expence."

In one part of a field where there were some stiles and gates, a big countryman caught a fat shopkeeper with the arms of the stile a terrible poke in the stomach; while the breath was knocked out of the poor man's stomach, and he was gasping with agony, the fellow set to laughing, and said to his companions, who were of the same class--

"I say, Jim, look at the grocer, he hasn't got any wind to spare, I'd run him for a wager, see how he gapes like a fish out of water."

The poor shopkeeper felt indeed like a fish out of water, and as he afterwards declared he felt just as if he had had a red hot clock weight thrust into the midst of his stomach and there left to cool.

However, the grocer would be revenged upon his tormentor, who had now lost sight of him, but the fat man, after a time, recovering his wind, and the pain in his stomach becoming less intense, he gathered himself up.

"My name ain't Jones," he muttered, "if I don't be one to his one for that; I'll do something that shall make him remember what it is to insult a respectable tradesman. I'll never forgive such an insult. It is dark, and that's why it is he has dared to do this."

Filled with dire thoughts and a spirit of revenge, he looked from side to side to see with what he could effect his object, but could espy nothing.

"It's shameful," he muttered; "what would I give for a little retort. I'd plaster his ugly countenance."

As he spoke, he placed his hands on some pales to rest himself, when he found that they stuck to them, the pales had that day been newly pitched.

A bright idea now struck him.

"If I could only get a handful of this stuff," he thought, "I should be able to serve him out for serving me out. I will, cost what it may; I'm resolved upon that. I'll not have my wind knocked out, and my inside set on fire for nothing. No, no; I'll be revenged on him."

With this view he felt over the pales, and found that he could scrape off a little only, but not with his hands; indeed, it only plastered them; he, therefore, marched about for something to scrape it off with.

"Ah; I have a knife, a large pocket knife, that will do, that is the sort of thing I want."

He immediately commenced feeling for it, but had scarcely got his hand into his pocket when he found there would be a great difficulty in either pushing it in further or withdrawing it altogether, for the pitch made it difficult to do either, and his pocket stuck to his hands like a glove.

"D--n it," said the grocer, "who would have thought of that? here's a pretty go, curse that fellow, he is the cause of all this; I'll be revenged upon him, if it's a year hence."

The enraged grocer drew his hand out, but was unable to effect his object in withdrawing the knife also; but he saw something shining, he stooped to pick it up, exclaiming as he did so, in a gratified tone of voice,

"Ah, here's something that will do better."

As he made a grasp at it, he found he had inserted his hand into something soft.

"God bless me! what now?"

He pulled his hand hastily away, and found that it stuck slightly, and then he saw what it was.

"Ay, ay, the very thing. Surely it must have been placed here on purpose by the people."

The fact was, he had placed his hand into a pot of pitch that had been left by the people who had been at work at pitching the pales, but had been attracted by the fire at Sir Francis Varney's, and to see which they had left their work, and the pitch was left on a smouldering peat fire, so that when Mr. Jones, the grocer, accidentally put his hand into it he found it just warm.

When he made this discovery he dabbed his hand again into the pitch-pot, exclaiming,--

"In for a penny, in for a pound."

And he endeavoured to secure as large a handful of the slippery and sticky stuff as he could, and this done he set off to come up with the big countryman who had done him so much indignity and made his stomach uncomfortable.

He soon came up with him, for the man had stopped rather behind, and was larking, as it is called, with some men, to whom he was a companion.

He had slipped down a bank, and was partially sitting down on the soft mud. In his bustle, the little grocer came down with a slide, close to the big countryman.

"Ah--ah! my little grocer," said the countryman, holding out his hand to catch him, and drawing him towards himself. "You will come and sit down by the side of your old friend."

As he spoke, he endeavoured to pull Mr. Jones down, too; but that individual only replied by fetching the countryman a swinging smack across the face with the handful of pitch.

"There, take that; and now we are quits; we shall be old friends after this, eh? Are you satisfied? You'll remember me, I'll warrant."

As the grocer spoke, he rubbed his hands over the face of the fallen man, and then rushed from the spot with all the haste he could make.

The countryman sat a moment or two confounded, cursing, and swearing, and spluttering, vowing vengeance, believing that it was mud only that had been plastered over his face; but when he put his hands up, and found out what it was, he roared and bellowed like a town-bull.

He cried out to his companions that his eyes were pitched: but they only laughed at him, thinking he was having some foolish lark with them.

It was next day before he got home, for he wandered about all night: and it took him a week to wash the pitch off by means of grease; and ever afterwards he recollected the pitching of his face; nor did he ever forget the grocer.

Thus it was the whole party returned a long while after dark across the fields, with all the various accidents that were likely to befal such an assemblage of people.

The vampyre hunting cost many of them dear, for clothes were injured on all sides: hats lost, and shoes missing in a manner that put some of the rioters to much inconvenience. Soon afterwards, the military retired to their quarters; and the townspeople at length became tranquil and nothing more was heard or done that night.

CHAPTER LVI

THE DEPARTURE OF THE BANNERWORTHS FROM THE HALL.--THE NEW ABODE.--JACK PRINGLE, PILOT

During that very evening, on which the house of Sir Francis Varney was fired by the mob, another scene, and one of different character, was enacted at Bannerworth Hall, where the owners of that ancient place were departing from it.

It was towards the latter part of the day, that Flora Bannerworth, Mrs. Bannerworth, and Henry Bannerworth, were preparing themselves to depart from the house of their ancestors. The intended proprietor was, as we have already been made acquainted with, the old admiral, who had taken the place somewhat mysteriously, considering the way in which he usually did business.

The admiral was walking up and down the lawn before the house, and looking up at the windows every now and then; and turning to Jack Pringle, he said,--

"Jack, you dog."

"Ay--ay, sir."

"Mind you convoy these women into the right port; do you hear? and no mistaking the bearings; do you hear?"

"Ay, ay, sir."

"These crafts want care; and you are pilot, commander, and all; so mind and keep your weather eye open."

"Ay, ay, sir. I knows the craft well enough, and I knows the roads, too; there'll be no end of foundering against the breakers to find where they lie."

"No, no, Jack; you needn't do that; but mind your bearings. Jack, mind your bearings."

"Never fear; I know 'em, well enough; my eyes ain't laid up in ordinary yet."

"Eh? What do you mean by that, you dog, eh?"

"Nothing; only I can see without helps to read, or glasses either; so I know one place from another."

There was now some one moving within; and the admiral, followed by Jack Pringle, entered the Hall. Henry Bannerworth was there. They were all ready to go when the coach came for them, which the admiral had ordered for them.

"Jack, you lubber; where are you?"

"Ay, ay, sir, here am I."

"Go, and station yourself up in some place where you can keep a good look-out for the coach, and come and report when you see it."

"Ay--ay, sir," said Jack, and away he went from the room, and stationed himself up in one of the trees, that commanded a good view of the main road for some distance.

"Admiral Bell," said Henry, "here we are, trusting implicitly to you; and in doing so, I am sure I am doing right."

"You will see that," said the admiral. "All's fair and honest as yet; and what is to come, will speak for itself."

"I hope you won't suffer from any of these nocturnal visits," said Henry.

"I don't much care about them; but old Admiral Bell don't strike his colours to an enemy, however ugly he may look. No, no; it must be a better craft than his own that'll take him; and one who won't run away, but that will grapple yard-arm and yard-arm, you know."

"Why, admiral, you must have seen many dangers in your time, and be used to all kinds of disturbances and conflicts. You have had a life of experience."

"Yes; and experience has come pretty thick sometimes, I can tell you, when it comes in the shape of Frenchmen's broadsides."

"I dare say, then, it must be rather awkward."

"Death by the law," said the admiral, "to stop one of them with your head, I assure you. I dare not make the attempt myself, though I have often seen it done."

"I dare say; but here are Flora and my mother."

As he spoke, Flora and her mother entered the apartment.

"Well, admiral, we are all ready; and, though I may feel somewhat sorry at leaving the old Hall, yet it arises from attachment to the place, and not any disinclination to be beyond the reach of these dreadful alarms."

"And I, too, shall be by no means sorry," said Flora; "I am sure it is some gratification to know we leave a friend here, rather than some others, who would have had the place, if they could have got it, by any means."

"Ah, that's true enough, Miss Flora," said the admiral; "but we'll run the enemy down yet, depend upon it. But once away, you will be free from these terrors; and now, as you have promised, do not let yourselves be seen any where at all."

"You have our promises, admiral; and they shall be religiously kept, I can assure you."

"Boat, ahoy--ahoy!" shouted Jack.

"What boat?" said the admiral, surprised; and then he muttered, "Confound you for a lubber! Didn't I tell you to mind your bearings, you dog-fish you?"

"Ay, ay, sir--and so I did."

"You did."

"Yes, here they are. Squint over the larboard bulk-heads, as they call walls, and then atween the two trees on the starboard side of the course, then straight ahead for a few hundred fathoms, when you come to a funnel as is smoking like the crater of Mount Vesuvius, and then in a line with that on the top of the hill, comes our boat."

"Well," said the admiral, "that'll do. Now go open the gates, and keep a bright look out, and if you see anybody near your watch, why douse their glim."

"Ay--ay, sir," said Jack, and he disappeared.

"Rather a lucid description," said Henry, as he thought of Jack's report to the admiral.

"Oh, it's a seaman's report. I know what he means; it's quicker and plainer than the land lingo, to my ears, and Jack can't talk any other, you see."

By this time the coach came into the yard, and the whole party descended into the court-yard, where they came to take leave of the old place.

"Farewell, admiral."

"Good bye," said the admiral. "I hope the place you are going to will be such as please you--I hope it will."

"I am sure we shall endeavour to be pleased with it, and I am pretty sure we shall."

"Good bye."

"Farewell, Admiral Bell," said Henry.

"You remember your promises?"

"I do. Good bye, Mr. Chillingworth."

"Good bye," said Mr. Chillingworth, who came up to bid them farewell; "a pleasant journey, and may you all be the happier for it."

"You do not come with us?"

"No; I have some business of importance to attend to, else I should have the greatest pleasure in doing so. But good bye; we shall not be long apart, I dare say."

"I hope not," said Henry.

The door of the carriage was shut by the admiral, who looked round, saying,--

"Jack--Jack Pringle, where are you, you dog?"

"Here am I," said Jack.

"Where have you been to?"

"Only been for pigtail," said Jack. "I forgot it, and couldn't set sail without it."

"You dog you; didn't I tell you to mind your bearings?"

"So I will," said Jack, "fore and aft--fore and aft, admiral."

"You had better," said the admiral, who, however, relaxed into a broad grin, which he concealed from Jack Pringle.

Jack mounted the coach-box, and away it went, just as it was getting dark. The old admiral had locked up all the rooms in the presence of Henry Bannerworth; and when the coach had gone out of sight, Mr. Chillingworth came back to the Hall, where he joined the admiral.

"Well," he said, "they are gone, Admiral Bell, and we are alone; we have a clear stage and no favour."

"The two things of all others I most desire. Now, they will be strangers where they are going to, and that will be something gained. I will endeavour to do some thing if I get yard-arm and yard-arm with these pirates. I'll make 'em feel the weight of true metal; I'll board 'em--d----e, I'll do everything."

"Everything that can be done."

"Ay--ay."

***

The coach in which the family of the Bannerworths were carried away continued its course without any let or hindrance, and they met no one on their road during the whole drive. The fact was, nearly everybody was at the conflagration at Sir Francis Varney's house.

Flora knew not which way they were going, and, after a time, all trace of the road was lost. Darkness set in, and they all sat in silence in the coach.

At length, after some time had been spent thus, Flora Bannerworth turned to Jack Pringle, and said,--

"Are we near, or have we much further to go?"

"Not very much, ma'am," said Jack. "All's right, however--ship in the direct course, and no breakers ahead--no lookout necessary; however there's a land-lubber aloft to keep a look out."

As this was not very intelligible, and Jack seemed to have his own reasons for silence, they asked him no further questions; but in about three-quarters of an hour, during which time the coach had been driving through the trees, they came to a standstill by a sudden pull of the check-string from Jack, who said,--

"Hilloa!--take in sails, and drop anchor."

"Is this the place?"

"Yes, here we are," said Jack; "we're in port now, at all events;" and he began to sing,--

"The trials and the dangers of the voyage is past,"

when the coach door opened, and they all got out and looked about them where they were.

"Up the garden if you please, ma'am--as quick as you can; the night air is very cold."

Flora and her mother and brother took the hint, which was meant by Jack to mean that they were not to be seen outside. They at once entered a pretty garden, and then they came to a very neat and picturesque cottage. They had no time to look up at it, as the door was immediately opened by an elderly female, who was intended to wait upon them.

Soon after, Jack Pringle and the coachman entered the passage with the small amount of luggage which they had brought with them. This was deposited in the passage, and then Jack went out again, and, after a few minutes, there was the sound of wheels, which intimated that the coach had driven off.

Jack, however, returned in a few minutes afterwards, having secured the wicket-gate at the end of the garden, and then entered the house, shutting the door carefully after him.

Flora and her mother looked over the apartments in which they were shown with some surprise. It was, in everything, such as they could wish; indeed, though it could not be termed handsomely or extravagantly furnished, or that the things were new, yet, there was all that convenience and comfort could require, and some little of the luxuries.

"Well," said Flora, "this is very thoughtful of the admiral. The place will really be charming, and the garden, too, delightful."

"Mustn't be made use of just now," said Jack, "if you please, ma'am; them's the orders at present."

"Very well," said Flora, smiling. "I suppose, Mr. Pringle, we must obey them."

"Jack Pringle, if you please," said Jack. "My commands only temporary. I ain't got a commission."

CHAPTER LVII

THE LONELY WATCH, AND THE ADVENTURE IN THE DESERTED HOUSE

It is now quite night, and so peculiar and solemn a stillness reigns in and about Bannerworth Hall and its surrounding grounds, that one might have supposed it a place of the dead, deserted completely after sunset by all who would still hold kindred with the living. There was not a breath of air stirring, and this circumstance added greatly to the impression of profound repose which the whole scene exhibited.

The wind during the day had been rather of a squally character, but towards nightfall, as is often usual after a day of such a character, it had completely lulled, and the serenity of the scene was unbroken even by the faintest sigh from a wandering zephyr.

The moon rose late at that period, and as is always the case at that interval between sunset and the rising of that luminary which makes the night so beautiful, the darkness was of the most profound character.

It was one of those nights to produce melancholy reflections--a night on which a man would be apt to review his past life, and to look into the hidden recesses of his soul to see if conscience could make a coward of him in the loneliness and stillness that breathed around.

It was one of those nights in which wanderers in the solitude of nature feel that the eye of Heaven is upon them, and on which there seems to be a more visible connection between the world and its great Creator than upon ordinary occasions.

The solemn and melancholy appear places once instinct with life, when deserted by those familiar forms and faces that have long inhabited them. There is no desert, no uninhabited isle in the far ocean, no wild, barren, pathless tract of unmitigated sterility, which could for one moment compare in point of loneliness and desolation to a deserted city.

Strip London, mighty and majestic as it is, of the busy swarm of humanity that throng its streets, its suburbs, its temples, its public edifices, and its private dwellings, and how awful would be the walk of one solitary man throughout its noiseless thoroughfares.

If madness seized not upon him ere he had been long the sole survivor of a race, it would need be cast in no common mould.

And to descend from great things to smaller--from the huge leviathan city to one mansion far removed from the noise and bustle of conventional life, we may imagine the sort of desolation that reigned through Bannerworth Hall, when, for the first time, after nearly a hundred and fifty years of occupation, it was deserted by the representatives of that family, so many members of which had lived and died beneath its roof. The house, and everything within, without, and around it, seemed actually to sympathize with its own desolation and desertion.

It seemed as if twenty years of continued occupation could not have produced such an effect upon the ancient edifice as had those few hours of neglect and desertion.

And yet it was not as if it had been stripped of those time-worn and ancient relics of ornament and furnishing that so long had appertained to it. No, nothing but the absence of those forms which had been accustomed quietly to move from room to room, and to be met here upon a staircase, there upon a corridor, and even in some of the ancient panelled apartments, which give it an air of dreary repose and listlessness.

The shutters, too, were all closed, and that circumstance contributed largely to the production of that gloomy effect which otherwise could not have ensued.

In fact, what could be done without attracting very special observation was done to prove to any casual observer that the house was untenanted.

But such was not really the case. In that very room where the much dreaded Varney the vampyre had made one of his dreaded appearances to Flora Bannerworth and her mother, sat two men.

It was from that apartment that Flora had discharged the pistol, which had been left to her by her brother, and the shot from which it was believed by the whole family had most certainly taken effect upon the person of the vampyre.

It was a room peculiarly accessible from the gardens, for it had long French windows opening to the very ground, and but a stone step intervened between the flooring of the apartment and a broad gravel walk which wound round that entire portion of the house.

It was in this room, then, that two men sat in silence, and nearly in darkness.

Before them, and on a table, were several articles of refreshment, as well of defence and offence, according as their intentions might be.

There were a bottle and three glasses, and lying near the elbow of one of the men was a large pair of pistols, such as might have adorned the belt of some desperate character, who wished to instil an opinion of his prowess into his foes by the magnitude of his weapons.

Close at hand, by the same party, lay some more modern fire arms, as well as a long dirk, with a silver mounted handle.

The light they had consisted of a large lantern, so constructed with a slide, that it could be completely obscured at a moment's notice; but now as it was placed, the rays that were allowed to come from it were directed as much from the window of the apartment, as possible, and fell upon the faces of the two men, revealing them to be Admiral Bell and Dr. Chillingworth.

It might have been the effect of the particular light in which he sat, but the doctor looked extremely pale, and did not appear at all at his ease.

The admiral, on the contrary, appeared in as placable a state of mind as possible and had his arms folded across his breast, and his head shrunk down between his shoulders as if he had made up his mind to something that was to last a long time, and, therefore he was making the best of it.

"I do hope," said Mr. Chillingworth, after a long pause, "that our efforts will be crowned with success--you know, my dear sir, that I have always been of your opinion, that there was a great deal more in this matter than met the eye."

"To be sure," said the admiral, "and as to our efforts being crowned with success, why, I'll give you a toast, doctor, 'may the morning's reflection provide for the evening's amusement.'"

"Ha! ha!" said Chillingworth, faintly; "I'd rather not drink any more, and you seem, admiral, to have transposed the toast in some way. I believe it runs, 'may the evening's amusement bear the morning's reflection.'"

"Transpose the devil!" said the admiral; "what do I care how it runs? I gave you my toast, and as to that you mention, it's another one altogether, and a sneaking, shore-going one too: but why don't you drink?"

"Why, my dear sir, medically speaking, I am strongly of opinion that, when the human stomach is made to contain a large quantity of alcohol, it produces bad effects upon the system. Now, I've certainly taken one glass of this infernally strong Hollands, and it is now lying in my stomach like the red-hot heater of a tea-urn."

"Is it? put it out with another, then."

"Ay, I'm afraid that would not answer, but do you really think, admiral, that we shall effect anything by waiting here, and keeping watch and ward, not under the most comfortable circumstances, this first night of the Hall being empty."

"Well, I don't know that we shall," said the admiral; "but when you really want to steal a march upon the enemy, there is nothing like beginning betimes. We are both of opinion that Varney's great object throughout has been, by some means or another, to get possession of the house."

"Yes; true, true."

"We know that he has been unceasing in his endeavours to get the Bannerworth family out of it; that he has offered them their own price to become its tenant, and that the whole gist of his quiet and placid interview with Flora in the garden, was to supply her with a new set of reasons for urging her mother and brother to leave Bannerworth Hall, because the old ones were certainly not found sufficient."

"True, true, most true," said Mr. Chillingworth, emphatically. "You know, sir, that from the first time you broached that view of the subject to me, how entirely I coincided with you."

"Of course you did, for you are a honest fellow, and a right-thinking fellow, though you are a doctor, and I don't know that I like doctors much better than I like lawyers--they're only humbugs in a different sort of way. But I wish to be liberal; there is such a thing as an honest lawyer, and, d----e, you're an honest doctor!"

"Of course I'm much obliged, admiral, for your good opinion. I only wish it had struck me to bring something of a solid nature in the shape of food, to sustain the waste of the animal economy during the hours we shall have to wait here."

"Don't trouble yourself about that," said the admiral. "Do you think I'm a donkey, and would set out on a cruise without victualling my ship? I should think not. Jack Pringle will be here soon, and he has my orders to bring in something to eat."

"Well," said the doctor, "that's very provident of you, admiral, and I feel personally obliged; but tell me, how do you intend to conduct the watch?"

"What do you mean?"

"Why, I mean, if we sit here with the window fastened so as to prevent our light from being seen, and the door closed, how are we by any possibility to know if the house is attacked or not?"

"Hark'ee, my friend," said the admiral; "I've left a weak point for the enemy."

"A what, admiral?"

"A weak point. I've taken good care to secure everything but one of the windows on the ground floor, and that I've left open, or so nearly open, that it will look like the most natural place in the world to get in at. Now, just inside that window, I've placed a lot of the family crockery. I'll warrant, if anybody so much as puts his foot in, you'll hear the smash;--and, d----e, there it is!"

There was a loud crash at this moment, followed by a succession of similar sounds, but of a lesser degree; and both the admiral and Mr. Chillingworth sprung to their feet.

"Come on," cried the former; "here'll be a precious row--take the lantern."

Mr. Chillingworth did so, but he did not seem possessed of a great deal of presence of mind; for, before they got out of the room, he twice accidentally put on the dark slide, and produced a total darkness.

"D--n!" said the admiral; "don't make it wink and wink in that way; hold it up, and run after me as hard as you can."

"I'm coming, I'm coming," said Mr. Chillingworth.

It was one of the windows of a long room, containing five, fronting the garden, which the admiral had left purposely unguarded; and it was not far from the apartment in which they had been sitting, so that, probably, not half a minute's time elapsed between the moment of the first alarm, and their reaching the spot from whence it was presumed to arise.

The admiral had armed himself with one of the huge pistols, and he dashed forward, with all the vehemence of his character, towards the window, where he knew he had placed the family crockery, and where he fully expected to meet the reward of his exertion by discovering some one lying amid its fragments.

In this, however, he was disappointed; for, although there was evidently a great smash amongst the plates and dishes, the window remained closed, and there was no indication whatever of the presence of any one.

"Well, that's odd," said the admiral; "I balanced them up amazingly careful, and two of 'em edgeways--d---e, a fly would have knocked them down."

"Mew," said, a great cat, emerging from under a chair.

"Curse you, there you are," said the admiral. "Put out the light, put out the light; here we're illuminating the whole house for nothing."

With, a click went the darkening slide over the lantern, and all was obscurity.

At that instant a shrill, clear whistle came from the garden.

CHAPTER LVIII

THE ARRIVAL OF JACK PRINGLE.--MIDNIGHT AND THE VAMPYRE.--THE MYSTERIOUS HAT

"Bless me! what is that?" said Mr. Chillingworth; "what a very singular sound."

"Hold your noise," said the admiral; "did you never hear that before?"

"No; how should I?"

"Lor, bless the ignorance of some people, that's a boatswain's call."

"Oh, it is," said Mr. Chillingworth; "is he going to call again?"

"D----e, I tell ye it's a boatswain's call."

"Well, then, d----e, if it comes to that," said Mr. Chillingworth, "what does he call here for?"

The admiral disdained an answer; but demanding the lantern, he opened it, so that there was a sufficient glimmering of light to guide him, and then walked from the room towards the front door of the Hall.

He asked no questions before he opened it, because, no doubt, the signal was preconcerted; and Jack Pringle, for it was he indeed who had arrived, at once walked in, and the admiral barred the door with the same precision with which it was before secured.

"Well, Jack," he said, "did you see anybody?"

"Ay, ay, sir," said Jack.

"Why, ye don't mean that--where?"

"Where I bought the grub; a woman--"

"D----e, you're a fool, Jack."

"You're another."

"Hilloa, ye scoundrel, what d'ye mean by talking to me in that way? is this your respect for your superiors?"

"Ship's been paid off long ago," said Jack, "and I ain't got no superiors. I ain't a marine or a Frenchman."

"Why, you're drunk."

"I know it; put that in your eye."

"There's a scoundrel. Why, you know-nothing-lubber, didn't I tell you to be careful, and that everything depended upon secrecy and caution? and didn't I tell you, above all this, to avoid drink?"

"To be sure you did."

"And yet you come here like a rum cask."

"Yes; now you've had your say, what then?"

"You'd better leave him alone," said Mr. Chillingworth; "it's no use arguing with a drunken man."

"Harkye, admiral," said Jack, steadying himself as well as he could. "I've put up with you a precious long while, but I won't no longer; you're so drunk, now, that you keeping bobbing up and down like the mizen gaff in a storm--that's my opinion--tol de rol."

"Let him alone, let him alone," urged Mr. Chillingworth.

"The villain," said the admiral; "he's enough to ruin everything; now, who would have thought that? but it's always been the way with him for a matter of twenty years--he never had any judgment in his drink. When it was all smooth sailing, and nothing to do, and the fellow might have got an extra drop on board, which nobody would have cared for, he's as sober as a judge; but, whenever there's anything to do, that wants a little cleverness, confound him, he ships rum enough to float a seventy-four."

"Are you going to stand anything to drink," said Jack, "my old buffer? Do you recollect where you got your knob scuttled off Beyrout--how you fell on your latter end and tried to recollect your church cateckis, you old brute?--I's ashamed of you. Do you recollect the brown girl you bought for thirteen bob and a tanner, at the blessed Society Islands, and sold her again for a dollar, to a nigger seven feet two, in his natural pumps? you're a nice article, you is, to talk of marines and swabs, and shore-going lubbers, blow yer. Do you recollect the little Frenchman that told ye he'd pull your blessed nose, and I advised you to soap it? do you recollect Sall at Spithead, as you got in at a port hole of the state cabin, all but her behind?"

"Death and the devil!" said the admiral, breaking from the grasp of Mr. Chillingworth.

"Ay," said Jack, "you'll come to 'em both one of these days, old cock, and no mistake."

"I'll have his life, I'll have his life," roared the admiral.

"Nay, nay, sir," said Mr. Chillingworth, catching the admiral round the waist. "My dear sir, recollect, now, if I may venture to advise you, Admiral Bell, there's a lot of that fiery hollands you know, in the next room; set firm down to that, and finish him off. I'll warrant him, he'll be quiet enough."

"What's that you say?" cried Jack--"hollands!--who's got any?--next to rum and Elizabeth Baker, if I has an affection, it's hollands."

"Jack!" said the admiral.

"Ay, ay, sir!" said Jack, instinctively.

"Come this way."

Jack staggered after him, and they all reached the room where the admiral and Mr. Chillingworth had been sitting before the alarm.

"There!" said the admiral, putting the light upon the table, and pointing to the bottle; "what do you think of that?"

"I never thinks under such circumstances," said Jack. "Here's to the wooden walls of old England!"

He seized the bottle, and, putting its neck into his mouth, for a few moments nothing was heard but a gurgling sound of the liquor passing down his throat; his head went further and further back, until, at last, over he went, chair and bottle and all, and lay in a helpless state of intoxication on the floor.

"So far, so good," said the admiral. "He's out of the way, at all events."

"I'll just loosen his neckcloth," said Mr. Chillingworth, "and then we'll go and sit somewhere else; and I should recommend that, if anywhere, we take up our station in that chamber, once Flora's, where the mysterious panelled portrait hangs, that bears so strong a resemblance to Varney, the vampyre."

"Hush!" said the admiral. "What's that?"

They listened for a moment intently; and then, distinctly, upon the gravel path outside the window, they heard a footstep, as if some person were walking along, not altogether heedlessly, but yet without any very great amount of caution or attention to the noise he might make.

"Hist!" said the doctor. "Not a word. They come."

"What do you say they for?" said the admiral.

"Because something seems to whisper me that Mr. Marchdale knows more of Varney, the vampyre, than ever he has chosen to reveal. Put out the light."

"Yes, yes--that'll do. The moon has risen; see how it streams through the chinks of the shutters."

"No, no--it's not in that direction, or our light would have betrayed us. Do you not see the beams come from that half glass-door leading to the greenhouse?"

"Yes; and there's the footstep again, or another."

Tramp, tramp came a footfall again upon the gravel path, and, as before, died away upon their listening ears.

"What do you say now," said Mr. Chillingworth--"are there not two?"

"If they were a dozen," said the admiral, "although we have lost one of our force, I would tackle them. Let's creep on through the rooms in the direction the footsteps went."

"My life on it," said Mr. Chillingworth as they left the apartment, "if this be Varney, he makes for that apartment where Flora slept, and which he knows how to get admission to. I've studied the house well, admiral, and to get to that window any one from here outside must take a considerable round. Come on--we shall be beforehand."

"A good idea--a good idea. Be it so."

Just allowing themselves sufficient light to guide them on the way from the lantern, they hurried on with as much precipitation as the intricacies of the passage would allow, nor halted till they had reached the chamber were hung the portrait which bore so striking and remarkable a likeness to Varney, the vampyre.

They left the lamp outside the door, so that not even a straggling beam from it could betray that there were persons on the watch; and then, as quietly as foot could fall, they took up their station among the hangings of the antique bedstead, which has been before alluded to in this work as a remarkable piece of furniture appertaining to that apartment.

"Do you think," said the admiral, "we've distanced them?"

"Certainly we have. It's unlucky that the blind of the window is down."

"Is it? By Heaven, there's a d----d strange-looking shadow creeping over it."

Mr. Chillingworth looked almost with suspended breath. Even he could not altogether get rid of a tremulous feeling, as he saw that the shadow of a human form, apparently of very large dimensions, was on the outside, with the arms spread out, as if feeling for some means of opening the window.

It would have been easy now to have fired one of the pistols direct upon the figure; but, somehow or another, both the admiral and Mr. Chillingworth shrank from that course, and they felt much rather inclined to capture whoever might make his appearance, only using their pistols as a last resource, than gratuitously and at once to resort to violence.

"Who should you say that was?" whispered the admiral.

"Varney, the vampyre."

"D----e, he's ill-looking and big enough for anything--there's a noise!"

There was a strange cracking sound at the window, as if a pane of glass was being very stealthily and quietly broken; and then the blind was agitated slightly, confusing much the shadow that was cast upon it, as if the hand of some person was introduced for the purpose of effecting a complete entrance into the apartment.

"He's coming in," whispered the admiral.

"Hush, for Heaven's sake!" said Mr. Chillingworth; "you will alarm him, and we shall lose the fruit of all the labour we have already bestowed upon the matter; but did you not say something, admiral, about lying under the window and catching him by the leg?"

"Why, yes; I did."

"Go and do it, then; for, as sure as you are a living man, his leg will be in in a minute."

"Here goes," said the admiral; "I never suggest anything which I'm unwilling to do myself."

Whoever it was that now was making such strenuous exertions to get into the apartment seemed to find some difficulty as regarded the fastenings of the window, and as this difficulty increased, the patience of the party, as well as his caution deserted him, and the casement was rattled with violence.

With a far greater amount of caution than any one from a knowledge of his character would have given him credit for, the admiral crept forward and laid himself exactly under the window.

The depth of wood-work from the floor to the lowest part of the window-frame did not exceed above two feet; so that any one could conveniently step in from the balcony outride on to the floor of the apartment, which was just what he who was attempting to effect an entrance was desirous of doing.

It was quite clear that, be he who he might, mortal or vampyre, he had some acquaintance with the fastening of the window; for now he succeeded in moving it, and the sash was thrown open.

The blind was still an obstacle; but a vigorous pull from the intruder brought that down on the prostrate admiral; and then Mr. Chillingworth saw, by the moonlight, a tall, gaunt figure standing in the balcony, as if just hesitating for a moment whether to get head first or feet first into the apartment.

Had he chosen the former alternative he would need, indeed, to have been endowed with more than mortal powers of defence and offence to escape capture, but his lucky star was in the ascendancy, and he put his foot in first.

He turned his side to the apartment and, as he did so, the blight moonlight fell upon his face, enabling Mr. Chillingworth to see, without the shadow of a doubt, that it was, indeed, Varney, the vampyre, who was thus stealthily making his entrance into Bannerworth Hall, according to the calculation which had been made by the admiral upon that subject. The doctor scarcely knew whether to be pleased or not at this discovery; it was almost a terrifying one, sceptical as he was upon the subject of vampyres, and he waited breathless for the issue of the singular and perilous adventure.

No doubt Admiral Bell deeply congratulated himself upon the success which was about to crown his stratagem for the capture of the intruder, be he who he might, and he writhed with impatience for the foot to come sufficiently near him to enable him to grasp it.

His patience was not severely tried, for in another moment it rested upon his chest.

"Boarders a hoy!" shouted the admiral, and at once he laid hold of the trespasser. "Yard-arm to yard-arm, I think I've got you now. Here's a prize, doctor! he shall go away without his leg if he goes away now. Eh! what! the light--d----e, he has--Doctor, the light! the light! Why what's this?--Hilloa, there!"

Dr. Chillingworth sprang into the passage, and procured the light--in another moment he was at the side of the admiral, and the lantern slide being thrown back, he saw at once the dilemma into which his friend had fallen.

There he lay upon his back, grasping, with the vehemence of an embrace that had in it much of the ludicrous, a long boot, from which the intruder had cleverly slipped his leg, leaving it as a poor trophy in the hands of his enemies.

"Why you've only pulled his boot off," said the doctor; "and now he's gone for good, for he knows what we're about, and has slipped through your fingers."

Admiral Bell sat up and looked at the boot with a rueful countenance.

"Done again!" he said.

"Yes, you are done," said the doctor; "why didn't you lay hold of the leg while you were about it, instead of the boot? Admiral, are these your tactics?"

"Don't be a fool," said the admiral; "put out the light and give me the pistols, or blaze away yourself into the garden; a chance shot may do something. It's no use running after him; a stern chase is a long chase; but fire away."

As if some parties below had heard him give the word, two loud reports from the garden immediately ensued, and a crash of glass testified to the fact that some deadly missile had entered the room.

"Murder!" said the doctor, and he fell flat upon his back. "I don't like this at all; it's all in your line, admiral, but not in mine."

"All's right, my lad," said the admiral; "now for it."

He saw lying in the moonlight the pistols which he and the doctor had brought into the room, and in another moment he, to use his own words, returned the broadside of the enemy.

"D--n it!" he said, "this puts me in mind of old times. Blaze away, you thieves, while I load; broadside to broadside. It's your turn now; I scorn to take an advantage. What the devil's that?"

Something very large and very heavy came bang against the window, sending it all into the room, and nearly smothering the admiral with the fragments. Another shot was then fired, and in came something else, which hit the wall on the opposite side of the room, rebounding from thence on to the doctor, who gave a yell of despair.

After that all was still; the enemy seemed to be satisfied that they had silenced the garrison. And it took the admiral a great deal of kicking and plunging to rescue himself from some superincumbent mass that was upon him, which seemed to him to be a considerable sized tree.

"Call this fair fighting," he shouted--"getting a man's legs and arms tangled up like a piece of Indian matting in the branches of a tree? Doctor, I say! hilloa! where are you?"

"I don't know," said the doctor; "but there's somebody getting into the balcony--now we shall be murdered in cold blood!"

"Where's the pistols?"

"Fired off, of course; you did it yourself."

Bang came something else into the room, which, from the sound it made, closely resembled a brick, and after that somebody jumped clean into the centre of the floor, and then, after rolling and writhing about in a most singular manner, slowly got up, and with various preliminary hiccups, said,--

"Come on, you lubbers, many of you as like. I'm the tar for all weathers."

"Why, d----e," said the admiral, "it's Jack Pringle."

"Yes, it is," said Jack, who was not sufficiently sober to recognise the admiral's voice. "I sees as how you've heard of me. Come on, all of you."

"Why, Jack, you scoundrel," roared the admiral, "how came you here? Don't you know me? I'm your admiral, you horse-marine."

"Eh?" said Jack. "Ay--ay, sir, how came you here?"

"How came you, you villain?"

"Boarded the enemy."

"The enemy who you boarded was us; and hang me if I don't think you haven't been pouring broadsides into us, while the enemy were scudding before the wind in another direction."

"Lor!" said Jack.

"Explain, you scoundrel, directly--explain."

"Well, that's only reasonable," said Jack; and giving a heavier lurch than usual, he sat down with a great bounce upon the floor. "You see it's just this here,--when I was a coming of course I heard, just as I was a going, that ere as made me come all in consequence of somebody a going, or for to come, you see, admiral."

"Doctor," cried the admiral, in a great rage, "just help me out of this entanglement of branches, and I'll rid the world from an encumbrance by smashing that fellow."

"Smash yourself!" said Jack. "You know you're drunk."

"My dear admiral," said Mr. Chillingworth, laying hold of one of his legs, and pulling it very hard, which brought his face into a lot of brambles, "we're making a mess of this business."

"Murder!" shouted the admiral; "you are indeed. Is that what you call pulling me out of it? You've stuck me fast."

"I'll manage it," said Jack. "I've seed him in many a scrape, and I've seed him out. You pull me, doctor, and I'll pull him. Yo hoy!"

Jack laid hold of the admiral by the scuff of the neck, and the doctor laid hold of Jack round the waist, the consequence of which was that he was dragged out from the branches of the tree, which seemed to have been thrown into the room, and down fell both Jack and the doctor.

At this instant there was a strange hissing sound heard below the window; then there was a sudden, loud report, as if a hand-grenade had gone off. A spectral sort of light gleamed into the room, and a tall, gaunt-looking figure rose slowly up in the balcony.

"Beware of the dead!" said a voice. "Let the living contend with the living, the dead with the dead. Beware!"

The figure disappeared, as did also the strange, spectral-looking light. A death-like silence ensued, and the cold moonbeams streamed in upon the floor of the apartment, as if nothing had occurred to disturb the wrapped repose and serenity of the scene.

CHAPTER LIX

THE WARNING.--THE NEW PLAN OF OPERATION.--THE INSULTING MESSAGE FROM VARNEY

So much of the night had been consumed in these operations, that by the time they were over, and the three personages who lay upon the floor of what might be called the haunted chamber of Bannerworth Hall, even had they now been disposed to seek repose, would have had a short time to do so before the daylight would have streamed in upon them, and roused them to the bustle of waking existence.

It may be well believed what a vast amount of surprise came over the three persons in that chamber at the last little circumstance that had occurred in connection with the night's proceedings.

There was nothing which had preceded that, that did not resemble a genuine attack upon the premises; but about that last mysterious appearance, with its curious light, there was quite enough to bother the admiral and Jack Pringle to a considerable effect, whatever might be the effect upon Mr. Chillingworth, whose profession better enabled him to comprehend, chemically, what would produce effects that, no doubt, astonished them amazingly.

What with his intoxication and the violent exercise he had taken, Jack was again thoroughly prostrate; while the admiral could not have looked more astonished had the evil one himself appeared in propria persona and given him notice to quit the premises.

He was, however, the first to speak, and the words he spoke were addressed to Jack, to whom he said,--

"Jack, you lubber, what do you think of all that?"

Jack, however, was too far gone even to say "Ay, ay, sir;" and Mr. Chillingworth, slowly getting himself up to his feet, approached the admiral.

"It's hard to say so much, Admiral Bell," he said, "but it strikes me that whatever object this Sir Francis Varney, or Varney, the vampyre, has in coming into Bannerworth Hall, it is, at all events, of sufficient importance to induce him to go any length, and not to let even a life to stand in the way of its accomplishment."

"Well, it seems so," said the admiral; "for I'll be hanged if I can make head or tail of the fellow."

"If we value our personal safety, we shall hesitate to continue a perilous adventure which I think can end only in defeat, if not in death."

"But we don't value our personal safety," said the admiral. "We've got into the adventure, and I don't see why we shouldn't carry it out. It may be growing a little serious; but what of that? For the sake of that young girl, Flora Bannerworth, as well as for the sake of my nephew, Charles Holland, I will see the end of this affair, let it be what it may; but mind you, Mr. Chillingworth, if one man chooses to go upon a desperate service, that's no reason why he should ask another to do so."

"I understand you," said Mr. Chillingworth; "but, having commenced the adventure with you, I am not the man to desert you in it. We have committed a great mistake."

"A mistake! how?"

"Why, we ought to have watched outside the house, instead of within it. There can be no doubt that if we had lain in wait in the garden, we should have been in a better position to have accomplished our object."

"Well, I don't know, doctor, but it seems to me that if Jack Pringle hadn't made such a fool of himself, we should have managed very well: and I don't know now how he came to behave in the manner he did."

"Nor I," said Mr. Chillingworth. "But, at all events, so far as the result goes, it is quite clear that any further watching, in this house, for the appearance of Sir Francis Varney, will now be in vain. He has nothing to do now but to keep quiet until we are tired out--a fact, concerning which he can easily obtain information--and then he immediately, without trouble, walks into the premises, to his own satisfaction."

"But what the deuce can he want upon the premises?"

"That question, admiral, induces me to think that we have made another mistake. We ought not to have attempted to surprise Sir Francis Varney in coming into Bannerworth Hall, but to catch him as he came out."

"Well, there's something in that," said the admiral. "This is a pretty night's business, to be sure. However, it can't be helped, it's done, and there's an end on't. And now, as the morning is near at hand, I certainly must confess I should like to get some breakfast, although I don't like that we should all leave the house together"

"Why," said Mr. Chillingworth, "as we have now no secret to keep with regard to our being here, because the principal person we wished to keep it from is aware of it, I think we cannot do better than send at once for Henry Bannerworth, tell him of the non-success of the effort we have made in his behalf, and admit him at once into our consultation of what is next to be done."

"Agreed, agreed, I think that, without troubling him, we might have captured this Varney; but that's over now, and, as soon as Jack Pringle chooses to wake up again, I'll send him to the Bannerworths with a message."

"Ay, ay, sir," said Jack, suddenly; "all's right."

"Why, you vagabond," said the admiral, "I do believe you've been shamming!"

"Shamming what?"

"Being drunk, to be sure."

"Lor! couldn't do it," said Jack; "I'll just tell you how it was. I wakened up and found myself shut in somewhere; and, as I couldn't get out of the door, I thought I'd try the window, and there I did get out. Well, perhaps I wasn't quite the thing, but I sees two people in the garden a looking up at this ere room; and, to be sure, I thought it was you and the doctor. Well, it warn't no business of mine to interfere, so I seed one of you climb up the balcony, as I thought, and then, after which, come down head over heels with such a run, that I thought you must have broken your neck. Well, after that you fired a couple of shots in, and then, after that, I made sure it was you, admiral."

"And what made you make sure of that?"

"Why, because you scuttled away like an empty tar-barrel in full tide."

"Confound you, you scoundrel!"

"Well, then, confound you, if it comes to that. I thought I was doing you good sarvice, and that the enemy was here, when all the while it turned out as you was and the enemy wasn't, and the enemy was outside and you wasn't."

"But who threw such a confounded lot of things into the room?"

"Why, I did, of course; I had but one pistol, and, when I fired that off, I was forced to make up a broadside with what I could."

"Was there ever such a stupid!" said the admiral; "doctor, doctor, you talked of us making two mistakes; but you forgot a third and worse one still, and that was the bringing such a lubberly son of a sea-cook into the place as this fellow."

"You're another," said Jack; "and you knows it."

"Well, well," said Mr. Chillingworth, "it's no use continuing it, admiral; Jack, in his way, did, I dare say, what he considered for the best."

"I wish he'd do, then, what he considers for the worst, next time."

"Perhaps I may," said Jack, "and then you will be served out above a bit. What 'ud become of you, I wonder, if it wasn't for me? I'm as good as a mother to you, you knows that, you old babby."

"Come, come, admiral," said Mr. Chillingworth: "come down to the garden-gate; it is now just upon daybreak, and the probability is that we shall not be long there before we see some of the country people, who will get us anything we require in the shape of refreshment; and as for Jack, he seems quite sufficiently recovered now to go to the Bannerworths'."

"Oh! I can go," said Jack; "as for that, the only thing as puts me out of the way is the want of something to drink. My constitution won't stand what they call temperance living, or nothing with the chill off."

"Go at once," said the admiral, "and tell Mr. Henry Bannerworth that we are here; but do not tell him before his sister or his mother. If you meet anybody on the road, send them here with a cargo of victuals. It strikes me that a good, comfortable breakfast wouldn't be at all amiss, doctor."

"How rapidly the day dawns," remarked Mr. Chillingworth, as he walked into the balcony from whence Varney, the vampire, had attempted to make good his entrance to the Hall.

Just as he spoke, and before Jack Pringle could get half way over to the garden gate, there came a tremendous ring at the bell which was suspended over it.

A view of that gate could not be commanded from the window of the haunted apartment, so that they could not see who it was that demanded admission.

As Jack Pringle was going down at any rate, they saw no necessity for personal interference; and he proved that there was not, by presently returning with a note which he said had been thrown over the gate by a lad, who then scampered off with all the speed he could make.

The note, exteriorly, was well got up, and had all the appearance of great care having been bestowed upon its folding and sealing.

It was duly addressed to "Admiral Bell, Bannerworth Hall," and the word "immediate" was written at one corner.

The admiral, after looking at it for some time with very great wonder, came at last to the conclusion that probably to open it would be the shortest way of arriving at a knowledge of who had sent it, and he accordingly did so.

The note was as follows:--

"My dear sir,--Feeling assured that you cannot be surrounded with those means and appliances for comfort in the Hall, in its now deserted condition, which you have a right to expect, and so eminently deserve, I flatter myself that I shall receive an answer in the affirmative, when I request the favour of your company to breakfast, as well as that of your learned friend. Mr. Chillingworth.

"In consequence of a little accident which occurred last evening to my own residence, I am, ad interim, until the county build it up for me again, staying at a house called Walmesley Lodge, where I shall expect you with all the impatience of one soliciting an honour, and hoping that it will be conferred upon him.

"I trust that any little difference of opinion on other subjects will not interfere to prevent the harmony of our morning's meal together.

"Believe me to be, my dear sir, with the greatest possible consideration, your very obedient, humble servant,

"FRANCIS VARNEY."

The admiral gasped again, and looked at Mr. Chillingworth, and then at the note, and then at Mr. Chillingworth again, as if he was perfectly bewildered.

"That's about the coolest piece of business," said Mr. Chillingworth, "that ever I heard of."

"Hang me," said the admiral, "if I sha'n't like the fellow at last. It is cool, and I like it because it is cool. Where's my hat? where's my stick!"

"What are you going to do?"

"Accept his invitation, to be sure, and breakfast with him; and, my learned friend, as he calls you, I hope you'll come likewise. I'll take the fellow at his word. By fair means, or by foul, I'll know what he wants here; and why he persecutes this family, for whom I have an attachment; and what hand he has in the disappearance of my nephew, Charles Holland; for, as sure as there's a Heaven above us, he's at the bottom of that affair. Where is this Walmesley Lodge?"

"Just in the neighbourhood; but--"

"Come on, then; come on."

"But, really, admiral, you don't mean to say you'll breakfast with--with--"

"A vampyre? Yes, I would, and will, and mean to do so. Here, Jack, you needn't go to Mr. Bannerworth's yet. Come, my learned friend, let's take Time by the forelock."

CHAPTER LX

THE INTERRUPTED BREAKFAST AT SIR FRANCIS VARNEY'S

Notwithstanding all Mr. Chillingworth could say to the contrary, the admiral really meant to breakfast with Sir Francis Varney.

The worthy doctor could not for some time believe but that the admiral must be joking, when he talked in such a strain; but he was very soon convinced to the contrary, by the latter actually walking out and once more asking him, Mr. Chillingworth, if he meant to go with him, or not.

This was conclusive, so the doctor said,--

"Well, admiral, this appears to me rather a mad sort of freak; but, as I have begun the adventure with you, I will conclude it with you."

"That's right," said the admiral; "I'm not deceived in you, doctor; so come along. Hang these vampyres, I don't know how to tackle them, myself. I think, after all, Sir Francis Varney is more in your line than line is in mine."

"How do you mean?"

"Why, couldn't you persuade him he's ill, and wants some physic? That would soon settle him, you know."

"Settle him!" said Mr. Chillingworth; "I beg to say that if I did give him any physic, the dose would be much to his advantage; but, however, my opinion is, that this invitation to breakfast is, after all, a mere piece of irony; and that, when we get to Walmesley Lodge, we shall not see anything of him; on the contrary, we shall probably find it's a hoax."

"I certainly shouldn't like that, but still it's worth the trying. The fellow has really behaved himself in such an extraordinary manner, that, if I can make terms with him I will; and there's one thing, you know, doctor, that I think we may say we have discovered."

"And what may that be? Is it, not to make too sure of a vampyre, even when you have him by the leg?"

"No, that ain't it, though that's a very good thing in its way: but it is just this, that Sir Francis Varney, whoever he is and whatever he is, is after Bannerworth Hall, and not the Bannerworth family. If you recollect, Mr. Chillingworth, in our conversation, I have always insisted upon that fact."

"You have; and it seems to me to be completely verified by the proceedings of the night. There, then, admiral, is the great mystery--what can he want at Bannerworth Hall that makes him take such a world of trouble, and run so many fearful risks in trying to get at it?"

"That is, indeed, the mystery; and if he really means this invitation to breakfast, I shall ask him plumply, and tell him, at the same time, that possibly his very best way to secure his object will be to be candid, vampyre as he is."

"But really, admiral, you do not still cling to that foolish superstition of believing that Sir Francis Varney is in reality a vampyre?"

"I don't know, and I can't say; if anybody was to give me a description of a strange sort of fish that I had never seen, I wouldn't take upon myself to say there wasn't such a thing; nor would you, doctor, if you had really seen the many odd ones that I have encountered at various times."

"Well, well, admiral, I'm certainly not belonging to that school of philosophy which declares the impossible to be what it don't understand; there may be vampyres, and there may be apparitions, for all I know to the contrary; I only doubt these things, because I think, if they were true, that, as a phenomena of nature, they would have been by this time established by repeated instances without the possibility of doubt or cavil."

"Well, there's something in that; but how far have we got to go now?"

"No further than to yon enclosure where you see those park-like looking gates, and that cedar-tree stretching its dark-green foliage so far into the road; that is Walmesley Lodge, whither you have been invited."

"And you, my learned friend, recollect that you were invited too; so that you are no intruder upon the hospitality of Varney the vampyre."

"I say, admiral," said Mr. Chillingworth, when they reached the gates, "you know it is not quite the thing to call a man a vampyre at his own breakfast-table, so just oblige me by promising not to make any such remark to Sir Francis."

"A likely thing!" said the admiral; "he knows I know what he is, and he knows I'm a plain man and a blunt speaker; however, I'll be civil to him, and more than that I can't promise. I must wring out of him, if I can, what has become of Charles Holland, and what the deuce he really wants himself."

"Well, well; come to no collision with him, while we're his guests."

"Not if I can help it."

The doctor rang at the gate bell of Walmesley Lodge, and was in a few moments answered by a woman, who demanded their business.

"Is Sir Francis Varney here?" said the doctor.

"Oh, ah! yes," she replied; "you see his house was burnt down, for something or other--I'm sure I don't know what--by some people--I'm sure I don't know who; so, as the lodge was to let, we have took him in till he can suit himself."

"Ah! that's it, is it?" said the admiral--"tell him that Admiral Bell and Dr. Chillingworth are here."

"Very well," said the woman; "you may walk in."

"Thank ye; you're vastly obliging, ma'am. Is there anything going on in the breakfast line?"

"Well, yes; I am getting him some breakfast, but he didn't say as he expected company."

The woman opened the garden gate, and they walked up a trimly laid out garden to the lodge, which was a cottage-like structure in external appearance, although within it boasted of all the comforts of a tolerably extensive house.

She left them in a small room, leading from the hall, and was absent about five minutes; then she returned, and, merely saying that Sir Francis Varney presented his compliments, and desired them to walk up stairs, she preceded them up a handsome flight which led to the first floor of the lodge.

Up to this moment, Mr. Chillingworth had expected some excuse, for, notwithstanding all he had heard and seen of Sir Francis Varney, he could not believe that any amount of impudence would suffice to enable him to receive people as his guests, with whom he must feel that he was at such positive war.

It was a singular circumstance; and, perhaps, the only thing that matched the cool impertinence of the invitation, was the acceptance of it under the circumstances by the admiral.

Sir Francis Varney might have intended it as a jest; but if he did so, in the first instance, it was evident he would not allow himself to be beaten with his own weapons.

The room into which they were shown was a longish narrow one; a very wide door gave them admission to it, at the end, nearest the staircase, and at its other extremity there was a similar door opening into some other apartments of the house.

Sir Francis Varney sat with his back towards this second door, and a table, with some chairs and other articles of furniture, were so arranged before him, that while they seemed but to be carelessly placed in the position they occupied, they really formed a pretty good barrier between him and his visitors.

The admiral, however, was too intent upon getting a sight of Varney, to notice any preparation of this sort, and he advanced quickly into the room.

And there, indeed, was the much dreaded, troublesome, persevering, and singular looking being who had caused such a world of annoyance to the family of the Bannerworths, as well as disturbing the peace of the whole district, which had the misfortune to have him as an inhabitant.

If anything, he looked thinner, taller, and paler than usual, and there seemed to be a slight nervousness of manner about him, as he slowly inclined his head towards the admiral, which was not quite intelligible.

"Well," said Admiral Bell, "you invited me to breakfast, and my learned friend; here we are."

"No two human beings," said Varney, "could be more welcome to my hospitality than yourself and Dr. Chillingworth. I pray you to be seated. What a pleasant thing it is, after the toils and struggles of this life, occasionally to sit down in the sweet companionship of such dear friends."

He made a hideous face as he spoke, and the admiral looked as if he were half inclined to quarrel at that early stage of the proceedings.

"Dear friends!" he said; "well, well--it's no use squabbling about a word or two; but I tell you what it is, Mr. Varney, or Sir Francis Varney, or whatever your d----d name is--"

"Hold, my dear sir," said Varney--"after breakfast, if you please--after breakfast."

He rang a hand-bell as he spoke, and the woman who had charge of the house brought in a tray tolerably covered with the materials for a substantial morning's meal. She placed it upon the table, and certainly the various articles that smoked upon it did great credit to her culinary powers.

"Deborah," said Sir Varney, in a mild sort of tone, "keep on continually bringing things to eat until this old brutal sea ruffian has satiated his disgusting appetite."

The admiral opened his eyes an enormous width, and, looking at Sir Francis Varney, he placed his two fists upon the table, and drew a long breath.

"Did you address those observations to me," he said, at length, "you blood-sucking vagabond?"

"Eh?" said Sir Francis Varney, looking over the admiral's head, as if he saw something interesting on the wall beyond.

"My dear admiral," said Mr. Chillingworth, "come away."

"I'll see you d----d first!" said the admiral. "Now, Mr. Vampyre, no shuffling; did you address those observations to me?"

"Deborah," said Sir Francis Varney, in silvery tones, "you can remove this tray and bring on the next."

"Not if I know it," said the admiral "I came to breakfast, and I'll have it; after breakfast I'll pull your nose--ay, if you were fifty vampyres, I'd do it."

"Dr. Chillingworth," said Varney, without paying the least attention to what the admiral said, "you don't eat, my dear sir; you must be fatigued with your night's exertions. A man of your age, you know, cannot be supposed to roll and tumble about like a fool in a pantomime with impunity. Only think what a calamity it would be if you were laid up. Your patients would all get well, you know."

"Sir Francis Varney," said Mr. Chillingworth, "we're your guests; we come here at your invitation to partake of a meal. You have wantonly attacked both of us. I need not say that by so doing you cast a far greater slur upon your own taste and judgment than you can upon us."

"Admirably spoken," said Sir Francis Varney, giving his hands a clap together that made the admiral jump again. "Now, old Bell, I'll fight you, if you think yourself aggrieved, while the doctor sees fair play."

"Old who?" shouted the admiral.

"Bell, Bell--is not your name Bell?--a family cognomen, I presume, on account of the infernal clack, clack, without any sense in it, that is the characteristic of your race."

"You'll fight me?" said the admiral, jumping up.

"Yes; if you challenge me."

"By Jove I do; of course"

"Then I accept it; and the challenged party, you know well, or ought to know, can make his own terms in the encounter."

"Make what terms you please; I care not what they are. Only say you will fight, and that's sufficient."

"It is well," said Sir Francis Varney, in a solemn tone.

"Nay, nay," interrupted Mr. Chillingworth; "this is boyish folly."

"Hold your row," said the admiral, "and let's hear what he's got to say."

"In this mansion," said Sir Francis Varney--"for a mansion it is, although under the unpretending name of a lodge--in this mansion there is a large apartment which was originally fitted up by a scientific proprietor of the place, for the purpose of microscopic and other experiments, which required a darkness total and complete, such a darkness as seems as if it could be felt--palpable, thick, and obscure as the darkness of the tomb, and I know what that is."

"The devil you do!" said this admiral "It's damp, too, ain't it?"

"The room?"

"No; the grave."

"Oh! uncommonly, after autumnal rains. But to resume--this room is large, lofty, and perfectly empty."

"Well?"

"I propose that we procure two scythes."

"Two what?"

"Scythes, with their long handles, and their convenient holding places."

"Well, I'll be hanged! What next do you propose?"

"You may be hanged. The next is, that with these scythes we be both of us placed in the darkened room, and the door closed, and doubly locked upon us for one hour, and that then and there we do our best each to cut the other in two. If you succeed in dismembering me, you will have won the day; but I hope, from my superior agility"--here Sir Francis jumped upon his chair, and sat upon the back of it--"to get the better of you. How do you like the plan I have proposed? Does it meet your wishes?"

"Curse your impudence!" said the admiral, placing his elbows upon the table and resting his chin in astonishment upon his two hands.

"Nay," interrupted Sir Francis, "you challenged me; and, besides, you'll have an equal chance, you know that. If you succeed in striking me first, down I go; whereas it I succeed in striking you first, down you go."

As he spoke, Sir Francis Varney stretched out his foot, and closed a small bracket which held out the flap of the table on which the admiral was leaning, and, accordingly, down the admiral went, tea-tray and all.

Mr. Chillingworth ran to help him up, and, when they both recovered their feet, they found they were alone.

CHAPTER LXI

THE MYSTERIOUS STRANGER.--THE PARTICULARS OF THE SUICIDE AT BANNERWORTH HALL

"Hilloa where the deuce is he?" said the admiral. "Was there ever such a confounded take-in?"

"Well, I really don't know," said Mr. Chillingworth; "but it seems to me that he must have gone out of that door that was behind him: I begin, do you know, admiral, to wish--"

"What?"

"That we had never come here at all; and I think the sooner we get out of it the better."

"Yes; but I am not going to be hoaxed and humbugged in this way. I will have satisfaction, but not with those confounded scythes and things he talks about in the dark room. Give me broad daylight and no favour; yardarm and yardarm; broadside and broadside; hand-grenades and marling-spikes."

"Well, but that's what he won't do. Now, admiral, listen to me."

"Well, go on; what next?"

"Come away at once."

"Oh, you said that before."

"Yes; but I'm going to say something else. Look round you. Don't you think this a large, scientific-looking room?"

"What of that?"

"Why, what if suppose it was to become as dark as the grave, and Varney was to enter with his scythe, that he talks of, and begin mowing about our legs."

"The devil! Come along!"

The door at which they entered was at this moment opened, and the old woman made her appearance.

"Please, sir," she said, "here's a Mr. Mortimer," in a loud voice. "Oh, Sir Francis ain't here! Where's he gone, gentlemen?"

"To the devil!" said the admiral. "Who may Mr. Mortimer be?"

There walked past the woman a stout, portly-looking man, well dressed, but with a very odd look upon his face, in consequence of an obliquity of vision, which prevented the possibility of knowing which way he was looking.

"I must see him," he said; "I must see him."

Mr. Chillingworth started back as if in amazement.

"Good God!" he cried, "you here!"

"Confusion!" said Mortimer; "are you Dr.---- Dr.----"

"The same. Hush! there is no occasion to betray--that is, to state my secret."

"And mine, too," said Chillingworth. "But what brings you here?"

"I cannot and dare not tell you. Farewell!"

He turned abruptly, and was leaving the room; but he ran against some one at the entrance, and in another moment Henry Bannerworth, heated and almost breathless by evident haste, made his appearance.

"Hilloa! bravo!" cried the admiral; "the more the merrier! Here's a combined squadron! Why, how came you here, Mr. Henry Bannerworth?"

"Bannerworth!" said Mortimer; "is that young man's name Bannerworth?"

"Yes," said Henry. "Do you know me, sir?"

"No, no; only I--I--must be off. Does anybody know anything of Sir Francis Varney?"

"We did know something of him," said the admiral, "a little while ago; but he's taken himself off. Don't you do so likewise. If you've got anything to say, stop and say it, like an Englishman."

"Stuff! stuff!" said Mortimer, impatiently. "What do you all want here?"

"Why, Sir Francis Varney," said Henry,--"and I care not if the whole world heard it--is the persecutor of my family."

"How? in what way?"

"He has the reputation of a vampyre; he has hunted me and mine from house and home."

"Indeed!"
"Yes," cried Dr. Chillingworth; "and, by some means or another, he seems determined to get possession of Bannerworth Hall."
"Well, gentlemen," said Mortimer, "I promise you that I will inquire into this. Mr. Chillingworth, I did not expect to meet you. Perhaps the least we say to each other is, after all, the better."
"Let me ask but one question," said Dr. Chillingworth, imploringly.
"Ask it."
"Did he live after--"
"Hush! he did."
"You always told me to the contrary."
"Yes; I had an object; the game is up. Farewell; and, gentlemen, as I am making my exit, let me do so with a sentiment:--Society at large is divided into two great classes."
"And what may they be?" said the admiral.
"Those who have been hanged, and those who have not. Adieu!"
He turned and left the room; and Mr. Chillingworth sunk into a chair, and said, in a low voice,--
"It's uncommonly true; and I've found out an acquaintance among the former."
"-D--n it! you seem all mad," said the admiral. "I can't make out what you are about. How came you here, Mr. Henry Bannerworth?"
"By mere accident I heard," said Henry, "that you were keeping watch and ward in the Hall. Admiral, it was cruel, and not well done of you, to attempt such an enterprise without acquainting me with it. Did you suppose for a moment that I, who had the greatest interest in this affair, would have shrunk from danger, if danger there be; or lacked perseverance, if that quality were necessary in carrying out any plan by which the safety and honour of my family might be preserved?"
"Nay, now, my young friend," said Mr. Chillingworth.
"Nay, sir; but I take it ill that I should have been kept out of this affair; and it should have been sedulously, as it were, kept a secret from me."
"Let him go on as he likes," said the admiral; "boys will be boys. After all, you know, doctor, it's my affair, and not yours. Let him say what he likes; where's the odds? It's of no consequence."
"I do not expect. Admiral Bell," said Henry, "that it is to you; but it is to me."
"Psha!"
"Respecting you, sir, as I do--"
"Gammon!"
"I must confess that I did expect--"
"What you didn't get; therefore, there's an end of that. Now, I tell you what, Henry, Sir Francis Varney is within this house; at least, I have reason to suppose so."
"Then," exclaimed Henry, impetuously, "I will wring from him answers to various questions which concern my peace and happiness."
"Please, gentlemen," said the woman Deborah, making her appearance, "Sir Francis Varney has gone out, and he says I'm to show you all the door, as soon as it is convenient for you all to walk out of it."
"I feel convinced," said Mr. Chillingworth, "that it will be a useless search now to attempt to find Sir Francis Varney here. Let me beg of you all to come away; and believe me that I do not speak lightly, or with a view to get you from here, when I say, that after I have heard something from you, Henry, which I shall ask you to relate to me, painful though it may be, I shall be able to suggest some explanation of many things which appear at present obscure, and to put you in a course of freeing you from the difficulties which surround you, which, Heaven knows, I little expected I should have it in my power to propose to any of you."
"I will follow your advice, Mr. Chillingworth," said Henry; "for I have always found that it has been dictated by good feeling as well as correct judgment. Admiral Bell, you will oblige me much by coming away with me now and at once."
"Well," remarked the admiral, "if the doctor has really something to say, it alters the appearance of things, and, of course, I have no objection."
Upon this, the whole three of them immediately left the place, and it was evident that Mr. Chillingworth had something of an uncomfortable character upon his mind. He was unusually silent and reserved, and, when he did speak, he seemed rather inclined to turn the conversation upon indifferent topics, than to add anything more to what he had said upon the deeply interesting one which held so foremost a place in all their minds.
"How is Flora, now," he asked of Henry, "since her removal?"
"Anxious still," said Henry; "but, I think, better."
"That is well. I perceive that, naturally, we are all three walking towards Bannerworth Hall,

and, perhaps, it is as well that on that spot I should ask of you, Henry, to indulge me with a confidence such as, under ordinary circumstances, I should not at all feel myself justified in requiring of you."

"To what does it relate?" said Henry. "You may be assured, Mr. Chillingworth, that I am not likely to refuse my confidence to you, whom I have so much reason to respect as an attached friend of myself and my family."

"You will not object, likewise, I hope," added Mr. Chillingworth, "to extend that confidence to Admiral Bell; for, as you well know, a truer and more warm-hearted man than he does not exist."

"What do you expect for that, doctor?" said the admiral.

"There is nothing," said Henry, "that I could relate at all, that I should shrink from relating to Admiral Bell."

"Well, my boy," said the admiral, "and all I can reply to that is, you are quite right; for there can be nothing that you need shrink from telling me, so far as regards the fact of trusting me with it goes."

"I am assured of that."

"A British officer, once pledging his word, prefers death to breaking it. Whatever you wish kept secret in the communication you make to me, say so, and it will never pass my lips."

"Why, sir, the fact is," said Henry, "that what I am about to relate to you consists not so much of secrets as of matters which would be painful to my feelings to talk of more than may be absolutely required."

"I understand you."

"Let me, for a moment," said Mr Chillingworth, "put myself right. I do not suspect, Mr. Henry Bannerworth, that you fancy I ask you to make a recital of circumstances which must be painful to you from any idle motive. But let me declare that I have now a stronger impulse, which induces me to wish to hear from your own lips those matters which popular rumour may have greatly exaggerated or vitiated."

"It is scarcely possible," remarked Henry, sadly, "that popular rumour should exaggerate the facts."

"Indeed!"

"No. They are, unhappily, of themselves, in their bare truthfulness, so full of all that can be grievous to those who are in any way connected with them, that there needs no exaggeration to invest them with more terror, or with more of that sadness which must ever belong to a recollection of them in my mind."

In suchlike discourse as this, the time was passed, until Henry Bannerworth and his friends once more reached the Hall, from which he, with his family, had so recently removed, in consequence of the fearful persecution to which they had been subjected.

They passed again into the garden which they all knew so well, and then Henry paused and looked around him with a deep sigh.

In answer to an inquiring glance from Mr. Chillingworth, he said,--

"Is it not strange, now, that I should have only been away from here a space of time which may be counted by hours, and yet all seems changed. I could almost fancy that years had elapsed since I had looked at it."

"Oh," remarked the doctor, "time is always by the imagination measured by the number of events which are crowded into a given space of it, and not by its actual duration. Come into the house; there you will find all just as you left it, Henry, and you can tell us your story at leisure."

"The air," said Henry, "about here is fresh and pleasant. Let us sit down in the summer-house yonder, and there I will tell you all. It has a local interest, too, connected with the tale."

This was agreed to, and, in a few moments, the admiral, Mr. Chillingworth, and Henry were seated in the same summer-house which had witnessed the strange interview between Sir Francis Varney and Flora Bannerworth, in which he had induced her to believe that he felt for the distress he had occasioned her, and was strongly impressed with the injustice of her sufferings.

Henry was silent for some few moments, and then he said, with a deep sigh, as he looked mournfully around him,--

"It was on this spot that my father breathed his last, and hence have I said that it has a local interest in the tale I have to tell, which makes it the most fitting place in which to tell it."

"Oh," said the admiral, "he died here, did he?"

"Yes, where you are now sitting."

"Very good, I have seen many a brave man die in my time, and I hope to see a few more, although, I grant you, the death in the heat of conflict, and fighting for our country, is a vastly different thing to some shore-going mode of leaving the world."

"Yes," said Henry, as if pursuing his own meditations, rather than listening to the admiral. "Yes, it was from this precise spot that my father took his last look at the ancient house of his race.

What we can now see of it, he saw of it with his dying eyes and many a time I have sat here and fancied the world of terrible thoughts that must at such a moment have come across his brain."

"You might well do so," said the doctor.

"You see," added Henry, "that from here the fullest view you have of any of the windows of the house is of that of Flora's room, as we have always called it, because for years she had had it as her chamber; and, when all the vegetation of summer is in its prime, and the vine which you perceive crawls over this summer-house is full of leaf and fruit, the view is so much hindered that it is difficult, without making an artificial gap in the clustering foliage, to see anything but the window."

"So I should imagine," replied Mr. Chillingworth.

"You, doctor," added Henry, "who know much of my family, need not be told what sort of man my father was."

"No, indeed."

"But you, Admiral Bell, who do not know, must be told, and, however grievous it may be to me to have to say so, I must inform you that he was not a man who would have merited your esteem."

"Well," said the admiral, "you know, my boy, that can make no difference as regards you in anybody's mind, who has got the brains of an owl. Every man's credit, character, and honour, to my thinking, is in his own most special keeping, and let your father be what he might, or who he might, I do not see that any conduct of his ought to raise upon your cheek the flush of shame, or cost you more uneasiness than ordinary good feeling dictates to the errors and feelings of a fellow creature."

"If all the world," said Henry, "would take such liberal and comprehensive views as you do, admiral, it would be much happier than it is; but such is not the case, and people are but too apt to blame one person for the evil that another has done."

"Ah, but," said Mr. Chillingworth, "it so happens that those are the people whose opinions are of the very least consequence."

"There is some truth in that," said Henry, sadly; "but, however, let me proceed; since I have to tell the tale, I could wish it over. My father, then, Admiral Bell, although a man not tainted in early life with vices, became, by the force of bad associates, and a sort of want of congeniality and sentiment that sprang up between him and my mother, plunged into all the excesses of his age."

"These excesses were all of that character which the most readily lay hold strongly of an unreflecting mind, because they all presented themselves in the garb of sociality.

"The wine cup is drained in the name of good fellowship; money which is wanted for legitimate purposes is squandered under the mask of a noble and free generosity, and all that the small imaginations of a number of persons of perverted intellects could enable them to do, has been done from time to time, to impart a kind of lustre to intemperance and all its dreadful and criminal consequences.

"My father, having once got into the company of what he considered wits and men of spirit, soon became thoroughly vitiated. He was almost the only one of the set among whom he passed what he considered his highly convivial existence, who was really worth anything, pecuniarily speaking. There were some among them who might have been respectable men, and perchance carved their way to fortune, as well as some others who had started in life with good patrimonies; but he, my father, at the time he became associated with them, was the only one, as I say, who, to use a phrase I have heard myself from his lips concerning them, had got a feather to fly with.

"The consequence of this was, that his society, merely for the sake of the animal gratification of drinking at his expense was courted, and he was much flattered, all of which he laid to the score of his own merits, which had been found out, and duly appreciated by these bon vivants, while he considered that the grave admonitions of his real friends proceeded from nothing in the world but downright envy and malice.

"Such a state of things as this could not last very long. The associates of my father wanted money as well as wine, so they introduced him to the gaming-table, and he became fascinated with the fearful vice to an extent which predicted his own destruction and the ruin of every one who was in any way dependent upon him.

"He could not absolutely sell Bannerworth Hall, unless I had given my consent, which I refused; but he accumulated debt upon debt, and from time to time stripped the mansion of all its most costly contents.

"With various mutations of fortune, he continued this horrible and baneful career for a long time, until, at last, he found himself utterly and irretrievably ruined, and he came home in an agony of despair, being so weak, and utterly ruined in constitution, that he kept his bed for many days.

"It appeared, however, that something occurred at this juncture which gave him actually, or all events awakened a hope that he should possess some money, and be again in a position to try his fortune at the gaming-table.

"He rose, and, fortifying himself once more with the strong stimulant of wine and spirits, he left his home, and was absent for about two months.

"What occurred to him during that time we none of us ever knew, but late one night he came home, apparently much flurried in manner, and seeming as if something had happened to drive him half mad.

"He would not speak to any one, but he shut himself up the whole of the night in the chamber where hangs the portrait that bears so strong a resemblance to Sir Francis Varney, and there he remained till the morning, when he emerged, and said briefly that he intended to leave the country.

"He was in a most fearful state of nervousness, and my mother tells me that he shook like one in an ague, and started at every little sound that occurred in the house, and glared about him so wildly that it was horrible to see him, or to sit in the same apartment with him.

"She says that the whole morning passed on in this way till a letter came to him, the contents of which appeared to throw him into a perfect convulsion of terror, and he retired again to the room with the portrait, where he remained some hours, and then he emerged, looking like a ghost, so dreadfully pale and haggard was he.

"He walked into the garden here, and was seen to sit down in this summer-house, and fix his eyes upon the window of that apartment."

Henry paused for a few moments, and then he added,--

"You will excuse me from entering upon any details of what next ensued in the melancholy history. My father here committed suicide. He was found dying, and all I he words he spoke were, 'The money is hidden!' Death claimed his victim, and, with a convulsive spasm, he resigned his spirit, leaving what he had intended to say hidden in the oblivion of the grave."

"That was an odd affair," said the admiral.

"It was, indeed. We have all pondered deeply, and the result was, that, upon the whole, we were inclined to come to an opinion that the words he so uttered were but the result of the mental disturbance that at such a moment might well be supposed to be ensuing in the mind, and that they related really to no foregone fact any more than some incoherent words uttered by a man in a dream might be supposed to do."

"It may be so."

"I do not mean," remarked Mr. Chillingworth, "for one moment to attempt to dispute, Henry, the rationality of such an opinion as you have just given utterance to; but you forget that another circumstance occurred, which gave a colour to the words used by your father."

"Yes; I know to what you allude."

"Be so good as to state it to the admiral."

"I will. On the evening of that same day there came a man here, who, in seeming ignorance of what had occurred, although by that time it was well known to all the neighbourhood, asked to see my father.

"Upon being told that he was dead, he started back, either with well acted or with real surprise, and seemed to be immensely chagrined. He then demanded to know if he had left any disposition of his property; but he got no information, and departed muttering the most diabolical oaths and curses that can be imagined. He mounted his horse, for he had ridden to the Hall and his last words were, as I am told--

"'Where, in the name of all that's damnable, can he have put the money!'"

"And did you never find out who this man was?" asked the admiral.

"Never."

"It is an odd affair."

"It is," said Mr. Chillingworth, "and full of mystery. The public mind was much taken up at the time with some other matters, or it would have made the death of Mr. Bannerworth the subject of more prolific comment than it did. As it was, however, a great deal was said upon the subject, and the whole comity was in a state of commotion for weeks afterwards."

"Yes," said Henry; "it so happened that about that very time a murder was committed in the neighbourhood of London, which baffled all the exertions of the authorities to discover the perpetrators of. It was the murder of Lord Lorne."

"Oh! I remember," said the admiral; "the newspapers were full of it for a long time."

"They were; and so, as Mr. Chillingworth says, the more exciting interest which that affair created drew off public attention, in a great measure, from my father's suicide, and we did not suffer so much from public remark and from impertinent curiosity as might have been expected."

"And, in addition," said Mr. Chillingworth, and he changed colour a little as he spoke, "there was an execution shortly afterwards."

"Yes," said Henry, "there was."

"The execution of a man named Angerstein," added Mr. Chillingworth, "for a highway robbery, attended with the most brutal violence."

"True; all the affairs of that period of time are strongly impressed upon my mind," said Henry; "but you do not seem well, Mr. Chillingworth."

"Oh, yes; I am quite well--you are mistaken."

Both the admiral and Henry looked scrutinizingly at the doctor, who certainly appeared to them to be labouring under some great mental excitement, which he found it almost beyond his power to repress.

"I tell you what it is, doctor," said the admiral; "I don't pretend, and never did, to see further through a tar-barrel than my neighbours; but I can see far enough to feel convinced that you have got something on your mind, and that it somehow concerns this affair."

"Is it so?" said Henry.

"I cannot if I would," said Mr. Chillingworth; "and I may with truth add, that I would not, if I could, hide from you that I have something on my mind connected with this affair; but let me assure you it would be premature of me to tell you of it."

"Premature be d----d!" said the admiral; "out with it."

"Nay, nay, dear sir; I am not now in a position to say what is passing through my mind."

"Alter your position, then, and be blowed!" cried Jack Pringle, suddenly stepping forward, and giving the doctor such a push, that he nearly went through one of the sides of the summer-house.

"Why, you scoundrel!" cried the admiral, "how came you here?"

"On my legs," said Jack. "Do you think nobody wants to know nothing but yourself? I'm as fond of a yarn as anybody."

"But if you are," said Mr. Chillingworth, "you had no occasion to come against me as if you wanted to move a house."

"You said as you wasn't in a position to say something as I wanted to hear, so I thought I'd alter it for you."

"Is this fellow," said the doctor, shaking his head, as he accosted the admiral, "the most artful or stupid?"

"A little of both," said Admiral Bell--"a little of both, doctor. He's a great fool and a great scamp."

"The same to you," said Jack; "you're another. I shall hate you presently, if you go on making yourself so ridiculous. Now, mind, I'll only give you a trial of another week or so, and if you don't be more purlite in your d--n language, I'll leave you."

Away strolled Jack, with his hands in his pockets, towards the house, while the admiral was half choked with rage, and could only glare after him, without the ability to say a word.

Under any other circumstances than the present one of trouble, and difficulty; and deep anxiety, Henry Bannerworth must have laughed at these singular little episodes between Jack and the admiral; but his mind was now by far too much harassed to permit him to do so.

"Let him go, let him go, my dear sir," said Mr. Chillingworth to the admiral, who showed some signs of an intention to pursue Jack; "he no doubt has been drinking again."

"I'll turn him off the first moment I catch him sober enough to understand me," said the admiral.

"Well, well; do as you please; but now let me ask a favour of both of you."

"What is it?"

"That you will leave Bannerworth Hall to me for a week."

"What for?"

"I hope to make some discoveries connected with it which shall well reward you for the trouble."

"It's no trouble," said Henry; "and for myself, I have amply sufficient faith, both in your judgment and in your friendship, doctor, to accede to any request which you may make to me."

"And I," said the admiral. "Be it so--be it so. For one week, you say?"

"Yes--for one week. I hope, by the end of that time, to have achieved something worth the telling you of; and I promise you that, if I am at all disappointed in my expectation, that I will frankly and freely communicate to you all I know and all I suspect."

"Then that's a bargain."

"It is."

"And what's to be done at once?"

"Why, nothing, but to take the greatest possible care that Bannerworth Hall is not left another hour without some one in it; and in order that such should be the case, I have to request that you two will remain here until I go to the town, and make preparations for taking quiet possession of it myself, which I will do in the course of two hours, at most."

"Don't be longer," said the admiral, "for I am so desperately hungry, that I shall certainly begin to eat somebody, if you are."

"Depend upon me."

"Very well," said Henry; "you may depend we will wait here until you come back."

The doctor at once hurried from the garden, leaving Henry and the admiral to amuse themselves as best they might, with conjectures as to what he was really about, until his return.

CHAPTER LXII

THE MYSTERIOUS MEETING IN THE RUIN AGAIN.--THE VAMPYRE'S ATTACK UPON THE CONSTABLE

It is now necessary that we return once more to that mysterious ruin, in the intricacies of which Varney, when pursued by the mob, had succeeded in finding a refuge which defied all the exertions which were made for his discovery. Our readers must be well aware, that, connected with that ruin, are some secrets of great importance to our story; and we will now, at the solemn hour of midnight, take another glance at what is doing within its recesses.

At that solemn hour it is not probable that any one would seek that gloomy place from choice. Some lover of the picturesque certainly might visit it; but such was not the inciting cause of the pilgrimage with those who were soon to stand within its gloomy precincts.

Other motives dictated their presence in that spot--motives of rapine; peradventure of murder itself.

As the neighbouring clocks sounded the hour of twelve, and the faint strokes were borne gently on the wind to that isolated ruin, there might have been seen a tall man standing by the porch of what had once been a large doorway to some portion of the ruin.

His form was enveloped in a large cloak, which was of such ample material that he seemed well able to wrap it several times around him, and then leave a considerable portion of it floating idly in the gentle wind.

He stood as still, as calm, and as motionless as a statue, for a considerable time, before any degree of impatience began to show itself.

Then he took from his pocket a large antique watch, the white face of which just enabled him to see what the time was, and, in a voice which had in it some amount of petulance and anger, he said,--

"Not come yet, and nearly half an hour beyond the time! What can have detained him? This is, indeed, trifling with the most important moments of a man's existence."

Even as he spoke, he heard, from some distance off, the sound of a short, quick footstep. He bent forwards to listen, and then, in a tone of satisfaction, he said,--

"He comes--he comes!"

But he who thus waited for some confederate among these dim and old grey ruins, advanced not a step to meet him. On the contrary, such seemed the amount of cold-blooded caution which he possessed, that the nearer the man--who was evidently advancing--got to the place, the further back did he who had preceded him shrink into the shadow of the dim and crumbling walls, which had, for some years now past, seemed to bend to the passing blast, and to be on the point of yielding to the destroying hand of time.

And yet, surely he needed not have been so cautious. Who was likely, at such an hour as that, to come to the ruins, but one who sought it by appointment?

And, moreover, the manner of the advancing man should have been quite sufficient to convince him who waited, that so much caution was unnecessary; but it was a part and parcel of his nature.

About three minutes more sufficed to bring the second man to the ruin, and he, at once, and fearlessly, plunged into its recesses.

"Who comes?" said the first man, in a deep, hollow voice.

"He whom you expect," was the reply.

"Good," he said, and at once he now emerged from his hiding-place, and they stood together in the nearly total darkness with which the place was enshrouded; for the night was a cloudy one, and there appeared not a star in the heavens, to shed its faint light upon the scene below.

For a few moments they were both silent, for he who had last arrived had evidently made great exertions to reach the spot, and was breathing laboriously, while he who was there first appeared, from some natural taciturnity of character, to decline opening the conversation.

At length the second comer spoke, saying,--

"I have made some exertion to get here to my time, and yet I am beyond it, as you are no doubt aware."

"Yes, yes."

"Well, such would not have been the case; but yet, I stayed to bring you some news of importance."

"Indeed!"

"It is so. This place, which we have, now for some time had as a quiet and perfectly eligible one of meeting, is about to be invaded by one of those restless, troublesome spirits, who are never happy but when they are contriving something to the annoyance of others who do not interfere with them."

"Explain yourself more fully."

"I will. At a tavern in the town, there has happened some strange scenes of violence, in consequence of the general excitement into which the common people have been thrown upon the dreadful subject of vampyres."

"Well."

"The consequence is, that numerous arrests have taken place, and the places of confinement for offenders against the laws are now full of those whose heated and angry imaginations have induced them to take violent steps to discover the reality or the falsehood of rumours which so much affected them, their wives, and their families, that they feared to lie down to their night's repose."

The other laughed a short, hollow, restless sort of laugh, which had not one particle of real mirth in it.

"Go on--go on," he said. "What did they do?"

"Immense excesses have been committed; but what made me, first of all, stay beyond my time, was that I overheard a man declare his intentions this night, from twelve till the morning, and for some nights to come, to hold watch and ward for the vampyre."

"Indeed!"

"Yes. He did but stay, at the earnest solicitation of his comrades, to take yet another glass, ere he came upon his expedition."

"He must be met. The idiot! what business is it of his?"

"There are always people who will make everything their business, whether it be so or not."

"There are. Let us retire further into the recesses of the ruin, and there consider as well what is to be done regarding more important affairs, as with this rash intruder here."

They both walked for some twenty paces, or so, right into the ruin, and then he who had been there first, said, suddenly, to his companion,--

"I am annoyed, although the feeling reaches no further than annoyance, for I have a natural love of mischief, to think that my reputation has spread so widely, and made so much noise."

"Your reputation as a vampyre, Sir Francis Varney, you mean?"

"Yes; but there is no occasion for you to utter my name aloud, even here where we are alone together."

"It came out unawares."

"Unawares! Can it be possible that you have so little command over yourself as to allow a name to come from your lips unawares?"

"Sometimes."

"I am surprised."

"Well, it cannot be helped. What do you now propose to do?"

"Nay, you are my privy councillor. Have you no deep-laid, artful project in hand? Can you not plan and arrange something which may yet have the effect of accomplishing what at first seemed so very simple, but which has, from one unfortunate circumstance and another, become full of difficulty and pregnant with all sorts of dangers?"

"I must confess I have no plan."

"I listen with astonishment."

"Nay, now, you are jesting."

"When did you ever hear of me jesting?"

"Not often, I admit. But you have a fertile genius, and I have always, myself, found it easier to be the executive than to plan an elaborate course of action for others."

"Then you throw it all on me?"

"I throw a weight, naturally enough, upon the shoulders which I think the best adapted to sustain it."

"Be it so, then--be it so."

"You are, I presume, from what you say, provided with a scheme of action which shall present better hopes of success, at less risk, I hope. Look what great danger we have already passed through."

"Yes, we have."

"I pray you avoid that in the next campaign."

"It is not the danger that annoys and troubles me, but it is that, notwithstanding it, the object is as far off as ever from being attained."

"And not only so, but, as is invariably the case under such circumstances, we have made it more difficult of execution because we have put those upon their guard thoroughly who are the most likely to oppose us."

"We have--we have."

"And placed the probability of success afar off indeed."

"And yet I have set my life upon the cast, and I will stand the hazard. I tell you I will accomplish this object, or I will perish in the attempt."

"You are too enthusiastic."

"Not at all. Nothing has been ever done, the execution of which was difficult, without enthusiasm. I will do what I intend, or Bannerworth Hall shall become a heap of ruins, where fire shall do its worst work of devastation, and I will myself find a grave in the midst."

"Well, I quarrel with no man for chalking out the course he intends to pursue; but what do you mean to do with the prisoner below here?"

"Kill him."

"What?"

"I say kill him. Do you not understand me?"

"I do, indeed."

"When everything else is secured, and when the whole of that which I so much court, and which I will have, is in my possession, I will take his life, or you shall. Ay, you are just the man for such a deed. A smooth-faced, specious sort of roan are you, and you like not danger. There will be none in taking the life of a man who is chained to the floor of a dungeon."

"I know not why," said the other, "you take a pleasure on this particular night, of all others, in saying all you can which you think will be offensive to me."

"Now, how you wrong me. This is the reward of confidence."

"I don't want such confidence."

"Why, you surely don't want me to flatter you."

"No; but--"

"Psha! Hark you. That admiral is the great stumbling-block in my way. I should ere this have had undisturbed possession of Bannerworth Hall but for him. He must be got out of the way somehow."

"A short time will tire him out of watching. He is one of those men of impulse who soon become wearied of inaction."

"Ay, and then the Bannerworths return to the Hall."

"It may be so."

"I am certain of it. We have been out-generalled in this matter, although I grant we did all that men could do to give us success."

"In what way would you get rid of this troublesome admiral?"

"I scarcely know. A letter from his nephew might, if well put together, get him to London."

"I doubt it. I hate him mortally. He has offended me more than once most grievously."

"I know it. He saw through you."

"I do not give him so much credit. He is a suspicious man, and a vain and a jealous one."

"And yet he saw through you. Now, listen to me. You are completely at fault, and have no plan of operations whatever in your mind. What I want you to do is, to disappear from the neighbourhood for a time, and so will I. As for our prisoner here below, I cannot see what else can be done with him than--than--"

"Than what? Do you hesitate?"

"I do."

"Then what is it you were about to say?"

"I cannot but feel that all we have done hitherto, as regards this young prisoner of ours, has failed. He has, with a determined obstinacy, set at naught, as well you know, all threats."

"He has."

"He has refused to do one act which could in any way aid me in my objects. In fact, from the first to the last, he has been nothing but an expense and an encumbrance to us both."

"All that is strictly true."

"And yet, although you, as well as I, know of a marvellously ready way of getting rid of such encumbrances, I must own, that I shrink with more than a feeling of reluctance from the murder of the youth."

"You contemplated it then?" asked the other.

"No; I cannot be said to have contemplated it. That is not the proper sort of expression to use."

"What is then?"

"To contemplate a deed seems to me to have some close connexion to the wish to do it."

"And you have no such wish?"

"I have no such wish, and what is more I will not do it."

"Then that is sufficient; and the only question that remains for you to confide, is, what you will do. It is far easier in all enterprises to decide upon what we will not do, than upon what we will. For my own part I must say that I can perceive no mode of extricating ourselves from this involvement with anything like safety."

"Then it must be done with something like danger."

"As you please."

"You say so, and your words bear a clear enough signification; but from your tone I can guess how much you are dissatisfied with the aspect of affairs."

"Dissatisfied!"

"Yes; I say, dissatisfied. Be frank, and own that which it is in vain to conceal from me. I know you too well; arch hypocrite as you are, and fully capable of easily deceiving many, you cannot deceive me."

"I really cannot understand you."

"Then I will take care that you shall."

"How?"

"Listen. I will not have the life of Charles Holland taken."

"Who wishes to take it?"

"You."

"There, indeed, you wrong me. Unless you yourself thought that such an act was imperatively called for by the state of affairs, do you think that I would needlessly bring down upon my head the odium as well as the danger of such a deed? No, no. Let him live, if you are willing; he may live a thousand years for all I care."

"'Tis well. I am, mark me, not only willing, but I am determined that he shall live so far as we are concerned. I can respect the courage that, even when he considered that his life was at stake, enabled him to say no to a proposal which was cowardly and dishonourable, although it went far to the defeat of my own plans and has involved me in much trouble."

"Hush! hush!"

"What is it?"

"I fancy I hear a footstep."

"Indeed; that were a novelty in such a place as this."

"And yet not more than I expected. Have you forgotten what I told you when I reached here to-night after the appointed hour?"

"Truly; I had for the moment. Do you think then that the footstep which now meets our ears, is that of the adventurer who boasted that he could keep watch for the vampyre?"

"In faith do I. What is to be done with such a meddling fool?"

"He ought certainly to be taught not to be so fond of interfering with other people's affairs."

"Certainly."

"Perchance the lesson will not be wholly thrown away upon others. It may be worth while to take some trouble with this poor valiant fellow, and let him spread his news so as to stop any one else from being equally venturous and troublesome."

"A good thought."

"Shall it be done?"

"Yes; if you will arrange that which shall accomplish such a result."

"Be it so. The moon rises soon."

"It does."

"Ah, already I fancy I see a brightening of the air as if the mellow radiance of the queen of night were already quietly diffusing itself throughout the realms of space. Come further within the ruins."

They both walked further among the crumbling walls and fragments of columns with which the place abounded. As they did so they paused now and then to listen, and more than once they both heard plainly the sound of certain footsteps immediately outside the once handsome and spacious building.

Varney, the vampyre, who had been holding this conversation with no other than Marchdale, smiled as he, in a whispered voice, told the latter what to do in order to frighten away from the place the foolhardy man who thought that, by himself, he should be able to accomplish anything against the vampyre.

It was, indeed, a hair-brained expedition, for whether Sir Francis Varney was really so awful and preternatural a being as so many concurrent circumstances would seem to proclaim, or not, he was not a likely being to allow himself to be conquered by anyone individual, let his powers or his courage be what they might.

What induced this man to become so ventursome we shall now proceed to relate, as well as what kind of reception he got in the old ruins, which, since the mysterious disappearance of Sir Francis Varney within their recesses, had possessed so increased a share of interest and attracted so much popular attention and speculation.

CHAPTER LXIII

THE GUESTS AT THE INN, AND THE STORY OF THE DEAD UNCLE

As had been truly stated by Mr. Marchdale, who now stands out in his true colours to the reader as the confidant and abettor of Sir Francis Varney, there had assembled on that evening a curious and a gossipping party at the inn where such dreadful and such riotous proceedings had taken place, which, in their proper place, we have already duly and at length recorded.

It was not very likely that, on that evening, or for many and many an evening to come, the conversation in the parlour of the inn would be upon any other subject than that of the vampyre.

Indeed, the strange, mysterious, and horrible circumstances which had occurred, bade fair to be gossipping stock in trade for many a year.

Never before had a subject presenting so many curious features arisen. Never, within the memory of that personage who is supposed to know everything, had there occurred any circumstance in the county, or set of circumstances, which afforded such abundant scope for conjecture and speculation.

Everybody might have his individual opinion, and be just as likely to be right as his neighbours; and the beauty of the affair was, that such was the interest of the subject itself, that there was sure to be a kind of reflected interest with every surmise that at all bore upon it.

On this particular night, when Marchdale was prowling about, gathering what news he could, in order that he might carry it to the vampyre, a more than usually strong muster of the gossips of the town took place.

Indeed, all of any note in the talking way were there, with the exception of one, and he was in the county gaol, being one of the prisoners apprehended by the military when they made the successful attack upon the lumber-room of the inn, after the dreadful desecration of the dead which had taken place.

The landlord of the inn was likely to make a good thing of it, for talking makes people thirsty; and he began to consider that a vampyre about once a-year would be no bad thing for the Blue Lion.

"It's shocking," said one of the guests; "it's shocking to think of. Only last night, I am quite sure I had such a fright that it added at least ten years to my age."

"A fright!" said several.

"I believe I speak English--I said a fright."

"Well, but had it anything to do with the vampyre?"

"Everything."

"Oh! do tell us; do tell us all about it. How was it? Did he come to you? Go on. Well, well."

The first speaker became immediately a very important personage in the room; and, when he saw that, he became at once a very important personage in his own eyes likewise; and, before he would speak another word, he filled a fresh pipe, and ordered another mug of ale.

"It's no use trying to hurry him," said one.

"No," he said, "it isn't. I'll tell you in good time what a dreadful circumstance has made me sixty-three to-day, when I was only fifty-three yesterday."

"Was it very dreadful?"

"Rather. You wouldn't have survived it at all."

"Indeed!"

"No. Now listen. I went to bed at a quarter after eleven, as usual. I didn't notice anything particular in the room."

"Did you peep under the bed?"

"No, I didn't. Well, as I was a-saying, to bed I went, and I didn't fasten the door; because, being a very sound sleeper, in case there was a fire, I shouldn't hear a word of it if I did."

"No," said another. "I recollect once--"

"Be so good as allow me to finish what I know, before you begin to recollect anything, if you please. As I was saying, I didn't lock the door, but I went to bed. Somehow or another, I did not feel at all comfortable, and I tossed about, first on one side, and then on the other; but it was all in vain; I only got, every moment, more and more fidgetty."

"And did you think of the vampyre?" said one of the listeners.

"I thought of nothing else till I heard my clock, which is on the landing of the stairs above my bed-room, begin to strike twelve."

"Ah! I like to hear a clock sound in the night," said one; "it puts one in mind of the rest of the world, and lets one know one isn't all alone."

"Very good. The striking of the clock I should not at all have objected to; but it was what followed that did the business."

"What, what?"

"Fair and softly; fair and softly. Just hand me a light, Mr. Sprigs, if you please. I'll tell you all, gentlemen, in a moment or two."

With the most provoking deliberation, the speaker re-lit his pipe, which had gone out while he was talking, and then, after a few whiffs, to assure himself that its contents had thoroughly ignited, he resumed,--

"No sooner had the last sound of it died away, than I heard something on the stairs."

"Yes, yes."

"It was as if some man had given his foot a hard blow against one of the stairs; and he would have needed to have had a heavy boot on to do it. I started up in bed and listened, as you may well suppose, not in the most tranquil state of mind, and then I heard an odd, gnawing sort of noise, and then another dab upon one of the stairs."

"How dreadful!"

"It was. What to do I knew not, or what to think, except that the vampyre had, by some means, got in at the attic window, and was coming down stairs to my room. That seemed the most likely. Then there was another groan, and then another heavy step; and, as they were evidently coming towards my door, I felt accordingly, and got out of bed, not knowing hardly whether I was on my head or my heels, to try and lock my door."

"Ah, to be sure."

"Yes; that was all very well, if I could have done it; but a man in such a state of mind as I was in is not a very sharp hand at doing anything. I shook from head to foot. The room was very dark, and I couldn't, for a moment or two, collect my senses sufficient really to know which way the door lay."

"What a situation!"

"It was. Dab, dab, dab, came these horrid footsteps, and there was I groping about the room in an agony. I heard them coming nearer and nearer to my door. Another moment, and they must have reached it, when my hand struck against the lock."

"What an escape!"

"No, it was not."

"No?"

"No, indeed. The key was on the outside, and you may well guess I was not over and above disposed to open the door to get at it."

"No, no."

"I felt regularly bewildered, I can tell you; it seemed to me as if the very devil himself was coming down stairs hopping all the way upon one leg."

"How terrific!"

"I felt my senses almost leaving me; but I did what I could to hold the door shut just as I heard the strange step come from the last stair on to the landing. Then there was a horrid sound, and some one began trying the lock of my door."

"What a moment!"

"Yes, I can tell you it was a moment. Such a moment as I don't wish to go through again. I held the door as close as I could, and did not speak. I tried to cry out help and murder, but I could not; my tongue stuck to the roof of my mouth, and my strength was fast failing me."

"Horrid, horrid!"

"Take a drop of ale."

"Thank you. Well, I don't think this went on above two or three minutes, and all the while some one tried might and main to push open the door. My strength left me all at once; I had only time to stagger back a step or two, and then, as the door opened, I fainted away."

"Well, well!"

"Ah, you wouldn't have said well, if you had been there, I can tell you."

"No; but what become of you. What happened next? How did it end? What was it?"

"Why, what exactly happened next after I fainted I cannot tell you; but the first thing I saw when I recovered was a candle."

"Yes, yes."

"And then a crowd of people."

"Ah, ah!"

"And then Dr. Web."

"Gracious!"

"And. Mrs. Bulk, my housekeeper. I was in my own bed, and when I opened my eyes I heard Dr. Webb say,--

"'He will be better soon. Can no one form any idea of what it is all about. Some sudden fright surely could alone have produced such an effect.'"

"'The Lord have mercy upon me!' said I.

"Upon this everybody who had been called in got round the bed, and wanted to know what had happened; but I said not a word of it; but turning to Mrs. Bulk, I asked her how it was she found out I had fainted.

"'Why, sir,' says she, 'I was coming up to bed as softly as I could, because I knew you had gone to rest some time before. The clock was striking twelve, and as I went past it some of my clothes, I suppose, caught the large weight, but it was knocked off, and down the stairs it rolled, going with such a lump from one to the other, and I couldn't catch it because it rolled so fast, that I made sure you would be awakened; so I came down to tell you what it was, and it was some time before I could get your room door open, and when I did I found you out of bed and insensible.'"

There was a general look of disappointment when this explanation was given, and one said,--

"Then it was not the vampire?"

"Certainly not."

"And, after all, only a clock weight."

"That's about it."

"Why didn't you tell us that at first?"

"Because that would have spoilt the story."

There was a general murmur of discontent, and, after a few moments one man said, with some vivacity,--

"Well, although our friend's vampyre has turned out, after all, to be nothing but a confounded clock-weight, there's no disputing the fact about Sir Francis Varney being a vampyre, and not a clock-weight."

"Very true--very true."

"And what's to be done to rid the town of such a man?"

"Oh, don't call him a man."

"Well, a monster."

"Ah, that's more like. I tell you what, sir, if you had got a light, when you first heard the noise in your room, and gone out to see what it was, you would have spared yourself much fright."

"Ah, no doubt; it's always easy afterwards to say, if you had done this, and if you had done the other, so and so would have been the effect; but there is something about the hour of midnight that makes men tremble."

"Well," said one, who had not yet spoken, "I don't see why twelve at night should be a whit more disagreeable than twelve at day."

"Don't you?"

"Not I."

"Now, for instance, many a party of pleasure goes to that old ruin where Sir Francis Varney so unaccountably disappeared in broad daylight. But is there any one here who would go to it alone, and at midnight?"

"Yes."

"Who?"

"I would."

"What! and after what has happened as regards the vampyre in connection with it?"

"Yes, I would."

"I'll bet you twenty shilling you won't."

"And I--and I," cried several.

"Well, gentlemen," said the man, who certainly shewed no signs of fear, "I will go, and not only will I go and take all your bets, but, if I do meet the vampyre, then I'll do my best to take him prisoner."

"And when will you go?"

"To-night," he cried, and he sprang to his feet; "hark ye all, I don't believe one word about vampyres. I'll go at once; it's getting late, and let any one of you, in order that you may be convinced I have been to the place, give me any article, which I will hide among the ruins; and tell you where to find it to-morrow in broad daylight."

"Well," said one, "that's fair, Tom Eccles. Here's a handkerchief of mine; I should know it again among a hundred others."

"Agreed; I'll leave it in the ruins."

The wagers were fairly agreed upon; several handkerchiefs were handed to Tom Eccles; and at eleven o'clock he fairly started, through the murky darkness of the night, to the old ruin where Sir Francis Varney and Marchdale were holding their most unholy conference.

It is one thing to talk and to accept wagers in the snug parlour of an inn, and another to go alone across a tract of country wrapped in the profound stillness of night to an ancient ruin which, in addition to the natural gloom which might well be supposed to surround it, has superadded associations which are anything but of a pleasant character.

Tom Eccles, as he was named, was one of those individuals who act greatly from impulse. He was certainly not a coward, and, perhaps, really as free from superstition as most persons, but he was human, and consequently he had nerves, and he had likewise an imagination.

He went to his house first before he started on his errand to the ruins. It was to get a horse-pistol which he had, and which he duly loaded and placed in his pocket. Then he wrapped himself up in a great-coat, and with the air of a man quite determined upon something desperate he left the town.

The guests at the inn looked after him as he walked from the door of that friendly establishment, and some of them, as they saw his resolved aspect, began to quake for the amount of the wagers they had laid upon his non-success.

However, it was resolved among them, that they would stay until half-past twelve, in the expectation of his return, before they separated.

To while away the time, he who had been so facetious about his story of the clock-weight, volunteered to tell what happened to a friend of his who went to take possession of some family property which he became possessed of as heir-at-law to an uncle who had died without a will, having an illegitimate family unprovided for in every shape.

"Ah! nobody cares for other people's illegitimate children, and, if their parents don't provide for them, why, the workhouse is open for them, just as if they were something different from other people."

"So they are; if their parents don't take care of them, and provide for them, nobody else will, as you say, neighbour, except when they have a Fitz put to their name, which tells you they are royal bastards, and of course unlike anybody else's."

"But go on--let's know all about it; we sha'n't hear what he has got to say at all, at this rate."

"Well, as I was saying, or about to say, the nephew, as soon as he heard his uncle was dead, comes and claps his seal upon everything in the house."

"But, could he do so?" inquired one of the guests.

"I don't see what was to hinder him," replied a third. "He could do so, certainly."

"But there was a son, and, as I take it, a son's nearer than a nephew any day."

"But the son is illegitimate."

"Legitimate, or illegitimate, a son's a son; don't bother me about distinction of that sort; why, now, there was old Weatherbit--"

"Order, order."

"Let's hear the tale."

"Very good, gentlemen, I'll go on, if I ain't to be interrupted; but I'll say this, that an illegitimate son is no son, in the eyes of the law; or at most he's an accident quite, and ain't what he is, and so can't inherit."

"Well, that's what I call making matters plain," said one of the guests, who took his pipe from his mouth to make room for the remark; "now that is what I likes."

"Well, as I have proved then," resumed the speaker, "the nephew was the heir, and into the house he would come. A fine affair it was too--the illegitimates looking the colour of sloes; but he knew the law, and would have it put in force."

"Law's law, you know."

"Uncommonly true that; and the nephew stuck to it like a cobbler to his last--he said they should go out, and they did go out; and, say what they would about their natural claims, he would not listen to them, but bundled them out and out in a pretty short space of time."

"It was trying to them, mind you, to leave the house they had been born in with very different expectations to those which now appeared to be their fate. Poor things, they looked ruefully enough, and well they might, for there was a wide world for them, and no prospect of a warm corner.

"Well, as I was saying, he had them all out and the house clear to himself.

"Now," said he, "I have an open field and no favour. I don't care for no--Eh! what?"

"There was a sudden knocking, he thought, the door, and went and opened it, but nothing was to be seen.

"Oh! I see--somebody next door; and if it wasn't, it don't matter. There's nobody here. I'm alone, and there's plenty of valuables in the house. That is what I call very good company. I wouldn't wish for better."

He turned about, looked over room after room, and satisfied himself that he was alone--that the house was empty.

At every room he entered he paused to think over the value--what it was worth, and that he was a very fortunate man in having dropped into such a good thing.

"Ah! there's the old boy's secretary, too--his bureau--there'll be something in that that will amuse me mightily; but I don't think I shall sit up late. He was a rum old man, to say the least of it--a very odd sort of man."

With that he gave himself a shrug, as if some very uncomfortable feeling had come over him.

"I'll go to bed early, and get some sleep, and then in daylight I can look after these papers. They won't be less interesting in the morning than they are now."

There had been some rum stories about the old man, and now the nephew seemed to think he might have let the family sleep on the premises for that night; yes, at that moment he could have found it in his heart to have paid for all the expense of their keep, had it been possible to have had them back to remain the night.

But that wasn't possible, for they would not have done it, but sooner have remained in the streets all night than stay there all night, like so many house-dogs, employed by one who stepped in between them and their father's goods, which were their inheritance, but for one trifling circumstance--a mere ceremony.

The night came on, and he had lights. True it was he had not been down stairs, only just to have a look. He could not tell what sort of a place it was; there were a good many odd sort of passages, that seemed to end nowhere, and others that did.

There were large doors; but they were all locked, and he had the keys; so he didn't mind, but secured all places that were not fastened.

He then went up stairs again, and sat down in the room where the bureau was placed.

"I'll be bound," said one of the guests, "he was in a bit of a stew, notwithstanding all his brag."

"Oh! I don't believe," said another, "that anything done that is dangerous, or supposed to be dangerous, by the bravest man, is any way wholly without some uncomfortable feelings. They may not be strong enough to prevent the thing proposed to be done from being done, but they give a disagreeable sensation to the skin."

"You have felt it, then?"

"Ha! ha! ha!"

"Why, at that time I slept in the churchyard for a wager, I must say I felt cold all over, as if my skin was walking about me in an uncomfortable manner."

"But you won your wager?"

"I did."

"And of course you slept there?"

"To be sure I did."

"And met with nothing?"

"Nothing, save a few bumps against the gravestones."

"Those were hard knocks, I should say."

"They were, I assure you; but I lay there, and slept there, and won my wager."

"Would you do it again?"

"No."

"And why not?"

"Because of the rheumatism."

"You caught that?"

"I did; I would give ten times my wager to get rid of them. I have them very badly."

"Come, order, order--the tale; let's hear the end of that, since it has begun."

"With all my heart. Come, neighbour."

"Well, as I said, he was fidgetty; but yet he was not a man to be very easily frightened or overcome, for he was stout and bold.

"When he shut himself up in the room, he took out a bottle of some good wine, and helped himself to drink; it was good old wine, and he soon felt himself warmed and, comforted. He could have faced the enemy.

"If one bottle produces such an effect," he muttered, "what will two do?"

This was a question that could only be solved by trying it, and this he proceeded to do.

But first he drew a brace of long barrelled pistols from his coat pocket, and taking a powder-flask and bullets from his pocket also, he loaded them very carefully.

"There," said he, "are my bull-dogs; and rare watch-dogs they are. They never bark but they bite. Now, if anybody does come, it will be all up with them. Tricks upon travellers ain't a safe game when I have these; and now for the other bottle."

He drew the other bottle, and thought, if anything, it was better than the first. He drank it rather quick, to be sure, and then he began to feel sleepy and tired.

"I think I shall go to bed," he said; "that is, if I can find my way there, for it does seem to me as if the door was travelling. Never mind, it will make a call here again presently, and then I'll get through."

So saying he arose. Taking the candle in his hand, he walked with a better step than might have been expected under the circumstance. True it was the candle wagged to and fro, and his shadow danced upon the wall; but still, when he got to the bed, he secured his door, put the light in a safe place, threw himself down, and was fast asleep in a few moments, or rather he fell into a doze instantaneously.

How long he remained in this state he knew not, but he was suddenly awakened by a loud bang, as though something heavy and flat had fallen upon the floor--such, for instance, as a door, or anything of that sort. He jumped up, rubbed his eyes, and could even then hear the reverberations through the house.

"What is that?" he muttered; "what is that?"

He listened, and thought he could hear something moving down stairs, and for a moment he was seized with an ague fit; but recollecting, I suppose, that there were some valuables down stairs that were worth fighting for, he carefully extinguished the light that still burned, and softly crept down stairs.

When he got down stairs he thought he could hear some one scramble up the kitchen stairs, and then into the room where the bureau was. Listening for a moment to ascertain if there were more than one, and then feeling convinced there was not, he followed into the parlour, when he heard the cabinet open by a key.

This was a new miracle, and one he could not understand; and then he heard the papers begin to rattle and rustle; so, drawing out one of the pistols, he cocked it, and walked in.

The figure instantly began to jump about; it was dressed in white--in grave-clothes. He was terribly nervous, and shook, so he feared to fire the pistol; but at length he did, and the report was followed by a fall and a loud groan.

This was very dreadful--very dreadful; but all was quiet, and he lit the candle again, and approached the body to examine it, and ascertain if he knew who it was. A groan came from it. The bureau was open, and the figure clutched firmly a will in his hand.

The figure was dressed in grave-clothes, and he started up when he saw the form and features of his own uncle, the man who was dead, who somehow or other had escaped his confinement, and found his way up, here. He held his will firmly; and the nephew was so horrified and stunned, that he threw down the light, and rushed out of the room with a shout of terror, and never returned again.

***

The narrator concluded, and one of the guests said,--

"And do you really believe it?"--"No, no--to be sure not."

"You don't?"--"Why should I? My friend was, out of all hand, one of the greatest liars I ever came near; and why, therefore, should I believe him? I don't, on my conscience, believe one word of it."

It was now half-past twelve, and, as Tom Eccles came not back, and the landlord did not feel disposed to draw any more liquor, they left the inn, and retired to their separate houses in a great state of anxiety to know the fate of their respective wagers.

CHAPTER LXIV

THE VAMPIRE IN THE MOONLIGHT.--THE FALSE FRIEND

Part of the distance being accomplished towards the old ruins, Tom Eccles began to feel that what he had undertaken was not altogether such child's-play as he had at first imagined it to be. Somehow or another, with a singular and uncomfortable sort of distinctness, there came across his mind every story that he had remembered of the wild and the wonderful. All the long-since forgotten tales of superstition that in early childhood he had learned, came now back upon him, suggesting to his mind a thousand uncomfortable fancies of the strangest description.

It was not likely that when once a man, under such circumstances, got into such a frame of mind, he would readily get out of it again, while he continued surrounded by such scenes as had first called them into existence.

No doubt, had he turned about, and faced the inn again instead of the old ruins he would soon have shaken off these "thick coming fancies;" but such a result was no to be expected, so long as he kept on towards the dismal place he had pledged himself to reach.

As he traversed meadow after meadow he began to ask himself some questions which he found that he could not answer exactly in a consolatory manner, under the present state of things.

Among these question was the very pertinent one of,--"It's no argument against vampyres, because I don't see the use of 'em--is it?" This he was compelled to answer as he had put it; and when, in addition, he began to recollect that, without the shadow of a doubt, Sir Francis Varney the supposed vampyre, had been chased across the fields to that very ruin whither he was bound, and had then and there disappeared, he certainly found himself in decidedly uncomfortable and most unpromising situation.

"No," he said, "no. Hang it, I won't go back now, to be made the laughing-stock of the whole town, which I should be. Come what may of it, I will go on as I have commenced; so I shall put on as stout a heart as I can."

Then, having come to this resolve, he strove might and main to banish from his mind those disagreeable reminiscences that had been oppressing him, to turn his attention to subjects of a different complexion.

During the progress of making this endeavour, which was rather futile, he came within sight of the ruins. Then he slackened his pace a little, telling himself, with a pardonable self-deceit, that it was common, ordinary caution only, which induced him to do so, and nothing at all in the shape of fear.

"Time enough," he remarked, "to be afraid, when I see anything to be afraid of, which I don't see as yet. So, as all's right, I may as well put a good face upon the matter."

He tried to whistle a tune, but it turned out only a melancholy failure; so he gave that up in despair, and walked on until he got within a hundred yards, or thereabouts, of the old ruins.

He thus proceeded, and bending his ear close to the ground, he listened attentively for several minutes. Somehow, he fancied that a strange, murmuring sound came to his ears; but he was not quite sure that it proceeded from the ruins, because it was just that sort of sound that might come from a long way off, being mellowed by distance, although, perhaps, loud enough at its source.

"Well, well," he whispered to himself, "it don't matter much, after all. Go I must, and hide the handkerchiefs somewhere, or else be laughed at, besides losing my wages. The former I don't like, and the latter I cannot afford."

Thus clinching the matter by such knock-down arguments, he walked on until he was almost within the very shadow of the ruins, and, probably, it was at this juncture that his footsteps may have been heard by Marchdale and Sir Francis Varney.

Then he paused again; but all was profoundly still, and he began to think that the strange sort of murmuring noise which he had heard must have come from far off and not at all from any person or persons within the ruins.

"Let me see," he said to himself; "I have five handkerchiefs to hide among the old ruins somewhere, and the sooner I do so the better, because then I will get away; for, as regards staying here to watch, Heaven knows how long, for Sir Francis Varney, I don't intend to do it, upon second thoughts and second thoughts, they say, are generally best."

With the most careful footsteps now, as if he were treading upon some fragile substance, which he feared to injure, he advanced until he was fairly within the precincts of the ancient place, which now bore so ill a reputation.

He then made to himself much the same remark that Sir Francis Varney had made to Marchdale, with respect to the brightening up of the sky, in consequence of its being near the time for the moon to rise from the horizon, and he saw more clearly around him, although he could not find any good place to hide the handkerchiefs in.

"I must and will," he said, "hide them securely; for it would, indeed, be remarkably unpleasant, after coming here and winning my wages, to have the proofs that I had done so taken away by some chance visitor to the place."

He at length saw a tolerably large stone, which stood, in a slant position, up against one of the walls. Its size attracted him. He thought, if his strength was sufficient to move it, that it would be a good thing to do so, and to place the handkerchiefs beneath it; for, at all events, it was so heavy that it could not be kicked aside, and no one, without some sort of motive to do so, beyond the mere love of labour, would set about moving it from its position.

"I may go further and fare worse," he said to himself; "so here shall all the handkerchiefs lie, to afford a proof that I have been here."

He packed them into a small compass, and then stooped to roll aside the heavy stone, when, at the moment, before he could apply his strength to that purpose, he heard some one, in his immediate neighbourhood, say,--"Hist!"

This was so sudden, and so utterly unexpected, that he not only ceased his exertions to move the stone, but he nearly fell down in his surprise.

"Hist--hist!" said the voice again.

"What--what," gasped Tom Eccles--"what are you?"--"Hush--hush--hush!"

The perspiration broke out upon his brow, and he leaned against the wall for support, as he managed to say, faintly,--

"Well, hush--what then?"--"Hist!"

"Well, I hear you. Where are you?"

"Here at hand. Who are you?"

"Tom Eccles. Who are you?"--"A friend. Have you seen anything?"

"No; I wish I could. I should like to see you if I could."--"I'm coming."

There was a slow and cautious footstep, and Marchdale advanced to where Tom Eccles was standing.

"Come, now," said the latter, when he saw the dusky-looking form stalking towards him; "till I know you better, I'll be obliged to you to keep off. I am well armed. Keep your distance, be you friend or foe."

"Armed!" exclaimed Marchdale, and he at once paused.--"Yes, I am."

"But I am a friend. I have no sort of objection frankly to tell you my errand. I am a friend of the Bannerworth family, and have kept watch here now for two nights, in the hopes of meeting with Varney, the vampyre."

"The deuce you have: and pray what may your name be?"--"Marchdale."

"If you be Mr. Marchdale, I know you by sight: for I have seen you with Mr. Henry Bannerworth several times. Come out from among the shadows, and let us have a look at you; but, till you do, don't come within arm's length of me. I am not naturally suspicious; but we cannot be too careful."

"Oh! certainly--certainly. The silver edge of the moon is now just peeping up from the east, and you will be able to see me well, if you step from the shadow of the wall by which you now are."

This was a reasonable enough proposition, and Tom Eccles at once acceded to it, by stepping out boldly into the partial moonlight, which now began to fall upon the open meadows, tinting the grass with a silvery refulgence, and rendering even minute objects visible. The moment he saw Marchdale he knew him, and, advancing frankly to him, he said,--

"I know you, sir, well."

"And what brings you here?"--"A wager for one thing, and a wish to see the vampyre for another."

"Indeed!"--"Yes; I must own I have such a wish, along with a still stronger one, to capture him, if possible; and, as there are now two of us, why may we not do it?"

"As for capturing him," said Marchdale, "I should prefer shooting him."--"You would?"

"I would, indeed. I have seen him once shot down, and he is now, I have no doubt, as well as ever. What were you doing with that huge stone I saw you bending over?"--"I have some handkerchiefs to hide here, as a proof that I have to-night really been to this place."

"Oh, I will show you a better spot, where there is a crevice in which you can place them with perfect safety. Will you walk with me into the ruins?"--"Willingly."

"It's odd enough," remarked Marchdale, after he had shown Tom Eccles where to hide the handkerchiefs, "that you and I should both be here upon so similar an errand."--"I'm very glad of it. It robs the place of its gloom, and makes it ten times more endurable than it otherwise would be. What do you propose to do if you see the vampyre?"

"I shall try a pistol bullet on him. You say you are armed?"--"Yes."

"With pistols?"--"One. Here it is."

"A huge weapon; loaded well, of course?"--"Oh, yes, I can depend upon it; but I did not intend to use it, unless assailed."

"'Tis well. What is that?"--"What--what?"

"Don't you see anything there? Come farther back. Look--look. At the corner of that wall there I am certain there is the flutter of a human garment."--"There is--there is."

"Hush! Keep close. It must be the vampyre."--"Give me my pistol. What are you doing with it?"

"Only ramming down the charge more firmly for you. Take it. If that be Varney the vampyre, I shall challenge him to surrender the moment he appears; and if he does not, I will fire upon him, and do you do so likewise."--"Well, I--I don't know."

"You have scruples?"--"I certainly have."

"Well, well--don't you fire, then, but leave it to me. There; look--look. Now have you any doubt? There he goes; in his cloak. It is--it is----"--"Varney, by Heavens!" cried Tom Eccles.

"Surrender!" shouted Marchdale.

At the instant Sir Francis Varney sprang forward, and made off at a rapid pace across the meadows.

"Fire after him--fire!" cried Marchdale, "or he will escape. My pistol has missed fire. He will be off."

On the impulse of the moment, and thus urged by the voice and the gesture of his companion, Tom Eccles took aim as well as he could, and fired after the retreating form of Sir Francis Varney. His conscience smote him as he heard the report and saw the flash of the large pistol amid the half sort of darkness that was still around.

The effect of the shot was then to him painfully apparent. He saw Varney stop instantly; then make a vain attempt to stagger forward a little, and finally fall heavily to the earth, with all the appearance of one killed upon the spot.

"You have hit him," said Marchdale--"you have hit him. Bravo!"--"I have--hit him."

"Yes, a capital shot, by Jove!"--"I am very sorry."

"Sorry! sorry for ridding the world of such a being! What was in your pistol?"--"A couple of slugs."

"Well, they have made a lodgment in him, that's quite clear. Let's go up and finish him at once."--"He seems finished."

"I beg your pardon there. When the moonbeams fall upon him he'll get up and walk away as if nothing was the matter."--"Will he?" cried Tom, with animation--"will he?"

"Certainly he will."--"Thank God for that. Now, hark you, Mr. Marchdale: I should not have fired if you had not at the moment urged me to do so. Now, I shall stay and see if the effect which you talk of will ensue; and although it may convince me that he is a vampyre, and that there are such things, he may go off, scot free, for me."

"Go off?"--"Yes; I don't want to have even a vampyre's blood upon my hands."

"You are exceedingly delicate."--"Perhaps I am; it's my way, though. I have shot him--not you, mind; so, in a manner of speaking, he belongs to me. Now, mark, me: I won't have him touched any more to-night, unless you think there's a chance of making a prisoner of him without violence."

"There he lies; you can go and make a prisoner of him at once, dead as he is; and if you take him out of the moonlight--"

"I understand; he won't recover."--"Certainly not."

"But, as I want him to recover, that don't suit me."--"Well, I cannot but honour your scruples, although I do not actually share in them; but I promise you that, since such is your wish, I will take no steps against the vampyre; but let us come up to him and see if he be really dead, or only badly wounded."

Tom Eccles hang back a little from this proposal; but, upon being urged again by Marchdale, and told that he need not go closer than he chose, he consented, and the two of them approached the prostrate form of Sir Francis Varney, which lay upon its face in the faint moonlight, which each moment was gathering strength and power.

"He lies upon his face," said Marchdale. "Will you go and turn him over?"--"Who--I? God forbid I should touch him."

"Well--well, I will. Come on."

They halted within a couple of yards of the body. Tom Eccles would not go a step farther; so Marchdale advanced alone, and pretended to be, with great repugnance, examining for the wound.

"He is quite dead," he said; "but I cannot see the hurt."--"I think he turned his head as I fired."

"Did he? Let us see."

Marchdale lifted up the head, and disclosed such a mass of clotted-looking blood, that Tom Eccles at once took to his heels, nor stopped until he was nearly as far off as the ruins. Marchdale followed him more slowly, and when he came up to him, he said,--

"The slugs have taken effect on his face."--"I know it--I know it. Don't tell me."

"He looks horrible."--"And I am a murderer."

"Psha! You look upon this matter too seriously. Think of who and what he was, and then you will soon acquit yourself of being open to any such charge."--"I am bewildered, Mr. Marchdale, and cannot now know whether he be a vampyre or not. If he be not, I have murdered, most unjustifiably, a fellow-creature."

"Well, but if he be?"--"Why, even then I do not know but that I ought to consider myself as guilty. He is one of God's creatures if he were ten times a vampyre."

"Well, you really do take a serious view of the affair."--"Not more serious than it deserves."

"And what do you mean to do?"--"I shall remain here to await the result of what you tell me will ensue, if he be a real vampire. Even now the moonbeams are full upon him, and each moment increasing in intensity. Think you he will recover?"

"I do indeed."--"Then here will I wait."

"Since that is you resolve, I will keep you company. We shall easily find some old stone in the ruins which will serve us for a seat, and there at leisure we can keep our eyes upon the dead body, and be able to observe if it make the least movement."

This plan was adopted, and they sat down just within the ruins, but in such a place that they had a full view of the dead body, as it appeared to be, of Sir Francis Varney, upon which the sweet moonbeams shone full and clear.

Tom Eccles related how he was incited to come upon his expedition, but he might have spared himself that trouble, as Marchdale had been in a retired corner of the inn parlour before he came to his appointment with Varney, and heard the business for the most part proposed.

Half-an-hour, certainly not more, might have elapsed; when suddenly Tom Eccles uttered an exclamation, partly of surprise and partly of terror,--

"He moves; he moves!" he cried. "Look at the vampyre's body."

Marchdale affected to look with an all-absorbing interest, and there was Sir Francis Varney, raising slowly one arm with the hand outstretched towards the moon, as if invoking that luminary to shed more of its beams upon him. Then the body moved slowly, like some one writhing in pain, and yet unable to move from the spot on which it lay. From the head to the foot, the whole frame seemed to be convulsed, and now and then as the ghastly object seemed to be gathering more strength, the limbs were thrown out with a rapid and a frightful looking violence.

It was truly to one, who might look upon it as a reality and no juggle, a frightful sight to see, and although Marchdale, of course, tolerably well preserved his equanimity, only now and then, for appearance sake, affecting to be wonderfully shocked, poor Tom Eccles was in such a state of horror and fright that he could not, if he would, have flown from the spot, so fascinated was he by the horrible spectacle.

This was a state of things which continued for many minutes, and then the body showed evident symptoms of so much returning animation, that it was about to rise from his gory bed and mingle once again with the living.

"Behold!" said Marchdale--"behold!"--"Heaven have mercy upon us!"

"It is as I said; the beams of the moon have revived the vampyre. You perceive now that there can be no doubt."--"Yes, yes, I see him; I see him."

Sir Francis Varney now, as if with a great struggle, rose to his feet, and looked up at the bright moon for some moments with such an air and manner that it would not have required any very great amount of imagination to conceive that he was returning to it some sort of thanksgiving for the good that it had done to him.

He then seemed for some moments in a state of considerable indecision as to which way he should proceed. He turned round several times. Then he advanced a step or two towards the house, but apparently his resolution changed again, and casting his eyes upon the ruins, he at once made towards them.

This was too much for the philosophy as well as for the courage of Tom Eccles. It was all very well to look on at some distance, and observe the wonderful and inexplicable proceedings of the vampyre; but when he showed symptoms of making a nearer acquaintance, it was not to be borne.

"Why, he's coming here," said Tom.--"He seems so indeed," remarked Marchdale.

"Do you mean to stay?"--"I think I shall."

"You do, do you?"--"Yes, I should much like to question him, and as we are two to one I think we really can have nothing to fear."

"Do you? I'm altogether of a different opinion. A man who has more lives than a cat don't much mind at what odds he fights. You may stay if you like."--"You do not mean to say that you will desert me?"

"I don't see a bit how you call it deserting you; if we had come out together on this adventure, I would have stayed it out with you; but as we came separate and independent, we may as well go back so."--"Well, but--"

"Good morning?" cried Tom, and he at once took to his heels towards the town, without staying to pay any attention to the remonstrances of Marchdale, who called after him in vain.

Sir Francis Varney, probably, had Tom Eccles not gone off so rapidly, would have yet taken another thought, and gone in another direction than that which led him to the ruins, and Tom, if he had had his senses fully about him, as well as all his powers of perception, would have seen that the progress of the vampyre was very slow, while he continued to converse with Marchdale, and that it was only when he went off at good speed that Sir Francis Varney likewise thought it prudent to do so.

"Is he much terrified?" said Varney, as he came up to Marchdale.--"Yes, most completely."

"This then, will make a good story in the town."--"It will, indeed, and not a little enhance your reputation."

"Well, well; it don't much matter now; but if by terrifying people I can purchase for myself anything like immunity for the past, I shall be satisfied."--"I think you may now safely reckon that you have done so. This man who has fled with so much precipitation, had courage."

"Unquestionably."--"Or else he would have shrunk from coming here at all."

"True, but his courage and presence arose from his strong doubts as to the existence of such beings as vampyres."--"Yes, and now that he is convinced, his bravery has evaporated along with his doubts; and such a tale as he has now to tell, will be found sufficient to convert even the most sceptical in the town."

"I hope so."--"And yet it cannot much avail you."

"Not personally, but I must confess that I am not dead to all human opinions, and I feel some desire of revenge against those dastards who by hundreds have hunted me, burnt down my mansion, and sought my destruction."--"That I do not wonder at."

"I would fain leave among them a legacy of fear. Such fear as shall haunt them and their children for years to come. I would wish that the name of Varney, the vampire, should be a sound of terror for generations."--"It will be so."

"It shall."--"And now, then, for a consideration of what is to be done with our prisoner. What is your resolve upon that point?"

"I have considered it while I was lying upon yon green sward waiting for the friendly moonbeams to fall upon my face, and it seems to me that there is no sort of resource but to----"--"Kill him?"

"No, no."--"What then?"

"To set him free."--"Nay, have you considered the immense hazard of doing so? Think again; I pray you think again. I am decidedly of opinion that he more than suspects who are his enemies; and, in that case, you know what consequences would ensue; besides, have we not enough already to encounter? Why should we add another young, bold, determined spirit to the band which is already arrayed against us?"

"You talk in vain, Marchdale; I know to what it all tends; you have a strong desire for the death of this young man."--"No; there you wrong me. I have no desire for his death, for its own sake; but, where great interests are at stake, there must be sacrifices made."

"So there must; therefore, I will make a sacrifice, and let this young prisoner free from his dungeon."--"If such be your determination, I know well it is useless to combat with it. When do you purpose giving him his freedom?"

"I will not act so heedlessly as that your principles of caution shall blame me. I will attempt to get from him some promise that he will not make himself an active instrument against me. Perchance, too, as Bannerworth Hall, which he is sure to visit, wears such an air of desertion, I may be able to persuade him that the Bannerworth family, as well as his uncle, have left this part of the country altogether; so that, without making any inquiry for them about the neighbourhood, he may be induced to leave at once."--"That would be well."

"Good; your prudence approves of the plan, and therefore it shall be done."--"I am rather inclined to think," said Marchdale, with a slight tone of sarcasm, "that if my prudence did not approve of the plan, it would still be done."

"Most probably," said Varney, calmly.--"Will you release him to-night?"

"It is morning, now, and soon the soft grey light of day will tint the east. I do not think I will release him till sunset again now. Has he provision to last him until then?"--"He has."

"Well, then, two hours after sunset I will come here and release him from his weary bondage, and now I must go to find some place in which to hide my proscribed head. As for Bannerworth Hall, I will yet have it in my power; I have sworn to do so, I will keep my oath."--"The accomplishment of our purpose, I regret to say, seems as far off as ever."

"Not so--not so. As I before remarked, we must disappear, for a time, so as to lull suspicion. There will then arise a period when Bannerworth Hall will neither be watched, as it is now, nor will it be inhabited,--a period before the Bannerworth family has made up its mind to go back to it, and when long watching without a result has become too tiresome to be continued at all; then we can at once pursue our object."--"Be it so."

"And now, Marchdale, I want more money."--"More money!"

"Yes; you know well that I have had large demands of late."--"But I certainly had an impression that you were possessed, by the death of some one, with very ample means."

"Yes, but there is a means by which all is taken from me. I have no real resources but what are rapidly used up, so I must come upon you again."--"I have already completely crippled myself as regards money matters in this enterprise, and I do certainly hope that the fruits will not be far distant. If they be much longer delayed, I shall really not know what to do. However, come to the lodge where you have been staying, and then I will give you, to the extent of my ability, whatever sum you think your present exigencies require."

"Come on, then, at once. I would certainly, of course, rather leave this place now, before daybreak. Come on, I say, come on."

Sir Francis Varney and Marchdale walked for some time in silence across the meadows. It was evident that there was not between these associates the very best of feelings. Marchdale was always smarting under an assumption of authority over him, on the part of Sir Francis Varney, while the latter scarcely cared to conceal any portion of the contempt with which he regarded his hypocritical companion.

Some very strong band of union, indeed, must surely bind these two strange persons together! It must be something of a more than common nature which induces Marchdale not only to obey the behests of his mysterious companion, but to supply him so readily with money as we perceive he promises to do.

And, as regards Varney, the vampyre, he, too, must have some great object in view to induce him to run such a world of risk, and take so much trouble as he was doing with the Bannerworth family.

What his object is, and what is the object of Marchdale, will, now that we have progressed so far in our story, soon appear, and then much that is perfectly inexplicable, will become clear and distinct, and we shall find that some strong human motives are at the bottom of it all.

CHAPTER LXV

VARNEY'S VISIT TO THE DUNGEON OF THE LONELY PRISONER IN THE RUINS

Evident it was that Marchdale was not near so scrupulous as Sir Francis Varney, in what he chose to do. He would, without hesitation, have sacrificed the life of that prisoner in the lonely dungeon, whom it would be an insult to the understanding of our readers, not to presume that they had, long ere this, established in their minds to be Charles Holland.

His own safety seemed to be the paramount consideration with Marchdale, and it was evident that he cared for nothing in comparison with that object.

It says much, however, for Sir Francis Varney, that he did not give in to such a blood-thirsty feeling, but rather chose to set the prisoner free, and run all the chances of the danger to which he might expose himself by such a course of conduct, than to insure safety, comparatively, by his destruction.

Sir Francis Varney is evidently a character of strangely mixed feelings. It is quite evident that he has some great object in view, which he wishes to accomplish almost at any risk; but it is equally evident, at the same time, that he wishes to do so with the least possible injury to others, or else he would never have behaved as he had done in his interview with the beautiful and persecuted Flora Bannerworth, or now suggested the idea of setting Charles Holland free from the dreary dungeon in which he had been so long confined.

We are always anxious and willing to give every one credit for the good that is in them; and, hence, we are pleased to find that Sir Francis Varney, despite his singular, and apparently preternatural capabilities, has something sufficiently human about his mind and feelings, to induce him to do as little injury as possible to others in the pursuit of his own objects.

Of the two, vampyre as he is, we prefer him much to the despicable and hypocritical, Marchdale, who, under the pretence of being the friend of the Bannerworth family, would freely have inflicted upon them the most deadly injuries.

It was quite clear that he was most dreadfully disappointed that Sir Francis Varney, would not permit him to take the life of Charles Holland, and it was with a gloomy and dissatisfied air that he left the ruins to proceed towards the town, after what we may almost term the altercation he had had with Varney the vampyre upon that subject.

It must not be supposed that Sir Francis Varney, however, was blind to the danger which must inevitably accrue from permitting Charles Holland once more to obtain his liberty.

What the latter would be able to state would be more than sufficient to convince the Bannerworths, and all interested in their fortunes, that something was going on of a character, which, however, supernatural it might seem to be, still seemed to have some human and ordinary objects for its ends.

Sir Francis Varney thought over all this before he proceeded, according to his promise, to the dungeon of the prisoner; but it would seem as if there was considerable difficulty, even to an individual of his long practice in all kinds of chicanery and deceit, in arriving at any satisfactory conclusion, as to a means of making Charles Holland's release a matter of less danger to himself, than it would be likely to be, if, unfettered by obligation, he was at once set free.

At the solemn hour of midnight, while all was still, that is, to say, on the night succeeding the one, on which he had had the interview with Marchdale, we have recorded, Sir Francis Varney alone sought the silent ruins. He was attired, as usual, in his huge cloak, and, indeed, the chilly air of the evening warranted such protection against its numerous discomforts.

Had any one seen him, however, that evening, they would have observed an air of great doubt, and irresolution upon his brow, as if he were struggling with some impulses which he found it extremely difficult to restrain.

"I know well," he muttered, as he walked among the shadow of the ruins, "that Marchdale's reasoning is coldly and horribly correct, when he says that there is danger in setting this youth free; but, I am about to leave this place, and not to show myself for some time, and I cannot reconcile myself to inflicting upon him the horror of a death by starvation, which must ensue."

It was a night of more than usual dullness, and, as Sir Francis Varney removed the massy stone, which hid the narrow and tortuous entrance to the dungeons, a chilly feeling crept over him, and he could not help supposing, that even then Marchdale might have played him false, and neglected to supply the prisoner food, according to his promise.

Hastily he descended to the dungeons, and with a step, which had in it far less of caution, than had usually characterised his proceedings, he proceeded onwards until he reached that particular dungeon, in which our young friend, to whom we wished so well, had been so long confined from the beautiful and cheering light of day, and from all that his heart's best affections most cling to.

"Speak," said Sir Francis Varney, as he entered the dungeon--"If the occupant of this dreary place live, let him answer one who is as much his friend as he has been his enemy."

"I have no friend," said Charles Holland, faintly; "unless it be one who would come and restore me to liberty."

"And how know you that I am not he?"

"Your voice sounds like that of one of my persecutors. Why do you not place the climax to your injuries by at once taking away life. I should be better pleased that you would do so, than that I should wear out the useless struggle of existence in so dreary and wretched an abode as this."

"Young man," said Sir Francis Varney, "I have come to you on a greater errand of mercy than, probably, you will ever give me credit for. There is one who would too readily have granted your present request, and who would at once have taken that life of which you profess to be so wearied; but which may yet present to you some of its sunniest and most beautiful aspects."

"Your tones are friendly," said Charles; "but yet I dread some new deception. That you are one of those who consigned me by stratagem, and by brute force, to this place of durance, I am perfectly well assured, and, therefore, any good that may be promised by you, presents itself to me in a very doubtful character."

"I cannot be surprised," said Sir Francis Varney, "at such sentiments arising from your lips; but, nevertheless, I am inclined to save you. You have been detained here because it was supposed by being so, a particular object would be best obtained by your absence. That object, however has failed, notwithstanding, and I do not feel further inclined to protract your sufferings. Have you any guess as to the parties who have thus confined you?"--"I am unaccustomed to dissemble, and, therefore I will say at once that I have a guess."

"In which way does it tend?"--

"Against Sir Francis Varney, called the vampyre."

"Does it not strike you that this may be a dangerous candour?"--"It may, or it may not be; I cannot help it. I know I am at the mercy of my foes, and I do not believe that anything I can say or do will make my situation worse or better."

"You are much mistaken there. In other hands than mine, it might make it much worse; but it happens to be one of my weaknesses, that I am charged with candour, and that I admire boldness of disposition."--"Indeed! and yet can behave in the manner you have done towards me."

"Yes. There are more things in heaven and on earth than are dreamt of in your philosophy. I am the more encouraged to set you free, because, if I procure from you a promise, which I intend to attempt, I am inclined to believe that you will keep it."--"I shall assuredly keep whatever promise I may make. Propound your conditions, and if they be such as honour and honesty will permit me to accede to, I will do so willingly and at once. Heaven knows I am weary enough of this miserable imprisonment."

"Will you promise me then, if I set you free, not to mention your suspicions that it is to Sir Francis Varney you owe this ill turn, and not to attempt any act of vengeance against him as a retaliation for it."--"I cannot promise so much as that. Freedom, indeed, would be a poor boon, if I were not permitted freely to converse of some of the circumstances connected with my captivity."

"You object?"--"I do to the former of your propositions, but not to the latter. I will promise not to go at all out of my way to execute any vengeance upon you; but I will not promise that I will not communicate the circumstances of my forced absence from them, to those friends whose opinion I so much value, and to return to whom is almost as dear to me as liberty itself."

Sir Francis Varney was silent for a few moments, and then he said, in a tone of deep solemnity,--

"There are ninety-nine persons out of a hundred who would take your life for the independence of your tongue; but I am as the hundredth one, who looks with a benevolent eye at your proceedings. Will you promise me, if I remove the fetters which now bind your limbs, that you will make no personal attack upon me; for I am weary of personal contention, and I have no disposition to endure it. Will you make me this promise?"--"I promise?"--"I will."

Without another word, but trusting implicitly to the promise which had been given to him, Sir Francis Varney produced a small key from his pocket, and unlocked with it a padlock which confined the chains about the prisoner.

With ease, Charles Holland was then enabled to shake them off, and then, for the first time, for some weeks, he rose to his feet, and felt all the exquisite relief of being comparatively free from bondage.

"This is delightful, indeed," he said.

"It is," said Sir Francis Varney--"it is but a foretaste of the happiness you will enjoy when you are entirely free. You see that I have trusted you."

"You have trusted me as you might trust me, and you perceive that I have kept my word."

"You have; and since you decline to make me the promise which I would fain have from you, to the effect that you would not mention me as one of the authors of your calamity, I must trust to your honour not to attempt revenge for what you have suffered."

"That I will promise. There can be but little difficulty to any generous mind in giving up such a feeling. In consequence of your sparing me what you might still further have inflicted, I will let the past rest, and as if it had never happened really to me; and speak of it to others, but as a circumstance which I wish not to revert to, but prefer should be buried in oblivion."

"It is well; and now I have a request to make of you, which, perhaps, you will consider the hardest of all."

"Name it. I feel myself bound to a considerable extent to comply with whatever you may demand of me, that is not contrary to honourable principle."

"Then it is this, that, comparatively free as you are, and in a condition, as you are, to assert your own freedom, you will not do so hastily, or for a considerable period; in fact, I wish and expect that you should wait yet awhile, until it shall suit me to say that it is my pleasure that you shall be free."

"That is, indeed, a hard condition to man who feels, as you yourself remark, that he can assert his freedom. It is one which I have still a hope you will not persevere in.

"Nay, young man, I think that I have treated you with generosity, to make you feel that I am not the worst of foes you could have had. All I require of you is, that you should wait here for about an hour. It is now nearly one o'clock; will you wait until you hear it strike two before you actually make a movement to leave this place?"

Charles Holland hesitated for some moments, and then he said,--

"Do not fancy that I am not one who appreciates the singular trust you have reposed in me; and, however repugnant to me it may be to remain here, a voluntary prisoner, I am inclined to do so, if it be but to convince you that the trust you have reposed in me is not in vain, and that I can behave with equal generosity to you as you can to me."

"Be it so," said Sir Francis Varney; "I shall leave you with a full reliance that you will keep your word; and now, farewell. When you think of me, fancy me rather one unfortunate than criminal, and tell yourself that even Varney the vampyre had some traits in his character, which, although they might not raise your esteem, at all events did not loudly call for your reprobation."

"I shall do so. Oh! Flora, Flora, I shall look upon you once again, after believing and thinking that I had bidden you a long and last adieu. My own beautiful Flora, it is joy indeed to think that I shall look upon that face again, which, to my perception, is full of all the majesty of loveliness."

Sir Francis Varney looked coldly on while Charles uttered this enthusiastic speech.

"Remember," he said, "till two o'clock;" and he walked towards the door of the dungeon. "You will have no difficulty in finding your way out from this place. Doubtless you already perceive the entrance by which I gained admission."

"Had I been free," said Charles, "and had the use of my limbs, I should, long ere this, have worked my way to life and liberty."

"'Tis well. Goodnight."

Varney walked from the place, and just closed the door behind him. With a slow and stately step he left the ruins, and Charles Holland found himself once more alone, but in a much more enviable condition than for many weeks he could have called his.

CHAPTER LXVI

FLORA BANNERWORTH'S APPARENT INCONSISTENCY.--THE ADMIRAL'S CIRCUMSTANCES AND ADVICE.--MR. CHILLINGWORTH'S MYSTERIOUS ABSENCE

For a brief space let us return to Flora Bannerworth, who had suffered so much on account of her affections, as well as on account of the mysterious attack that had been made upon her by the reputed vampyre.

After leaving Bannerworth Hall for a short time, she seemed to recover her spirits; but this was a state of things which did not last, and only showed how fallacious it was to expect that, after the grievous things that had happened, she would rapidly recover her equanimity.

It is said, by learned physiologists, that two bodily pains cannot endure at the same space of time in the system; and, whether it be so or not, is a question concerning which it would be foreign to the nature of our work, to enter into anything like an elaborate disquisition.

Certainly, however, so far as Flora Bannerworth was concerned, she seemed inclined to show that, mentally, the observation was a true one, for that, now she became released from a continued dread of the visits of the vampyre, her mind would, with more painful interest than ever, recur to the melancholy condition, probably, of Charles Holland, if he were alive, and to soul-harrowing reflections concerning him, if he were dead.

She could not, and she did not, believe, for one moment, that his desertion of her had been of a voluntary character. She knew, or fancied she knew, him by far too well for that; and she more than once expressed her opinion, to the effect that she was perfectly convinced his disappearance was a part and parcel of all that train of circumstances which had so recently occurred, and produced such a world of unhappiness to her, as well as to the whole of the Bannerworth family.

"If he had never loved me," she said to her brother Henry, "he would have been alive and well; but he has fallen a victim to the truth of a passion, and to the constancy of an affection which, to my dying day, I will believe in."

Now that Mr. Marchdale had left the place there was no one to dispute this proposition with Flora, for all, as well as she, were fully inclined to think well of Charles Holland.

It was on the very morning which preceded that evening when Sir Francis Varney called upon Charles Holland in the manner we have related, with the gratifying news that, upon certain conditions, he might be released, that Flora Bannerworth, when the admiral came to see them, spoke to him of Charles Holland, saying,--

"Now, sir, that I am away from Bannerworth Hall, I do not, and cannot feel satisfied; for the thought that Charles may eventually come back, and seek us there, still haunts me. Fancy him, sir, doing so, and seeing the place completely deserted."

"Well, there's something in that," said the admiral; "but, however, he's hardly such a goose, if it were so to happen, to give up the chase--he'd find us out somehow."

"You think he would, sir? or, do you not think that despair would seize upon him, and that, fancying we had all left the spot for ever, he might likewise do so; so that we should lose him more effectually than we have done at present?"

"No; hardly," said the admiral; "he couldn't be such a goose as that. Why, when I was of his age, if I had secured the affections of a young girl like you, I'd have gone over all the world, but I'd have found out where she was; and what I mean to say is, if he's half such a goose as you think him, he deserves to lose you."

"Did you not tell me something, sir, of Mr. Chillingworth talking of taking possession of the Hall for a brief space of time?"

"Why, yes, I did; and I expect he is there now; in fact, I'm sure he's there, for he said he would be."

"No, he ain't," said Jack Pringle, at that moment entering the room; "you're wrong again, as you always are, somehow or other."

"What, you vagabond, are you here, you mutinous rascal?"--"Ay, ay, sir; go on; don't mind me. I wonder what you'd do, sir, if you hadn't somebody like me to go on talking about."

"Why, you infernal rascal, I wonder what you'd do if you had not an indulgent commander, who puts up even with real mutiny, and says nothing about it. But where have you been? Did you go as I directed you, and take some provisions to Bannerworth Hall?"

"Yes, I did; but I brought them back again; there's nobody there, and don't seem likely to be, except a dead body."

"A dead body! Whose body can that be!"--"Tom somebody; for I'm d----d if it ain't a great he cat."

"You scoundrel, how dare you alarm me in such a way? But do you mean to tell me that you did not see Dr. Chillingworth at the Hall?"--"How could I see him, if he wasn't there?"

"But he was there; he said he would be there."--"Then he's gone again, for there's nobody there that I know of in the shape of a doctor. I went through every part of the ship--I mean the house--and the deuce a soul could I find; so as it was rather lonely and uncomfortable, I came away again. 'Who knows,' thought I, 'but some blessed vampyre or another may come across me.'"

"This won't do," said the old admiral, buttoning up his coat to the chin; "Bannerworth Hall must not be deserted in this way. It is quite clear that Sir Francis Varney and his associates have some particular object in view in getting possession of the place. Here, you Jack."--"Ay, ay, sir."

"Just go back again, and stay at the Hall till somebody comes to you. Even such a stupid hound as you will be something to scare away unwelcome visitors. Go back to the Hall, I say. What are you staring at?"--"Back to Bannerworth Hall!" said Jack. "What! just where I've come from; all that way off, and nothing to eat, and, what's worse, nothing to drink. I'll see you d----d first."

The admiral caught up a table-fork, and made a rush at Jack; but Henry Bannerworth interfered.

"No, no," he said, "admiral; no, no--not that. You must recollect that you yourself have given this, no doubt, faithful fellow of your's liberty to do and say a great many things which don't look like good service; but I have no doubt, from what I have seen of his disposition, that he would risk his life rather than, that you should come to any harm."

"Ay, ay," said Jack; "he quite forgets when the bullets were scuttling our nobs off Cape Ushant, when that big Frenchman had hold of him by the skirf of his neck, and began pummelling his head, and the lee scuppers were running with blood, and a bit of Joe Wiggins's brains had come slap in my eye, while some of Jack Marling's guts was hanging round my neck like a nosegay, all in consequence of grape-shot--then he didn't say as I was a swab, when I came up, and bored a hole in the Frenchman's back with a pike. Ay, it's all very well now, when there's peace, and no danger, to call Jack Pringle a lubberly rascal, and mutinous. I'm blessed if it ain't enough to make an old pair of shoes faint away."

"Why, you infernal scoundrel," said the admiral, "nothing of the sort ever happened, and you know it. Jack, you're no seaman."--"Werry good," said Jack; "then, if I ain't no seaman, you are what shore-going people calls a jolly fat old humbug."

"Jack, hold your tongue," said Henry Bannerworth; "you carry these things too far. You know very well that your master esteems you, and you should not presume too much upon that fact."--"My master!" said Jack; "don't call him my master. I never had a master, and don't intend. He's my admiral, if you like; but an English sailor don't like a master."

"I tell you what it is, Jack," said the admiral; "you've got your good qualities, I admit."--"Ay, ay, sir--that's enough; you may as well leave off well while you can."

"But I'll just tell you what you resemble more than anything else."--"Chew me up! what may that be, sir?"

"A French marine."--"A what! A French marine! Good-bye. I wouldn't say another word to you, if you was to pay me a dollar a piece. Of all the blessed insults rolled into one, this here's the worstest. You might have called me a marine, or you might have called me a Frenchman, but to make out that I'm both a marine and a Frenchman, d--me, if it isn't enough to make human nature stand on an end! Now, I've done with you."

"And a good job, too," said the admiral. "I wish I'd thought of it before. You're worse than a third day's ague, or a hot and a cold fever in the tropics."--"Very good," said Jack; "I only hope Providence will have mercy upon you, and keep an eye upon you when I'm gone, otherwise, I wonder what will become of you? It wasn't so when young Belinda, who you took off the island of Antiggy, in the Ingies, jumped overboard, and I went after her in a heavy swell. Howsomdever, never mind, you shook hands with me then; and while a bushel of the briny was weeping out of the corner of each of your blinkers, you says, says you,--"

"Hold!" cried the admiral, "hold! I know what I said, Jack. It's cut a fathom deep in my memory. Give us your fist, Jack, and--and--"--"Hold yourself," said Jack; "I know what you're going to say, and I won't hear you say it--so there's an end of it. Lor bless you! I knows you. I ain't a going to leave you. Don't be afraid; I only works you up, and works you down again, just to see if there's any of that old spirit in you when we was aboard the Victory. Don't you recollect, admiral?"

"Yes--yes; enough, Jack."--"Why, let me see--that was a matter of forty years ago, nearly, when I was a youngster."

"There--there, Jack--that'll do. You bring the events of other years fresh upon my memory. Peace--peace. I have not forgotten; but still, to hear what you know of them, if recited, would give the old man a pang."--"A pang," said Jack; "I suppose that's some dictionary word for a punch in the eye. That would be mutiny with a vengeance; so I'm off."

"Go, go."--"I'm a going; and just to please you, I'll go to the Hall, so you sha'n't say that you told me to do anything that I didn't."

Away went Jack, whistling an air, that might have been popular when he and the admiral were young, and Henry Bannerworth could not but remark that an appearance of great sadness came over the old man, when Jack was gone.

"I fear, sir," he said, "that heedless sailor has touched upon some episode in your existence, the wounds of which are still fresh enough to give you pain."--"It is so," said the old admiral; "just look at me, now. Do I look like the hero of a romantic love story?"

"Not exactly, I admit."--"Well, notwithstanding that, Jack Pringle has touched a chord that vibrates in my heart yet," replied the admiral.

"Have you any objection to tell me of it?"--"None, whatever; and perhaps, by the time I have done, the doctor may have found his way back again, or Jack may bring us some news of him. So here goes for a short, but a true yarn."

CHAPTER LXVII

THE ADMIRAL'S STORY OF THE BEAUTIFUL BELINDA

Just at this moment Flora Bannerworth stole into the room from whence she had departed a short time since; but when she saw that old Admiral Bell was looking so exceedingly serious, and apparently about to address Henry upon some very important subject, she would have retired, but he turned towards her, and said,--

"My story, my dear, I've no objection to your hearing, and, like all women folks, a love story never comes amiss to you; so you may as well stay and hear it."--"A love story," said Flora; "you tell a love story, sir?"

"Yes, my dear, and not only tell it, but be the hero of it, likewise; ain't you astonished?"--"I am, indeed."

"Well, you'll be more astonished then before I've done; so just listen. As Jack Pringle says, it was the matter of about somewhere forty years ago, that I was in command of the Victory frigate, which was placed upon the West Indian station, during a war then raging, for the protection of our ports and harbours in that vicinity. We'd not a strong force in that quarter, therefore, I had to cut about from place to place, and do the best I could. After a time, though, I rather think that we frightened off the enemy, during which time I chiefly anchored off the island of Antigua, and was hospitably received at the house of a planter, of the name of Marchant, who, in fact, made his house my home, and introduced me to all the elite of the society of the island. Ah! Miss Flora, you've no idea, to look at me now, what I was then; I held a captain's commission, and was nearly the youngest man in the service, with such a rank. I was as slender, ay, as a dancing master. These withered and bleached locks were black as the raven's plume. Ay, ay, but no matter: the planter had a daughter."

"And you loved her?" said Flora--"Loved her," said the old man, and the flush of youthful animation come to his countenance; "loved her, do you say! I adored her; I worshipped her; she was to me--but what a d----d old fool, I am; we'll skip that if you please."

"Nay, nay," said Flora; "that is what I want to hear."--"I haven't the least doubt of that, in the world; but that's just what you won't hear; none of your nonsense, Miss Flora; the old man may be a fool, but he isn't quite an idiot."

"He's neither," said Flora; "true feelings can never disgrace any one."--"Perhaps not; but, however, to make a long story short, somehow or other, one day, Belinda was sitting alone, and I rudely pounced upon her; I rather think then I must have said something that I oughtn't to have said, for it took her so aback; I was forced, somehow or other, to hold her up, and then I--I--yes; I'm sure I kissed her; and so, I told her I loved her; and then, what do you think she said?"

"Why," said Flora, "that she reciprocated the passion."--"D--n my rags," said Jack, who at the moment came into the room, "I suppose that's the name of some shell or other."

"You here, you villain!" said the admiral; "I thought you were gone."--"So I was," said Jack, "but I came back for my hat, you see."

Away he went again, and the admiral resumed his story.

"Well, Miss Flora," he said, "you haven't made a good guess, as she didn't say anything at all, she only clung to me like some wild bird to its mother's breast, and cried as if her heart would break."--"Indeed!"

"Yes; I didn't know the cause of her emotion, but at last I got it out of her."--"What was it?"

"Oh, a mere trifle; she was already married to somebody else, that's all; some d----d fellow, who had gone trading about the islands, a fellow she didn't care a straw about, that was old enough to be her father."

"And you left her?"--"No, I didn't. Guess again. I was a mad-headed youngster. I only felt--I didn't think. I persuaded her to come away with me. I took her aboard my ship, and set sail with her. A few weeks flew like hours; but one day we were hailed by a vessel, and when we neared her, she manned a boat and brought a letter on board, addressed to Belinda. It was from her father, written in his last moments. It began with a curse and ended with a blessing. There was a postscript in another hand, to say the old man died of grief. She read it by my side on the quarter-deck. It dropped from her grasp, and she plunged into the sea. Jack Pringle went after her; but I never saw her again."

"Gracious Heavens! what a tragedy!"--"Yes, tolerable," said the old man.

He arose and took his hat and placed it on his head. He gave the crown of it a blow that sent it nearly over his eyes. He thrust his hands deep into his breeches pockets, clenched his teeth, and muttered something inaudible as he strode from the apartment.

"Who would have thought, Henry," said Flora, "that such a man as Admiral Bell had been the hero of such an adventure?"--"Ay, who indeed; but it shows that we never can judge from appearances, Flora; and that those who seem to us the most heart-whole may have experienced the wildest vicissitudes of passion."

"And we must remember, likewise, that this was forty years ago, Henry, which makes a material difference in the state of the case as regards Admiral Bell."

"It does indeed--more than half a lifetime; and yet how evident it was that his old feelings clung to him. I can well imagine the many hours of bitter regret which the memory of this his lost love must have given him."

"True--true. I can feel something for him; for have I not lost one who loved me--a worse loss, too, than that which Admiral Bell relates; for am I not a prey to all the horrors of uncertainty? Whereas he knew the worst, and that, at all events, death had claimed its victim, leaving nothing to conjecture in the shape of suffering, so that the mind had nothing to do but to recover slowly, but surely, as it would from the shock which it had received."

"That is worse than you, Flora; but rather would I have you cherish hope of soon beholding Charles Holland, probably alive and well, than fancy any great disaster has come over him."

"I will endeavour to do so," replied Flora.

"I long to hear what has become of Dr. Chillingworth. His disappearance is most singular; for I fully suspected that he had some particular object in view in getting possession for a short time of Bannerworth Hall; but now, from Jack Pringle's account, he appears not to be in it, and, in fact, to have disappeared completely from the sight of all who knew him."

"Yes," said Flora; "but he may have done that, brother, still in furtherance of his object."

"It may be so, and I will hope that it is so. Keep yourself close, sister, and see no one, while I proceed to his house to inquire if they have heard anything of him. I will return soon, be assured; and, in the meantime, should you see my brother, tell him I shall be at home in an hour or so, and not to leave the cottage; for it is more than likely that the admiral has gone to Bannerworth Hall, so that you may not see anything of him for some time."

CHAPTER LXVIII

MARCHDALE'S ATTEMPTED VILLANY, AND THE RESULT

Varney the vampyre left the dungeon of Charles Holland amid the grey ruins, with a perfect confidence the young man would keep his word, and not attempt to escape from that place until the time had elapsed which he had dictated to him.

And well might he have that confidence, for having once given his word that he would remain until he heard the clock strike two from a neighbouring church, Charles Holland never dreamt for a moment of breaking it.

To be sure it was a weary time to wait when liberty appeared before him; but he was the soul of honour, and the least likely man in all the world to infringe in the slightest upon the condition which he had, of his own free will, acceded to.

Sir Francis Varney walked rapidly until he came nearly to the outskirts of the town, and then he slackened his pace, proceeding more cautiously, and looking carefully about him, as if he feared to meet any one who might recognise him.

He had not proceeded far in this manner, when he became conscious of the cautious figure of a man gliding along in the opposite direction to that which he was taking.

A suspicion struck him, from the general appearance, that it was Marchdale, and if so he wondered to see him abroad at such a time. Still he would not be quite certain; but he hurried forward, so as to meet the advancing figure, and then his suspicions were confirmed; and Marchdale, with some confusion in his looks and manners, accosted him.

"Ah, Sir Francis Varney," he said, "you are out late."--

"Why, you know I should be out late," said Varney, "and you likewise know the errand upon which I was to be out."

"Oh, I recollect; you were to release your prisoner."--

"Yes, I was."

"And have you done so?"--

"Oh, no."

"Oh, indeed. I--I am glad you have taken better thoughts of it. Good night--good night; we shall meet to-morrow."--

"Adieu," said Sir Francis Varney; and he watched the retreating figure of Marchdale, and then he added, in a low tone to himself,--

"I know his object well. His craven spirit shrinks at the notion, a probable enough one, I will admit, that Charles Holland has recognised him, and that, if once free, he would denounce him to the Bannerworths, holding him up to scorn in his true colours, and bringing down upon his head, perhaps, something more than detestation and contempt. The villain! he is going now to take the life of the man whom he considers chained to the ground. Well, well, they must fight it out together. Charles Holland is sufficiently free to take his own part, although Marchdale little thinks that such is the case."

Marchdale walked on for some little distance, and then he turned and looked after Sir Francis Varney.

"Indeed!" he said; "so you have not released him to-night, but I know well will do so soon. I do not, for my part, admire this romantic generosity which sets a fox free at the moment that he's the most dangerous. It's all very well to be generous, but it is better to be just first, and that I consider means looking after one's self first. I have a poniard here which will soon put an end to the troubles of the prisoner in his dungeon--its edge is keen and sharp, and will readily find a way to his heart."

He walked on quite exultingly and carelessly now, for he had got into the open country, and it was extremely unlikely that he would meet anybody on his road to the ruins.

It did not take many minutes, sharp walking now to bring him close to the spot which he intended should become such a scene of treacherous slaughter, and just then he heard from afar off something like the muttering of thunder, as if Heaven itself was proclaiming its vengeance against the man who had come out to slay one of its best and noblest creatures.

"What is that'" said Marchdale, shrinking back a moment; "what is that--an approaching storm? It must be so, for, now I recollect me, the sun set behind a bank of clouds of a fiery redness, and as the evening drew in there was every appearance in the heavens of some ensuing strife of the elements."

He listened for a few moments, and fixed his eyes intently in the direction of the horizon from where the muttering sounds had proceeded.

He had not long to wait before he saw a bright flash of blue lightning, which for one instant illumined the sky; then by the time he could have counted twelve there came the thunder which the flash preceded, and he felt terribly anxious to complete his enterprize, so that he might get back to the town and be safely housed before the storm, which was evidently approaching, should burst upon him.

"It is sweeping on apace," he said; "why did I not come earlier?"

Even as he spoke he plunged among the recesses of the ruins, and searching about for the old stone which covered the entrance to the dungeon, he was surprised to find it rolled from its place, and the aperture open.

"What is the meaning of this?" he said; "how negligent of Sir Francis Varney; or perhaps, after all, he was only jesting with me, and let the prisoner go. If that should be the case, I am foiled indeed; but surely he could not be so full of indiscretion."

Again came a dazzling flash of lightning, which now, surrounded by the ruins as he was, made him shrink back and cover his eyes for a moment; and then followed a peal of thunder with not half the duration of time between it and the flash which had characterized the previous electric phenomenon.

"The storm approaches fast," said Marchdale; "I must get my work done quickly, if indeed my victim be here, which I begin seriously to doubt."

He descended the intricate winding passage to the vault below, which served the purpose of a dungeon, and when he got very nearly into the depth of its recesses, he called aloud, saying,--

"Ho! what ho! is there any one here?"--"Yes," said Charles Holland, who fancied it might be his former visitor returned. "Have you come to repent of your purpose?"

"Ah!" said Marchdale to himself, "Sir Francis, after all, has told me the truth--the prisoner is still here."

The light from without was not near sufficient to send the least ray into the depths of that dungeon; so that Marchdale, when he entered the place, could see nothing but an absolute blackness.

It was not so, however, with Charles Holland, whose eyes had been now so long accustomed to the place that he could see in it as if a dim twilight irradiated it, and he at once, in his visitor, saw his worst foe, and not the man who had comparatively set him free.

He saw, too, that the hand of his visitor grasped a weapon, which Marchdale thought that, favoured by the darkness, he might carry openly in perfect security.

"Where are you?" said Marchdale; "I cannot see you."--"Here!" said Charles, "you may feel my grip;" and he sprung upon him in an instant.

The attack was so sudden and so utterly unexpected, that Marchdale was thrown backwards, and the dagger wrested from his grasp, during the first impulse which Charles Holland had thrown into his attack.

Moreover, his head struck with such violence against the earthern floor, that it produced a temporary confusion of his faculties, so that, had Charles Holland been so inclined, he might, with Marchdale's own weapon, have easily taken his life.

The young man did, on the impulse of the moment, raise it in his hand, but, on the impulse of another thought, he cast it from him, exclaiming--

"No, no! not that; I should be as bad as he, or nearly so. This villain has come to murder me, but yet I will not take his life for the deed. What shall I do with him? Ha! a lucky thought--chains!"

He dragged Marchdale to the identical spot of earth on which he had lain so long; and, as Sir Francis Varney had left the key of the padlock which bound the chains together in it, he, in a few moments, had succeeded in placing the villain Marchdale in the same durance from which he had himself shortly since escaped.

"Remain there," he said, "until some one comes to rescue you. I will not let you starve to death, but I will give you a long fast; and, when I come again, it shall be along with some of the Bannerworth family, to show them what a viper they have fostered in their hearts."

Marchdale was just sufficiently conscious now to feel all the realities of his situation. In vain he attempted to rise from his prostrate position. The chains did their duty, keeping down a villain with the same means that they had held in ignominious confinement a true man.

He was in a perfect agony, inasmuch as he considered that he would be allowed to remain there to starve to death, thus achieving for himself a more horrible death than any he had ever thought of inflicting.

"Villain!" exclaimed Charles Holland, "you shall there remain; and, let you have what mental sufferings you may, you richly deserve them."

He heeded not the cries of Marchdale--he heeded not his imprecations any more than he did his prayers; and the arch hypocrite used both in abundance. Charles was but too happy once more to look upon the open sky, although it was then in darkness, to heed anything that Marchdale, in the agony to which he was now reduced, might feel inclined to say; and, after glancing around him for some few moments, when he was free of the ruins, and inhaling with exquisite delight the free air of the surrounding meadows, he saw, by the twinkling of the lights, in which direction the town lay, and knowing that by taking a line in that path, and then after a time diverging a little to the right, he should come to Bannerworth Hall, he walked on, never in his whole life probably feeling such an enjoyment of the mere fact of existence as at such a moment as that of exquisite liberty.

Our readers may with us imagine what it is to taste the free, fresh air of heaven, after being long pent up, as he, Charles Holland, had been, in a damp, noisome dungeon, teeming with unwholesome exhalations. They may well suppose with what an amount of rapture he now found himself unrestrained in his movements by those galling fetters which had hung for so long a period upon his youthful limbs, and which, not unfrequently in the despair of his heart, he had thought he should surely die in.

And last, although not least in his dear esteem, did the rapturous thought of once more looking in the sweet face of her he loved come cross him with a gush of delight.

"Yes!" he exclaimed, as he quickened his pace; "yes! I shall be able to tell Flora Bannerworth how well and how truly I love her. I shall be able to tell her that, in my weary and hideous imprisonment, the thought alone of her has supported me."

As he neared the Hall, he quickened his pace to such an extent, that soon he was forced to pause altogether, as the exertion he had undertaken pretty plainly told him that the imprisonment, scanty diet, and want of exercise, which had been his portion for some time past, had most materially decreased his strength.

His limbs trembled, and a profuse perspiration bedewed his brow, although the night was rather cold than otherwise.

"I am very weak," he said; "and much I wonder now that I succeeded in overcoming that villain Marchdale; who, if I had not done so, would most assuredly have murdered me."

And it was a wonder; for Marchdale was not an old man, although he might be considered certainly as past the prime of life, and he was of a strong and athletic build. But it was the suddenness of his attack upon him which had given Charles Holland the great advantage, and had caused the defeat of the ruffian who came bent on one of the most cowardly and dastardly murders that could be committed--namely, upon an unoffending man, whom he supposed to be loaded with chains, and incapable of making the least efficient resistance.

Charles soon again recovered sufficient breath and strength to proceed towards the Hall, and now warned, by the exhaustion which had come over him that he had not really anything like strength enough to allow him to proceed rapidly, he walked with slow and deliberate steps.

This mode of proceeding was more favourable to reflection than the wild, rapid one which he had at first adopted, and in all the glowing colours of youthful and ingenious fancy did he depict to himself the surprise and the pleasure that would beam in the countenance of his beloved Flora when she should find him once again by her side.

Of course, he, Charles, could know nothing of the contrivances which had been resorted to, and which the reader may lay wholly to the charge of Marchdale, to blacken his character, and to make him appear faithless to the love he had professed.

Had he known this, it is probable that indignation would have added wings to his progress, and he would not have been able to proceed at the leisurely pace he felt that his state of physical weakness dictated to him.

And now he saw the topmost portion at Bannerworth Hall pushing out from amongst the trees with which the ancient pile was so much surrounded, and the sight of the home of his beloved revived him, and quickened the circulation of the warm blood in his veins.

"I shall behold her now," he said--"I shall behold her how! A few minutes more, and I shall hold her to my heart--that heart which has been ever hers, and which carried her image enshrined in its deepest recesses, even into the gloom of a dungeon!"

But let us, while Charles Holland is indulging in these delightful anticipations--anticipations which, we regret, in consequence of the departure of the Bannerworths from the Hall, will not be realized so soon as he supposes--look back upon the discomfited hypocrite and villain, Marchdale, who occupies his place in the dungeon of the old ruins.

Until Charles Holland actually had left the strange, horrible, and cell-like place, he could scarcely make up his mind that the young man entertained a serious intention of leaving him there.

Perhaps he did not think any one could be so cruel and so wicked as he himself; for the reader will no doubt recollect that his, Marchdale's, counsel to Varney, was to leave Charles Holland to his fate, chained down as he was in the dungeon, and that fate would have been the horrible one of being starved to death in the course of a few days.

When now, however, he felt confident that he was deserted--when he heard the sound of Charles Holland's retreating footsteps slowly dying away in the distance, until not the faintest echo of them reached his ears, he despaired indeed; and the horror he experienced during the succeeding ten minutes, might be considered an ample atonement for some of his crimes. His brain was in a complete whirl; nothing of a tangible nature, but that he was there, chained down, and left to starve to death, came across his intellect. Then a kind of madness, for a moment or two, took possession of him; he made a tremendous effort to burst asunder the bands that held him.

But it was in vain. The chains--which had been placed upon Charles Holland during the first few days of his confinement, when he had a little recovered from the effects of the violence which had been committed upon him at the time when he was captured--effectually resisted Marchdale.

They even cut into his flesh, inflicting upon him some grievous wounds; but that was all he achieved by his great efforts to free himself, so that, after a few moments, bleeding and in great pain, he, with a deep groan, desisted from the fruitless efforts he had better not have commenced.

Then he remained silent for a time, but it was not the silence of reflection; it was that of exhaustion, and, as such, was not likely to last long; nor did it, for, in the course of another five minutes, he called out loudly.

Perhaps he thought there might be a remote chance that some one traversing the meadows would hear him; and yet, if he had duly considered the matter, which he was not in a fitting frame of mind to do, he would have recollected that, in choosing a dungeon among the underground vaults of these ruins, he had, by experiment, made certain that no cry, however loud, from where he lay, could reach the upper air. And thus had this villain, by the very precautions which he had himself taken to ensure the safe custody of another, been his own greatest enemy.

"Help! help! help!" he cried frantically "Varney! Charles Holland! have mercy upon me, and do not leave me here to starve! Help, oh, Heaven! Curses on all your heads--curses! Oh, mercy--mercy--mercy!"

In suchlike incoherent expressions did he pass some hours, until, what with exhaustion and a raging thirst that came over him, he could not utter another word, but lay the very picture of despair and discomfited malice and wickedness.

CHAPTER LXIX

FLORA BANNERWORTH AND HER MOTHER.--THE EPISODE OF CHIVALRY

Gladly we turn from such a man as Marchdale to a consideration of the beautiful and accomplished Flora Bannerworth, to whom we may, without destroying in any way the interest of our plot, predict a much happier destiny than, probably, at that time, she considers as at all likely to be hers.

She certainly enjoyed, upon her first removal from Bannerworth Hall, greater serenity of mind than she had done there; but, as we have already remarked of her, the more her mind was withdrawn, by change of scene, from the horrible considerations which the attack of the vampyre had forced upon her, the more she reverted to the fate of Charles Holland, which was still shrouded in so much gloom.

She would sit and converse with her mother upon that subject until she worked up her feelings to a most uncomfortable pitch of excitement, and then Mrs. Bannerworth would get her younger brother to join them, who would occasionally read to her some compositions of his own, or of some favourite writer whom he thought would amuse her.

It was on the very evening when Sir Francis Varney had made up his mind to release Charles Holland, that young Bannerworth read to his sister and his mother the following little chivalric incident, which he told them he had himself collated from authentic sources:--

"The knight with the green shield," exclaimed one of a party of men-at-arms, who were drinking together at an ancient hostel, not far from Shrewsbury--"the knight with the green shield is as good a knight as ever buckled on a sword, or wore spurs."--"Then how comes it he is not one of the victors in the day's tournament?" exclaimed another.--"By the bones of Alfred!" said a third, "a man must be judged of by his deserts, and not by the partiality of his friends. That's my opinion, friends."--"And mine, too," said another.

"That is all very true, and my opinion would go with yours, too; but not in this instance. Though you may accuse me of partiality, yet I am not so; for I have seen some of the victors of to-day by no means forward in the press of battle-men who, I will not say feared danger, but who liked it not so well but they avoided it as much as possible."

"Ay, marry, and so have I. The reason is, 'tis much easier to face a blunted lance, than one with a spear-head; and a man may practise the one and thrive in it, but not the other; for the best lance in the tournament is not always the best arm in the battle."

"And that is the reason of my saying the knight with the green shield was a good knight. I have seen him in the midst of the melee, when men and horses have been hurled to the ground by the shock; there he has behaved himself like a brave knight, and has more than once been noticed for it."

"But how canne he to be so easily overthrown to-day? That speaks something."--"His horse is an old one."

"So much the better," said another; "he's used to his work, and as cunning as an old man."--"But he has been wounded more than once, and is weakened very much: besides, I saw him lose his footing, else he had overthrown his opponent.

"He did not seem distressed about his accident, at all events, but sat contented in the tent."--"He knows well that those who know him will never attribute his misadventure either to want of courage or conduct; moreover, he seems to be one of those who care but little for the opinion of men who care nothing for him."

"And he's right. Well, dear comrades, the health of Green Knight, or the Knight with a Green Shield, for that's his name, or the designation he chooses to go by."--"A health to the Knight with the Green Shield!" shouted the men-at-arms, as they lifted their cups on high.

"Who is he?" inquired one of the men-at-arms, of him who had spoken favourably of the stranger.--"I don't know."

"And yet you spoke favourably of him a few seconds back, and said what a brave knight he was!"--"And so I uphold him to be; but, I tell you what, friend, I would do as much for the greatest stranger I ever met. I have seen him fight where men and horses have bit the dust in hundreds; and that, in my opinion, speaks out for the man and warrior; he who cannot, then, fight like a soldier, had better tilt at home in the castle-yard, and there win ladies' smiles, but not the commendation of the leader of the battle."

"That's true: I myself recollect very well Sir Hugh de Colbert, a very accomplished knight in the castle-yard; but his men were as fine a set of fellows as ever crossed a horse, to look at, but they proved deficient at the moment of trial; they were broken, and fled in a moment, and scarce one of them received a scratch."

"Then they hadn't stood the shock of the foeman?"--"No; that's certain."

"But still I should like to know the knight,--to know his name very well."--"I know it not; he has some reason for keeping it secret, I suppose; but his deeds will not shame it, be it what it may. I can bear witness to more than one foeman falling beneath his battle-axe."

"Indeed!"--"Yes; and he took a banner from the enemy in the last battle that was fought."

"Ah, well! he deserves a better fortune to-morrow. Who is to be the bridegroom of the beautiful Bertha, daughter of Lord de Cauci?"--"That will have to be decided: but it is presumed that Sir Guthrie de Beaumont is the intended."

"Ah! but should he not prove the victor?"--"It's understood; because it's known he is intended by the parents of the lady, and none would be ungallant enough to prevail against him,--save on such conditions as would not endanger the fruits of victory."

"No?"--"Certainly not; they would lay the trophies at the foot of the beauty worshipped by the knights at the tournament."

"So, triumphant or not, he's to be the bridegroom; bearing off the prize of valour whether or no,--in fact, deserve her or not,--that's the fact."--"So it is, so it is."

"And a shame, too, friends; but so it is now; but yet, if the knight's horse recovers from the strain, and is fit for work to-morrow, it strikes me that the Green Shield will give some work to the holiday knight."

***

There had been a grand tournament held near Shrewsbury Castle, in honour of the intended nuptials of the beautiful Lady Bertha de Cauci. She was the only daughter of the Earl de Cauci, a nobleman of some note; he was one of an ancient and unblemished name, and of great riches.

The lady was beautiful, but, at the same time, she was an unwilling bride,--every one could see that; but the bridegroom cared not for that. There was a sealed sorrow on her brow,--a sorrow that seemed sincere and lasting; but she spoke not of it to any one,--her lips were seldom parted. She loved another. Yes; she loved one who was far away, fighting in the wars of his country,--one who was not so rich in lands as her present bridegroom.

When he left her, she remembered his promise; it was, to fight on till he earned a fortune, or name that should give him some right to claim her hand, even from her imperious father. But alas! he came not; and what could she do against the commands of one who would be obeyed? Her mother, too, was a proud, haughty woman, one whose sole anxiety was to increase the grandeur and power of her house by such connections.

Thus it was pressed on by circumstances, she could no longer hold out, more especially as she heard nothing of her knight. She knew not where he was, or indeed if he were living or dead. She knew not he was never named. This last circumstance, indeed, gave her pain; for it assured her that he whom she loved had been unable to signalize himself from among other men. That, in fact, he was unknown in the annals of fame, as well as the probability that he had been slain in some of the earlier skirmishes of the war. This, if it had happened, caused her some pain to think upon; not but such events were looked upon with almost indifference by females, save in such cases where their affections were engaged, as on this occasion. But the event was softened by the fact that men were continually falling by the hand of man in such encounters, but at the same time it was considered an honourable and praiseworthy death for a soldier. He was wounded, but not with the anguish we now hear of; for the friends were consoled by the reflection that the deceased warrior died covered with glory.

Bertha, however, was young, and as yet she knew not the cause of her absent knight's silence, or why he had not been heard of among the most forward in the battle.

"Heaven's will be done," she exclaimed; "what can I do? I must submit to my father's behests; but my future life will be one of misery and sorrow."

She wept to think of the past, and to dream of the future; both alike were sorrowful to think upon--no comfort in the past and no joy in the future.

Thus she wept and sorrowed on the night of the first tournament; there was to be a second, and that was to be the grand one, where her intended bridegroom was to show himself off in her eyes, and take his part in the sport.

***

Bertha sat late--she sat sorrowing by the light of the lamps and the flickering flame of the fire, as it rose and fell on the hearth and threw dancing shadows on the walls.

"Oh, why, Arthur Home, should you thus be absent? Absent, too, at such a time when you are more needed than ever. Alas, alas! you may no longer be in the land of the living. Your family is great and your name known--your own has been spoken with commendation from the lips of your friend; what more of fame do you need? but I am speaking without purpose. Heaven have mercy on me."

As she spoke she looked up and saw one of her women in waiting standing by.

"Well, what would you?"--"My lady, there is one who would speak with you," said the handmaiden.

"With me?"--"Yes, my lady; he named you the Lady Bertha de Cauci."

"Who and what is he?" she inquired, with something like trepidation, of the maiden.--"I know not, my lady."

"But gave he not some token by which I might know who I admit to my chamber?"--"None," replied the maiden.

"And what does he bear by way of distinguishing himself? What crest or device doth he bear?"--"Merely a green shield."

"The unsuccessful knight in the tournament to-day. Heaven's! what can he desire with me; he is not--no, no, it cannot be--it cannot be."--"Will you admit him, lady?"

"Indeed, I know not what to do; but yet he may have some intelligence to give me. Yes, yes, admit him; but first throw some logs on the fire."

The attendant did as she was desired, and then quitted the room for the purpose of admitting the stranger knight with the green shield. In a few moments she could hear the stride of the knight as he entered the apartment, and she thought the step was familiar to her ear--she thought it was the step of Sir Arthur Home, her lover. She waited anxiously to see the door open, and then the stranger entered. His form and bearing was that of her lover, but his visor was down, and she was unable to distinguish the features of the stranger.

His armour was such as had seen many a day's hard wear, and there were plenty of marks of the battle about him. His travel-worn accoutrements were altogether such as bespoke service in the field.

"Sir, you desired to see me; say wherefore you do so, and if it is news you bring." The knight answered not, but pointed to the female attendant, as if he desired she would withdraw. "You may retire," said Bertha; "be within call, and let me know if I am threatened with interruption."

The attendant retired, and then the knight and lady were left alone. The former seemed at a loss how to break silence for some moments, and then he said,--

"Lady ----" "Oh, Heavens! 'tis he!" exclaimed Bertha, as she sprang to her feet; "it is Sir Arthur Home!"

"It is," exclaimed the knight, pulling up his visor, and dropping on one knee he encircled his arm round the waist of the lady, and at the same moment he pressed her lips to his own.

The first emotion of joy and surprise over, Bertha checked her transports, and chid the knight for his boldness.

"Nay, chide me not, dear Bertha; I am what I was when I left you, and hope to find you the same."

"Am I not?" said Bertha.--"Truly I know not, for you seem more beautiful than you were then; I hope that is the only change."

"If there be a change, it is only such as you see. Sorrow and regret form the principal causes."--"I understand you."

"My intended nuptials ----" "Yes, I have heard all. I came here but late in the morning; and my horse was jaded and tired, and my impatience to attend the tournament caused me a disaster which it is well it came not on the second day."

"It is, dear Arthur. How is it I never heard your name mentioned, or that I received no news from any one about you during the wars that have ended?"--"I had more than one personal enemy, Bertha; men who would have been glad to see me fall, and who, in default of that, would not have minded bribing an assassin to secure my death for them at any risk whatever."

"Heavens! and how did you escape such a death from such people, Arthur?"--"By adopting such a device as that I wear. The Knight of the Green Shield I'm called."

"I saw you to-day in the tournament."--"And there my tired and jaded horse gave way; but to-morrow I shall have, I hope, a different fortune."

"I hope so too."--"I will try; my arm has been good in battle, and I see not why it should be deficient in peaceful jousts."

"Certainly not. What fortune have you met with since you left England?"--"I was of course known but to a few; among those few were the general under whom I served and my more immediate officers, who I knew would not divulge my secret."

"And they did not?"--"No; kept it nobly, and kept their eyes upon me in battle; and I have reaped a rich harvest in force, honour, and riches, I assure you."

"Thank Heaven!" said Bertha.--"Bertha, if I be conqueror, may I claim you in the court-yard before all the spectators?"

"You may," said Bertha, and she hung her head.--"Moreover," said Sir Arthur, "you will not make a half promise, but when I demand you, you will at once come down to me and accept me as your husband; if I be the victor then he cannot object to the match."

"But he will have many friends, and his intended bride will have many more, so that you may run some danger among so many enemies."--"Never fear for me, Bertha, because I shall have many friends of distinction there too--many old friends who are tried men in battle, and whose deeds are a glory and honour to them; besides, I shall have my commander and several gentlemen who would at once interfere in case any unfair advantage was attempted to be taken of my supposed weakness."

"Have you a fresh horse?" inquired Bertha.--"I have, or shall have by the morning; but promise me you will do what I ask you, and then my arm will be nerved to its utmost, and I am sure to be victorious."

"I do promise," said Bertha; "I hope you may be as successful as you hope to be, Arthur; but suppose fortune should declare against you; suppose an accident of any kind were to happen, what could be done then?"--"I must be content to hide myself for ever afterwards, as a defeated knight; how can I appear before your friends as the claimant of your hand?"

"I will never have any other."--"But you will be forced to accept this Guthrie de Beaumont, your father's chosen son-in-law."

"I will seek refuge in a cloister."--"Will you fly with me, Bertha, to some sequestered spot, where we can live in each others society?"

"Yes," said Bertha, "anything, save marriage with Guthrie de Beaumont."--"Then await the tournament of to-morrow," said Sir Arthur, "and then this may be avoided; in the meantime, keep up a good heart and remember I am at hand."

***

These two lovers parted for the present, after a protracted interview, Bertha to her chamber, and the Knight of the Green Shield to his tent.

The following morning was one of great preparation; the lists had been enlarged, and the seats made more commodious, for the influx of visitors appeared to be much greater than had been anticipated.

Moreover, there were many old warriors of distinction to be present, which made the bridegroom look pale and feel uncomfortable as to the results of the tournament. The tilting was to begin at an early hour, and then the feasting and revelry would begin early in the evening, after the tilting had all passed off.

In that day's work there were many thrown from their saddles, and many broke their lances. The bridegroom tilted with several knights, and came off victorious, or without disadvantage to either.

The green knight, on the contrary, tilted with but few, and always victorious, and such matches were with men who had been men of some name in the wars, or at least in the tilt yard.

The sports drew to a close, and when the bridegroom became the challenger, the Knight of the Green Shield at once rode out quietly to meet him. The encounter could not well be avoided, and the bridegroom would willingly have declined the joust with a knight who had disposed of his enemies so easily, and so unceremoniously as he had.

The first encounter was enough; the bridegroom was thrown to a great distance, and lay insensible on the ground, and was carried out of the field. There was an immediate sensation among the friends of the bridegroom, several of whom rode out to challenge the stranger knight for his presumption.

In this, however, they had misreckoned the chances, for the challenged accepted their challenges with alacrity and disposed of them one by one with credit to himself until the day was concluded. The stranger was then asked to declare who he was, upon which he lifted his visor, and said,

"I am Sir Arthur Home, and claim the Lady Bertha as my bride, by the laws of arms, and by those of love."

***

Again the tent was felled, and again the hostelry was tenanted by the soldier, who declared for one side and then for the other, as the cups clanged and jingled together.

"Said I not," exclaimed one of the troopers, "that the knight with a green shield was a good knight?"--"You did," replied the other.

"And you knew who he was?" said another of the troopers.--"Not I, comrades; I had seen him fight in battle, and, therefore, partly guessed how it would be if he had any chance with the bridegroom. I'm glad he has won the lady."

It was true, the Lady Bertha was won, and Sir Arthur Home claimed his bride, and then they attempted to defeat his claim; yet Bertha at once expressed herself in his favour, to strongly that they were, however reluctantly compelled, to consent at last.

At this moment, a loud shout as from a multitude of persons came upon their ears and Flora started from her seat in alarm. The cause of the alarm we shall proceed to detail.

CHAPTER LXX

THE FUNERAL OF THE STRANGER OF THE INN.--THE POPULAR COMMOTION, AND MRS. CHILLINGWORTH'S APPEAL TO THE MOB.--THE NEW RIOT.--THE HALL IN DANGER

As yet the town was quiet; and, though there was no appearance of riot or disturbance, yet the magistracy had taken every precaution they deemed needful, or their position and necessities warranted, to secure the peace of the town from the like disturbance to that which had been, of late, a disgrace and terror of peaceably-disposed persons.

The populace were well advertised of the fact, that the body of the stranger was to be buried that morning in their churchyard; and that, to protect the body, should there be any necessity for so doing, a large body of constables would be employed.

There was no disposition to riot; at least, none was visible. It looked as if there was some event about to take place that was highly interesting to all parties, who were peaceably assembling to witness the interment of nobody knew who.

The early hour at which persons were assembling, at different points, clearly indicated that there was a spirit of curiosity about the town, so uncommon that none would have noticed it but for the fact of the crowd of people who hung about the streets, and there remained, listless and impatient.

The inn, too, was crowded with visitors, and there were many who, not being blessed with the strength of purse that some were, were hanging about in the distance, waiting and watching the motions of those who were better provided.

"Ah!" said one of the visitors, "this is a disagreeable job in your house, landlord."--"Yes, sir; I'd sooner it had happened elsewhere, I assure you. I know it has done me no good."

"No; no man could expect any, and yet it is none the less unfortunate for that."--"I would sooner anything else happen than that, whatever it might be. I think it must be something very bad, at all events; but I dare say I shall never see the like again."

"So much the better for the town," said another; "for, what with vampyres and riots, there has been but little else stirring than mischief and disturbances of one kind and another."

"Yes; and, what between Varneys and Bannerworths, we have had but little peace here."

"Precisely. Do you know it's my opinion that the least thing would upset the whole town. Any one unlucky word would do it, I am sure," said a tall thin man.

"I have no doubt of it," said another; "but I hope the military would do their duty under such circumstances, for people's lives and property are not safe in such a state of things."--"Oh, dear no."

"I wonder what has become of Varney, or where he can have gone to."--"Some thought he must have been burned when they burned his house," replied the landlord.

"But I believe it generally understood he's escaped, has he not? No traces of his body were found in the ruins."--"None. Oh! he's escaped, there can be no doubt of that. I wish I had some fortune depending upon the fact; it would be mine, I am sure."

"Well, the lord keep us from vampyres and suchlike cattle," said an old woman. "I shall never sleep again in my bed with any safety. It frightens one out of one's life to think of it. What a shame the men didn't catch him and stake him!"

The old woman left the inn as soon as she had spoke this Christian speech.

"Humane!" said a gentleman, with a sporting coat on. "The old woman is no advocate for half measures!"

"You are right, sir," said the landlord; "and a very good look-out she keeps upon the pot, to see it's full, and carefully blows the froth off!"--"Ah! I thought as much."

"How soon will the funeral take place, landlord?" inquired a person, who had at that moment entered the inn.--"In about an hour's time, sir."

"Oh! the town seems pretty full, though it is very quiet. I suppose it is more as a matter of curiosity people congregate to see the funeral of this stranger?"

"I hope so, sir."

"The time is wearing on, and if they don't make a dust, why then the military will not be troubled."

"I do not expect anything more, sir," said the landlord; "for you see they must have had their swing out, as the saying is, and be fully satisfied. They cannot have much more to do in the way of exhibiting their anger or dislike to vampyres--they all have done enough."

"So they have--so they have."

"Granted," said an old man with a troublesome cough; "but when did you ever know a mob to be satisfied? If they wanted the moon and got it, they'd find out it would be necessary to have the stars also."

"That's uncommonly true," said the landlord. "I shouldn't be surprised if they didn't do something worse than ever."--"Nothing more likely," said the little old man. "I can believe anything of a mob--anything--no matter what."

The inn was crowded with visitors, and several extra hands were employed to wait upon the customers, and a scene of bustle and activity was displayed that was never before seen. It would glad the heart of a landlord, though he were made of stone, and landlords are usually of much more malleable materials than that.

However, the landlord had hardly time to congratulate himself, for the bearers were come now, and the undertaker and his troop of death-following officials.

There was a stir among the people, who began now to awaken from the lethargy that seemed to have come over them while they were waiting for the moment when it should arrive, that was to place the body under the green sod, against which so much of their anger had been raised. There was a decent silence that pervaded the mob of individuals who had assembled.

Death, with all its ghastly insignia, had an effect even upon the unthinking multitude, who were ever ready to inflict death or any violent injury upon any object that came in their way--they never hesitated; but even these, now the object of their hatred was no more, felt appalled.

'Tis strange what a change comes over masses of men as they gaze upon a dead body. It may be that they all know that to that complexion they must come at last. This may be the secret of the respect offered to the dead.

The undertakers are men, however, who are used to the presence of death--it is their element; they gain a living by attending upon the last obsequies of the dead; they are used to dead bodies, and care not for them. Some of them are humane men, that is, in their way; and even among them are men who wouldn't be deprived of the joke as they screwed down the last screw. They could not forbear, even on this occasion, to hold their converse when left alone.

"Jacobs," said one who was turning a long screw, "Jacobs, my boy, do you take the chair to-night?"--"Yes," said Jacobs who was a long lugubrious-looking man, "I do take the chair, if I live over this blessed event."

"You are not croaking, Jacobs, are you? Well, you are a lively customer, you are."--"Lively--do you expect people to be lively when they are full dressed for a funeral? You are a nice article for your profession. You don't feel like an undertaker, you don't."

"Don't, Jacobs, my boy. As long as I look like one when occasion demands; when I have done my job I puts my comfort in my pocket, and thinks how much more pleasanter it is to be going to other people's funerals than to our own, and then only see the difference as regards the money."

"True," said Jacobs with a groan; "but death's a melancholy article, at all events."--"So it is."

"And then when you come to consider the number of people we have buried--how many have gone to their last homes--and how many more will go the same way."--"Yes, yes; that's all very well, Jacob. You are precious surly this morning. I'll come to-night. You're brewing a sentimental tale as sure as eggs is eggs."

"Well, that is pretty certain; but as I was saying how many more are there--"

"Ah, don't bother yourself with calculations that have neither beginning nor end, and which haven't one point to go. Come, Jacob, have you finished yet?"--"Quite," said Jacob.

They now arranged the pall, and placed all in readiness, and returned to a place down stairs where they could enjoy themselves for an odd half hour, and pass that time away until the moment should arrive when his reverence would be ready to bury the deceased, upon consideration of the fees to be paid upon the occasion.

The tap-room was crowded, and there was no room for the men, and they were taken into the kitchen, where they were seated, and earnestly at work, preparing for the ceremony that had so shortly to be performed.

"Any better, Jacobs?"--"What do you mean?" inquired Jacobs, with a groan. "It's news to me if I have been ill."

"Oh, yes, you were doleful up stairs, you know."--"I've a proper regard for my profession--that's the difference between you and I, you know."

"I'll wager you what you like, now, that I'll handle a corpse and drive a screw in a coffin as well as you, now, although you are so solid and miserable."--"So you may--so you may."

"Then what do you mean by saying I haven't a proper regard for my profession?"--"I say you haven't, and there's the thing that shall prove it--you don't look it, and that's the truth."

"I don't look like an undertaker! indeed I dare say I don't if I ain't dressed like one."--"Nor when you are," reiterated Jacob.

"Why not, pray?"--"Because you have always a grin on your face as broad as a gridiron--that's why."

This ended the dispute, for the employer of the men suddenly put his head in, saying,--

"Come, now, time's up; you are wanted up stairs, all of you. Be quick; we shall have his reverence waiting for us, and then we shall lose his recommendation."

"Ready sir," said the round man, taking up his pint and finishing it off at a draught, at the same moment he thrust the remains of some bread and cheese into his pocket.

Jacob, too, took his pot, and, having finished it, with great gravity followed the example of his more jocose companion, and they all left the kitchen for the room above, where the corpse was lying ready for interment.

There was an unusual bustle; everybody was on the tip-top of expectation, and awaiting the result in a quiet hurry, and hoped to have the first glimpse of the coffin, though why they should do so it was difficult to define. But in this fit of mysterious hope and expectation they certainly stood.

"Will they be long?" inquired a man at the door of one inside,--"will they be long before they come?"--"They are coming now," said the man. "Do you all keep quiet; they are knocking their heads against the top of the landing. Hark! There, I told you so."

The man departed, hearing something, and being satisfied that he had got some information.

"Now, then," said the landlord, "move out of the way, and allow the corpse to pass out. Let me have no indecent conduct; let everything be as it should be."

The people soon removed from the passage and vicinity of the doorway, and then the mournful procession--as the newspapers have it--moved forward. They were heard coming down stairs, and thence along the passage, until they came to the street, and then the whole number of attendants was plainly discernible.

How different was the funeral of one who had friends. He was alone; none followed, save the undertaker and his attendants, all of whom looked solemn from habit and professional motives. Even the jocose man was as supernaturally solemn as could be well imagined; indeed, nobody knew he was the same man.

"Well," said the landlord, as he watched them down the street, as they slowly paced their way with funereal, not sorrowful, solemnity--"well, I am very glad that it is all over."

"It has been a sad plague to you," said one.

"It has, indeed; it must be to any one who has had another such a job as this. I don't say it out of any disrespect to the poor man who is dead and gone--quite the reverse; but I would not have such another affair on my hands for pounds."

"I can easily believe you, especially when we come to consider the disagreeables of a mob."

"You may say that. There's no knowing what they will or won't do, confound them! If they'd act like men, and pay for what they have, why, then I shouldn't care much about them; but it don't do to have other people in the bar."

"I should think not, indeed; that would alter the scale of your profits, I reckon."

"It would make all the difference to me. Business," added the landlord, "conducted on that scale, would become a loss; and a man might as well walk into a well at once."

"So I should say. Have many such occurrences as these been usual in this part of the country?" inquired the stranger.

"Not usual at all," said the landlord; "but the fact is, the whole neighbourhood has run distracted about some superhuman being they call a vampyre."

"Indeed!"--"Yes; and they suspected the unfortunate man who has been lying up-stairs, a corpse, for some days."

"Oh, the man they have just taken in the coffin to bury?" said the stranger.

"Yes, sir, the same."

"Well, I thought perhaps somebody of great consequence had suddenly become defunct."--"Oh, dear no; it would not have caused half the sensation; people have been really mad."

"It was a strange occurrence, altogether, I believe, was it?" inquired the stranger.--"Indeed it was, sir. I hardly know the particulars, there have been so many tales afloat; though they all concur in one point, and that is, it has destroyed the peace of one family."

"Who has done so?"--"The vampyre."

"Indeed! I never heard of such an animal, save as a fable, before; it seems to me extraordinary."

"So it would do to any one, sir, as was not on the spot, to see it; I'm sure I wouldn't."

***

In the meantime, the procession, short as it was of itself, moved along in slow time through a throng of people who ran out of their houses on either side of the way, and lined the whole length of the town.

Many of these closed in behind, and followed the mourners until they were near the church, and then they made a rush to get into the churchyard.

As yet all had been conducted with tolerable propriety, the funeral met with no impediment. The presence of death among so many of them seemed some check upon the licence of the mob, who bowed in silence to the majesty of death.

Who could bear ill-will against him who was now no more? Man, while he is man, is always the subject of hatred, fear, or love. Some one of these passions, in a modified state, exists in all men, and with such feelings they will regard each other; and it is barely possible that any one should not be the object of some of these, and hence the stranger's corpse was treated with respect.

In silence the body proceeded along the highway until it came to the churchyard, and followed by an immense multitude of people of all grades.

The authorities trembled; they knew not what all this portended. They thought it might pass off; but it might become a storm first; they hoped and feared by turns, till some of them fell sick with apprehension.

There was a deep silence observed by all those in the immediate vicinity of the coffin, but those farther in the rear found full expression for their feelings.

"Do you think," said an old man to another, "that he will come to life again, eh?"--"Oh, yes, vampyres always do, and lay in the moonlight, and then they come to life again. Moonlight recovers a vampyre to life again."

"And yet the moonlight is cold."--"Ah, but who's to tell what may happen to a vampyre, or what's hot or what's cold?"

"Certainly not; oh, dear, no."--"And then they have permission to suck the blood of other people, to live themselves, and to make other people vampyres, too."

"The lord have mercy upon us!"--"Ay, but they have driven a stake through this one, and he can't get in moonlight or daylight; it's all over--he's certainly done for; we may congratulate ourselves on this point."

"So we may--so we may."

They now neared the grave, the clergyman officiating as usual on such occasions. There was a large mob of persons on all sides, with serious faces, watching the progress of the ceremony, and who listened in quietness.

There was no sign of any disturbance amongst the people, and the authorities were well pleased; they congratulated themselves upon the quietness and orderliness of the assemblage.

The service was ended and the coffin lowered, and the earth was thrown on the coffin-lid with a hollow sound. Nobody could hear that sound unmoved. But in a short while the sound ceased as the grave became filled; it was then trodden carefully down.

There were no relatives there to feel affected at the last scene of all. They were far away, and, according to popular belief upon the subject, they must have been dead some ages.

***

The mob watched the last shovel-full of earth thrown upon the coffin, and witnessed the ramming down of the soil, and the heaping of it over at top to make the usual monument; for all this was done speedily and carefully, lest there should be any tendency to exhume the body of the deceased.

The people were now somewhat relieved, as to their state of solemnity and silence. They would all of them converse freely on the matter that had so long occupied their thoughts.

They seemed now let loose, and everybody found himself at liberty to say or do something, no matter if it were not very reasonable; that is not always required of human beings who have souls, or, at least it is unexpected; and were it expected, the expectation would never be realized.

The day was likely to wear away without a riot, nay, even without a fight; a most extraordinary occurrence for such a place under the existing circumstances; for of late the populace, or, perhaps, the townspeople, were extremely pugnacious, and many were the disputes that were settled by the very satisfactory application of the knuckles to the head of the party holding a contrary opinion.

Thus it was they were ready to take fire, and a hubbub would be the result of the slightest provocation. But, on the present occasion, there was a remarkable dearth of, all subjects of the nature described.

Who was to lead Israel out to battle? Alas! no one on the present occasion.

Such a one, however, appeared, at least, one who furnished a ready excuse for a disturbance.

Suddenly, Mrs Chillingworth appeared in the midst of a large concourse of people. She had just left her house, which was close at hand, her eyes red with weeping, and her children around her on this occasion.

The crowd made way for her, and gathered round her to see what was going to happen.

"Friends and neighbours," she said "can any of you relieve the tears of a distressed wife and mother, have any of you seen anything of my husband, Mr. Chillingworth?"

"What the doctor?" exclaimed one.--"Yes; Mr. Chillingworth, the surgeon. He has not been home two days and a night. I'm distracted!--what can have become of him I don't know, unless--"

Here Mrs Chillingworth paused, and some person said,--

"Unless what, Mrs Chillingworth? there are none but friends here, who wish the doctor well, and would do anything to serve him--unless what? speak out."

"Unless he's been destroyed by the vampyre. Heaven knows what we may all come to! Here am I and my children deprived of our protector by some means which we cannot imagine. He never, in all his life, did the same before."

"He must have been spirited away by some of the vampyres. I'll tell you what, friend," said one to another, "that something must be done; nobody's safe in their bed."

"No; they are not, indeed. I think that all vampyres ought to be burned and a stake run through them, and then we should be safe."

"Ay; but you must destroy all those who are even suspected of being vampyres, or else one may do all the mischief."--"So he might."

"Hurrah!" shouted the mob. "Chillingworth for ever! We'll find the doctor somewhere, if we pull down the whole town."

There was an immense commotion among the populace, who began to start throwing stones, and do all sorts of things without any particular object, and some, as they said, to find the doctor, or to show how willing they were to do so if they knew how.

Mrs. Chillingworth, however, kept on talking to the mob, who continued shouting; and the authorities anticipated an immediate outbreak of popular opinion, which is generally accompanied by some forcible demonstration, and on this occasion some one suggested the propriety of burning down Bannerworth Hall; because they had burned down the vampyre's home, and they might as well burn down that of the injured party, which was carried by acclamation; and with loud shouts they started on their errand.

This was a mob's proceeding all over, and we regret very much to say, that it is very much the characteristic of English mobs. What an uncommonly strange thing it is that people in multitudes seem completely to get rid of all reason--all honour--all common ordinary honesty; while, if you were to take the same people singly, you would find that they were reasonable enough, and would shrink with a feeling quite approaching to horror from anything in the shape of very flagrant injustice.

This can only be accounted for by a piece of cowardice in the human race, which induces them when alone, and acting with the full responsibility of their actions, to shrink from what it is quite evident they have a full inclination to do, and will do when, having partially lost their individuality in a crowd, they fancy, that to a certain extent they can do so with impunity.

The burning of Sir Francis Varney's house, although it was one of those proceedings which would not bear the test of patient examination, was yet, when we take all the circumstances into consideration, an act really justifiable and natural in comparison with the one which was now meditated.

Bannerworth Hall had never been the residence even of anyone who had done the people any injury or given them any offence, so that to let it become a prey to the flames was but a gratuitous act of mischief.

It was, however, or seemed to be, doomed, for all who have had any experience in mobs, must know how extremely difficult it is to withdraw them from any impulse once given, especially when that impulse, as in the present instance, is of a violent character.

"Down with Bannerworth Hall!" was the cry. "Burn it--burn it," and augmented by fresh numbers each minute, the ignorant, and, in many respects, ruffianly assemblage, soon arrived within sight of what had been for so many years the bane of the Bannerworths, and whatever may have been the fault of some of that race, those faults had been of a domestic character, and not at all such as would interfere with the public weal.

The astonished, and almost worn-out authorities, hastily, now, after having disposed of their prisoners, collected together what troops they could, and by the time the misguided, or rather the not guided at all populace, had got halfway to Bannerworth Hall, they were being outflanked by some of the dragoons, who, by taking a more direct route, hoped to reach Bannerworth Hall first, and so perhaps, by letting the mob see that it was defended, induce them to give up the idea of its destruction on account of the danger attendant upon the proceeding by far exceeding any of the anticipated delight of the disturbance.

CHAPTER LXXI

THE STRANGE MEETING AT THE HALL BETWEEN MR. CHILLINGWORTH AND THE MYSTERIOUS FRIEND OF VARNEY

When we praise our friend Mr. Chillingworth for not telling his wife where he was going, in pursuance of a caution and a discrimination so highly creditable to him, we are quite certain that he has no such excuse as regards the reader. Therefore we say at once that he had his own reasons now for taking up his abode at Bannerworth Hall for a time. These reasons seemed to be all dependant upon the fact of having met the mysterious man at Sir Francis Varney's; and although we perhaps would have hoped that the doctor might have communicated to Henry Bannerworth all that he knew and all that he surmised, yet have we no doubt that what he keeps to himself he has good reasons for so keeping, and that his actions as regards it are founded upon some very just conclusions.

He has then made a determination to take possession of, and remain in, Bannerworth Hall according to the full and free leave which the admiral had given him so to do. What results he anticipated from so lonely and so secret a watch we cannot say, but probably they will soon exhibit themselves. It needed no sort of extraordinary discrimination for any one to feel it once that not the least good, in the way of an ambuscade, was likely to be effected by such persons as Admiral Bell or Jack Pringle. They were all very well when fighting should actually ensue, but they both were certainly remarkably and completely deficient in diplomatic skill, or in that sort of patience which should enable them at all to compete with the cunning, the skill, and the nice discrimination of such a man as Sir Francis Varney.

If anything were to be done in that way it was unquestionably to be done by some one alone, who, like the doctor, would, and could, remain profoundly quiet and await the issue of events, be they what they might, and probably remain a spy and attempt no overt act which should be of a hostile character. This unquestionably was the mode, and perhaps we should not be going too far when we say it was the only mode which could be with anything like safety relied upon as one likely to lead really to a discovery of Sir Francis Varney's motives in making such determined exertions to get possession of Bannerworth Hall.

That night was doomed to be a very eventful one, indeed; for on it had Charles Holland been, by a sort of wild impulsive generosity of Sir Francis Varney, rescued from the miserable dungeon in which he had been confined, and on that night, too, he, whom we cannot otherwise describe than as the villain Marchdale, had been, in consequence of the evil that he himself meditated, and the crime with which he was quite willing to stain his soul, been condemned to occupy Charles's position.

On that night, too, had the infuriated mob determined upon the destruction of Bannerworth Hall, and on that night was Mr. Chillingworth waiting with what patience he could exert, at the Hall, for whatever in the chapter of accidents might turn up of an advantageous character to that family in whose welfare and fortunes he felt so friendly and so deep an interest.

Let us look, then, at the worthy doctor as he keeps his solitary watch.

He did not, as had been the case when the admiral shared the place with him in the hope of catching Varney on that memorable occasion when he caught only his boot, sit in a room with a light and the means and appliances for making the night pass pleasantly away; but, on the contrary, he abandoned the house altogether, and took up a station in that summer-house which has been before mentioned as the scene of a remarkable interview between Flora Bannerworth and Varney the vampyre.

Alone and in the dark, so that he could not be probably seen, he watched that one window of the chamber where the first appearance of the hideous vampyre had taken place, and which seemed ever since to be the special object of his attack.

By remaining from twilight, and getting accustomed to the gradually increasing darkness of the place, no doubt the doctor was able to see well enough without the aid of any artificial light whether any one was in the place besides himself.

"Night after night," he said, "will I watch here until I have succeeded in unravelling this mystery; for that there is some fearful and undreamt of mystery at the bottom of all these proceedings I am well convinced."

When he made such a determination as this, Dr. Chillingworth was not at all a likely man to break it, so there, looking like a modern statue in the arbour, he sat with his eyes fixed upon the balcony and the window of what used to be called Flora's room for some hours.

The doctor was a contemplative man, and therefore he did not so acutely feel the loneliness of his position as many persons would have done; moreover, he was decidedly not of a superstitious turn of mind, although certainly we cannot deny an imagination to him. However, if he really had harboured some strange fears and terrors they would have been excusable, when we consider how many circumstances had combined to make it almost a matter of demonstration that Sir Francis Varney was something more than mortal.

What quantities of subjects the doctor thought over during his vigil in that garden it is hard to say, but never in his whole life, probably, had he such a glorious opportunity for the most undisturbed contemplation of subjects requiring deep thought to analyze, than as he had then. At least he felt that since his marriage he had never been so thoroughly quiet, and left so completely to himself.

It is to be hoped that he succeeded in settling any medical points of a knotty character that might be hovering in his brain, and certain it is that he had become quite absorbed in an abstruse matter connected with physiology, when his ears were startled, and he was at once aroused to a full consciousness of where he was, and why he had come there, by the distant sound of a man's footstep.

It was a footstep which seemed to be that of a person who scarcely thought it at all necessary to use any caution, and the doctor's heart leaped within him as in the lowest possible whisper he said to himself,--

"I am successful--I am successful. It is believed now that the Hall is deserted, and no doubt that is Sir Francis Varney come with confidence, to carry out his object in so sedulously attacking it, be that object what it may."

Elated with this idea, the doctor listened intently to the advancing footstep, which each moment sounded more clearly upon his ears.

It was evidently approaching from the garden entrance towards the house, and he thought, by the occasional deadened sound of the person's feet, be he whom he might, that he could not see his way very well, and, consequently, frequently strayed from the path, on to some of the numerous flower-beds which were in the way.

"Yes," said the doctor, exultingly, "it must be Varney; and now I have but to watch him, and not to resist him; for what good on earth is it to stop him in what he wishes to do, and, by such means, never wrest his secret from him. The only way is to let him go on, and that will I do, most certainly."

Now he heard the indistinct muttering of the voice of some one, so low that he could not catch what words were uttered; but he fancied that, in the deep tones, he recognised, without any doubt, the voice of Sir Francis Varney.

"It must be he," he said, "it surely must be he. Who else would come here to disturb the solitude of an empty house? He comes! he comes!"

Now the doctor could see a figure emerge from behind some thick beeches, which had before obstructed his vision, and he looked scrutinisingly about, while some doubts stole slowly over his mind now as to whether it was the vampyre or not. The height was in favour of the supposition that it was none other than Varney; but the figure looked so much stouter, that Mr. Chillingworth felt a little staggered upon the subject, and unable wholly to make up his mind upon it.

The pausing of this visitor, too, opposite that window where Sir Francis Varney had made his attempts, was another strong reason why the doctor was inclined to believe it must be him, and yet he could not quite make up his mind upon the subject, so as to speak with certainty.

A very short time, however, indeed, must have sufficed to set such a question as that at rest; and patience seemed the only quality of mind necessary under those circumstances for Mr. Chillingworth to exert.

The visitor continued gazing either at that window, or at the whole front of the house, for several minutes, and then he turned away from a contemplation of it, and walked slowly along, parallel with the windows of that dining-room, one of which had been broken so completely on the occasion of the admiral's attempt to take the vampyre prisoner.

The moment the stranger altered his position, from looking at the window, and commenced walking away from it, Mr. Chillingworth's mind was made up. It was not Varney--of that he felt now most positively assured, and could have no doubt whatever upon the subject.

The gait, the general air, the walk, all were different; and then arose the anxious question of who could it be that had intruded upon that lonely place, and what could be the object of any one else but Varney the vampyre to do so.

The stranger looked a powerful man, and walked with a firm tread, and, altogether he was an opponent that, had the doctor been ever so belligerently inclined, it would have been the height of indiscretion for him to attempt to cope with.

It was a very vexatious thing, too, for any one to come there at such a juncture, perhaps only from motives of curiosity, or possibly just to endeavour to commit some petty depredations upon the deserted building, if possible; and most heartily did the doctor wish that, in some way, he could scare away the intruder.

The man walked along very slowly, indeed, and seemed to be quite taking his time in making his observations of the building; and this was the more provoking, as it was getting late, and if having projected a visit at all, it would surely soon be made, and then, when he found any one there, of course, he would go.

Amazed beyond expression, the doctor felt about on the ground at his feet, until he found a tolerably large stone, which he threw at the stranger with so good an aim, that it hit him a smart blow on the back, which must have been anything but a pleasant surprise.

That it was a surprise, and that, too, a most complete one, was evident from the start which the man gave, and then he uttered a furious oath, and rubbed his back, as he glanced about him to endeavour to ascertain from whence the missile had come.

"I'll try him again with that," thought the doctor; "it may succeed in scaring him away;" and he stooped to watch for another stone.

It was well that he did so at that precise moment; for, before he rose again, he heard the sharp report of a pistol, and a crashing sound among some of the old wood work of which the summer-house was composed, told him that a shot had there taken effect. Affairs were now getting much too serious; and, accordingly, Dr. Chillingworth thought that, rather than stay there to be made a target of, he would face the intruder.

"Hold--hold!" he cried. "Who are you, and what do you mean by that?"--"Oh! somebody is there," cried the man, as he advanced. "My friend, whoever you are, you were very foolish to throw a stone at me."

"And, my friend, whoever you are," responded the doctor, "you were very spiteful to fire a pistol bullet at me in consequence."--

"Not at all."

"But I say yes; for, probably, I can prove a right to be here, which you cannot."--"Ah!" said the stranger, "that voice--why--you are Dr. Chillingworth?"

"I am; but I don't know you," said the doctor, as he emerged now from the summer-house, and confronted the stranger who was within a few paces of the entrance to it. Then he started, as he added,--

"Yes, I do know you, though. How, in the name of Heaven, came you here, and what purpose have you in so coming?"

"What purpose have you? Since we met at Varney's, I have been making some inquiries about this neighbourhood, and learn strange things."--"That you may very easily do here; and, what is more extraordinary, the strange things are, for the most part, I can assure you, quite true."

The reader will, from what has been said, now readily recognise this man as Sir Francis Varney's mysterious visitor, to whom he gave, from some hidden cause or another, so large a sum of money, and between whom and Dr. Chillingworth a mutual recognition had taken place, on the occasion when Sir Francis Varney had, with such cool assurance, invited the admiral to breakfast with him at his new abode.

"You, however," said the man, "I have no doubt, are fully qualified to tell me of more than I have been able to learn from other people; and, first of all, let me ask you why you are here?"--"Before I answer you that question, or any other," said the doctor, "let me beg of you to tell me truly, is Sir Francis Varney--"

The doctor whispered in the ear of the stranger some name, as if he feared, even there, in the silence of that garden, where everything conspired to convince him that he could not be overheard, to pronounce it in an audible tone.

"He is," said the other.--"You have no manner of doubt of it?"

"Doubt?--certainly not. What doubt can I have? I know it for a positive certainty, and he knows, of course, that I do know it, and has purchased my silence pretty handsomely, although I must confess that nothing but my positive necessities would have induced me to make the large demands upon him that I have, and I hope soon to be able to release him altogether from them."

The doctor shook his head repeatedly, as he said,--

"I suspected it; I suspected it, do you know, from the first moment that I saw you there in his house. His face haunted me ever since--awfully haunted me; and yet, although I felt certain that I had once seen it under strange circumstances, I could not identify it with--but no matter, no matter.

I am waiting here for him."

"Indeed!"--"Ay, that I am; and I flung a stone at you, not knowing you, with hope that you would be, by such means, perhaps, scared away, and so leave the coast clear for him."

"Then you have an appointment with him?"--"By no means; but he has made such repeated and determined attacks upon this house that the family who inhabited it were compelled to leave it, and I am here to watch him, and ascertain what can possibly be his object."

"It is as I suspected, then," muttered this man. "Confound him! Now can I read, as if in a book, most clearly, the game that he is playing!"

"Can you?" cried the doctor, energetically--"can you? What is it? Tell me, for that is the very thing I want to discover."--"You don't say so?"

"It is, indeed; and I assure you that it concerns the peace of a whole family to know it. You say you have made inquiries about this neighbourhood, and, if you have done so, you have discovered how the family of the Bannerworths have been persecuted by Varney, and how, in particular, Flora Bannerworth, a beautiful and intelligent girl, has been most cruelly made to suffer."

"I have heard all that, and I dare say with many exaggerations."--"It would be difficult for any one really to exaggerate the horrors that have taken place in this house, so that any information which you can give respecting the motives of Varney will tend, probably, to restore peace to those who have been so cruelly persecuted, and be an act of kindness which I think not altogether inconsistent with your nature."

"You think so, and yet know who I am."--"I do, indeed."

"And what I am. Why, if I were to go into the market-place of yon town, and proclaim myself, would not all shun me--ay, even the very lowest and vilest; and yet you talk of an act of kindness not being altogether inconsistent with my nature!"--"I do, because I know something more of you than many."

There was a silence of some moments' duration, and then the stranger spoke in a tone of voice which looked as if he were struggling with some emotion.

"Sir, you do know more of me than many. You know what I have been, and you know how I left an occupation which would have made me loathed. But you--even you--do not know what made me take to so terrible a trade."--"I do not."

"Would it suit you for me now to tell you?"--"Will you first promise me that you will do all you can for this persecuted family of the Bannerworths, in whom I take so strange an interest?"

"I will. I promise you that freely. Of my own knowledge, of course, I can say but little concerning them, but, upon that warranting, I well believe they deserve abundant sympathy, and from me they shall have it."

"A thousand thanks! With your assistance, I have little doubt of being able to extricate them from the tangled web of dreadful incidents which has turned them from their home; and now, whatever you may choose to tell me of the cause which drove you to be what you became, I shall listen to with abundant interest. Only let me beseech you to come into this summer-house, and to talk low."

"I will, and you can pursue your watch at the same time, while I beguile its weariness."--"Be it so."

"You knew me years ago, when I had all the chances in the world of becoming respectable and respected. I did, indeed; and you may, therefore, judge of my surprise when, some years since, being in the metropolis, I met you, and you shunned my company."--"Yes; but, at last, you found out why it was that I shunned your company."

"I did. You yourself told me once that I met you, and would not leave you, but insisted upon your dining with me. Then you told me, when you found that I would take no other course whatever, that you were no other than the--the----"--

"Out with it! I can bear to hear it now better than I could then! I told you that I was the common hangman of London!"

"You did, I must confess, to my most intense surprise."

"Yes, and yet you kept to me; and, but that I respected you too much to allow you to do so, you would, from old associations, have countenanced me; but I could not, and I would not, let you do so. I told you then that, although I held the terrible office, that I had not been yet called upon to perform its loathsome functions. Soon--soon--come the first effort--it was the last!"

"Indeed! You left the dreadful trade?"

"I did--I did. But what I want to tell you, for I could not then, was why I went ever to it. The wounds my heart had received were then too fresh to allow me to speak of them, but I will tell you now. The story is a brief one, Mr. Chillingworth. I pray you be seated."

CHAPTER LXXII

THE STRANGE STORY.--THE ARRIVAL OF THE MOB AT THE HALL, AND THEIR DISPERSION

"You will find that the time which elapsed since I last saw you in London, to have been spent in an eventful, varied manner."--"You were in good circumstances then," said Mr. Chillingworth.--"I was, but many events happened after that which altered the prospect; made it even more gloomy than you can well imagine: but I will tell you all candidly, and you can keep watch upon Bannerworth Hall at the same time. You are well aware that I was well to do, and had ample funds, and inclination to spend them."--"I recollect: but you were married then, surely?"--"I was," said the stranger, sadly, "I was married then."--"And now?"--"I am a widower." The stranger seemed much moved, but, after a moment or so, he resumed--"I am a widower now; but how that event came about is partly my purpose to tell you. I had not married long--that is very long--for I have but one child, and she is not old, or of an age to know much more than what she may be taught; she is still in the course of education. I was early addicted to gamble; the dice had its charms, as all those who have ever engaged in play but too well know; it is perfectly fascinating."--"So I have heard," said Mr. Chillingworth; "though, for myself, I found a wife and professional pursuits quite incompatible with any pleasure that took either time or resources."--

"It is so. I would I had never entered one of those houses where men are deprived of their money and their own free will, for at the gambling-table you have no liberty, save that in gliding down the stream in company with others. How few have ever escaped destruction--none, I believe--men are perfectly fascinated; it is ruin alone that enables a man to see how he has been hurried onwards without thought or reflection; and how fallacious were all the hopes he ever entertained! Yes, ruin, and ruin alone, can do this; but, alas! 'tis then too late--the evil is done. Soon after my marriage I fell in with a Chevalier St. John. He was a man of the world in every sense of the word, and one that was well versed in all the ways of society. I never met with any man who was so perfectly master of himself, and of perfect ease and self-confidence as he was. He was never at a loss, and, come what would, never betrayed surprise or vexation--two qualities, he thought, never ought to be shown by any man who moved in society."--

"Indeed!"--"He was a strange man--a very strange man."--

"Did he gamble?"--

"It is difficult to give you a correct and direct answer. I should say he did, and yet he never lost or won much; but I have often thought he was more connected with those who did than was believed."--

"Was that a fact?" inquired Mr. Chillingworth.--

"You shall see as we go on, and be able to judge for yourself. I have thought he was. Well, he first took me to a handsome saloon, where gambling was carried on. We had been to the opera. As we came out, he recommended that we should sup at a house where he was well known, and where he was in the habit of spending his evenings after the opera, and before he retired. I agreed to this. I saw no reason why I should not. We went there, and bitterly have I repented of so doing for years since, and do to this day."--

"Your repentance has been sincere and lasting," said Mr. Chillingworth; "the one proves the other."--"It does; but I thought not so then. The place was glittering, and the wine good. It was a kind of earthly paradise; and when we had taken some wine, the chevalier said to me,--

"'I am desirous of seeing a friend backwards; he is at the hazard-table. Will you go with me?'--I hesitated. I feared to see the place where a vice was carried on. I knew myself inclined to prudential motives. I said to him,--'No, St. John, I'll wait here for you; it may be as well--the wine is good, and it will content me?'

"'Do so,' he said, smiling; 'but remember I seldom or never play myself, nor is there any reason why you should.'--'I'll go, but I will not play.'--'Certainly not; you are free alike to look on, play, or quit the place at any moment you please, and not be noticed, probably, by a single soul.'

"I arose, and we walked backwards, having called one of the men who were waiting about, but who were watchers and door-keepers of the 'hell.' We were led along the passage, and passed through the pair of doors, which were well secured and rendered the possibility of a surprise almost impossible. After these dark places, we were suddenly let into a place where we were dazzled by the light and brilliancy of the saloon. It was not so large as the one we left, but it was superior to it in all its appointments.

"At first I could not well see who was, or who was not, in the room where we were. As soon, however, as I found the use of my eyes, I noticed many well-dressed men, who were busily engaged in play, and who took no notice of any one who entered. We walked about for some minutes without speaking to any one, but merely looking on. I saw men engaged in play; some with earnestness, others again with great nonchalance, and money changed hands without the least remark. There were but few who spoke, and only those in play. There was a hum of conversation; but you could not distinguish what was said, unless you paid some attention to, and was in close vicinity with, the individual who spoke.

"'Well,' said St. John, 'what do you think of this place?'--'Why,' I replied, 'I had no notion of seeing a place fitted up as this is.'

"'No; isn't it superb?'--'It is beautifully done. They have many visitors,' said I, 'many more than I could have believed.'

"'Yes, they are all bona fide players; men of stamp and rank--none of your seedy legs who have only what they can cheat you out of.'--'Ah!'--'And besides,' he added, 'you may often form friendships here that lead to fortune hereafter. I do not mean in play, because there is no necessity for your doing so, or, if you do so, in going above a stake which you know won't hurt you.'--'Exactly.'

"'Many men can never approach a table like this, and sit down to an hour's play, but, if they do, they must stake not only more than they can afford, but all their property, leaving themselves beggars.' 'They do?" said I.

"'But men who know themselves, their resources, and choose to indulge for a time, may often come and lay the foundation to a very pretty fortune.'

"'Do you see your friend?' I inquired.--'No, I do not; but I will inquire if he has been here--if not, we will go.'

"He left me for a moment or two to make some inquiry, and I stood looking at the table, where there were four players, and who seemed to be engaged at a friendly game; and when one party won they looked grave, and when the other party lost they smiled and looked happy. I walked away, as the chevalier did not return immediately to me; and then I saw a gentleman rise up from a table. He had evidently lost. I was standing by the seat, unconsciously holding the back in my hand. I sat down without thinking or without speaking, and found myself at the hazard table.

"'Do you play, sir?'--'Yes,' I said. I had hardly uttered the words when I was sorry for them; but I could not recall them. I sat down, and play at once commenced.

"In about ten or fifteen minutes, often losing and then winning, I found myself about a hundred and twenty pounds in pocket, clear gain by the play.

"'Ah!' said the chevalier, who came up at that moment, 'I thought you wouldn't play.'--'I really don't know how it happened,' said I, 'but I suddenly found myself here without any previous intention.'

"'You are not a loser, I hope?'--'Indeed I am not,' I replied; 'but not much a gainer.'

"'Nor need you desire to be. Do you desire to give your adversary his revenge now, or take another opportunity.'--'At another time,' I replied.

"'You will find me here the day after to-morrow, when I shall be at your service;' then bowing, he turned away.

"'He is a very rich man whom you have been playing with,' said the chevalier.--"

"Indeed!"

"'Yes, and I have known him to lose for three days together; but you may take his word for any amount; he is a perfect gentleman and man of honour.'--"Tis well to play with such,' I replied; 'but I suppose you are about to leave.'

"'Yes, it grows late, and I have some business to transact to-morrow, so I must leave.'--'I will accompany you part of the way home,' said I, 'and then I shall have finished the night.'

"I did leave with him, and accompanied him home, and then walked to my own home."

***

"This was my first visit, and I thought a propitious beginning, but it was the more dangerous. Perhaps a loss might have effectually deterred me, but it is doubtful to tell how certain events might have been altered. It is just possible that I might have been urged on by my desire to retrieve any loss I might have incurred, and so made myself at once the miserable being it took months to accomplish in bringing me to.

"I went the day but one after this, to meet the same individual at the gambling-table, and played some time with varied success, until I left off with a trifling loss upon the night's play, which was nothing of any consequence.

"Thus matters went on; I sometimes won and sometimes lost, until I won a few hundreds, and this determined me to play for higher stakes than any I had yet played for.

"It was no use going on in the peddling style I had been going on; I had won two hundred and fifty pounds in three months, and had I been less fearful I might have had twenty-five thousand pounds. Ah! I'll try my fortune at a higher game.

"Having once made this resolution, I was anxious to begin my new plan, which I hoped would have the effect of placing me far above my then present position in society, which was good, and with a little attention it would have made me an independent man; but then it required patience, and nothing more. However, the other method was so superior since it might all be done with good luck in a few months. Ah! good luck; how uncertain is good luck; how changeful is fortune; how soon is the best prospect blighted by the frosts of adversity. In less than a month I had lost more than I could pay, and then I gambled on for a living.

"My wife had but one child; her first and only one; an infant at her breast; but there was a change came over her; for one had come over me--a fearful one it was too--one not only in manner but in fortune too. She would beg me to come home early; to attend to other matters, and leave the dreadful life I was then leading.

"'Lizzy,' said I, 'we are ruined.'--'Ruined!' she exclaimed, and staggered back, until she fell into a seat. 'Ruined!'

"'Ay, ruined. It is a short word, but expressive.'--'No, no, we are not ruined. I know what you mean, you would say, we cannot live as we have lived; we must retrench, and so we will, right willingly.'

"'You must retrench most wonderfully,' I said, with desperate calmness, 'for the murder must out.'--'And so we will; but you will be with us; you will not go out night after night, ruining your health, our happiness, and destroying both peace and prospects.'

"'No, no, Lizzy, we have no chance of recovering ourselves; house and home--all gone--all, all.'--'My God!' she exclaimed.

"'Ay, rail on,' said I; 'you have cause enough; but, no matter--we have lost all.'--'How--how?'

"'It is useless to ask how; I have done, and there is an end of the matter; you shall know more another day; we must leave this house for a lodging.'--'It matters little,' she said; 'all may be won again, if you will but say you will quit the society of those who have ruined you.'

"'No one,' said I, 'has ruined me; I did it; it was no fault of any one else's; I have not that excuse.'--'I am sure you can recover.'

"'I may; some day fortune will shower her favours upon me, and I live on in that expectation.'--'You cannot mean that you will chance the gaming-table? for I am sure you must have lost all there?'

"'I have.'--'God help me,' she said; 'you have done your child a wrong, but you may repair it yet.'

"'Never!'--''Tis a long day! let me implore you, on my knees, to leave this place, and adopt some other mode of life; we can be careful; a little will do, and we shall, in time, be equal to, and better than what we have been.'

"'We never can, save by chance.'--'And by chance we never shall,' she replied; 'if you will exert yourself, we may yet retrieve ourselves.'

"'And exert myself I will.'--'And quit the gaming-table?'

"'Ask me to make no promises,' said I; 'I may not be able to keep them; therefore, ask me to make none.'--'I do ask you, beg of, entreat of you to promise, and solemnly promise me that you will leave that fearful place, where men not only lose all their goods, but the feelings of nature also.'

"'Say no more, Lizzy; if I can get a living elsewhere I will, but if not, I must get it there.'

"She seemed to be cast down at this, and she shed tears. I left the room, and again went to the gambling-house, and there that night, I won a few pounds, which enabled me to take my wife and child away from the house they had so long lived in, and took them afterwards to a miserable place,--one room, where, indeed, there were a few articles of furniture that I had saved from the general wreck of my own property.

"She took things much less to heart than I could have anticipated; she seemed cheerful and happy,--she endeavoured to make my home as comfortable as she could.

"Her whole endeavour was to make me as much as possible, forget the past. She wanted, as much as possible, to wean me away from my gambling pursuits, but that was impossible. I had no hope, no other prospect.

"Thus she strove, but I could see each day she was getting paler, and more pale; her figure, before round, was more thin, and betrayed signs of emaciation. This preyed upon me; and, when fortune denied me the means of carrying home that which she so much wanted, I could never return for two days at a time. Then I would find her shedding tears, and sighing; what could I say? If I had anything to take her, then I used to endeavour to make her forget that I had been away.

"'Ah!' she would exclaim, 'you will find me dead one of these days; what you do now for one or two days, you will do by-and-bye for many days, perhaps weeks.'--'Do not anticipate evil.'

"'I cannot do otherwise; were you in any other kind of employment but that of gambling,' she said, 'I should have some hope of you; but, as it is, there is none.'--'Speak not of it; my chances may turn out favourable yet, and you may be again as you were.'

"'Never.'--'But fortune is inconstant, and may change in my favour as much as she has done in others.'

"'Fortune is indeed constant, but misfortune is as inconstant.'--'You are prophetic of evil."

"'Ah! I would to Heaven I could predict good; but who ever yet heard of a ruined gambler being able to retrieve himself by the same means that he was ruined?'

"Thus we used to converse, but our conversation was usually of but little comfort to either of us, for we could give neither any comfort to the other; and as that was usually the case, our interviews became less frequent, and of less duration. My answer was always the same.

"'I have no other chance; my prospects are limited to that one place; deprive me of that, and I never more should be able to bring you a mouthful of bread.'

"Day after day,--day after day, the same result followed, and I was as far from success as ever I was, and ever should be; I was yet a beggar.

"The time flew by; my little girl was nearly four years old, but she knew not the misery her father and mother had to endure. The poor little thing sometimes went without more than a meal a day; and while I was living thus upon the town, upon the chances of the gaming-table, many a pang did she cause me, and so did her mother. My constant consolation was this,--

"'It is bad luck now,' I would say; 'but will be better by-and-bye; things cannot always continue thus. It is all for them--all for them.'

"I thought that by continuing constantly in one course, I must be at land at the ebb of the tide. 'It cannot always flow one way,' I thought. I had often heard people say that if you could but have the resolution to play on, you must in the end seize the turn of fortune.

"'If I could but once do that, I would never enter a hell again as long as I drew breath.'

"This was a resolve I could not only make but keep, because I had suffered so much that I would never run through the same misery again that I had already gone through. However, fortune never seemed inclined to take the turn I had hoped for; fortune was as far off as ever, and had in no case given me any opportunity of recovering myself.

"A few pounds were the utmost I could at any time muster, and I had to keep up something of an appearance, and seem as if I had a thousand a year; when, God knows, I could not have mustered a thousandth part of that sum, were all done and paid for.

"Day after day passed on, and yet no change. I had almost given myself up to despair, when one night when I went home I saw my wife was more than usually melancholy and sad, and perhaps ill; I didn't look at her--I seldom did, because her looks were always a reproach to me; I could not help feeling them so.

"'Well,' said I, 'I have come home to you because I have something to bring you; not what I ought--but what I can--you must be satisfied!'--'I am,' she said.

"'I know also you want it; how is the child, is she quite well?'--'Yes, quite.'

"'Where is she?' inquired I, looking round the room, but I didn't see her; she used to be up.--'She has gone to bed,' she said.

"'It is very early.'--'Yes, but she cried so for food that I was obliged to get her to sleep to forget her hunger: poor thing, she has wanted bread very badly.'

"'Poor thing!' I said, 'let her be awakened and partake of what I have brought home.'

"With that my wife waked her up, and the moment she opened her eyes she again began to cry for food, which I immediately gave her and saw her devour with the utmost haste and hunger. The sight smote my heart, and my wife sat by watching, and endeavouring to prevent her from eating so fast.

"'This is bad,' I said.--'Yes, but I hope it may be the worst,' she replied, in a deep and hollow voice.

"'Lizzy,' I exclaimed, 'what is the matter--are you ill?'--'Yes, very ill.'

"'What is the matter with you? For God's sake tell me,' I said, for I was alarmed.--'I am very ill,' she said, 'very ill indeed; I feel my strength decreasing every day. I must drink.'

"You, too, want food?'--'I have and perhaps do, though the desire to eat seems almost to have left me.'

"'For Heaven's sake eat,' said I; 'I will bring you home something more by to-morrow; eat and drink Lizzy. I have suffered; but for you and your child's sake, I will do my best.'--'Your best,' she said, 'will kill us both; but, alas, there is no other aid at hand. You may one day, however, come here too late to find us living.'

"'Say no more, Lizzy, you know not my feelings when you speak thus; alas, I have no hope--no aid--no friend.'--'No,' she replied, 'your love of gaming drove them from you, because they would not aid a gambler.'

"'Say no more, Lizzy,' I said; 'if there be not an end to this life soon, there will be an end to me. In two days more I shall return to you. Good bye; God bless you. Keep up your heart and the child.'--'Good bye,' she said, sorrowfully. She shed tears, and wrung her hands bitterly. I hastened away--my heart was ready to burst, and I could not speak.

"I walked about to recover my serenity, but could not do so sufficiently well to secure anything like an appearance that would render me fit to go to the gaming-house. That night I remained away, but I could not avoid falling into a debauch to drown my misfortunes, and shift the scene of misery that was continually before my eyes."

***

"The next night I was at the gaming-house. I went there in better than usual spirits. I saw, I thought, a change in fortune, and hailed that as the propitious moment of my life, when I was to rise above my present misfortunes.

"I played and won--played and lost--played and won, and then lost again; thus I went on, fluctuating more and more, until I found I was getting money in my pocket. I had, at one moment more than three hundred pounds in my pocket, and I felt that then was my happy moment--then the tide of fortune was going in my favour. I ought to have left off with that--to have been satisfied with such an amount of money; but the demon of avarice seemed to have possessed me, and I went on and on with fluctuating fortune, until I lost the whole of it.

"I was mad--desperate, and could have destroyed myself; but I thought of the state my wife and child were in; I thought that that night they would want food; but they could not hurt for one day--they must have some, or would procure some.

"I was too far gone to be able to go to them, even if I were possessed of means; but I had none, and daylight saw me in a deep sleep, from which I awoke not until the next evening let in, and then I once more determined that I would make a desperate attempt to get a little money. I had always paid, and thought my word would be taken for once; and, if I won, all well and good; if not, then I was no worse off than before.

"This was easy to plan, but not to execute. I went there, but there were none present in whom I had sufficient interest to dare make the attempt. I walked about, and felt in a most uncomfortable state. I feared I should not succeed at all, then what was to become of me--of my wife and child? This rendered me almost mad. I could not understand what I was to do, what to attempt, or where to go. One or two persons came up, and asked me if I were ill. My answers were, that I was well enough. Good God! how far from the truth was that; but I found I must place more control on my feelings, else I should cause much conversation, and then I should lose all hope of recovering myself, and all prospect of living, even.

"At length some one did come in, and I remarked I had been there all the evening and had not played. I had an invitation to play with him, which ended, by a little sleight of hand, in my favour; and on that I had calculated as much as on any good fortune I might meet. The person I played with observed it not, and, when we left off playing, I had some six or seven pounds in pocket. This, to me, was a very great sum; and, the moment I could decently withdraw myself, I ran off home.

"I was fearful of the scene that awaited me. I expected something; worse than I had yet seen. Possibly Lizzy might be angry, and scold as well as complain. I therefore tapped at the door gently, but heard no one answer; but of this I took no notice, as I believed that they might be, and were, most probably, fast asleep. I had provided myself with a light, and I therefore opened the door, which was not fastened.

"'Lizzy!' said I, 'Lizzy!' There was no answer given, and I paused. Everything was as still as death. I looked on the bed--there lay my wife with her clothes on.

"'Lizzy! Lizzy!' said I. But still she did not answer me.

"'Well,' said I, 'she sleeps sound;' and I walked towards the bed, and placed my hand upon her shoulder, and began to shake her, saying, as I did so,--

"'Lizzy! Lizzy! I'm come home.' But still no answer, or signs of awaking.

"I went on the other side of the bed to look at her face, and some misgivings overtook me. I trembled much. She lay on the bed, with her back towards the spot where I stood.

"I came towards her face. My hand shook violently as I endeavoured to look at her. She had her eyes wide open, as if staring at me.

"'Lizzy,' said I. No answer was returned. I then placed my hand upon her cheek. It was enough, and I started back in great horror. She was dead!

"This was horror itself. I staggered back and fell into a chair. The light I placed down, Heaven knows how or why; but there I sat staring at the corpse of my unfortunate wife. I can hardly tell you the tremendous effect this had upon me. I could not move. I was fascinated to the spot. I could not move and could not turn."

***

"It was morning, and the rays of the sun illumined the apartment; but there sat I, still gazing upon the face of my unfortunate wife, I saw, I knew she was dead; but yet I had not spoken, but sat looking at her.

"I believe my heart was as cold as she was; but extreme horror and dread had dried up all the warm blood in my body, and I hardly think there was a pulsation left. The thoughts of my child never once seemed to cross my mind. I had, however, sat there long--some hours before I was discovered, and this was by the landlady.

"I had left the door open behind me, and she, in passing down, had the curiosity to peep, and saw me sitting in what she thought to be a very strange attitude, and could hear no sounds.

"After some time she discovered my wife was dead, and, for some time, she thought me so, too. However, she was convinced to the contrary, and then began to call for assistance. This awoke the child, which was nearly famished. The landlady, to become useful, and to awaken me from my lethargy, placed the child in my hands, telling me I was the best person now to take care of it.

"And so I was; there was no doubt of the truth of that, and I was compelled to acknowledge it. I felt much pride and pleasure in my daughter, and determined she should, if I starved, have the benefit of all I could do for her in the way of care, &c."

***

"The funeral over, I took my child and carried it to a school, where I left her, and paid in advance, promising to do so as often as the quarter came round. My wife I had seen buried by the hands of man, and I swore I would do the best for my child, and to keep this oath was a work of pleasure.

"I determined also I would never more enter a gaming-house, be the extremity what it might; I would suffer even death before I would permit myself to enter the house in which it took place.

"'I will,' I thought, 'obtain some employment of some kind or other. I could surely obtain that. I have only to ask and I have it, surely--something, however menial, that would keep me and my child. Yes, yes--she ought, she must have her charges paid at once."

"The effect of my wife's death was a very great shock to me, and such a one I could not forget--one I shall ever remember, and one that at least made a lasting impression upon me."

***

"Strange, but true, I never entered a gambling-house; it was my horror and my aversion. And yet I could obtain no employment. I took my daughter and placed her at a boarding-school, and tried hard to obtain bread by labour; but, do what would, none could be had; if my soul depended upon it, I could find none. I cared not what it was--anything that was honest.

"I was reduced low--very low; gaunt starvation showed itself in my cheeks; but I wandered about to find employment; none could be found, and the world seemed to have conspired together to throw me back to the gaming-table.

"But this I would not. At last employment was offered; but what was it? The situation of common hangman was offered me. The employment was disgusting and horrible; but, at the same time, it was all I could get, and that was a sufficient inducement for me to accept of it. I was, therefore, the common executioner; and in that employment for some time earned a living. It was terrible; but necessity compelled me to accept the only thing I could obtain. You now know the reason why I became what I have told you."

CHAPTER LXXIII

THE VISIT OF THE VAMPIRE.--THE GENERAL MEETING

The mysterious friend of Mr. Chillingworth finished his narrative, and then the doctor said to him,--

"And that, then, is the real cause why you, a man evidently far above the position of life which is usually that of those who occupy the dreadful post of executioner, came to accept of it."--"The real reason, sir. I considered, too, that in holding such a humiliating situation that I was justly served for the barbarity of which I had been guilty; for what can be a greater act of cruelty than to squander, as I did, in the pursuit of mad excitement, those means which should have rendered my home happy, and conduced to the welfare of those who were dependant upon me?"

"I do not mean to say that your self-reproaches are unjust altogether, but--What noise is that? do you hear anything?"--

"Yes--yes."

"What do you take it to be?"--"It seemed like the footsteps of a number of persons, and it evidently approaches nearer and nearer. I know not what to think."

"Shall I tell you?" said a deep-toned voice, and some one, through the orifice in the back of the summer-house, which, it will be recollected, sustained some damage at the time that Varney escaped from it, laid a hand upon Mr. Chillingworth's shoulder. "God bless me!" exclaimed the doctor; "who's that?" and he sprang from his seat with the greatest perturbation in the world.

"Varney, the vampyre!" added the voice, and then both the doctor and his companion recognised it, and saw the strange, haggard features, that now they knew so well, confronting them. There was a pause of surprise, for a moment or two, on the part of the doctor, and then he said, "Sir Francis Varney, what brings you here? I conjure you to tell me, in the name of common justice and common feeling, what brings you to this house so frequently? You have dispossessed the family, whose property it is, of it, and you have caused great confusion and dismay over a whole county. I implore you now, not in the language of menace or as an enemy, but as the advocate of the oppressed, and one who desires to see justice done to all, to tell me what it is you require."

"There is no time now for explanation," said Varney, "if explanations were my full and free intent. You wished to know what noise was that you heard?"

"I did; can you inform me?"--"I can. The wild and lawless mob which you and your friends first induced to interfere in affairs far beyond their or your control, are now flushed with the desire of riot and of plunder. The noise you hear is that of their advancing footsteps; they come to destroy Bannerworth Hall."

"Can that be possible? The Bannerworth family are the sufferers from all that has happened, and not the inflictors of suffering."--"Ay, be it so; but he who once raises a mob has raised an evil spirit, which, in the majority of cases, it requires a far more potent spell than he is master of to quell again."

"It is so. That is a melancholy truth; but you address me, Sir Francis Varney, as if I led on the mob, when in reality I have done all that lay in my power, from the very first moment of their rising on account of this affair, which, in the first instance, was your work, to prevent them from proceeding to acts of violence."--"It may be so; but if you have now any regard for your own safety you will quit this place. It will too soon become the scene of a bloody contention. A large party of dragoons are even now by another route coming towards it, and it will be their duty to resist the aggressions of the mob; then should the rioters persevere, you can guess the result."--"I can, indeed."

"Retire then while you may, and against the bad deeds of Sir Francis Varney at all events place some of his good ones, that he may not seem wholly without one redeeming trait."--"I am not accustomed," said the doctor, "to paint the devil blacker than he really is; but yet the cruel persecutions that the Bannerworth family have endured call aloud for justice. You still, with a perseverance which shows you regardless of what others suffer so that you compass your own ends, hover round a spot which you have rendered desolate."

"Hark, sir; do you not hear the tramp of horses' feet?"--"I do."

The noise made by the feet of the insurgents was now almost drowned in the louder and more rapid tramp of the horses' feet of the advancing dragoons, and, in a few moments more, Sir Francis Varney waved his arm, exclaiming,--

"They are here. Will you not consult your safety by flight?"--"No," said Mr. Chillingworth's companion; "we prefer remaining here at the risk even of whatever danger may accrue to us."

"Fools, would you die in a chance melee between an infuriated populace and soldiery?"--"Do not leave," whispered the ex-hangman to Mr. Chillingworth; "do not leave, I pray you. He only wants to have the Hall to himself."

There could be no doubt now of the immediate appearance of the cavalry, and, before Sir Francis Varney could utter another word, a couple of the foremost of the soldiers cleared the garden fence at a part where it was low, and alighted not many feet from the summer-house in which this short colloquy was taking place. Sir Francis Varney uttered a bitter oath, and immediately disappeared in the gloom.

"What shall we do?" said the hangman.--"You can do what you like, but I shall avow my presence to the military, and claim to be on their side in the approaching contest, if it should come to one, which I sincerely hope it will not."

The military detachment consisted of about twenty-five dragoons, who now were all in the gardens. An order was given by the officer in command for them to dismount, which was at once obeyed, and the horses were fastened by their bridles to the various trees with which the place abounded.

"They are going to oppose the mob on foot, with their carbines," said the hangman; "there will be sad work here I am afraid."--"Well, at all events," said Mr. Chillingworth, "I shall decline acting the part of a spy here any longer; so here goes."

"Hilloa! a friend,--a friend here, in the summer-house!"

"Make it two friends," cried the hangman, "if you please, while you are about it."

A couple of the dragoons immediately appeared, and the doctor, with his companion, were marched, as prisoners, before the officer in command.

"What do you do here?" he said; "I was informed that the Hall was deserted. Here, orderly, where is Mr. Adamson, the magistrate, who came with me?"--"Close at hand sir, and he says he's not well."

"Well, or ill, he must come here, and do something with these people."

A magistrate of the district who had accompanied the troops, and been accommodated with a seat behind one of the dragoons, which seemed very much to have disagreed with him, for he was as pale as death, now stepped forward.

"You know me, Mr. Adamson?" said the doctor; "I am Mr. Chillingworth."--"Oh! yes; Lord bless you! how came you here?"

"Never mind that just now; you can vouch for my having no connection with the rioters."--"Oh! dear, yes; certainly. This is a respectable gentleman, Captain Richardson, and a personal friend of mine."

"Oh! very good."--"And I," said the doctor's companion, "am likewise a respectable and useful member of society, and a great friend of Mr. Chillingworth."

"Well, gentlemen," said the captain in command, "you may remain here, if you like, and take the chances, or you may leave."

They intimated that they preferred remaining, and, almost at the moment that they did so, a loud shout from many throats announced the near approach of the mob.--"Now, Mr. Magistrate, if you please," said the officer; "you will be so good as to tell the mob that I am here with my troop, under your orders, and strongly advise them to be off while they can, with whole skins, for if they persevere in attacking the place, we must persevere in defending it; and, if they have half a grain of sense among them, they can surely guess what the result of that will be."

"I will do the best I can, as Heaven is, my judge," said the magistrate, "to produce a peaceable recall,--more no man can do."

"Hurrah! hurrah!"' shouted the mob, "down with the Vampyre! down with the Hall!" and then one, more candid than his fellows, shouted,--"Down with everything and everybody!"

"Ah!" remarked the officer; "that fellow now knows what he came about."

A great number of torches and links were lighted by the mob, but the moment the glare of light fell upon the helmets and accoutrements of the military, there was a pause of consternation on the part of the multitude, and Mr. Adamson, urged on by the officer, who, it was evident, by no means liked the service he was on, took advantage of the opportunity, and, stepping forward, he said,--

"My good people, and fellow townsmen, let me implore you to listen to reason, and go to your homes in peace. If you do not, but, on the contrary, in defiance of law and good order, persist in attacking this house, it will become my painful duty to read the riot act, and then the military and you will have to fight it out together, which I beg you will avoid, for you know that some of you will be killed, and a lot more of you receive painful wounds. Now disperse, let me beg of you, at once."

There seemed for a moment a disposition among the mob to give up the contest, but there were others among them who were infuriated with drink, and so regardless of all consequences. Those set up a shout of "Down with the red coats; we are Englishmen, and will do what we like." Some one then threw a heavy stone, which struck one of the soldiers, and brought blood from his cheek. The officer saw it, but he said at once,--

"Stand firm, now, stand firm. No anger--steady."

"Twenty pounds for the man who threw that stone," said the magistrate.--"Twenty pound ten for old Adamson, the magistrate," cried a voice in the crowd, which, no doubt came from him who had cast the missile.

Then, at least fifty stones were thrown, some of which hit the magistrate, and the remainder came rattling upon the helmets of the dragoons, like a hail shower.

"I warn you, and beg of you to go," said Mr. Adamson; "for the sake of your wives and families, I beg of you not to pursue this desperate game."

Loud cries now arose of "Down with the soldiers; down with the vampyre. He's in Bannerworth Hall. Smoke him out." And then one or two links were hurled among the dismounted dragoons. All this was put up with patiently; and then again the mob were implored to leave, which being answered by fresh taunts, the magistrate proceeded to read the riot act, not one word of which was audible amid the tumult that prevailed.

"Put out all the lights," cried a voice among the mob. The order was obeyed, and the same voice added; "they dare not fire on us. Come on:" and a rush was made at the garden wall.

"Make ready--present," cried the officer. And then he added, in an under tone, "above their heads, now--fire."

There was a blaze of light for a moment, a stunning noise, a shout of dismay from the mob, and in another moment all was still.

"There," said Dr. Chillingworth, "that this is, at all events, a bloodless victory."

"You may depend upon that," said his companion; "but is not there some one yet remaining? Look there, do you not see a figure clambering over the fence?"

"Yes, I do, indeed. Ah, they have him a prisoner, at all events. Those two dragoons have him, fast enough; we shall now, perhaps, hear from this fellow who is the actual ringleader in such an affair, which, but for the pusillanimity of the mob, might have turned out to be really most disastrous."

It was strange how one man should think it expedient to attack the military post after the mob had been so completely routed at the first discharge of fire-arms, but so it was. One man did make an attempt to enter the garden, and it was so rapid and so desperate an one, that he rather seemed to throw himself bodily at the fence, which separated it from the meadows without, than to clamber over it, as any one under ordinary circumstances, who might wish to effect an entrance by that means, would have done.

He was no sooner, however, perceived, than a couple of the dismounted soldiers stepped forward and made a prisoner of him.

"Good God!" exclaimed Mr. Chillingworth, as they approached nearer with him. "Good God! what is the meaning of that? Do my eyes deceive me, or are they, indeed, so blessed?"

"Blessed by what?" exclaimed the hangman.

"By a sight of the long lost, deeply regretted Charles Holland. Charles--Charles, is that indeed you, or some unsubstantial form in your likeness?"

Charles Holland, for it was, indeed, himself, heard the friendly voice of the doctor, and he called out to him.

"Speak to me of Flora. Oh, speak to me of Flora, if you would not have me die at once of suspense, and all the torture of apprehension."

"She lives and is well."

"Thank Heaven. Do with me what you please."

Dr. Chillingworth sprang forward, and addressing the magistrate, he said,--

"Sir, I know this gentleman. He is no one of the rioters, but a dear friend of the family of the Bannerworths. Charles Holland, what in the name of Heaven had become of you so long, and what brought you here at such a juncture as this?"

"I am faint," said Charles; "I--I only arrived as the crowd did. I had not strength to fight my way through them, and was compelled to pause until they had dispersed Can--can you give me water?"

"Here's something better," said one of the soldiers, as he handed a flask to Charles, who partook of some of the contents, which greatly revived him, indeed.

"I am better now," he said. "Thank you kindly. Take me into the house. Good God! why is it made a point of attack? Where are Flora and Henry? Are they all well? And my uncle? Oh! what must you all have thought of my absence! But you cannot have endured a hundredth part of what I have suffered. Let me look once again upon the face of Flora. Take me into the house."

"Release him," said the officer, as he pointed to his head, and looked significantly, as much as to say, "Some mad patient of yours, I suppose."

"You are much mistaken, sir," said Dr. Chillingworth; "this gentleman has been cruelly used, I have no doubt. He has, I am inclined to believe, been made the victim, for a time, of the intrigues of that very Sir Francis Varney, whose conduct has been the real cause of all the serious disturbances that have taken place in the country."

"Confound Sir Francis Varney," muttered the officer; "he is enough to set a whole nation by the ears. However, Mr. Magistrate, if you are satisfied that this young man is not one of the rioters, I have, of course, no wish to hold him a prisoner."

"I can take Mr. Chillingworth's word for more than that," said the magistrate.

Charles Holland was accordingly released, and then the doctor, in hurried accents, told him the principal outlines of what had occurred.

"Oh! take me to Flora," he said; "let me not delay another moment in seeking her, and convincing her that I could not have been guilty of the baseness of deserting her."

"Hark you, Mr. Holland, I have quite made up my mind that I will not leave Bannerworth Hall yet; but you can go alone, and easily find them by the directions which I will give you; only let me beg of you not to go abruptly into the presence of Flora. She is in an extremely delicate state of health, and although I do not take upon myself to say that a shock of a pleasurable nature would prove of any paramount bad consequence to her, yet it is as well not to risk it."

"I will be most careful, you may depend."

At this moment there was a loud ringing at the garden bell, and, when it was answered by one of the dragoons, who was ordered to do so by his officer, he came back, escorting no other than Jack Pringle, who had been sent by the admiral to the Hall, but who had solaced himself so much on the road with divers potations, that he did not reach it till now, which was a full hour after the reasonable time in which he ought to have gone the distance.

Jack was not to say dumb, but he had had enough to give him a very jolly sort of feeling of independence, and so he came along quarrelling with the soldier all the way, the latter only laughing and keeping his temper admirably well, under a great deal of provocation.

"Why, you land lubbers," cried Jack, "what do you do here, all of you, I wonder! You are all wamphighers, I'll be bound, every one of you. You mind me of marines, you do, and that's quite enough to turn a proper seaman's stomach, any day in the week."

The soldier only laughed, and brought Jack up to the little group of persons consisting of Dr. Chillingworth, the hangman, Charles Holland, and the officer.

"Why, Jack Pringle," said Dr. Chillingworth, stepping before Charles, so that Jack should not see him,--"why, Jack Pringle, what brings you here?"

"A slight squall, sir, to the nor'west. Brought you something to eat."

Jack produced a bottle.

"To drink, you mean?"

"Well, it's all one; only in this here shape, you see, it goes down better, I'm thinking, which does make a little difference somehow."

"How is the admiral?"

"Oh, he's as stupid as ever; Lord bless you, he'd be like a ship without a rudder without me, and would go swaying about at the mercy of winds and waves, poor old man. He's bad enough as it is, but if so be I wasn't to give the eye to him as I does, bless my heart if I thinks as he'd be above hatches long. Here's to you all."

Jack took the cork from the bottle he had with him, and there came from it a strong odour of rum. Then he placed it to his lips, and was enjoying the pleasant gurgle of the liquor down his throat, when Charles stepped up to him, and laying hold of the lower end of the bottle, he dragged it from his mouth, saying,--

"How dare you talk in the way you have of my uncle, you drunken, mutinous rascal, and behind his back too!"

The voice of Charles Holland was as well known to Jack Pringle as that of the admiral, and his intense astonishment at hearing himself so suddenly addressed by one, of whose proximity he had not the least idea, made some of the rum go, what is popularly termed, the wrong way, and nearly choked him.

He reeled back, till he fell over some obstruction, and then down he sat on a flower bed, while his eyes seemed ready to come out of his head.

"Avast heavings," he cried, "Who's that?"

"Come, come," said Charles Holland, "don't pretend you don't know me; I will not have my uncle spoken of in a disrespectful manner by you."

"Well, shiver my timbers, if that ain't our nevey. Why, Charley, my boy, how are you? Here we are in port at last. Won't the old commodore pipe his eye, now. Whew! here's a go. I've found our nevey, after all."

"You found him," said Dr. Chillingworth; "now, that is as great a piece of impudence as ever I heard in all my life. You mean that he has found you, and found you out, too, you drunken fellow. Jack, you get worse and worse every day."

"Ay, ay, sir."

"What, you admit it?"

"Ay, ay, sir. Now, Master Charley, I tell you what it is, I shall take you off to your old uncle, you shore going sneak and you'll have to report what cruise you've been upon all this while, leaving the ship to look after itself. Lord love you all, if it hadn't been for me I don't know what anybody would have done."

"I only know of the result," said Dr Chillingworth, "that would ensue, if it were not for you, and that would consist in a great injury to the revenue, in consequence of the much less consumption of rum and other strong liquors."

"I'll be hanged up at the yard if I understands what you mean," said Jack; "as if I ever drunk anything--I, of all people in the world. I am ashamed of you. You are drunk."

Several of the dragoons had to turn aside to keep themselves from laughing, and the officer himself could not forbear from a smile as he said to the doctor,--

"Sir, you seem to have many acquaintances, and by some means or another they all have an inclination to come here to-night. If, however, you consider that you are bound to remain here from a feeling that the Hall is threatened with any danger, you may dismiss that fear, for I shall leave a picquet here all night."

"No, sir," replied Dr. Chillingworth, "it is not that I fear now, after the manner in which they have been repulsed, any danger to the Hall from the mob; but I have reasons for wishing to be in it or near it for some time to come."

"As you please."

"Charles, do not wait for or accept the guidance of that drunken fellow, but go yourself with a direction which I will write down for you in a leaf of my pocket-book."

"Drunken fellow," exclaimed Jack, who had now scrambled to his feet, "who do you call a drunken fellow?"

"Why you, unquestionably."

"Well, now, that is hard. Come along, nevey; I'll shew you where they all are. I could walk a plank on any deck with any man in the service, I could. Come along, my boy, come along."

"You can accept of him as a guide if you like, of course," said the doctor; "he may be sober enough to conduct you."

"I think he can," said Charles. "Lead on, Jack; but mark me, I shall inform my uncle of this intemperance, as well as of the manner in which you let your tongue wag about him behind his back, unless you promise to reform."

"He is long past all reformation," remarked Dr. Chillingworth; "it is out of the question."

"And I am afraid my uncle will not have courage to attempt such an ungrateful task, when there is so little chance of success," replied Charles Holland, shaking the worthy doctor by the hand. "Farewell, for the present, sir; the next time I see you, I hope we shall both be more pleasantly situated."

"Come along, nevey," interrupted Jack Pringle; "now you've found your way back, the first thing you ought to do, is to report yourself as having come aboard. Follow me, and I'll soon show yer the port where the old hulk's laid hisself up."

Jack walked on first, tolerably steady, if one may take into account his divers deep potations, and Charles Holland, anticipating with delight again looking upon the face of his much loved Flora, followed closely behind him.

We can well imagine the world of delightful thoughts that came crowding upon him when Jack, after rather a long walk, announced that they were now very near the residence of the object of his soul's adoration.

We trust that there is not one of our readers who, for one moment, will suppose that Charles Holland was the sort of man to leave even such a villain and double-faced hypocrite as Marchdale, to starve amid the gloomy ruins where he was immured.

Far from Charles's intentions was any such thing; but he did think that a night passed there, with no other company than his own reflections, would do him a world of good, and was, at all events, no very great modicum of punishment for the rascality with which he had behaved.

Besides, even during that night there were refreshments in the shape of bread and water, such as had been presented to Charles himself, within Marchdale's reach as they had been within his.

That individual now, Charles thought, would have a good opportunity of testing the quality of that kind of food, and of finding out what an extremely light diet it was for a strong man to live upon.

But in the morning it was Charles's intention to take Henry Bannerworth and the admiral with him to the ruins, and then and there release the wretch from his confinement, on condition that he made a full confession of his villanies before those persons.

Oh, how gladly would Marchdale have exchanged the fate which actually befell him for any amount of personal humiliation, always provided that it brought with it a commensurate amount of personal safety.

But that fate was one altogether undreamt of by Charles Holland, and wholly without his control.

It was a fate which would have been his, but for the murderous purpose which had brought Marchdale to the dungeon, and those happy accidents which had enabled Charles to change places with him, and breathe the free, cool, fresh air; while he left his enemy loaded with the same chains that had encumbered his limbs so cruelly, and lying on that same damp dungeon floor, which he thought would be his grave.

We mentioned that as Charles left the ruins, the storm, which had been giving various indications of its coming, seemed to be rapidly approaching.

It was one of these extremely local tempests which expend all their principal fury over a small space of country; and, in this instance, the space seemed to include little more than the river, and the few meadows which immediately surrounded it, and lent it so much of its beauty.

Marchdale soon found that his cries were drowned by the louder voices of the elements. The wailing of the wind among the ancient ruins was much more full of sound than his cries; and, now and then, the full-mouthed thunder filled the air with such a volume of roaring, and awakened so many echoes among the ruins, that, had he possessed the voices of fifty men, he could not have hoped to wage war with it.

And then, although we know that Charles Holland would have encountered death himself, rather than he would have willingly left anything human to expire of hunger in that dungeon, yet Marchdale, judging of others by himself, felt by no means sure of any such thing, and, in his horror of apprehension, fancied that that was just the sort of easy, and pleasant, and complete revenge that it was in Charles Holland's power to take, and just the one which would suggest itself, under the circumstances, to his mind.

Could anything be possibly more full of horror than such a thought? Death, let it come in any shape it may, is yet a most repulsive and unwelcome guest; but, when it comes, so united with all that can add to its terrors, it is enough to drive reason from its throne, and fill the mind with images of absolute horror.

Tired of shrieking, for his parched lips and clogged tongue would scarcely now permit him to utter a sound higher than a whisper. Marchdale lay, listening to the furious storm without, in the last abandonment of despair.

"Oh! what a death is this," he groaned. "Here, alone--all alone--and starvation to creep on me by degrees, sapping life's energies one by one. Already do I feel the dreadful sickening weakness growing on me. Help, oh! help me Heav--no, no! Dare I call on Heaven to help me? Is there no fiend of darkness who now will bid me a price for a human soul? Is there not one who will do so--not one who will rescue me from the horror that surrounds me, for Heaven will not? I dare not ask mercy there."

The storm continued louder and louder. The wind, it is true, was nearly hushed, but the roar and the rattle of the echo-awakening thunder fully made up for its cessation, while, now and then, even there, in that underground abode, some sudden reflection of the vivid lightning's light would find its way, lending, for a fleeting moment, sufficient light to Marchdale, wherewith he could see the gloomy place in which he was.

At times he wept, and at times he raved, while ever and anon he made such frantic efforts to free himself from the chains that were around him, that, had they not been strong, he must have succeeded; but, as it was, he only made deep indentations into his flesh, and gave himself much pain.

"Charles Holland!" he shouted; "oh! release me! Varney! Varney! why do you not come to save me? I have toiled for you most unrequitedly--I have not had my reward. Let it all consist in my release from this dreadful bondage. Help! help! oh, help!"

There was no one to hear him. The storm continued, and now, suddenly, a sudden and a sharper sound than any awakened by the thunder's roar came upon his startled ear, and, in increased agony, he shouted,--

"What is that? oh! what is that? God of heaven, do my fears translate that sound aright? Can it be, oh! can it be, that the ruins which have stood for so many a year are now crumbling down before the storm of to-night?"

The sound came again, and he felt the walls of the dungeon in which he was shake. Now there could be no doubt but that the lightning had struck some part of the building, and so endangered the safety of all that was above ground. For a moment there came across his brain such a rush of agony, that he neither spoke nor moved. Had that dreadful feeling continued much longer, he must have lapsed into insanity; but that amount of mercy--for mercy it would have been--was not shown to him. He still felt all the accumulating horrors of his situation, and then, with such shrieks as nothing but a full appreciation of such horrors could have given him strength to utter, he called upon earth, upon heaven and upon all that was infernal, to save him from his impending doom.

All was in vain. It was an impending doom which nothing but the direct interposition of Heaven could have at all averted; and it was not likely that any such perversion of the regular laws of nature would take place to save such a man as Marchdale.

Again came the crashing sound of falling stones, and he was certain that the old ruins, which had stood for so many hundred years the storm, and the utmost wrath of the elements, was at length yielding, and crumbling down.

What else could he expect but to be engulphed among the fragments--fragments still weighty and destructive, although in decay. How fearfully now did his horrified imagination take in at one glance, as it were, a panoramic view of all his past life, and how absolutely contemptible, at that moment, appeared all that he had been striving for.

But the walls shake again, and this time the vibration is more fearful than before. There is a tremendous uproar above him--the roof yields to some superincumbent pressure--there is one shriek, and Marchdale lies crushed beneath a mass of masonry that it would take men and machinery days to remove from off him.

All is over now. That bold, bad man--that accomplished hypocrite--that mendacious, would-be murderer was no more. He lies but a mangled, crushed, and festering corpse.

May his soul find mercy with his God!

The storm, from this moment, seemed to relax in its violence, as if it had accomplished a great purpose, and, consequently, now, need no longer "vex the air with its boisterous presence." Gradually the thunder died away in the distance. The wind no longer blew in blustrous gusts, but, with a gentle murmuring, swept around the ancient pile, as if singing the requiem of the dead that lay beneath--that dead which mortal eyes were never to look upon.

CHAPTER LXXIV

THE MEETING OF CHARLES AND FLORA

Charles Holland followed Jack Pringle for some time in silence from Bannerworth Hall; his mind was too full of thought concerning the past to allow him to indulge in much of that kind of conversation in which Jack Pringle might be fully considered to be a proficient.

As for Jack, somehow or another, he had felt his dignity offended in the garden of Bannerworth Hall, and he had made up his mind, as he afterwards stated in his own phraseology, not to speak to nobody till somebody spoke to him.

A growing anxiety, however, to ascertain from one who had seen her lately, how Flora had borne his absence, at length induced Charles Holland to break his self-imposed silence.

"Jack," he said, "you have had the happiness of seeing her lately, tell me, does Flora Bannerworth look as she was wont to look, or have all the roses faded from her cheeks?"

"Why, as for the roses," said Jack, "I'm blowed if I can tell, and seeing as how she don't look at me much, I doesn't know nothing about her; I can tell you something, though, about the old admiral that will make you open your eyes."

"Indeed, Jack, and what may that be?"

"Why, he's took to drink, and gets groggy about every day of his life, and the most singular thing is, that when that's the case with the old man, he says it's me."

"Indeed, Jack! taken to drinking has my poor old uncle, from grief, I suppose, Jack, at my disappearance."

"No, I don't think it's grief," said Jack; "it strikes me it's rum-and-water."

"Alas, alas, I never could have imagined he could have fallen into that habit of yours; he always seemed so far from anything of this kind."

"Ay, ay, sir," said Jack, "I know'd you'd be astonished. It will be the death of him, that's my opinion; and the idea, you know, Master Charles, of accusing me when he gets drunk himself."

"I believe that is a common delusion of intemperate persons," said Charles.

"Is it, sir; well, it's a very awkward I thing, because you know, sir, as well as most people, that I'm not the fellow to take a drop too much."

"I cannot say, Jack, that I know so much, for I have certainly heard my uncle accuse you of intoxication."

"Lor', sir, that was all just on account of his trying it hisself; he was a thinking on it then, and wanted to see how I'd take it."

"But tell me of Flora; are you quite certain that she has had no more alarms from Varney?"

"What, that ere vampyre fellow? not a bit of it, your honour. Lor' bless you, he must have found out by some means or another that I was on the look out, and that did the business. He'll never come near Miss Flora again, I'll be bound, though to be sure we moved away from the Hall on account of him; but not that I saw the good of cruising out of one's own latitude, but somehow or another you see the doctor and the admiral got it into their heads to establish a sort of blockade, and the idea of the thing was to sail away in the night quite quiet, and after that take up a position that would come across the enemy on the larboard tack, if so be as he made his appearance."

"Oh, you allude to watching the Hall, I presume?"

"Ay, ay, sir, just so; but would you believe it, Master Charlie, the admiral and the doctor got so blessed drunk that I could do nothing with 'em."

"Indeed!"

"Yes, they did indeed, and made all kinds of queer mistakes, so that the end of all that was, that the vampyre did come; but he got away again."

"He did come then; Sir Francis Varney came again after the house was presumed to be deserted?"

"He did, sir."

"That is very strange; what on earth could have been his object? This affair is most inexplicably mysterious. I hope the distance, Jack, is not far that you're taking me, for I'm incapable of enduring much fatigue."

"Not a great way, your honour; keep two points to the westward, and sail straight on; we'll soon come to port. My eye, won't there be a squall when you get in. I expect as Miss Flora will drop down as dead as a herring, for she doesn't think you're above the hatches."

"A good thought, Jack; my sudden appearance may produce alarm. When we reach the place of abode of the Bannerworths, you shall precede me, and prepare them in some measure for my reception."

"Very good, sir; do you see that there little white cottage a-head, there in the offing?"

"Yes, yes; is that the place?"

"Yes, your honour, that's the port to which we are bound."

"Well, then, Jack, you hasten a-head, and see Miss Flora, and be sure you prepare her gently and by degrees, you know, Jack, for my appearance, so that she shall not be alarmed."

"Ay, ay, sir, I understand; you wait here, and I'll go and do it; there would be a squall if you were to make your appearance, sir, all at once. She looks upon you as safely lodged in Davy's locker; she minds me, all the world, of a girl I knew at Portsmouth, called Bet Bumplush. She was one of your delicate little creatures as don't live long in this here world; no, blow me; when I came home from a eighteen months' cruise, once I seed her drinking rum out of a quart pot, so I says, 'Hilloa, what cheer?' And only to think now of the wonderful effect that there had upon her; with that very pot she gives the fellow as was standing treat a knobber on the head as lasted him three weeks. She was too good for this here world, she was, and too rummantic. 'Go to blazes,' she says to him, 'here's Jack Pringle come home.'"

"Very romantic indeed," said Charles.

"Yes, I believe you, sir; and that puts me in mind of Miss Flora and you."

"An extremely flattering comparison. Of course I feel much obliged."

"Oh, don't name it, sir. The British tar as can't oblige a feller-cretor is unworthy to tread the quarter-deck, or to bear a hand to the distress of a woman."

"Very well," said Charles. "Now, as we are here, precede me, if you please, and let me beg of you to be especially cautious in your manner of announcing me."

"Ay, ay, sir," said Jack: and away he walked towards the cottage, leaving Charles some distance behind.

Flora and the admiral were sitting together conversing. The old man, who loved her as if she had been a child of his own, was endeavouring, to the extent of his ability, to assuage the anguish of her thoughts, which at that moment chanced to be bent upon Charles Holland.

"Nevermind, my dear," he said; "he'll turn up some of these days, and when he does, I sha'n't forget to tell him that it was you who stood out for his honesty and truth, when every one else was against him, including myself, an old wretch that I was."

"Oh, sir, how could you for one moment believe that those letters could have been written by your nephew Charles? They carried, sir, upon the face of them their own refutation; and I'm only surprised that for one instant you, or any one who knew him, could have believed him capable of writing them."

"Avast, there," said the admiral; "that'll do. I own you got the better of the old sailor there. I think you and Jack Pringle were the only two persons who stood out from the first."

"Then I honour Jack for doing so."

"And here he is," said the admiral, "and you'd better tell him. The mutinous rascal! he wants all the honour he can get, as a set-off against his drunkenness and other bad habits."

Jack walked into the room, looked about him in silence for a moment, thrust his hands in his breeches pockets, and gave a long whistle.

"What's the matter now?" said the admiral.

"D--me, if Charles Holland ain't outside, and I've come to prepare you for the blessed shock," said Jack. "Don't faint either of you, because I'm only going to let you know it by degrees, you know."

A shriek burst from Flora's lips, and she sprung to the door of the apartment.

"What!" cried the admiral, "my nephew--my nephew Charles! Jack, you rascal, if you're joking, it's the last joke you shall make in this world; and if it's true, I--I--I'm an old fool, that's all."

"Ay, ay, sir," said Jack; "didn't you know that afore?"

"Charles--Charles!" cried Flora. He heard the voice. Her name escaped his lips, and rang with a pleasant echo through the house.

In another moment he was in the room, and had clasped her to his breast.

"My own--my beautiful--my true!"

"Charles, dear Charles!"

"Oh, Flora, what have I not endured since last we met; but this repays me--more than repays me for all."

"What is the past now," cried Flora--"what are all its miseries placed against this happy,

happy moment?"

"D--me, nobody thinks of me," said the admiral.

"My dear uncle," said Charles, looking over Flora's shoulder, as he still held her in his arms, "is that you?"

"Yes, yes, swab, it is me, and you know it; but give us your five, you mutinous vagabond; and I tell you what, I'll do you the greatest favour I've had an opportunity of doing you some time--I'll leave you alone, you dog. Come along, Jack."

"Ay, ay, sir," said Jack; and away they went out of the apartment.

And now those two loving hearts were alone--they who had been so long separated by malignant destiny, once again were heart to heart, looking into each other's faces with all the beaming tenderness of an affection of the truest, holiest character.

The admiral had done a favour to them both to leave them alone, although we much doubt whether his presence, or the presence of the whole world, would have had the effect of controlling one generous sentiment of noble feeling.

They would have forgotten everything but that they were together, and that once again each looked into the other's eyes with all the tenderness of a love purer and higher than ordinarily belongs to mortal affections.

Language was weak to give utterance to the full gust of happy feelings that now were theirs. It was ecstasy enough to feel, to know that the evil fortune which had so long separated them, depriving each existence of its sunniest aspect, was over. It was enough for Charles Holland to feel that she loved him still. It was enough for Flora Bannerworth to know, as she looked into his beaming countenance, that that love was not misplaced, but was met by feelings such as she herself would have dictated to be the inhabitants of the heart of him whom she would have chosen from the mass of mankind as her own.

"Flora--dear Flora," said Charles, "and you have never doubted me?"

"I've never doubted, Charles, Heaven or you. To doubt one would have been, to doubt both."

"Generous and best of girls, what must you have thought of my enforced absence! Oh! Flora, I was unjust enough to your truth to make my greatest pang the thought that you might doubt me, and cast me from your heart for ever."

"Ah! Charles, you ought to have known me better. I stood amid sore temptation to do so much. There were those who would have urged me on to think that you had cast me from your heart for ever. There were those ready and willing to place the worst construction upon your conduct, and with a devilish ingenuity to strive to make me participate in such a feeling; but, no, Charles, no--I loved you, and I trusted you, and I could not so far belie my own judgment as to tell you other than what you always seemed to my young fancy."

"And you are right, my Flora, right; and is it not a glorious triumph to see that love--that sentiment of passion--has enabled you to have so enduring and so noble a confidence in aught human?"

"Ay, Charles, it is the sentiment of passion, for our love has been more a sentiment than a passion. I would fain think that we had loved each other with an affection not usually known, appreciated, or understood, and so, in the vanity of my best affections, I would strive to think them something exclusive, and beyond the common feelings of humanity."

"And you are right, my Flora; such love as yours is the exception; there may be preferences, there may be passions, and there may be sentiments, but never, never, surely, was there a heart like yours."

"Nay, Charles, now you speak from a too poetical fancy; but is it possible that I have had you here so long, with your hand clasped in mine, and asked you not the causes of your absence?"

"Oh, Flora, I have suffered much--much physically, but more mentally. It was the thought of you that was at once the bane and the antidote of my existence."

"Indeed, Charles! Did I present myself in such contradictory colours to you?"

"Yes, dearest, as thus. When I thought of you, sometimes, in the deep seclusion of a dungeon, that thought almost goaded me to madness, because it brought with it the conviction--a conviction peculiar to a lover--that none could so effectually stand between you and all evil as myself."

"Yes, yes, Charles; most true."

"It seemed to me as if all the world in arms could not have protected you so well as this one heart, clad in the triple steel of its affections, could have shielded you from evil."

"Ay, Charles; and then I was the bane of your existence, because I filled you with apprehension?"

"For a time, dearest; and then came the antidote; for when exhausted alike in mind and body--when lying helpless, with chains upon my limbs--when expecting death at every visit of those who had dragged me from light and from liberty, and from love; it was but the thought of thy beauty and thy affection that nerved me, and gave me a hope even amidst the cruellest disaster."

"And then--and then, Charles?"

"You were my blessing, as you have ever been--as you are, and as you will ever be--my own Flora, my beautiful--my true!"

We won't go so far as to say it is the fact; but, from a series of singular sounds which reached even to the passage of the cottage, we have our own private opinion to the effect, that Charles began kissing Flora at the top of her forehead, and never stopped, somehow or another, till he got down to her chin--no, not her chin--her sweet lips--he could not get past them. Perhaps it was wrong; but we can't help it--we are faithful chroniclers. Reader, if you be of the sterner sex, what would you have done?--if of the gentler, what would you have permitted?

CHAPTER LXXV

MUTUAL EXPLANATIONS, AND THE VISIT TO THE RUINS

During the next hour, Charles informed Flora of the whole particulars of his forcible abduction; and to his surprise he heard, of course, for the first time, of those letters, purporting to be written by him, which endeavoured to give so bad an aspect to the fact of his sudden disappearance from Bannerworth Hall.

Flora would insist upon the admiral, Henry, and the rest of the family, hearing all that Charles had to relate concerning Mr. Marchdale; for well she knew that her mother, from early associations, was so far impressed in the favour of that hypocritical personage, that nothing but damning facts, much to his prejudice, would suffice to convince her of the character he really was.

But she was open to conviction, and when she really found what a villain she had cherished and given her confidence to, she shed abundance of tears, and blamed herself exceedingly as the cause of some of the misfortunes which had fallen upon her children.

"Very good," said the admiral; "I ain't surprised a bit. I knew he was a vagabond from the first time I clapped eyes upon him. There was a down look about the fellow's figure-head that I didn't like, and be hanged to him, but I never thought he would have gone the length he has done. And so you say you've got him safe in the ruins, Charles?"

"I have, indeed, uncle."

"And then there let him remain, and a good place, too, for him."

"No, uncle, no. I'm sure you speak without thought. I intend to release him in a few hours, when I have rested from my fatigues. He could not come to any harm if he were to go without food entirely for the time that I leave him; but even that he will not do, for there is bread and water in the dungeon."

"Bread and water! that's too good for him. But, however, Charles, when you go to let him out, I'll go with you, just to tell him what I think of him, the vagabond."

"He must suffer amazingly, for no doubt knowing well, as he does, his own infamous intentions, he will consider that if I were to leave him to starve to death, I should be but retailing upon him the injuries he would have inflicted upon me."

"The worst of it is," said the admiral, "I can't think what to do with him."

"Do nothing, uncle, but just let him go; it will be a sufficient punishment for such a man to feel that, instead of succeeding in his designs, he has only brought upon himself the bitterest contempt of those whom he would fain have injured. I can have no desire for revenge on such a man as Marchdale."

"You are right, Charles," said Flora; "let him go, and let him go with a feeling that he has acquired the contempt of those whose best opinions might have been his for a far less amount of trouble than he has taken to acquire their worst."

Excitement had kept up Charles to this point, but now, when he arose and expressed his intention of going to the ruins, for the purpose of releasing Marchdale, he exhibited such unequivocal symptoms of exhaustion and fatigue that neither his uncle nor Flora would permit him to go, so, in deference to them, he gave up the point, and commissioned the admiral and Jack, with Henry, to proceed to the place, and give the villain his freedom; little suspecting what had occurred since he had himself left the neighbourhood of those ruins.

Of course Charles Holland couldn't be at all accountable for the work of the elements, and it was not for him to imagine that when he left Marchdale in the dungeon that so awful a catastrophe as that we have recorded to the reader was to ensue.

The distance to the ruins was not so great from this cottage even as it was from Bannerworth Hall, provided those who went knew the most direct and best road to take; so that the admiral was not gone above a couple of hours, and when he returned he sat down and looked at Charles with such a peculiar expression, that the latter could not for the life of him tell what to make of it.

"Something has happened, uncle," he said, "I am certain; tell me at once what it is."

"Oh! nothing, nothing," said the admiral, "of any importance."

"Is that what you call your feelings?" said Jack Pringle. "Can't you tell him as there came on a squall last night, and the ruins have come in with a dab upon old Marchdale, crushing his guts, so that we smelt him as soon as we got nigh at hand?"

"Good God!" said Charles, "has such a catastrophe occurred?"

"Yes, Charles, that's just about the catastrophe that has occurred. He's dead; and rum enough it is that it should happen on the very night that you escaped."

"Rum!" said Jack, suddenly; "my eye, who mentions rum? What a singular sort of liquor rum must be. I heard of a chap as used to be fond of it once on board a ship; I wonder if there's any in the house."

"No!" said the admiral; "but there's a fine pump of spring water outside if you feel a little thirsty, Jack; and I'll engage it shall do you more good than all the rum in the world."

"Uncle," said Charles, "I'm glad to hear you make that observation."

"What for?"

"Why, to deal candidly with you, uncle, Jack informed me that you had lately taken quite a predilection for drinking."

"Me!" cried the admiral; "why the infernal rascal, I've had to threaten him with his discharge a dozen times, at least, on that very ground, and no other."

"There's somebody calling me," said Jack. "I'm a coming! I'm a coming!" and, so he bolted out of the room, just in time to escape an inkstand, which the admiral caught up and flung after him.

"I'll strike that rascal off the ship's books this very day," muttered Admiral Bell. "The drunken vagabond, to pretend that I take anything, when all the while it's himself!"

"Well, well, I ought certainly to have suspected the quarter from whence the intelligence came; but he told it to me so circumstantially, and with such an apparent feeling of regret for the weakness into which he said you had fallen, that I really thought there might be some truth in it."

"The rascal! I've done with him from this moment; I have put up with too much from him for years past."

"I think now that you have given him a great deal of liberty, and that, with a great deal more he has taken, makes up an amount which you find it difficult to endure."

"And I won't endure it."

"Let me talk to him, and I dare say I shall be able to convince him that he goes too far, and when he finds that such is the case he will mend."

"Speak to him, if you like, but I have done with such a mutinous rascal, I have. You can take him into your service, if you like, till you get tired of him; and that won't be very long."

"Well, well, we shall see. Jack will apologise to you I have no doubt; and then I shall intercede for him, and advise you to give him another trial."

"If you get him into the apology, then there's no doubt about me giving him another trial. But I know him too well for that; he's as obstinate as a mule, he is, and you won't get a civil word out of him; but never mind that, now. I tell you what, Master Charley, it will take a good lot of roast beef to get up your good looks again."

"It will, indeed, uncle; and I require, now, rest, for I am thoroughly exhausted. The great privations I have undergone, and the amount of mental excitement which I have experienced, in consequence of the sudden and unexpected release from a fearful confinement, have greatly weakened all my energies. A few hours' sleep will make quite a different being of me."

"Well, my boy, you know best," returned the admiral; "and I'll take care, if you sleep till to-morrow, that you sha'n't be disturbed. So now be off to bed at once."

The young man shook his uncle's hand in a cordial manner, and then repaired to the apartment which had been provided for him.

Charles Holland did, indeed, stand in need of repose; and for the first time now for many days he laid down with serenity at his heart, and slept for many hours. And was there not now a great and a happy change in Flora Bannerworth! As if by magic, in a few short hours, much of the bloom of her before-fading beauty returned to her. Her step again recovered its springy lightness; again she smiled upon her mother, and suffered herself to talk of a happy future; for the dread even of the vampyre's visitations had faded into comparative insignificance against the heart's deep dejection which had come over her at the thought that Charles Holland must surely be murdered, or he would have contrived to come to her.

And what a glorious recompense she had now for the trusting confidence with which she had clung to a conviction of his truth! Was it not great, now, to feel that when he was condemned by others, and when strong and unimpeachable evidence seemed to be against him, she had clung to him and declared her faith in his honour, and wept for him instead of condemning?

Yes, Flora; you were of that order of noble minds that, where once confidence is given, give it fully and completely, and will not harbour a suspicion of the faith of the loved one, a happy disposition when verified, as in this instance, by an answering truthfulness.

But when such a heart trusts not with judgment--when that pure, exalted, and noble confidence is given to an object unworthy of it--then comes, indeed, the most fearful of all mental struggles; and if the fond heart, that has hugged to its inmost core so worthless a treasure, do not break in the effort to discard it, we may well be surprised at the amount of fortitude that has endured so much.

Although the admiral had said but little concerning the fearful end Marchdale had come to, it really did make some impression upon him; and, much as he held in abhorrence the villany of Marchdale's conduct, he would gladly in his heart have averted the fate from him that he had brought upon himself.

On the road to the ruins, he calculated upon taking a different kind of vengeance.

When they had got some distance from the cottage, Admiral Bell made a proposal to Henry to be his second while he fought Marchdale, but Henry would not hear of it for a moment.

"My dear sir," he said, "could I, do you think, stand by and see a valuable, revered, and a respected life like yours exposed to any hazard merely upon the chance of punishing a villain? No, no; Marchdale is too base now to be met in honourable encounter. If he is dealt with in any way let it be by the laws."

This was reasonable enough, and after some argument the admiral coincided in it, and then they began to wonder how, without Charles, they should be able to get an entrance to the dungeons, for it had been his intention originally, had he not felt so fatigued, to go with them.

As soon, however, as they got tolerably near to the ruins, they saw what had happened. Neither spoke, but they quickened their pace, and soon stood close to the mass of stone-work which now had assumed so different a shape to what it had a few short hours before.

It needed little examination to let them feel certain that whoever might have been in any of the underground dungeons must have been crushed to death.

"Heaven have mercy upon his soul!" said Henry.

"Amen!" said the admiral.

They both turned away, and for some time they neither of them spoke, for their thoughts were full of reflection upon the horrible death which Marchdale must have endured. At length the admiral said--

"Shall we tell this or not?"

"Tell it at once," said Henry; "let us have no secrets."

"Good. Then I will not make one you may depend. I only wish that while he was about it, Charley could have popped that rascal Varney as well in the dungeon, and then there would have been an end and a good riddance of them both."

CHAPTER LXXVI

THE SECOND NIGHT-WATCH OF MR. CHILLINGWORTH AT THE HALL

The military party in the morning left Bannerworth Hall, and the old place resumed its wonted quiet. But Dr. Chillingworth found it difficult to get rid of his old friend, the hangman, who seemed quite disposed to share his watch with him.

The doctor, without being at all accused of being a prejudiced man, might well object to the continued companionship of one, who, according to his own account, was decidedly no better than he should be, if he were half so good.

Moreover, it materially interfered with the proceedings of our medical friend, whose object was to watch the vampyre with all imaginable quietness and secrecy, in the event of his again visiting Bannerworth Hall.

"Sir," he said, to the hangman, "now that you have so obligingly related to me your melancholy history, I will not detain you."

"Oh, you are not detaining me."

"Yes, but I shall probably remain here for a considerable time."

"I have nothing to do; and one place is about the same as another to me."

"Well, then, if I must speak plainly, allow me to say, that as I came here upon a very important and special errand, I desire most particularly to be left alone. Do you understand me now?"

"Oh! ah!--I understand; you want me to go?"

"Just so."

"Well, then, Dr. Chillingworth, allow me to tell you, I have come here on a very special errand likewise."

"You have?"

"I have. I have been putting one circumstance to another, and drawing a variety of conclusions from a variety of facts, so that I have come to what I consider an important resolve, namely, to have a good look at Bannerworth Hall, and if I continue to like it as well as I do now, I should like to make the Bannerworth family an offer for the purchase of it."

"The devil you would! Why all the world seems mad upon the project of buying this old building, which really is getting into such a state of dilapidation, that it cannot last many years longer."

"It is my fancy."

"No, no; there is something more in this than meets the eye. The same reason, be it what may, that has induced Varney the vampyre to become so desirous of possessing the Hall, actuates you."

"Possibly."

"And what is that reason? You may as well be candid with me."

"Yes, I will, and am. I like the picturesque aspect of the place."

"No, you know that that is a disingenuous answer, that you know well. It is not the aspect of the old Hall that has charms for you. But I feel, only from your conduct, more than ever convinced, that some plot is going on, having the accomplishment of some great object as its climax, a something of which you have guessed."

"How much you are mistaken!"

"No, I am certain I am right; and I shall immediately advise the Bannerworth family to return, and to take up their abode again here, in order to put an end to the hopes which you, or Varney, or any one else may have, of getting possession of the place."

"If you were a man," said the hangman, "who cared a little more for yourself, and a little less for others, I would make a confidant of you."

"What do you mean?"

"Why, I mean, candidly, that you are not selfish enough to be entitled to my confidence."

"That is a strange reason for withholding confidence from any man."

"It is a strange reason; but, in this case, a most abundantly true one. I cannot tell you what I would tell you, because I cannot make the agreement with you that I would fain make."

"You talk in riddles."

"To explain which, then, would be to tell my secret."

Dr. Chillingworth was, evidently, much annoyed, and yet he was in an extremely helpless condition; for as to forcing the hangman to leave the Hall, if he did not feel disposed to do so, that was completely out of the question, and could not be done. In the first place, he was a much more powerful man than the doctor, and in the second, it was quite contrary to all Mr. Chillingworth's habits, to engage in anything like personal warfare.

He could only, therefore, look his vexation, and say,--

"If you are determined upon remaining, I cannot help it; but, when some one, as there assuredly will, comes from the Bannerworths, here, to me, or I shall be under the necessity of stating candidly that you are intruding."

"Very good. As the morning air is keen, and as we now are not likely to be as good company to each other as we were, I shall go inside the house."

This was a proposition which the doctor did not like, but he was compelled to submit to it; and he saw, with feelings of uneasiness, the hangman make his way into the Hall by one of the windows.

Then Dr. Chillingworth sat down to think. Much he wondered what could be the secret of the great desire which Varney, Marchdale, and even this man had, all of them to be possessors of the old Hall.

That there was some powerful incentive he felt convinced, and he longed for some conversation with the Bannerworths, or with Admiral Bell, in order that he might state what had now taken place. That some one would soon come to him, in order to bring fresh provisions for the day, he was certain, and all he could do, in the interim, was, to listen to what the hangman was about in the Hall.

Not a sound, for a considerable time, disturbed the intense stillness of the place; but, now, suddenly, Mr. Chillingworth thought he heard a hammering, as if some one was at work in one of the rooms of the Hall.

"What can be the meaning of that?" he said, and he was about to proceed at once to the interior of the building, through the same window which had enabled the hangman to gain admittance, when he heard his own name pronounced by some one at the back of the garden fence, and upon casting his eyes in that direction, he, to his great relief, saw the admiral and Henry Bannerworth.

"Come round to the gate," said the doctor. "I am more glad to see you than I can tell you just now. Do not make more noise than you can help; but, come round to the gate at once."

They obeyed the injunction with alacrity, and when the doctor had admitted them, the admiral said, eagerly,--

"You don't mean to tell us that he is here?"

"No, no, not Varney; but he is not the only one who has taken a great affection for Bannerworth Hall; you may have another tenant for it, and I believe at any price you like to name."

"Indeed!"

"Hush! creep along close to the house, and then you will not be seen. There! do you hear that noise in the hall?"

"Why it sounds," said the admiral, "like the ship's carpenter at work."

"It does, indeed, sound like a carpenter; it's only the new tenant making, I dare say, some repairs."

"D--n his impudence!"

"Why, it certainly does look like a very cool proceeding, I must admit."

"Who, and what is he?"

"Who he is now, I cannot tell you, but he was once the hangman of London, at a time when I was practising in the metropolis, and so I became acquainted with him. He knows Sir Francis Varney, and, if I mistake not, has found out the cause of that mysterious personage's great attachment to Bannerworth Hall, and has found the reasons so cogent, that he has got up an affection for it himself."

"To me," said Henry, "all this is as incomprehensible as anything can possibly be. What on earth does it all mean?"

"My dear Henry," said the doctor, "will you be ruled by me?"

"I will be ruled by any one whom I know I can trust; for I am like a man groping his way in the dark."

"Then allow this gentleman who is carpentering away so pleasantly within the house, to do so to his heart's content, but don't let him leave it. Show yourselves now in the garden, he has sufficient prudence to know that three constitute rather fearful odds against one, and so he will be careful, and remain where he is. If he should come out, we need not let him go until we thoroughly ascertain what he has been about."

"You shall command the squadron, doctor," said the admiral, "and have it all your own way, you know, so here goes! Come along, Henry, and let's show ourselves; we are both armed too!"

They walked out into the centre of the garden, and they were soon convinced that the hangman saw them, for a face appeared at the window, and was as quickly withdrawn again.

"There," said the doctor, "now he knows he is a prisoner, and we may as well place ourselves in some position which commands a good view of the house, as well as of the garden gate, and so see if we cannot starve him out, though we may be starved out ourselves."

"Not at all!" said Admiral Bell, producing from his ample pockets various parcels,--"we came to bring you ample supplies."

"Indeed!"

"Yes; we have been as far as the ruins."

"Oh, to release Marchdale. Charles told me how the villain had fallen into the trap he had laid for him."

"He has, indeed, fallen into the trap, and it's one he won't easily get out of again. He's dead."

"Dead!--dead!"

"Yes; in the storm of last night the ruins have fallen, and he is by this time as flat as a pancake."

"Good God! and yet it is but a just retribution upon him. He would have assassinated poor Charles Holland in the cruelest and most cold-blooded manner, and, however we may shudder at the manner of his death, we cannot regret it."

"Except that he has escaped your friend the hangman," said the admiral.

"Don't call him my friend, if you please," said Dr. Chillingworth, "but, hark how he is working away, as if he really intended to carry the house away piece by piece, as opportunity may serve, if you will not let it to him altogether, just as it stands."

"Confound him! he is evidently working on his own account," said the admiral, "or he would not be half so industrious."

There was, indeed, a tremendous amount of hammering and noise, of one sort and another, from the house, and it was quite clear that the hangman was too heart and soul in his work, whatever may have been the object of it, to care who was listening to him, or to what conjecture he gave rise.

He thought probably that he could but he stopped in what he was about, and, until he was so, that he might as well go on.

And on he went, with a vengeance, vexing the admiral terribly, who proposed so repeatedly to go into the house and insist upon knowing what he was about, that his, wishes were upon the point of being conceded to by Henry, although they were combatted by the doctor, when, from the window at which he had entered, out stepped the hangman.

"Good morning, gentlemen! good morning," he said, and he moved towards the garden gate. "I will not trouble you any longer. Good morning!"

"Not so fast," said the admiral, "or we may bring you up with a round turn, and I never miss my mark when I can see it, and I shall not let it get out of sight, you may depend."

He drew a pistol from his pocket, as he spoke, and pointed it at the hangman, who, thereupon paused and said:--

"What! am I not to be permitted to go in peace? Why it was but a short time since the doctor was quarrelling with me because I did not go, and now it seems that I am to be shot if I do."

"Yes," said the admiral, "that's it."

"Well! but,--"

"You dare," said he, "stir another inch towards the gate, and you are a dead man!"

The hangman hesitated a moment, and looked at Admiral Bell; apparently the result of the scrutiny was, that he would keep his word, for he suddenly turned and dived in at the window again without saying another word.

"Well; you have certainly stopped him from leaving," said Henry; "but what's to be done now?"

"Let him be, let him be," said the doctor; "he must come out again, for there are no provisions in the place, and he will be starved out."

"Hush! what is that?" said Henry.

There was a very gentle ring at the bell which hung over the garden gate.

"That's an experiment, now, I'll be bound," said the doctor, "to ascertain if any one is here; let us hide ourselves, and take no notice."

The ring in a few moments was repeated, and the three confederates hid themselves effectually behind some thick laurel bushes and awaited with expectation what might next ensue.

Not long had they occupied their place of concealment, before they heard a heavy fall upon the gravelled pathway, immediately within the gate, as if some one had clambered to the top from the outside, and then jumped down.

That this was the case the sound of footsteps soon convinced them, and to their surprise as well as satisfaction, they saw through the interstices of the laurel bush behind which they were concealed, no less a personage that Sir Francis Varney himself.

"It is Varney," said Henry.

"Yes, yes," whispered the doctor. "Let him be, do not move for any consideration, for the first time let him do just what he likes."

"D--n the fellow!" said the admiral; "there are some points about him that like, after all, and he's quite an angel compared to that rascal Marchdale."

"He is,--he saved Charles."

"He did, and not if I know it shall any harm come to him, unless he were terribly to provoke it by becoming himself the assailant."

"How sad he looks!"

"Hush! he comes nearer; it is not safe to talk. Look at him."

CHAPTER LXXVII

VARNEY IN THE GARDEN.--THE COMMUNICATION OF DR. CHILLINGWORTH TO THE ADMIRAL AND HENRY

Kind reader, it was indeed Varney who had clambered over the garden wall, and thus made his way into the garden of Bannerworth Hall; and what filled those who looked at him with the most surprise was, that he did not seem in any particular way to make a secret of his presence, but walked on with an air of boldness which either arose from a feeling of absolute impunity, from his thinking there was no one there, or from an audacity which none but he could have compassed.

As for the little party that was there assembled, and who looked upon him, they seemed thunderstricken by his presence; and Henry, probably, as well as the admiral, would have burst out into some sudden exclamation, had they not been restrained by Dr. Chillingworth, who, suspecting that they might in some way give an alarm, hastened to speak first, saying in a whisper,--

"For Heaven's sake, be still, fortune, you see, favours us most strangely. Leave Varney alone. You have no other mode whatever of discovering what he really wants at Bannerworth Hall."

"I am glad you have spoken," said Henry, as he drew a long breath. "If you had not, I feel convinced that in another moment I should have rushed forward and confronted this man who has been the very bane of my life."

"And so should I," said the admiral; "although I protest against any harm being done to him, on account of some sort of good feeling that he has displayed, after all, in releasing Charles from that dungeon in which Marchdale has perished."

"At the moment," said Henry, "I had forgotten that; but I will own that his conduct has been tinctured by a strange and wild kind of generosity at times, which would seem to bespeak, at the bottom of his heart, some good feelings, the impulses of which were only quenched by circumstances."

"That is my firm impression of him, I can assure you," said Dr. Chillingworth.

They watched Varney now from the leafy covert in which they were situated, and, indeed, had they been less effectually concealed, it did not seem likely that the much dreaded vampyre would have perceived them; for not only did he make no effort at concealment himself, but he took no pains to see if any one was watching him in his progress to the house.

His footsteps were more rapid than they usually were, and there was altogether an air and manner about him, as if he were moved to some purpose which of itself was sufficiently important to submerge in its consequences all ordinary risks and all ordinary cautions.

He tried several windows of the house along that terrace of which we have more than once had occasion to speak, before he found one that opened; but at length he did succeed, and stepped at once into the Hall, leaving those, who now for some moments in silence had regarded his movements, to lose themselves in a fearful sea of conjecture as to what could possibly be his object.

"At all events," said the admiral, "I'm glad we are here. If the vampyre should have a fight with that other fellow, that we heard doing such a lot of carpentering work in the house, we ought, I think, to see fair play."

"I, for one," said the doctor, "would not like to stand by and see the vampyre murdered; but I am inclined to think he is a good match for any mortal opponent."

"You may depend he is," said Henry.

"But how long, doctor, do you purpose that we should wait here in such a state of suspense as to what is going on within the house?"

"I hope not long; but that something will occur to make us have food for action. Hark! what is that?"

There was a loud crash within the building, as of broken glass. It sounded as if some window had been completely dashed in; but although they looked carefully over the front of the building, they could see no evidences of such a thing having happened, and were compelled, consequently, to come to the opinion that Varney and the other man must have met in one of the back rooms, and that the crash of glass had arisen from some personal conflict in which they had engaged.

"I cannot stand this," said Henry.

"Nay, nay," said the doctor; "be still, and I will tell you something, than which there can be no more fitting time than this to reveal it."

"Refers it to the vampyre?"

"It does--it does."

"Be brief, then; I am in an agony of impatience."

"It is a circumstance concerning which I can be brief; for, horrible as it is, I have no wish to dress it in any adventitious colours. Sir Francis Varney, although under another name, is an old acquaintance of mine."

"Acquaintance!" said Henry.

"Why, you don't mean to say you are a vampyre?" said the admiral; "or that he has ever visited you?"

"No; but I knew him. From the first moment that I looked upon him in this neighbourhood, I thought I knew him; but the circumstance which induced me to think so was of so terrific a character, that I made some efforts to chase it from my mind. It has, however, grown upon me day by day, and, lately, I have had proof sufficient to convince me of his identity with one whom I first saw under most singular circumstances of romance."

"Say on,--you are agitated."

"I am, indeed. This revelation has several times, within the last few days, trembled on my lips, but now you shall have it; because you ought to know all that it is possible for me to tell you of him who has caused you so serious an amount of disturbance."

"You awaken, doctor," said Henry, "all my interest."

"And mine, too," remarked the admiral. "What can it be all about? and where, doctor, did you first see this Varney the vampyre?"

"In his coffin."

Both the admiral and Henry gave starts of surprise as, with one accord, they exclaimed,--

"Did you say coffin?"

"Yes: I tell you, on my word of honour, that the first time in my life I saw ever Sir Francis Varney, was in his coffin."

"Then he is a vampyre, and there can be no mistake," said the admiral.

"Go on, I pray you, doctor, go on," said Henry, anxiously.

"I will. The reason why he became the inhabitant of a coffin was simply this:--he had been hanged,--executed at the Old Bailey, in London, before ever I set eyes upon that strange countenance of his. You know that I was practising surgery at the London schools some years ago, and that, consequently, as I commenced the profession rather late in life, I was extremely anxious to do the most I could in a very short space of time."

"Yes--yes."

"Arrived, then, with plenty of resources, which I did not, as the young men who affected to be studying in the same classes as myself, spend in the pursuit of what they considered life in London, I was indefatigable in my professional labours, and there was nothing connected with them which I did not try to accomplish.

"At that period, the difficulty of getting a subject for anatomization was very great, and all sorts of schemes had to be put into requisition to accomplish so desirable, and, indeed, absolutely necessary a purpose.

"I became acquainted with the man who, I have told you, is in the Hall, at present, and who then filled the unenviable post of public executioner. It so happened, too, that I had read a learned treatise, by a Frenchman, who had made a vast number of experiments with galvanic and other apparatus, upon persons who had come to death in different ways, and, in one case, he asserted that he had actually recovered a man who had been hanged, and he had lived five weeks afterwards.

"Young as I then was, in comparison to what I am now, in my profession, this inflamed my imagination, and nothing seemed to me so desirable as getting hold of some one who had only recently been put to death, for the purpose of trying what I could do in the way of attempting a resuscitation of the subject. It was precisely for this reason that I sought out the public executioner, and made his acquaintance, whom every one else shunned, because I thought he might assist me by handing over to me the body of some condemned and executed man, upon whom I could try my skill.

"I broached the subject to him, and found him not averse. He said, that if I would come forward and claim, as next of kin and allow the body to be removed to his house, the body of the criminal who was to be executed the first time, from that period, that he could give me a hint that I should have no real next of kin opponents, he would throw every facility in my way.

"This was just what I wanted; and, I believe, I waited with impatience for some poor wretch to be hurried to his last account by the hands of my friend, the public executioner.

"At length a circumstance occurred which favoured my designs most effectually,--A man was apprehended for a highway robbery of a most aggravated character. He was tried, and the evidence against him was so conclusive, that the defence which was attempted by his counsel, became a mere matter of form.

"He was convicted, and sentenced. The judge told him not to flatter himself with the least notion that mercy would be extended to him. The crime of which he had been found guilty was on the increase it was highly necessary to make some great public example, to show evil doers that they could not, with impunity, thus trample upon the liberty of the subject, and had suddenly, just as it were, in the very nick of time, committed the very crime, attended with all the aggravated circumstances which made it easy and desirable to hang him out of hand.

"He heard his sentence, they tell me unmoved. I did not see him, but he was represented to me as a man of a strong, and well-knit frame, with rather a strange, but what some would have considered a handsome expression of countenance, inasmuch as that there was an expression of much haughty resolution depicted on it.

"I flew to my friend the executioner.

"'Can you,' I said, 'get me that man's body, who is to be hanged for the highway robbery, on Monday?'

"'Yes,' he said; 'I see nothing to prevent it. Not one soul has offered to claim even common companionship with him,--far less kindred. I think if you put in your claim as a cousin, who will bear the expense of his decent burial, you will have every chance of getting possession of the body.'

"I did not hesitate, but, on the morning before the execution, I called upon one of the sheriffs.

"I told him that the condemned man, I regretted to say, was related to me; but as I knew nothing could be done to save him on the trial, I had abstained from coming forward; but that as I did not like the idea of his being rudely interred by the authorities, I had come forward to ask for the body, after the execution should have taken place, in order that I might, at all events, bestow upon it, in some sequestered spot, a decent burial, with all the rites of the church.

"The sheriff was a man not overburthened with penetration. He applauded my pious feelings, and actually gave me, without any inquiry, a written order to receive the body from the hands of the hangman, after it had hung the hour prescribed by the law.

"I did not, as you may well suppose, wish to appear more in the business than was absolutely necessary; but I gave the executioner the sheriff's order for the body, and he promised that he would get a shell ready to place it in, and four stout men to carry it at once to his house, when he should cut it down.

"'Good!' I said; 'and now as I am not a little anxious for the success of my experiment, do you not think that you can manage so that the fall of the criminal shall not be so sudden as to break his neck?'

"'I have thought of that,' he said, 'and I believe that I can manage to let him down gently, so that he shall die of suffocation, instead of having his neck put out of joint. I will do my best."

"'If you can but succeed in that,' said I, for I was quite in a state of mania upon the subject, 'I shall be much indebted to you, and will double the amount of money which I have already promised.'

"This was, as I believed it would be, a powerful stimulus to him to do all in his power to meet my wishes, and he took, no doubt, active measures to accomplish all that I desired.

"You can imagine with what intense impatience I waited the result. He resided in an old ruinous looking house, a short distance on the Surrey side of the river, and there I had arranged all my apparatus for making experiments upon the dead man, in an apartment the windows of which commanded a view of the entrance."

"I was completely ready by half-past eight, although a moment's consideration of course told me that at least another hour must elapse before there could be the least chance of my seeing him arrive, for whom I so anxiously longed.

"I can safely say so infatuated was I upon the subject, that no fond lover ever looked with more nervous anxiety for the arrival of the chosen object of his heart, than I did for that dead body, upon which I proposed to exert all the influences of professional skill, to recall back the soul to its earthly dwelling-place.

"At length I heard the sound of wheels. I found that my friend the hangman had procured a cart, in which he brought the coffin, that being a much quicker mode of conveyance than by bearers so that about a quarter past nine o'clock the vehicle, with its ghastly content, stopped at the door of his house.

"In my impatience I ran down stairs to meet that which ninety-nine men out of a hundred would have gone some distance to avoid the sight of, namely, a corpse, livid and fresh from the gallows. I, however, heralded it as a great gift, and already, in imagination I saw myself imitating the learned Frenchman, who had published such an elaborate treatise on the mode of restoring life under all sorts of circumstances, to those who were already pronounced by unscientific persons to be dead.

"To be sure, a sort of feeling had come over me at times, knowing as I did that the French are a nation that do not scruple at all to sacrifice truth on the altar of vanity, that it might be after all a mere rhodomontade; but, however, I could only ascertain so much by actually trying, so the suspicion that such might, by a possibility, be the end of the adventure, did not deter me.

"I officiously assisted in having the coffin brought into the room where I had prepared everything that was necessary in the conduction of my grand experiment; and then, when no one was there with me but my friend the executioner, I, with his help, the one of us taking the head and the other the feet, took the body from the coffin and laid it upon a table.

"Hastily I placed my hand upon the region of the heart, and to my great delight I found it still warm. I drew off the cap that covered the face, and then, for the first time, my eyes rested upon the countenance of him who now calls himself--Heaven only knows why--Sir Francis Varney."

"Good God!" said Henry, "are you certain?"

"Quite."

"It may have been some other rascal like him," said the admiral.

"No, I am quite sure now; I have, as I have before mentioned to you, tried to get out of my own conviction upon the subject, but I have been actually assured that he is the man by the very hangman himself."

"Go on, go on! Your tale certainly is a strange one, and I do not say it either to compliment you or to cast a doubt upon you, but, except from the lips of an old, and valued friend, such as you yourself are, I should not believe it.'

"I am not surprised to hear you say that," replied the doctor; "nor should I be offended even now if you were to entertain a belief that I might, after all, be mistaken."

"No, no; you would not be so positive upon the subject, I well know, if there was the slightest possibility of an error."

"Indeed I should not."

"Let us have the sequel, then."

"It is this. I was most anxious to effect an immediate resuscitation, if it were possible, of the hanged man. A little manipulation soon convinced me that the neck was not broken, which left me at once every thing to hope for. The hangman was more prudent than I was, and before I commenced my experiments, he said,--

"'Doctor, have you duly considered what you mean to do with this fellow, in case you should be successful in restoring him to life?'

"'Not I,' said I.

"'Well,' he said, 'you can do as you like; but I consider that it is really worth thinking of.'

"I was headstrong on the matter, and could think of nothing but the success or the non-success, in a physiological point of view, of my plan for restoring the dead to life; so I set about my experiments without any delay, and with a completeness and a vigour that promised the most completely successful results, if success could at all be an ingredient in what sober judgment would doubtless have denominated a mad-headed and wild scheme.

"For more than half an hour I tried in vain, by the assistance of the hangman, who acted under my directions. Not the least symptom of vitality presented itself; and he had a smile upon his countenance, as he said in a bantering tone,--

"'I am afraid, sir, it is much easier to kill than to restore their patients with doctors.'

"Before I could make him any reply, for I felt that his observation had a good amount of truth in it, joined to its sarcasm the hanged man uttered a loud scream, and opened his eyes.

"I must own I was myself rather startled; but I for some moments longer continued the same means which had produced such an effect, when suddenly he sprang up and laid hold of me, at the same time exclaiming,--

"'Death, death, where is the treasure?'

"I had fully succeeded--too fully; and while the executioner looked on with horror depicted in his countenance, I fled from the room and the house, taking my way home as fast as I possibly could.

"A dread came over me, that the restored man would follow me if he should find out, to whom it was he was indebted for the rather questionable boon of a new life. I packed up what articles I set the greatest store by, bade adieu to London, and never have I since set foot within that city."

"And you never met the man you had so resuscitated?"

"Not till I saw Varney, the vampyre; and, as I tell you, I am now certain that he is the man."

"That is the strangest yarn that ever I heard," said the admiral.

"A most singular circumstance," said Henry.

"You may have noticed about his countenance," said Dr. Chillingworth, "a strange distorted look?"

"Yes, yes."

"Well, that has arisen from a spasmodic contraction of the muscles, in consequence of his having been hanged. He will never lose it, and it has not a little contributed to give him the horrible look he has, and to invest him with some of the seeming outward attributes of the vampyre."

"And that man who is now in the hall with him, doctor," said Henry, "is the very hangman who executed him?"

"The same. He tells me that after I left, he paid attention to the restored man, and completed what I had nearly done. He kept him in his house for a time, and then made a bargain with him, for a large sum of money per annum, all of which he has regularly been paid, although he tells me he has no more idea where Varney gets it, than the man in the moon."

"It is very strange; but, hark! do you not hear the sound of voices in angry altercation?"

"Yes, yes, they have met. Let us approach the windows now. We may chance to hear something of what they say to each other."

CHAPTER LXXVIII

THE ALTERCATION BETWEEN VARNEY AND THE EXECUTIONER IN THE HALL.--THE MUTUAL AGREEMENT

There was certainly a loud wrangling in the Hall, just as the doctor finished his most remarkable revelation concerning Sir Francis Varney, a revelation which by no means attacked the fact of his being a vampyre or not; but rather on the contrary, had a tendency to confirm any opinion that might arise from the circumstance of his being restored to life after his execution, favourable to that belief.

They all three now carefully approached the windows of the Hall, to listen to what was going on, and after a few moments they distinctly heard the voice of the hangman, saying in loud and rather angry accents,--

"I do not deny but that you have kept your word with me--our bargain has been, as you say, a profitable one: but, still I cannot see why that circumstance should give you any sort of control over my actions."

"But what do you here?" said Varney, impatiently.

"What do you?" cried the other.

"Nay, to ask another question, is not to answer mine. I tell you that I have special and most important business in this house; you can have no motive but curiosity."

"Can I not, indeed? What, too, if I have serious and important business here?"

"Impossible."

"Well, I may as easily use such a term as regards what you call important business, but here I shall remain."

"Here you shall not remain."

"And will you make the somewhat hazardous attempt to force me to leave?"

"Yes, much as I dislike lifting my hand against you, I must do so; I tell you that I must be alone in this house. I have most special reasons--reasons which concern my continued existence.

"Your continued existence you talk of.--Tell me, now, how is it that you have acquired so frightful a reputation in this neighbourhood? Go where I will, the theme of conversation is Varney, the vampyre! and it is implicitly believed that you are one of those dreadful characters that feed upon the life-blood of others, only now and then revisiting the tomb to which you ought long since to have gone in peace."

"Indeed!"

"Yes; what, in the name of all that's inexplicable, has induced you to enact such a character?"

"Enact it! you say. Can you, then, from all you have heard of me, and from all you know of me, not conceive it possible that I am not enacting any such character? Why may it not be real? Look at me. Do I look like one of the inhabitants of the earth?"

"In sooth, you do not."

"And yet I am, as you see, upon it. Do not, with an affected philosophy, doubt all that may happen to be in any degree repugnant to your usual experiences."

"I am not one disposed to do so; nor am I prepared to deny that such dreadful beings may exist as vampyres. However, whether or not you belong to so frightful a class of creatures, I do not intend to leave here; but, I will make an agreement with you."

Varney was silent; and after a few moments' pause, the other exclaimed,--

"There are people, even now, watching the place, and no doubt you have been seen coming into it."

"No, no, I was satisfied no one was here but you."

"Then you are wrong. A Doctor Chillingworth, of whom you know something, is here; and him, you have said, you would do no harm to, even to save your life."

"I do know him. You told me that it was to him that I was mainly indebted for my mere existence; and although I do not consider human life to be a great boon, I cannot bring myself to raise my hand against the man who, whatever might have been the motives for the deed, at all events, did snatch me from the grave."

"Upon my word," whispered the admiral, "there is something about that fellow that I like, after all."

"Hush!" said Henry, "listen to them. This would all have been unintelligible to us, if you had not related to us what you have."

"I have just told you in time," said Chillingworth, "it seems."

"Will you, then," said the hangman, "listen to proposals?"

"Yes," said Varney.

"Come along, then, and I will show you what I have been about; and I rather think you have already a shrewd guess as to my motive. This way--this way."

They moved off to some other part of the mansion, and the sound of their voices gradually died away, so that after all, the friends had not got the least idea of what that motive was, which still induced the vampyre and the hangman, rather than leave the other on the premises, to make an agreement to stay with each other.

"What's to be done now?" said Henry.

"Wait," said Dr. Chillingworth, "wait, and watch still. I see nothing else that can be done with any degree of safety."

"But what are we to wait for?" said the admiral.

"By waiting, we shall, perhaps, find out," was the doctor's reply; "but you may depend that we never shall by interfering."

"Well, well, be it so. It seems that we have no other resource. And when either or both of those fellows make their appearance, and seem about to leave, what is to be done with them?"

"They must be seized then, and in order that that may be done without any bloodshed, we ought to have plenty of force here. Henry, could you get your brother, and Charles, if he be sufficiently recovered, to come?"

"Certainly, and Jack Pringle."

"No," said the admiral, "no Jack Pringle for me; I have done with him completely, and I have made up my mind to strike him off the ship's books, and have nothing more to do with him."

"Well, well," added the doctor, "we will not have him, then; and it is just as well, for, in all likelihood, he would come drunk, and we shall be--let me see--five strong without him, which ought to be enough to take prisoners two men."

"Yes," said Henry, "although one of them may be a vampyre."

"That makes no difference," said the admiral. "I'd as soon take a ship manned with vampyres as with Frenchmen."

Henry started off upon his errand, certainly leaving the admiral and the doctor in rather a critical situation while he was gone; for had Varney the vampyre and the hangman chosen, they could certainly easily have overcome so inefficient a force.

The admiral would, of course, have fought, and so might the doctor, as far as his hands would permit him; but if the others had really been intent upon mischief, they could, from their downright superior physical power, have taken the lives of the two that were opposed to them.

But somehow the doctor appeared to have a great confidence in the affair. Whether that confidence arose from what the vampyre had said with regard to him, or from any hidden conviction of his own that they would not yet emerge from the Hall, we cannot say; but certain it is, he waited the course of events with great coolness.

No noise for some time came from the house; but then the sounds, as if workmen were busy within it, were suddenly resumed, and with more vigour than before.

It was nearly two hours before Henry made the private signal which had been agreed upon as that which should proclaim his return; and then he and his brother, with Charles, who, when he heard of the matter, would, notwithstanding the persuasions of Flora to the contrary, come, got quietly over the fence at a part of the garden which was quite hidden from the house by abundant vegetation, and the whole three of them took up a position that tolerably well commanded a view of the house, while they were themselves extremely well hidden behind a dense mass of evergreens.

"Did you see that rascal, Jack Pringle?" said the admiral.

"Yes," said Henry; "he is drunk."

"Ah, to be sure."

"And we had no little difficulty in shaking him off. He suspected where we were going; but I think, by being peremptory, we got fairly rid of him."

"The vagabond! if he comes here, I'll brain him, I will, the swab. Why, lately he's done nothing but drink. That's the way with him. He'll go on sometimes for a year and more, and not take more than enough to do him good, and then all at once, for about six or eight weeks, he does nothing but drink."

"Well, well, we can do without him," said Henry.

"Without him! I should think so. Do you hear those fellows in the Hall at work? D--n me, if I haven't all of a sudden thought what the reason of it all is."

"What--what?" said the doctor, anxiously.

"Why, that rascal Varney, you know, had his house burnt down."

"Yes; well?"

"Yes, well. I dare say he didn't think it well. But, however, he no doubt wants another; so, you see, my idea is, that he's stealing the material from Bannerworth Hall."

"Oh, is that your notion?"

"Yes, and a very natural one, I think, too, Master Doctor, whatever you may think of it. Come, now, have you a better?"

"Oh, dear, no, certainly not; but I have a notion that something to eat would comfort the inward man much."

"And so would something to drink, blow me if it wouldn't," said Jack Pringle, suddenly making his appearance.

The admiral made a rush upon him; but he was restrained by the others, and Jack, with a look of triumph, said,--

"Why, what's amiss with you now? I ain't drunk now. Come, come, you have something dangerous in the wind, I know, so I've made up my mind to be in it, so don't put yourself out of the way. If you think I don't know all about it, you are mistaken, for I do. The vampyre is in the house yonder, and I'm the fellow to tackle him, I believe you, my boys."

"Good God!" said the doctor, "what shall we do?"

"Nothing," said Jack, as he took a bottle from his pocket and applied the neck of it to his lips--"nothing--nothing at all."

"There's something to begin with," said the admiral, as with his stick he gave the bottle a sudden blow that broke it and spilt all its contents, leaving Jack petrified, with the bit of the neck of it still in his mouth.

"My eye, admiral," he said, "was that done like a British seaman? My eye--was that the trick of a lubber, or of a thorough-going first-rater? first-rater? My eye--"

"Hold your noise, will you; you are not drunk yet, and I was determined that you should not get so, which you soon would with that rum-bottle, if I had not come with a broadside across it. Now you may stay; but, mark me, you are on active service now, and must do nothing without orders."

"Ay, ay, your honour," said Jack, as he dropped the neck of the bottle, and looked ruefully upon the ground, from whence arose the aroma of rum--"ay, ay; but it's a hard case, take it how you will, to have your grog stopped; but, d--n it, I never had it stopped yet when it was in my mouth."

Henry and Charles could not forbear a smile at Jack's discomfiture, which, however, they were very glad of, for they knew full well his failing, and that in the course of another half hour he would have been drunk, and incapable of being controlled, except, as on some former occasions, by the exercise of brute force.

But Jack was evidently displeased, and considered himself to be grievously insulted, which, after all, was the better, inasmuch as, while he was brooding over his wrongs, he was quiet; when, otherwise, it might have been a very difficult matter to make him so.

They partook of some refreshments, and, as the day advanced, the brothers Bannerworth, as well as Charles Holland, began to get very anxious upon the subject of the proceedings of Sir Francis Varney in the Hall.

They conversed in low tones, exhausting every, as they considered, possible conjecture to endeavour to account for his mysterious predilection for that abode, but nothing occurred to them of a sufficiently probable motive to induce them to adopt it as a conclusion.

They more than suspected Dr. Chillingworth, because he was so silent, and hazarded no conjecture at all of knowing something, or of having formed to himself some highly probable hypothesis upon the subject; but they could not get him to agree that such was the case.

When they challenged him upon the subject, all he would say was,--

"My good friends, you perceive that, there is a great mystery somewhere, and I do hope that to-night it will be cleared up satisfactorily."

With this they were compelled to be satisfied; and now the soft and sombre shades of evening began to creep over the scene, enveloping all objects in the dimness and repose of early night.

The noise from the house had ceased, and all was profoundly still. But more than once Henry fancied he heard footsteps outside the garden.

He mentioned his suspicions to Charles Holland, who immediately said,--

"The same thing has come to my ears."

"Indeed! Then it must be so; we cannot both of us have merely imagined such a thing. You may depend that this place is beleaguered in some way, and that to-night will be productive of events which will throw a great light upon the affairs connected with this vampyre that have hitherto baffled conjecture."

"Hush!" said Charles; "there, again; I am quite confident I heard a sound as of a broken twig outside the garden-wall. The doctor and the admiral are in deep discussion about something,--shall we tell them?"

"No; let us listen, as yet."

They bent all their attention to listening, inclining their ears towards the ground, and, after a few moments, they felt confident that more than one footstep was creeping along, as cautiously as possible, under the garden wall. After a few moments' consultation, Henry made up his mind--he being the best acquainted with the localities of the place--to go and reconnoitre, so he, without saying anything to the doctor or the admiral, glided from where he was, in the direction of a part of the fence which he knew he could easily scale.

CHAPTER LXXIX

THE VAMPYRE'S DANGER.--THE LAST REFUGE.--THE RUSE OF HENRY BANNERWORTH

Yet knowing to what deeds of violence the passions of a lawless mob will sometimes lead them, and having the experience of what had been attempted by the alarmed and infuriated populace on a former occasion, against the Hall, Henry Bannerworth was, reasonably enough, not without his fears that something might occur of a nature yet highly dangerous to the stability of his ancient house.

He did not actually surmount the fence, but he crept so close to it, that he could get over in a moment, if he wished; and, if any one should move or speak on the other side, he should be quite certain to hear them.

For a few moments all was still, and then suddenly he heard some one say, in a low voice,

"Hist! hist! did you hear nothing?"

"I thought I did," said another; "but I now am doubtful."

"Listen again."

"What," thought Henry, "can be the motives of these men lying secreted here? It is most extraordinary what they can possibly want, unless they are brewing danger for the Hall."

Most cautiously now he raised himself, so that his eyes could just look over the fence, and then, indeed, he was astonished.

He had expected to see two or three persons, at the utmost; what was his surprise! to find a compact mass of men crouching down under the garden wall, as far as his eye could reach.

For a few moments, he was so surprised, that he continued to gaze on, heedless of the danger there might be from a discovery that he was playing the part of a spy upon them.

When, however, his first sensations of surprise were over, he cautiously removed to his former position, and, just as he did, so, he heard those who had before spoken, again, in low tones, breaking the stillness of the night.

"I am resolved upon it," said one; "I am quite determined. I will, please God, rid the country of that dreadful man."

"Don't call him a man," said the oilier.

"Well, well; it is a wrong name to apply to a vampyre."

"It is Varney, after all, then," said Henry. Bannerworth, to himself;--"it is his life that they seek. What can be done to save him?--for saved he shall be if I can compass such an object. I feel that there is yet a something in his character which is entitled to consideration, and he shall not be savagely murdered while I have an arm to raise in his defence. But if anything is now to be done, it must be done by stratagem, for the enemy are, by far, in too great force to be personally combatted with."

Henry resolved to take the advice of his friends, and with that view he went silently and quietly back to where they were, and communicated to them the news that he had so unexpectedly discovered.

They were all much surprised, and then the doctor said,

"You may depend, that since the disappointment of the mob in the destruction of this place, they have had their eye upon Varney. He has been dogged here by some one, and then by degrees that assemblage has sought the spot."

"He's a doomed man, then," remarked the admiral; "for what can save him from a determined number of persons, who, by main force, will overcome us, let us make what stand we may in his defence."

"Is there no hiding-place in the house," said Charles, "where you might, after warning him of his danger, conceal him?"

"There are plenty, but of what avail would that be, if they burn down the Hall, which in all probability they will!"

"None, certainly."

"There is but one chance," said Henry, "and that is to throw them off the scent, and induce them to think that he whom they seek is not here; I think that may possibly be done by boldness."

"But how!"

"I will go among them and make the effort."

He at once left the friends, for he felt that there might be no time to lose, and hastening to the same part of the wall, over which he had looked so short a time before, he clambered over it, and cried, in a loud voice,

"Stop the vampyre! stop the vampyre!"

"Where, where?" shouted a number of persons at once, turning their eyes eagerly towards the spot where Henry stood.

"There, across the fields," cried Henry. "I have lain in wait for him long; but he has eluded me, and is making his way again towards the old ruins, where I am sure he has some hiding-place that he thinks will elude all search. There, I see his dusky form speeding onwards."

"Come on," cried several; "to the ruins! to the ruins! We'll smoke him out if he will not come by fair means: we must have him, dead or alive."

"Yes, to the ruins!" shouted the throng of persons, who up to this time had preserved so cautious a silence, and, in a few moments more, Henry Bannerworth had the satisfaction of finding that his ruse had been perfectly successful, for Bannerworth Hall and its vicinity were completely deserted, and the mob, in a straggling mass, went over hedge and ditch towards those ruins in which there was nothing to reward the exertions they might choose to make in the way of an exploration of them, but the dead body of the villain Marchdale, who had come there to so dreadful, but so deserved a death.

CHAPTER LXXX

THE DISCOVERY OF THE BODY OF MARCHDALE IN THE RUINS BY THE MOB.--THE BURNING OF THE CORPSE.--THE MURDER OF THE HANGMAN

The mob reached the ruins of Bannerworth Hall, and crowded round it on all sides, with the view of ascertaining if a human creature, dead or alive, were there; various surmises were afloat, and some were for considering that everybody but themselves, or their friends, must be nothing less than vampyres. Indeed, a strange man, suddenly appearing among them, would have caused a sensation, and a ring would no doubt have been formed round him, and then a hasty council held, or, what was more probable, some shout, or word uttered by some one behind, who could not understand what was going on in front, would have determined them to commit some desperate outrage, and the sacrifice of life would have been the inevitable result of such an unfortunate concurrence of circumstances.

There was a pause before anyone ventured among the ruins; the walls were carefully looked to, and in more than one instance, but they were found dangerous, what were remaining; some parts had been so completely destroyed, that there were nothing but heaps of rubbish.

However, curiosity was exerted to such an extraordinary pitch that it overcame the fear of danger, in search of the horrible; for they believed that if there were any one in the ruins he must be a vampyre, of course, and they were somewhat cautious in going near such a creature, lest in so doing they should meet with some accident, and become vampyres too.

This was a dreadful reflection, and one that every now and then impressed itself upon the individuals composing the mob; but at the same time any new impulse, or a shout, and they immediately became insensible to all fear; the mere impulse is the dominant one, and then all is forgotten.

The scene was an impressive one; the beautiful house and grounds looked desolate and drear; many of the trees were stripped and broken down, and many scorched and burned, while the gardens and flower beds, the delight of the Bannerworth family, were rudely trodden under foot by the rabble, and all those little beauties so much admired and tended by the inhabitants, were now utterly destroyed, and in such a state that their site could not even be detected by the former owners.

It was a sad sight to see such a sacrilege committed,--such violence done to private feelings, as to have all these places thrown open to the scrutiny of the brutal and vulgar, who are incapable of appreciating or understanding the pleasures of a refined taste.

The ruins presented a remarkable contrast to what the place had been but a very short time before; and now the scene of desolation was complete, there was no one spot in which the most wretched could find shelter.

To be sure, under the lee of some broken and crumbling wall, that tottered, rather than stood, a huddled wretch might have found shelter from the wind, but it would have been at the risk of his life, and not there complete.

The mob became quiet for some moments, but was not so long; indeed, a mob of people,--which is, in fact, always composed of the most disorderly characters to be found in a place, is not exactly the assembly that is most calculated for quietness; somebody gave a shout, and then somebody else shouted, and the one wide throat of the whole concourse was opened, and sent forth a mighty yell.

After this exhibition of power, they began to run about like mad,--traverse the grounds from one end to the other, and then the ruins were in progress of being explored.

This was a tender affair, and had to be done with some care and caution by those who were so engaged; and they walked over crumbling and decayed masses.

In one or two places, they saw what appeared to be large holes, into which the building materials had been sunk, by their own weight, through the flooring, that seemed as roofs to some cellars or dungeons.

Seeing this, they knew not how soon some other part might sink in, and carry their precious bodies down with the mass of rubbish; this gave an interest to the scene,--a little danger is a sort of salt to an adventure, and enables those who have taken part in it to talk of their exploits, and of their dangers, which is pleasant to do, and to hear in the ale-house, and by the inglenook in the winter.

However, when a few had gone some distance, others followed, when they saw them enter the place in safety: and at length the whole ruins were covered with living men, and not a few women, who seemed necessary to make up the elements of mischief in this case.

There were some shouting and hallooing from one to the other as they hurried about the ruins.

At length they had explored the ruins nearly all over, when one man, who had stood a few minutes upon a spot, gazing intently upon something, suddenly exclaimed,--

"Hilloa! hurrah! here we are, altogether,--come on,--I've found him,--I've found--recollect it's me, and nobody else has found,--hurrah!"

Then, with a wild kind of frenzy, he threw his hat up into the air, as if to attract attention, and call others round him, to see what it was he had found.

"What's the matter, Bill?" exclaimed one who came up to him, and who had been close at hand.

"The matter? why, I've found him; that's the matter, old man," replied the first.

"What, a whale?

"No, a wampyre; the blessed wampyre! there he is,--don't you see him under them ere bricks?"

"Oh, that's not him; he got away."

"I don't care," replied the other, "who got away, or who didn't; I know this much, that he's a wampyre,--he wouldn't be there if he warn't."

This was an unanswerable argument, and nobody could deny it; consequently, there was a cessation of talk, and the people then came up, as the two first were looking at the body.

"Whose is it?" inquired a dozen voices.

"Not Sir Francis Varney's!" said the second speaker; "the clothes are not his--"

"No, no; not Sir Francis's"

"But I tell you what, mates," said the first speaker; "that if it isn't Sir Francis Varney's, it is somebody else's as bad. I dare say, now, he's a wictim."

"A what!"

"A wictim to the wampyre; and, if he sees the blessed moonlight, he will be a wampyre hisself, and so shall we be, too, if he puts his teeth into us."

"So we shall,--so we shall," said the mob, and their flesh begin to run cold, and there was a feeling of horror creeping over the whole body of persons within hearing.

"I tell you what it is; our only plan will be to get him out of the ruins, then, remarked another.

"What!" said one; "who's going to handle such cattle? if you've a sore about you, and his blood touches you, who's to say you won't be a vampyre, too!"

"No, no you won't," said an old woman.

"I won't try," was the happy rejoinder; "I ain't a-going to carry a wampyre on my two legs home to my wife and small family of seven children, and another a-coming."

There was a pause for a few moments, and then one man more adventurous than the rest, exclaimed,--

"Well, vampyre, or no vampyre, his dead body can harm no one; so here goes to get it out, help me who will; once have it out, and then we can prevent any evil, by burning it, and thus destroying the whole body.

"Hurrah!" shouted three or four more, as they jumped down into the hole formed by the falling in of the materials which had crushed Marchdale to death, for it was his body they had discovered.

They immediately set to work to displace such of the materials as lay on the body, and then, having cleared it of all superincumbent rubbish, they proceeded to lift it up, but found that it had got entangled, as they called it, with some chains: with some trouble they got them off, and the body was lifted out to a higher spot.

"Now, what's to be done?" inquired one.

"Burn it," said another.

"Hurrah!" shouted a female voice; "we've got the wampyre! run a stake through his body, and then place him upon some dry wood,--there's plenty to be had about here, I am sure,--and then burn him to a cinder."

"That's right, old woman,--that's right," said a man; "nothing better: the devil must be in him if he come to life after that, I should say."

There might be something in that, and the mob shouted its approbation, as it was sure to do as anything stupid or senseless, and the proposal might be said to have been carried by acclamation, and it required only the execution.

This was soon done. There were plenty of laths and rafters, and the adjoining wood furnished an abundant supply of dry sticks, so there was no want of fuel.

There was a loud shout as each accession of sticks took place, and, as each individual threw his bundle into the heap, each man felt all the self-devotion to the task as the Scottish chieftain who sacrificed himself and seven sons in the battle for his superior; and, when one son was cut down, the man filled up his place with the exclamation,--"Another for Hector," until he himself fell as the last of his race.

Soon now the heap became prodigious, and it required an effort to get the mangled corpse upon this funeral bier; but it was then a shout from the mob that rent the air announced, both the fact and their satisfaction.

The next thing to be done was to light the pile--this was no easy task; but like all others, it was accomplished, and the dead body of the vampyre's victim was thrown on to prevent that becoming a vampyre too, in its turn.

"There, boys," said one, "he'll not see the moonlight, that's certain, and the sooner we put a light to this the better; for it may be, the soldiers will be down upon us before we know anything of it; so now, who's got a light?"

This was a question that required a deal of searching; but, at length one was found by one of the mob coming forward, and after drawing his pipe vigorously for some moments, he collected some scraps of paper upon which he emptied the contents of the pipe, with the hope they would take fire.

In this, however, he was doomed to disappointment; for it produced nothing but a deal of smoke, and the paper burned without producing any flame.

This act of disinterestedness, however was not without its due consequences, for there were several who had pipes, and, fired with the hope of emulating the first projector of the scheme for raising the flame, they joined together, and potting the contents of their pipes together on some paper, straw, and chips, they produced, after some little trouble, a flame.

Then there was a shout, and the burning mass was then placed in a favourable position nearer the pile of materials collected for burning, and then, in a few moments, it began to take light; one piece communicated the fire to another, until the whole was in a blaze.

When the first flame fairly reached the top, a loud and tremendous shout arose from the mob, and the very welkin re-echoed with its fulness.

Then the forked flames rushed through the wood, and hissed and crackled as they flew, throwing up huge masses of black smoke, and casting a peculiar reflection around. Not a sound was heard save the hissing and roaring of the flames, which seemed like the approaching of a furious whirlwind.

At length there was nothing to be seen but the blackened mass; it was enveloped in one huge flame, that threw out a great heat, so much so, that those nearest to it felt induced to retire from before it.

"I reckon," said one, "that he's pretty well done by this time--he's had a warm berth of it up there."

"Yes," said another, "farmer Walkings's sheep he roasted whole at last harvest-home hadn't such a fire as this, I'll warrant; there's no such fire in the county--why, it would prevent a frost, I do believe it would."

"So it would, neighbour," answered another.

"Yes," replied a third, "but you'd want such a one corner of each field though."

***

There was much talk and joking going on among the men who stood around, in the midst of which, however, they were disturbed by a loud shout, and upon looking in the quarter whence it came, they saw stealing from among the ruins, the form of a man.

He was a strange, odd looking man, and at the time it was very doubtful among the mob as to whom it was--nobody could tell, and more than one looked at the burning pile, and then at the man who seemed to be so mysteriously present, as if they almost imagined that the body had got away.

"Who is it?" exclaimed one.

"Danged if I knows," said another, looking very hard, and very white at the same time;--"I hope it ain't the chap what we've burned here jist now."

"No," said the female, "that you may be sure of, for he's had a stake through his body, and as you said, he can never get over that, for as the stake is consumed, so are his vitals, and that's a sure sign he's done for."

"Yes, yes, she's right--a vampyre may live upon blood, but cannot do without his inside."

This was so obvious to them all, that it was at once conceded, and a general impression pervaded the mob that it might be Sir Francis Varney: a shout ensued.

"Hurrah!--After him--there's a vampyre--there he goes!--after him--catch him--burn him!"

And a variety of other exclamations were uttered, at the same time; the victim of popular wrath seemed to be aware that he was now discovered, and made off with all possible expedition, towards some wood.

Away went the mob in pursuit, hooting and hallooing like demons, and denouncing the unfortunate being with all the terrors that could be imagined, and which naturally added greater speed to the unfortunate man.

However, some among the mob, seeing that there was every probability of the stranger's escaping at a mere match of speed, brought a little cunning to bear upon matter, and took a circuit round, and thus intercepted him.

This was not accomplished without a desperate effort, and by the best runners, who thus reached the spot he made for, before he could get there.

When the stranger saw himself thus intercepted, he endeavoured to fly in a different direction; but was soon secured by the mob, who made somewhat free with his person, and commenced knocking him about.

"Have mercy on me," said the stranger. "What do you want? I am not rich; but take all I have."

"What do you do here?" inquired twenty voices. "Come, tell us that--what do you do here, and who are you?"

"A stranger, quite a stranger to these parts."

"Oh, yes! he's a stranger; but that's all the worse for him--he's a vampyre--there's no doubt about that."

"Good God," said the man, "I am a living and breathing man like yourselves. I have done no wrong, and injured no man--be merciful unto me; I intend no harm."

"Of course not; send him to the fire--take him back to the ruins--to the fire."

"Ay, and run a stake through his body, and then he's safe for life. I am sure he has something to do with the vampyre; and who knows, if he ain't a vampyre, how soon he may become one?"

"Ah! that's very true; bring him back to the fire, and we'll try the effects of the fire upon his constitution."

"I tell you what, neighbour, it's my opinion, that as one fool makes many, so one vampyre makes many."

"So it does, so it does; there's much truth and reason in that neighbour; I am decidedly of that opinion, too."

"Come along then," cried the mob, cuffing and pulling the unfortunate stranger with them.

"Mercy, mercy!"

But it was useless to call for mercy to men whose superstitious feelings urged them on; for when the demon of superstition is active, no matter what form it may take, it always results in cruelty and wickedness to all.

Various were the shouts and menaces of the mob, and the stranger saw no hope of life unless he could escape from the hands of the people who surrounded him.

They had now nearly reached the ruins, and the stranger, who was certainly a somewhat odd and remarkable looking man, and who appeared in their eyes the very impersonation of their notions of a vampyre, was thrust from one to the other, kicked by one, and then cuffed by the other, as if he was doomed to run the gauntlet.

"Down with the vampyre!" said the mob.

"I am no vampyre," said the stranger; "I am new to these parts, and I pray you have mercy upon me. I have done you no wrong. Hear me,--I know nothing of these people of whom you speak."

"That won't do; you've come here to see what you can do, I dare say; and, though you may have been hurt by the vampyre, and may be only your misfortune, and not your fault, yet the mischief is as great as ever it was or can be, you become, in spite of yourself, a vampyre, and do the same injury to others that has been done to you--there's no help for you."

"No help,--we can't help it," shouted the mob; "he must die,--throw him on the pile."

"Put a stake through him first, though," exclaimed the humane female; "put a stake through him, and then he's safe."

This horrible advice had an electric effect on the stranger, who jumped up, and eluded the grasp of several hands that were stretched forth to seize him.

"Throw him upon the burning wood!" shouted one.

"And a stake through his body," suggested the humane female again, who seemed to have this one idea in her heart, and no other, and, upon every available opportunity, she seemed to be anxious to give utterance to the comfortable notion.

"Seize him!" exclaimed one.

"Never let him go," said another; "we've gone too far to hang back now; and, if he escape, he will visit us in our sleep, were it only out of spite."

The stranger made a dash among the ruins, and, for a moment, out-stripped his pursuers; but a few, more adventurous than the rest, succeeded in driving him into an angle formed by two walls, and the consequence was, he was compelled to come to a stand.

"Seize him--seize him!" exclaimed all those at a distance.

The stranger, seeing he was now nearly surrounded, and had no chance of escape, save by some great effort, seized a long piece of wood, and struck two of his assailants down at once, and then dashed through the opening.

He immediately made for another part of the ruins, and succeeded in making his escape for some short distance, but was unable to keep up the speed that was required, for his great exertion before had nearly exhausted him, and the fear of a cruel death before his eyes was not enough to give him strength, or lend speed to his flight. He had suffered too much from violence, and, though he ran with great speed, yet those who followed were uninjured, and fresher,--he had no chance.

They came very close upon him at the corner of a field, which he endeavoured to cross, and had succeeded in doing, and he made a desperate attempt to scramble up the bank that divided the field from the next, but he slipped back, almost exhausted, into the ditch, and the whole mob came up.

However, he got on the bank, and leaped into the next field, and then he was immediately surrounded by those who pursued him, and he was struck down.

"Down with the vampyre!--kill him,--he's one of 'em,--run a stake through him!" were a few of the cries of the infuriated mob of people, who were only infuriated because he attempted to escape their murderous intentions.

It was strange to see how they collected in a ring as the unfortunate man lay on the ground, panting for breath, and hardly able to speak--their infuriated countenances plainly showing the mischief they were intent upon.

"Have mercy upon me!" he exclaimed, as he lay on the earth; "I have no power to help myself."

The mob returned no answer, but stood collecting their numbers as they came up.

"Have mercy on me! it cannot be any pleasure to you to spill my blood. I am unable to resist--I am one man among many,--you surely cannot wish to beat me to death?"

"We want to hurt no one, except in our own defence, and we won't be made vampyres of because you don't like to die."

"No, no; we won't be vampyres," exclaimed the mob, and there arose a great shout from the mob.

"Are you men--fathers?--have you families? if so, I have the same ties as you have; spare me for their sakes,--do not murder me,--you will leave one an orphan if you do; besides, what have I done? I have injured no one."

"I tell you what, friends, if we listen to him we shall all be vampyres, and all our children will all be vampyres and orphans."

"So we shall, so we shall; down with him!"

The man attempted to get up, but, in doing so, he received a heavy blow from a hedge-stake, wielded by the herculean arm of a peasant. The sound of the blow was heard by those immediately around, and the man fell dead. There was a pause, and those nearest, apparently fearful of the consequences, and hardly expecting the catastrophe, began to disperse, and the remainder did so very soon afterwards.

CHAPTER LXXXI

THE VAMPYRE'S FLIGHT.--HIS DANGER, AND THE LAST PLACE OF REFUGE

Leaving the disorderly and vicious mob, who were thus sacrificing human life to their excited passions, we return to the brothers Bannerworth and the doctor, who together with Admiral Bell, still held watch over the hall.

No indication of the coming forth of Varney presented itself for some time longer, and then, at least they thought, they heard a window open; and, turning their eyes in the direction whence the sound proceeded, they could see the form of a man slowly and cautiously emerging from it.

As far as they could judge, from the distance at which they were, that form partook much of the appearance and the general aspect of Sir Francis Varney, and the more they looked and noticed its movements, the more they felt convinced that such was the fact.

"There comes your patient, doctor," said the admiral.

"Don't call him my patient," said the doctor, "if you please."

"Why you know he is; and you are, in a manner of speaking, bound to look after him. Well, what is to be done?"

"He must not, on any account," said Dr. Chillingworth, "be allowed to leave the place. Believe me, I have the very strongest reasons for saying so."

"He shall not leave it then," said Henry.

Even as he spoke, Henry Bannerworth darted forward, and Sir Francis Varney dropped from the window, out of which he had clambered, close to his feet.

"Hold!" cried Henry, "you are my prisoner."

With the most imperturbable coolness in the world, Sir Francis Varney turned upon him, and replied,--

"And pray, Henry Bannerworth, what have I done to provoke your wrath?"

"What have you done?--have you not, like a thief, broken into my house? Can you ask what you have done?"

"Ay," said the vampyre, "like a thief, perchance, and yet no thief. May I ask you, what there is to steal, in the house?"

By the time this short dialogue had been uttered, the rest of the party had come up, and Varney was, so far as regarded numbers, a prisoner.

"Well, gentlemen," he said, with that strange contortion of countenance which, now they all understood, arose from the fact of his having been hanged, and restored to life again. "Well, gentlemen, now that you have beleaguered me in such a way, may I ask you what it is about?"

"If you will step aside with me, Sir Francis Varney, for a moment," said Dr. Chillingworth, "I will make to you a communication which will enable you to know what it is all about."

"Oh, with pleasure," said the vampyre. "I am not ill at present; but still, sir, I have no objection to hear what you have to say."

He stepped a few paces on one side with the doctor, while the others waited, not without some amount of impatience for the result of the communication. All that they could hear was, that Varney said, suddenly--

"You are quite mistaken."

And then the doctor appeared to be insisting upon something, which the vampyre listened to patiently; and, at the end, burst out with,--

"Why, doctor, you must be dreaming."

At this, Dr. Chillingworth at once left him, and advancing to his friends, he said,--

"Sir Francis Varney denies in toto all that I have related to you concerning him; therefore, I can say no more than that I earnestly recommend you, before you let him go, to see that he takes nothing of value with him."

"Why, what can you mean?" said Varney.

"Search him," said the doctor; "I will tell you why, very shortly."

"Indeed--indeed!" said Sir Francis Varney. "Now, gentlemen, I will give you a chance of behaving justly and quietly, so saving yourself the danger of acting otherwise. I have made repeated offers to take this house, either as a tenant or as a purchaser, all of which offers have been declined, upon, I dare say, a common enough principle, namely, one which induces people to enhance the value of anything they have for disposal, if it be unique, by making it difficult to come at. Seeing that you had deserted the place, I could make no doubt but that it was to be had, so I came here to make a thorough examination of its interior, to see if it would suit me. I find that it will not; therefore, I have only to apologise for the intrusion, and to wish you a remarkably good evening."

"That won't do," said the doctor.

"What won't do, sir?"

"This excuse will not do, Sir Francis Varney. You are, although you deny it, the man who was hanged in London some years ago for a highway robbery."

Varney laughed, and held up his hands, exclaiming,--

"Alas! alas! our good friend, the doctor, has studied too hard; his wits, probably, at the best of times, none of the clearest, have become hopelessly entangled."

"Do you deny," said Henry, "then, that you are that man?"

"Most unequivocally."

"I assert it," said the doctor, "and now, I will tell you all, for I perceive you hesitate about searching, Sir Francis Varney, I tell you all why it is that he has such an affection for Bannerworth Hall."

"Before you do," said Varney, "there is a pill for you, which you may find more nauseous and harder of digestion, than any your shop can furnish."

As Varney uttered these words, he suddenly drew from his pocket a pistol, and, levelling it at the unfortunate doctor, he fired it full at him.

The act was so sudden, so utterly unexpected, and so stunning, that it was done before any one could move hand or foot to prevent it. Henry Bannerworth and his brother were the furthest off from the vampyre; and, unhappily, in the rush which they, as soon us possible, made towards him, they knocked down the admiral, who impeded them much; and, before they could spring over, or past him, Sir Francis Varney was gone.

So sudden, too, had been his departure, that they had not the least idea in which direction he had gone; so that to follow him would have been a work of the greatest possible difficulty.

Notwithstanding, however, both the difficulty and the danger, for no doubt the vampyre was well enough armed, Henry and his brother both rushed after the murderer, as they now believed him to be, in the route which they thought it was most probable he would take, namely, that which led towards the garden gate.

They reached that spot in a few moments, but all was profoundly still. Not the least trace of any one could be seen, high or low, and they were compelled, after a cursory examination, to admit that Sir Francis Varney had again made his escape, despite the great odds that were against him in point of numbers.

"He has gone," said Henry. "Let us go back, and see into the state of poor Dr. Chillingworth, who, I fear, is a dead man."

They hurried back to the spot, and there they found the admiral looking as composed as possible, and solacing himself with a pinch of snuff, as he gazed upon the apparently lifeless form at his feet.

"Is he dead?" said Henry.

"I should say he was," replied the admiral; "such a shot as that was don't want to be repeated. Well, I liked the doctor with all his faults. He only had one foolish way with him, and that was, that he shirked his grog."

"This is an awful catastrophe," said Henry, as he knelt down by the side of the body. "Assist me, some of you. Where is Charles?"

"I'll be hanged," said the admiral, "if I know. He disappeared somewhere."

"This is a night of mystery as well as terror. Alas! poor Dr. Chillingworth! I little thought that you would have fallen a victim to the man whom you preserved from death. How strange it is that you should have snatched from the tomb the very individual who was, eventually, to take your own life."

The brothers gently raised the body of the doctor, and carried it on to the glass plot, which was close at hand.

"Farewell, kind and honest-hearted Chillingworth," said Henry; "I shall, many and many a time, feel your loss; and now I will rest not until I have delivered up to justice your murderer. All consideration, or feeling, for what seemed to be latent virtues in that strange and inexplicable man, Varney, shall vanish, and he shall reap the consequences of the crime he has now committed."

"It was a cold blooded, cowardly murder," said his brother.

"It was; but you may depend the doctor was about to reveal something to us, which Varney so much dreaded, that he took his life as the only effectual way, at the moment, of stopping him."

"It must be so," said Henry.

"And now," said the admiral, "it's too late, and we shall not know it at all. That's the way. A fellow saves up what he has got to tell till it is too late to tell it, and down he goes to Davy Jones's locker with all his secrets aboard."

"Not always," said Dr. Chillingworth, suddenly sitting bolt upright--"not always."

Henry and his brother started back in amazement, and the admiral was so taken by surprise, that had not the resuscitated doctor suddenly stretched out his hand and laid hold of him by the ankle, he would have made a precipitate retreat.

"Hilloa! murder!" he cried. "Let me go! How do I know but you may be a vampyre by now, as you were shot by one."

Henry soonest recovered from the surprise of the moment, and with the most unfeigned satisfaction, he cried,--

"Thank God you are unhurt, Dr. Chillingworth! Why he must have missed you by a miracle."

"Not at all," said the doctor. "Help me up--thank you--all right. I'm only a little singed about the whiskers. He hit me safe enough."

"Then how have you escaped?"

"Why from the want of a bullet in the pistol, to be sure. I can understand it all well enough. He wanted to create sufficient confusion to cover a desperate attempt to escape, and he thought that would be best done by seeming so shoot me. The suddenness of the shock, and the full belief, at the moment, that he had sent a bullet into my brains, made me fall, and produced a temporary confusion of ideas, amounting to insensibility."

"From which you are happily recovered. Thank Heaven that, after all, he is not such a villain as this act would have made him."

"Ah!" said the admiral, "it takes people who have lived a little in these affairs to know the difference in sound between a firearm with a bullet in it, and one without. I knew it was all right."

"Then why did you not say so, admiral?"

"What was the use? I thought the doctor might be amused to know what you should say of him, so you see I didn't interfere; and, as I am not a good hand at galloping after anybody, I didn't try that part of the business, but just remained where I was."

"Alas! alas!" cried the doctor, "I much fear that, by his going, I have lost all that I expected to be able to do for you, Henry. It's of not the least use now telling you or troubling you about it. You may now sell or let Bannerworth Hall to whomever you please, for I am afraid it is really worthless."

"What on earth do you mean?" said Henry. "Why, doctor, will you keep up this mystery among us? If you have anything to say, why not say it at once?"

"Because, I tell you it's of no use now. The game is up, Sir Francis Varney has escaped; but still I don't know that I need exactly hesitate."

"There can be no reason for your hesitating about making a communication to us," said Henry. "It is unfriendly not to do so."

"My dear boy, you will excuse me for saying that you don't know what you are talking about."

"Can you give any reason?"

"Yes; respect for the living. I should have to relate something of the dead which would be hurtful to their feelings."

Henry was silent for a few moments, and then he said,--

"What dead? And who are the living?"

"Another time," whispered the doctor to him; "another time, Henry. Do not press me now. But you shall know all another time."

"I must be content. But now let us remember that another man yet lingers in Bannerworth Hall. I will endure suspense on his account no longer. He is an intruder there; so I go at once to dislodge him."

No one made any opposition to this move, not even the doctor; so Henry preceded them all to the house. They passed through the open window into the long hall, and from thence into every apartment of the mansion, without finding the object of their search. But from one of the windows up to which there grew great masses of ivy, there hung a rope, by which any one might easily have let himself down; and no doubt, therefore, existed in all their minds that the hangman had sufficiently profited by the confusion incidental to the supposed shooting of the doctor, to make good his escape from the place.

"And so, after all," said Henry, "we are completely foiled?"

"We may be," said Dr. Chillingworth; "but it is, perhaps, going too far to say that we actually are. One thing, however, is quite clear; and that is, no good can be done here."

"Then let us go home," said the admiral. "I did not think from the first that any good would be done here."

They all left the garden together now; so that almost for the first time, Bannerworth Hall was left to itself, unguarded and unwatched by any one whatever. It was with an evident and a marked melancholy that the doctor proceeded with the party to the cottage-house of the Bannerworths; but, as after what he had said, Henry forbore to question him further upon those subjects which he admitted he was keeping secret; and as none of the party were much in a cue for general conversation, the whole of them walked on with more silence than usually characterised them.

CHAPTER LXXXII

CHARLES HOLLAND'S PURSUIT OF THE VAMPYRE.--THE DANGEROUS INTERVIEW

It will be recollected that the admiral had made a remark about Charles Holland having suddenly disappeared; and it is for us now to account for that disappearance and to follow him to the pathway he had chosen.

The fact was, that he, when Varney fired the shot at the doctor, or what was the supposed shot, was the farthest from the vampyre; and he, on that very account, had the clearest and best opportunity of marking which route he took when he had discharged the pistol.

He was not confused by the smoke, as the others were; nor was he stunned by the noise of the discharge; but he distinctly saw Varney dart across one of the garden beds, and make for the summer-house, instead of for the garden gate, as Henry had supposed was the most probable path he had chosen.

Now, Charles Holland either had an inclination, for some reasons of his own, to follow the vampyre alone; or, on the spur of the moment, he had not time to give an alarm to the others; but certain it is that he did, unaided, rush after him. He saw him enter the summer-house, and pass out of it again at the back portion of it, as he had once before done, when surprised in his interview with Flora.

But the vampyre did not now, as he had done on the former occasion, hide immediately behind the summer-house. He seemed to be well aware that that expedient would not answer twice; so he at once sped onwards, clearing the garden fence, and taking to the meadows.

It formed evidently no part of the intentions of Charles Holland to come up with him. He was resolved upon dogging his footsteps, to know where he should go; so that he might have a knowledge of his hiding-place, if he had one.

"I must and will," said Charles to himself, "penetrate the mystery that hangs about this most strange and inexplicable being. I will have an interview with him, not in hostility, for I forgive him the evil he has done me, but with a kindly spirit; and I will ask him to confide in me."

Charles, therefore, did not keep so close upon the heels of the vampyre as to excite any suspicions of his intention to follow him; but he waited by the garden paling long enough not only for Varney to get some distance off, but long enough likewise to know that the pistol which had been fired at the doctor had produced no real bad effects, except singing some curious tufts of hair upon the sides of his face, which the doctor was pleased to call whiskers.

"I thought as much," was Charles's exclamation when he heard the doctor's voice. "It would have been strikingly at variance with all Varney's other conduct, if he had committed such a deliberate and heartless murder."

Then, as the form of the vampyre could be but dimly seen, Charles ran on for some distance in the direction he had taken, and then paused again; so that if Varney heard the sound of footsteps, and paused to listen they had ceased again probably, and nothing was discernible.

In this manner he followed the mysterious individual, if we may really call him such, for above a mile; and then Varney made a rapid detour, and took his way towards the town.

He went onwards with wonderful precision now in a right line, not stopping at any obstruction, in the way of fences, hedges, or ditches, so that it took Charles some exertion, to which, just then, he was scarcely equal, to keep up with him.

At length the outskirts of the town were gained, and then Varney paused, and looked around him, scarcely allowing Charles, who was now closer to him than he had been, time to hide himself from observation, which, however, he did accomplish, by casting himself suddenly upon the ground, so that he could not be detected against the sky, which then formed a back ground to the spot where he was.

Apparently satisfied that he had completely now eluded the pursuit, if any had been attempted, of those whom he had led in such a state of confusion, the vampyre walked hastily towards a house that was to let, and which was only to be reached by going up an avenue of trees, and then unlocking a gate in a wall which bounded the premises next to the avenue. But the vampyre appeared to be possessed of every facility for effecting an entrance to the place and, producing from his pocket a key, he at once opened the gate, and disappeared within the precincts of those premises.

He, no doubt, felt that he was hunted by the mob of the town, and hence his frequent change of residence, since his own had been burnt down, and, indeed, situated as he was, there can be no manner of doubt that he would have been sacrificed to the superstitious fury of the populace, if they could but have got hold of him.

He had, from his knowledge, which was no doubt accurate and complete, of what had been done, a good idea of what his own fate would be, were he to fall into the hands of that ferocious multitude, each individual composing which, felt a conviction that there would be no peace, nor hope of prosperity or happiness, on the place, until he, the arch vampyre of all the supposed vampyres, was destroyed.

Charles did pause for a few moments, after having thus become roused, to consider whether he should then attempt to have the interview he had resolved upon having by some means or another, or defer it, now that he knew where Varney was to be found, until another time.

But when he came to consider how extremely likely it was that, even in the course of a few hours, Varney might shift his abode for some good and substantial reasons, he at once determined upon attempting to see him.

But how to accomplish such a purpose was not the easiest question in the world to answer. If he rung the bell that presented itself above the garden gate, was it at all likely that Varney, who had come there for concealment, would pay any attention to the summons?

After some consideration, he did, however, think of a plan by which, at all events, he could ensure effecting an entrance into the premises, and then he would take his chance of finding the mysterious being whom he sought, and who probably might have no particular objection to meeting with him, Charles Holland, because their last interview in the ruins could not be said to be otherwise than of a peaceable and calm enough character.

He saw by the board, which was nailed in the front of the house, that all applications to see it were to be made to a Mr. Nash, residing close at hand; and, as Charles had the appearance of a respectable person, he thought he might possibly have the key entrusted to him, ostensibly to look at the house, preparatory possibly to taking it, and so he should, at all events, obtain admission.

He, accordingly, went at once to this Mr. Nash, and asked about the house; of course he had to affect an interest in its rental and accommodations, which he did not feel, in order to lull any suspicion, and, finally, he said,--

"I should like to look over it if you will lend me the key, which I will shortly bring back to you."

There was an evident hesitation about the agent when this proposal was communicated by Charles Holland, and he said,--

"I dare say, sir, you wonder that I don't say yes, at once; but the fact is there came a gentleman here one day when I was out, and got a key, for we have two to open the house, from my wife, and he never came back again."

That this was the means by which Varney, the vampyre, had obtained the key, by the aid of which Charles had seen him effect so immediate an entrance to the house, there could be no doubt.

"How long ago were you served that trick?" he said.

"About two days ago, sir."

"Well, it only shows how, when one person acts wrongly, another is at once suspected of a capability to do so likewise. There is my name and my address; I should like rather to go alone to see the house, because I always fancy I can judge better by myself of the accommodation, and I can stay as long as I like, and ascertain the sizes of all the rooms without the disagreeable feeling upon my mind, which no amount of complaisance on your part, could ever get me over, that I was most unaccountably detaining somebody from more important business of their own."

"Oh, I assure you, sir," said Mr. Nash, "that I should not be at all impatient. But if you would rather go alone--"

"Indeed I would."

"Oh, then, sir, there is the key. A gentleman who leaves his name and address, of course, we can have no objection to. I only told you of what happened, sir, in the mere way of conversation, and I hope you won't imagine for a moment that I meant to insinuate that you were going to keep the key."

"Oh, certainly not--certainly not," said Charles, who was only too glad to get the key upon any terms. "You are quite right, and I beg you will say no more about it; I quite understand."

He then walked off to the empty house again, and, proceeding to the avenue, he fitted the key to the lock, and had the satisfaction of finding the gate instantly yield to him.

When he passed through it, and closed the door after him, which he did carefully, he found himself in a handsomely laid-out garden, and saw the house a short distance in front of him, standing upon a well got-up lawn.

He cared not if Varney should see him before he reached the house, because the fact was sufficiently evident to himself that after all he could not actually enforce an interview with the vampyre. He only hoped that as he had found him out it would be conceded to him.

He, therefore, walked up the lawn without making the least attempt at concealment, and when he reached the house he allowed his footsteps to make what noise they would upon the stone steps which led up to it. But no one appeared; nor was there, either by sight or by sound, any indication of the presence of any living being in the place besides himself.

Insensibly, as he contemplated the deserted place around him, the solemn sort of stillness began to have its effect upon his imagination, and, without being aware that he did so, he had, with softness and caution, glided onwards, as if he were bent on some errand requiring the utmost amount of caution and discrimination in the conduction of it.

And so he entered the hall of the house, where he stood some time, and listened with the greatest attention, without, however, being able to hear the least sound throughout the whole of the house.

"And yet he must be here," thought Charles to himself; "I was not gone many minutes, and it is extremely unlikely that in so short a space of time he has left, after taking so much trouble, by making such a detour around the meadows to get here, without being observed. I will examine every room in the place, but I will find him."

Charles immediately commenced going from room to room of that house in his search for the vampyre. There were but four apartments upon the ground floor, and these, of course, he quickly ran through. Nothing whatever at all indicative of any one having been there met his gaze, and with a feeling of disappointment creeping over him, he commenced the ascent of the staircase.

The day had now fairly commenced, so that there was abundance of light, although, even for the country, it was an early hour, and probably Mr. Nash had been not a little surprised to have a call from one whose appearance bespoke no necessity for rising with the lark at such an hour.

All these considerations, however, sank into insignificance in Charles's mind, compared with the object he had in view, namely, the unravelling the many mysteries that hung around that man. He ascended to the landing of the first story, and then, as he could have no choice, he opened the first door that his eyes fell upon, and entered a tolerably large apartment. It was quite destitute of furniture, and at the moment Charles was about to pronounce it empty; but then his eyes fell upon a large black-looking bundle of something, that seemed to be lying jammed up under the window on the floor--that being the place of all others in the room which was enveloped in the most shadow.

He started back involuntarily at the moment, for the appearance was one so shapeless, that there was no such thing as defining, from even that distance, what it really was.

Then he slowly and cautiously approached it, as we always approach that of the character of which we are ignorant, and concerning the powers of which to do injury we can consequently have no defined idea.

That it was a human form there, was the first tangible opinion he had about it; and from its profound stillness, and the manner in which it seemed to be laid close under the window, he thought that he was surely upon the point of finding out that some deed of blood had been committed, the unfortunate victim of which was now lying before him.

Upon a nearer examination, he found that the whole body, including the greater part of the head and face, was wrapped in a large cloak; and there, as he gazed, he soon found cause to correct his first opinion at to the form belonging to the dead, for he could distinctly hear the regular breathing, as of some one in a sound and dreamless sleep.

Closer he went, and closer still. Then, as he clasped his hands, he said, in a voice scarcely above a whisper,--

"It is--it is the vampyre."

Yes, there could be no doubt of the fact. It was Sir Francis Varney who lay there, enveloped in the huge horseman's cloak, in which, on two or three occasions during the progress of this narrative, he had figured. There he lay, at the mercy completely of any arm that might be raised against him, apparently so overcome by fatigue that no ordinary noise would have awakened him.

Well might Charles Holland gaze at him with mingled feelings. There lay the being who had done almost enough to drive the beautiful Flora Bannerworth distracted--the being who had compelled the Bannerworth family to leave their ancient house, to which they had been bound by every description of association. The same mysterious existence, too, who, the better to carry on his plots and plans, had, by dint of violence, immured him, Charles, in a dungeon, and loaded him with chains. There he lay sleeping, and at his mercy.

"Shall I awaken him," said Charles, "or let him sleep off the fatigue, which, no doubt, is weighing down his limbs, and setting heavily on his eyelids. No, my business with him is too urgent."

He then raised his voice, and cried,--

"Varney, Varney, awake!"

The sound disturbed, without altogether breaking up, the deep slumber of the vampyre, and he uttered a low moan, and moved one hand restlessly. Then, as if that disturbance of the calm and deep repose which had sat upon him, had given at once the reins to fancy, he begin to mutter strange words in his sleep, some of which could be heard by Charles distinctly, while others were too incoherently uttered to be clearly understood.

"Where is it?" he said; "where--where hidden?--Pull the house down!--Murder! No, no, no! no murder!--I will not, I dare not. Blood enough is upon my hands.--The money!--the money! Down, villains! down! down! down!"

What these incoherent words alluded to specifically, Charles, of course, could not have the least idea, but he listened attentively, with a hope that something might fall from his lips that would afford a key to some of the mysterious circumstances with which he was so intimately connected.

Now, however, there was a longer silence than before, only broken occasionally by low moans; but suddenly, as Charles was thinking of again speaking, he uttered some more disjointed sentences.

"No harm," he said, "no harm,--Marchdale is a villain!--Not a hair of his head injured--no, no. Set him free--yes, I will set him free. Beware! beware, Marchdale! and you Mortimer. The scaffold! ay, the scaffold! but where is the bright gold? The memory of the deed of blood will not cling to it. Where is it hidden? The gold! the gold! the gold! It is not in the grave--it cannot be there--no, no, no!--not there, not there! Load the pistols. There, there! Down, villain, down!--down, down!"

Despairing, now, of obtaining anything like tangible information from these ravings, which, even if they did, by accident, so connect themselves together as to seem to mean something, Charles again cried aloud,--

"Varney, awake, awake!"

But, as before, the sleeping man was sufficiently deaf to the cry to remain, with his eyes closed, still in a disturbed slumber, but yet a slumber which might last for a considerable time.

"I have heard," said Charles, "that there are many persons whom no noise will awaken, while the slightest touch rouses them in an instant. I will try that upon this slumbering being."

As he spoke, he advanced close to Sir Francis Varney, and touched him slightly with the toe of his boot.

The effect was as startling as it was instantaneous. The vampyre sprang to his feet, as he had been suddenly impelled up by some powerful machinery; and, casting his cloak away from his arms, so as to have them at liberty, he sprang upon Charles Holland, and hurled him to the ground, where he held him with a giant's gripe, as he cried,--

"Rash fool! be you whom you may. Why have you troubled me to rid the world of your intrusive existence?"

The attack was so sudden and so terrific, that resistance to it, even if Charles had had the power, was out of the question. All he could say, was,--

"Varney, Varney! do you not know me? I am Charles Holland. Will you now, in your mad rage, take the life you might more easily have taken when I lay in the dungeon from which you released me?"

The sound of his voice at once convinced Sir Francis Varney of his identity; and it was with a voice that had some tones of regret in it, that he replied,--

"And wherefore have you thought proper, when you were once free and unscathed, to cast yourself into such a position of danger as to follow me to my haunt?"

"I contemplated no danger," said Charles, "because I contemplated no evil. I do not know why you should kill me."

"You came here, and yet you say you do not know why I should kill you. Young man, have you a dozen lives that you can afford to tamper with them thus? I have, at much chance of imminence to myself, already once saved you, when another, with a sterner feeling, would have gladly taken your life; but now, as if you were determined to goad me to an act which I have shunned committing, you will not let me close my eyes in peace."

"Take your hand from off my throat, Varney, and I will then tell you what brought me here."

Sir Francis Varney did so.

"Rise," he said--"rise; I have seen blood enough to be sickened at the prospect of more; but you should not have come here and tempted me."

"Nay, believe me, I came here for good and not for evil. Sir Francis Varney, hear me out, and then judge for yourself whether you can blame the perseverance which enabled me to find out this secret place of refuge; but let me first say that now it is as good a place of concealment to you as before it was, for I shall not betray you."

"Go on, go on. What is it you desire?"

"During the long and weary hours of my captivity, I thought deeply, and painfully too, as may be well imagined, of all the circumstances connected with your appearance at Bannerworth Hall, and your subsequent conduct. Then I felt convinced that there was something far more than met the eye, in the whole affair, and, from what I have been informed of since, I am the more convinced that some secret, some mystery, which it is in your power only perhaps to explain, lurks at the bottom of all your conduct."

"Well, proceed," said Varney.

"Have I not said enough now to enable you to divine the object of my visit? It is that you should shake off the trammels of mystery in which you have shrouded yourself, and declare what it is you want, what it is you desire, that has induced you to set yourself up as such a determined foe of the Bannerworth family."

"And that, you say, is the modest request that brings you here?"

"You speak as if you thought it was idle curiosity that prompts me, but you know it is not. Your language and manner are those of a man of too much sagacity not to see that I have higher notions."

"Name them."

"You have yourself, in more than one instance, behaved with a strange sort of romantic generosity, as if, but for some great object which you felt impelled to seek by any means, and at any sacrifice, you would be a something in character and conduct very different from what you are. One of my objects, then, is to awaken that better nature which is slumbering within you, only now and then rousing itself to do some deed which should be the character of all your actions--for your own sake I have come."

"But not wholly?"

"Not wholly, as you say. There is another than whom, the whole world is not so dear to me. That other one was serene as she was beautiful. Happiness danced in her eyes, and she ought--for not more lovely is the mind that she possesses than the glorious form that enshrines it--to be happy. Her life should have passed like one long summer's day of beauty, sunshine, and pure heavenly enjoyment. You have poisoned the cup of joy that the great God of nature had permitted her to place to her lips and taste of mistrustingly. Why have you done this? I ask you--why have you done this?"

"Have you said all that you came to say?"

"I have spoken the substance of my message. Much could I elaborate upon such a theme; but it is not one, Varney, which is congenial to my heart; for your sake, however, and for the sakes of those whom I hold most dear, let me implore you to act in this matter with a kindly consideration. Proclaim your motives; you cannot say that they are not such as we may aid you in."

Varney was silent for several moments; he seemed perceptibly moved by the manner of the young man, as well as by the matter of his discourse. In fact, one would suppose that Charles Holland had succeeded in investing what he said with some sort of charm that won much upon the fancy of Sir Francis Varney, for when he ceased to speak, the latter said in a low voice,--

"Go on, go on; you have surely much more to say."

"No, Varney; I have said enough, and not thus much would I have said had I not been aware, most certainly and truly aware, without the shadow of a doubt, by your manner, that you were most accessible to human feeling."

"I accessible to human feeling! know you to whom you speak? Am I not he before whom all men shudder, whose name has been a terror and a desolation; and yet you can talk of my human feelings. Nay, if I had had any, be sure they would have been extinguished by the persecutions I have endured from those who, you know, with savage ferocity have sought my life."

"No, Varney; I give you credit for being a subtler reasoner than thus to argue; you know well that you were the aggressor to those parties who sought your life; you know well that with the greatest imaginable pains you held yourself up to them as a thing of great terror."

"I did--I did."

"You cannot, then, turn round upon ignorant persons, and blame them because your exertions to make yourself seem what you wish were but too successful."

"You use the word seem," said Varney, with a bitterness of aspect, "as if you would imply a doubt that I am that which thousands, by their fears, would testify me to be."

"Thousands might," said Charles Holland; "but not among them am I, Varney; I will not be made the victim of superstition. Were you to enact before my very eyes some of those feats which, to the senses of others, would stamp you as the preternatural being you assume to be, I would doubt the evidence of my own senses ere I permitted such a bugbear to oppress my brain."

"Go," said Sir Francis Varney, "go: I have no more words for you; I have nothing to relate to you."

"Nay, you have already listened sufficiently to me to give me a hope that I had awakened some of the humanity that was in your nature. Do not, Sir Francis Varney, crush that hope, even as it was budding forth; not for my own sake do I ask you for revelations; that may, perhaps--must be painful for you; but for the sake of Flora Bannerworth, to whom you owe abundance of reparation."

"No, no."

"In the name of all that is great, and good, and just, I call upon you for justice."

"What have I to do with such an invocation? Utter such a sentiment to men who, like yourself, are invested with the reality as well as the outward show of human nature."

"Nay, Sir Francis Varney, now you belie yourself. You have passed through a long, and, perchance, a stormy life. Can you look back upon your career, and find no reminiscences of the past that shall convince you that you are of the great family of man, and have had abundance of human feelings and of human affections?"

"Peace, peace!"

"Nay, Sir Francis Varney, I will take your word, and if you will lay your hand upon your heart, and tell me truly that you never felt what it was to love--to have all feeling, all taste, and all hope of future joy, concentrated in one individual, I will despair, and leave you. If you will tell me that never, in your whole life, you have felt for any fair and glorious creature, as I now feel for Flora Bannerworth, a being for whom you could have sacrificed not only existence, but all the hopes of a glorious future that bloom around it--if you will tell me, with the calm, dispassionate aspect of truth, that you have held yourself aloof from such human feelings, I will no longer press you to a disclosure which I shall bring no argument to urge."

The agitation of Sir Francis Varney's countenance was perceptible, and Charles Holland was about to speak again, when, striking him upon the breast with his clinched hand, the vampyre checked him, saying--

"Do you wish to drive me mad, that you thus, from memory's hidden cells, conjure up images of the past?"

"Then there are such images to conjure up--there are such shadows only sleeping, but which require only, as you did even now, but a touch to awaken them to life and energy. Oh, Sir Francis Varney, do not tell me that you are not human."

The vampyre made a furious gesture, as if he would have attacked Charles Holland; but then he sank nearly to the floor, as if soul-stricken by some recollection that unnerved his arm; he shook with unwonted emotion, and, from the frightful livid aspect of his countenance, Charles dreaded some serious accession of indisposition, which might, if nothing else did, prevent him from making the revelation he so much sought to hear from his lips.

"Varney," he cried, "Varney, be calm! you will be listened to by one who will draw no harsh--no hasty conclusions; by one, who, with that charity, I grieve to say, is rare, will place upon the words you utter the most favourable construction. Tell me all, I pray you, tell me all."

"This is strange," said the vampyre. "I never thought that aught human could thus have moved me. Young man, you have touched the chords of memory; they vibrate throughout my heart, producing cadences and sounds of years long past. Bear with me awhile."

"And you will speak to me?"

"I will."

"Having your promise, then, I am content, Varney."

"But you must be secret; not even in the wildest waste of nature, where you can well presume that naught but Heaven can listen to your whisperings, must you utter one word of that which I shall tell to you."

"Alas!" said Charles, "I dare not take such a confidence; I have said that it is not for myself; I seek such knowledge of what you are, and what you have been, but it is for another so dear to me, that all the charms of life that make up other men's delights, equal not the witchery of one glance from her, speaking as it does of the glorious light from that Heaven which is eternal, from whence she sprung."

"And you reject my communication," said Varney, "because I will not give you leave to expose it to Flora Bannerworth?"

"It must be so."

"And you are most anxious to hear that which I have to relate?"

"Most anxious, indeed--indeed, most anxious."

"Then have I found in that scruple which besets your mind, a better argument for trusting you, than had ye been loud in protestation. Had your promises of secrecy been but those which come from the lip, and not from the heart, my confidence would not have been rejected on such grounds. I think that I dare trust you."

"With leave to tell to Flora that which you shall communicate."

"You may whisper it to her, but to no one else, without my special leave and licence."

"I agree to those terms, and will religiously preserve them."

"I do not doubt you for one moment; and now I will tell to you what never yet has passed my lips to mortal man. Now will I connect together some matters which you may have heard piecemeal from others."

"What others are they?"

"Dr. Chillingworth, and he who once officiated as a London hangman."

"I have heard something from those quarters."

"Listen then to me, and you shall better understand that which you have heard. Some years ago, it matters not the number, on a stormy night, towards the autumn of the year, two men sat alone in poverty, and that species of distress which beset the haughty, profligate, daring man, who has been accustomed all his life to its most enticing enjoyments, but never to that industry which alone ought to produce them, and render them great and magnificent."

"Two men; and who were they?"

"I was one. Look upon me! I was of those men; and strong and evil passions were battling in my heart."

"And the other!"

"Was Marmaduke Bannerworth."

"Gracious Heaven! the father of her whom I adore; the suicide."

"Yes, the same; that man stained with a thousand vices--blasted by a thousand crimes--the father of her who partakes nothing of his nature, who borrows nothing from his memory but his name--was the man who there sat with me, plotting and contriving how, by fraud or violence, we were to lead our usual life of revelry and wild audacious debauch."

"Go on, go on; believe me, I am deeply interested."

"I can see as much. We were not nice in the various schemes which our prolific fancies engendered. If trickery, and the false dice at the gaming-table, sufficed not to fill our purses, we were bold enough for violence. If simple robbery would not succeed, we could take a life."

"Murder?"

"Ay, call it by its proper name, a murder. We sat till the midnight hour had passed, without arriving at a definite conclusion; we saw no plan of practicable operation, and so we wandered onwards to one of those deep dens of iniquity, a gaming-house, wherein we had won and lost thousands.

"We had no money, but we staked largely, in the shape of a wager, upon the success of one of the players; we knew not, or cared not, for the consequence, if we had lost; but, as it happened, we were largely successful, and beggars as we had walked into that place, we might have left it independent men.

"But when does the gambler know when to pause in his career? If defeat awakens all the raging passions of humanity within his bosom, success but feeds the great vice that has been there engendered. To the dawn of morn we played; the bright sun shone in, and yet we played--the midday came, and went--the stimulant of wine supported us, and still we played; then came the shadows of evening, stealing on in all their beauty. But what were they to us, amid those mutations of fortune, which, at one moment, made us princes, and placed palaces at our control, and, at another, debased us below the veriest beggar, that craves the stinted alms of charity from door to door.

"And there was one man who, from the first to the last, stayed by us like a very fiend; more than man, I thought he was not human. We won of all, but of him. People came and brought their bright red gold, and laid it down before us, but for us to take it up, and then, by a cruel stroke of fortune, he took it from us.

"The night came on; we won, and he won of us; the clock struck twelve--we were beggars. God knows what was he.

"We saw him place his winnings about his person--we saw the smile that curved the corners of his lips; he was calm, and we were maddened. The blood flowed temperately through his veins, but in ours it was burning lava, scorching as it went through every petty artery, and drying up all human thought--all human feeling.

"The winner left, and we tracked his footsteps. When he reached the open air, although he had taken much less than we of the intoxicating beverages that are supplied gratis to those who frequent those haunts of infamy, it was evident that some sort of inebriation attacked him; his steps were disordered and unsteady, and, as we followed him, we could perceive, by the devious track that he took, that he was somewhat uncertain of his route.

"We had no fixed motive in so pursuing this man. It was but an impulsive proceeding at the best; but as he still went on and cleared the streets, getting into the wild and open country, and among the hedge-rows, we began to whisper together, and to think that what we did not owe to fortune, we might to our own energy and courage at such a moment.

"I need not hesitate to say so, since, to hide the most important feature of my revelation from you, would be but to mock you; we resolved upon robbing him.

"And was that all?"

"It was all that our resolution went to. We were not anxious to spill blood; but still we were resolved that we would accomplish our purpose, even if it required murder for its consummation. Have you heard enough?"

"I have not heard enough, although I guess the rest."

"You may well guess it, from its preface. He turned down a lonely pathway, which, had we chosen it ourselves, could not have been more suitable for the attack we meditated.

"There were tall trees on either side, and a hedge-row stretching high up between them. We knew that that lane led to a suburban village, which, without a doubt, was the object of his destination.

"Then Marmaduke Bannerworth spoke, saying,--

"'What we have to do, must be done now or never. There needs not two in this adventure. Shall you or I require him to refund what he has won from us?'

"'I care not,' I said; 'but if we are to accomplish our purpose without arousing even a shadow of resistance, it is better to show him its futility by both appearing, and take a share in the adventure.'

"This was agreed upon, and we hastened forward. He heard footsteps pursuing him and quickened his pace. I was the fleetest runner, and overtook him. I passed him a pace or two, and then turning, I faced him, and impeded his progress.

"The lane was narrow, and a glance behind him showed him Marmaduke Bannerworth; so that he was hemmed in between two enemies, and could move neither to the right nor to the left, on account of the thick brushwood that intervened between the trees.

"Then, with an assumed courage, that sat but ill upon him, he demanded of us what we wanted, and proclaimed his right to pass despite the obstruction we placed in his way.

"The dialogue was brief. I, being foremost, spoke to him.

"'Your money,' I said; 'your winnings at the gaming-table. We cannot, and we will not lose it.'

"So suddenly, that he had nearly taken my life, he drew a pistol from his pocket, and levelling it at my head, he fired upon me.

"Perhaps, had I moved, it might have been my death; but, as it was, the bullet furrowed my cheek, leaving a scar, the path of which is yet visible in a white cicatrix.

"I felt a stunning sensation, and thought myself a dead man. I cried aloud to Marmaduke Bannerworth, and he rushed forward. I knew not that he was armed, and that he had the power about him to do the deed which he then accomplished; but there was a groan, a slight struggle, and the successful gamester fell upon the green sward, bathed in his blood."

"And this is the father of her whom I adore?"

"It is. Are you shocked to think of such a neat relationship between so much beauty and intelligence and a midnight murderer? Is your philosophy so poor, that the daughter's beauty suffers from the commission of a father's crime?"

"No, no, It is not so. Do not fancy that, for one moment, I can entertain such unworthy opinions. The thought that crossed me was that I should have to tell one of such a gentle nature that her father had done such a deed."

"On that head you can use your own discretion. The deed was done; there was sufficient light for us to look upon the features of the dying man. Ghastly and terrific they glared upon us; while the glazed eyes, as they were upturned to the bright sky, seemed appealing to Heaven for vengeance against us, for having done the deed.

"Many a day and many an hour since at all times and all seasons, I have seen those eyes, with the glaze of death upon them, following me, and gloating over the misery they had the power to make. I think I see them now."

"Indeed!"

"Yes; look--look--see how they glare upon me--with what a fixed and frightful stare the bloodshot pupils keep their place--there, there! oh! save me from such a visitation again. It is too horrible. I dare not--I cannot endure it; and yet why do you gaze at me with such an aspect, dread visitant? You know that it was not my hand that did the deed--who laid you low. You know that not to me are you able to lay the heavy charge of your death!"

"Varney, you look upon vacancy," said Charles Holland.

"No, no; vacancy it may be to you, but to me 'tis full of horrible shapes."

"Compose yourself; you have taken me far into your confidence already; I pray you now to tell me all. I have in my brain no room for horrible conjectures such as those which might else torment me."

Varney was silent for a few minutes, and then he wiped from his brow the heavy drops of perspiration that had there gathered, and heaved a deep sigh.

"Speak to me," added Charles; "nothing will so much relieve you from the terrors of this remembrance as making a confidence which reflection will approve of, and which you will know that you have no reason to repent."

"Charles Holland," said Varney, "I have already gone too far to retract--much too far, I know, and can well understand all the danger of half confidence. You already know so much, that it is fit you should know more."

"Go on then, Varney, I will listen to you."

"I know not if, at this juncture, I can command myself to say more. I feel that what next has to be told will be most horrible for me to tell--most sad for you to hear told."

"I can well believe, Varney, from your manner of speech, and from the words you use, that you have some secret to relate beyond this simple fact of the murder of this gamester by Marmaduke Bannerworth."

"You are right--such is the fact; the death of that man could not have moved me as you now see me moved. There is a secret connected with his fate which I may well hesitate to utter--a secret even to whisper to the winds of heaven--I--although I did not do the deed, no, no--I--I did not strike the blow--not I--not I!"

"Varney, it is astonishing to me the pains you take to assure yourself of your innocence of this deed; no one accuses you, but still, were it not that I am impressed with a strong conviction that you're speaking to me nothing but the truth, the very fact of your extreme anxiety to acquit yourself, would engender suspicion."

"I can understand that feeling, Charles Holland; I can fully understand it. I do not blame you for it--it is a most natural one; but when you know all, you will feel with me how necessary it must have been to my peace to seize upon every trivial circumstance that can help me to a belief in my own innocence."

"It may be so; as yet, you well know, I speak in ignorance. But what could there have been in the character of that gambler, that has made you so sympathetic concerning his decease?"

"Nothing--nothing whatever in his character. He was a bad man; not one of those free, open spirits which are seduced into crime by thoughtlessness--not one of those whom we pity, perchance, more than we condemn; but a man without a redeeming trait in his disposition--a man so heaped up with vices and iniquities, that society gained much by his decease, and not an individual could say that he had lost a friend."

"And yet the mere thought of the circumstances connected with his death seems almost to drive you to the verge of despair."

"You are right; the mere thought has that effect."

"You have aroused all my curiosity to know the causes of such a feeling."

Varney paced the apartment in silence for many minutes. He seemed to be enduring a great mental struggle, and at length, when he turned to Charles Holland and spoke, there were upon his countenance traces of deep emotion.

"I have said, young man, that I will take you into my confidence. I have said that I will clear up many seeming mysteries, and that I will enable you to understand what was obscure in the narrative of Dr. Chillingworth, and of that man who filled the office of public executioner, and who has haunted me so long."

"It is true, then, as the doctor states, that you were executed in London?"

"I was."

"And resuscitated by the galvanic process, put into operation by Dr. Chillingworth?"

"As he supposed; but there are truths connected with natural philosophy which he dreamed not of. I bear a charmed life, and it was but accident which produced a similar effect upon the latent springs of my existence in the house to which the executioner conducted me, to what would have been produced had I been sufficed, in the free and open air, to wait until the cool moonbeams fell upon me."

"Varney, Varney," said Charles Holland, "you will not succeed in convincing me of your supernatural powers. I hold such feelings and sensations at arm's length. I will not--I cannot assume you to be what you affect."

"I ask for no man's belief. I know that which I know, and, gathering experience from the coincidences of different phenomena, I am compelled to arrive at certain conclusions. Believe what you please, doubt what you please; but I say again that I am not as other men."

"I am in no condition to depute your proposition; I wish not to dispute it; but you are wandering, Varney, from the point. I wait anxiously for a continuation of your narrative."

"I know that I am wandering from it--I know well that I am wandering from it, and that the reason I do so is that I dread that continuation."

"That dread will nor be the less for its postponement."

"You are right; but tell me, Charles Holland, although you are young you have been about in the great world sufficiently to form correct opinions, and to understand that which is related to you, drawing proper deductions from certain facts, and arriving possibly at more correct conclusions than some of maturer years with less wisdom."

"I will freely answer, Varney, any question you may put to me."

"I know it; tell me then what measure of guilt you attach to me in the transaction I have noticed to you."

"It seems then to me that, not contemplating the man's murder, you cannot be accused of the act, although a set of fortuitous circumstances made you appear an accomplice to its commission."

"You think I may be acquitted?"

"You can acquit yourself, knowing that you did not contemplate the murder."

"I did not contemplate it. I know not what desperate deed I should have stopped short at then, in the height of my distress, but I neither contemplated taking that man's life, nor did I strike the blow which sent him from existence."

"There is even some excuse as regards the higher crime for Marmaduke Bannerworth."

"Think you so?"

"Yes; he thought that you were killed, and impulsively he might have struck the blow that made him a murderer."

"Be it so. I am willing, extremely willing that anything should occur that should remove the odium of guilt from any man. Be it so, I say, with all my heart; but now, Charles Holland, I feel that we must meet again ere I can tell you all; but in the meantime let Flora Bannerworth rest in peace--she need dread nothing from me. Avarice and revenge, the two passions which found a home in my heart, are now stifled for ever."

"Revenge! did you say revenge?"

"I did; whence the marvel, am I not sufficiently human for that?"

"But you coupled it with the name of Flora Bannerworth."

"I did, and that is part of my mystery."

"A mystery, indeed, to imagine that such a being as Flora could awaken any such feeling in your heart--a most abundant mystery."

"It is so. I do not affect to deny it: but yet it is true, although so greatly mysterious, but tell her that although at one time I looked upon her as one whom I cared not if I injured, her beauty and distress changed the current of my thoughts, and won upon me greatly, From the moment I found I had the power to become the bane of her existence, I ceased to wish to be so, and never again shall she experience a pang of alarm from Varney, the vampyre."

"Your message shall be faithfully delivered, and doubt not that it will be received with grateful feelings. Nevertheless I should have much wished to have been in a position to inform her of more particulars."

"Come to me here at midnight to-morrow, and you shall know all. I will have no reservation with you, no concealments; you shall know whom I have had to battle against, and how it is that a world of evil passions took possession of my heart and made me what I am."

"Are you firm in this determination, Varney--will you indeed tell me no more to-night?"

"No more, I have said it. Leave me now. I have need of more repose, for of late sleep has seldom closed my eyelids."

Charles Holland was convinced, from the positive manner in which he spoke, that nothing more in the shape of information, at that time, was to be expected from Varney; and being fearful that if he urged this strange being too far, at a time when he did not wish it, he might refuse all further communication, he thought it prudent to leave him, so he said to him,--

"Be assured, Varney, I shall keep the appointment you have made, with an expectation when we do meet of being rewarded by a recital of some full particulars."

"You shall not be disappointed; farewell, farewell!"

Charles Holland bade him adieu, and left the place.

Although he had now acquired all the information he hoped to take away with him when Varney first began to be communicative, yet, when he came to consider how strange and unaccountable a being he had been in communication with, Charles could not but congratulate himself that he had heard so much, for, from the manner of Varney, he could well suppose that that was, indeed, the first time he had been so communicative upon subjects which evidently held so conspicuous a place in his heart.

And he had abundance of hope, likewise, from what had been said by Varney, that he would keep his word, and communicate to him fully all else that he required to know; and when he recollected those words which Varney had used, signifying that he knew the danger of half confidences, that hope grew into a certainty, and Charles began to have no doubt but that on the next evening all that was mysterious in the various affairs connected with the vampyre would become clear and open to the light of day.

He strolled down the lane in which the lone house was situated, revolving these matters in his mind, and when he arrived at its entrance, he was rather surprised to see a throng of persons hastily moving onward, with come appearance of dismay about them, and anxiety depicted upon their countenances.

He stopped a lad, and inquired of him the cause of the seeming tumult.

"Why, sir, the fact is," said the boy, "a crowd from the town's been burning down Bannerworth Hall, and they've killed a man."

"Bannerworth Hall! you must be mistaken."

"Well, sir, I ought not to call it Bannerworth Hall, because I mean the old ruins in the neighbourhood that are supposed to have been originally Bannerworth Hall before the house now called such was built; and, moreover, as the Bannerworths have always had a garden there, and two or three old sheds, the people in the town called it Bannerworth Hall in common with the other building."

"I understand. And do you say that all have been destroyed?"

"Yes, sir. All that was capable of being burnt has been burnt, and, what is more, a man has been killed among the ruins. We don't know who he is, but the folks said he was a vampyre, and they left him for dead."

"When will these terrible outrages cease? Oh! Varney, Varney, you have much to answer for; even if in your conscience you succeed in acquitting yourself of the murder, some of the particulars concerning which you have informed me of."

CHAPTER LXXXIII

THE MYSTERIOUS ARRIVAL AT THE INN.--THE HUNGARIAN NOBLEMAN.--THE LETTER TO VARNEY

While these affairs are proceeding, and when there seems every appearance of Sir Francis Varney himself quickly putting an end to some of the vexatious circumstances connected with himself and the Bannerworth family, it is necessary that we should notice an occurrence which took place at the same inn which the admiral had made such a scene of confusion upon the occasion of his first arrival in the town.

Not since the admiral had arrived with Jack Pringle, and so disturbed the whole economy of the household, was there so much curiosity excited as on the morning following the interview which Charles Holland had had with Varney, the vampyre.

The inn was scarcely opened, when a stranger arrived, mounted on a coal-black horse, and, alighting, he surrendered the bridle into the hands of a boy who happened to be at the inn-door, and stalked slowly and solemnly into the building.

He was tall, and of a cadaverous aspect; in attire he was plainly apparelled, but there was no appearance of poverty about him; on the contrary, what he really had on was of a rich and costly character, although destitute of ornament.

He sat down in the first room that presented itself, and awaited the appearance of the landlord, who, upon being informed that a guest of apparently ample means, and of some consequence, had entered the place, hastily went to him to receive his commands.

With a profusion of bows, our old friend, who had been so obsequious to Admiral Bell, entered the room, and begged to know what orders the gentleman had for him.

"I presume," said the stranger, in a deep, solemn voice, "I presume that you have no objection, for a few days that I shall remain in this town, to board and lodge me for a certain price which you can name to me at once?"

"Certainly, sir," said the landlord; "any way you please; without wine, sir, I presume?"

"As you please; make your own arrangements."

"Well, sir, as we can't tell, of course, what wine a gentleman may drink, but when we come to consider breakfast, dinner, tea, and supper, and a bed, and all that sort of thing, and a private sitting-room, I suppose, sir?"

"Certainly."

"You would not, then, think, sir, a matter of four guineas a week will be too much, perhaps."

"I told you to name your own charge. Let it be four guineas; if you had said eight I should have paid it."

"Good God!" said the publican, "here's a damned fool that I am. I beg your pardon, sir, I didn't mean you. Now I could punch my own head--will you have breakfast at once, sir, and then we shall begin regular, you know, sir?"

"Have what?"

"Breakfast, breakfast, you know, sir; tea, coffee, cocoa, or chocolate; ham, eggs, or a bit of grilled fowl, cold sirloin of roast beef, or a red herring--anything you like, sir."

"I never take breakfast, so you may spare yourself the trouble of providing anything for me."

"Not take breakfast, sir! not take breakfast! Would you like to take anything to drink then, sir? People say it's an odd time, at eight o'clock in the morning, to drink; but, for my part, I always have thought that you couldn't begin a good thing too soon."

"I live upon drink," said the stranger; "but you have none in the cellar that will suit me."

"Indeed, sir."

"No, no, I am certain."

"Why, we've got some claret now, sir," said the landlord.

"Which may look like blood, and yet not be it."

"Like what, sir?--damn my rags!"

"Begone, begone."

The stranger uttered these words so peremptorily that the landlord hastily left the room, and going into his own bar, he gave himself so small a tap on the side of the head, that it would not have hurt a fly, as he said,--

"I could punch myself into bits, I could tear my hair out by the roots;" and then he pulled a little bit of his hair, so gently and tenderly that it showed what a man of discretion he was, even in the worst of all his agony of passion.

"The idea," he added, "of a fellow coming here, paying four guineas a week for board and lodging, telling me he would not have minded eight, and then not wanting any breakfast; it's enough to aggravate half a dozen saints; but what an odd fish he looks."

At this moment the ostler came in, and, standing at the bar, he wiped his mouth with his sleeve, as he said,--

"I suppose you'll stand a quart for that, master?"

"A quart for what, you vagabond? A quart because I've done myself up in heaps; a quart because I'm fit to pull myself into fiddlestrings?"

"No," said the ostler; "because I've just put up the gentleman's horse."

"What gentleman's horse?"

"Why, the big-looking fellow with the white face, now in the parlour."

"What, did he come on a horse, Sam? What sort of a looking creature is it? you may judge of a man from the sort of horse-company he keeps."

"Well, then, sir, I hardly know. It's coal black, and looks as knowing as possible; it's tried twice to get a kick at me, but I was down upon him, and put the bucket in his way. Howsomdever, I don't think it's a bad animal, as a animal, mind you, sir, though a little bit wicious or so."

"Well," said the publican, as he drew the ostler half a pint instead of a quart, "you're always drinking; take that."

"Blow me," said the ostler, "half a pint, master!"

"Plague take you, I can't stand parleying with you, there's the parlour bell; perhaps, after all, he will have some breakfast."

While the landlord was away the ostler helped himself to a quart of the strongest ale, which, by a singular faculty that he had acquired, he poured down his throat without any effort at swallowing, holding his head back, and the jug at a little distance from his mouth.

Having accomplished this feat, he reversed the jug, giving it a knowing tap with his knuckles as though he would have signified to all the world that it was empty, and that he had accomplished what he desired.

In the meantime, the landlord had made his way to his strange guest, who said to him, when he came into the room,

"Is there not one Sir Francis Varney residing in this town?"

"The devil!" thought the landlord; "this is another of them, I'll bet a guinea. Sir Francis Varney, sir, did you say? Why, sir, there was a Sir Francis Varney, but folks seem to think as how he's no better than he should be--a sort of vampyre, sir, if you know what that is."

"I have, certainly, heard of such things; but can you not tell me Varney's address? I wish to see him."

"Well, then, sir, I cannot tell it to you, for there's really been such a commotion and such a riot about him that he's taken himself off, I think, altogether, and we can hear nothing of him. Lord bless you, sir, they burnt down his house, and hunted him about so, that I don't think that he'll ever show his face here again."

"And cannot you tell me where he was seen last?"

"That I cannot, sir; but, if anybody knows anything about him, it's Mr. Henry Bannerworth, or perhaps Dr. Chillingworth, for they have had more to do with him than anybody else."

"Indeed; and can you tell me the address of the former individual?"

"That I can't, sir, for the Bannerworths have left the Hall. As for the doctor, sir, you'll see his house in the High-street, with a large brass plate on the door, so that you cannot mistake it. It's No. 9, on the other side of the way."

"I thank you for so much information," said the stranger, and rising, he walked to the door. Before, however, he left, he turned, and added,--"You can say, if you should by chance meet Mr. Bannerworth, that a Hungarian nobleman wishes to speak to him concerning Sir Francis Varney, the vampyre?"

"A what, sir?"

"A nobleman from Hungary," was the reply.

"The deuce!" said the landlord, as he looked after him. "He don't seem at all hungry here, not thirsty neither. What does he mean by a nobleman from Hungary? The idea of a man talking about hungry, and not taking any breakfast. He's queering me. I'll be hanged if I'll stand it. Here I clearly lose four guineas a week, and then get made game of besides. A nobleman, indeed! I think I see him. Why, he isn't quite so big as old Slaney, the butcher. It's a do. I'll have at him when he comes back."

Meanwhile, the unconscious object of this soliloquy passed down the High-street, until he came to Dr. Chillingworth's, at whose door he knocked.

Now Mrs. Chillingworth had been waiting the whole night for the return of the doctor, who had not yet made his appearance, and, consequently, that lady's temper had become acidulated to an uncommon extent and when she heard a knock at the door, something possessed her that it could be no other than her spouse, and she prepared to give him that warm reception which she considered he had a right, as a married man, to expect after such conduct.

She hurriedly filled a tolerably sized hand-basin with not the cleanest water in the world, and then, opening the door hurriedly with one hand, she slouced the contents into the face of the intruder, exclaiming,--

"Now you've caught it!"

"D--n!" said the Hungarian nobleman, and then Mrs. Chillingworth uttered a scream, for she feared she had made a mistake.

"Oh, sir! I'm very sorry: but I thought it was my husband."

"But if you did," said the stranger, "there was no occasion to drown him with a basin of soap-suds. It is your husband I want, madam, if he be Dr. Chillingworth."

"Then, indeed, you must go on wanting him, sir, for he's not been to his own home for a day and a night. He takes up all his time in hunting after that beastly vampyre."

"Ah! Sir Francis Varney, you mean."

"I do; and I'd Varney him if I caught hold of him."

"Can you give me the least idea of where he can be found?"

"Of course I can."

"Indeed! where?" said the stranger, eagerly.

"In some churchyard, to be sure, gobbling up the dead bodies."

With this Mrs. Chillingworth shut the door with a bang that nearly flattened the Hungarian's nose with his face, and he was fain to walk away, quite convinced that there was no information to be had in that quarter.

He returned to the inn, and having told the landlord that he would give a handsome reward to any one who would discover to him the retreat of Sir Francis Varney, he shut himself up in an apartment alone, and was busy for a time in writing letters.

Although the sum which the stranger offered was an indefinite one, the landlord mentioned the matter across the bar to several persons; but all of them shook their heads, believing it to be a very perilous adventure indeed to have anything to do with so troublesome a subject as Sir Francis Varney. As the day advanced, however, a young lad presented himself, and asked to see the gentleman who had been inquiring for Varney.

The landlord severely questioned and cross-questioned him, with the hope of discovering if he had any information: but the boy was quite obdurate, and would speak to no one but the person who had offered the reward, so that mine host was compelled to introduce him to the Hungarian nobleman, who, as yet, had neither eaten nor drunk in the house.

The boy wore upon his countenance the very expression of juvenile cunning, and when the stranger asked him if he really was in possession of any information concerning the retreat of Sir Francis Varney, he said,--

"I can tell you where he is, but what are you going to give?"

"What sum do you require?" said the stranger.

"A whole half-crown."

"It is your's; and, if your information prove correct, come to-morrow, and I'll add another to it, always provided, likewise, you keep the secret from any one else."

"Trust me for that," said the boy. "I live with my grandmother; she's precious old, and has got a cottage. We sell milk and cakes, sticky stuff, and pennywinkles."

"A goodly collection. Go on."

"Well, sir, this morning, there comes a man in with a bottle, and he buys a bottle full of milk and a loaf. I saw him, and I knew it was Varney, the vampyre."

"You followed him?"

"Of course I did, sir; and he's staying at the house that's to let down the lane, round the corner, by Mr. Biggs's, and past Lee's garden, leaving old Slaney's stacks on your right hand, and so cutting on till you come to Grants's meadow, when you'll see old Madhunter a brick-field staring of you in the face; and, arter that--"

"Peace--peace!--you shall yourself conduct me. Come to this place at sunset; be secret, and, probably, ten times the reward you have already received may be yours," said the stranger.

"What, ten half-crowns?"

"Yes, I will keep my word with you."

"What a go! I know what I'll do. I'll set up as a show man, and what a glorious treat it will be, to peep through one of the holes all day myself, and get somebody to pull the strings up and down, and when I'm tired of that, I can blaze away upon the trumpet like one o'clock. I think I see me. Here you sees the Duke of Marlborough a whopping of everybody, and here you see the Frenchmen flying about like parched peas in a sifter."

CHAPTER LXXXIV

THE EXCITED POPULACE.--VARNEY HUNTED.--THE PLACE OF REFUGE

There seemed, now a complete lull in the proceedings as connected with Varney, the vampyre. We have reason to believe that the executioner who had been as solicitous as Varney to obtain undisputed possession of Bannerworth Hall, has fallen a victim to the indiscriminating rage of the mob. Varney himself is a fugitive, and bound by the most solemn ties to Charles Holland, not only to communicate to him such particulars of the past, as will bring satisfaction to his mind, but to abstain from any act which, for the future, shall exercise a disastrous influence upon the happiness of Flora.

The doctor and the admiral, with Henry, had betaken themselves from the Hall as we had recorded, and, in due time, reached the cottage where Flora and her mother had found a temporary refuge.

Mrs. Bannerworth was up; but Flora was sleeping, and, although the tidings they had to tell were of a curious and mixed nature, they would not have her disturbed to listen to them.

And, likewise, they were rather pleased than otherwise, since they knew not exactly what had become of Charles Holland, to think that they would probably be spared the necessity of saying they could not account for his absence.

That he had gone upon some expedition, probably dangerous, and so one which he did not wish to communicate the particulars of to his friends, lest they should make a strong attempt to dissuade him from it, they were induced to believe.

But yet they had that confidence in his courage and active intellectual resources, to believe that he would come through it unscathed, and, probably, shortly show himself at the cottage.

In this hope they were not disappointed, for in about two hours Charles made his appearance; but, until he began to be questioned concerning his absence by the admiral, he scarcely considered the kind of dilemma he had put himself into by the promise of secrecy he had given to Varney, and was a little puzzled to think how much he might tell, and how much he was bound in honour to conceal.

"Avast there!" cried the admiral; "what's become of your tongue, Charles? You've been on some cruize, I'll be bound. Haul over the ship's books, and tell us what's happened."

"I have been upon an adventure," said Charles, "which I hope will be productive of beneficial results to us all; but, the fact is, I have made a promise, perhaps incautiously, that I will not communicate what I know."

"Whew!" said the admiral, "that's awkward; but, however, if a man said under sealed instructions, there's an end of it. I remember when I was off Candia once---"

"Ha!" interposed Jack, "that was the time you tumbled over the blessed binnacle, all in consequence of taking too much Madeira. I remember it, too--it's an out and out good story, that 'ere. You took a rope's end, you know, and laid into the bowsprit; and, says you, 'Get up, you lubber,' says you, all the while a thinking, I supposes, as it was long Jack Ingram, the carpenter's mate, laying asleep. What a lark!"

"This scoundrel will be the death of me," said the admiral; "there isn't one word of truth in what he says. I never got drunk in all my life, as everybody knows. Jack, affairs are getting serious between you and I--we must part, and for good. It's a good many times that I've told you you've forgot the difference between the quarter-deck and the caboose. Now, I'm serious--you're off the ship's books, and there's an end of you."

"Very good," said Jack; "I'm willing I'll leave you. Do you think I want to keep you any longer? Good bye, old bloak--I'll leave you to repent, and when old grim death comes yard-arm and yard-arm with you, and you can't shake off his boarding-tackle, you'll say, 'Where's Jack Pringle?' says you; and then what's his mane--oh ah! echo you call it--echo'll say, it's d----d if it knows."

Jack turned upon his heel, and, before the admiral could make any reply he left the place.

"What's the rascal up to now?" said the admiral. "I really didn't think he'd have taken me at my word."

"Oh, then, after all, you didn't mean it, uncle?" said Charles.

"What's that to you, you lubber, whether I mean it, or not, you shore-going squab? Of course I expect everybody to desert an old hulk, rats and all--and now Jack Pringle's gone; the vagabond, couldn't he stay, and get drunk as long as he liked! Didn't he say what he pleased, and do what he pleased, the mutinous thief? Didn't he say I run away from a Frenchman off Cape Ushant, and didn't I put up with that?"

"But, my dear uncle, you sent him away yourself."

"I didn't, and you know I didn't; but I see how it is, you've disgusted Jack among you. A better seaman never trod the deck of a man-of-war."

"But his drunkenness, uncle?"

"It's a lie. I don't believe he ever got drunk. I believe you all invented it, and Jack's so good-natured, he tumbled about just to keep you in countenance."

"But his insolence, uncle; his gross insolence towards you--his inventions, his exaggerations of the truth?"

"Avast, there--avast, there--none of that, Master Charlie; Jack couldn't do anything of the sort; and I means to say this, that if Jack was here now, I'd stick up for him, and say he was a good seaman.

"Tip us your fin, then," said Jack, darting into the room; "do you think I'd leave you, you d----d old fool? What would become of you, I wonder, if I wasn't to take you in to dry nurse? Why, you blessed old babby, what do you mean by it?"

"Jack, you villain!"

"Ah! go on and call me a villain as much as you like. Don't you remember when the bullets were scuttling our nobs?"

"I do, I do, Jack; tip us your fin, old fellow. You've saved my life more than once."

"It's a lie."

"It ain't. You did, I say."

"You bed----d!"

And thus was the most serious misunderstanding that these two worthies ever had together made up. The real fact is, that the admiral could as little do without Jack, as he could have done without food; and as for Pringle, he no more thought of leaving the old commodore, than of--what shall we say? forswearing him. Jack himself could not have taken a stronger oath.

But the old admiral had suffered so much from the idea that Jack had actually left him, that although he abused him as usual often enough, he never again talked of taking him off the ship's books; and, to the credit of Jack be it spoken, he took no advantage of the circumstance, and only got drunk just as usual, and called his master an old fool whenever it suited him.

CHAPTER LXXXV

THE HUNGARIAN NOBLEMAN GETS INTO DANGER.--HE IS FIRED AT, AND SHOWS SOME OF HIS QUALITY

Considerably delighted was the Hungarian, not only at the news he had received from the boy, but as well for the cheapness of it. Probably he did not conceive it possible that the secret of the retreat of such a man as Varney could have been attained so easily.

He waited with great impatience for the evening, and stirred not from the inn for several hours; neither did he take any refreshment, notwithstanding he had made so liberal an arrangement with the landlord to be supplied.

All this was a matter of great excitement and speculation in the inn, so much so, indeed, that the landlord sent for some of the oldest customers of his house, regular topers, who sat there every evening, indulging in strong drinks, and pipes and tobacco, to ask their serious advice as to what he should do, as if it were necessary he should do anything at all.

But, somehow or another, these wiseacres who assembled at the landlord's bidding, and sat down, with something strong before them, in the bar parlour, never once seemed to think that a man might, if he choosed, come to an inn, and agree to pay four guineas a week for board and lodging, and yet take nothing at all.

No; they could not understand it, and therefore they would not have it. It was quite monstrous that anybody should attempt to do anything so completely out of the ordinary course of proceeding. It was not to be borne; and as in this country it happens, free and enlightened as we are, that no man can commit a greater social offence than doing something that his neighbours never thought of doing themselves, the Hungarian nobleman was voted a most dangerous character, and, in fact, not to be put up with.

"I shouldn't have thought so much of it" said the landlord; "but only look at the aggravation of the thing. After I have asked him four guineas a week, and expected to be beaten down to two, to be then told that he would not have cared if it had been eight. It is enough to aggravate a saint."

"Well, I agree with you there," said another; "that's just what it is, and I only wonder that a man of your sagacity has not quite understood it before."

"Understood what?"

"Why, that he is a vampyre. He has heard of Sir Francis Varney, that's the fact, and he's come to see him. Birds of a feather, you know, flock together, and now we shall have two vampyres in the town instead of one."

The party looked rather blank at this suggestion, which, indeed, seemed rather uncomfortable probably. The landlord had just opened his mouth to make some remark, when he was stopped by the violent ringing of what he now called the vampyre's bell, since it proceeded from the room where the Hungarian nobleman was.

"Have you an almanack in the house?" was the question of the mysterious guest.

"An almanack, sir? well, I really don't know. Let me see, an almanack."

"But, perhaps, you can tell me. I was to know the moon's age."

"The devil!" thought the landlord; "he's a vampyre, and no mistake. Why, sir, as to the moon's age, it was a full moon last night, very bright and beautiful, only you could not see it for the clouds."

"A full moon last night," said the mysterious guest, thoughtfully; "it may shine, then, brightly, to-night, and if so, all will be well. I thank you,--leave the room."

"Do you mean to say, sir, you don't want anything to eat now?"

"What I want I'll order."

"But you have ordered nothing."

"Then presume that I want nothing."

The discomfited landlord was obliged to leave the room, for there was no such a thing as making any answer to this, and so, still further confirmed in his opinion that the stranger was a vampyre that came to see Sir Francis Varney from a sympathetic feeling towards him, he again reached the bar-parlour.

"You may depend," he said, "as sure as eggs is eggs, that he is a vampyre. Hilloa! he's going off,--after him--after him; he thinks we suspect him. There he goes--down the High-street."

The landlord ran out, and so did those who were with him, one of whom carried his brandy and water in his hand, which, being too hot for him to swallow all at once, he still could not think of leaving behind.

It was now gelling rapidly dark, and the mysterious stranger was actually proceeding towards the lane to keep his appointment with the boy who had promised to conduct him to the hiding-place of Sir Francis Varney.

He had not proceeded far, however, before he began to suspect that he was followed, as it was evident on the instant that he altered his course; for, instead of walking down the lane, where the boy was waiting for him, he went right on, and seemed desirous of making his way into the open country between the town and Bannerworth Hall.

His pursuers--for they assumed that character--when they saw this became anxious to intercept him; and thinking that the greater force they had the better, they called out aloud as they passed a smithy, where a man was shoeing a horse,--

"Jack Burdon, here is another vampyre!"

"The deuce there is!" said the person who was addressed. "I'll soon settle him. Here's my wife gets no sleep of a night as it is, all owing to that Varney, who has been plaguing us so long. I won't put up with another."

So saying, he snatched from a hook on which it hung, an old fowling-piece, and joined the pursuit, which now required to be conducted with some celerity, for the stranger had struck into the open country, and was getting on at good speed.

The last remnants of the twilight were fading away, and although the moon had actually risen, its rays were obscured by a number of light, fleecy clouds, which, although they did not promise to be of long continuance, as yet certainly impeded the light.

"Where is he going?" said the blacksmith. "He seems to be making his way towards the mill-stream."

"No," said another; "don't you see he is striking higher up towards the old ford, where the stepping-stones are!"

"He is--he is," cried the blacksmith. "Run on--run on; don't you see he is crossing it now? Tell me, all of you, are you quite sure he is a vampyre, and no mistake? He ain't the exciseman, landlord, now, is he?"

"The exciseman, the devil! Do you think I want to shoot the exciseman?"

"Very good--then here goes," exclaimed the Smith.

He stooped, and just as the brisk night air blew aside the clouds from before the face of the moon, and as the stranger was crossing the slippery stones, he fired at him.

***

How silently and sweetly the moon's rays fall upon the water, upon the meadows, and upon the woods. The scenery appeared the work of enchantment, some fairy land, waiting the appearance of its inhabitants. No sound met the ear; the very wind was hushed; nothing was there to distract the sense of sight, save the power of reflection.

This, indeed, would aid the effect of such a scene. A cloudless sky, the stars all radiant with beauty, while the moon, rising higher and higher in the heavens, increasing in the strength and refulgence of her light, and dimming the very stars, which seemed to grow gradually invisible as the majesty of the queen of night became more and more manifest.

The dark woods and the open meadows contrasted more and more strongly; like light and shade, the earth and sky were not more distinct and apart; and the ripling stream, that rushed along with all the impetuosity of uneven ground.

The banks are clothed with verdure; the tall sedges, here and there, lined the sides; beds of bulrushes raised their heads high above all else, and threw out their round clumps of blossoms like tufts, and looked strange in the light of the moon.

Here and there, too, the willows bent gracefully over the stream, and their long leaves were wafted and borne up and down by the gentler force of the stream.

Below, the stream widened, and ran foaming over a hard, stony bottom, and near the middle is a heap of stones--of large stones, that form the bed of the river, from which the water has washed away all earthy particles, and left them by themselves.

These stones in winter could not be seen, they were all under water, and the stream washed over in a turbulent and tumultuous manner. But now, when the water was clear and low, they are many of them positively out of the water, the stream running around and through their interstices; the water-weeds here and there lying at the top of the stream, and blossoming beautifully.

The daisy-like blossoms danced and waved gently on the moving flood, at the same time they shone in the moonlight, like fairy faces rising from the depths of the river, to receive the principle of life from the moon's rays.

'Tis sweet to wander in the moonlight at such an hour, and it is sweet to look upon such a scene with an unruffled mind, and to give way to the feelings that are engendered by a walk by the river side.

See, the moon is rising higher and higher, the shadows grow shorter and shorter; the river, which in places was altogether hidden by the tall willow trees, now gradually becomes less and less hidden, and the water becomes more and more lit up.

The moonbeams play gracefully on the rippling surface, here and there appearing like liquid silver, that each instant changed its position and surface exposed to the light.

Such a moment--such a scene, were by far too well calculated to cause the most solemn and serious emotions of the mind, and he must have been but at best insensible, who could wander over meadow and through grove, and yet remain untouched by the scene of poetry and romance in which he breathed and moved.

At such a time, and in such a place, the world is alive with all the finer essences of mysterious life. 'Tis at such an hour that the spirits quit their secret abodes, and visit the earth, and whirl round the enchanted trees.

'Tis now the spirits of earth and air dance their giddy flight from flower to flower. 'Tis now they collect and exchange their greetings; the wood is filled with them, the meadows teem with them, the hedges at the river side have them hidden among the deep green leaves and blades.

But what is that yonder, on the stones, partially out of the water--what can it be? The more it is looked at, the more it resembles the human form--and yet it is still and motionless on the hard stones--and yet it is a human form. The legs are lying in the water, the arms appear to be partially in and partially out, they seem moved by the stream now and then, but very gently--so slightly, indeed, that it might well be questioned if it moved at all.

The moon's rays had not yet reached it; the bank on the opposite side of the stream was high, and some tall trees rose up and obscured the moon. But she was rising higher and higher each moment, and, finally, when it has reached the tops of those trees, then the rays will reach the middle of the river, and then, by degrees, it will reach the stones in the river, and, finally, the body that lies there so still and so mysteriously.

How it came there it would be difficult to say. It appeared as though, when the waters were high, the body had floated down, and, at the subsidence of the waters, it had been left upon the stones, and now it was exposed to view.

It was strange and mysterious, and those who might look upon such a sight would feel their blood chill, and their body creep, to contemplate the remains of humanity in such a place, and in such a condition as that must be in.

A human life had been taken! How? Who could tell? Perhaps accident alone was the cause of it; perhaps some one had taken a life by violent means, and thrown the body in the waters to conceal the fact and the crime.

The waters had brought it down, and deposited it there in the middle of the river, without any human creature being acquainted with the fact.

But the moon rises--the beams come trembling through the tree tops and straggling branches, and fall upon the opposite bank, and there lies the body, mid stream, and in comparative darkness.

By the time the river is lit up by the moon's rays, then the object on the stones will be visible, then it can be ascertained what appears now only probable, namely, is the dark object a human form or not?

In the absence of light it appears to be so, but when the flood of silver light falls upon it, it would be placed then beyond a doubt.

The time is approaching--the moon each moment approaches her meridian, and each moment do the rays increase in number and in strength, while the shadows shorten.

The opposite bank each moment becomes more and more distinct, and the side of the stream, the green rushes and sedges, all by degrees come full into view.

Now and then a fish leaps out of the stream, and just exhibits itself, as much as to say, "There are things living in the stream, and I am one of them."

The moment is one of awe--the presence of that mysterious and dreadful-looking object, even while its identity remains doubt, chills the heart--it contracts the expanding thoughts to that one object--all interest in the scene lies centered in that one point.

What could it be? What else but a human body? What else could assume such a form? But see, nearly half the stream is lit by the moonbeams struggling through the tree tops, and now rising above them. The light increases, and the shadows shorten.

The edge of the bed of stones now becomes lit up by the moonlight; the rippling stream, the bubbles, and the tiny spray that was caused by the rush of water against the stones, seemed like sparkling flashes of silver fire.

Then came the moonbeams upon the body, for it was raised above the level of the water, and shewed conspicuously; for the moonbeams reached the body before they fell on the surrounding water; for that reason then it was the body presented a strange and ghastly object against a deep, dark background, by which it was surrounded.

But this did not last long--the water in another minute was lit up by the moon's pale beams, and then indeed could be plainly enough seen the body of a man lying on the heap of stones motionless and ghastly.

The colourless hue of the moonlight gave the object a most horrific and terrible appearance! The face of the dead man was turned towards the moon's rays, and the body seemed to receive all the light that could fall upon it.

It was a terrible object to look upon, and one that added a new and singular interest to the scene! The world seemed then to be composed almost exclusively of still life, and the body was no impediment to the stillness of the scene.

It was, all else considered, a calm, beautiful scene, lovely the night, gorgeous the silvery rays that lit up the face of nature; the hill and dale, meadow, and wood, and river, all afforded contrasts strong, striking, and strange.

But strange, and more strange than any contrast in nature, was that afforded to the calm beauty of the night and place by the deep stillness and quietude imposed upon the mind by that motionless human body.

The moon's rays now fell upon its full length; the feet were lying in the water, the head lay back, with its features turned towards the quarter of the heavens where the moon shone from; the hair floated on the shallow water, while the face and body were exposed to all influences, from its raised and prominent position.

The moonbeams had scarcely settled upon it--scarce a few minutes--when the body moved. Was it the water that moved it? it could not be, surely, that the moonbeams had the power of recalling life into that inanimate mass, that lay there for some time still and motionless as the very stones on which it lay.

It was endued with life; the dead man gradually rose up, and leaned himself upon his elbow; he paused a moment like one newly recalled to life; he seemed to become assured he did live. He passed one hand through his hair, which was wet, and then rose higher into a sitting posture, and then he leaned on one hand, inclining himself towards the moon.

His breast heaved with life, and a kind of deep inspiration, or groan, came from him, as he first awoke to life, and then he seemed to pause for a few moments. He turned gradually over, till his head inclined down the stream.

Just below, the water deepened, and ran swiftly and silently on amid meads and groves of trees. The vampyre was revived; he awoke again to a ghastly life; he turned from the heap of stones, he gradually allowed himself to sink into deep water, and then, with a loud plunge, he swam to the centre of the river.

Slowly and surely did he swim into the centre of the river, and down the stream he went. He took long, but easy strokes, for he was going down the stream, and that aided him.

For some distance might he be heard and seen through the openings in the trees, but he became gradually more and more indistinct, till sound and sight both ceased, and the vampyre had disappeared.

During the continuance of this singular scene, not one word had passed between the landlord and his companions. When the blacksmith fired the fowling-piece, and saw the stranger fall, apparently lifeless, upon the stepping-stones that crossed the river, he became terrified at what he had done, and gazed upon the seeming lifeless form with a face on which the utmost horror was depicted.

They all seemed transfixed to the spot, and although each would have given worlds to move away, a kind of nightmare seemed to possess them, which stunned all their faculties, and brought over them a torpidity from which they found it impossible to arouse themselves.

But, when the apparently dead man moved again, and when, finally, the body, which appeared so destitute of life, rolled into the stream, and floated away with the tide, their fright might be considered to have reached its climax. The absence of the body, however, had seemingly, at all events, the effect of releasing them from the mental and physical thraldom in which they were, and they were enabled to move from the spot, which they did immediately, making their way towards the town with great speed.

As they got near, they held a sort of council of war as to what they should do under the circumstances, the result of which was, that they came to a conclusion to keep all that they had done and seen to themselves; for, if they did not, they might be called upon for some very troublesome explanations concerning the fate of the supposed Hungarian nobleman whom they had taken upon themselves to believe was a vampyre, and to shoot accordingly, without taking the trouble to inquire into the legality of such an act.

How such a secret was likely to be kept, when it was shared amongst seven people, it is hard to say; but, if it were so kept, it could only be under the pressure of a strong feeling of self-preservation.

They were forced individually, of course, to account for their absence during the night at their respective homes, and how they managed to do that is best known to themselves.

As to the landlord, he felt compelled to state that, having his suspicions of his guest aroused, he followed him on a walk that he pretended to take, and he had gone so far, that at length he had given up the chase, and lost his own way in returning.

Thus was it, then, that this affair still preserved all its mystery, with a large superadded amount of fear attendant upon it; for, if the mysterious guest were really anything supernatural, might he not come again in a much more fearful shape, and avenge the treatment he had received?

The only person who fell any disappointment in the affair, or whose expectations were not realised, was the boy who had made the appointment with the supposed vampyre at the end of the lane, and who was to have received what he considered so large a reward for pointing out the retreat of Sir Francis Varney.

He waited in vain for the arrival of the Hungarian nobleman, and, at last, indignation got the better of him, and he walked away. Feeling that he had been jilted, he resolved to proceed to the public-house and demand the half-crowns which had been so liberally promised him; but when he reached there he found that the party whom he sought was not within, nor the landlord either, for that was the precise time when that worthy individual was pursuing his guest over meadow and bill, through brake and through briar, towards the stepping stones on the river.

What the boy further did on the following day, when he found that he was to reap no more benefit for the adventure, we shall soon perceive.

As for the landlord, he did endeavour to catch a few hours' brief repose; but as he dreamed that the Hungarian nobleman came in the likeness of a great toad, and sat upon his chest, feeling like the weight of a mountain, while he, the landlord, tried to scream and cry for help, but found that he could neither do one thing nor the other, we may guess that his repose did not at all invigorate him.

As he himself expressed it, he got up all of a shake, with a strong impression that he was a very ill-used individual, indeed, to have had the nightmare in the day time.

And now we will return to the cottage where the Bannerworth family were at all events, making themselves quite as happy as they did at their ancient mansion, in order to see what is there passing, and how Dr. Chillingworth made an effort to get up some evidence of something that the Bannerworth family knew nothing of, therefore could not very well be expected to render him much assistance. That he did, however, make what he considered an important discovery, we shall perceive in the course of the ensuing chapter, in which it will be seen that the best hidden things will, by the merest accident, sometimes come to light, and that, too, when least expected by any one at all connected with the result.

CHAPTER LXXXVI

THE DISCOVERY OF THE POCKET BOOK OF MARMADUKE BANNERWORTH.--ITS MYSTERIOUS CONTENTS

The little episode had just taken place which we have recorded between the old admiral and Jack Pringle, when Henry Bannerworth and Charles Holland stepped aside to converse.

"Charles," said Henry, "it has become absolutely necessary that I should put an end to this state of dependence in which we all live upon your uncle. It is too bad to think, that because, through fighting the battles of his country, he has amassed some money, we are to eat it up."

"My dear friend," said Charles, "does it not strike you, that it would be a great deal worse than too bad, if my uncle could not do what he liked with his own?"

"Yes; but, Charles, that is not the question."

"I think it is, though I know not what other question you can make of it."

"We have all talked it over, my mother, my brother, and Flora; and my brother and I have determined, if this state of things should last much longer, to find out some means of honourable exertion by which we may, at all events, maintain ourselves without being burdensome to any."

"Well, well, we will talk of that another time."

"Nay, but hear me; we were thinking that if we went into some branch of the public service, your uncle would have the pleasure, such we are quite sure it would be to him, of assisting us greatly by his name and influence."

"Well, well, Henry, that's all very well; but for a little time do not throw up the old man and make him unhappy. I believe I am his only relative in the world, and, as he has often said, he intended leaving me heir to all he possesses, you see there is no harm done by you receiving a small portion of it beforehand."

"And," said Henry, "by that line of argument, we are to find an excuse for robbing your uncle; in the fact, that we are robbing you likewise."

"No, no; indeed, you do not view the matter rightly."

"Well, all I can say is, Charles, that while I feel, and while we all feel, the deepest debt of gratitude towards your uncle, it is our duty to do something. In a box which we have brought with us from the Hall, and which has not been opened since our father's death, I have stumbled over some articles of ancient jewellery and plate, which, at all events, will produce something."

"But which you must not part with."

"Nay, but, Charles, these are things I knew not we possessed, and most ill-suited do they happen to be to our fallen fortunes. It is money we want, not the gewgaws of a former state, to which we can have now no sort of pretension."

"Nay, I know you have all the argument; but still is there something sad and uncomfortable to one's feelings in parting with such things as those which have been in families for many years."

"But we knew not that we had them; remember that, Charles. Come and look at them. Those relics of a bygone age may amuse you, and, as regards myself, there are no circumstances whatever associated with them that give them any extrinsic value; so laugh at them or admire them, as you please, I shall most likely be able to join with you in either feeling."

"Well, be it so--I will come and look at them; but you must think better of what you say concerning my uncle, for I happen to know--which you ought likewise by this time--how seriously the old man would feel any rejection on your part of the good he fancies he is doing you. I tell you, Henry, it is completely his hobby, and let him have earned his money with ten times the danger he has, he could not spend it with anything like the satisfaction that he does, unless he were allowed to dispose of it in this way."

"Well, well; be it so for a time."

"The fact is, his attachment to Flora is so great--which is a most fortunate circumstance for me--that I should not be at all surprised that she cuts me out of one half my estate, when the old man dies. But come, we will look at your ancient bijouterie."

Henry led Charles into an apartment of the cottage where some of the few things had been placed that were brought from Bannerworth Hall, which were not likely to be in constant and daily use.

Among these things happened to be the box which Henry had mentioned, and from which he had taken a miscellaneous assortment of things of an antique and singular character.

There were old dresses of a season and of a taste long gone by; ancient articles of defence; some curiously wrought daggers; and a few ornaments, pretty, but valueless, along with others of more sterling pretensions, which Henry pointed out to Charles.

"I am almost inclined to think," said the latter, "that some of these things are really of considerable value; but I do not I profess to be an accurate judge, and, perhaps, I am more taken with the beauty of an article, than the intrinsic worth. What is that which you have just taken from the box?"

"It seems a half-mask," said Henry, "made of silk; and here are initial letters within it--M. B."

"To what do they apply?"

"Marmaduke Bannerworth, my father."

"I regret I asked you."

"Nay, Charles, you need not. Years have now elapsed since that misguided man put a period to his own existence, in the gardens of Bannerworth Hall. Of course, the shock was a great one to us all, although I must confess that we none of us knew much of a father's affections. But time reconciles one to these dispensations, and to a friend, like yourself, I can talk upon these subjects without a pang."

He laid down the mask, and proceeded further in his search in the old box.

Towards the bottom of it there were some books, and, crushed in by the side of them, there was an ancient-looking pocket-book, which Charles pointed out, saying,--

"There, Henry, who knows but you may find a fortune when you least expect it?"

"Those who expect nothing," said Henry, "will not be disappointed. At all events, as regards this pocket-book, you see it is empty."

"Not quite. A card has fallen from it."

Charles took up the card, and read upon it the name of Count Barrare.

"That name," he said, "seems familiar to me. Ah! now I recollect, I have read of such a man. He flourished some twenty, or five-and-twenty years ago, and was considered a roue of the first water--a finished gamester; and, in a sort of brief memoir I read once of him, it said that he disappeared suddenly one day, and was never again heard of."

"Indeed! I'm not puzzled to think how his card came into my father's pocket-book. They met at some gaming-house; and, if some old pocket-book of the Count Barrare's were shaken, there might fall from it a card, with the name of Mr. Marmaduke Bannerworth upon it."

"Is there nothing further in the pocket-book--no memoranda?"

"I will look. Stay! here is something upon one of the leaves--let me see--'Mem., twenty-five thousand pounds! He who robs the robber, steals little; it was not meant to kill him: but it will be unsafe to use the money for a time--my brain seems on fire--the remotest hiding-place in the house is behind the picture."

"What do you think of that?" said Charles.

"I know not what to think. There is one thing though, that I do know."

"And what is that?"

"It is my father's handwriting. I have many scraps of his, and his peculiar hand is familiar to me."

"It's very strange, then, what it can refer to."

"Charles--Charles! there is a mystery connected with our fortunes, that I never could unravel; and once or twice it seemed as if we were upon the point of discovering all; but something has ever interfered to prevent us, and we have been thrown back into the realms of conjecture. My father's last words were, 'The money is hidden;' and then he tried to add something; but death stopped his utterance. Now, does it not almost seem that this memorandum alluded to the circumstance?"

"It does, indeed."

"And then, scarcely had my father breathed his last, when a man comes and asks for him at the garden-gate, and, upon hearing that he is dead, utters some imprecations, and walks away."

"Well, Henry, you must trust to time and circumstances to unravel these mysteries. For myself, I own that I cannot do so; I see no earthly way out of the difficulty whatever. But still it does appear to me as if Dr. Chillingworth knew something or had heard something, with which he really ought to make you acquainted."

"Do not blame the worthy doctor; he may have made an error of judgment, but never one of feeling; and you may depend, if he is keeping anything from me, that he is doing so from some excellent motive: most probably because he thinks it will give me pain, and so will not let me endure any unhappiness from it, unless he is quite certain as regards the facts. When he is so, you may depend he will be communicative, and I shall know all that he has to relate. But, Charles, it is evident to me that you, too, are keeping something."

"I!"

"Yes; you acknowledge to having had an interview, and a friendly one, with Varney; and you likewise acknowledge that he had told you things which he has compelled you to keep secret."

"I have promised to keep them secret, and I deeply regret the promise that I have made. There cannot be anything to my mind more essentially disagreeable than to have one's tongue tied in one's interview with friends. I hate to hear anything that I may not repeat to those whom I take into my own confidence."

"I can understand the feeling; but here comes the worthy doctor."

"Show him the memorandum."

"I will."

As Dr. Chillingworth entered the apartments Henry handed him the memorandum that had been found in the old pocket-book, saying as he did so,--

"Look at that, doctor, and give us your candid opinion upon it."

Dr. Chillingworth fitted on his spectacles, and read the paper carefully. At its conclusion, he screwed up his mouth into an extremely small compass, and doubling up the paper, he put it into his capacious waistcoat pocket, saying as he did so,--

"Oh! oh! oh! oh! hum!"

"Well, doctor," said Henry; "we are waiting for your opinion."

"My opinion! Well, then, my dear boy, I must say, my opinion, to the best of my belief is, that I really don't know anything about it."

"Then, perhaps, you'll surrender us the memorandum," said Charles; "because, if you don't know anything, we may as well make a little inquiry."

"Ha!" said the worthy doctor; "we can't put old heads upon young shoulders, that's quite clear. Now, my good young men, be patient and quiet; recollect, that what you know you're acquainted with, and that that which is hidden from you, you cannot very well come to any very correct conclusion upon. There's a right side and a wrong one you may depend, to every question; and he who walks heedlessly in the dark, is very apt to run his head against a post. Good evening, my boys--good evening."

Away bustled the doctor.

"Well," said Charles, "what do you think of that, Mr. Henry?"

"I think he knows what he's about."

"That may be; but I'll be hanged if anybody else does. The doctor is by no means favourable to the march of popular information; and I really think he might have given us some food for reflection, instead of leaving us so utterly and entirely at fault as he has; and you know he's taken away your memorandum even."

"Let him have it, Charles--let him have it; it is safe with him. The old man may be, and I believe is, a little whimsical and crotchety; but he means abundantly well, and he's just one of those sort of persons, and always was, who will do good his own way, or not at all; so we must take the good with the bad in those cases, and let Dr. Chillingworth do as he pleases."

"I cannot say it is nothing to me, although those words were rising to my lips, because you know, Henry, that everything which concerns you or yours is something to me; and therefore it is that I feel extremely anxious for the solution of all this mystery. Before I hear the sequel of that which Varney, the vampyre, has so strongly made me a confidant of, I will, at all events, make an effort to procure his permission to communicate it to all those who are in any way beneficially interested in the circumstances. Should he refuse me that permission, I am almost inclined myself to beg him to withhold his confidence."

"Nay, do not do so, Charles--do not do that, I implore you. Recollect, although you cannot make us joint recipients with you in your knowledge, you can make use of it, probably, to our advantage, in saving us, perchance, from the different consequences, so that you can make what you know in some way beneficial to us, although not in every way."

"There is reason in that, and I give in at once. Be it so, Henry. I will wait on him, and if I cannot induce him to change his determination, and allow me to tell some other as well as Flora, I must give in, and take the thing as a secret, although I shall not abandon a hope, even after he has told me all he has to tell, that I may induce him to permit me to make a general confidence, instead of the partial one he has empowered me to do."

"It may be so; and, at all events, we must not reject a proffered good because it is not quite so complete as it might be."

"You are right; I will keep my appointment with him, entertaining the most sanguine hope that our troubles and disasters--I say our, because I consider myself quite associated in thought, interest, and feelings with your family--may soon be over."

"Heaven grant it may be so, for your's and Flora's sake; but I feel that Bannerworth Hall will never again be the place it was to us. I should prefer that we sought for new associations, which I have no doubt we may find, and that among us we get up some other home that would be happier, because not associated with so many sad scenes in our history."

"Be it so; and I am sure that the admiral would gladly give way to such an arrangement. He has often intimated that he thought Bannerworth Hall a dull place; consequently, although he pretends to have purchased it of you, I think he will be very glad to leave it."

"Be it so, then. If it should really happen that we are upon the eve of any circumstances that will really tend to relieve us from our misery and embarrassments, we will seek for some pleasanter abode than the Hall, which you may well imagine, since it became the scene of that dreadful tragedy that left us fatherless, has borne but a distasteful appearance to all our eyes."

"I don't wonder at that, and am only surprised that, after such a thing had happened any of you liked to inhabit the place."

"We did not like, but our poverty forced us. You have no notion of the difficulties through which we have struggled; and the fact that we had a home rent free was one of so much importance to us, that had it been surrounded by a thousand more disagreeables than it was, we must have put up with it; but now that we owe so much to the generosity of your uncle, I suppose we can afford to talk of what we like and of what we don't like."

"You can, Henry, and it shall not be my fault if you do not always afford to do so; and now, as the time is drawing on, I think I will proceed at once to Varney, for it is better to be soon than late, and get from him the remainder of his story."

***

There were active influences at work, to prevent Sir Francis Varney from so quickly as he had arranged to do, carrying out his intention of making Charles Holland acquainted with the history of the eventful period of his life, which had been associated with Marmaduke Bannerworth.

One would have scarcely thought it possible that anything now would have prevented Varney from concluding his strange narrative; but that he was prevented, will appear.

The boy who had been promised such liberal payment by the Hungarian nobleman, for betraying the place of Varney's concealment, we have already stated, felt bitterly the disappointment of not being met, according to promise, at the corner of the lane, by that individual.

It not only deprived him of the half-crowns, which already in imagination he had laid out, but it was a great blow to his own importance, for after his discovery of the residence of the vampyre, he looked upon himself as quite a public character, and expected great applause for his cleverness.

But when the Hungarian nobleman came not, all these dreams began to vanish into thin air, and, like the unsubstantial fabric of a vision, to leave no trace behind them.

He got dreadfully aggravated, and his first thought was to go to Varney, and see what he could get from him, by betraying the fact that some one was actively in search of him.

That seemed, however, a doubtful good, and perhaps there was some personal dread of the vampyre mixed up with the rejection of this proposition. But reject it he did, and then he walked moodily into the town without any fixed resolution of what he should do.

All that he thought of was a general idea that he should like to create some mischief, if possible--what it was he cared not, so long as it made a disturbance.

Now, he knew well that the most troublesome and fidgetty man in the town was Tobias Philpots, a saddler, who was always full of everybody's business but his own, and ever ready to hear any scandal of his neighbours.

"I have a good mind," said the boy, "to go to old Philpots, and tell him all about it, that I have."

The good mind soon strengthened itself into a fixed resolution, and full of disdain and indignation at the supposed want of faith of the Hungarian nobleman, he paused opposite the saddler's door.

Could he but for a moment have suspected the real reason why the appointment had not been kept with him, all his curiosity would have been doubly aroused, and he would have followed the landlord of the inn and his associate upon the track of the second vampyre that had visited the town.

But of this he knew nothing, for that proceeding had been conducted with amazing quietness; and the fact of the Hungarian nobleman, when he found that he was followed, taking a contrary course to that in which Varney was concealed, prevented the boy from knowing anything of his movements.

Hence the thing looked to him like a piece of sheer neglect and contemptuous indifference, which he felt bound to resent.

He did not pause long at the door of the saddler's, but, after a few moments, he walked boldly in, and said,--

"Master Philpots, I have got something extraordinary to tell you, and you may give me what you like for telling you."

"Go on, then," said the saddler, "that's just the price I always likes to pay for everything."

"Will you keep it secret?" said the boy.

"Of course I will. When did you ever hear of me telling anything to a single individual?"

"Never to a single individual, but I have heard you tell things to the whole town."

"Confound your impudence. Get out of my shop directly."

"Oh! very good. I can go and tell old Mitchell, the pork-butcher."

"No, I say--stop; don't tell him. If anybody is to know, let it be me, and I'll promise you I'll keep it secret."

"Very good," said the boy, returning, "you shall know it; and, mind, you have promised me to keep it secret, so that if it gets known, you know it cannot be any fault of mine."

The fact was, the boy was anxious it should be known, only that in case some consequences might arise, he thought he would quiet his own conscience, by getting a promise of secrecy from Tobias Philpots, which he well knew that individual would not think of keeping.

He then related to him the interview he had had with the Hungarian nobleman at the inn, how he had promised a number of half-crowns, but a very small instalment of which he had received.

All this Master Philpots cared very little for, but the information that the dreaded Varney, the vampyre, was concealed so close to the town was a matter of great and abounding interest, and at that part of the story he suddenly pricked up his ears amazingly.

"Why, you don't mean to say that?" he exclaimed. "Are you sure it was he?"

"Yes, I am quite certain. I have seen I him more than once. It was Sir Francis Varney, without any mistake."

"Why, then you may depend he's only waiting until it's very dark, and then he will walk into somebody, and suck his blood. Here's a horrid discovery! I thought we had had enough of Master Varney, and that he would hardly show himself here again, and now you tell me he is not ten minutes' walk off."

"It's a fact," said the boy. "I saw him go in, and he looks thinner and more horrid than ever. I am sure he wants a dollop of blood from somebody."

"I shouldn't wonder."

"Now there is Mrs. Philpots, you know, sir; she's rather big, and seems most ready to burst always; I shouldn't wonder if the vampyre came to her to-night."

"Wouldn't you?" said Mrs. Philpots, who had walked into the shop, and overheard the whole conversation; "wouldn't you, really? I'll vampyre you, and teach you to make these remarks about respectable married women. You young wretch, take that, will you!"

She gave the boy such a box on the ears, that the place seemed to spin round with him. As soon as he recovered sufficiently to be enabled to walk, he made his way from the shop with abundance of precipitation, much regretting that he had troubled himself to make a confidant of Master Philpots.

But, however, he could not but tell himself that if his object was to make a general disturbance through the whole place, he had certainly succeeded in doing so.

He slunk home perhaps with a feeling that he might be called upon to take part in something that might ensue, and at all events be compelled to become a guide to the place of Sir Francis Varney's retreat, in which case, for all he knew, the vampyre might, by some more than mortal means, discover what a hand he had had in the matter, and punish him accordingly.

The moment he hid left the saddler's Mrs. Philpots, after using some bitter reproaches to her husband for not at once sacrificing the boy upon the spot for the disrespectful manner in which he had spoken of her, hastily put on her bonnet and shawl, and the saddler, although it was a full hour before the usual time, began putting up the shutters of his shop.

"Why, my dear," he said to Mrs. Philpots, when she came down stairs equipped for the streets, "why, my dear, where are you going?"

"And pray, sir, what are you shutting up the shop for at this time of the evening!"

"Oh! why, the fact is, I thought I'd just go to the Rose and Crown, and mention that the vampyre was so near at hand."

"Well, Mr. Philpots, and in that case there can be no harm in my calling upon some of my acquaintance and mentioning it likewise."

"Why, I don't suppose there would be much harm; only remember, Mrs. Philpots, remember if you please---"

"Remember what?"

"To tell everybody to keep it secret."

"Oh, of course I will; and mind you do it likewise."

"Most decidedly."

The shop was closed, Mr. Philpots ran off to the Rose and Crown, and Mrs, Philpots, with as much expedition as she could, purposed making the grand tour of all her female acquaintance in the town, just to tell them, as a great secret, that the vampyre, Sir Francis Varney, as he called himself, had taken refuge at the house that was to let down the lane leading to Higgs's farm.

"But by no means," she said, "let it go no further, because it is a very wrong thing to make any disturbance, and you will understand that it's quite a secret."

She was listened to with breathless attention, as may well be supposed, and it was a singular circumstance that at every house she left some other lady put on her bonnet and shawl, and ran out to make the circle of her acquaintance, with precisely the same story, and precisely the same injunctions to secrecy.

And, as Mr. Philpots pursued an extremely similar course, we are not surprised that in the short space of one hour the news should have spread through all the town, and that there was scarcely a child old enough to understand what was being talked about, who was ignorant of the fact, that Sir Francis Varney was to be found at the empty house down the lane.

It was an unlucky time, too, for the night was creeping on, a period at which people's apprehension of the supernatural becomes each moment stronger and more vivid--a period at which a number of idlers are let loose for different employments, and when anything in the shape of a row or a riot presents itself in pleasant colours to those who have nothing to lose and who expect, under the cover of darkness, to be able to commit outrages they would be afraid to think of in the daytime, when recognition would be more easy.

Thus was it that Sir Francis Varney's position, although he knew it not, became momentarily one of extreme peril, and the danger he was about to run, was certainly greater than any he had as yet experienced. Had Charles Holland but known what was going on, he would undoubtedly have done something to preserve the supposed vampyre from the mischief that threatened him, but the time had not arrived when he had promised to pay him a second visit, so he had no idea of anything serious having occurred.

Perhaps, too, Mr. and Mrs. Philpots scarcely anticipated creating so much confusion, but when they found that the whole place was in an uproar, and that a tumultuous assemblage of persons called aloud for vengeance upon Varney, the vampyre, they made their way home again in no small fright.

And, now, what was the result of all these proceedings will be best known by our introducing the reader to the interior of the house in which Varney had found a temporary refuge, and following in detail his proceedings as he waited for the arrival of Charles Holland.

CHAPTER LXXXVII

THE HUNT FOR VARNEY.--THE HOUSE-TOPS.--THE MIRACULOUS ESCAPE.--THE LAST PLACE OF REFUGE.--THE COTTAGE

On the tree tops the moon shines brightly, and the long shadows are shooting its rays down upon the waters, and the green fields appear clothed in a flood of silver light; the little town was quiet and tranquil--nature seemed at rest.

The old mansion in which Sir Francis Varney had taken refuge, stood empty and solitary; it seemed as though it were not associated with the others by which it was surrounded. It was gloomy, and in the moonlight it reminded one of things long gone by, existences that had once been, but now no longer of this present time--a mere memento of the past.

Sir Francis Varney reclined upon the house-top; he gazed upon the sky, and upon the earth; he saw the calm tranquillity that reigned around, and could not but admire what he saw; he sighed, he seemed to sigh, from a pleasure he felt in the fact of his security; he could repose there without fear, and breathe the balmy air that fanned his cheek.

"Certainly," he muttered, "things might have been worse, but not much worse; however, they might have been much better; the ignorant are away--the most to be feared, because they have no guide and no control, save what can be exerted over them by their fears and their passions."

He paused to look again over the scene, and, as far as the eye could reach, and that, moonlight as it was, was many miles, the country was diversified with hill and dale, meadow and ploughed land; the open fields, and the darker woods, and the silvery stream that ran at no great distance, all presented a scene that was well calculated to warm the imagination, and to give the mind that charm which a cultivated understanding is capable of receiving.

There was but one thing wanted to make such a scene one of pure happiness, and that was all absence of care of fears for the future and the wants of life.

Suddenly there was a slight sound that came from the town. It was very slight, but the ears of Sir Francis Varney were painfully acute of late; the least sound that came across him was heard in a moment, and his whole visage was changed to one of listening interest.

The sound was hushed; but his attention was not lulled, for he had been placed in circumstances that made all his vigilance necessary for his own preservation. Hence it was, what another would have passed over, or not heard at all, he both heard and noticed. He was not sure of the nature of the sound, it was so slight and so indistinct.

There it was again! Some persons were moving about in the town. The sounds that came upon the night air seemed to say that there was an unusual bustle in the town, which was, to Sir Francis Varney, ominous in the extreme.

What could people in such a quiet, retired place require out at such an hour at night? It must be something very unusual--something that must excite them to a great degree; and Sir Francis began to feel very uneasy.

"They surely," he muttered to himself--"they surely cannot have found out my hiding place, and intend to hunt me from it, the blood-thirsty hounds! they are never satisfied. The mischief they are permitted to do on one occasion is but the precursor to another. The taste has caused the appetite for more, and nothing short of his blood can satisfy it."

The sounds increased, and the noise came nearer and nearer, and it appeared as though a number of men had collected together and were coming towards him. Yes, they were coming down the lane towards the deserted mansion where he was.

For once in his life, Sir Francis Varney trembled; he felt sick at heart, though no man was less likely to give up hope and to despair than he; yet this sign of unrelenting hatred and persecution was too unequivocal and too stern not to produce its effect upon even his mind; for he had no doubt but that they were coming with the express purpose of seeking him.

How they could have found him out was a matter he could not imagine. The Bannerworths could not have betrayed him--he was sure of that; and yet who could have seen him, so cautious and so careful as he had been, and so very sparing had he lived, because he would not give the slightest cause for all that was about to follow. He hoped to have hidden himself; but now he could hear the tramp of men distinctly, and their voices came now on the night air, though it was in a subdued tone, as if they were desirous of approaching unheard and unseen by their victim.

Sir Francis Varney stirred not from his position. He remained silent and motionless. He appeared not to heed what was going on; perhaps he hoped to see them go by--to be upon some false scent; or, if they saw no signs of life, they might leave the place, and go elsewhere.

Hark! they stop at the house--they go not by; they seem to pause, and then a thundering knock came at the door, which echoed and re-echoed through the empty and deserted house, on the top of which sat, in silent expectation, the almost motionless Sir Francis Varney, the redoubted vampyre.

The knock which came so loud and so hard upon the door caused Sir

Francis to start visibly, for it seemed his own knell. Then, as if the mob were satisfied with their knowledge of his presence, and of their victory, and of his inability to escape them, they sent up a loud shout that filled the whole neighbourhood with its sound.

It seemed to come from below and around the house; it rose from all sides, and that told Sir Francis Varney that the house was surrounded and all escape was cut off; there was no chance of his being able to rush through such a multitude of men as that which now encircled him.

With the calmest despair, Sir Francis Varney lay still and motionless on the house-top, and listened to the sounds that proceeded from below. Shout after shout arose on the still, calm air of the night; knock after knock came upon the stout old door, which awakened responsive echoes throughout the house that had for many years lain dormant, and which now seemed disturbed, and resounded in hollow murmurs to the voices from without.

Then a loud voice shouted from below, as if to be heard by any one who might be within,--

"Sir Francis Varney, the vampyre, come out and give yourself up at discretion! If we have to search for you, you may depend it will be to punish you; you will suffer by burning. Come out and give yourself up."

There was a pause, and then a loud shout.

Sir Francis Varney paid no attention to this summons, but sat, motionless, on the house-top, where he could hear all that passed below in the crowd.

"He will not come out," said one.

"Ah! he's much too cunning to be caught in such a trap. Why, he knows what you would do with him; he knows you would stake him, and make a bonfire about him."

"So he has no taste for roasting," remarked another; "but still, it's no use hiding; we have too many hands, and know the house too well to be easily baffled."

"That may be; and, although he don't like burning, yet we will unearth the old fox, somehow or other; we have discovered his haunt at last, and certainly we'll have him out."

"How shall we get in?"

"Knock in the door--break open the door! the front door--that is the best, because it leads to all parts of the house, and we can secure any one who attempts to move from one to the other, as they come down."

"Hurrah!" shouted several men in the crowd.

"Hurrah!" echoed the mob, with one accord, and the shout rent the air, and disturbed the quietude and serenity that scarce five minutes before reigned through the place.

Then, as if actuated by one spirit, they all set to work to force the door in. It was strong, and capable of great defence, and employed them, with some labour, for fifteen or twenty minutes, and then, with a loud crash, the door fell in.

"Hurrah!" again shouted the crowd.

These shouts announced the fall of the door, and then, and not until then, did Sir Francis Varney stir.

"They have broken in the door," he muttered, "well, if die I must, I will sell my life dearly. However, all is not yet lost, and, in the struggle for life, the loss is not so much felt."

He got up, and crept towards the trap that led into the house, or out of it, as the occasion might require.

"The vampyre! the vampyre!" shouted a man who stood on a garden wall, holding on by the arm of an apple-tree.

"Varney, the vampyre!" shouted a second.

"Hurrah! boys, we are on the right scent; now for a hunt; hurrah! we shall have him now."

They rushed in a tumultuous riot up the stone steps, and into the hall. It was a large, spacious place, with a grand staircase that led up to the upper floor, but it had two ends, and then terminated in a gallery.

It could not be defended by one man, save at the top, where it could not long be held, because the assailants could unite, and throw their whole weight against the entrance, and thus storm it. This actually happened.

They looked up, and, seeing nobody, they rushed up, some by one stair, and some by the other; but it was dark; there were but few of the moon's rays that pierced the gloom of that place, and those who first reached the place which we have named, were seized with astonishment, staggered, and fell.

Sir Francis Varney had met them; he stood there with a staff--something he had found about the house--not quite so long as a broom-handle, but somewhat thicker and heavier, being made of stout ash.

This formidable weapon, Sir Francis Varney wielded with strength and resolution; he was a tall man, and one of no mean activity and personal strength, and such a weapon, in his hands, was one of a most fearful character, and, for the occasion, much better than his sword.

Man after man fell beneath the fearful brace of these blows, for though they could not see Sir Francis, yet he could see them, or the hall-lights were behind them at the time, while he stood in the dark, and took advantage of this to deal murderous blows upon his assailants.

This continued for some minutes, till they gave way before such a vigorous defence, and paused.

"On, neighbours, on," cried one; "will you be beaten off by one man? Rush in at once and you must force him from his position--push him hard, and he must give way."

"Ay," said one fellow who sat upon the ground rubbing his head; "it's all very well to say push him hard, but if you felt the weight of that d----d pole on your head, you wouldn't be in such a blessed hurry."

However true that might be, there was but little attention paid to it, and a determined rush was made at the entrance to the gallery, and they found that it was unoccupied; and that was explained by the slamming of a door, and its being immediately locked upon them; and when the mob came to the door, they found they had to break their way through another door.

This did not take long in effecting; and in less than five minutes they had broken through that door which led into another room; but the first man who entered it fell from a crashing blow on the head from the ashen staff of Sir Francis Varney, who hurried and fled, closely pursued, until he came to another door, through which he dashed.

Here he endeavoured to make a stand and close it, but was immediately struck and grappled with; but he threw his assailant, and turned and fled again.

His object had been to defend each inch of the ground as long as he was able; but he found they came too close upon his steps, and prevented his turning in time to try the strength of his staff upon the foremost.

He dashed up the first staircase with surprising rapidity, leaving his pursuers behind; and when he had gained the first landing, he turned upon those who pursued him, who could hardly follow him two abreast.

"Down with the vampyre!" shouted the first, who rushed up heedless of the staff.

"Down with a fool!" thundered Varney, as he struck the fellow a terrific blow, which covered his face with blood, and he fell back into the arms of his companions.

A bitter groan and execration arose from them below, and again they shouted, and rushed up headlong.

"Down with the vampyre!" was again shouted, and met by a corresponding, but deep guttural sound of--

"Down with a fool!"

And sure enough the first again came to the earth without any preparation, save the application of an ashen stick to his skull, which, by-the-bye, no means aided the operation of thinking.

Several more shared a similar fate; but they pressed hard, and Sir Francis was compelled to give ground to keep them at the necessary length from him, as they rushed on regardless of his blows, and if he had not he would soon have been engaged in a personal struggle, for they were getting too close for him to use the staff.

"Down with the vampyre!" was the renewed cry, as they drove him from spot to spot until he reached the roof of the house, and then he ran up the steps to the loft, which he had just reached when they came up to the bottom.

Varney attempted to draw the ladder up but four or five stout men held that down; then by a sudden turn, as they were getting up, he turned it over, threw those on it down, and the ladder too, upon the heads of those who were below.

"Down with the vampyre!" shouted the mob, as they, with the most untiring energy, set the ladder, or steps, against the loft, and as many as could held it, while others rushed up to attack Varney with all the ferocity and courage of so many bull dogs.

It was strange, but the more they were baffled the more enraged and determined they rushed on to a new attack, with greater resolution than ever.

On this occasion, however, they were met with a new kind of missile, for Sir Francis had either collected and placed there for the occasion, or they had been left there for years, a number of old bricks, which lay close at hand. These he took, one by one, and deliberately took aim at them, and flung them with great force, striking down every one they hit.

This caused them to recoil; the bricks caused fearful gashes in their heads, and the wounds were serious, the flesh being, in many places, torn completely off. They however, only paused, for one man said,--

"Be of good heart, comrades, we can do as he does; he has furnished us with weapons, and we can thus attack him in two ways, and he must give way in the end."

"Hurrah! down with the vampyre!" sounded from all sides, and the shout was answered by a corresponding rush.

It was true; Sir Francis had furnished them with weapons to attack himself, for they could throw them back at him, which they did, and struck him a severe blow on the head, and it covered his face with blood in a moment.

"Hurrah!" shouted the assailants; "another such a blow, and all will be over with the vampyre."

"He's got--"

"Press him sharp, now," cried another man, as he aimed another blow with a brick, which struck Varney on the arm, causing him to drop the brick he held in his hand. He staggered back, apparently in great pain.

"Up! up! we have him now; he cannot get away; he's hurt; we have him--we have him."

And up they went with all the rapidity they could scramble up the steps; but this had given Varney time to recover himself; and though his right arm was almost useless, yet he contrived, with his left, to pitch the bricks so as to knock over the first three or four, when, seeing that he could not maintain his position to advantage, he rushed to the outside of the house, the last place he had capable of defence.

There was a great shout by those outside, when they saw him come out and stand with his staff, and those who came first got first served, for the blows resounded, while he struck them, and sent them over below.

Then came a great shout from within and without, and then a desperate rush was made at the door, and, in the next instant, Varney was seen flying, followed by his pursuers, one after the other, some tumbling over the tiles, to the imminent hazard of their necks.

Sir Francis Varney rushed along with a speed that appeared by far too great to admit of being safely followed, and yet those who followed appeared infected by his example, and appeared heedless of all consequences by which their pursuit might be attended to themselves.

"Hurrah!" shouted the mob below.

"Hurrah!" answered the mob on the tiles.

Then, over several housetops might be seen the flying figure of Sir Francis Varney, pursued by different men at a pace almost equal to his own.

They, however, could keep up the same speed, and not improve upon it, while he kept the advantage he first obtained in the start.

Then suddenly he disappeared.

It seemed to the spectators below that he had dropped through a house, and they immediately surrounded the house, as well as they could, and then set up another shout.

This took place several times, and as often was the miserable man hunted from his place of refuge only to seek another, from which he was in like manner hunted by those who thirsted for his blood.

On one occasion, they drove him into a house which was surrounded, save at one point, which had a long room, or building in it, that ran some distance out, and about twenty feet high.

At the entrance to the roof of this place, or leads, he stood and defended himself for some moments with success; but having received a blow himself, he was compelled to retire, while the mob behind forced those in front forward faster than he could by any exertion wield the staff that had so much befriended him on this occasion.

He was, therefore, on the point of being overwhelmed by numbers, when he fled; but, alas! there was no escape; a bare coping stone and rails ran round the top of that.

There was not much time for hesitation, but he jumped over the rails and looked below. It was a great height, but if he fell and hurt himself, he knew he was at the mercy of the bloodhounds behind him, who would do anything but show him any mercy, or spare him a single pang.

He looked round and beheld his pursuers close upon him, and one was so close to him that he seized upon his arm, saying, as he shouted to his companions,--

"Hurrah, boys! I have him."

With an execration, Sir Francis wielded his staff with such force, that he struck the fellow on the head, crushing in his hat as if it had been only so much paper. The man fell, but a blow followed from some one else which caused Varney to relax his hold, and finding himself falling, he, to save himself, sprang away.

The rails, at that moment, were crowded with men who leaned over to ascertain the effect of the leap.

"He'll be killed," said one.

"He's sure to be smashed," said another.

"I'll lay any wager he'll break a limb!" said a third.

Varney came to the earth--for a moment he lay stunned, and not able to move hand or foot.

"Hurrah!" shouted the mob.

Their triumph was short, for just as they shouted Varney arose, and after a moment or two's stagger he set off at full speed, which produced another shout from the mob; and just at that moment, a body of his pursuers were seen scaling the walls after him.

There was now a hunt through all the adjoining fields--from cover after cover they pursued him until he found no rest from the hungry wolves that beset him with cries, resembling beasts of prey rather than any human multitude.

Sir Francis heard them, at the same time, with the despair of a man who is struggling for life, and yet knows he is struggling in vain; he knew his strength was decaying--his immense exertions and the blows he had received, all weakened him, while the number and strength of his foes seemed rather to increase than to diminish.

Once more he sought the houses, and for a moment he believed himself safe, but that was only a momentary deception, for they had traced him.

He arrived at a garden wall, over which he bounded, and then he rushed into the house, the door of which stood open, for the noise and disturbance had awakened most of the inhabitants, who were out in all directions.

He took refuge in a small closet on the stairs, but was seen to do so by a girl, who screamed out with fear and fright,

"Murder! murder!--the wampyre!--the wampyre!" with all her strength, and in the way of screaming that was no little, and then she went off into a fit.

This was signal enough, and the house was at once entered, and beset on all sides by the mob, who came impatient of obtaining their victim who had so often baffled them.

"There he is--there he is," said the girl, who came to as soon as other people came up.

"Where?--where?"

"In that closet," she said, pointing to it with her finger. "I see'd him go in the way above."

Sir Francis, finding himself betrayed, immediately came out of the closet, just as two or three were advancing to open it, and dealt so hard a blow on the head of the first that came near him that he fell without a groan, and a second shared the same fate; and then Sir Francis found himself grappled with, but with a violent effort he relieved himself and rushed up stairs.

"Oh! murder--the wampyre! what shall I do--fire--fire!"

These exclamations were uttered in consequence of Varney in his haste to get up stairs, having inadvertently stepped into the girl's lap with one foot, while he kicked her in the chin with the other, besides scratching her nose till it bled.

"After him--stick to him," shouted the mob, but the girl kicked and sprawled so much they were impeded, till, regardless of her cries, they ran over her and pursued Varney, who was much distressed with the exertions he had made.

After about a minute's race he turned upon the head of the stair, not so much with the hope of defending it as of taking some breathing time: but seeing his enemies so close, he drew his sword, and stood panting, but prepared.

"Never mind his toasting-fork," said one bulky fellow, and, as he spoke, he rushed on, but the point of the weapon entered his heart and he fell dead.

There was a dreadful execration uttered by those who came up after him, and there was a momentary pause, for none liked to rush on to the bloody sword of Sir Francis Varney, who stood so willing and so capable of using it with the most deadly effect. They paused, as well they might, and this pause was the most welcome thing next to life to the unfortunate fugitive, for he was dreadfully distressed and bleeding.

"On to him boys! He can hardly stand. See how he pants. On to him, I say--push him hard."

"He pushes hard, I tell you," said another. "I felt the point of his sword, as it came through Giles's back.".

"I'll try my luck, then," said another, and he rushed up; but he was met by the sword of Sir Francis, who pierced it through his side, and he fell back with a groan.

Sir Francis, fearful of stopping any longer to defend that point, appeared desirous of making good his retreat with some little advantage, and he rushed up stairs before they had recovered from the momentary consternation into which they had been thrown by the sudden disaster they had received.

But they were quickly after him, and before he, wearied as he was, could gain the roof, they were up the ladder after him.

The first man who came through the trap was again set upon by Varney, who made a desperate thrust at him, and it took effect; but the sword snapped by the handle.

With an execration, Sir Francis threw the hilt at the head of the next man he saw; then rushing, with headlong speed, he distanced his pursuers for some house tops.

But the row of houses ended at the one he was then at, and he could go no further. What was to be done? The height was by far too great to be jumped; death was certain. A hideous heap of crushed and mangled bones would be the extent of what would remain of him, and then, perhaps, life not extinct for some hours afterwards.

He turned round; he saw them coming hallooing over the house tops, like a pack of hounds. Sir Francis struck his hands together, and groaned. He looked round, and perceived some ivy peeping over the coping-stone. A thought struck him, and he instantly ran to the spot and leaned over.

"Saved--saved!" he exclaimed.

Then, placing his hand over, he felt for the ivy; then he got over, and hung by the coping-stone, in a perilous position, till he found a spot on which he could rest his foot, and then he grasped the ivy as low down as he could, and thus he lowered himself a short way, till he came to where the ivy was stronger and more secure to the wall, as the upper part was very dangerous with his weight attached to it.

The mob came on, very sure of having Sir Francis Varney in their power, and they did not hurry on so violently, as their position was dangerous at that hour of the night.

"Easy, boys, easy," was the cry. "The bird is our own; he can't get away, that's very certain."

They, however, came on, and took no time about it hardly; but what was their amazement and rage at finding he had disappeared.

"Where is he?" was the universal inquiry, and "I don't know," an almost universal answer.

There was a long pause, while they searched around; but they saw no vestige of the object of their search.

"There's no trap door open," remarked one; "and I don't think he could have got in at any one."

"Perhaps, finding he could not get away, he has taken the desperate expedient of jumping over, and committing suicide, and so escape the doom he ought to be subjected to."

"Probably he has; but then we can run a stake through him and burn him all the same."

They now approached the extreme verge of the houses, and looked over the sides, but they could see nothing. The moon was up, and there was light enough to have seen him if he had fallen to the earth, and they were quite sure that he could not have got up after such a fall as he must have received.

"We are beaten after all, neighbours."

"I am not so sure of that," was the reply. "He may now be hidden about, for he was too far spent to be able to go far; he could not do that, I am sure."

"I think not either."

"Might he not have escaped by means of that ivy, yonder?" said one of the men, pointing to the plant, as it climbed over the coping-stones of the wall.

"Yes; it may be possible," said one; "and yet it is very dangerous, if not certain destruction to get over."

"Oh, yes; there is no possibility of escape that way. Why, it wouldn't bear a cat, for there are no nails driven into the wall at this height."

"Never mind," said another, "we may as well leave no stone unturned, as the saying is, but at once set about looking out for him."

The individual who spoke now leant over the coping stone, for some moments, in silence. He could see nothing, but yet he continued to gaze for some moments.

"Do you see him?" inquired one.

"No," was the answer.

"Ay, ay, I thought as much," was the reply. "He might as well have got hold of a corner of the moon, which, I believe, is more likely--a great deal more likely."

"Hold still a moment," said the man, who was looking over the edge of the house.

"What's the matter now? A gnat flew into your eye?"

"No; but I see him--by Jove, I see him!"

"See who--see who?"

"Varney, the vampyre!" shouted the man. "I see him about half-way down clinging, like a fly, to the wall. Odd zounds! I never saw the like afore!"

"Hurrah! after him then, boys!"

"Not the same way, if you please. Go yourself, and welcome; but I won't go that way."

"Just as you please," said the man; "but what's good for the goose is good for the gander is an old saying, and so is Jack as good as his master."

"So it may be; but cuss me if you ain't a fool if you attempt that!"

The man made no reply, but did as Varney had done before, got over the coping stone, and then laid hold of the ivy; but, whether his weight was heavier than Varney's, or whether it was that the latter had loosened the hold of the ivy or not, but he had no sooner left go of the coping stone than the ivy gave way, and he was precipitated from the height of about fifty feet to the earth--a dreadful fall!

There was a pause--no one spoke. The man lay motionless and dead--he had dislocated his neck!

The fall had not, however, been without its effect upon Varney, for the man's heels struck him so forcibly on his head as he fell, that he was stunned, and let go his hold, and he, too, fell to the earth, but not many feet.

He soon recovered himself, and was staggering away, when he was assailed by those above with groans, and curses of all kinds, and then by stones, and tiles, and whatever the mob could lay their hands upon.

Some of these struck him, and he was cut about in various places, so that he could hardly stand.

The hoots and shouts of the mob above had now attracted those below to the spot where Sir Francis Varney was trying to escape, but he had not gone far before the loud yells of those behind him told him that he was again pursued.

Half dead, and almost wholly spent, unarmed, and defenceless, he scarce knew what to do; whether to fly, or to turn round and die as a refuge from the greater evil of endeavouring to prolong a struggle which seemed hopeless. Instinct, however, urged him on, at all risks, and though he could not go very far, or fast, yet on he went, with the crowd after him.

"Down with the vampyre!--seize him--hold him--burn him! he must be down presently, he can't stand!"

This gave them new hopes, and rendered Varney's fate almost certain. They renewed their exertions to overtake him, while he exerted himself anew, and with surprising agility, considering how he had been employed for more than two hours.

There were some trees and hedges now that opposed the progress of both parties. The height of Sir Francis Varney gave him a great advantage, and, had he been fresh, he might have shown it to advantage in vaulting over the hedges and ditches, which he jumped when obliged, and walked through when he could.

Every now and then, the party in pursuit, who had been behind him some distance, now they gained on him; however, they kept, every now and then, losing sight of him among the trees and shrubs, and he made direct for a small wood, hoping that when there, he should to be able to conceal himself for some time, so as to throw his pursuers off the track.

They were well aware of this, for they increased their speed, and one or two swifter of foot than the others, got a-head of them and cried out aloud as they ran,--

"Keep up! keep up! he's making for the wood."

"He can't stop there long; there are too many of us to beat that cover without finding our game. Push, lads, he's our own now, as sure as we know he's on a-head."

They did push on, and came in full sight as they saw Sir Francis enter the wood, with what speed he could make; but he was almost spent. This was a cheering sight to them, and they were pretty certain he would not leave the wood in the state he was then--he must seek concealment.

However, they were mistaken, for Sir Francis Varney, as soon as he got into the wood, plunged into the thickest of it, and then paused to gain breath.

"So far safe," he muttered; "but I have had a narrow escape; they are not yet done, though, and it will not be safe here long. I must away, and seek shelter and safety elsewhere, if I can;--curses on the hounds that run yelping over the fields!"

He heard the shouts of his pursuers, and prepared to quit the wood when he thought the first had entered it.

"They will remain here some time in beating about," he muttered; "that is the only chance I have had since the pursuit; curse them! I say again. I may now get free; this delay must save my life, but nothing else will."

He moved away, and, at a slow and lazy pace, left the wood, and then made his way across some fields, towards some cottages, that lay on the left.

The moon yet shone on the fields; he could hear the shouts of the mob, as various parties went through the wood from one covert to another, and yet unable to find him.

Then came a great shout upon his ears, as though they had found out he had left the wood. This caused him to redouble his speed, and, fearful lest he should be seen in the moonlight, he leaped over the first fence that he came to, with almost the last effort he could make, and then staggered in at an open door--through a passage--into a front parlour, and there fell, faint, and utterly spent and speechless, at the feet of Flora Bannerworth.

CHAPTER LXXXVIII

THE RECEPTION OF THE VAMPYRE BY FLORA.--VARNEY SUBDUED

We must say that the irruption into the house of the Bannerworths by Sir Francis Varney, was certainly unpremeditated by him, for he knew not into whose house he had thus suddenly rushed for refuge from the numerous foes who were pursuing him with such vengeful ire. It was a strange and singular incident, and one well calculated to cause the mind to pause before it passed it by, and consider the means to an end which are sometimes as wide of the mark, as it is in nature possible to be.

But truth is stronger than fiction by far, and the end of it was, that, pressed on all sides by danger, bleeding, faint, and exhausted, he rushed into the first house he came to, and thus placed himself in the very house of those whom he had brought to such a state of misfortune.

Flora Bannerworth was seated at some embroidery, to pass away an hour or so, and thus get over the tedium of time; she was not thinking, either, upon the unhappy past; some trifling object or other engaged her attention. But what was her anguish when she saw a man staggering into the room bleeding, and bearing the marks of a bloody contest, and sinking at her feet.

Her astonishment was far greater yet, when she recognised that man to be Sir Francis Varney.

"Save me!--save me! Miss Bannerworth, save me!--only you can save me from the ruthless multitude which follows, crying aloud for my blood."

As he spoke, he sank down speechless. Flora was so much amazed, not to say terrified, that she knew not what to do. She saw Sir Francis a suppliant at her feet, a fugitive from his enemies, who would show him no mercy--she saw all this at a moment's glance; and yet she had not recovered her speech and presence of mind enough to enable her to make any reply to him.

"Save me! Miss Flora Bannerworth, save me!" he again said, raising himself on his hands. "I am beset, hunted like a wild beast--they seek my life--they have pursued me from one spot to another, and I have unwittingly intruded upon you. You will save me: I am sure your kindness and goodness of heart will never permit me to be turned out among such a crew of blood-thirsty butchers as those who pursue me are."

"Rise, Sir Francis Varney," said Flora, after a moment's hesitation; "in such an extremity as that which you are in, it would be inhuman indeed to thrust you out among your enemies."

"Oh! it would," said Varney. "I had thought, until now, I could have faced such a mob, until I was in this extremity; and then, disarmed and thrown down, bruised, beaten, and incapable of stemming such a torrent, I fled from one place to another, till hunted from each, and then instinct alone urged me to greater exertion than before, and here I am--this is now my last and only hope."

"Rise, Sir Francis."

"You will not let me be torn out and slaughtered like an ox. I am sure you will not."

"Sir Francis, we are incapable of such conduct; you have sought refuge here, and shall find it as far as we are able to afford it to you."

"And your brother--and--"

"Yes--yes--all who are here will do the same; but here they come to speak for themselves."

As she spoke, Mrs. Bannerworth entered, also Charles Holland, who both started on seeing the vampyre present, Sir Francis Varney, who was too weak to rise without assistance.

"Sir Francis Varney," said Flora, speaking to them as they entered, "has sought refuge here; his life is in peril, and he has no other hope left; you will, I am sure, do what can be done for him."

"Mr. Holland," said Sir Francis, "I am, as you may see by my condition, a fugitive, and have been beaten almost to death; instinct alone urged me on to save my life, and I, unknowingly, came in here."

"Rise, Sir Francis," said Charles Holland; "I am not one who would feel any pleasure in seeing you become the victim of any brutal mob. I am sure there are none amongst us who would willingly do so. You have trusted to those who will not betray you."

"Thank you," said Sir Francis, faintly. "I thank you; your conduct is noble, and Miss Bannerworth's especially so."

"Are you much hurt, Sir Francis?" inquired Charles.

"I am much hurt, but not seriously or dangerously; but I am weak and exhausted."

"Let me assist you to rise," said Charles Holland.

"Thank you," said Sir Francis, as he accepted of the assistance, and when he stood up, he found how incapable he really was, for a child might have grappled with him.

"I have been sore beset, Mrs. Bannerworth," he said, endeavouring to bow to that lady; "and I have suffered much ill-usage. I am not in such a plight as I could wish to be seen in by ladies; but my reasons for coming will be an excuse for my appearance in such disorder."

"We will not say anything about that," said Charles Holland; "under the circumstances, it could not be otherwise."

"It could not," said Sir Francis, as he took the chair Miss Flora Bannerworth placed for him.

"I will not ask you for any explanation as to how this came about; but you need some restorative and rest."

"I think I suffer more from exhaustion than anything else. The bruises I have, of course, are not dangerous."

"Can you step aside a few moments?" said Mrs. Bannerworth. "I will show you where you can remove some of those stains, and make yourself more comfortable."

"Thank you, madam--thank you. It will be most welcome to me, I assure you."

Sir Francis rose up, and, with the aid of Charles Holland, he walked to the next room, where he washed himself, and arranged his dress as well as it would admit of its being done.

"Mr. Holland," he said, "I cannot tell you how grateful I feel for this. I have been hunted from the house where you saw me. From what source they learned my abode--my place of concealment--I know not; but they found me out."

"I need hardly say, Sir Francis, that it could not have occurred through me," said Charles Holland.

"My young friend," said Sir Francis, "I am quite sure you were not; and, moreover, I never, for one moment, suspected you. No, no; some accidental circumstance alone has been the cause. I have been very cautious--I may say extremely so--but at the same time, living, as I have, surrounded by enemies on all sides, it is not to be wondered at that I should be seen by some one, and thus traced to my lair, whither they followed me at their leisure."

"They have been but too troublesome in this matter. When they become a little reasonable, it will be a great miracle; for, when their passions and fears are excited, there is no end to the extremes they will perpetrate."

"It is so," said Varney, "as the history of these last few days amply testifies to me. I could never have credited the extent to which popular excitement could be carried, and the results it was likely to produce."

"It is an engine of very difficult control," pursued Charles Holland; "but what will raise it will not allay it, but add fuel to the fire that burns so fiercely already."

"True enough," said Sir Francis.

"If you have done, will you again step this way?"

Sir Francis Varney followed Charles Holland into the sitting-room, and sat down with them, and before him was spread a light supper, with some good wine.

"Eat, Sir Francis," said Mrs. Bannerworth. "Such a state as that in which you are, must, of necessity, produce great exhaustion, and you must require food and drink."

Sir Francis bowed as well as he was able, and even then, sore and bruised as he was, fugitive as he had been, he could not forget his courtesy; but it was not without an effort. His equanimity was, however, much disturbed, by finding himself in the midst of the Bannerworths.

"I owe you a relation," he said, "of what occurred to drive me from my place of concealment."

"We should like to hear it, if you are not too far fatigued to relate it," said Charles.

"I will. I was sitting at the top of that house in which I sought to hide myself, when I heard sounds come that were of a very suspicious nature; but did not believe that it could happen that they had discovered my lurking-place; far from it; though, of late, I had been habitually cautious and suspicious, yet I thought I was safe, till I heard the noise of a multitude coming towards me. I could not be mistaken in it, for the sounds are so peculiar that they are like nothing else. I heard them coming.

"I moved not; and when they surrounded the house as far as was practicable, they gave an immense shout, and made the welkin ring with the sound."

"I heard a confused noise at a distance," remarked Flora; "but I had no idea that anything serious was contemplated. I imagined it was some festival among some trade, or portion of the townspeople, who were shouting from joy."

"Oh, dear no," said Sir Francis; "but I am not surprised at the mistake, because there are such occurrences occasionally; but whenever the mob gained any advantage upon me they shouted, and when I was able to oppose them with effect, they groaned at me most horribly."

"The deuce," said Charles; "the sound, suppose, serves to express their feelings, and to encourage each other."

"Something of the sort, I dare say," said Varney: "but at length, after defending the house with all the desperation that despair imparted to me, I was compelled to fly from floor to floor, until I had reached the roof; there they followed me, and I was compelled again to fly. House after house they followed me to, until I could go no farther," said Varney.

"How did you escape?"

"Fortunately I saw some ivy growing and creeping over the coping-stones, and by grasping that I got over the side, and so let myself down by degrees, as well as I was able."

"Good heavens! what a dreadful situation," exclaimed Flora; "it is really horrible!"

"I could not do it again, under, I think, any circumstances."

"Not the same?" said Mrs. Bannerworth.

"I really doubt if I could," said Varney. "The truth is, the excitement of the moment was great, and I at that moment thought of nothing but getting away.

"The same circumstances, the same fear of death, could hardly be produced in me again, and I am unable to account for the phenomenon on this occasion."

"Your escape was very narrow indeed," said Flora; "it makes me shudder to think of the dangers you have gone through; it is really terrible to think of it."

"You," said Sir Francis, "are young and susceptible, and generous in your disposition, You can feel for me, and do; but how little I could have expected it, it is impossible to say; but your sympathy sinks into my mind and causes such emotions as never can be erased from my soul.

"But to proceed. You may guess how dreadful was my position, by the fact that the first man who attempted to get over tore the ivy away and fell, striking me in his fall; he was killed, and I thrown down and stunned. I then made for the wood, closely pursued and got into it; then I baffled them: they searched the wood, and I went through it. I then ran across the country to these houses here; I got over the fence, and in at the back door."

"Did they see you come?" inquired Charles Holland.

"I cannot say, but I think that they did not; I heard them give a loud shout more than once when on this side of the wood."

"You did? How far from here were you when you heard the shouts?" inquired Mrs. Bannerworth.

"I was close here; and, as I jumped over the fence, I heard them shout again; but I think they cannot see so far; the night was moonlight, to be sure, but that is all; the shadow of the hedge, and the distance together, would make it, if not impossible, at least very improbable."

"That is very likely," said Mrs. Bannerworth.

"In that case," said Charles Holland, "you are safe here; for none will suspect your being concealed here."

"It is the last place I should myself have thought of," said Varney; "and I may say the last place I would knowingly have come to; but had I before known enough of you, I should have been well assured of your generosity, and have freely come to claim your aid and shelter, which accident has so strangely brought me to be a candidate for, and which you have so kindly awarded me."

"The night is wearing away," said Flora, "and Sir Francis is doubtless fatigued to an excess; sleep, I dare say, will be most welcome to him."

"It will indeed, Miss Bannerworth," said Varney; "but I can do that under any circumstances; do not let me put you to any inconvenience; a chair, and at any hour, will serve me for sleep."

"We cannot do for you what we would wish," said Flora, looking at her mother; "but something better than that, at all events, we can and will provide for you."

"I know not how to thank you," said Sir Francis Varney; "I assure you, of late I have not been luxuriously lodged, and the less trouble I give you the greater I shall esteem the favour."

The hour was late, and Sir Francis Varney, before another half hour had elapsed, was consigned to his own reflections, in a small but neat room, there to repose his bruised and battered carcass, and court the refreshing influence of sleep.

His reflections were, for nearly an hour, of the most contradictory character; some one passion was trying to overcome the other; but he seemed quite subdued.

"I could not have expected this," he muttered; "Flora Bannerworth has the soul of a heroine. I deserved not such a reception from them; and yet, in my hour of utmost need, they have received me like a favoured friend; and yet all their misfortunes have taken their origin from me; I am the cause of all."

Filled with these thoughts, he fell asleep; he slept till morning broke. He was not disturbed; it seemed as though the influence of sleep was sweeter far there, in the cottage of the Bannerworths, than ever he had before received.

It was late on that morning before Sir Francis rose, and then only through hearing the family about, and, having performed his toilet, so far as circumstances permitted, he descended, and entered the front-parlour, the room he had been in the night before.

Flora Bannerworth was already there; indeed, breakfast was waiting the appearance of Sir Francis Varney.

"Good morning, Miss Bannerworth," said Sir Francis, bowing with his usual dignified manner, but in the kindest and sincerest way he was able to assume.

"Good morning, Sir Francis," said Flora, rising to receive him; and she could not avoid looking at him as he entered the room. "I hope you have had a pleasant night?"

"It has been the best night's rest I have had for some time, Miss Bannerworth. I assure you I have to express my gratitude to you for so much kindness. I have slept well, and soundly."

"I am glad to hear it."

"I think yet I shall escape the search of these people who have hunted me from so many places."

"I hope you may, indeed, Sir Francis."

"You, Miss Bannerworth! and do you hope I may escape the vengeance of these people--the populace?"

"I do, Sir Francis, most sincerely hope so. Why should I wish evil to you, especially at their hands?"

Sir Francis did not speak for a minute or two, and then he said, turning full upon Flora--

"I don't know why, Miss Bannerworth, that I should think so, but perhaps it is because there are peculiar circumstances connected with myself, that have made me feel conscious that I have not deserved so much goodness at your hands."

"You have not deserved any evil. Sir Francis, we could not do that if it were in our power; we would do you a service at any time."

"You have done so, Miss Bannerworth--the greatest that can be performed. You have saved my life."

At that moment Charles Holland entered, and Sir Francis bowed, as he said,--

"I hope you, Mr. Holland, have slept as well, and passed as good a night as I have passed?"

"I am glad you, at least, have passed a quiet one," said Charles Holland; "you, I dare say, feel all the better for it? How do you feel yourself? Are you much hurt?"

"Not at all, not at all," said Sir Francis Varney. "Only a few bruises, and so forth, some of which, as you may perceive, do not add to one's personal appearance. A week or two's quiet would rid me of them. At all events, I would it may do the same with my enemies."

"I wish they were as easily gotten rid of myself," said Charles; "but as that cannot be, we must endeavour to baffle them in the best way we may."

"I owe a debt to you I shall never be able to repay; but where there is a will, they say there is a way; and if the old saying be good for anything, I need not despair, though the way is by no means apparent at present."

"Time is the magician," said Flora, "whose wand changes all things--the young to the aged, and the aged to nothing."

"Certainly, that is true," said Varney, "and many such changes have I seen. My mind is stored with such events; but this is sadness, and I have cause to rejoice."

***

The breakfast was passed off in pleasing conversation, and Varney found himself much at home with the Bannerworths, whose calm and even tenour was quite new to him.

He could not but admit the charms of such a life as that led by the Bannerworths; but what it must have been when they were supplied by ample means, with nothing to prey upon their minds, and no fearful mystery to hang on and weigh down their spirits, he could scarcely imagine.

They were amiable, accomplished; they were in the same mind at all times, and nothing seemed to ruffle them; and when night came, he could not but acknowledge to himself that he had never formed half the opinion of them they were deserving of.

Of course during that day he was compelled to lie close, so as not to be seen by any one, save the family. He sat in a small room, which was overlooked by no other in the neighbourhood, and he remained quiet, sometimes conversing, and sometimes reading, but at the same time ever attentive to the least sound that appeared at all of a character to indicate the approach of persons for any purpose whatever.

At supper time he spoke to Flora and to Charles Holland, saying,--

"There are certain matters connected with myself--I may say with you now--sure all that has happened will make it so--of which you would be glad to hear some thing."

"You mean upon the same subject upon which I had some conversation with you a day or two back?"

"Yes, the same. Allow me one week, and you shall know all. I will then relate to you that which you so much desire to know--one week, and all shall be told."

"Well," said Charles Holland, "this has not been exacted from you as the price of your safety, but you can choose your own time, of course; what you promise is most desired, for it will render those happy who now are much worse than they were before these occurrences took place."

"I am aware of all that; grant me but one week, and then you shall be made acquainted with all."

"I am satisfied, Sir Francis," said Flora; "but while here under our roof, we should never have asked you a question."

"Of this, Miss Bannerworth, the little I have seen of you assures me you would not do so; however, I am the more inclined to make it--I am under so deep an obligation to you all, that I can never repay it."

***

Sir Francis Varney retired to rest that night--his promise to the Bannerworths filled his mind with many reflections--the insecurity of his own position, and the frail tenure which he even held in the hands of those whom he had most injured.

This produced a series of reflections of a grave and melancholy nature, and he sat by his window, watching the progress of the clouds, as they appeared to chase each other over the face of the scene--now casting a shade over the earth, and then banishing the shadows, and throwing a gentle light over the earth's surface, which was again chased away, and shadows again fell upon the scene below.

How long he had sat there in melancholy musing he knew not; but suddenly he was aroused from his dreams by a voice that shook the skies, and caused him to start to his feet.

"Hurrah!--hurrah!--hurrah!" shouted the mob, which had silently collected around the cottage of the Bannerworths.

"Curses!" muttered Sir Francis, as he again sank in his chair, and struck his head with his hand. "I am hunted to death--they will not leave me until my body has graced a cross-road."

"Hurrah!--down with the vampyre--pull him out!"

Then came an instant knocking at the doors, and the people on the outside made so great a din, that it seemed as though they contemplated knocking the house down at once, without warning the inmates that they waited there.

There was a cessation for about a minute, when one of the family hastened to the door, and inquired what was wanted.

"Varney, the vampyre," was the reply.

"You must seek him elsewhere."

"We will search this place before we go further," replied a man.

"But he is not here."

"We have reason to believe otherwise. Open the door, and let us in--no one shall be hurt, or one single object in the house; but we must come in, and search for the vampyre."

"Come to-morrow, then."

"That will not do," said the voice; "open, or we force our way in without more notice."

At the same a tremendous blow was bestowed upon the door, and then much force was used to thrust it in. A consultation was suddenly held among the inmates, as to what was to be done, but no one could advise, and each was well aware of the utter impossibility of keeping the mob out.

"I do not see what is to become of me," said Sir Francis Varney, suddenly appearing before them. "You must let them in; there is no chance of keeping them off, neither can you conceal me. You will have no place, save one, that will be sacred from their profanation."

"And which is that?"

"Flora's own room."

All started at the thought that Flora's chamber could in any way be profaned by any such presence as Sir Francis Varney's.

However, the doors below were suddenly burst open, amid loud cries from the populace, who rushed in in great numbers, and began to search the lower rooms, immediately.

"All is lost!" said Sir Francis Varney, as he dashed away and rushed to the chamber of Flora, who, alarmed at the sounds that were now filling the house, stood listening to them.

"Miss Bannerworth--" began Varney.

"Sir Francis!"

"Yes, it is indeed I, Miss Bannerworth; hear me, for one moment."

"What is the matter?"

"I am again in peril--in more imminent peril than before; my life is not worth a minute's purchase, unless you save me. You, and you alone, can now save me. Oh! Miss Bannerworth, if ever pity touched your heart, save me from those only whom I now fear. I could meet death in any shape but that in which they will inflict it upon me. Hear their execrations below!"

"Death to the vampyre! death to Varney! burn him! run a stake through his body!"

"What can I do, Sir Francis?"

"Admit me to your chamber."

"Sir Francis, are you aware of what you are saying?"

"I am well. It is a request which you would justly scorn to reply to, but now my life--recollect you have saved me once--my life,--do not now throw away the boon you have so kindly bestowed. Save me, Miss Bannerworth."

"It is not possible. I--"

"Nay, Miss Bannerworth, do you imagine this is a time for ceremony, or the observances of polished life! On my honour, you run no risk of censure."

"Where is Varney? Where is the vampyre? He ain't far off."

"Hear--hear them, Miss Bannerworth. They are now at the foot of the stairs. Not a moment to lose. One minute more, and I am in the hands of a crew that has no mercy."

"Hurrah! upstairs! He's not below. Upstairs, neighbours, we shall have him yet!"

These words sounded on the stairs: half-a-dozen more steps, and Varney would be seen. It was a miracle he was not heard begging for his life.

Varney cast a look of despair at the stairhead and felt for his sword, but it was not there, he had lost it. He struck his head with his clenched hand, and was about to rush upon his foes, when he heard the lock turn; he looked, and saw the door opened gently, and Flora stood there; he passed in, and sank cowering into a chair, at the other end of the room, behind some curtains.

The door was scarcely shut ere some tried to force it, and then a loud knocking came at the door.

"Open! open! we want Varney, the vampyre. Open! or we will burst it open."

Flora did open it, but stood resolutely in the opening, and held up her hand to impose silence.

"Are you men, that you can come thus to force yourselves upon the privacy of a female? Is there nothing in the town or house, that you must intrude in numbers into a private apartment? Is no place sacred from you?"

"But, ma'am--miss--we only want Varney, the vampyre."

"And can you find him nowhere but in a female's bedroom? Shame on you! shame on you! Have you no sisters, wives, or mothers, that you act thus?"

"He's not there, you may be sure of that, Jack," said a gruff voice. "Let the lady be in quiet; she's had quite enough trouble with him to sicken her of a vampyre. You may be sure that's the last place to find him in."

With this they all turned away, and Flora shut the door and locked it upon them, and Varney was safe.

"You have saved me," said Varney.

"Hush!" said Flora. "Speak not; there maybe some one listening."

Sir Francis Varney stood in the attitude of one listening most anxiously to catch some sounds; the moon fell across his face, and gave it a ghastly hue, that, added to his natural paleness and wounds, gave him an almost unearthly aspect.

The sounds grew more and more distant; the shouts and noise of men traversing the apartments subsided, and gradually the place became restored to its original silence. The mob, after having searched every other part of the house, and not finding the object of their search, they concluded that he was not there, but must have made his escape before.

***

This most desperate peril of Sir Francis Varney seemed to have more effect upon him than anything that had occurred during his most strange and most eventful career.

When he was assured that the riotous mob that had been so intent upon his destruction was gone, and that he might emerge from his place of concealment, he did so with an appearance of such utter exhaustion that the Bannerworth family could not but look upon him as a being who was near his end.

At any time his countenance, as we long have had occasion to remark, was a strange and unearthly looking one; but when we come to superadd to the strangeness of his ordinary appearance the traces of deep mental emotion, we may well say that Varney's appearance was positively of the most alarming character.

When he was seated in the ordinary sitting apartment of the Bannerworths, he drew a long sighing breath, and placing his hand upon his heart, he said, in a faint tone of voice,--

"It beats now laboriously, but it will soon cease its pulsations for ever."

These words sounded absolutely prophetic, there was about them such a solemn aspect, and he looked at the same time that he uttered them so much like one whose mortal race was run, and who was now a candidate for the grave.

"Do not speak so despairingly," said Charles Holland; "remember, that if your life has been one of errors hitherto, how short a space of time may suffice to redeem some of them at least, and the communication to me which you have not yet completed may to some extent have such an effect."

"No, no. It may contribute to an act of justice, but it can do no good to me. And yet do not suppose that because such is my impression that I mean to hesitate in finishing to you that communication."

"I rejoice to hear you say so, and if you would, now that you must be aware of what good feelings towards you we are all animated with, remove the bar of secrecy from the communication, I should esteem it a great favour."

Varney appeared to be considering for a few moments, and then he said,--

"Well, well. Let the secrecy no longer exist. Have it removed at once. I will no longer seek to maintain it. Tell all, Charles Holland--tell all."

Thus empowered by the mysterious being, Charles Holland related briefly what Varney had already told him, and then concluded by saying,--

"That is all that I have myself as yet been made aware of, and I now call upon Sir Francis Varney to finish his narration."

"I am weak," said Varney, "and scarcely equal to the task; but yet I will not shrink from the promise that I have made. You have been the preservers of my life, and more particularly to you, Flora Bannerworth, am I indebted for an existence, which otherwise must have been sacrificed upon the altar of superstition."

"But you will recollect, Master Varney," said the admiral, who had sat looking on for some time in silent wonder, "you must recollect, Master Varney, that the people are, after all, not so much to blame for their superstition, because, whether you are a vampyre or not, and I don't pretend to come to a positive opinion now, you took good care to persuade them you were."

"I did," said Varney, with a shudder; "but why did I?"

"Well, you know best."

"It was, then, because I did believe, and do believe, that there is something more than natural about my strangely protracted existence; but we will waive that point, and, before my failing strength, for it appears to me to be failing, completely prevents me from doing so, let me relate to you the continued particulars of the circumstances that made me what I am."

Flora Bannerworth, although she had heard before from the lips of Charles Holland the to her dreadful fact, that her father, in addition to having laid violent hands upon his own life, was a murderer, now that that fearful circumstance was related more publicly, felt a greater pang than she had done when it was whispered to her in the accents of pure affection, and softened down by a gentleness of tone, which Charles Holland's natural delicacy would not allow him to use even to her whom he loved so well in the presence of others.

She let her beautiful face be hidden by her hands, and she wept as she listened to the sad detail.

Varney looked inquiringly in the countenance of Charles Holland, because, having given him leave to make Flora acquainted with the circumstance, he was rather surprised at the amount of emotion which it produced in her.

Charles Holland answered the appealing look by saying,--

"Flora is already aware of the facts, but it naturally affects her much to hear them now repeated in the presence of others, and those too, towards whom she cannot feel--"

What Charles Holland was going to say was abruptly stopped short by the admiral, who interposed, exclaiming,--

"Why, what do you mean, you son of a sea cook? The presence of who do you mean? Do you mean to say that I don't feel for Miss Flora, bless her heart! quite as much as a white-faced looking swab like you? Why, I shall begin to think you are only fit for a marine."

"Nay, uncle, now do not put yourself out of temper. You must be well aware that I could not mean anything disrespectful to you. You should not suppose such a state of things possible; and although, perhaps, I did not express myself so felicitously as I might, yet what I intended to say, was--"

"Oh, bother what you intended to say. You go on, Mr. Vampyre, with your story. I want to know what became of it all; just you get on as quick as you can, and let us know what you did after the man was murdered."

"When the dreadful deed was committed," said Varney, "and our victim lay weltering in his blood, and had breathed his last, we stood like men who for the first time were awakened to the frightful consequences of what they had done.

"I saw by the dim light that hovered round us a great change come over the countenance of Marmaduke Bannerworth, and he shook in every limb.

"This soon passed away, however, and the powerful and urgent necessity which arose of avoiding the consequences of the deed that we had done, restored us to ourselves. We stooped and took from the body the ill-gotten gains of the gambler. They amounted to an immense sum, and I said to Marmaduke Bannerworth,--

"'Take you the whole of this money and proceed to your own home with it, where you will be least suspected. Hide it in some place of great secrecy, and to-morrow I will call upon you, when we will divide it, and will consider of some means of safely exchanging the notes for gold.'

"He agreed to this, and placed the money in his pocket, after which it became necessary that we should dispose of the body, which, if we did not quickly remove, must in a few hours be discovered, and so, perchance, accompanied by other criminating circumstances, become a frightful evidence against us, and entail upon us all those consequences of the deed which we were so truly anxious to escape from.

"It is ever the worst part of the murderer's task, that after he has struck the blow that has deprived his victim of existence, it becomes his frightful duty to secrete the corpse, which, with its dead eyes, ever seems to be glaring upon him such a world of reproach.

"That it is which should make people pause ere they dipped their hands in the blood of others, and that it is which becomes the first retribution that the murderer has to endure for the deep crime that he has committed.

"We tore two stakes from a hedge, and with their assistance we contrived to dig a very superficial hole, such a hole as was only sufficient, by placing a thin coating of earth over it, to conceal the body of the murdered man.

"And then came the loathsome task of dragging him into it--a task full of horror, and from which we shrunk aghast; but it had to be done, and, therefore, we stooped, and grasping the clothes as best we might, we dragged the body into the chasm we had prepared for its reception. Glad were we then to be enabled to throw the earth upon it and to stamp upon it with such vehemence as might well be supposed to actuate men deeply anxious to put out of sight some dangerous and loathsome object.

"When we had completed this, and likewise gathered handsfull of dust from the road, and dry leaves, and such other matter, to sprinkle upon the grave, so as to give the earth an appearance of not having been disturbed, we looked at each other and breathed from our toil.

"Then, and not till then, was it that we remembered that among other things which the gambler had won of Marmaduke were the deeds belonging to the Dearbrook property."

"The Dearbrook property!" exclaimed Henry Bannerworth; "I know that there was a small estate going by that name, which belonged to our family, but I always understood that long ago my father had parted with it."

"Yes; it was mortgaged for a small sum--a sum not a fourth part of its value--and it had been redeemed by Marmaduke Bannerworth, not for the purpose of keeping it, but in order that he might sell it outright, and so partially remedy his exhausted finances."

"I was not aware of that," returned Henry.

"Doubtless you were not, for of late--I mean for the twelve months or so preceding your father's death--you know he was much estranged from all the family, so that you none of you knew much of what he was doing, except that he was carrying on a very wild and reckless career, such as was sure to end in dishonour and poverty; but I tell you he had the title deeds of the Dearbrook property, and that they were only got from him, along with everything else of value that he possessed, at the gaming-table, by the man who paid such a fearful penalty for his success.

"It was not until after the body was completely buried, and we had completed all our precautions for more effectually hiding it from observation, that we recollected the fact of those important papers being in his possession. It was Marmaduke Bannerworth who first remembered it, and he exclaimed,--

"'By Heaven, we have buried the title deeds of the property, and we shall have again to exhume the corpse for the purpose of procuring them.'

"Now those deeds were nothing to me, and repugnant as I had felt from the first to having anything whatever to do with the dead body, it was not likely that I would again drag it from the earth for such an object.

"'Marmaduke Bannerworth,' I said, 'you can do what you please, and take the consequences of what you do, but I will not again, if I can help it, look upon the face of that corpse. It is too fearful a sight to contemplate again. You have a large sum of money, and what need you care now for the title deeds of a property comparatively insignificant?'

"'Well, well,' he said, 'I will not, at the present time, disturb the remains; I will wait to see if anything should arise from the fact of the murder; if it should turn out that no suspicion of any kind is excited, but that all is still and quiet, I can then take measures to exhume the corpse, and recover those papers, which certainly are important.'

"By this time the morning was creeping on apace, and we thought it prudent to leave the spot. We stood at the end of the lane for a few moments conversing, and those moments were the last in which I ever saw Marmaduke Bannerworth."

"Answer me a question," said Henry.

"I will; ask me what you please, I will answer it."

"Was it you that called at Bannerworth Hall, after my father's melancholy death, and inquired for him?"

"I did; and when I heard of the deed that he had done, I at once left, in order to hold counsel with myself as to what I should do to obtain at least a portion of the property, one-half of which, it was understood, was to have been mine. I heard what had been the last words used by Marmaduke Bannerworth on the occasion of his death, and they were amply sufficient to let me know what had been done with the money--at all events, so far as regards the bestowal of it in some secret place; and from that moment the idea of, by some means or another, getting the exclusive possession of it, never forsook my mind.

"I thought over the matter by day and, by night; and with the exception of having a knowledge of the actual hiding-place of the money, I could see, in the clearest possible manner, how the whole affair had been transacted. There can be no doubt but that Marmaduke Bannerworth had reached home safely with the large sum of which he had become possessed, and that he had hidden it securely, which was but an ordinary measure of precaution, when we come to consider how the property had been obtained.

"Then I suspect that, being alone, and left to the gloom of his own miserable thoughts, they reverted so painfully to the past that he was compelled to drink deeply for the purpose of drowning reflection.

"The natural consequence of this, in his state, was, that partial insanity supervened, and at a moment when frenzy rose far above reflection, he must have committed the dreadful act which hurried him instantaneously to eternity."

"Yes," said Henry; "it must have been so; you have guessed truly. He did on that occasion drink an immense quantity of wine; but instead of stilling the pangs of remorse it must have increased them, and placed him in such a frenzied condition of intellect, that he found it impossible to withstand the impulse of it, unless by the terrific act which ended his existence."

"Yes, and which at once crushed all my expectations of the large fortune which was to have been mine; for even the one-half of the sum which had been taken from the gamester's pocket would have been sufficient to have enabled me to live for the future in affluence.

"I became perfectly maddened at the idea that so large a sum had passed out of my hands. I constantly hovered about Bannerworth Hall, hoping and expecting that something might arise which would enable me to get admittance to it, and make an active search through its recesses for the hidden treasure.

"All my exertions were in vain. I could hit upon no scheme whatever; and at length, wearied and exhausted, I was compelled to proceed to London for the sake of a subsistence. It is only in that great metropolis that such persons as myself, destitute of real resources, but infinitely reckless as regards the means by which they acquire a subsistence, can hope to do so. Once again, therefore, I plunged into the vortex of London life, and proceeded, heedless of the criminality of what I was about, to cater for myself by robbery, or, indeed, in any manner which presented a prospect of success. It was during this career of mine, that I became associated with some of the most desperate characters of the time; and the offences we committed were of that daring character that it could not be wondered at eventually so formidable a gang of desperadoes must be by force broken up.

"It so occurred, but unknown to us, that the police resolved upon making one of the most vigorous efforts to put an end to the affair, and in consequence a watch was set upon every one of our movements.

"The result of this was, as might have been expected, our complete dispersion, and the arrest of some our members, and among them myself.

"I knew my fate almost from the first. Our depredations had created such a sensation, that the legislature, even, had made it a matter of importance that we should be suppressed, and it was an understood thing among the judges, that the severest penalties of the law should be inflicted upon any one of the gang who might be apprehended and convicted.

"My trial scarcely occupied an hour, and then I was convicted and sentenced to execution, with an intimation from the judge that it would be perfectly absurd of me to dream, for one moment, of a remission of that sentence.

"In this state of affairs, and seeing nothing but death before me, I gave myself up to despair, and narrowly missed cheating the hangman of his victim.

"More dead than alive, I was, however, dragged out to be judicially murdered, and I shall never forget the crowd of frightful sensations that came across my mind upon that terrific occasion.

"It seemed as if my fate had then reached its climax, and I have really but a dim recollection of the terrible scene.

"I remember something of the confused murmur arising from an immense throng of persons. I remember looking about me, and seeing nothing but what appeared to me an immense sea of human heads, and then suddenly I heard a loud roar of execration burst from the multitude.

"I shrunk back terrified, and it did, indeed, seem to me a brutal thing thus to roar and shout at a man who was brought out to die. I soon, however, found that the mob who came to see such a spectacle was not so debased as I imagined, but that it was at the hangman, who had suddenly made his appearance on the scaffold, at whom they raised that fearful yell.

"Some one--I think it was one of the sheriffs--must have noticed that I was labouring under the impression that the cry from the mob was levelled at me, for he spoke, saying,--

"'It is at the hangman they shout,' and he indicated with his finger that public functionary. In my mind's eye I think I see him now, and I am certain that I shall never forget the expression of his face. It was perfectly fearful; and afterwards, when I learned who and what he was, I was not surprised that he should feel so acutely the painfully degrading office which he had to perform.

"The fatal rope was in a few minutes adjusted to my neck. I felt its pressure, and I heard the confused sounds of the monotonous voice of the clergyman, as he muttered some prayers, that I must confess sounded to me at the time like a mockery of human suffering.

"Then suddenly there was a loud shout--I felt the platform give way beneath my feet--I tried to utter a yell of agony, but could not--it seemed to me as if I was encompassed by fire, and then sensation left me, and I knew no more.

***

"The next feelings of existence that came over me consisted in a frightful tingling sensation throughout my veins, and I felt myself making vain efforts to scream. All the sensations of a person suffering from a severe attack of nightmare came across me, and I was in such an agony, that I inwardly prayed for death to release me from such a cruel state of suffering. Then suddenly the power to utter a sound came to me, and I made use of it well, for the piercing shriek I uttered, must have struck terror into the hearts of all who heard it, since it appalled even myself.

"Then I suppose I must have fainted, but when I recovered consciousness again, I found myself upon a couch, and a man presenting some stimulus to me in a cup. I could not distinguish objects distinctly, but I heard him say, 'Drink, and you will be better.'

"I did drink, for a raging thirst consumed me, and then I fell into a sound sleep, which, I was afterwards told, lasted nearly twenty-four hours, and when I recovered from that, I heard again the same voice that had before spoken to me, asking me how I was.

"I turned in the direction of the sound, and, as my vision was now clearer, I could see that it was the hangman, whose face had made upon the scaffold such an impression upon me--an impression which I then considered my last in this world, but which turned out not to be such by many a mingled one of pain and pleasure since.

"It was some time before I could speak, and when I did, it was only in a few muttered words, to ask what had happened, and where I was.

"'Do you not remember,' he said, 'that you were hanged?'

"'I do--I do,' was my reply. 'Is this the region of damned souls?'

"'No; you are still in this world, however strange you may think it. Listen to me, and I will briefly tell you how it is that you have come back again, as it were, from the very grave, to live and walk about among the living."

"I listened to him with a strange and rapt attention, and then he told how a young and enthusiastic medical man had been anxious to try some experiments with regard to the restoration of persons apparently dead, and he proceeded to relate how it was that he had given ear to the solicitations of the man, and had consented to bring my body after it was hung for him to experiment upon. He related how the doctor had been successful, but how he was so terrified at his own success, that he hastily fled, and had left London, no one knowing whither he had gone.

"I listened to this with the most profound attention, and then he concluded, by saying to me,--

"'There can be no doubt but my duty requires of me to give you up again to the offended laws of your country. I will not, however, do that, if you will consent to an arrangement that I shall propose to you.'

"I asked him what the arrangement was, and he said that if I would solemnly bind myself to pay to him a certain sum per annum, he would keep my secret, and forsaking his calling as hangman, endeavour to do something that should bring with it pleasanter results. I did so solemnly promise him, and I have kept my word. By one means or another I have succeeded in procuring the required amount, and now he is no more."

"I believe," cried Henry, "that he has fallen a victim to the blind fury of the populace."

"You are right, he has so, and accordingly I am relieved from the burden of those payments; but it matters little, for now I am so near the tomb myself, that, together with all my obligations, I shall soon be beyond the reach of mortal cavilling."

"You need not think so, Varney; you must remember that you are at present suffering from circumstances, the pressure of which will soon pass away, and then you will resume your wonted habits."

"What did you do next?" said the admiral.--"Let's know all while you are about it."

"I remained at the hangman's house for some time, until all fear of discovery was over, and then he removed me to a place of greater security, providing me from his own resources with the means of existence, until I had fully recovered my health, and then he told me to shift for myself.

"During my confinement though, I had not been idle mentally, for I concocted a plan, by which I should be enabled not only to live well myself, but to pay to the hangman, whose name was Mortimore, the annual sum I had agreed upon. I need not go into the details of this plan. Of course it was neither an honest nor respectable one, but it succeeded, and I soon found myself in a position to enable me thereby to keep my engagement, as well as to supply me with means of plotting and planning for my future fortunes.

"I had never for a moment forgotten that so large a sum of money was somewhere concealed about Bannerworth Hall, and I still looked forward to obtaining it by some means or another.

"It was in this juncture of affairs, that one night I was riding on horseback through a desolate part of England. The moon was shining sweetly, as I came to a broad stream of water, across which, about a mile further on, I saw that there was a bridge, but being unwilling to waste time by riding up to it, and fancying, by the lazy ripple of the waters, that the river was not shallow, I plunged my horse boldly into the stream.

"When we reached its centre, some sudden indisposition must have seized the horse, for instead of swimming on well and gallantly as it had done before, it paused for a moment, and then plunged headlong into the torrent.

"I could not swim, and so, for a second time, death, with all its terrors, appeared to be taking possession of me. The waters rolled over my head, gurgling and hissing in my ears, and then all was past. I know no more, until I found myself lying upon a bright green meadow, and the full beams of the moon shining upon me.

"I was giddy and sick, but I rose, and walked slowly away, each moment gathering fresh strength, and from that time to this, I never discovered how I came to be rescued from the water, and lying upon that green bank. It has ever been a mystery to me, and I expect it ever will.

"Then from that moment the idea that I had a sort of charmed life came across me, and I walked about with an impression that such was the case, until I came across a man who said that he was a Hungarian, and who was full of strange stories of vampyres. Among other things, he told me that a vampyre could not be drowned, for that the waters would cast him upon its banks, and, if the moonbeams fell upon him, he would be restored to life.

"This was precisely my story, and from that moment I believed myself to be one of those horrible, but charmed beings, doomed to such a protracted existence. The notion grew upon me day by day, and hour by hour, until it became quite a fixed and strong belief, and I was deceiving no one when I played the horrible part that has been attributed to me."

"But you don't mean to say that you believe you are a vampyre now?" said the admiral.

"I say nothing, and know not what to think. I am a desperate man, and what there is at all human in me, strange to say, all of you whom I sought to injure, have awakened."

"Heed not that," said Henry, "but continue your narrative. We have forgiven everything, and that ought to suffice to quiet your mind upon such a subject."

"I will continue; and, believe me, I will conceal nothing from you. I look upon the words I am now uttering as a full, candid, and free confession; and, therefore, it shall be complete.

"The idea struck me that if, by taking advantage of my supposed preternatural gifts, I could drive you from Bannerworth Hall, I should have it to myself to hunt through at my leisure, and possibly find the treasure. I had heard from Marmaduke Bannerworth some slight allusion to concealing the money behind a picture that was in a bed-room called the panelled chamber. By inquiry, I ascertained that in that bed-room slept Flora Bannerworth.

"I had resolved, however, at first to try pacific measures, and accordingly, as you are well aware, I made various proposals to you to purchase or to rent Bannerworth Hall, the whole of which you rejected; so that I found myself compelled to adopt the original means that had suggested themselves to me, and endeavour to terrify you from the house.

"By prowling about, I made myself familiar with the grounds, and with all the plan of the residence, and then one night made my appearance in Flora's chamber by the window."

"But how do you account," said Charles Holland, "for your extraordinary likeness to the portrait?"

"It is partly natural, for I belong to a collateral branch of the family; and it was previously arranged. I had seen the portrait in Marmaduke Bannerworth's time, and I knew some of its peculiarities and dress sufficiently well to imitate them. I calculated upon producing a much greater effect by such an imitation; and it appears that I was not wrong, for I did produce it to the full."

"You did, indeed," said Henry; "and if you did not bring conviction to our minds that you were what you represented yourself to be, you at least staggered our judgments upon the occasion, and left us in a position of great doubt and difficulty."

"I did; I did all that, I know I did; and, by pursuing that line of conduct, I, at last, I presume, entirely forced you from the house."

"That you did."

"Flora fainted when I entered her chamber; and the moment I looked upon her sweet countenance my heart smote me for what I was about; but I solemnly aver, that my lips never touched her, and that, beyond the fright, she suffered nothing from Varney, the vampyre."

"And have you succeeded," said Henry, "in your object now?"

"No; the treasure has yet to be found. Mortimore, the hangman, followed me into the house, guessing my intention, and indulging a hope that he would succeed in sharing with me its proceeds. But he, as well as myself, was foiled, and nothing came of the toilsome and anxious search but disappointment and bitterness."

"Then it is supposed that the money is still concealed?"

"I hope so; I hope, as well, that it will be discovered by you and yours; for surely none can have a better right to it than you, who have suffered so much on its account."

"And yet," remarked Henry, "I cannot help thinking it is too securely hidden from us. The picture has been repeatedly removed from its place, and produced no results; so that I fear we have little to expect from any further or more protracted research."

"I think," said Varney, "that you have everything to expect. The words of the dying Marmaduke Bannerworth, you may depend, were not spoken in vain; and I have every reason to believe that, sooner or later, you must, without question, become the possessors of that sum."

"But ought we rightly to hold it?"

"Who ought more rightly to hold it?" said Varney; "answer me that."

"That's a sensible enough idea of your's," said the admiral; "and if you were twice over a vampyre, I would tell you so. It's a very sensible idea; I should like to know who has more right to it than those who have had such a world of trouble about it."

"Well, well," said Henry, "we must not dispute, as yet, about a sum of money that may really never come to hand. For my own part, I have little to hope for in the matter; but, certainly, nothing shall be spared, on my part, to effect such a thorough search of the Hall as shall certainly bring it to light, if it be in existence."

"I presume, Sir Francis Varney," said Charles Holland, "that you have now completed your narrative?"

"I have. After events are well known to you. And, now, I have but to lie down and die, with the hope of finding that rest and consolation in the tomb which has been denied me hitherto in this world. My life has been a stormy one, and full of the results of angry passions. I do hope now, that, for the short time I have to live, I shall know something like serenity, and die in peace."

"You may depend, Varney, that, as long as you have an asylum with us," said the admiral--"and that you may have as long as you like,--you may be at peace. I consider that you have surrendered at discretion, and, under such circumstances, an enemy always deserves honourable treatment, and always gets it on board such a ship as this."

"There you go again," said Jack, "calling the house a ship."

"What's that to you, if I were to call it a bowsprit? Ain't I your captain, you lubber, and so, sure to be right, while you are wrong, in the natural order of things? But you go and lay down, Master Varney, and rest yourself, for you seem completely done up."

Varney did look fearfully exhausted; and, with the assistance of Henry and Charles, he went into another apartment, and laid down upon a couch, showing great symptoms of debility and want of power.

And now it was a calm; Varney's stay at the cottage of the Bannerworths was productive of a different mood of mind than ever he had possessed before. He looked upon them in a very different manner to what he had been used to. He had, moreover, considerably altered prospects; there could not be the same hopes and expectations that he once had. He was an altered man. He saw in the Bannerworths those who had saved his life, and who, without doubt, had possessed an opinion, not merely obnoxious to him, but must have had some fearful misgivings concerning his character, and that, too, of a nature that usually shuts out all hope of being received into any family.

But, in the hour of his need, when his life was in danger, no one else would have done what they had done for him, especially when so relatively placed.

Moreover, he had been concealed, when to do so was both dangerous and difficult; and then it was done by Flora Bannerworth herself.

Time flew by. The mode of passing time at the cottage was calm and serene. Varney had seldom witnessed anything like it; but, at the same time, he felt more at ease than ever he had; he was charmed with the society of Flora--in fact, with the whole of the little knot of individuals who there collected together; from what he saw he was gratified in their society; and it seemed to alleviate his mental disquiet, and the sense he must feel of his own peculiar position. But Varney became ill. The state of mind and body he had been in for some time past might be the cause of it. He had been much harassed, and hunted from place to place. There was not a moment in which his life was not in danger, and he had, moreover, more than one case, received some bodily injuries, bruises, and contusions of a desperate character; and yet he would take no notice of them, but allow them to get well again, as best they could.

His escapes and injuries had made a deep impression upon his mind, and had no doubt a corresponding effect upon his body, and Varney became very ill.

Flora Bannerworth did all that could be done for one in his painful position, and this greatly added to the depths of thought that occasionally beset him, and he could scarcely draw one limb after the other.

He walked from room to room in the twilight, at which time he had more liberty permitted him than at any other, because there was not the same danger in his doing so; for, if once seen, there could be no manner of doubt but he would have been pursued until he was destroyed, when no other means of escape were at hand; and Varney himself felt that there could be no chance of his again escaping from them, for his physical powers were fast decaying; he was not, in fact, the same man.

He came out into the parlour from the room in which he had been seated during the day. Flora and her mother were there, while Charles Holland and Henry Bannerworth had both at that moment entered the apartment.

"Good evening, Miss Bannerworth," said Sir Francis, bowing to her, and then to her mother, Mrs. Bannerworth; "and you, Mr. Holland, I see, have been out enjoying the free breeze that plays over the hot fields. It must be refreshing."

"It is so, sir," said Charles. "I wish we could make you a partaker in our walks."

"I wish you could with all my heart," said Varney.

"Sir Francis," said Flora, "must be a prisoner for some short time longer yet."

"I ought not to consider it in any such light. It is not imprisonment. I have taken sanctuary. It is the well spring of life to me," said Varney.

"I hope it may prove so; but how do you find yourself this evening, Sir Francis Varney?"

"Really, it is difficult to say--I fluctuate. At times, I feel as though I should drop insensible on the earth, and then I feel better than I have done for some time previously."

"Doctor Chillingworth will be here bye and bye, no doubt; and he must see what he can do for you to relieve you of these symptoms," said Flora.

"I am much beholden to you--much beholden to you; but I hope to be able to do without the good doctor's aid in this instance, though I must admit I may appear ungrateful."

"Not at all--not at all."

"Have you heard any news abroad to-day?" inquired Varney.

"None, Sir Francis--none; there is nothing apparently stirring; and now, go out when you would, you would find nothing but what was old, quiet, and familiar."

"We cannot wish to look upon anything with mere charms for a mind at ease, than we can see under such circumstances; but I fear there are some few old and familiar features that I should find sad havoc in."

"You would, certainly, for the burnings and razings to the ground of some places, have made some dismal appearances; but time may efface that, and then the evil may die away, and the future will become the present, should we be able to allay popular feeling."

"Yes," said Sir Francis; "but popular prejudices, or justice, or feeling, are things not easily assuaged. The people when once aroused go on to commit all kinds of excess, and there is no one point at which they will step short of the complete extirpation of some one object or other that they have taken a fancy to hunt."

"The hubbub and excitement must subside."

"The greater the ignorance the more persevering and the more brutal they are," said Sir Francis; "but I must not complain of what is the necessary consequence of their state."

"It might be otherwise."

"So it might, and no mischief arise either; but as we cannot divert the stream, we may as well bend to the force of a current too strong to resist."

"The moon is up," said Flora, who wished to turn the conversation from that to another topic. "I see it yonder through the trees; it rises red and large--it is very beautiful--and yet there is not a cloud about to give it the colour and appearance it now wears."

"Exactly so," said Sir Francis Varney; "but the reason is the air is filled with a light, invisible vapour, that has the effect you perceive. There has been much evaporation going on, and now it shows itself in giving the moon that peculiar large appearance and deep colour."

"Ay, I see; it peeps through the trees, the branches of which cut it up into various portions. It is singular, and yet beautiful, and yet the earth below seems dark."

"It is dark; you would be surprised to find it so if you walked about. It will soon be lighter than it is at this present moment."

"What sounds are those?" inquired Sir Francis Varney, as he listened attentively.

"Sounds! What sounds?" returned Henry.

"The sounds of wheels and horses' feet," said Varney.

"I cannot even hear them, much less can I tell what they are," said Henry.

"Then listen. Now they come along the road. Cannot you hear them now?" said Varney.

"Yes, I can," said Charles Holland; "but I really don't know what they are, or what it can matter to us; we don't expect any visitors."

"Certainly, certainly," said Varney. "I am somewhat apprehensive of the approach of strange sounds."

"You are not likely to be disturbed here," said Charles.

"Indeed; I thought so when I had succeeded in getting into the house near the town, and so far from believing it was likely I should be discovered, that I sat on the house-top while the mob surrounded it."

"Did you not hear them coming?"

"I did."

"And yet you did not attempt to escape from them?"

"No, I could not persuade them I was not there save by my utter silence. I allowed them to come too close to leave myself time to escape--besides, I could hardly persuade myself there could be any necessity for so doing."

"It was fortunate it was as it happened afterwards, that you were able to reach the wood, and get out of it unperceived by the mob."

"I should have been in an unfortunate condition had I been in their hands long. A man made of iron would not be able to resist the brutality of those people."

As they were speaking, a gig, with two men, drove up, followed by one on horseback. They stopped at the garden-gate, and then tarried to consult with each other, as they looked at the house.

"What can they want, I wonder?" inquired Henry; "I never saw them before."

"Nor I," said Charles Holland.

"Do you not know them at all?" inquired Varney.

"No," replied Flora; "I never saw them, neither can I imagine what is their object in coming here."

"Did you ever see them before?" inquired Henry of his mother, who held up her hand to look more carefully at the strangers; then, shaking her head, she declared she had never seen such persons as those.

"I dare say not," said Charles Holland. "They certainly are not gentlemen; but here they come; there is some mistake, I daresay--they don't want to come here."

As they spoke, the two strangers got down; after picking up a topcoat they had let fall, they turned round, and deliberately put it into the chaise again; they walked up the path to the door, at which they knocked.

The door was opened by the old woman, when the two men entered.

"Does Francis Beauchamp live here?"

"Eh?" said the old woman, who was a little deaf, and she put her hand behind her ear to catch the sounds more distinctly--"eh?--who did you say?"

Sir Francis Varney started as the sounds came upon his ear, but he sat still an attentive listener.

"Are there any strangers in the house?" inquired the other officer, impatiently. "Who is here?"

"Strangers!" said the old woman; "you are the only strangers that I have seen here."

"Come," said the officer to his companion, "come this way; there are people in this parlour.

Our business must be an apology for any rudeness we may commit."

As he spoke he stepped by the old woman, and laying his hand upon the handle of the door, entered the apartment, at the same time looking carefully around the room as if he expected some one.

"Ladies," said the stranger, with an off-hand politeness that had something repulsive in it, though it was meant to convey a notion that civility was intended; "ladies, I beg pardon for intruding, but I am looking for a gentleman."

"You shall hear from me again soon," said Sir Francis, in an almost imperceptible whisper.

"What is the object of this intrusion?" demanded Henry Bannerworth, rising and confronting the stranger. "This is a strange introduction."

"Yes, but not an unusual one," said the stranger, "in these cases--being unavoidable, at the least."

"Sir," said Charles Holland, "if you cannot explain quickly your business here, we will proceed to take those measures which will at least rid ourselves of your company."

"Softly, sir. I mean no offence--not the least; but I tell you I do not come for any purpose that is at all consonant to my wishes. I am a Bow-street officer in the execution of my duty--excuse me, therefore."

"Whom do you want?"

"Francis Beauchamp; and, from the peculiarity of the appearance of this individual here, I think I may safely request the pleasure of his company."

Varney now rose, and the officer made a rush at him, when he saw him do so, saying,--

"Surrender in the king's name."

Varney, however, paid no attention to that, but rushed past, throwing his chair down to impede the officer, who could not stay himself, but fell over it, while Varney made a rush towards the window, which he cleared at one bound, and crossing the road, was lost to sight in a few seconds, in the trees and hedges on the other side.

"Accidents will happen," said the officer, as he rose to his feet; "I did not think the fellow would have taken the window in that manner; but we have him in view, and that will be enough."

"In heaven's name," said Henry, "explain all about this; we cannot understand one word of it--I am at a loss to understand one word of it."

"We will return and do so presently," said the officer as he dashed out of the house after the fugitive at a rapid and reckless speed, followed by his companion.

The man who had been left with the chaise, however, was the first in the chase; seeing an escape from the window, he immediately guessed that he was the man wanted, and, but for an accident, he would have met Varney at the gate, for, as he was getting out in a hurry, his foot became entangled with the reins, and he fell to the ground, and Varney at the same moment stepped over him.

"Curse his infernal impudence, and d--n these reins!" muttered the man in a fury at the accident, and the aggravating circumstance of the fugitive walking over him in such a manner, and so coolly too--it was vexing.

The man, however, quickly released himself, and rushed after Varney across the road, and kept on his track for some time. The moon was still rising, and shed but a gloomy light around. Everything was almost invisible until you came close to it. This was the reason why Varney and his pursuer met with several severe accidents--fumbles and hard knocks against impediments which the light and the rapid flight they were taking did not admit of their avoiding very well.

They went on for some time, but it was evident Varney knew the place best, and could avoid what the man could not, and that was the trees and the natural impediments of the ground, which Varney was acquainted with.

For instance, at full speed across a meadow, a hollow would suddenly present itself, and to an accustomed eye the moonlight might enable it to be distinguished at a glance what it was, while to one wholly unaccustomed to it, the hollow would often look like a hillock by such a light. This Varney would clear at a bound, which a less agile and heavier person would step into, lifting up his leg to meet an impediment, when he would find it come down suddenly some six or eight inches lower than he anticipated, almost dislocating his leg and neck, and producing a corresponding loss of breath, which was not regained by the muttered curse upon such a country where the places were so uneven.

Having come to one of these places, which was a little more perceptible than the others, he made a desperate jump, but he jumped into the middle of the hole with such force that he sprained his ankle, besides sinking into a small pond that was almost dry, being overgrown with rushes and aquatic plants.

"Well?" said the other officer coming up--"well?"

"Well, indeed!" said the one who came first; "it's anything but well. D--n all country excursions say I."

"Why, Bob, you don't mean to say as how you are caught in a rat-trap?"

"Oh, you be d----d! I am, ain't I?"

"Yes; but are you going to stop there, or coming out, eh? You'll catch cold."

"I have sprained my ankle."

"Well?"

"It ain't well, I tell you; here have I a sprained foot, and my wind broken for a month at least. Why were you not quicker? If you had been sharper we should have had the gentleman, I'll swear!"

"I tumbled down over the chair, and he got out of the window, and I come out of the door."

"Well, I got entangled in the reins; but I got off after him, only his long legs carried him over everything. I tell you what, Wilkinson, if I were to be born again, and intended to be a runner, I would bespeak a pair of long legs."

"Why?"

"Because I should be able to get along better. You have no idea of how he skimmed along the ground; it was quite beautiful, only it wasn't good to follow it."

"A regular sky scraper!"

"Yes, or something of that sort; he looked like a patent flying shadow."

"Well, get up and lead the way; we'll follow you."

"I dare say you will--when I lead the way back there; for as to going out yonder, it is quite out of the question. I want supper to-night and breakfast to-morrow morning."

"Well, what has that to do with it?"

"Just this much: if you follow any farther, you'll get into the woods, and there you'll be, going round and round, like a squirrel in a cage, without being able to get out, and you will there get none of the good things included under the head of those meals."

"I think so too," said the third.

"Well, then, let's go back; we needn't run, though it might be as well to do so."

"It would be anything but well. I don't gallop back, depend upon it."

The three men now slowly returned from their useless chase, and re-trod the way they had passed once in such a hurry that they could hardly recognize it.

"What a dreadful bump I came against that pole standing there," said one.

"Yes, and I came against a hedge-stake, that was placed so as the moon didn't show any light on it. It came into the pit of my stomach. I never recollect such a pain in my life; for all the world like a hot coal being suddenly and forcibly intruded into your stomach."

"Well, here's the road. I must go up to the house where I started him from. I promised them some explanation. I may as well go and give it to them at once."

"Do as you will. I will wait with the horse, else, perhaps, that Beauchamp will again return and steal him."

The officer who had first entered the house now returned to the Bannerworths, saying,

"I promised you I would give you some explanation as to what you have witnessed."

"Yes," said Henry; "we have been awaiting your return with some anxiety and curiosity. What is the meaning of all this? I am, as we are all, in perfect ignorance of the meaning of what took place."

"I will tell you. The person whom you have had here, and goes by the name of Varney, is named Francis Beauchamp."

"Indeed! Are you assured of this?"

"Yes, perfectly assured of it; I have it in my warrant to apprehend him by either name."

"What crime had he been guilty of?"

"I will tell you: he has been hanged."

"Hanged!" exclaimed all present.

"What do you mean by that?" added Henry; "I am at a loss to understand what you can mean by saying he was hanged."

"What I say is literally true."

"Pray tell us all about it. We are much interested in the fact; go on, sir."

"Well, sir, then I believe it was for murder that Francis Beauchamp was hanged--yes, hanged; a common execution, before a multitude of people, collected to witness such an exhibition."

"Good God!" exclaimed Henry Bannerworth. "And was--but that is impossible. A dead man come to life again! You must be amusing yourself at our expense."

"Not I," replied the officer. "Here is my warrant; they don't make these out in a joke."

And, as he spoke, he produced the warrant, when it was evident the officer spoke the truth.

"How was this?"

"I will tell you, sir. You see that this Varney was a regular scamp, gamester, rogue, and murderer. He was hanged, and hung about the usual time; he was cut down and the body was given to some one for dissection, when a surgeon, with the hangman, one Montgomery, succeeded in restoring the criminal to life."

"But I always thought they broke the neck when they were hanged; the weight of the body would alone do that."

"Oh, dear, no, sir," said the officer; "that is one of the common every day mistakes; they don't break the neck once in twenty times."

"Indeed!"

"No; they die of suffocation only; this man, Beauchamp, was hanged thus, but they contrived to restore him, and then he assumed a new name, and left London."

"But how came you to know all this?"

"Oh! it came to us, as many things usually do, in a very extraordinary manner, and in a manner that appears most singular and out of the way; but such it was.

"The executioner who was the means of his being restored, or one of them, wished to turn him to account, and used to draw a yearly sum of money from him, as hush money, to induce them to keep the secret; else, the fact of his having escaped punishment would subject him to a repetition of the same punishment; when, of course, a little more care would be taken that he did not escape a second time."

"I dare say not."

"Well, you see, Varney, or rather Beauchamp, was to pay a heavy sum to this man to keep him quiet, and to permit him to enjoy the life he had so strangely become possessed of."

"I see," said Holland.

"Well, this man, Montgomery, had always some kind of suspicion that Varney would murder him."

"Murder him! and be the means of saving his life; surely he could not be so bad as that."

"Why, you see, sir, this hangman drew a heavy sum yearly from him; thus making him only a mine of wealth to himself; this, no doubt, would rankle in the other's heart, to think he should be so beset, and hold life upon such terms."

"I see, now."

"Yes; and then came the consideration that he did not do it from any good motive, merely a selfish one, and he was consequently under no obligation to him for what he had done; besides, self-preservation might urge him on, and tell him to do the deed.

"However that may be, Montgomery dreaded it, and was resolved to punish the deed if he could not prevent it. He, therefore, left general orders with his wife, whenever he went on a journey to Varney, if he should be gone beyond a certain time, she was to open a certain drawer, and take out a sealed packet to the magistrate at the chief office, who would attend to it.

"He has been missing, and his wife did as she was desired, and now we have found what he there mentioned to be true; but, now, sir, I have satisfied you and explained to you why we intruded upon you, we must now leave and seek for him elsewhere."

"It is most extraordinary, and that is the reason why his complexion is so singular."

"Very likely."

They poured out some wine, which was handed to the officers, who drank and then quitted the house, leaving the inmates in a state of stupefaction, from surprise and amazement at what they had heard from the officers.

There was a strange feeling came over them when they recollected the many occurrences they had witnessed, and even the explanation of the officers; it seemed as if some mist had enveloped objects and rendered them indistinct, but which was fast rising, and they were becoming plainer and more distinct every moment in which they were regarded.

There was a long pause, and Flora was about to speak, when suddenly there came the sound of a footstep across the garden. It was slow but unsteady, and paused between whiles until it came close beneath the windows. They remained silent, and then some one was heard to climb up the rails of the veranda, and then the curtains were thrust aside, but not till after the person outside had paused to ascertain who was there.

Then the curtains were opened, and the visage of Sir Francis Varney appeared, much altered; in fact, completely worn and exhausted.

It was useless to deny it, but he looked ghastly--terrific; his singular visage was as pallid as death; his eyes almost protruding, his mouth opened, and his breathing short, and laboured in the extreme.

He climbed over with much difficulty, and staggered into the room, and would have spoken, but he could not; befell senseless upon the floor, utterly exhausted and motionless.

There was a long pause, and each one present looked at each other, and then they gazed upon the inanimate body of Sir Francis Varney, which lay supine and senseless in the middle of the floor.

***

The importance of the document, said to be on the dead body, was such that it would admit of no delay before it was obtained, and the party determined that it should be commenced instanter. Lost time would be an object to them; too much haste could hardly be made; and now came the question of, "should it be to-night, or not?"

"Certainly," said Henry Bannerworth; "the sooner we can get it, the sooner all doubt and distress will be at an end; and, considering the turn of events, that will be desirable for all our sakes; besides, we know not what unlucky accident may happen to deprive us of what is so necessary."

"There can be none," said Mr. Chillingworth; "but there is this to be said, this has been such an eventful history, that I cannot say what might or what might not happen."

"We may as well go this very night," said Charles Holland. "I give my vote for an immediate exhumation of the body. The night is somewhat stormy, but nothing more; the moon is up, and there will be plenty of light."

"And rain," said the doctor.

"Little or none," said Charles Holland. "A few gusts of wind now and then drive a few heavy plashes of rain against the windows, and that gives a fearful sound, which is, in fret, nothing, when you have to encounter it; but you will go, doctor?"

"Yes, most certainly. We must have some tools."

"Those may be had from the garden," said Henry. "Tools for the exhumation, you mean?"

"Yes; pickaxe, mattocks, and a crowbar; a lantern, and so forth," said the doctor. "You see I am at home in this; the fact is, I have had more than one affair of this kind on my hands before now, and whilst a student I have had more than one adventure of a strange character."

"I dare say, doctor," said Charles Holland, "you have some sad pranks to answer for; you don't think of it then, only when you find them accumulated in a heap, so that you shall not be able to escape them; because they come over your senses when you sleep at night."

"No, no," said Chillingworth; "you are mistaken in that. I have long since settled all my accounts of that nature; besides, I never took a dead body out of a grave but in the name of science, and never for my own profit, seeing I never sold one in my life, or got anything by it."

"That is not the fact," said Henry; "you know, doctor, you improved your own talents and knowledge."

"Yes, yes; I did."

"Well, but you profited by such improvements?"

"Well, granted, I did. How much more did the public not benefit then," said the doctor, with a smile.

"Ah, well, we won't argue the question," said Charles; "only it strikes me that the doctor could never have been a doctor if he had not determined upon following a profession."

"There may be a little truth in that," said Chillingworth; "but now we had better quit the house, and make the best of our way to the spot where the unfortunate man lies buried in his unhallowed grave."

"Come with me into the garden," said Henry Bannerworth; "we shall there be able to suit ourselves to what is required. I have a couple of lanterns."

"One is enough," said Chillingworth; "we had better not burden ourselves more than we are obliged to do; and we shall find enough to do with the tools."

"Yes, they are not light; and the distance is by far too great to make walking agreeable and easy; the wind blows strong, and the rain appears to be coming up afresh, and, by the time we have done, we shall find the ground will become slippy, and bad for walking."

"Can we have a conveyance?"

"No, no," said the doctor; "we could, but we must trouble the turnpike man; besides, there is a shorter way across some fields, which will be better and safer."

"Well, well," said Charles Holland; "I do not mind which way it is, as long as you are satisfied yourselves. The horse and cart would have settled it all better, and done it quicker, besides carrying the tools."

"Very true, very true," said the doctor; "all that is not without its weight, and you shall choose which way you would have it done; for my part, I am persuaded the expedition on foot is to be preferred for two reasons."

"And what are they?"

"The first is, we cannot obtain a horse and cart without giving some detail as to what you want it for, which is awkward, on account of the hour. Moreover, you could not get one at this moment in time."

"That ought to settle the argument," said Henry Bannerworth; "an impossibility, under the circumstances, at once is a clincher, and one that may be allowed to have some weight."

"You may say that," said Charles.

"Besides which, you must go a greater distance, and that, too, along the main road, which is objectionable."

"Then we are agreed," said Charles Holland, "and the sooner we are off the better; the night grows more and more gloomy every hour, and more inclement."

"It will serve our purpose the better," said Chillingworth. "What we do, we may as well do now."

"Come with me to the garden," said Henry, "and we will take the tools. We can go out the back way; that will preclude any observation being made."

They all now left the apartment, wrapped up in great overcoats, to secure themselves against the weather, and also for the purpose of concealing themselves from any chance passenger.

In the garden they found the tools they required, and having chosen them, they took a lantern, with the mean of getting a light when they got to their journey's end, which they would do in less than an hour.

After having duly inspected the state of their efficiency, they started away on their expedition.

The night had turned gloomy and windy; heavy driving masses of clouds obscured the moon, which only now and then was to be seen, when the clouds permitted her to peep out. At the same time, there were many drifting showers, which lasted but a few minutes, and then the clouds were carried forwards by some sudden gust of wind so that, altogether, it was a most uncomfortable night as well could be imagined.

However, there was no time to lose, and, under all circumstances, they could not have chosen a better night for their purpose than the one they had; indeed, they could not desire another night to be out on such a purpose.

They spoke not while they were within sight of the houses, though at the distance of many yards, and, at the same time, there was a noise through the trees that would have carried their voices past every object, however close; but they would make assurance doubly sure.

"I think we are fairly away now," said Henry, "from all fear of being recognized."

"To be sure you are. Who would recognize us now, if we were met?"

"No one."

"I should think not; and, moreover, there would be but small chance of any evil coming from it, even if it were to happen that we were to be seen and known. Nobody knows what we are going to do, and, if they did, there is no illegality in the question."

"Certainly not; but we wish the matter to be quite secret, therefore, we don't wish to be seen by any one while upon this adventure."

"Exactly," said Chillingworth; "and, if you'll follow my guidance, you shall meet nobody."

"We will trust you, most worthy doctor. What have you to say for our confidence?"

"That you will find it is not misplaced."

Just as the doctor had uttered the last sound, there came a hearty laugh upon the air, which, indeed, sounded but a few paces in advance of them. The wind blew towards them, and would, therefore, cause the sounds to come to them, but not to go away in the direction they were going.

The whole party came to a sudden stand still; there was something so strange in hearing a laugh at that moment, especially as Chillingworth was, at that moment, boasting of his knowledge of the ground and the certainty of their meeting no one.

"What is that?" inquired Henry.

"Some one laughing, I think," said Chillingworth.

"Of that there can be little or no doubt," said Charles Holland; "and, as people do not usually laugh by themselves so heartily, it may be presumed there are, at least, two."

"No doubt of it."

"And, moreover, their purpose cannot be a very good one, at this hour of the night, and of such a night, too. I think we had better be cautious."

"Hush! Follow me silently," said Henry.

As he spoke, he moved cautiously from the spot where he stood, and, at the same time, he was followed by the whole party, until they came to the hedge which skirted a lane, in which were seated three men.

They had a sort of tent erected, and that was hung upon a part of the hedge which was to windward of them, so that it sheltered them from wind and rain.

Henry and Chillingworth both peeped over the bank, and saw them seated beneath this kind of canopy. They were shabby, gipsy-looking men, who might be something else--sheep-stealers, or horse-stealers, in fact, anything, even to beggars.

"I say, Jack," said one; "it's no bottle to-night."

"No; there's nobody about these parts to-night. We are safe, and so are they."

"Exactly."

"Besides, you see, those who do happen to be out are not worth talking to."

"No cash."

"None, not enough to pay turnpike for a walking-slick, at the most."

"Besides, it does us no good to take a few shillings from a poor wretch, who has more in family than he has shillings in pocket."

"Ay, you are right, quite right. I don't like it myself, I don't; besides that, there's fresh risk in every man you stop, and these poor fellows will fight hard for a few shillings, and there is no knowing what an unlucky blow may do for a man."

"That is very true. Has anything been done to-night?"

"Nothing," said one.

"Only three half crowns," said the other; "that is the extent of the common purse to-night."

"And I," said the third, "I have got a bottle of bad gin from the Cat and Cabbage-stump."

"How did you manage it?"

"Why, this way. I went in, and had some beer, and you know I can give a long yarn when I want; but it wants only a little care to deceive these knowing countrymen, so I talked and talked, until they got quite chatty, and then I put the gin in my pocket."

"Good."

"Well, then, the loaf and beef I took out of the safe as I came by, and I dare say they know they have lost it by this time."

"Yes, and so do we. I expect the gin will help to digest the beef, so we mustn't complain of the goods."

"No; give us another glass, Jim."

Jim held the glass towards him, when the doctor, animated by the spirit of mischief, took a good sized pebble, and threw it into the glass, smashing it, and spilling the contents.

In a moment there was a change of scene; the men were all terrified, and started to their feet, while a sudden gust of wind caused their light to go out; at the same time their tent-cloth was thrown down by the wind, and fell across their heads.

"Come along," said the doctor.

There was no need of saying so, for in a moment the three were as if animated by one spirit, and away they scudded across the fields, with the speed of a race horse.

In a few minutes they were better than half a mile away from the spot.

"In absence of all authentic information," said the doctor, speaking as well as he could, and blowing prodigiously between each word, as though he were fetching breath all the way from his heels, "I think we may conclude we are safe from them. We ought to thank our stars we came across them in the way we did."

"But, doctor, what in the name of Heaven induced you to make such a noise, to frighten them, in fact, and to tell them some one was about?"

"They were too much terrified to tell whether it was one, or fifty. By this time they are out of the county; they knew what they were talking about."

"And perhaps we may meet them on the road where we are going, thinking it a rare lonely spot where they can hide, and no chance of their being found out."

"No," said the doctor; "they will not go to such a place; it has by far too bad a name for even such men as those to go near, much less stop in."

"I can hardly think that," said Charles Holland, "for these fellows are too terrified for their personal safety, to think of the superstitious fears with which a place may be regarded; and these men, in such a place as the one you speak of, they will be at home."

"Well, well, rather than be done, we must fight for it; and when you come to consider we have one pick and two shovels, we shall be in full force."

"Well said, doctor; how far have we to go?"

"Not more than a quarter of a mile."

They pursued their way through the fields, and under the hedge-rows, until they came to a gate, where they stopped awhile, and began to consult and to listen.

"A few yards up here, on the left," said the doctor; "I know the spot; besides, there is a particular mark. Now, then, are you all ready?"

"Yes, all."

"Here," said the doctor, pointing out the marks by which the spot might be recognized; "here is the spot, and I think we shall not be half a foot out of our reckoning."

"Then let us begin instanter," said Henry, as he seized hold of the pickaxe, and began to loosen the earth by means of the sharp end.

"That will do for the present," said Chillingworth; "now let me and Charles take a turn with our shovels, and you will get on again presently. Throw the earth up on the bank in one heap, so that we can put it on again without attracting any attention to the spot by its being left in clods and uneven."

"Exactly," said Henry, "else the body will be discovered."

They began to shovel away, and continued to do so, after it had been picked up, working alternately, until at length Charles stuck his pick-axe into something soft, and upon pulling it up, he found it was the body.

A dreadful odour now arose from the spot, and they were at no loss to tell where the body lay. The pick-axe had stuck into the deceased's ribs and clothing, and thus lifted it out of its place.

"Here it is," said the doctor; "but I needn't tell you that; the charnel-house smell is enough to convince you of the fact of where it is."

"I think so; just show a light upon the subject, doctor, and then we can see what we are about--do you mind, doctor--you have the management of the lantern, you know?"

"Yes, yes," said Chillingworth; "I see you have it--don't be in a hurry, but do things deliberately and coolly whatever you do--you will not be so liable to make mistakes, or to leave anything undone."

"There will be nothing of any use to you here, doctor, in the way of dissection, for the flesh is one mass of decay. What a horrible sight, to be sure!"

"It is; but hasten the search."

"Well, I must; though, to confess the truth, I'd sooner handle anything than this."

"It is not the most pleasant thing in the world, for there is no knowing what may be the result--what creeping thing has made a home of it."

"Don't mention anything about it."

Henry and Charles Holland now began to search the pockets of the clothes of the dead body, in one of which was something hard, that felt like a parcel.

"What have you got there?" said Chillingworth, as he held his lantern up so that the light fell upon the ghastly object that they were handling.

"I think it is the prize," said Charles Holland; "but we have not got it out yet, though I dare say it won't be long first, if this wind will but hold good for about five minutes, and keep the stench down."

They now tore open the packet and pulled out the papers, which appeared to have been secreted upon his person.

"Be sure there are none on any other part of the body," said Chillingworth, "because what you do now, you had better do well, and leave nothing to after thought, because it is frequently impracticable."

"The advice is good," said Henry, who made a second search, but found nothing.

"We had better re-bury him," said the doctor; "it had better be done cleanly. Well, it is a sad hole for a last resting-place, and yet I do not know that it matters--it is all a matter of taste--the fashion of the class, or the particular custom of the country."

There was but little to be said against such an argument, though the custom of the age had caused them to look upon it more as a matter of feeling than in such a philosophical sense as that in which the doctor had put it.

"Well, there he is now--shovel the earth in, Charles," said Henry Bannerworth, as he himself set the example, which was speedily and vigorously followed by Charles Holland, when they were not long before the earth was thrown in and covered up with care, and trodden down so that it should not appear to be moved.

"This will do, I think," said Henry.

"Yes; it is not quite the same, but I dare say no one will try to make any discoveries in this place; besides, if the rain continues to come down very heavy, why, it will wash much of it away, and it will make it look all alike."

There was little inducement to hover about the spot, but Henry could not forbear holding up the papers to the light of the lantern to ascertain what they were.

"Are they all right?" inquired the doctor.

"Yes," replied Henry, "yes. The Dearbrook estate. Oh! yes; they are the papers I am in want of."

"It is singularly fortunate, at least, to be successful in securing them. I am very glad a living person has possession of them, else it would have been very difficult to have obtained it from them."

"So it would; but now homeward is the word, doctor; and on my word there is reason to be glad, for the rain is coming on very fast now, and there is no moon at all--we had better step out."

They did, for the three walked as fast as the nature of the soil would permit them, and the darkness of the night.

CHAPTER LXXXIX

TELLS WHAT BECAME OF THE SECOND VAMPYRE WHO SOUGHT VARNEY

We left the Hungarian nobleman swimming down the stream; he swam slowly, and used but little exertion in doing so. He appeared to use his hands only as a means of assistance.

The stream carried him onwards, and he aided himself so far that he kept the middle of the stream, and floated along.

Where the stream was broad and shallow, it sometimes left him a moment or two, without being strong enough to carry him onwards; then he would pause, as if gaining strength, and finally he would, when he had rested, and the water came a little faster, and lifted him, make a desperate plunge, and swim forward, until he again came in deep water, and then he went slowly along with the stream, as he supported himself.

It was strange thus to see a man going down slowly, and without any effort whatever, passing through shade and through moonlight--now lost in the shadow of the tall trees, and now emerging into that part of the stream which ran through meadows and cornfields, until the stream widened, and then, at length, a ferry-house was to be seen in the distance.

Then came the ferryman out of his hut, to look upon the beautiful moonlight scene. It was cold, but pure, and brilliantly light. The chaste moon was sailing through the heavens, and the stars diminished in their lustre by the power of the luminous goddess of night.

There was a small cottage--true, it was somewhat larger than was generally supposed by any casual observer who might look at it. The place was rambling, and built chiefly of wood; but in it lived the ferryman, his wife, and family; among these was a young girl about seventeen years of age, but, at the same time, very beautiful.

They had been preparing their supper, and the ferryman himself walked out to look at the river and the shadows of the tall trees that stood on the hill opposite.

While thus employed, he heard a plashing in the water, and on turning towards the quarter whence the sound proceeded for a few yards, he came to the spot where he saw the stranger struggling in the stream.

"Good God!" he muttered to himself, as he saw the struggle continued; "good God! he will sink and drown."

As he spoke, he jumped into his boat and pushed it off, for the purpose of stopping the descent of the body down the stream, and in a moment or two it came near to him. He muttered,--

"Come, come--he tries to swim; life is not gone yet--he will do now, if I can catch hold of him. Swimming with one's face under the stream doesn't say much for his skill, though it may account for the fact that he don't cry out."

As the drowning man neared, the ferryman held on by the boat-hook, and stooping down, he seized the drowning man by the hair of the head, and then paused.

After a time, he lifted him up, and placed him across the edge of the boat, and then, with some struggling of his own, he was rolled over into the boat.

"You are safe now," muttered the ferryman.

The stranger spoke not, but sat or leaned against the boat's head, sobbing and catching at his breath, and spitting off his stomach the water it might be presumed he had swallowed.

The ferryman put back to the shore, when he paused, and secured his boat, and then pulled the stranger out, saying,--

"Do you feel any better now?"

"Yes," said the stranger; "I feel I am living--thanks to you, my good friend; I owe you my life."

"You are welcome to that," replied the ferryman; "it costs me nothing; and, as for my little trouble, I should be sorry to think of that, when a fellow-being's life was in danger."

"You have behaved very well--very well, and I can do little more now than thank you, for I have been robbed of all I possessed about me at the moment."

"Oh! you have been robbed?"

"Aye, truly, I have, and have been thrown into the water, and thus I have been nearly murdered."

"It is lucky you escaped from them without further injury," said the ferryman; "but come in doors, you must be mad to stand here in the cold."

"Thank you; your hospitality is great, and, at this moment, of the greatest importance to me."

"Such as we have," said the honest ferryman, "you shall be welcome to. Come in--come in."

He turned round and led the way to the house, which he entered, saying--as he opened the small door that led into the main apartment, where all the family were assembled, waiting for the almost only meal they had had that day, for the ferryman had not the means, before the sun had set, of sending for food, and then it was a long way before it could be found, and then it was late before they could get it,--

"Wife, we have a stranger to sleep with us to-night, and for whom we must prepare a bed."

"A stranger!" echoed the wife--"a stranger, and we so poor!"

"Yes; one whose life I have saved, and who was nearly drowned. We cannot refuse hospitality upon such an occasion as that, you know, wife."

The wife looked at the stranger as he entered the room, and sat down by the fire.

"I am sorry," he said, "to intrude upon you; but I will make you amends for the interruption and inconvenience I may cause you; but it is too late to apply elsewhere, and yet I am doubtful, if there were, whether I could go any further."

"No, no," said the ferryman; "I am sure a man who has been beaten and robbed, and thrown into a rapid and, in some parts, deep stream, is not fit to travel at this time of night."

"You are lonely about here," said the stranger, as he shivered by the fire.

"Yes, rather; but we are used to it."

"You have a family, too; that must help to lighten the hours away, and help you over the long evenings."

"So you may think, stranger, and, at times, so it is; but when food runs short, it is a long while to daylight, before any more money can be had. To be sure, we have fish in the river, and we have what we can grow in the garden; but these are not all the wants that we feel, and those others are sometimes pinching. However, we are thankful for what we have, and complain but little when we can get no more; but sometimes we do repine--though I cannot say we ought--but I am merely relating the fact, whether it be right or wrong."

"Exactly. How old is your daughter?"

"She is seventeen come Allhallow's eve."

"That is not far hence," said the stranger. "I hope I may be in this part of the country--and I think I shall--I will on that eve pay you a visit; not one on which I shall be a burden to you, but one more useful to you, and more consonant to my character."

"The future will tell us all about that," said the ferryman; "at present we will see what we can do, without complaining, or taxing anybody."

The stranger and the ferryman sat conversing for some time before the fire, and then the latter pointed out to him which was his bed--one made up near the fire, for the sake of its warmth; and then the ferryman retired to the next room, a place which was merely divided by an imperfect partition.

However, they all fell soundly asleep. The hours on that day had been longer than usual; there was not that buoyancy of spirit; when they retired, they fell off into a heavy, deep slumber.

From this they were suddenly aroused by loud cries and piercing screams from one of the family.

So loud and shrill were the cries, that they all started up, terrified and bewildered beyond measure, unable to apply their faculties to any one object.

"Help--help, father!--help!" shrieked the voice of the young girl whom we have before noticed.

The ferryman jumped up, and rushed to the spot where his daughter lay.

"Fanny," he said--"Fanny, what ails thee--what ails thee? Tell me, my dear child."

"Oh!" she exclaimed, almost choked--"oh, father! are we all alone? I am terrified."

"What ails thee--what ails thee? Tell me what caused you to scream out in such a manner?"

"I--I--that is I, father, thought--but no, I am sure it was reality. Where is the stranger?"

"A light--a light!" shouted the fisherman.

In another moment a light was brought him, and he discovered the stranger reclining in his bed, but awake, and looking around him, as if in the utmost amazement.

"What has happened?" he said--"what has happened?"

"That is more than I know as yet," the man replied. "Come, Fanny," he added, "tell me what it is you fear. What caused you to scream out in that dreadful manner?"

"Oh, father--the vampyre!"

"Great God! what do you mean, Fanny, by that?"

"I hardly know, father. I was fast asleep, when I thought I felt something at my throat; but being very sound asleep, I did not immediately awake. Presently I felt the sharp pang of teeth being driven into the flesh of my neck--I awoke, and found the vampyre at his repast. Oh, God! oh, God! what shall I do?"

"Stay, my child, let us examine the wound," said the fisherman, and he held the candle to the spot where the vampyre's teeth had been applied. There, sure enough, were teeth marks, such as a human being's would make were they applied, but no blood had been drawn therefrom.

"Come, come, Fanny; so far, by divine Providence, you are not injured; another moment, and the mischief would have been done entire and complete, and you would have been his victim."

Then turning to the stranger, he said,--

"You have had some hand in this. No human being but you could come into this place. The cottage door is secured. You must be the vampyre."

"I!"

"Yes; who else could?"

"I!--As Heaven's my judge--but there, it's useless to speak of it; I have not been out of my bed. In this place, dark as it is, and less used to darkness than you, I could not even find my way about.--It is impossible."

"Get out of your bed, and let me feel," said the ferryman, peremptorily--"get out, and I will soon tell."

The stranger arose, and began to dress himself, and the ferryman immediately felt the bed on which he had been lying; but it was ice cold--so cold that he started upon his legs in an instant, exclaiming with vehemence,--

"It is you, vile wretch! that has attempted to steal into the cottage of the poor man, and then to rob him of his only child, and that child of her heart's blood, base ingrate!"

"My friend, you are wrong, entirely wrong. I am not the creature you believe me. I have slept, and slept soundly, and awoke not until your daughter screamed."

"Scoundrel!--liar!--base wretch! you shall not remain alive to injure those who have but one life to lose."

As he spoke, the ferryman made a desperate rush at the vampyre, and seized him by the throat, and a violent struggle ensued, in which the superior strength of the ferryman prevailed, and he brought his antagonist to the earth, at the same time bestowing upon him some desperate blows.

"Thou shall go to the same element from which I took thee," said the ferryman, "and there swim or sink as thou wilt until some one shall drag thee ashore, and when they do, may they have a better return than I."

As he spoke, he dragged along the stranger by main force until they came to the bank of the river, and then pausing, to observe the deepest part, he said,--

"Here, then, you shall go."

The vampyre struggled, and endeavoured to speak, but he could not; the grasp at his throat prevented all attempts at speech; and then, with a sudden exertion of his strength, the ferryman lifted the stranger up, and heaved him some distance into the river.

Then in deep water sank the body.

The ferryman watched for some moments, and farther down the stream he saw the body again rise upon the current and struggling slightly, as for life--now whirled around and around, and then carried forward with the utmost velocity.

This continued as far as the moonlight enabled the ferryman to see, and then, with a slow step and clouded brow, he returned to his cottage, which he entered, and closed the door.

CHAPTER XC

DR. CHILLINGWORTH AT THE HALL.--THE ENCOUNTER OF MYSTERY.--THE CONFLICT.--THE RESCUE, AND THE PICTURE

There have been many events that have passed rapidly in this our narrative; but more have yet to come before we can arrive at that point which will clear up much that appears to be most mysterious and unaccountable.

Doctor Chillingworth, but ill satisfied with the events that had yet taken place, determined once more upon visiting the Hall, and there to attempt a discovery of something respecting the mysterious apartment in which so much has already taken place.

He communicated his design to no one; he resolved to prosecute the inquiry alone. He determined to go there and await whatever might turn up in the shape of events. He would not for once take any companion; such adventures were often best prosecuted alone--they were most easily brought to something like an explanatory position, one person can often consider matters more coolly than more. At all events, there is more secrecy than under any other circumstances.

Perhaps this often is of greater consequence than many others; and, moreover, when there is more than one, something is usually overdone. Where one adventurous individual will rather draw back in a pursuit, more than one would induce them to urge each other on.

In fact, one in such a case could act the part of a spy--a secret observer; and in that case can catch people at times when they could not under any other circumstances be caught or observed at all.

"I will go," he muttered; "and should I be compelled to run away again, why, nobody knows anything about it and nobody will laugh at me."

This was all very well; but Mr. Chillingworth was not the man to run away without sufficient cause. But there was so much mystery in all this that he felt much interested in the issue of the affair. But this issue he could not command; at the same time he was determined to sit and watch, and thus become certain that either something or nothing was to take place.

Even the knowledge of that much--that some inexplicable action was still going on--was far preferable to the uncertainty of not knowing whether what had once been going on was still so or not, because, if it had ceased, it was probable that nothing more would ever be known concerning it, and the mystery would still be a mystery to the end of time.

"It shall be fathomed if there be any possibility of its being discovered," muttered Chillingworth. "Who would have thought that so quiet and orderly a spot as this, our quiet village, would have suffered so much commotion and disturbance? Far from every cause of noise and strife, it is quite as great a matter of mystery as the vampyre business itself.

"I have been so mixed up in this business that I must go through with it. By the way, of the mysteries, the greatest that I have met with is the fact of the vampyre having anything to do with so quiet a family as the Bannerworths."

Mr. Chillingworth pondered over the thought; but yet he could make nothing of it. It in no way tended to elucidate anything connected with the affair, and it was much too strange and singular in all its parts to be submitted to any process of thought, with any hope of coming to anything like a conclusion upon the subject--that must remain until some facts were ascertained, and to obtain them Mr. Chillingworth now determined to try.

This was precisely what was most desirable in the present state of affairs; while things remained in the present state of uncertainty, there would be much more of mystery than could ever be brought to light.

One or two circumstances cleared up, the minor ones would follow in the same train, and they would be explained by the others; and if ever that happy state of things were to come about, why, then there would be a perfect calm in the town.

As Mr. Chillingworth was going along, he thought he observed two men sitting inside a hedge, close to a hay-rick, and thinking neither of them had any business there, he determined to listen to their conversation, and ascertain if it had any evil tendency, or whether it concerned the late event.

Having approached near the gate, and they being on the other side, he got over without any noise, and, unperceived by either of them, crept close up to them.

"So you haven't long come from sea?"

"No; I have just landed."

"How is it you have thrown aside your seaman's clothes and taken to these?"

"Just to escape being found out."

"Found out! what do you mean by that? Have you been up to anything?"

"Yes, I have, Jack. I have been up to something, worse luck to me; but I'm not to be blamed either."

"What is it all about?" inquired his companion. "I always thought you were such a steady-going old file that there was no going out of the even path with you."

"Nor would there have been, but for one simple circumstance."

"What was that?"

"I will tell you, Jack--I will tell you; you will never betray me, I am sure."

"Never, by heavens!"

"Well, then, listen--it was this. I had been some time aboard our vessel. I had sailed before, but the captain never showed any signs of being a bad man, and I was willing enough to sail with him again.

"He knew I was engaged to a young woman in this country, and that I was willing to work hard to save money to make up a comfortable home for us both, and that I would not sail again, but that I intended to remain ashore, and make up my mind to a shore life."

"Well, you would have a house then?"

"Exactly; and that's what I wished to do. Well, I made a small venture in the cargo, and thought, by so doing, that I should have a chance of realizing a sum of money that would put us both in a comfortable line of business.

"Well, we went on very smoothly until we were coming back. We had disposed of the cargo, and I had received some money, and this seemed to cause our captain to hate me, because I had been successful; but I thought there was something else in it than that, but I could not tell what it was that made him so intolerably cross and tyrannous.

"Well, I found out, at length, he knew my intended wife. He knew her very well, and at the same time he made every effort he could to induce me to commit some act of disobedience and insubordination; but I would not, for it seemed to me he was trying all he could to prevent my doing my duty with anything like comfort.

"However, I learned the cause of all this afterwards. It was told me by one of the crew.

"'Bill,' said my mate, 'look out for yourself.'

"'What's in the wind?' said I.

"'Only the captain has made a dead set at you, and you'll be a lucky man if you escape.'

"'What's it all about?' said I. 'I cannot understand what he means. I have done nothing wrong. I don't see why I should suddenly be treated in this way.'

"'It's all about your girl, Bill.'

"'Indeed!' said I. 'What can that have to do with the captain? he knows nothing of her.'

"'Oh, yes, he does,' he said. 'If it were not for you he would have the girl himself.'

"'I see now,' said I.

"'Ay, and so can a blind man if you open his eyes; but he wants to make you do wrong--to goad you on to do something that will give him the power of disgracing you, and, perhaps, of punishing you.'

"'He won't do that,' said I.

"'I am glad to hear you say so, Bill; for, to my mind, he has made up his mind to go the whole length against you. I can't make it out, unless he wishes you were dead.'

"'I dare say he does,' said I; 'but I will take care I will live to exact a reckoning when he comes ashore.'

"'That is the best; and when we are paid off, Bill, if you will take it out of him, and pay him off, why, I don't care if I lend you a hand.'

"'We'll say more about that, Dick,' said I, 'when we get ashore and are paid off. If we are overheard now, it will be said that we are conspiring, or committing mutiny, or something of that sort.'

"'You are right, Bill,' he said--'you are right. We'll say no more about this now, but you may reckon upon me when we are no longer under his orders.'

"'Then there's no danger, you know.'

"Well, we said nothing about this, but I thought of it, and I had cause enough, too, to think of it; for each day the captain grew more and more tyrannous and brutal. I knew not what to do, but kept my resolution of doing my duty in spite of all he could do, though I don't mind admitting I had more than one mind to kill him and myself afterwards.

"However, I contrived to hold out for another week or two, and then we came into port, and were released from his tyranny. I got paid off, and then I met my messmate, and we had some talk about the matter.

"'The worst of it is,' said I, 'we shall have some difficulty to catch him; and, if we can, I'll be sworn we shall give him enough to last him for at least a voyage or two.'

"'He ought to have it smart,' said my messmate; 'and I know where he is to be found.'

"'Do you?--at what hour?'

"'Late at night, when he may be met with as he comes from a house where he spends his evenings."

"'That will be the best time in the world, when we shall have less interference than at any other time in the day. But we'll have a turn to-night if you will be with me, as he will be able to make too good a defence to one. It will be a fight, and not a chastisement.'

"'It will. I will be with you; you know where to meet me. I shall be at the old spot at the usual time, and then we will go.'

"We parted; and, in the evening, we both went together, and sought the place where we should find him out, and set upon him to advantage.

"He was nearly two hours before he came; but when he did come, we saluted him with a rap on the head, that made him hold his tongue; and then we set to, and gave him such a tremendous drubbing, that we left him insensible; but he was soon taken away by some watchmen, and we heard that he was doing well; but he was dreadfully beaten; indeed, it would take him some weeks before he could be about in his duties.

"He was fearfully enraged, and offered fifty pounds reward to any one who could give him information as to who it was that assaulted him.

"I believe he had a pretty good notion of who it was; but he could not swear to me; but still, seeing he was busying himself too much about me, I at once walked away, and went on my way to another part of the country."

"To get married?"

"Ay, and to get into business."

"Then, things are not quite so bad as I thought for at first."

"No--no, not so bad but what they might have been worse a great deal; only I cannot go to sea any more, that's quite certain."

"You needn't regret that."

"I don't know."

"Why not know? Are you not going to be married?--ain't that much better?"

"I can't say," replied the sailor; "there's no knowing how my bargain may turn out; if she does well, why, then the cruising is over; but nothing short of that will satisfy me; for if my wife is at all not what I wish her to be, why, I shall be off to sea."

"I don't blame you, either; I would do so too, if it were possible; but you see, we can't do so well on land as you do at sea; we can be followed about from pillar to post, and no bounds set to our persecution."

"That's true enough," said the other; "we can cut and run when we have had enough of it. However, I must get to the village, as I shall sleep there to-night, if I find my quarters comfortable enough."

"Come on, then, at once," said his companion; "it's getting dark now; and you have no time to lose."

These two now got up, and walked away towards the village; and Chillingworth arose also, and pursued his way towards the Hall, while he remarked to himself,--

"Well--well, they have nothing to do with that affair at all events. By-the-bye, I wonder what amount of females are deserted in the navy; they certainly have an advantage over landsmen, in the respect of being tied to tiresome partners; they can, at least, for a season, get a release from their troubles, and be free at sea."

However, Mr. Chillingworth got to the Hall, and unobserved, for he had been especially careful not to be seen; he had watched on all sides, and no signs of a solitary human being had he seen, that could in any way make the slightest observation upon him.

Indeed, he had sheltered himself from observation at every point of his road, especially so when near Bannerworth Hall, where there were plenty of corners to enable him to do so; and when he arrived there, he entered at the usual spot, and then sat down a few moments in the bower.

"I will not sit here," he muttered. "I will go and have a watch at that mysterious picture; there is the centre of attraction, be it what it may."

As he spoke, he arose and walked into the house, and entered the same apartment which has been so often mentioned to the reader.

Here he took a chair, and sat down full before the picture, and began to contemplate it.

"Well, for a good likeness, I cannot say I ever saw anything more unprepossessing. I am sure such a countenance as that could never have won a female heart. Surely, it is more calculated to terrify the imagination, than to soothe the affections of the timid and shrinking female.

"However, I will have an inspection of the picture, and see if I can make anything of it."

As he spoke, he put his hand upon the picture with the intention of removing it, when it suddenly was thrust open, and a man stepped down.

The doctor was for a moment completely staggered, it was so utterly unexpected, and he stepped back a pace or two in the first emotion of his surprise; but this soon passed by, and he prepared to close with his antagonist, which he did without speaking a word.

There was a fair struggle for more than two or three minutes, during which the doctor struggled and fought most manfully; but it was evident that Mr. Chillingworth had met with a man who was his superior in point of strength, for he not only withstood the utmost force that Chillingworth could bring against him, but maintained himself, and turned his strength against the doctor.

Chillingworth panted with exertion, and found himself gradually losing ground, and was upon the point of being thrown down at the mercy of his adversary, who appeared to be inclined to take all advantages of him, when an occurrence happened that altered the state of affairs altogether.

While they were struggling, the doctor borne partially to the earth--but yet struggling, suddenly his antagonist released his hold, and staggered back a few paces.

"There, you swab--take that; I am yard-arm and yard-arm with you, you piratical-looking craft--you lubberly, buccaneering son of a fish-fag."

Before, however, Jack Pringle, for it was he who came so opportunely to the rescue of Doctor Chillingworth, could find time to finish the sentence, he found himself assailed by the very man who, but a minute before, he had, as he thought, placed hors de combat.

A desperate fight ensued, and the stranger made the greatest efforts to escape with the picture, but found he could not get off without a desperate struggle. He was, at length, compelled to relinquish the hope of carrying that off, for both Mr. Chillingworth and Jack Pringle were engaged hand to hand; but the stranger struck Jack so heavy a blow on the head, that made him reel a few yards, and then he escaped through the window, leaving Jack and Mr. Chillingworth masters of the field, but by no means unscathed by the conflict in which they had been engaged.

CHAPTER XCI

THE GRAND CONSULTATION BROKEN UP BY MRS. CHILLINGWORTH, AND THE DISAPPEARANCE OF VARNEY

Remarkable was the change that had taken place in the circumstances of the Bannerworth family. From a state of great despondency, and, indeed, absolute poverty, they had suddenly risen to comfort and independence.

It seemed as if the clouds that had obscured their destiny, had now, with one accord, dissipated, and that a brighter day was dawning. Not only had the circumstances of mental terror which had surrounded them given way in a great measure to the light of truth and reflection, but those pecuniary distresses which had pressed upon them for a time, were likewise passing away, and it seemed probable that they would be in a prosperous condition.

The acquisition of the title deeds of the estate, which they thought had passed away from the family for ever, became to them, in their present circumstances, an immense acquisition, and brought to their minds a feeling of great contentment.

Many persons in their situation would have been extremely satisfied at having secured so strong an interest in the mind of the old admiral, who was very wealthy, and who, from what he had already said and done, no doubt fully intended to provide handsomely for the Bannerworth family.

And not only had they this to look forward to, if they had chosen to regard it as an advantage, but they knew that by the marriage of Flora with Charles Holland she would have a fortune at her disposal, while he (Charles) would be the last man in the world to demur at any reasonable amount of it being lavished upon her mother and her brothers.

But all this did not suit the high and independent spirit of Henry Bannerworth. He was one who would rather have eaten the dust that he procured for himself by some meritorious exertion, than have feasted on the most delicate viands placed before him from the resources of another.

But now that he knew this small estate, the title deeds of which had been so singularly obtained, had once really belonged to the family, but had been risked and lost at the gaming-table, he had no earthly scruple in calling such property again his own.

As to the large sum of money which Sir Francis Varney in his confessions had declared to have found its way into the possession of Marmaduke Bannerworth, Henry did not expect, and scarcely wished to become possessed of wealth through so tainted a source.

"No," he said to himself frequently; "no--I care not if that wealth be never forthcoming, which was so badly got possession of. Let it sink into the earth, if, indeed, it be buried there; or let it rot in some unknown corner of the old mansion. I care not for it."

In this view of the case he was not alone, for a family more unselfish, or who cared so little for money, could scarcely have been found; but Admiral Bell and Charles Holland argued now that they had a right to the amount of money which Marmaduke Bannerworth had hidden somewhere, and the old admiral reasoned upon it rather ingeniously, for he said,--

"I suppose you don't mean to dispute that the money belongs to somebody, and in that case I should like to know who else it belonged to, if not to you? How do you get over that, master Henry?"

"I don't attempt to get over it at all," said Henry; "all I say is, that I do dislike the whole circumstances connected with it, and the manner in which it was come by; and, now that we have a small independence, I hope it will not be found. But, admiral, we are going to hold a family consultation as to what we shall do, and what is to become of Varney. He has convinced me of his relationship to our family, and, although his conduct has certainly been extremely equivocal, he has made all the amends in his power; and now, as he is getting old, I do not like to throw him upon the wide world for a subsistence."

"You don't contemplate," said the admiral, "letting him remain with you, do you?"

"No; that would be objectionable for a variety of reasons; and I could not think of it for a moment."

"I should think not. The idea of sitting down to breakfast, dinner, tea, and supper with a vampyre, and taking your grog with a fellow that sucks other people's blood!"

"Really, admiral, you do not really still cling to the idea that Sir Francis Varney is a vampyre."

"I really don't know; he clings to it himself, that's all I can say; and I think, under those circumstances, I might as well give him the benefit of his own proposition, and suppose that he is a vampyre."

"Really, uncle," said Charles Holland, "I did think that you had discarded the notion."

"Did you? I have been thinking of it, and it ain't so desirable to be a vampyre, I am sure, that any one should pretend to it who is not; therefore, I take the fellow upon his own showing. He is a vampyre in his own opinion, and so I don't see, for the life of me, why he should not be so in ours."

"Well," said Henry, "waving all that, what are we to do with him? Circumstances seem to have thrown him completely at our mercy. What are we to do with him, and what is to become of him for the future?"

"I'll tell you what I'll do," said the admiral. "If he were ten times a vampyre, there is some good in the fellow; and I will give him enough to live upon if he will go to America and spend it. They will take good care there that he sucks no blood out of them; for, although an American would always rather lose a drop of blood than a dollar, they keep a pretty sharp look out upon both."

"The proposal can be made to him," said Henry, "at all events. It is one which I don't dislike, and probably one that he would embrace at once; because he seems, to me, to have completely done with ambition, and to have abandoned those projects concerning which, at one time, he took such a world of trouble."

"Don't you trust to that," said the admiral. "What's bred in the bone don't so easily get out of the flesh; and once or twice, when Master Varney has been talking, I have seen those odd looking eyes of his flash up for a moment, as if he were quite ready to begin his old capers again, and alarm the whole country side."

"I must confess," said Charles Holland, "that I myself have had the impression once or twice that Varney was only subdued for a time, and that, with a proper amount of provocation, he would become again a very serious fellow, and to the full as troublesome as he has been."

"Do you doubt his sincerity?" said Henry.

"No, I do not do that, Henry: I think Varney fully means what he says; but I think, at the same time, that he has for so long lead a strange, wild, and reckless life, that he will find it very far from easy, if indeed possible, to shake off his old habits and settle down quietly, if not to say comfortably."

"I regret," said Henry, "that you have such an impression; but, while I do so, I cannot help admitting that it is, to a considerable extent, no more than a reasonable one; and perhaps, after all, my expectation that Varney will give us no more trouble, only amounts to a hope that he will not do so, and nothing more. But let us consider; there seems to be some slight difference of opinion among us, as to whether we should take up our residence at this new house of ours, which we did not know we owned, at Dearbrook, or proceed to London, and there establish ourselves, or again return to Bannerworth Hall, and, by a judicious expenditure of some money, make that a more habitable place than it has been for the last twenty years."

"Now, I'll tell you what," said the admiral, "I would do. It's quite out of the question for any body to live long unless they see a ship; don't you think so, Miss Flora?"

"Why, how can you ask Flora such a question, uncle," said Charles Holland, "when you know she don't care a straw about ships, and only looks upon admirals as natural curiosities?"

"Excepting one," said Flora, "and he is an admiral who is natural but no curiosity, unless it be that you, can call him such because he is so just and generous, and, as for ships, who can help admiring them; and if Admiral Bell proposes that we live in some pleasant, marine villa by the sea-coast, he shall have my vote and interest for the proceeding."

"Bravo! Huzza!" cried the admiral. "I tell you what it is, Master Charley--you horse marine,--I have a great mind to cut you out, and have Miss Flora myself."

"Don't, uncle," said Charles; "that would be so very cruel, after she has promised me so faithfully. How do you suppose I should like it; come now, be merciful."

At this moment, and before any one could make another remark, there came rather a sharp ring at the garden-gate bell, and Henry exclaimed,--

"That's Mr. Chillingworth, and I am glad he has come in time to join our conference. His advice is always valuable; and, moreover, I rather think he will bring us some news worth the hearing."

The one servant who they had to wait upon them looked into the room, and said,--"If you please, here is Mrs. Chillingworth."

"Mistress? you mean Mr."

"No; it is Mrs. Chillingworth and her baby."

"The devil!" said the admiral; "what can she want?"

"I'll come and let you know," said Mrs. Chillingworth, "what I want;" and she darted into the room past the servant. "I'll soon let you know, you great sea crab. I want my husband; and what with your vampyre, and one thing and another, I haven't had him at home an hour for the past three weeks. What am I to do? There is all his patients getting well as fast as they can without him; and, when they find that out, do you think they will take any more filthy physic? No, to be sure not; people ain't such fools as to do anything of the sort."

"I'll tell you what we will do, ma'am," said the admiral; "we'll all get ill at once, on purpose to oblige ye; and I'll begin by having the measles."

"You are an old porpoise, and I believe it all owing to you that my husband neglects his wife and family. What's vampyres to him, I should like to know, that he should go troubling about them? I never heard of vampyres taking draughts and pills."

"No, nor any body else that had the sense of a goose," said the admiral; "but if it's your husband you want, ma'am, it's no use your looking for him here, for here he is not."

"Then where is he? He is running after some of your beastly vampyres somewhere, I'll be bound, and you know where to send for him."

"Then you are mistaken; for, indeed, we don't. We want him ourselves, ma'am, and can't find him--that's the fact."

"It's all very well talking, sir, but if you were a married woman, with a family about you, and the last at the breast, you'd feel very different from what you do now."

"I'm d----d if I don't suppose I should," said the admiral; "but as for the last, ma'am, I'd soon settle that. I'd wring its neck, and shove it overboard."

"You would, you brute? It's quite clear to me you never had a child of your own."

"Mrs. Chillingworth," said Henry, "I think you have no right to complain to us of your domestic affairs. Where your husband goes, and what he does, is at his own will and pleasure, and, really, I don't see that we are to be made answerable as to whether he is at home or abroad; to say nothing of the bad taste--and bad taste it most certainly is, of talking of your private affairs to other people."

"Oh, dear!" said Mrs. Chillingworth; "that's your idea, is it, you no-whiskered puppy?"

"Really, madam, I cannot see what my being destitute of whiskers has to do with the affair; and I am inclined to think my opinion is quite as good without them as with them."

"I will speak," said Flora, "to the doctor, when I see him."

"Will you, Miss Doll's-eyes? Oh, dear me! you'll speak to the doctor, will you?"

"What on earth do you want?" said Henry. "For your husband's sake, whom we all respect, we wish to treat you with every imaginable civility; but we tell you, candidly, that he is not here, and, therefore, we cannot conceive what more you can require of us."

"Oh, it's a row," said the admiral; "that's what she wants--woman like. D----d a bit do they care what it's about as long as there's a disturbance. And now, ma'am, will you sit down and have a glass of grog?"

"No, I will not sit down; and all I can say is, that I look upon this place as a den full of snakes and reptiles. That's my opinion; so I'll not stay any longer; but, wishing that great judgments may some day come home to you all, and that you may know what it is to be a mother, with five babies, and one at the breast, I despise you all and leave you."

So saying, Mrs. Chillingworth walked from the place, feeling herself highly hurt and offended at what had ensued; and they were compelled to let her go just as she was, without giving her any information, for they had a vivid recollection of the serious disturbance she had created on a former occasion, when she had actually headed a mob, for the purpose of hunting out Varney, the vampyre, from Bannerworth Hall, and putting an end consequently, as she considered, to that set of circumstances which kept the doctor so much from his house, to the great detriment of a not very extensive practice.

"After all," said Flora, "Mrs. Chillingworth, although she is not the most refined person in the world, is to be pitied."

"What!" cried the admiral; "Miss Doll's-eyes, are you taking her part?"

"Oh, that's nothing. She may call me what she likes."

"I believe she is a good wife to the doctor," said Henry, "notwithstanding his little eccentricities; but suppose we now at once make the proposal we were thinking of to Sir Francis Varney, and so get him to leave England as quickly as possible and put an end to the possibility of his being any more trouble to anybody."

"Agreed--agreed. It's the best thing that can be done, and it will be something gained to get his consent at once."

"I'll run up stairs to him," said Charles, "and call him down at once. I scarcely doubt for a moment his acquiescence in the proposal."

Charles Holland rose, and ran up the little staircase of the cottage to the room which, by the kindness of the Bannerworth family, had been devoted to the use of Varney. He had not been gone above two minutes, when he returned, hastily, with a small scrap of paper in his hand, which he laid before Henry, saying,--

"There, what think you of that?"

Henry, upon taking up the paper, saw written upon it the words,--

"The Farewell of Varney the Vampyre."

"He is gone," said Charles Holland. "The room is vacant. I saw at a glance that he had removed his hat, and cloak, and all that belonged to him. He's off, and at so short a warning, and in so abrupt a manner, that I fear the worst."

"What can you fear?"

"I scarcely know what; but we have a right to fear everything and anything from his most inexplicable being, whose whole conduct has been of that mysterious nature, as to put him past all calculation as regards his motives, his objects, or his actions. I must confess that I would have hailed his departure from England with feelings of satisfaction; but what he means now, by this strange manoeuvre, Heaven, and his own singular intellect, can alone divine."

"I must confess," said Flora, "I should not at all have thought this of Varney. It seems to me as if something new must have occurred to him. Altogether, I do not feel any alarm concerning his actions as regards us. I am convinced of his sincerity, and, therefore, do not view with sensations of uneasiness this new circumstance, which appears at present so inexplicable, but for which we may yet get some explanation that will be satisfactory to us all."

"I cannot conceive," said Henry, "what new circumstances could have occurred to produce this effect upon Varney. Things remain just as they were; and, after all, situated as he is, if any change had taken place in matters out of doors, I do not see how he could become acquainted with them, so that his leaving must have been a matter of mere calculation, or of impulse at the moment--Heaven knows which--but can have nothing to do with actual information, because it is quite evident he could not get it."

"It is rather strange," said Charles Holland, "that just as we were speculating upon the probability of his doing something of this sort, he should suddenly do it, and in this singular manner too."

"Oh," said the old admiral, "I told you I saw his eye, that was enough for me. I knew he would do something, as well as I know a mainmast from a chain cable. He can't help it; it's in the nature of the beast, and that's all you can say about it."

CHAPTER XCII

THE MISADVENTURE OF THE DOCTOR WITH THE PICTURE

The situation of Dr. Chillingworth and Jack Pringle was not of that character that permitted much conversation or even congratulation. They were victors it was true, and yet they had but little to boast of besides the victory.

Victory is a great thing; it is like a gilded coat, it bewilders and dazzles. Nobody can say much when you are victorious. What a sound! and yet how much misery is there not hidden beneath it.

This victory of the worthy doctor and his aid amounted to this, they were as they were before, without being any better, but much the worse, seeing they were so much buffetted that they could hardly speak, but sat for some moments opposite to each other, gasping for breath, and staring each other in the face without speaking.

The moonlight came in through the window and fell upon the floor, and there were no sounds that came to disturb the stillness of the scene, nor any object that moved to cast a shadow upon the floor. All was still and motionless, save the two victors, who were much distressed and bruised.

"Well!" said Jack Pringle, with a hearty execration, as he wiped his face with the back of his hand; "saving your presence, doctor, we are masters of the field, doctor; but it's plaguey like capturing an empty bandbox after a hard fight."

"But we have got the picture, Jack--we have got the picture, you see, and that is something. I am sure we saved that."

"Well, that may be; and a pretty d----d looking picture it is after all. Why, it's enough to frighten a lady into the sulks. I think it would be a very good thing if it were burned."

"Well," said the doctor, "I would sooner see it burned than in the hands of that--"

"What?" exclaimed Jack.

"I don't know," said Mr. Chillingworth; "but thief I should say, for it was somewhat thief-like to break into another man's house and carry off the furniture."

"A pirate--a regular land shark."

"Something that is not the same as an honest man, Jack; but, at all events, we have beaten him back this time."

"Yes," said Jack, "the ship's cleared; no company is better than bad company, doctor."

"So it is, and yet it don't seem clear in terms. But, Jack, it you hadn't come in time, I should have been but scurvily treated. He was too powerful for me; I was as nigh being killed as ever I have been; but you were just in time to save me."

"Well, he was a large, ugly fellow, sure enough, and looked like an old tree."

"Did you see him?"

"Yes, to be sure I did."

"Well, I could not catch a glimpse of his features. In fact, I was too much employed to see anything, and it was much too dark to notice anything particular, even if I had had leisure."

"Why, you had as much to do as you could well manage, I must say that, at all events. I didn't see much of him myself; only he was a tall, out-of-the-way sort of chap--a long-legged shark. He gave me such a dig or two as I haven't had for a long while, nor don't want to get again; though I don't care if I face the devil himself. A man can't do more than do his best, doctor."

"No, Jack; but there are very few who do do their best, and that's the truth. You have, and have done it to some purpose too. But I have had enough for one day; he was almost strong enough to contend against us both."

"Yes, so he was."

"And, besides that, he almost carried away the picture--that was a great hindrance to him. Don't you think we could have held him if we had not been fighting over the picture?"

"Yes, to be sure we could; we could have gone at him bodily, and held him. He would not have been able to use his hands. We could have hung on him, and I am sure if I came to grapple yard-arm and yard-arm, he would have told a different tale; however, that is neither here nor there. How long had you been here?"

"Not very long," replied the doctor, whose head was a little confused by the blows which he had received. "I can't now tell how long, but only a short time, I think."

"Where did he come from?" inquired Jack.

"Come from, Jack?"

"Yes, doctor, where did he came from?--the window, I suppose--the same way he went out, I dare say--it's most likely."

"Oh, no, no; he come down from behind the picture. There's some mystery in that picture, I'll swear to it; it's very strange he should make such a desperate attempt to carry it away."

"Yes; one would think," said Jack, "there was more in it than we can see--that it is worth more than we can believe; perhaps somebody sets particular store by it."

"I don't know," said Mr. Chillingworth, shaking his head, "I don't know how that may be; but certain it is, the picture was the object of his visit here--that is very certain."

"It was; he was endeavouring to carry it off," said Jack; "it would be a very good ornament to the black hole at Calcutta."

"The utility of putting it where it cannot be seen," remarked Mr. Chillingworth, "I cannot very well see; though I dare say it might be all very well."

"Yes--its ugly features would be no longer seen; so far, it would be a good job. But are you going to remain here all night, and so make a long watch of it, doctor?"

"Why, Jack," said the doctor, "I did intend watching here; but now the game is disturbed, it is of no use remaining here. We have secured the picture, and now there will be no need of remaining in the house; in fact, there is no fear of robbery now."

"Not so long as we are here," said Jack Pringle; "the smugglers won't show a head while the revenue cutter is on the look out."

"Certainly not, Jack," said Mr. Chillingworth; "I think we have scared them away--the picture is safe."

"Yes--so long as we are here."

"And longer, too, I hope."

Jack shook his head, as much as to intimate that he had many doubts upon such a point, and couldn't be hurried into any concession of opinion of the safety of such a picture as that--much as he disliked it, and as poor an opinion as he had of it.

"Don't you think it will be safe?"

"No," said Jack.

"And why not?" said Mr. Chillingworth, willing to hear what Jack could advance against the opinion he had expressed, especially as he had disturbed the marauder in the very act of robbery.

"Why, you'll be watched by this very man; and when you are gone, he will return in safety, and take this plaguey picture away with him."

"Well, he might do so," said Mr. Chillingworth, after some thought; "he even endangered his own escape for the purpose of carrying it off."

"He wants it," said Jack.

"What, the picture?"

"Aye, to be sure; do you think anybody would have tried so hard to get away with it? He wants it; and the long and the short of it is, he will have it, despite all that can be done to prevent it; that's my opinion."

"Well, there is much truth in that; but what to do I don't know."

"Take it to the cottage," suggested Jack. "The picture must be more than we think for; suppose we carry it along."

"That is no bad plan of yours, Jack," said Mr. Chillingworth; "and, though a little awkward, yet it is not the worst I have heard; but--but--what will they say, when they see this frightful face in that quiet, yet contented house?"

"Why, they'll say you brought it," said Jack; "I don't see what else they can say, but that you have done well; besides, when you come to explain, you will make the matter all right to 'em."

"Yes, yes," said Chillingworth; "and, as the picture now seems to be the incomprehensible object of attack, I will secure that, at all events."

"I'll help you."

"Thank you, Jack; your aid will be welcome; at least, it was so just now."

"All right, doctor," said Jack. "I may be under your hands some day."

"I'll physic you for nothing," said Mr. Chillingworth. "You saved my life. One good turn deserves another; I'll not forget."

"Thank you," said Jack, as he made a wry face. "I hope you won't have occasion. I'd sooner have a can of grog than any bottle of medicine you can give me; I ain't ungrateful, neither."

"You needn't name it; I am getting my breath again. I suppose we had better leave this place, as soon as we conveniently can."

"Exactly. The sooner the better; we can take it the more leisurely as we go."

The moon was up; there were no clouds now, but there was not a very strong light, because the moon was on the wane. It was one of those nights during which an imperceptible vapour arises, and renders the moon somewhat obscure, or, at least, it robs the earth of her rays; and then there were shadows cast by the moon, yet they grew fainter, and those cast upon the floor of the apartment were less distinct than at first.

There seemed scarce a breath of air stirring; everything was quiet and still; no motion--no sound, save that of the breathing of the two who sat in that mysterious apartment, who gazed alternately round the place, and then in each other's countenances. Suddenly, the silence of the night was disturbed by a very slight, but distinct noise, which struck upon them with peculiar distinctness; it was a gentle tap, tap, at the window, as if some one was doing it with their fingernail.

They gazed on each other, for some moments, in amazement, and then at the window, but they saw nothing; and yet, had there been anything, they must have seen it, but there was not even a shadow.

"Well," said Mr. Chillingworth, after he had listened to the tap, tap, several times, without being able to find out or imagine what it could arise from, "what on earth can it be?"

"Don't know," said Jack, very composedly, squinting up at the window. "Can't see anything."

"Well, but it must be something," persisted Mr. Chillingworth; "it must be something."

"I dare say it is; but I don't see anything. I can't think what it can be, unless--"

"Unless what? Speak out," said the doctor, impatiently.

"Why, unless it is Davy Jones himself, tapping with his long finger-nails, a-telling us as how we've been too long already here."

"Then, I presume, we may as well go; and yet I am more disposed to deem it some device of the enemy to dislodge us from this place, for the purpose of enabling them to effect some nefarious scheme or other they have afloat."

"It may be, and is, I dare say, a do of some sort or other," said Jack; "but what' can it be?"

"There it is again," said the doctor; "don't you hear it? I can, as plain as I can hear myself."

"Yes," said Jack; "I can hear it plain enough, and can see it, too; and that is more. Yes, yes, I can tell all about it plain enough."

"You can? Well, then, shew me," said the doctor, as he strode up to the window, before which Jack was standing gazing upon one particular spot of the shattered window with much earnestness. "Where is it?"

"Look there," said Jack, pointing with his finger to a particular spot, to which the doctor directed his attention, expecting to see a long, skinny hand tapping against the glass; but he saw nothing.

"Where is it?"

"Do you see that twig of ivy, or something of the sort?" inquired Jack.

"Yes, I do."

"Very well, watch that; and when the wind catches it--and there is but very little--it lifts it up, and then, falling down again, it taps the glass."

Just as he spoke, there came a slight gust of wind; and it gave a practical illustration to his words; for the tapping was heard as often as the plant was moved by the wind.

"Well," said Mr. Chillingworth, "however simple and unimportant the matter may be, yet I cannot but say I am always well pleased to find a practical explanation of it, so that there will be no part left in doubt."

"There is none about that," said Jack.

"None. Well, we are not beset, then. We may as well consider of the manner of our getting clear of this place. What sort of burthen this picture may be I know not; but I will make the attempt to carry it."

"Avast, there," said Jack; "I will carry it: at all events, I'll take the first spell, and, if I can't go on, we'll turn and turn about."

"We can divide the weight from the first, and then neither of us will be tired at all."

"Just as you please, sir," said Jack Pringle. "I am willing to obey orders; and, if we are to get in to-night before they are all a-bed, we had better go at once; and then we shall not disturb them."

"Good, Jack," said Mr. Chillingworth; "very good: let us begin to beat our retreat at once."

"Very good," said Jack.

They both rose and approached the picture, which stood up in one corner, half reclining against the wall; the light, at least so much as there was, fell upon it, and gave it a ghastly and deathly hue, which made Mr. Chillingworth feel an emotion he could not at all understand; but, as soon as he could, he withdrew his eyes from off the picture, and they proceeded to secure it with some cord, so that they might carry it between them the easier--with less trouble and more safety.

These preparations did not take long in making, and, when completed, they gave another inquiring look round the chamber, and Mr. Chillingworth again approached the window, and gazed out upon the garden below, but saw nothing to attract his attention.

Turning away, he came to the picture, with which Jack Pringle had been standing. They proceeded towards the stairs, adopting every precaution they could take to prevent any surprise and any attempt upon the object of their solicitude.

Then they came to the great hall, and, having opened the door, they carried it out; then shutting the door, they both stood outside of Bannerworth Hall; and, before taking the picture up in their hands, they once more looked suspiciously around them.

There was nothing to be seen, and so, shouldering the ominous portrait, they proceeded along the garden till they conveyed it into the roadway.

"Now," said Jack, "we are off; we can scud along under press of sail, you know."

"I would rather not," said the doctor, "for two reasons; one of which is, I can't do it myself, and the other is, we should run the risk of injuring the picture; besides this, there is no reason for so doing."

"Very well," said Jack, "make it agreeable to yourself, doctor. See you, Jack's alive, and I am willing to do all I can to help you."

"I am very glad of your aid," said Mr. Chillingworth; "so we will proceed slowly. I shall be glad when we are there; for there are few things more awkward than this picture to carry."

"It is not heavy," said Jack, giving it a hitch up, that first pulled the doctor back, and then pushed him forward again.

"No; but stop, don't do that often, Jack, or else I shall be obliged to let go, to save myself from falling," said the doctor.

"Very sorry," said Jack; "hope it didn't inconvenience you; but I could carry this by myself."

"And so could I," returned Mr. Chillingworth; "but the probability is there would be some mischief done to it, and then we should be doing more harm than good."

"So we should," said Jack.

They proceeded along with much care and caution. It was growing late now, and no one was about--at least, they met none. People did not roam about much after dark, especially since the reports of the vampyre became current, for, notwithstanding all their bravery and violence while in a body, yet to meet and contend with him singly, and unseen, was not at all a popular notion among them; indeed, they would sooner go a mile out of their way, or remain in doors, which they usually did.

The evening was not precisely dark, there was moonlight enough to save it from that, but there was a mist hanging about, that rendered objects, at a short distance, very indistinct.

Their walk was uninterrupted by any one, and they had got through half the distance without any disturbance or interruption whatever.

When they arrived at the precincts of the village, Jack Pringle said to Dr. Chillingworth, "Do you intend going through the village, doctor?"

"Why not? there will be nobody about, and if there should be, we shall be safe enough from any molestation, seeing there are none here who would dare to harm us; it is the shortest way, too."

"Very good," said Jack; "I am agreeable, and as for any one harming me, they know better; but, at all events, there's company, and there's less danger, you know, doctor; though I'm always company to myself, but haven't any objection to a messmate, now and then."

They pursued their way in silence, for some distance, the doctor not caring about continuing the talk of Jack, which amounted to nothing; besides, he had too much to do, for, notwithstanding the lightness of the picture, which Jack had endeavoured to persuade the doctor of, he found it was heavy and ungainly; indeed, had he been by himself he would have had some trouble to have got it away.

"We are nearly there," said Jack, putting down his end of the picture, which brought Doctor Chillingworth to a standstill.

"Yes, we are; but what made you stop?"

"Why, you see," said Jack, giving his trowsers a hitch, "as I said before, we are nearly there."

"Well, what of that? we intended to go there, did we not?" inquired Chillingworth.

"Yes, exactly; that is, you intended to do so, I know, but I didn't."

"What do you mean by that?" inquired Chillingworth; "you are a complete riddle to-night, Jack; what is the matter with you?"

"Nothing; only, you see, I don't want to go into the cottage, 'cause, you see, the admiral and I have had what you may call a bit of a growl, and I am in disgrace there a little, though I don't know why, or wherefore; I always did my duty by him, as I did by my country. The ould man, however, takes fits into his head; at the same time I shall take some too; Jack's as good as his master, ashore, at all events."

"Well, then, you object to go in?" said Chillingworth.

"That is the state of the case; not that I'm afraid, or have any cause to be ashamed of myself; but I don't want to make anybody else uncomfortable, by causing black looks."

"Very well, Jack," said the doctor. "I am much obliged to you, and, if you don't like to come, I won't press you against your inclination."

"I understand, doctor. I will leave you here, if you can manage the rest of the way by yourself; there are not two hundred yards now to go, so you are all safe; so good bye."

"Good bye, Jack," said Doctor Chillingworth, who stood wiping his forehead, whilst the picture was standing up against the poles.

"Do you want a hand up first?"

"No, thank you; I can get it up very well without any trouble--it's not so heavy."

"Good bye, then," said Jack; and, in a few moments more, Jack Pringle was out of sight, and the doctor was alone with the ominous picture. He had not far to go, and was within hail of the cottage; but it was late, and yet he believed he should find them up, for the quietude and calmness of the evening hour was that which most chimed with their feelings. At such a time they could look out upon the face of nature, and the freedom of thought appeared the greater, because there was no human being to clash with the silence and stillness of the scene.

"Well," muttered Chillingworth, "I'll go at once to the cottage with my burthen. How they will look at me, and wonder what could induce me to bring this away. I can hardly help smiling at the thought of how they will look at the apparition I shall make."

Thus filled with notions that appeared to please him, the doctor shouldered the picture, and walked slowly along until he reached the dead wall that ran up to the entrance, or nearly so, of the gardens.

There was a plantation of young trees that overhung the path, and cast a deep shadow below--a pleasant spot in hot weather.

The doctor had been carrying the picture, resting the side of it on the small of his arm, and against his shoulder; but this was an inconvenient posture, because the weight of the picture cut his arm so much, that he was compelled to pause, and shift it more on his shoulder.

"There," he muttered, "that will do for the present, and last until I reach the cottage garden."

He was proceeding along at a slow and steady pace, bestowing all his care and attention to the manner of holding the picture, when he was suddenly paralysed by the sound of a great shout of such a peculiar character, that he involuntarily stopped, and the next moment, something heavy came against him with great force, just as if a man had jumped from the wall on to him.

This was the truth, for, in another moment, and before he could recover himself, he found that there was an attempt to deprive him of the picture.

This at once aroused him, and he made an instant and a vigorous defence; but he was compelled to let go his hold of the picture, and turn to resist the infuriated attack that was now commenced upon himself.

For some moments it was doubtful who would be the victor; but the wind and strength of the doctor were not enough to resist the powerful adversary against whom he had to contend, and the heavy blows that were showered down upon him.

At first he was enabled to bear up against this attack; and then he returned many of the blows with interest; but the stunning effect of the blows he received himself, was such that he could not help himself, and felt his senses gradually failing, his strength becoming less and less.

In a short time, he received such a blow, that he was laid senseless on the earth in an instant.

How long he remained thus he could not say; but it could not have been long, for all around him seemed just as it was before he was attacked.

The moon had scarcely moved, and the shadows, such as they were, were falling in the same direction as before.

"I have not been long here," he muttered, after a few moments' reflection; "but--but--"

He stopped short; for, on looking around him, he saw the object of his solicitude was gone. The picture was nowhere to be seen. It had been carried off the instant he had been vanquished.

"Gone!" he said, in a low, disconsolate tone; "and after all I have done!"

He wiped his hand across his brow, and finding it cut, he looked at the back of his hand, and saw by the deep colour that it was blood, indeed, he could now feel it trickle down his face.

What to do he hardly knew; he could stand, and after having got upon his feet, he staggered back against the wall, against which he leaned for support, and afterwards he crept along with the aid of its support, until he came to the door.

He was observed from the window, where Henry and Charles Holland, seeing him come up with such an unsteady gait, rushed to the door to ascertain what was the matter.

"What, doctor!" exclaimed Henry Bannerworth; "what is the matter?"

"I am almost dead, I think," said Chillingworth. "Lend me your arm, Henry."

Henry and Charles Holland immediately stepped out, and took him between them into the parlour, and placed him upon a couch.

"What on earth has happened, doctor?--have you got into disgrace with the populace?"

"No, no; give me some drink--some water, I am very faint--very faint."

"Give him some wine, or, what's better, some grog," said the admiral. "Why, he's been yard-arm with some pirate or other, and he's damaged about the figure-head. You ain't hurt in your lower works, are you, doctor?" said the admiral.

But the doctor took no notice of the inquiry; but eagerly sipped the contents of a glass that Charles Holland had poured out of a bottle containing some strong Hollands, and which appeared to nerve him much.

"There!" said the admiral, "that will do you good. How did all this damage to your upper works come about, eh?"

"Let him wash his face and hands first; he will be better able to talk afterwards."

"Oh, thank you," said Chillingworth. "I am much better; but I have had some hard bruises."

"How did it happen?"

"I went by myself to watch in the room where the picture was in Bannerworth Hall."

"Where the picture was!" said Henry; "where it is, you mean, do you not, doctor?"

"No; where it was, and where it is not now."

"Gone!"

"Yes, gone away; I'll tell you all about it. I went there to watch, but found nobody or nothing there; but suddenly a man stepped out from behind the picture, and we had a fight over it; after which, just as I was getting the worst of it, Jack Pringle came in."

"The dog!" muttered the admiral.

"Yes, he came in just in time, I believe, to save my life; for the man, whoever he was, would not have hesitated about it."

"Well, Jack is a good man," said the admiral; "there may be worse, at least."

"Well, we had a desperate encounter for some minutes, during which this fellow wanted to carry off the picture."

"Carry off the picture?"

"Yes; we had a struggle for that; but we could not capture him; he was so violent that he broke away and got clear off."

"With the picture?"

"No, he left the picture behind. Well, we were very tired and bruised, and we sat down to recover ourselves from our fatigue, and to consider what was best to be done; but we were some time before we could leave, and then we determined that we would take the picture away with us, as it seemed to be coveted by the robber, for what object we cannot tell."

"Well, well--where is the picture?"

"You shall hear all about it in a minute, if you'll let me take my time. I am tired and sore. Well, we brought the picture out, and Jack helped me carry it till he came within a couple of hundred yards of the cottage, and there left me."

"The lubber!" said the admiral, interjectionally.

"Well, I rested awhile, and then taking the picture on my shoulders, I proceeded along with it until I came to the wall, when suddenly I heard a great shout, and then down came something heavy upon me, just as if a man had jumped down upon me."

"And--and--"

"Yes," said the doctor, "it was--"

"Was what?" inquired the admiral.

"Just what you all seemed to anticipate; you are all before me, but that was it."

"A man?"

"Yes; I had a struggle with him, and got nearly killed, for I am not equal to him in strength. I was sadly knocked about, and finally all the senses were knocked out of me, and I was, I suppose, left for dead."

"And what became of the picture?"

"I don't know; but I suppose it was taken away, as, when I came to myself, it was gone; indeed, I have some faint recollection of seeing him seize the portrait as I was falling."

There was a pause of some moments, during which all the party appeared to be employed with their own thoughts, and the whole were silent.

"Do you think it was the same man who attacked you in the house that obtained the picture?" at last inquired Henry Bannerworth.

"I cannot say, but I think it most probable that it was the same; indeed, the general appearance, as near as I could tell in the dark, was the same; but what I look upon as much stronger is, the object appears to be the same in both cases."

"That is very true," said Henry Bannerworth--"very true; and I think it more than probable myself. But come, doctor, you will require rest and nursing after your dangers."

CHAPTER XCIII

THE ALARM AT ANDERBURY.--THE SUSPICIONS OF THE BANNERWORTH FAMILY, AND THE MYSTERIOUS COMMUNICATION

About twenty miles to the southward of Bannerworth Hall was a good-sized market-town, called Anderbury. It was an extensive and flourishing place, and from the beauty of its situation, and its contiguity to the southern coast of England, it was much admired; and, in consequence, numerous mansions and villas of great pretension had sprang up in its immediate neighbourhood.

Betides, there were some estates of great value, and one of these, called Anderbury-on-the-Mount, in consequence of the mansion itself, which was of an immense extent, being built upon an eminence, was to be let, or sold.

This town of Anderbury was remarkable not only for the beauty of its aspect, but likewise for the quiet serenity of its inhabitants, who were a prosperous, thriving race, and depended very much upon their own resources.

There were some peculiar circumstances why Anderbury-on-the-Mount was to let. It had been for a great number of years in possession of a family of the name of Milltown, who had resided there in great comfort and respectability, until an epidemic disorder broke out, first among the servants, and then spreading to the junior branches of the family, and from them to their seniors, produced such devastation, that in the course of three weeks there was but one young man left of the whole family, and he, by native vigour of constitution, had baffled the disorder, and found himself alone in his ancestral halls, the last of his race.

Soon a settled melancholy took possession of him, and all that had formerly delighted him now gave him pain, inasmuch as it brought to his mind a host of recollections of the most agonising character.

In vain was it that the surrounding gentry paid him every possible attention, and endeavoured to do all that was in their power to alleviate the unhappy circumstances in which he was placed. If he smiled, it was in a sad sort, and that was very seldom; and at length he announced his intention of leaving the neighbourhood, and seeking abroad, and in change of scene, for that solace which he could not expect to find in his ancestral home, after what had occurred within its ancient walls.

There was not a chamber but which reminded him of the past--there was not a tree or a plant of any kind or description but which spoke to him plainly of those who were now no more, and whose merry laughter had within his own memory made that ancient place echo with glee, filling the sunny air with the most gladsome shouts, such as come from the lips of happy youth long before the world has robbed it of any of its romance or its beauty.

There was a general feeling of regret when this young man announced the fact of his departure to a foreign land; for he was much respected, and the known calamities which he had suffered, and the grief under which he laboured, invested his character with a great and painful interest.

An entertainment was given to him upon the eve of his departure, and on the next day he was many miles from the place, and the estate of Anderbury-on-the-Mount was understood to be sold or let.

The old mansion had remained, then, for a year or two vacant, for it was a place of too much magnitude, and required by far too expensive an establishment to keep it going, to enable any person whose means were not very large to think of having anything to do with it.

So, therefore, it remained unlet, and wearing that gloomy aspect which a large house, untenanted, so very quickly assumes.

It was quite a melancholy thing to look upon it, and to think what it must have once been, and what it might be still, compared to what it actually was; and the inhabitants of the neighbourhood had made up their minds that Anderbury-on-the-Mount would remain untenanted for many a year to come, and, perhaps, ultimately fall into ruin and decay.

But in this they were doomed to be disappointed, for, on the evening of a dull and gloomy day, about one week after the events we have recorded as taking place at Bannerworth Hall and its immediate neighbourhood, a travelling carriage, with four horses and an out-rider, came dashing into the place, and drew up at the principal inn in the town, which was called the Anderbury Arms.

The appearance of such an equipage, although not the most unusual thing in the world, in consequence of the many aristocratic families who resided in the neighbourhood, caused, at all events, some sensation, and, perhaps, the more so because it drove up to the inn instead of to any of the mansions of the neighbourhood, thereby showing that the stranger, whoever he was, came not as a visitor, but either merely baited in the town, being on his road somewhere else, or had some special business in it which would soon be learned.

The out-rider, who was in handsome livery, had gallopped on in advance of the carriage a short distance, for the purpose of ordering the best apartments in the inn to be immediately prepared for the reception of his master.

"Who is he?" asked the landlord.

"It's the Baron Stolmuyer Saltsburgh."

"Bless my heart, I never heard of him before; where did he come from--somewhere abroad I suppose?"

"I can't tell you anything of him further than that he is immensely rich, and is looking for a house. He has heard that there is one to let in this immediate neighbourhood, and that's what has brought him from London, I suppose."

"Yes, there is one; and it is called Anderbury-on-the-Mount."

"Well, he will very likely speak to you about it himself, for here he comes."

By this time the carriage had halted at the door of the hotel, and, the door being opened, and the steps lowered, there alighted from it a tall man attired in a kind of pelisse, or cloak, trimmed with rich fur, the body of it being composed of velvet. Upon his head he wore a travelling cap, and his fingers, as he grasped the cloak around him, were seen to be covered with rings of great value.

Such a personage, coming in such style, was, of course, likely to be honoured in every possible way by the landlord of the inn, and accordingly he was shown most obsequiously to the handsomest apartment in the house, and the whole establishment was put upon the alert to attend to any orders he might choose to give.

He had not been long in the place when he sent for the landlord, who, hastily scrambling on his best coat, and getting his wife to arrange the tie of his neckcloth, proceeded to obey the orders of his illustrious guest, whatever they might chance to be.

He found the Baron Stolmuyer reclining upon a sofa, and having thrown aside his velvet cloak, trimmed with rich fur, he showed that underneath it he wore a costume of great richness and beauty, although, certainly, the form it covered was not calculated to set it off to any great advantage, for the baron was merely skin and bone, and looked like a man who had just emerged from a long illness, for his face was ghastly pale, and the landlord could not help observing that there was a strange peculiarity about his eyes, the reason of which he could not make out.

"You are the landlord of this inn, I presume," said the baron, "and, consequently, no doubt well acquainted with the neighbourhood?"

"I have the honour to be all that, sir. I have been here about sixteen years, and in that time I certainly ought to know something of the neighbourhood."

"'Tis well; some one told me there was a little cottage sort of place to let here, and as I am simple and retired in my habits I thought that it might possibly suit me."

"A little cottage, sir! There are certainly little cottages to let, but not such as would suit you; and if I might have presumed, sir, to think, I should have considered Anderbury-on-the-Mount, which is now to let, would have been the place for you. It is a large place, sir, and belonged to a good family, although they are now all dead and gone, except one, and it's he who wants to let the old place."

"Anderbury-on-the-Mount," said the baron, "was the name of the place mentioned to me; but I understood it was a little place."

"Oh! sir, that is quite a mistake; who told you so? It's the largest place about here; there are a matter of twenty-seven rooms in it, and it stands altogether upon three hundred acres of ground."

"And have you the assurance," said the baron, "to call that anything but a cottage, when the castle of the Stolmuyers, at Saltzburgh, has one suite of reception rooms thirty in number, opening into each other, and the total number of apartments in the whole building is two hundred and sixty, it is surrounded by eight miles of territory."

"The devil!" said the landlord. "I beg your pardon, sir, but when I am astonished, I generally say the devil. They want eight hundred pounds a year for Anderbury-on-the-Mount."

"A mere trifle. I will sleep here to-night, and in the morning I will go and look at the place. It is near the sea?"

"Half a mile, sir, exactly, from the beach; and one of the most curious circumstances of all connected with it is, that there is a subterranean passage from the grounds leading right away down to the sea-coast. A most curious place, sir, partly cut out of the cliff, with cellars in it for wine, and other matters, that in the height of summer are kept as cool as in the deep winter time. It's more for curiosity than use, such a place; and the old couple, that now take care of the house, make a pretty penny, I'll be bound, though they won't own it, by showing that part of the place."

"It may suit me, but I shall be able to give a decisive answer when I see it on the morrow. You will let my attendants have what they require, and see that my horses be well looked to."

"Certainly, oh! certainly, sir, of course; you might go far, indeed, sir, before you found an inn where everything would be done as things are done here. Is there anything in particular, sir, you would like for dinner?"

"How can I tell that, idiot, until the dinner time arrives?"

"Well, but, sir, in that case, you know, we scarcely know what to do, because you see, sir, you understand--"

"It is very strange to me that you can neither see nor understand your duty. I am accustomed to having the dinner tables spread with all that money can procure; then I choose, but not before, what it suits me to partake of."

"Wil, sir, that is a very good way, and perhaps we ain't quite so used to that sort of thing as we ought to be in these parts; but another time, sir, we shall know better what we are about, without a doubt, and I only hope, sir, that we shall have you in the neighbourhood for a long time; and so, sir, putting one thing to another, and then drawing a conclusion from both of them, you see, sir, you will be able to understand."

"Peace! begone! what is the use of all this bellowing to me--I want it not--I care not for it."

The baron spoke these words so furiously, that the landlord was rather terrified than otherwise, and left the room hastily, muttering to himself that he had never come across such a tiger, and wondering where the baron could have possibly come from, and what amount of wealth he could be possessed of, that would enable him to live in such a princely style as he mentioned.

If the Baron Stolmuyer of Saltzburgh had wished ever so much to impress upon the minds of all persons in the neighbourhood the fact of his wealth and importance, he could not have adopted a better plan to accomplish that object than by first of all impressing such facts upon the mind of the landlord of the Anderbury Arms, for in the course of another hour it was tolerably well spread all over the town, that never had there been such a guest at the Anderbury Arms; and that he called Anderbury-on-the-Mount, with all its rooms--all its outbuildings, and its three hundred acres of ground, a cottage.

This news spread like wildfire, awaking no end of speculation, and giving rise to the most exaggerated rumours, so that a number of persons came to the inn on purpose to endeavour to get a look at the baron; but he did not stir from his apartments, so that these wondermongers were disappointed, and even forced to go away as wise as they came; but in the majority of cases they made up their minds that in the morning they should surely be able to obtain a glimpse of him, which was considered a great treat, for a man with an immense income is looked upon in England as a natural curiosity.

The landlord took his guest at his word as regards the dinner, and provided such a repast as seldom, indeed, graced the board at the Anderbury Arms--a repast sufficient for twenty people, and certainly which was a monstrous thing to set before one individual.

The baron, however, made no remark, but selected a portion from some of the dishes, and those dishes that he did select from, were of the simplest kind, and not such as the landlord expected him to take, so that he really paid about one hundred times the amount he ought to have done for what actually passed his lips.

And then what a fidget the landlord was in about his wines, for he doubted not but such a guest would be extremely critical and hard to please; but, to his great relief, the baron declined taking any wine, merely washing down his repast with a tumbler of cool water; and then, although the hour was very early, he retired at once to rest.

The landlord was not disposed to disregard the injunction which the baron had given him to attend carefully on his servants and horses, and after giving orders that nothing should be stinted as regarded the latter, he himself looked to the creature-comforts of the former, and he did this with a double motive, for not only was he anxious to make the most he could out of the baron in the way of charges, but he was positively panting with curiosity to know more about so singular a personage, and he thought that surely the servants must be able to furnish him with some particulars regarding their eccentric master.

In this, however, he was mistaken, for although they told him all they knew, that amounted to so little as really not to be worth the learning.

They informed him that they had been engaged all in the last week, and that they knew nothing of the baron whatever, or where he came from, or what he was, excepting that he paid them most liberal wages, and was not very exacting in the service he required of them.

This was very unsatisfactory, and when the landlord started on a mission, which he considered himself bound to perform, to a Mr. Leek, in the town, who had the letting of Anderbury-on-the-Mount, he was quite vexed to think what a small amount of information he was able to carry to him.

"I can tell him," he said to himself as he went quickly towards the agent's residence; "I can tell him the baron's name, and that in the morning he wants to look at Anderbury-on-the-Mount; but that's all I know of him, except that he is a most extraordinary man--indeed, the most extraordinary that I ever came near."

Mr. Leek, the house agent, notwithstanding the deficiency of the facts contained in the landlord's statement, was well enough satisfied to hear that any one of apparent wealth was inquiring after the large premises to let, for, as he said truly to the landlord,--

"The commission on letting and receiving the rentals of such a property is no joke to me."

"Precisely," said the landlord. "I thought it was better to come and tell you at once, for there can be no doubt that he is enormously rich."

"If that be satisfactorily proved, it's of no consequence what he is, or who he is, and you may depend I shall be round to the inn early in the morning to attend upon him; and in that case, perhaps, if you have any conversation with him, you will be so good as to mention that I will show him over the premises at his own hour, and you shall not be forgotten, you may depend, if any arrangement is actually come to. It will be just as well for you to tell him what a nice property it is, and that it is to be let for eight hundred a year, or sold outright for eight thousand pounds."

"I will, you may depend, Mr. Leek. A most extraordinary man you will find him; not the handsomest in the world, I can tell you, but handsome is as handsome does, say I; and, if he takes Anderbury-on-the-Mount, I have no doubt but he will spend a lot of money in the neighbourhood, and we shall all be the better of that, of course, as you well know, sir."

This then was thoroughly agreed upon between these high contracting powers, and the landlord returned home very well satisfied, indeed, with the position in which he had put the affair, and resolved upon urging on the baron, as far as it lay within his power so to do, to establish himself in the neighbourhood, and to allow him to be purveyor-in-general to his household, which, if the baron continued in his liberal humour, would be unquestionably a very pleasant post to occupy.

CHAPTER XCIV

THE VISITOR, AND THE DEATH IN THE SUBTERRANEAN PASSAGE

About an hour and a half after the baron had retired to rest, and while the landlord was still creeping about enjoining silence on the part of the establishment, so that the slumbers of a wealthy and, no doubt, illustrious personage should not be disturbed, there arrived a horseman at the Anderbury Arms.

He was rather a singular-looking man, with a shifting, uneasy-looking glance, as if he were afraid of being suddenly pounced upon and surprised by some one; and although his apparel was plain, yet it was good in quality, and his whole appearance was such as to induce respectful attention.

The only singular circumstance was, that such a traveller, so well mounted, should be alone; but that might have been his own fancy, so that the absence of an attendant went for nothing. Doubtless, if the whole inn had not been in such a commotion about the illustrious and wealthy baron, this stranger would have received more consideration and attention than he did.

Upon alighting, he walked at once into what is called the coffee-room of the hotel, and after ordering some refreshments, of which he partook but sparingly, he said, in a mild but solemn sort of tone, to the waiter who attended upon him,--

"Tell the Baron Stolmuyer, of Saltzburgh, that there is one here who wants to see him."

"I beg your pardon, sir," said the waiter, "but the baron is gone to bed."

"It matters not to me. If you nor no one else in this establishment will deliver the message I charge you with, I must do so myself."

"I'll speak to my master, sir; but the baron is a very great gentleman indeed, and I don't think my master would like to have him disturbed."

The stranger hesitated for a time, and then he said,--

"Show me the baron's apartment. Perhaps I ought not to ask any one person connected with this establishment to disturb him, when I am quite willing to do so myself. Show me the way."

"Well, but, sir, the baron may get in a rage, and say, very naturally, that we had no business to let anybody walk up to his room and disturb him, because we wouldn't do so ourselves. So that you see, sir, when you come to consider, it hardly seems the right sort of thing."

"Since," said the stranger, rising, "I cannot procure even the common courtesy of being shown to the apartment of the person whom I seek, I must find him myself."

As he spoke he walked out of the room, and began ascending the staircase, despite the remonstrances of the waiter, who called after him repeatedly, but could not induce him to stop; and when he found that such was the case, he made his way to the landlord, to give the alarm that, for all he knew to the contrary, some one had gone up stairs to murder the baron.

This information threw the landlord into such a fix, that he knew not what to be at. At one moment he was for rushing up stairs and endeavouring to interfere, and at another he thought the best plan would be to pretend that he knew nothing about it.

While he was in this state of uncertainty, the stranger succeeded in making his way up stairs to the floor from which proceeded the bedrooms, and, apparently, having no fear whatever of the Baron Stolmuyer's indignation before his eyes, he opened door after door, until he came to one which led him into the apartment occupied by that illustrious individual.

The baron, half undressed only, lay in an uneasy slumber upon the bed, and the stranger stood opposite to him for some minutes, as if considering what he should do.

"It would be easy," he said, "to kill him; but it will pay me better to spare him. I may be wrong in supposing that he has the means which I hope he has; but that I shall soon discover by his conversation."

Stretching out, his hand, he tapped the baron lightly on the shoulder, who thereupon opened his eyes and sprang to his feet instantly, glancing with fixed earnestness at the intruder, upon whose face shone the light of a lamp which was burning in the apartment.

Then the baron shrunk back, and the stranger, folding his arms, said,--

"You know me. Let our interview be as brief as possible. There needs no explanations between us, for we both know all that could be said. By some accident you have become rich, while I continue quite otherwise. It matters not how this has occurred, the fact is everything. I don't know the amount of your possessions; but, from your style of living, they must be great, and therefore it is that I make no hesitation in asking of you, as a price for not exposing who and what you are, a moderate sum."

"I thought that you were dead."

"I know you did; but you behold me here, and, consequently, that delusion vanishes."

"What sum do you require, and what assurance can I have that, when you get it, the demand will not be repeated on the first opportunity?"

"I can give you no such assurance, perhaps, that would satisfy you entirely; but, for more reasons than I choose to enter into, I am extremely anxious to leave England at once and forever. Give me the power to do so that I require, and you will never hear of me again."

The baron hesitated for some few seconds, during which he looked scrutinizingly at his companion, and then he said, in a tone of voice that seemed as if he were making the remark to himself rather than to the other,--

"You look no older than you did when last we parted, and that was years ago."

"Why should I look older? You know as well as I that I need not. But, to be brief, I do not wish to interfere with any plans or projects you may have on hand. I do not wish to be a hindrance to you. Let me have five thousand pounds, and I am off at once and forever, I tell you."

"Five thousand! the man raves--five thousand pounds! Say one thousand, and it is yours."

"No; I have fixed my price; and if you do not consent, I now tell you that I will blazon forth, even in this house, who and what you are; and, let your schemes of ambition or of cupidity be what they may, you may be assured that I will blast them all."

"This is no place in which to argue such a point; come out into the open air; 'walls have ears;' but come out, and I will give you such special reasons why you should not now press your claim at all, that you shall feel much beholden to me for them, and not regret your visit."

"If that we come to terms, I no more desire than you can do that any one should overhear our conversation. I prefer the open air for any conference, be it whatever it may--much prefer it; and therefore most willingly embrace your proposition. Come out."

The baron put on his travelling cap, and the rich velvet cloak, edged with fur, that he possessed, and leaving his chamber a few paces in advance of his strange visitor, he descended the staircase, followed by him. In the hall of the hotel they found the landlord and almost the whole of the establishment assembled, in deep consultation as to whether or not any one was to go up stairs and ascertain if the stranger who had sought the baron's chamber was really a friend or an enemy.

But when they saw the two men coming down, at all events apparently amicably, it was a great relief, and the landlord rushed forward and opened the door, for which piece of service he got a very stately bow from the baron, and a slight inclination of the head from his visitor, and then they both passed out.

"I have ascertained," said the man who came on horseback, "that for the last week in London you have lived in a style of the most princely magnificence, and that you came down here, attended as if you were one of the first nobles of the land."

"These things amuse the vulgar," said the baron. "I do not mind admitting to you that I contemplate residing on this spot, and perhaps contracting a marriage."

"Another marriage?"

"And why not? If wives will die suddenly, and no one knows why, who is to help it. I do not pretend to control the fates."

"This, between us, is idle talk indeed--most idle; for we know there are certain circumstances which account for the strangest phenomena; but what roaring sound is that which comes so regularly and steadily upon the ear."

"It is the sea washing upon the coast. The tide is no doubt advancing, and, as the eddying surges roll in upon the pebbly shore, they make what, to my mind, is this pleasant music."

"I did not think we were so near the ocean. The moon is rising; let us walk upon the beach, and as that sound is such pleasant music, you shall hear it while I convince you what unpleasant consequences will arise from a refusal of the modest and moderate terms I offer you."

"We shall see, we shall see; but I must confess it does seem to me most extraordinary that you ask of me a positive fortune, for fear you should deprive me of a portion of one; but you cannot mean what you say."

While they were talking they reached a long strip of sand which was by the seashore, at the base of some cliffs, through which was excavated the passage from the coast into the grounds of Anderbury House, and which had been so expatiated upon by the landlord of the inn, in his description of the advantages attendant upon that property.

There were some rude steps, leading to a narrow arched door-way, which constituted an entrance to this subterraneous region; and as the moonlight streamed over the wide waste of waters, and fell upon this little door-way in the face of the cliff, he became convinced that it was the entrance to that excavation, and he eyed it curiously.

"What place is that?" said his companion.

"It is a private entrance to the grounds of a mansion in this neighbourhood."

"Private enough, I should presume; for if there be any other means of reaching the house, surely no one would go through such a dismal hole as that towards it; but come, make up your mind at once. There need be no quarrelling upon the subject of our conference, but let it be a plain matter of yes or no. Is it worth your while to be left alone in peace, or is it not?"

"It is worth my while, but not at such a price as that you mentioned; and I cannot help thinking that some cheaper mode of accomplishing the same object will surely present itself very shortly."

"I do not understand you; you talk ambiguously."

"But my acts," said the baron, "shall be clear and plain enough, as you shall see. Could you believe it possible that I was the sort of person to submit tamely to any amount of extortion you chose to practise upon me. There was a time when I thought you possessed great sense and judgment when I thought that you were a man who weighed well the chances of what you were about; but now I know to the contrary; and I think for less than a thousand pounds I may succeed in ridding myself of you."

"I do not understand you; you had better beware how you tamper with me, for I am not one who will be calmly disposed to put up with much. The sense, tact, and worldly knowledge which you say you have before, from time to time, given me credit for, belongs to me still, and I am not likely easily to commit myself."

"Indeed; do you think you bear such a charmed life that nothing can shake it?"

"I think nothing of the sort; but I know what I can do--I am armed."

"And I; and since it comes to this, take the reward of your villany; for it was you who made me what I am, and would now seek to destroy my every hope of satisfaction."

As the baron spoke he drew from his breast a small pistol, which, with the quickness of thought, he held full in the face of his companion, and pulled the trigger.

There can be no doubt on earth that his intention was to commit the murder, but the pistol missed fire, and he was defeated in his intention at that moment. Then the stranger laughed scornfully, and drawing a pistol from his pocket, he presented it at the baron's head, saying,--

"Do I not bear a charmed life? If I had not, should I have escaped death from you now? No, I could not; but you perceive that even a weapon that might not fail you upon another occasion is harmless against me; and can you expect that I will hesitate now to take full and ample revenge upon you for this dastardly attempt?"

These words were spoken with great volubility, so much so, indeed, that they only occupied a few very brief seconds in delivering; and then, perhaps, the baron's career might have ended, for it seemed to be fully the intention of the other to conclude what he said by firing the pistol in his face; but the wily aspect of the baron's countenance was, after all, but a fair index of the mind, and, just as the last words passed the lips of his irritated companion, he suddenly dropped in a crouching position to the ground, and, seizing his legs, threw him over his head in an instant.

The pistol was discharged, at the same moment, and then, with a shout of rage and satisfaction, the baron sprang upon his foe, and, kneeling upon his breast, he held aloft in his hand a glittering dagger, the highly-polished blade of which caught the moonbeams, and reflected them into the dazzled eyes of the conquered man, whose fate now appeared to be certain.

"Fool!" said the baron, "you must needs, then, try conclusions with me, and, not content with the safety of insignificance, you must be absurd enough to think it possible you could extort from me whatever sums your fancy dictated, or with any effect threaten me, if I complied not with your desires."

"Have mercy upon me. I meant not to take your life; and, therefore, why should you take mine?"

"You would have taken it, and, therefore, you shall die. Know, too, as this is your last moment, that, vampyre as you are, and as I, of all men, best know you to be, I will take especial care that you shall be placed in some position after death where the revivifying moonbeams may not touch you, so that this shall truly be your end, and you shall rot away, leaving no trace behind of your existence, sufficient to contain the vital principle."

"No--no! you cannot--will not. You will have mercy."

"Ask the famished tiger for mercy, when you intrude upon his den."

As he spoke the baron ground his teeth together with rage, and, in an instant, buried the poniard in the throat of his victim. The blade went through to the yellow sand beneath, and the murderer still knelt upon the man's chest, while he who had thus received so fatal a blow tossed his arms about with agony, and tried in vain to shriek.

The nature of the wound, however, prevented him from uttering anything but a low gurgling sound, for he was nearly choked with his own blood, and soon his eyes became fixed and of a glassy appearance; he stretched out his two arms, and dug his fingers deep into the sand.

The baron drew forth the poniard, and a gush of blood immediately followed it, and then one deep groan testified to the fact, that the spirit, if there be a spirit, had left its mortal habitation, and winged its flight to other realms, if there be other realms for it to wing its flight to.

"He is dead," said the baron, and, at the same moment, a roll of the advancing tide swept over the body, drenching the living, as well as the dead, with the brine of the ocean.

The baron stooped and rinsed the dagger in the advancing tide from the clotted blood which had clung to it, and then, wiping it carefully, he returned it to its sheath, which was hidden within the folds of his dress; and, rising from his kneeling posture upon the body, he stood by its side, with folded arms, gazing upon it, for some minutes, in silence, heedless of the still advancing water, which was already considerably above his feet.

Then he spoke in his ordinary accents, and evidently caring nothing for the fact that he had done such a deed.

"I must dispose of this carcase," he said, "which now seems so lifeless, for the moon is up, and if its beams fall upon it, I know, from former experience, what will happen; it will rise again, and walk the earth, seeking for vengeance upon me, and the thirst for that vengeance will become such a part of its very nature, that it will surely accomplish something, if not all that it desires."

After a few moments' consideration, he stooped, and, with more strength than one would have thought it possible a man reduced almost, as he was, to a skeleton could have exerted, he lifted the body, and carried it rapidly up the beach towards the cliffs. He threw it down upon the stone steps that led to the small door of the excavation in the cliff, and it fell upon them with a sickening sound, as if some of the bones were surely broken by the fall.

The object, then, of the baron seemed to be to get this door open, if he possibly could; but that was an object easier to be desired than carried into effect, for, although he exerted his utmost power, he did not succeed in moving it an inch, and he began evidently to think that it would be impossible to do so.

But yet he did not give up the attempt at once, but looking about upon the beach, until he found a large heavy stone, he raised it in his arms, and, approaching the door, he flung it against it with such tremendous force, that it flew open instantly, disclosing within a dark and narrow passage.

Apparently rejoiced that he had accomplished this much, he stopped cautiously within the entrance, and then, taking from a concealed pocket that was in the velvet cloak which he wore a little box, he produced from it some wax-lights and some chemical matches, which, by the slightest effort, he succeeded in igniting, and then, with one of the lights in his hand to guide him on his way, he went on exploring the passage, and treading with extreme caution as he went, for fear of falling into any of the ice-wells which were reported to be in that place.

After proceeding about twenty yards, and finding that there was no danger, he became less cautious; but, in consequence of such less caution, he very nearly sacrificed his life, for he came upon an ice-well which seemed a considerable depth, and into which he had nearly plunged headlong.

He started back with some degree of horror; but that soon left him, and then, after a moment's thought, he sought for some little nook in the wall, in which he might place the candle, and soon finding one that answered the purpose well, he there left it, having all the appearance of a little shrine, while he proceeded again to the mouth of that singular and cavernous-looking place. He had, evidently, quite made up his mind what to do, for, without a moment's hesitation, he lifted the body again, and carried it within the entrance, walking boldly and firmly, now that he knew there was no danger between him and the light, which shed a gleam through the darkness of the place of a very faint and flickering character.

He reached it rapidly, and when he got to the side of the well, he, without a moment's hesitation, flung it headlong down, and, listening attentively, he heard it fall with a slight plash, as if there was some water at the bottom of the pit.

It was an annoyance, however, for him to find that the distance was not so deep as he had anticipated, and when he took the light from the niche where he had placed it, and looked earnestly down, he could see the livid, ghastly-looking face of the dead man, for the body had accidentally fallen upon its back, which was a circumstance he had not counted upon, and one which increased the chances greatly of its being seen, should any one be exploring, from curiosity, that not very inviting place.

This was annoyance, but how could it be prevented, unless, indeed, he chose to descend, and make an alteration in the disposition of the corpse? But this was evidently what he did not choose to do; so, after muttering to himself a few words expressive of his intention to leave it where it was, he replaced the candle, after extinguishing it, in the box from whence he had taken it, and carefully walked out of the dismal place.

The moonbeams were shining very brightly and beautifully upon the face of the cliffs, when he emerged from the subterranean passage, so that he could see the door, the steps, and every object quite distinctly; and, to his gratification, he found that he had not destroyed any fastening that was to the door, but that when it was slammed shut, it struck so hard and fast, that the strength of one man could not possibly move it, even the smallest fraction of an inch.

"I shall be shown all this to-morrow," he said; "and if I take this house I must have an alteration made in this door, so that it may open with a lock, instead of by main violence, as at present; but if, in the morning, when I view Anderbury House, I can avoid an entrance into this region, I will do so, and at my leisure, if I become the possessor of the estate, I can explore every nook and cranny of it."

He then folded his cloak about him, after pulling the door as closely as he could. He walked slowly and thoughtfully back to the inn. It was quite evident that the idea of the murder he had committed did not annoy him in the least, and that in his speculations upon the subject he congratulated himself much upon having so far succeeded in getting rid of certainly a most troublesome acquaintance.

"'Tis well, indeed," he said, "that just at this juncture he should throw himself in my way, and enable me so easy to feel certain that I shall never more be troubled with him. Truly, I ran some risk, and when my pistol missed fire, it seemed as if my evil star was in its ascendant, and that I was doomed myself to become the victim of him whom I have laid in so cold a grave. But I have been victorious, and I am willing to accept the circumstance as an omen of the past--that my fortunes are on the change. I think I shall be successful now, and with the ample means which I now possess, surely, in this country, where gold is loved so well, I shall be able to overcome all difficulties, and to unite myself to some one, who--but no matter, her fate is an after consideration."

CHAPTER XCV

THE MARRIAGE IN THE BANNERWORTH FAMILY ARRANGED

After the adventure of the doctor with regard to the picture about which such an air of mystery and interest has been thrown, the Bannerworth family began to give up all hopes of ever finding a clue to those circumstances concerning which they would certainly have liked to have known the truth, but of which it was not likely they would ever hear anything more.

Dr. Chillingworth now had no reserve, and when he had recovered sufficiently to feel that he could converse without an effort, he took an opportunity, while the whole of the family were present, to speak of what had been his hopes and his expectations.

"You are all aware," he said, "now, of the story of Marmaduke Bannerworth, and what an excessively troublesome person he was, with all deference, to you, Henry; first of all, as to spending all his money at the gaming-table, and leaving his family destitute; and then, when he did get a lump of money which might have done some good to those he left behind him--hiding it somewhere where it could not be found at all, and so leaving you all in great difficulty and distress, when you might have been independent."

"That's true enough, doctor," said Henry; "but you know the old proverb,--that ill-gotten wealth never thrives; so that I don't regret not finding this money, for I am sure we should have been none the happier with it, and perhaps not so happy."

"Oh, bother the old proverb; thirty or forty thousand pounds is no trifle to be talked lightly of, or the loss of which to be quietly put up with, on account of a musty proverb. It's a large sum, and I should like to have placed it in your hands."

"But as you cannot, doctor, there can be no good possibly done by regretting it."

"No, certainly; I don't mean that; utter regret is always a very foolish thing; but it's questionable whether something might not be done in the matter, after all, for you, as it appears, by all the evidence we can collect, that it must have been Varney, after all, who jumped down upon me from the garden-wall in so sudden a manner: and, if the picture be valuable to him, it must be valuable to us."

"But how are we to get it, and if we could, I do not see that it would be of much good to anybody, for, after all, it is but a painting."

"There you go again," said the doctor, "depreciating what you know nothing about; now, listen to me, Master Henry, and I will tell you. That picture evidently had some sort of lining at the back, over the original canvas; and do you think I would have taken such pains to bring it away with me if that lining had not made me suspect that between it and the original picture the money, in bank notes, was deposited?"

"Had you any special reason for supposing such was the case?"

"Yes; most unquestionably I had; for when I got the picture fairly down, I found various inequalities in the surface of the back, which led me to believe that rolls of notes were deposited, and that the great mistake we had all along made was in looking behind the picture, instead of at the picture itself. I meant immediately to have cut it to pieces when I reached here with it; but now it has got into the hands of somebody else, who knows, I suspect, as much I do."

"It is rather provoking."

"Rather provoking! is that the way to talk of the loss of Heaven knows how many thousands of pounds! I am quite aggravated myself at the idea of the thing, and it puts me in a perfect fever to think of it, I can assure you."

"But what can we do?"

"Oh! I propose an immediate crusade against Varney, the vampyre, for who but he could have made such an attack upon me, and force me to deliver up such a valuable treasure?"

"Never heed it, doctor," said Flora; "let it go; we have never had or enjoyed that money, so it cannot matter, and it is not to be considered as the loss of an actual possession, because we never did actually possess it."

"Yes," chimed in the admiral; "bother the money! what do we care about it; and, besides, Charley Holland is going to be very busy."

"Busy!" said the doctor, "how do you mean?"

"Why, isn't he going to be married directly to Flora, here, and am not I going to settle the whole of my property upon him on condition that he takes the name of Bell instead of Holland? for, you see, his mother was my sister, and of course her name was Bell. As for his father Holland, it can't matter to him now what Charley is called; and if he don't take the name of Bell I shall be the last in the family, for I am not likely to marry, and have any little Bells about me."

"No," said the doctor; "I should say not; and that's the reason why you want to ring the changes upon Charles Holland's name. Do you see the joke, admiral?"

"I can't say I do--where is it? It's all very well to talk of jokes, but if I was like Charles, going to be married, I shouldn't be in any joking humour, I can tell you, but quite the reverse; and as for you and your picture, if you want it, doctor, just run after Varney yourself for it; or, stay--I have a better idea than that--get your wife to go and ask him for it, and if she makes half such a clamour about his ears that she did about ours, he will give it her in a minute, to get rid of her."

"My wife!--you don't mean to say she has been here?"

"Yes, but she has though. And now, doctor, I can tell you I have seen a good deal of service in all parts of the world, and, of course, picked up a little experience; and, if I were you, some of these days, when Mrs. Chillingworth ain't very well, I'd give her a composing draught that would make her quiet enough."

"Ah! that's not my style of practice, admiral; but I am sorry to hear that Mrs. Chillingworth has annoyed you so much."

"Pho, pho, man!--pho, pho! do you think she could annoy me? Why, I have encountered storms and squalls in all latitudes, and it isn't a woman's tongue now that can do anything of an annoying character, I can tell you; far from it--very far from it; so don't distress yourself upon that head. But come, doctor, we are going to have the wedding the day after to-morrow."

"No, no," said Flora; "the week after next, you mean,"

"Is it the week after next? I'll be hanged if I didn't think it was the day after to-morrow; but of course you know best, as you have settled it all among you. I have nothing to do with it."

"Of course, I shall, with great pleasure," returned the doctor, "be present on the interesting occasion; but do you intend taking possession of Bannerworth Hall again?"

"No, certainly not," said Henry; "we propose going to the Dearbrook estate, and there remaining for a time to see how we all like it. We may, perchance, enjoy it very much, for I have heard it spoken of as an attractive little property enough, and one that any one might fancy, after being resident a short time upon it."

"Well," said the admiral; "that is, I believe, settled among us, but I am sure we sha'n't like it, on account of the want of the sea. Why, I tell you, I have not seen a ship myself for this eighteen months; there's a state of things, you see, that won't do to last, because one would get dry-mouldy: it's a shocking thing to see nothing but land, land, wherever you go."

From the preceding conversation may be gathered what were the designs of the Bannerworth family, and what progress had been made in carrying them out. From the moment they had discovered the title-deeds of the Dearbrook property, they had ceased to care about the large sum of money which Marmaduke Bannerworth had been supposed to have hidden in some portion of Bannerworth Hall.

They had already passed through quite enough of the busy turmoils of existence to be grateful for anything that promised ease and competence, and that serenity of mind which is the dearest possession which any one can compass.

Consequently was it, that, with one accord, they got rid of all yearning after the large sum which the doctor was so anxious to procure for them, and looked forward to a life of great happiness and contentment. On the whole, too, when they came to talk the matter over quietly among themselves, they were not sorry that Varney had taken himself off in the way he had, for really it was a great release; and, as he had couched his farewell in words which signified it was a final one, they were inclined to think that he must have left England, and that it was not likely they should ever again encounter him, under any circumstances whatever.

It was to be considered quite as a whim of the old admiral's, the changing of Charles Holland's name to Bell; but, as Charles himself said when the subject was broached to him,--"I am so well content to be called whatever those to whom I feel affection think proper, that I give up my name of Holland without a pang, willingly adopting in its stead one that has always been hallowed in my remembrance with the best and kindest recollections."

And thus this affair was settled, much to the satisfaction of Flora, who was quite as well content to be called Mrs. Bell as to be called Mrs. Holland, since the object of her attachment remained the same. The wedding was really fixed for the week after that which followed the conversation we have recorded; but the admiral was not at all disposed to allow Flora and his nephew Charles to get through such an important period of their lives without some greater demonstration and show than could be made from the little cottage where they dwelt; and consequently he wished that they should leave that and proceed at once to a larger mansion, which he had his eye upon a few miles off, and which was to be had furnished for a time, at the pleasure of any one.

"And we won't shut ourselves up," said the admiral; "but we will find out all the Christian-like people in the neighbourhood, and invite them to the wedding, and we will have a jolly good breakfast together, and lots of music, and a famous lunch; and, after that, a dinner, and then a dance, and all that sort of thing; so that there shall be no want of fun."

As may be well supposed, both Charles and Flora shrunk from so public an affair; but, as the old man had evidently set his heart upon it, they did not like to say they positively would not; so, after a vain attempt to dissuade him from removing at all from the cottage until they removed for good, they gave up the point to him, and he had it all his own way.

He took the house, for one month, which had so taken his fancy, and certainly a pretty enough place it was, although they found out afterwards, that why it was he was so charmed with it consisted in the fact that it bore the name of a vessel which he had once commanded; but this they did not know until a long time afterwards, when it slipped out by mere accident.

They stipulated with the admiral that there should not be more than twenty guests at the breakfast which was to succeed the marriage ceremony; and to that he acceded; but Henry whispered to Charles Holland,--

"I know this public wedding to be distasteful to you, and most particularly do I know it is distasteful to Flora; so, if you do not mind playing a trick upon the old man, I can very easily put you in the way of cheating him entirely."

"Indeed; I should like to hear, and, what is more, I should like to practise, if you think it will not so entirely offend him as to make him implacable."

"Not at all, not at all; he will laugh himself, when he comes to know it, as much as any of us; the present difficulty will be to procure Flora's connivance; but that we must do the best way we can by persuasion."

What this scheme was will ultimately appear; but, certain it is, that the old admiral had no suspicion of what was going on, and proceeded to make all his arrangements accordingly.

From his first arrival in the market town--in the neighbourhood of which was Bannerworth Hall--it will be recollected that he had taken a great fancy to the lawyer, in whose name a forged letter had been sent him, informing him of the fact that his nephew, Charles Holland, intended marrying into a family of vampyres.

It was this letter, as the reader is aware, which brought the old admiral and Jack Pringle into the neighbourhood of the Hall; and, although it was a manoeuvre to get rid of Charles Holland, which failed most signally, there can be no doubt but that such a letter was the production of Sir Francis Varney, and that he wrote it for the express purpose of getting rid of Charles from the Hall, who had begun materially to interfere with his plans and projects there.

After some conversation with himself, the admiral thought that this lawyer would be just the man to recommend the proper sort of people to be invited to the wedding of Charles and Flora; so he wrote to him, inviting himself to dinner, and received back a very gracious reply from the lawyer, who declared that the honour of entertaining a gentleman whom he so much respected as Admiral Bell, was greater than he had a right to expect by a great deal, and that he should feel most grateful for his company, and await his coming with the greatest impatience.

"A devilish civil fellow, that attorney," said the admiral, as he put the letter in his pocket, "and almost enough to put one in conceit of lawyers."

"Yes," said Jack Pringle, who had overheard the admiral read the letter.

"Yes, we will honour him; and I only hope he will have plenty of grog; because, you see, if he don't--D--n it! what's that? Can't you keep things to yourself?"

This latter exclamation arose from the fact that the admiral was so indignant at Jack for listening to what he had been saying, as to throw a leaden inkstand, that happened to be upon the table, at his head.

"You mutinous swab!" he said, "cannot a gentleman ask me to dinner, or cannot I ask myself, without you putting your spoke in the windlass, you vagabond?"

"Oh! well," said Jack, "if you are out of temper about it, I had better send my mark to the lawyer, and tell him that we won't come, as it has made some family differences."

"Family, you thief!" said the admiral. "What do you mean? What family do you think would own you? D--n me, if I don't think you came over in some strange ship. But, I tell you what it is, if you interfere in this matter, I'll be hanged if I don't blow your brains out."

"And you'll be hanged if you do," said Jack, as he walked out of the room; "so it's all one either way, old fizgig."

"What!" roared the admiral, as he sprang up and ran after Jack. "Have I lived all these years to be called names in my own ship--I mean my own house? What does the infernal rascal mean by it?"

The admiral, no doubt, would have pursued Jack very closely, had not Flora intercepted him, and, by gentle violence, got him back to the room. No one else could have ventured to have stopped him, but the affection he had for her was so great that she could really accomplish almost anything with him; and, by listening quietly to his complaints of Jack Pringle--which, however, involved a disclosure of the fact which he had intended to keep to himself, that he had sought the lawyer's advice--she succeeded in soothing him completely, so that he forgot his anger in a very short time.

But the old man's anger, although easily aroused, never lasted very long; and, upon the whole, it was really astonishing what he put up with from Jack Pringle, in the way of taunts and sneers, of all sorts and descriptions, and now and then not a little real abuse.

And, probably, he thought likewise that Jack Pringle did not mean what he said, on the same principle that he (the admiral), when he called Jack a mutinous swab and a marine, certainly did not mean that Jack was those things, but merely used them as expletives to express a great amount of indignation at the moment, because, as may be well supposed, nothing in the world could be worse, in Admiral Bell's estimation, that to be a mutinous swab or a marine.

It was rather a wonder, though, that, in his anger some day, he did not do Jack some mischief; for, as we have had occasion to notice in one or two cases, the admiral was not extremely particular as to what sorts of missiles he used when he considered it necessary to throw something at Jack's head.

It would not have been a surprising thing if Jack had really made some communication to the lawyer; but he did stop short at that amount of pleasantry, and, as he himself expressed it, for once in a way he let the old man please himself.

The admiral soon forgot this little dispute, and then pleased himself with the idea that he should pass a pleasant day with the attorney.

"Ah! well," he said; "who would have thought that ever I should have gone and taken dinner with a lawyer--and not only done that, but invited myself too! It shows us all that there may be some good in all sorts of men, lawyers included; and I am sure, after this, I ought to begin to think what I never thought before, and that is, that a marine may actually be a useful person. It shows that, as one gets older, one gets wiser."

It was an immense piece of liberality for a man brought up, as Admiral Bell had been, in decidedly one of the most prejudiced branches of the public service, to make any such admissions as these. A very great thing it was, and showed a liberality of mind such as, even at the present time, is not readily found.

It is astonishing, as well as amusing, to find how the mind assimilates itself to the circumstances in which it is placed, and how society, being cut up into small sections, imagines different things merely as a consequence of their peculiar application. We shall find that even people, living at different ends of a city, will look with a sort of pity and contempt upon each other; and it is much to be regretted that public writers are found who use what little ability they may possess in pandering to their feelings.

It was as contemptible and silly as it was reprehensible for a late celebrated novelist to pretend that he believed there was at place called Bloomsbury-square, but he really did not know; because that was merely done for the purpose of raising a silly laugh among persons who were neither respectable on account of their abilities or their conduct.

But to return from this digression. The admiral, attired in his best suit, which always consisted of a blue coat, the exact colour of the navy uniform, an immense pale primrose coloured waistcoat, and white kerseymere continuations, went to the lawyer's as had been arranged.

If anything at all could flatter the old man's vanity successfully, it certainly would be the manner in which he was received at the lawyer's house, where everything was done that could give him satisfaction.

A very handsome repast was laid before him, and, when the cloth was removed, the admiral broached the subject upon which he wished to ask the advice of his professional friend. After telling him of the wedding that was to come off, he said,--

"Now, I have bargained to invite twenty people; and, of course, as that is exclusive of any of the family, and as I don't know any people about this neighbourhood except yourself, I want you and your family to come to start with, and then I want you to find me out some more decent people to make up the party."

"I feel highly flattered," said the attorney, "that, in such a case as this, you should have come to me, and my only great fear is, that I should not be able to give you satisfaction."

"Oh! you needn't be afraid of that; there is no fear on that head; so I shall leave it all to you to invite the folks that you think proper."

"I will endeavour, certainly, admiral, to do my best. Of course, living in the town, as I have for many years, I know some very nice people as well as some very queer ones."

"Oh! we don't want any of the queer ones; but let those who are invited be frank, hearty, good-tempered people, such as one will be glad to meet over and over again without any ceremony--none of your simpering people, who are afraid to laugh for fear of opening their mouths too wide, but who are so mighty genteel that they are afraid to enjoy anything for fear it should be vulgar."

"I understand you, admiral, perfectly, and shall endeavour to obey your instructions to the very letter; but, if I should unfortunately invite anybody you don't like, you must excuse me for making such a mistake."

"Oh, of course--of course. Never mind that; and, if any disagreeable fellow comes, we will smother him in some way."

"It would serve him right, for no one ought to make himself disagreeable, after being honoured with an invitation from you; but I will be most especially careful, and I hope that such a circumstance will not occur."

"Never mind. If it should, I'll tell you what I'll do; I'll set Jack Pringle upon him, and if he don't worry his life out it will be a strange thing to me."

"Oh," said the lawyer, "I am glad you have mentioned him, for it gives me an opportunity of saying that I have done all in my power to make him comfortable."

"All in your power to make him comfortable! What do you mean?"

"I mean that I have placed such a dinner before him as will please him; I told him to ask for just whatever he likes."

The admiral looked at the lawyer with amazement, for a few moments, in silence, and then he said,

"D--n it! why, you don't mean to tell me, that that rascal is here."

"Oh, yes; he came about ten minutes I before you arrived, and said you were coming, and he has been down stairs feasting all the while since."

"Stop a bit. Do you happen to have any loaded fire arms in the house?"

"We have got an old bunderbuss; but what for, admiral?"

"To shoot that scoundrel, Pringle. I'll blow his brains out, as sure as fate. The impudence of his coming here, directly against my orders, too."

"My dear sir, calm yourself, and think nothing of it; it's of no consequence whatever."

"No consequence; where is that blunderbuss of yours? Do you mean to tell me that mutiny is of no consequence? Give me the blunderbuss."

"But, my clear sir, we only keep it in terrorem, and have no bullets."

"Never mind that, we can cram in a handful of nails, or brass buttons, or hammer up a few halfpence--anything of that sort will do to settle his business with."

"How do you get on, old Tarbarrel?" said Jack, putting his head in at the door. "Are you making yourself comfortable? I'll be hanged if I don't think you have a drop too much already, you look so precious red about the gills. I have been getting on famous, and I thought I'd just hop up for a minute to make your mind easy about me, and tell you so."

It was quite evident that Jack had done justice to the good cheer of the lawyer, for he was rather unsteady, and had to hold by the door-post to support himself, while there was such a look of contentment upon his countenance as contrasted with the indignation that was manifest upon the admiral's face that, as the saying is, it would have made a cat laugh to see them.

"Be off with ye, Jack," said the lawyer; "be off with ye. Go down stairs again and enjoy yourself. Don't you see that the admiral is angry with you."

"Oh, he be bothered," said Jack; "I'll soon settle him if he comes any of his nonsense; and mind, Mr. Lawyer, whatever you do, don't you give him too much to drink."

The lawyer ran to the door, and pushed Jack out, for he rightly enough suspected that the quietness of the admiral was only that calm which precedes a storm of more than usual amount and magnitude, so he was anxious to part them at once.

He then set about appeasing, as well as he could, the admiral's anger, by attributing the perseverance of Jack, in following him wherever he went, to his great affection for him, which, combined with his ignorance, might make him often troublesome when he had really no intention of being so.

This was certainly the best way of appeasing the old man; and, indeed, the only way in which it could be done successfully, and the proof that it was so, consisted in the fact, that the admiral did consent, at the suggestion of the attorney, to forgive Jack once more for the offence he had committed.

CHAPTER XCVI

THE BARON TAKES ANDERBURY HOUSE, AND DECIDES UPON GIVING A GRAND ENTERTAINMENT

It was not considered anything extraordinary that, although the Baron Stolmuyer of Saltzburgh went out with the mysterious stranger who had arrived at the Anderbury Arms to see him, he should return without him for certainly he was not bound to bring him back, by any means whatever.

Moreover, he entered the inn so quietly, and with such an appearance of perfect composure, that no one could have suspected for a moment that he had been guilty really of the terrific crime which had been laid to his charge--a crime which few men could have committed in so entirely unmoved and passionless a manner as he had done it.

But he seemed to consider the taking of a human life as a thing not of the remotest consequence, and not to be considered at all as a matter which was to put any one out of the way, but as a thing to be done when necessity required, with all the ease in the world, without arousing or awaking any of those feelings of remorse which one would suppose ought to find a place in the heart of a man who had been guilty of such monstrous behaviour.

He walked up to his own apartment again, and retired to rest with the same feeling, apparently, of calmness, and the same ability to taste of the sweets of repose as had before characterized him.

The stranger's horse, which was a valuable and beautiful animal, remained in the stable of the inn, and as, of course, that was considered a guarantee for his return, the landlord, when he himself retired to rest, left one of his establishment sitting up to let in the man who now lay so motionless and so frightful in appearance in one of the ice-wells of the mysterious passage leading from the base of the cliff, to the grounds of Anderbury House.

But the night wore on, and the man who had been left to let the stranger in, after making many efforts to keep himself awake, dropped into sound repose, which he might just as well have done in the first instance, inasmuch as, although he knew it not, he was engaged in the vain task of waiting for the dead.

The morning was fresh and beautiful, and, at a far earlier hour than a person of his quality was expected to make his appearance, the baron descended from his chamber; for, somehow or other, by common consent, it seems to be agreed that great personages must be late in rising, and equally late in going to bed.

But the baron was evidently not so disposed to turn night into day, and the landlord congratulated himself not a little upon the fact that he was ready for his illustrious guest when he descended so unexpectedly from his chamber as he did.

An ample breakfast was disposed of; that is to say, it was placed upon the table, and charged to the baron, who selected from it what he pleased; and when the meal was over the landlord ventured to enter the apartment, and said to him, with all due humility,--

"If you please, sir, Mr. Leek, who has the letting of Anderbury-on-the-Mount, that is, Anderbury House, as it is usually called, is here, sir, and would be happy to take your orders as to when you would be pleased to look at those premises?"

"I shall be ready to go in half a hour," said the baron; "and, as the distance is not great, I will walk from here to the mansion."

This message was duly communicated to Mr. Leek, who thereupon determined upon waiting until the baron should announce his readiness to depart upon the expedition; and he was as good as his word, for, in about half-an-hour afterwards, he descended to the hall, and then Mr. Leek was summoned, who came out of the bar with such a grand rush, that he fell over a mat that was before him, and saluted the baron by digging his head into his stomach, and then falling sprawling at his feet, and laying hold of his ankle.

This little incident was duly apologised for, and explained; after which Mr. Leek walked on through the town, towards Anderbury-on-the-Mount, followed by the illustrious personage whom he sincerely hoped he should be able to induce to take it.

It was a curious thing to see how they traversed the streets together; for while the baron walked right on, and with a solemn and measured step, Mr. Leek managed to get along a few paces in front of him, sideways, so that he could keep up a sort of conversation upon the merits of Anderbury House, and the neighbourhood in general, without much effort; to which remarks the baron made such suitable and dignified replies as a baron would be supposed to make.

"You will find, sir," said Mr. Leek, "that everything about Anderbury is extremely select, and amazingly correct; and I am sure a more delightful place to live in could not be found."

"Ah!" said the baron; "very likely."

"It's lively, too," continued Mr. Leek; "very lively; and there are two chapels of ease, besides the church."

"That's a drawback," said the baron.

"A drawback, sir! well, I am sorry I mentioned it; but perhaps you are a Roman Catholic, sir, and, in that case, the chapels of ease have no interest for you."

"Not the slightest; but do not, sir, run away with any assumption concerning my religious opinions, for I am not a Roman Catholic."

"No, sir, no, sir; nor more am I; and, as far as I think, and my opinion goes, I say, why shouldn't a gentleman with a large fortune be what he likes, or nothing, if he likes that better? but here we are, sir, close to one of the entrances of Anderbury House. There are three principal entrances, you understand, sir, on three sides of the estate, and the fourth side faces the sea, where there is that mysterious passage that leads down from the grounds to the beach, which, perhaps, you have heard of, sir."

"The landlord of the inn mentioned it."

"We consider it a great curiosity, sir, I can assure you, in these parts--a very great curiosity; and it's an immense advantage to the house, because, you see, sir, in extremely hot weather, all sorts of provisions can be taken down there, and kept at such a very low temperature as to be quite delightful."

"That is an advantage."

Mr. Leek rang the bell that hung over one of the entrances, and his summons for admission was speedily answered by the old couple who had charge of the premises, and then, with a view of impressing them with a notion of the importance of the personage whom he had brought to look at the place, he said, aloud,--

"The Baron Stoltmayor, of Saltsomething, has come to look at the premises."

This announcement was received with all due deference and respect, and the task of showing the baron the premises at once fairly commenced.

"Here you have," said Mr. Leek, assuming an oratorical attitude--"here you have the umbrageous trees stooping down to dip their leaves in the purling waters; here you have the sweet foliage lending a delicious perfume to the balmy air; here you have the murmuring waterfalls playing music of the spheres to the listening birds, who sit responsive upon the dancing boughs; here you have all the fragrance of the briny ocean, mingling with the scent of a bank of violets, and wrapping the senses in Elysium; here you may never tire of an existence that presents never-ending charms, and that, in the full enjoyment of which, you may live far beyond the allotted span of man."

"Enough--enough," said the baron.

"Here you have the choicest exotics taking kindly to a soil gifted by nature with the most extraordinary powers of production; and all that can pamper the appetite or yield delight to the senses, is scattered around by nature with a liberal hand. It is quite impossible that royalty should come near the favoured spot without visiting it as a thing of course; and I forgot to mention that a revenue is derived from some cottages, which, although small, is yet sufficient to pay the tithe on the whole estate."

"There, there--that will do."

"Here you have purling rills and cascades, and fish-ponds so redundant with the finny tribe, that you have but to wish for sport, and it is yours; here you have in the mansion, chambers that vie with the accommodation of a palace--ample dormitories and halls of ancient grandeur; here you have--"

"Stop," said the baron, "stop; I cannot be pestered in this way with your description. I have no patience to listen to such mere words--show me the house at once, and let me judge for myself."

"Certainly, sir; oh! certainly; only I thought it right to give you a slight description of the place as it really was: and now, sir, that we have reached the house, I may remark that here we have--"

"Silence!" said the baron; "if you begin with here we have, I know not when you will leave off. All I require of you is to show me the place, and to answer any question which I may put to you concerning it. I will draw my own conclusions, and nothing you can say, one way or another, will affect my imagination."

"Certainly, sir, certainly; I shall only be too happy to answer any questions that may be put to me by a person of your lordship's great intelligence; and all I can remark is, that when you reach the drawing-room floor, any person may truly say, here you have--I really beg your pardon, sir--I had not the slightest intention of saying here you have, I assure you; but the words came out quite unawares, I assure you."

"Peace--peace!" cried again the baron; "you disturb me by this incessant clatter."

Thus admonished, Mr. Leek was now quiet, and allowed the baron in his own way to make what investigation he pleased concerning Anderbury House.

The investigation was not one that could be gone over in ten minutes; for the house was extremely extensive, and the estate altogether presented so many features of beauty and interest, that it was impossible not to linger over it for a considerable period of time.

The grounds were most extensive, and planted with such a regard to order and regularity, everything being in its proper place, that it was a pleasure to see an estate so well kept. And although the baron was not a man who said much, it was quite evident, by what little he did utter, that he was very well pleased with Anderbury-on-the-Mount.

"And now," said Mr. Leek, "I will do myself the pleasure, sir, of showing your grace the subterranean passage."

At this moment a loud ring at one of the entrance gates was heard, and upon the man who had charge of the house answering the summons for admission, he found that it was a gentleman, who gave a card on which was the name of Sir John Westlake, and who desired to see the premises.

"Sir John Westlake," said Mr. Leek; "oh! I recollect he did call at my office, and say that he thought of taking Anderbury-on-the-Mount. A gentleman of great and taste is Sir John, but I must tell him, baron, that you have the preference if you choose to embrace it."

At this moment the stranger advanced, and when he saw the baron, he bowed courteously, upon which Mr. Leek said,--

"I regret, Sir John, that if you should take a fancy to the place, I am compelled first of all to give this gentleman the refusal of it."

"Certainly," said Sir John Westlake; "do not let me interfere with any one. I have nearly made up my mind, and came to look over the property again; but of course, if this gentleman is beforehand with me, I must be content. I wish particularly to go down to the subterranean passage to the beach, if it is not too much trouble."

"Trouble! certainly not, sir. Here, Davis, get some links, and we can go at once; and as this gentleman likewise has seen everything but that strange excavation, he will probably descend with us."

"Certainly," said the baron; "I shall have great pleasure;" and he said it with so free and unembarrassed an air, that no one could have believed for a moment in the possibility that such a subject of fearful interest to him was there to be found.

The entrance from the grounds into this deep cavernous place was in a small but neat building, that looked like a summer-house; and now, torches being procured, and one lit, a door was opened, which conducted at once into the commencement of the excavation; and Mr. Leek heading the way, the distinguished party, as that gentleman loved afterwards to call it in his accounts of the transaction, proceeded into the very bowels of the earth, as it were, and quickly lost all traces of the daylight.

The place did not descend by steps, but by a gentle slope, which it required some caution to traverse, because, being cut in the chalk, which in some places was worn very smooth, it was extremely slippery; but this was a difficulty that a little practice soon overcame, and as they went on the place became more interesting every minute.

Even the baron allowed Mr. Leek to make a speech upon the occasion, and that gentleman said,--

"You will perceive that this excavation must have been made, at a great expense, out of the solid cliff, and in making it some of the most curious specimens of petrifaction and fossil remains were found. You see that the roof is vaulted, and that it is only now and then a lump of chalk has fallen in, or a great piece of flint; and now we come to one of the ice-wells."

They came to a deep excavation, down which they looked, and when the man held the torch beneath its surface, they could dimly see the bottom of it, where there was a number of large pieces of flint stone, and, apparently, likewise, the remains of broken bottles.

"There used to be a windlass at the top of this," said Mr. Leek, "and the things were let down in a basket. They do say that ice will keep for two years in one of these places."

"And are there more of these excavations?" said the baron.

"Oh, dear, yes, sir; there are five or six of them for different purposes; for when the family that used to live in Anderbury House had grand entertainments, which they sometimes had in the summer season, they always had a lot of men down here, cooling wines, and passing them up from hand to hand to the house."

From the gradual slope of this passage down to the cliffs, and the zigzag character of it, it may be well supposed that it was of considerable extent. Indeed, Mr. Leek asserted that it was half a mile in actual measured length.

The baron was not at all anxious to run any risk of a discovery of the dead body which he had cast into that ice-well which was nearest to the opening on to the beach, so, as he went on, he negatived the different proposals that were made to look down into the excavations, and succeeded in putting a stop to that species of inquiry in the majority of instances, but he could not wholly do so.

Perhaps it would have been better for his purpose if he had encouraged a look into every one of the ice-wells; for, in that case, their similarity of appearance might have tired out Sir John Westlake before they got to the last one; but as it was, when they reached the one down which the body had been precipitated, he had the mortification to hear Mr. Leek say,--

"And now, Sir John, and you, my lord baron, as we have looked at the first of these ice wells and at none of the others, suppose we look at the last."

The baron was afraid to say anything; because, if the body were discovered, and identified as that of the visitor at the inn, and who had been seen last with him, any reluctance on his part to have that ice-well examined, might easily afterwards be construed into a very powerful piece of circumstantial evidence against him.

He therefore merely bowed his assent, thinking that the examination would be but a superficial one, and that, in consequence, he should escape easily from any disagreeable consequences.

But this the fates ordained otherwise; and there seemed no hope of that ice-well in particular escaping such an investigation as was sure to induce some uncomfortable results.

"Davis," said Mr. Leek, "these places are not deep, you see, and I was thinking that if you went down one of them, it would be as well; for then you would be able to tell the gentlemen what the bottom was fairly composed of, you understand."

"Oh, I don't mind, sir," said Davis. "I have been down one of them before to-day, I can tell you, sir."

"I do not see the necessity," said Sir John Westlake, "exactly, of such a thing; but still if you please, and this gentleman wishes--"

"I have no wish upon the occasion," said the baron; "and, like yourself, cannot see the necessity."

"Oh, there is no trouble," said Mr. Leek; "and it's better, now you are here, that you see and understand all about it. How can you get down, Davis?"

"Why, sir, it ain't above fourteen feet altogether; so I sha'n't have any difficulty, for I can hang by my hands about half the distance, and drop the remainder."

As he spoke he took off his coat, and then stuck the link he carried into a cleft of the rock, that was beside the brink of the excavation.

The baron now saw that there would be no such thing as avoiding a discovery of the fact of the dead body being in that place, and his only hope was, that in its descent it might have become so injured as to defy identification.

But this was a faint hope, because he recollected that he had himself seen the face, which was turned upwards, and the period after death was by far too short for him to have any hope that decomposition could have taken place even to the most limited extent.

The light, which was stuck in a niche, shed but a few inefficient rays down into the pit, and, as the baron stood, with folded arms, looking calmly on, he expected each moment a scene of surprise and terror would ensue.

Nor was he wrong; for scarcely had the man plunged down into that deep place, than he uttered a cry of alarm and terror, and shouted,--

"Murder! murder! Lift me out. There is a dead man down here, and I have jumped upon him."

"A dead man!" cried Mr. Leek and Sir John Westlake in a breath.

"How very strange!" said the baron.

"Lend me a hand," cried Davis; "lend me a hand out; I cannot stand this, you know. Lend me a hand out, I say, at once."

This was easier to speak of than to do, and Mr. Davis began to discover that it was easier by far to get into a deep pit, than to get out of one, notwithstanding that his assertion of having been down into those places was perfectly true; but then he had met with nothing alarming, and had been able perfectly at his leisure to scramble out the best way he could.

Now, however, his frantic efforts to release himself from a much more uncomfortable situation than he had imagined it possible for him to get into, were of so frantic a nature, that he only half buried himself in pieces of chalk, which he kept pulling down with vehemence from the sides of the pit, and succeeded in accomplishing nothing towards his rescue.

"Oh! the fellow is only joking," said the baron, "and amusing himself at our expense."

But the manner in which the man cried for help, and the marked terror which was in every tone, was quite sufficient to prove that he was not acting; for if he were, a more accomplished mimic could not have been found on the stage than he was.

"This is serious," said Sir John Westlake, "and cannot be allowed. Have you any ropes here by which we can assist him from the pit? Don't be alarmed, my man, for if there be a dead body in the pit, it can't harm you. Take your time quietly and easily, and you will assuredly get out."

"Aye," said the baron, "the more haste, the worst speed, is an English proverb, and in this case it will be fully exemplified. This man would easily leave the pit, if he would have the patience, with care and quietness, to clamber up its sides."

It would appear that Davis felt the truth of these exhortations, for although he trembled excessively, he did begin to make some progress in his ascent, and get so high, that Mr. Leek was enabled to get hold of his hand, and give him a little assistance, so that, in another minute or so, he was rescued from his situation, which was not one of peril, although it was certainly one of fright.

He trembled so excessively, and stuttered and stammered, that for some minutes no one could understand very well what he said; but at length, upon making himself intelligible, he exclaimed,--

"There has been a murder! there has been a murder committed, and the body thrown into the ice pit. I felt that I jumped down upon something soft, and when I put down my hand to feel what it was, it came across a dead man's face, and then, of course, I called out."

"You certainly did call out."

"Yes, and so would anybody, I think, under such circumstances. I suppose I shall be hung now, because I had charge of the house?"

"That did not strike me until this moment," said the baron; "but if there be a dead body in that pit, it certainly places this man in a very awkward position."

"What the deuce do you mean?" said Davis; "I don't know no more about it than the child unborn. There is a dead man in the ice-well, and that is all I know about it; but whether he has been there a long time, or a short time, I don't know any more than the moon, so it's no use bothering me about it."

"My good man," said the baron, "it would be very wrong indeed to impute to you any amount of criminality in this business, since you may be entirely innocent; and I, for one, believe that you are so, for I cannot think that any guilty man would venture into the place where he had put the body of his victim, in the way that you ventured into that pit. I say I cannot believe it possible, and therefore I think you innocent, and will take care to see that no injustice is done you; but at the same time I cannot help adding, that I think, of course, you will find yourself suspected in some way."

"I am very much obliged to you, sir," said Davis; "but as I happen to be quite innocent, I am very easy about it, and don't care one straw what people say. I have not been in this excavation for Heaven knows how long."

"But what's to be done?" said Mr. Leek. "I suppose it's our duty to do something, under such circumstances."

"Unquestionably," said the baron; "and the first thing to be done, is to inform the police of what has happened, so that the body may be got up; and as I have now seen enough of the estate to satisfy me as regards its capabilities, I decide at once upon taking it, if I can agree upon the conditions of the tenancy, and I will purchase it, if the price be such as I think suitable."

"Well," said Mr. Leek, "if anything could reconcile me to the extraordinary circumstance that has just occurred, it certainly is, baron, the having so desirable a tenant for Anderbury-on-the-Mount as yourself. But we need not traverse all this passage again, for it is much nearer now to get out upon the sea-coast at once, as we are so close to the other opening upon the beach. It seems to me that we ought to proceed at once to the town, and give information to the authorities of the discovery which we have made."

"It is absolutely necessary," said the baron, "so to do; so come along at once. I shall proceed to my inn, and as, of course, I have seen nothing more than yourselves, and consequently could only repeat your evidence, I do not see that my presence is called for. Nevertheless, of course, if the justices think it absolutely necessary that I should appear, I can have no possible objection to so do."

This was as straightforward as anything that could be desired, and, moreover, it was rather artfully put together, for it seemed to imply that he, Mr. Leek, would be slighted, if his evidence was not considered sufficient.

"Of course," said Mr. Leek; "I don't see at all why, as you, sir, have only the same thing to say as myself, I should not be sufficient."

"Don't call upon me on any account," said Sir John Westlake.

"Oh! no, no," cried Mr. Leek; "there is no occasion. I won't, you may depend, if it can be helped."

Sir John, in rather a nervous and excited manner, bade them good day, before they got quite into the town, and hurried off; while the baron, with a dignified bow, when he reached the door of his hotel, said to Mr. Leek,--

"Of course I do not like the trouble of judicial investigations more than anybody else, and therefore, unless it is imperatively necessary that I should appear, I shall take it as a favour to be released from such a trouble."

"My lord baron," said Mr. Leek, "you may depend that I shall mention that to the magistrates and the coroner, and all those sort of people;" and then Mr. Leek walked away, but he muttered to himself, as he did so, "They will have him, as sure as fate, just because he is a baron; and his name will look well in the 'County Chronicle.'"

Mr. Leek then repaired immediately to the house of one of the principal magistrates, and related what had occurred, to the great surprise of that gentleman, who suggested immediately the propriety of making the fact known to the coroner of the district, as it was more his business, than a magistrate's, in the first instance, since nobody was accused of the offence.

This suggestion was immediately followed, and that functionary directed that the body should be removed from where it was to the nearest public-house, and immediately issued his precept for an inquiry into the case.

By this time the matter had begun to get bruited about in the town, and of course it went from mouth to mouth with many exaggerations; and although it by no means did follow that a murder had been committed because a dead body had been found, yet, such was the universal impression; and the matter began to be talked about as the murder in the subterranean passage leading to Anderbury House, with all the gusto which the full particulars of some deed of blood was calculated to inspire. And how it spread about was thus:--

The fact was, that Mr. Leek was so anxious to let Anderbury-on-the-Mount to the rich Baron Stolmuyer, of Saltzburgh, that he got a friend of his to come and personate Sir John Westlake, while he, the baron, was looking at the premises, in order to drive him at once to a conclusion upon the matter; so that what made Sir John so very anxious that he should not be called forward in the matter, consisted in the simple fact that he was nothing else than plain Mr. Brown, who kept a hatter's shop in the town; but he could not keep his own counsel, and, instead of holding his tongue, as he ought to have done, about the matter, he told it to every one he met, so that in a short time it was generally known that something serious and startling had occurred in the subterranean passage to Anderbury House, and a great mob of persons thronged the beach in anxious expectation of getting more information on the matter.

The men, likewise, who had been ordered by the coroner to remove the body, soon reached the spot, and they gave an increased impetus to the proceedings, by opening the door of the subterranean passage, and then looking earnestly along the beach as if in expectation of something or somebody of importance.

When eagerly questioned by the mob, for the throng of persons now assembled quite amounted to a mob, to know what they waited for, one of them said,--

"A coffin was to have been brought down to take the body in."

This announcement at once removed anything doubtful that might be in the minds of any of them upon the subject, and at once proclaimed the fact not only that there was a dead body, but that if they looked out they would see it forthwith.

The throng thickened, and by the time two men were observed approaching with a coffin on their shoulders, there was scarcely anybody left in the town, except a few rare persons, indeed, who were not so curious as their neighbours.

It was not an agreeable job, even to those men who were not the most particular in the world, to be removing so loathsome a spectacle as that which they were pretty sure to encounter in the ice-well; but they did not shrink from it, and, by setting about it as a duty, they got through it tolerably well.

They took with them several large torches, and then, one having descended into the pit, fastened a rope under the arms of the dead man, and so he was hauled out, and placed in the shell that was ready to receive him.

They were all surprised at the fresh and almost healthful appearance of the countenance, and it was quite evident to everybody that if any one had known him in life, they could not have the least possible difficulty in recognising him now that he was no more.

And the only appearance of injury which he exhibited was in that dreadful wound which had certainly proved his death, and which was observable in his throat the moment they looked upon him.

The crush to obtain a sight of the body was tremendous at the moment it was brought out, and a vast concourse of persons followed it in procession to the town, where the greatest excitement prevailed. It was easily discovered that no known person was missing, and some who had caught a sight of the body, went so far as to assert that it must have been in the ice-well for years, and that the extreme cold had preserved it in all its original freshness.

The news, of course, came round, although not through the baron, for he did not condescend to say one word about it at the inn, and it was the landlord who first started the suggestion of-- "What suppose it is the gentleman who left his horse here?"

This idea had no sooner got possession of his brain, than it each moment seemed to him to assume a more reasonable and tangible form, and without saying any more to any one else about it, he at once started off to where the body lay awaiting an inquest, to see if his suspicions were correct.

When he arrived at the public-house and asked to see the body, he was at once permitted to do so; for the landlord knew him, and was as curious as he could be upon the subject by any possibility. One glance, of course, was sufficient, and the landlord at once said,--

"Yes, I have seen him before, though I don't know his name. He came to my house last night, and left his horse there; and, although I only saw him for a moment as he passed through the hall, I am certain I am not mistaken. I dare say all my waiters will recognise him, as well as the Baron Stolmuyer of Saltzburgh, who is staying with me, and who no doubt knows very well who he is, for he went out with him late and came home alone, and I ordered one of my men to wait up all night in order to let in this very person who is now lying dead before us."

"The deuce you did! But you don't suppose the baron murdered him, do you?"

"It's a mystery to me altogether--quite a profound mystery. It's very unlikely, certainly; and what's the most extraordinary part of the whole affair is, how the deuce could he come into one of the ice-wells belonging to Anderbury House. That's what puzzles me altogether."

"Well, it will all come out, I hope, at the inquest, which is to be held at four o'clock to day. There must have been foul play somewhere, but the mystery is where, and that Heaven only knows, perhaps."

"I shall attend," said the landlord, "of course, to identify him; and I suppose, unless anybody claims the horse, I may as well keep possession of it."

"Don't you flatter yourself that you will get the horse out of the transaction. Don't you know quite well that the government takes possession of everything as don't belong to nobody?"

"Yes; but I have got him, and possession, you know, is nine points of the law."

"It may be so; but their tenth point will get the better of you for all that. You take my word for it, the horse will be claimed of you; but I don't mind, as an old acquaintance, putting you up to a dodge."

"In what way?"

"Why, I'll tell you what happened with a friend of mine; but don't think it was me for if it was I would tell you at once, so don't think it. He kept a country public-house; and, one day, an elderly gentleman came in, and appeared to be unwell. He just uttered a word or two, and then dropped down dead. He happened to have in his fob a gold repeater, that was worth, at least a hundred guineas, and my friend, before anybody came, took it out, and popped in, in its stead, an old watch that he had, which was not worth a couple of pounds."

"It was running a risk."

"It was; but it turned out very well, because the old gentleman happened to be a very eccentric person, and was living alone, so that his friends really did not know what he had, or what he had not, but took it for granted that any watch produced belonged to him. So, if I were you in this case, when the gentleman's horse is claimed. I'd get the d--dest old screw I could, and let them have that."

"You would?"

"Indeed would I, and glory in it, too, as the very best thing that could be done. Now, a horse is of use to you?"

"I believe ye, it is."

"Exactly; but what's the use of it to government? and, what's more, if it went to the government, there might be some excuse; but the government will know no more about it, and make not so much as I shall. Some Jack-in-office will lay hold of it as a thing of course and a perquisite, when you might just as well, and a great deal better, too, keep it yourself, for it would do you some good, as you say, and none to them."

"I'll do it; it is a good and a happy thought. There is no reason on earth why I shouldn't do it, and I will. I have made up my mind to it now."

"Well, I am glad you have. What do you think now the dead man's horse is worth?"

"Oh! fifty or sixty guineas value."

"Then very good. Then, when the affair is all settled, I will trouble you for twenty pounds.

"You?"

"Yes, to be sure. Who else do you suppose is going to interfere with you? One is enough, ain't it, at a time; and I think, after giving you such advice as I have, that I am entitled, at all events, to something."

"I tell you what," said the landlord of the hotel, "taking all things into consideration, I have altered my mind rather, and won't do it."

"Very good. You need not; only mind, if you do, I am down upon you like a shot."

The excitement contingent upon the inquest was very great; indeed, the large room in the public-house, where it was held, was crowded to suffocation with persons who were anxious to be present at the proceedings. When the landlord reached home, of course he told his guest, the baron, of the discovery he had made, that the murdered man was the strange visitor of the previous night; for now, from the frightful wound he had received in his throat, the belief that he was murdered became too rational a one to admit of any doubts, and was that which was universally adopted in preference to any other suggestion upon the occasion; although, no doubt, people would be found who would not scruple to aver that he had cut his own throat, after making his way into the well belonging to Anderbury House.

The landlord had his own misgivings concerning his guest, the baron, now that something had occurred of such an awful and mysterious a nature to one who was evidently known to him. It did not seem to be a pleasant thing to have such an intimate friend of a man who had been murdered in one's house, especially when it came to be considered that he was the last person seen in his company, and that, consequently, he was peculiarly called upon to give an explanation of how, and under what circumstances, he had parted with him.

The baron was sitting smoking in the most unconcerned manner in the world, when the landlord came to bring him this intelligence, and, when he had heard him to an end, the remark he made was,--

"Really, you very much surprise me; but, perhaps, as you are better acquainted with the town than I am, you can tell me who he was?"

"Why, sir, that is what we hoped you would be able to tell us."

"How should I tell you? He introduced himself to me as a Mr. Mitchell, a surveyor, and he said that, hearing I talked of purchasing or renting Anderbury-on-the-Mount, he came to tell me that the principal side wall, that you could see from the beach, was off the perpendicular."

"Indeed, sir!"

"Yes; and as this was a very interesting circumstance to me, considering that I really did contemplate such a purchase or renting, and do so still, as it was a moonlight night, and he said he could show me in a minute what he meant if I would accompany him, I did so; but when we got there, and on the road, I heard quite enough of him to convince me that he was a little out of his senses, and, consequently, I paid no more attention to what he said, but walked home and left him on the beach."

"It's a most extraordinary circumstance, sir; there is no such person, I assure you, as Mitchell, a surveyor, in the town; so I can't make it out in the least."

"But, I tell you, I consider the man out of his senses, and perhaps that may account for the whole affair."

"Oh, yes, sir, that would, certainly; but still, it's a very odd thing, because we don't know of such a person at all, and it does seem so extraordinary that he should have made his appearance, all of a sudden, in this sort of way. I suppose, sir, that you will attend the inquest, now, that's to be held upon him?"

"Oh, yes; I have no objection whatever to that; indeed, I feel myself bound to do so, because I suppose mine is the latest evidence that can be at all produced concerning him."

"Unquestionably, sir; our coroner is a very clever man, and you will be glad to know him--very glad to know him, sir, and he will be glad to know you, so I am sure it will be a mutual gratification. It's at four o'clock the inquest is to be, and I dare say, sir, if you are there by half-past, it will be time enough."

"No doubt of that; but I will be punctual."

We have already said the room in which the inquest was to be held was crowded almost to suffocation, and not only was that the case, but the lower part of the house was crammed with people likewise; and there can be very little doubt but the baron would have shrunk from such an investigation from a number of curious eyes, if he could have done so; while the landlord of the house would have had no objection, as far as his profit was concerned in the sale of a great quantity of beer and spirits, to have had such an occurrence every day in the week, if possible.

The body lay still in the shell where it had been originally placed. After it had been viewed by the jury, and almost every one had remarked upon the extraordinary fresh appearance it wore, they proceeded at once to the inquiry, and the first witness who appeared was Mr. Leek, who deposed to have been in company with some gentlemen viewing Anderbury House, and to have found the body in one of the ice-wells of that establishment.

This evidence was corroborated by that of Davis, who had so unexpectedly jumped into the well, without being aware that it contained already so disagreeable a visitor as it did in the person of the murdered man, regarding the cause of whose death the present inquiry was instituted.

Then the landlord identified the body as that of a gentleman who had come to his house on horseback, and who had afterwards walked out with Baron Stolmuyer of Saltzburgh, who was one of his guests.

"Is that gentleman in attendance?" said the coroner.

"Yes, sir, he is; I told him about it, and he has kindly come forward to give all the evidence in his power concerning it."

There was a general expression of interest and curiosity when the baron stepped forward, attired in his magnificent coat, trimmed with fur, and tendered his evidence to the coroner, which, of course, was precisely the same as the statement he had made to the landlord of the house; for, as he had made up such a well connected story, he was not likely to prevaricate or to depart from it in the smallest particular.

He was listened to with breathless attention, and, when he had concluded, the coroner, with a preparatory hem! said to him,

"And you have reason to suppose, sir, that this person was out of his senses?"

"It seemed to me so; he talked wildly and incoherently, and in such a manner as to fully induce such a belief."

"You left him on the beach?"

"I did. I found when I got there that it was only a very small portion, indeed, of Anderbury House that was visible; and, although the moon shone brightly, I must confess I did not see, myself, any signs of deviation from the perpendicular; and, such being the case, I left the spot at once, because I could have no further motive in staying; and, moreover, it was not pleasant to be out at night with a man whom I thought was deranged. I regretted, after making this discovery, that I had come from home on such a fool's errand; but as, when one is going to invest a considerable sum of money in any enterprise, one is naturally anxious to know all about it, I went, little suspecting that the man was insane."

"Did you see him after that?"

"Certainly not, until to-day, when I recognised in the body that has been exhibited to me the same individual."

"Gentlemen," said the coroner to the jury, "it appears to me that this is a most mysterious affair; the deceased person has a wound in his throat, which, I have no doubt, you will hear from a medical witness has been the cause of death; and the most singular part of the affair is, how, if he inflicted it upon himself, he has managed to dispose of the weapon with which he did the deed."

"The last person seen in his company," said one of the jury, "was the baron, and I think he is bound to give some better explanation of the affair."

"I am yet to discover," said the baron, "that the last person who acknowledges to having been in the company of a man afterwards murdered, must, of necessity, be the murderer?"

"Yes; but how do you account, sir, for there being no weapon found by which the man could have done the deed himself?"

"I don't account for it at all--how do you?"

"This is irregular," said the coroner; "call the next witness."

This was a medical man, who briefly stated that he had seen the deceased, and that the wound in his throat was amply sufficient to account for his death; that it was inflicted with a sharp instrument having an edge on each side.

This, then, seemed to conclude the case, and the coroner remarked,--

"Gentlemen of the jury,--I think this is one of those peculiar cases in which an open verdict is necessary, or else an adjournment without date, so that the matter can be resumed at any time, if fresh evidence can be procured concerning it. There is no one accused of the offence, although it appears to me impossible that the unhappy man could have committed the act himself. We have no reason to throw the least shade of suspicion or doubt upon the evidence of the Baron Stolmuyer of Saltzburgh; for as far as we know anything of the matter, the murdered man may have been in the company of a dozen people after the baron left him."

A desultory conversation ensued, which ended in an adjournment of the inquest, without any future day being mentioned for its re-assembling, and so the Baron Stolmuyer entirely escaped from what might have been a very serious affair to him.

It did not, however, appear to shake him in his resolution of taking Anderbury-on-the-Mount, although Mr. Leek very much feared it would; but he announced to that gentleman his intention fully of doing so, and told him to get the necessary papers drawn up forthwith.

"I hope," he said, "within a few weeks' time to be fairly installed in that mansion, and then I will trouble you, Mr. Leek, to give me a list of the names of all the best families in the neighbourhood; for I intend giving an entertainment on a grand scale in the mansion and grounds."

"Sir," said Mr. Leek, "I shall, with the greatest pleasure, attend upon you in every possible way in this affair. This is a very excellent neighbourhood, and you will have no difficulty, I assure you, sir, in getting together an extremely capital and creditable assemblage of persons. There could not be a better plan devised for at once introducing all the people who are worth knowing, to you."

"I thank you," said the baron; "I think the place will suit me well; and, as the Baroness Stolmuyer of Saltzburgh is dead, I have some idea of marrying again; and therefore it becomes necessary and desirable that I should be well acquainted with the surrounding families of distinction in this neighbourhood."

This was a hint not at all likely to be thrown away upon Mr. Leek, who was the grand gossip-monger of the place, and he treasured it up in order to see if he could not make something of it which would be advantageous to himself.

He knew quite enough of the select and fashionable families in that neighbourhood, to be fully aware that neither the baron's age nor his ugliness would be any bar to his forming a matrimonial alliance.

"There is not one of them," he said to himself, "who would not marry the very devil himself and be called the Countess Lucifer, or any name of the kind, always provided there was plenty of money: and that the baron has without doubt, so it is equally without doubt he may pick and choose where he pleases."

This was quite correct of Mr. Leek, and showed his great knowledge of human nature; and we entertain with him a candid opinion, that if the Baron Stolmuyer of Saltzburgh had been ten times as ugly as he was, and Heaven knows that was needless, he might pick and choose a wife almost when he pleased.

This is a general rule; and as, of course, to all general rules there are exceptions, this one cannot be supposed to be free from them. Under all circumstances, and in all classes of society, there are single-minded beings who consult the pure dictates of their own hearts, and who, disdaining those things which make up the amount of the ambition of meaner spirits, stand aloof as bright and memorable examples to the rest of human nature.

Such a being was Flora Bannerworth. She would never have been found to sacrifice herself to the fancied advantages of wealth and station, but would have given her heart and hand to the true object of her affection, although a sovereign prince had made the endeavour to wean her from it.

www.ingramcontent.com/pod-product-compliance
Lightning Source LLC
Chambersburg PA
CBHW030927020726
47498CB00001B/140

9781773560465